D1134290

GILBERT MORRIS

APPOMATTOX SAGA

(PART 2)

1861-1863

ADVENTURE AND ROMANCE THRIVE

DURING THE WAR BETWEEN THE STATES

THREE BOOKS IN ONE
1) LAND OF THE SHADOW
2) OUT OF THE WHIRLWIND
3) THE SHADOW OF HIS WINGS

BARBOUR
PUBLISHING

Land of the Shadow © 1993 by Gilbert Morris
Out of the Whirlwind © 1994 by Gilbert Morris
The Shadow of His Wings © 1994 by Gilbert Morris

ISBN 978-1-60260-179-6

All scripture quotations are taken from the King James Version of the Bible.

This book is a work of fiction. Names, characters, places, and incidents are either products of the author's imagination or used fictitiously. Any similarity to actual people, organizations, and/or events is purely coincidental.

Published by Barbour Publishing, Inc., P.O. Box 719, Uhrichsville, Ohio 44683, www.barbourbooks.com

Our mission is to publish and distribute inspirational products offering exceptional value and biblical encouragement to the masses.

 Member of the
Evangelical Christian
Publishers Association

Printed in the United States of America.

GENEALOGY OF THE ROCKLIN FAMILY

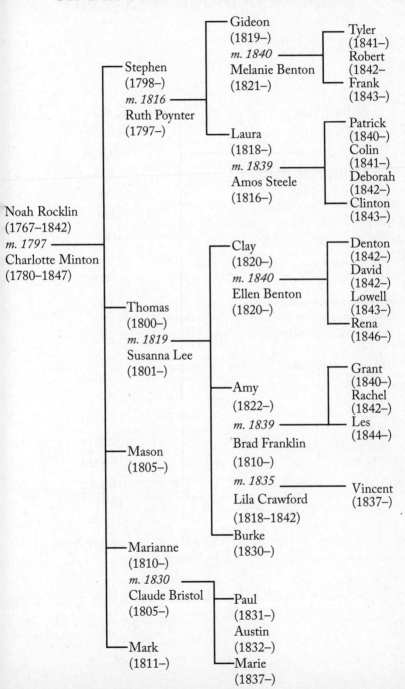

Noah Rocklin
(1767–1842)
m. 1797
Charlotte Minton
(1780–1847)

Stephen
(1798–)
m. 1816
Ruth Poynter
(1797–)

Gideon
(1819–)
m. 1840
Melanie Benton
(1821–)

Tyler
(1841–)
Robert
(1842–)
Frank
(1843–)

Laura
(1818–)
m. 1839
Amos Steele
(1816–)

Patrick
(1840–)
Colin
(1841–)
Deborah
(1842–)
Clinton
(1843–)

Thomas
(1800–)
m. 1819
Susanna Lee
(1801–)

Clay
(1820–)
m. 1840
Ellen Benton
(1820–)

Denton
(1842–)
David
(1842–)
Lowell
(1843–)
Rena
(1846–)

Amy
(1822–)
m. 1839
Brad Franklin
(1810–)
m. 1835
Lila Crawford
(1818–1842)

Grant
(1840–)
Rachel
(1842–)
Les
(1844–)

Vincent
(1837–)

Burke
(1830–)

Mason
(1805–)

Marianne
(1810–)
m. 1830
Claude Bristol
(1805–)

Paul
(1831–)
Austin
(1832–)
Marie
(1837–)

Mark
(1811–)

GENEALOGY OF THE YANCY FAMILY

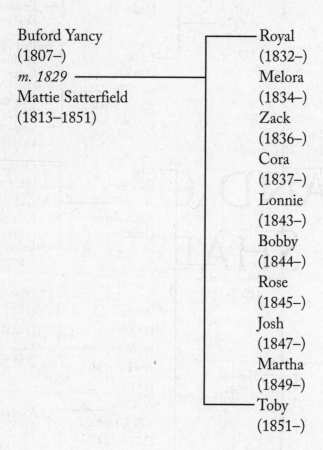

Buford Yancy
(1807–)
m. 1829
Mattie Satterfield
(1813–1851)

Royal
(1832–)
Melora
(1834–)
Zack
(1836–)
Cora
(1837–)
Lonnie
(1843–)
Bobby
(1844–)
Rose
(1845–)
Josh
(1847–)
Martha
(1849–)
Toby
(1851–)

LAND OF THE SHADOW

Editor's Note:

This book begins shortly after the family reunion that
takes place in chapter 15 of book 3, *Where Honor Dwells.*

PART ONE

The Outsider—November 1861

CHAPTER 1

RETURN OF THE PRODIGAL

Paul Bristol was an expert in three distinct areas: painting, horses—and women.

It was the latter of these that enabled Bristol to understand exactly what had brought Luci DeSpain to the party at his parents' house one November evening. He had descended the beautifully constructed curving stairway expecting to find only his own family, but his father met him, saying, "The DeSpains are joining us tonight, Paul."

Instantly a tiny alarm went off inside Paul Bristol's head, a warning device that had enabled him, at the ripe old age of thirty-one, to still be single. He said nothing about this, however, and spent the evening never more than a few feet away from the beautiful and charming Luci. And somehow, between visiting with the DeSpains and dinner, he found himself alone with her in the long gallery, examining the family portraits. Luci, he knew, had seen all the portraits before, but she stopped to examine each one, sometimes touching Paul's arm when one of them impressed her.

It was when the couple paused under a fine portrait of Noah Rocklin, Paul's grandfather on his mother's side, that the tiny alarm began to ring more insistently. Luci was petite and had to look up to Paul as she said, "What a fine-looking man, Paul. . . ." She had not seemed to move, yet somehow her body pressed against Paul, and as she looked up, her blue eyes were bright and her lips softly pursed, saying, "All you Rocklin men are such tall fellows!"

Ah, the chase was on. . . . Paul held back the smile of amusement that wanted to curve his lips and simply spoke his lines, as smoothly as any actor in a play: "And you DeSpain women are all beautiful." He needed no stage direction to know what came next, and so he took her in his arms and kissed her thoroughly. It was a long kiss, and Bristol was somewhat surprised at Luci's eager response. But only somewhat surprised.

As the kiss ended, he knew she would pull away and rebuke him soundly, all the while giving him the impression that she was not really angry.

"Paul—you mustn't do that!" Luci cried, pushing him away. Paul almost applauded and said, "Bravo!" so well did the girl perform. Unfortunately for Luci, however, his attention had been drawn away from her by the image reflected in the full-length mirror just to Luci's left. There Paul saw a fine-looking couple embracing—but it brought back memories of other images he'd seen in that same mirror. The same man but different girls. . .several different girls, all playing their parts beautifully, all determined to convince Paul he could not live without them.

This has always been a good hunting ground, he thought sardonically. His gaze went back to Luci, who was watching him with a slight frown. He had missed his cue, and it would take some quick thinking to keep the girl from growing miffed. He smiled at her, a smile full of both apology and promise, and said, "I beg your pardon, Luci. But you don't know what a beautiful girl like you can do to a man!"

That ought to brighten her up, he thought and once again almost applauded when she lowered her lashes demurely, a slight smile playing at her beautifully shaped lips. "I do fear, Paul, that you've been spoiled by all those terrible women in Europe," Luci said, pursing her mouth into a pout. "I've heard all about them, about how free they are with their favors." She looked up suddenly and met his eyes. "Do you think so?" she demanded.

Ah no, my dear, you won't catch me in any careless admissions, he thought, and he looked at her blankly. "Do I think you've heard about them?"

Luci laughed. She did it so well—with a fine, tinkling sound—that Paul suspected she practiced the thing. "No, silly! I mean, do you think the women over there are. . .I mean, do they. . . ?"

Paul enjoyed Luci's inability to ask straight out what was on her mind, and took full advantage of this opportunity to tease her. "Yes, I'm afraid they do," he remarked rather piously. "I must say that it's wonderful to be back in America with respectable ladies again—ladies such as yourself, my dear, who would never dream of employing such coquettish ways."

Luci paused for a moment, and her eyes narrowed just the slightest bit at the faint irony in Paul's tone. Surely he wasn't implying that she was the least bit like those loose women! What she wanted at that moment, more than anything else, was to go deeper into the "coquettish ways" of those women, but before she could think of a way to broach the subject, Bristol forestalled her.

"I think I heard the dinner chime, Luci," he said, extending his elbow gallantly. She had no choice but to slip her hand through it and follow as he led her out of the gallery and down the hall. As the two of them took their places, side by side, at the long cherry table, Luci had the distinct sense she'd just been bested at her own game. But, never one to give up too easily, she put on a bright smile and exclaimed at the beautiful setting before her, remarking over the fine white tablecloth and the way the table all but sparkled with crystal glasses and gleaming silver. From the corner of her eye, she caught Paul's admiring expression. (She would not have felt quite so pleased by it, however, had she realized it stemmed not so much from his appreciation of her charm and beauty as from his appreciation of her ability to regroup so quickly.)

Paul's father spoke his usual rather oratorical blessing, and for the next hour the talk flowed around the table freely.

There were only eight at the meal, including Paul's parents, his sister, Marie, and his brother, Austin—plus Luci and her parents. They were all old friends and knew everything there was to know about each other. Paul, having been in Europe for a good part of the last three years, found himself feeling like a foreigner. He listened to Luci's conversation and decided he'd be as surprised if she uttered a single brilliant and unusual speech as if his mare, Queenie, were to turn and speak to him on their morning ride!

Not that Luci was an ignorant person, far from it. But her world was bounded by invisible strands that circled Richmond. If an event didn't happen in Richmond, then—to Luci and her friends—it might as well take place on the moon!

Paul's lips thinned as he listened to the conversation so common in polite society. He could usually hold his own in such conversation by drawing on one of his three areas of expertise. However, the mere thought of doing so bored him to distraction. For all his well-developed social graces, only his experiences with fast horses had brought him much satisfaction. He was admired as an expert breeder and had made quite a bit of cash riding his own races. As for his other two areas of involvement, he had gained little money and only slight recognition as a painter. . .and his extensive success with women had made him slightly contemptuous of most females.

Perhaps most people secretly despise what comes too easily, and Paul Bristol had experienced few rebuffs from the women of Richmond. The corps of mothers in that city—those with eligible daughters—had practically flung their female offspring at Bristol. As for the gaggle of perfumed, powdered, and polished young women, they themselves were more than willing to be flung.

There was, of course, a sociological factor in this eager sacrifice: What else was a young daughter of Southern aristocracy to do except marry well? Women in the lower classes might become schoolteachers, but the daughters of high society were taught as soon as they were able to function that the acquisition of a husband was their single hope of happiness.

Paul Bristol had the dubious distinction of being one of those young men who met every requirement of both hawk-eyed mothers and dewy-eyed maidens. His family was good, for the Bristols were of that part of the aristocracy that—though not rich like the Hugers, Lees, and Wainscots of Virginia—owned fine plantations and had exactly the *proper* number of slaves. That is, enough to be impressive and do the work, but not so many that they got underfoot or made the family seem showy. Claude Bristol, Paul's father, was ornamental and fairly useless, but his wife, the former Marianne Rocklin, was capable enough to keep the plantation from disaster. She saw to it that enough cotton was grown to pay for her husband's fine clothes, horses, and gambling losses—in addition, she made sure there was enough extra to enable her family to keep up the style of living demanded by the Southern aristocracy. This being the case, Paul Bristol easily met the requirements set by parents who sought suitable husbands for their daughters.

Paul himself provided an enticing opportunity for the young women. He was handsome, witty, and wicked—that, combined with his family and money, made Paul an irresistible combination guaranteed to flutter a young woman's heart. The trouble was, Paul had yet to find even one woman who stirred within him more than a passing interest. He glanced again at Luci DeSpain and sighed. Perhaps he was looking for something that didn't exist. . . .

The turkey had been devastated, and house slaves started carrying in freshly made pies—pecan, pumpkin, apple, and cherry. House Mary—so called to set her off from Field Mary—knew Paul well enough to bring him a wedge of cherry, his favorite. "You thinking this pie will get you a Christmas gift, House Mary?" Paul teased the servant. "Well, I think it might work." He grinned as she protested, then hewed off the tip of the wedge, placed it carefully in his mouth, and chewed slowly. His mother was watching him with a smile, and he winked at her.

"Mother, this piece of pie is worth the trip home from France!" Waving his fork in a salute, he added, "Nothing in Europe to beat it!"

Marianne Bristol's black hair showed traces of gray, but at the age of fifty-one she was still a strikingly beautiful woman. Her eyes were royal blue, and when she smiled, as she did now at her eldest son, dimples appeared on each side of her shapely mouth. "Tell us about the king and queen," she said. Paul smiled at his mother, studying her for a moment. She was wearing a

13

green silk dress and a pair of jade earrings, and Paul thought she was one of the most beautiful women he'd ever seen—and perhaps one of ten women he'd ever known from the land of his birth who could discuss something besides cotton and new dresses.

But as Paul started to repeat the story of his visit at Windsor Castle, his brother, Austin, interrupted. "Paul, never mind all that—what about recognition from England?" Austin was twenty-nine years old, short and strong with his father's brown hair and eyes. He was caught up in the war that had begun at Fort Sumter in April 1861. Now he was staring defiantly at Paul and added, "England will *have* to recognize the Confederacy! Everybody knows England exists on her looms—and she can't run her looms without cotton!"

"I expect you're right, Austin," Luci's father, Clarence DeSpain, agreed. "England can get along without the North, but not without King Cotton!" DeSpain was a tall, portly man, handsome in a florid way, and had been a secessionist for years.

"Well, sir," Paul said cautiously, "England does have many mills and has used American cotton for a long time."

"So they'll *have* to recognize us, won't they?" Austin insisted.

Paul didn't answer, preferring not to get involved in what he knew would be a less-than-satisfying discussion, but his father asked him directly, "Well, isn't your brother right, Paul? If we don't let England have our cotton, they'll go broke! Isn't that a fact?"

"I'm no expert on British economy," Paul protested, but when he saw that the others would not let him off, he shrugged. His mother was watching him carefully, and he saw something in her expression—a warning of some kind. As tactfully as he could, he began to speak of the situation as he'd seen it when in Europe, knowing all the time his views would find little approval from those who waited so expectantly to hear what he would say.

"I was busy painting while I was in Europe, but what I heard from those who seemed to know the situation isn't too encouraging for the South." He picked up his glass, drank a few swallows, then set the glass down and looked at the circle of faces. "What they say is that England has been having a devil of a time financially, and many of the mills have been forced to close. One fellow who worked for the government told me that there are at least half a million bales of cotton on hand right now—enough to do the British for a long time. He also said that the government has gotten very interested in Egyptian cotton."

"They grow cotton in Egypt?" Paul's sister, Marie, who was seated at his right hand, drew his attention. "I didn't know that."

"Well, they do, and it's long staple, better than our cotton."

"I don't believe it!" Austin said heatedly. Paul listened quietly as Austin and Clarence DeSpain spoke at great length on how England *would* buy American cotton. Neither offered any evidence but spoke what many in the South considered to be truth as solid as the sun rising in the east.

Marianne sat quietly, paying almost no heed to the arguments mouthed by DeSpain and her younger son. She had been somewhat embarrassed at first that her husband and son had had little interest in the war. Now, however, they seemed to grow more interested with each passing day—and to echo the sentiments expressed by so many in the South. Why, she had even heard such declarations once from the lips of Jefferson Davis, the president of the Confederate States of America, himself. So none of this surprised or concerned her.

Of more concern to Marianne was this youngest son of hers, Austin, who lounged across the table from her. She knew him better than he knew himself—for he was an openhearted young man, easy enough to read. And she was proud of him, for he had been a good son, hardworking and happy in making his life at their plantation, Hartsworth. He knew every foot of the plantation, knew the slaves, and was sensitive to the seasons— so much so that Wiley Otes, the overseer, paid him the highest compliment in his power: "Mister Austin, he *knows* when to plant cotton!"

Marianne considered her son thoughtfully. *Austin will marry one day, and he'll bring his bride to Hartsworth. And someday he'll be buried along with his people.* Marianne felt a sudden flush of joy, for she was a woman who loved stability and loathed change. This was one reason she never sought to change her husband or their situation. Though she had long known that her husband was weaker than she, rather than try to change anything, she simply became adept at working behind the scenes, taking care of business, making up for Claude's lacks without drawing attention to herself. She was a proud woman, this Marianne Bristol, and would accept pity from neither man nor woman—especially over her husband's weaknesses, which were legion.

But even Claude she could understand—and forgive. He had been unfaithful to her more than once, and little remained of the fervent love she'd had for him in her youth. He drank too much and cared little for the things that made a plantation profitable. Yet underneath the shallow veneer of manners and charm, Marianne still believed that something of the man she'd fallen in love with remained.

If only he were as fine as he looks! The thought had come often to her, for Claude Bristol was indeed handsome, even at the age of fifty-six. Not tall, but erect, with a pair of sharp brown eyes and evidence of the classic lines of his French blood in his smooth, unlined face. His was not a strong face, but it certainly was an attractive one.

Marie, their only daughter, was a fine combination of the best of her parents. She carried Claude's fine looks, with curly brown hair and large, almost luminous brown eyes, and her mother's common sense and delight in living. Marianne let her gaze rest on Marie, suddenly grateful that her daughter had more substance than Luci DeSpain—indeed, more than any girl she'd ever known.

But Paul! What and who was he, this eldest son of hers? He

17

had been gone for almost three years, but even before he had returned, bringing with him a slightly foreign air, Marianne had found no key to understanding him. He was turned now to face Clarence DeSpain, and slowly she analyzed her son's face. She felt pleasure at his good looks but was perplexed by what lay behind the smooth expression Paul always seemed to wear. She studied his wedge-shaped face, which tapered from a broad forehead and over smooth olive-tinted cheeks to a strong, almost defiant chin. A small scar—the result of a fall during a horse race—marked his chin. A thin black mustache traced the upper lip, and the lower lip was almost too full for a man. She studied the deep-set blue eyes, covered by a shelf of bone capped by black brows. Eyes that could grow tender—at least, that had been so when he was a young boy—or that could blaze with a fierce anger that made one want to step back.

I don't know him at all, Marianne thought. *He's like a stranger. And an unhappy stranger, at that! Even when he smiles, there's some sort of sadness in his eyes.* She tried to think back, to remember when she'd last seen Paul completely happy—but she could not recall such a time.

Marianne's gaze shifted to Luci, and the sight of the girl both pleased and troubled her. *She'd be a fine wife—beautiful and from a good family. And yet. . .* Though she couldn't explain how she knew it, Marianne was certain this wasn't enough for Paul. She frowned. *I wish Luci was interested in Austin.* The thought jumped into her brain, and she shook it away, feeling somehow that there was something disloyal about it. At the same time, she became aware that Mrs. DeSpain was speaking to Paul with a thinly veiled annoyance in her voice:

"But, Paul, surely you see that we *must* fight?" Lillian DeSpain was somewhat overweight and given to wearing dresses that were too young for her, and she was also outspoken at times. She had a round face with light blue eyes and spoke in pronounced tones, accenting her words with short motions of her hands. "What else can we do? The Yankees have put that dreadful embargo on agricultural products, so planters must do something or we'll all go to the poorhouse! And besides, after we gave the Yankees such a thrashing at Bull Run, why, I don't think we'll have to worry about our brave boys!"

"Exactly right, Mrs. DeSpain!" Austin nodded, his face beaming with excitement.

Marianne could not help herself. "Well then, you won't have to enlist, will you, Austin? If the war is really over, there's no need of it, is there?"

Paul grinned at his mother, allowing one eye to droop in a slight wink. She was a knowing woman, quick-witted and capable of a biting satire when she was so inclined. Austin flushed, then stammered, "Well. . .I mean, after all—there'll be *some* more fighting, Mother! And I want to get in on it before the Yankees turn tail and head back to Washington!" He saw the smile on Paul's lips, and it angered him. He had been cautioned by his mother not to meddle in his brother's business, but he was a man who could keep nothing back. "Are *you* going to join up, Paul?"

"No, I'm not."

Paul's quick reply struck all of them forcefully. Ever since Fort Sumter had been fired on and the war had become a certainty, a fever had swept the South. Though it was strong everywhere, it was especially virulent in Virginia. Young men—and some not so young—were now stirred by the sound of bugles. Every town began to raise a company. It was exciting, this going off to war! Much more thrilling than clerking in a store or following a mule! And it would soon be over, in maybe six months at the most. It'd be a shame to miss it, to have to stand back while the other young fellows took all the good-looking girls!

Bull Run had proved the war was going to be a short affair, at least to the South. An article in the *Richmond Examiner* had spoken ecstatically of "the sprightly running of the Yankees." Indeed, there was some truth in this, for the North had gone to war in a picnic spirit. The Union soldiers had marched toward Bull Run with flowers inserted in the barrels of their muskets, and the congressmen and their wives and families had packed picnic lunches and gone to see their men put the Rebels to flight.

Somehow, though, it hadn't gone that way. The Rebels had been fierce; the battle bloody and ugly—and the Union troops had panicked, fleeing back to Washington. The same newspapers that had been screaming "On to Richmond!" began calling for peace at any cost.

Abraham Lincoln had been one of the few to see the thing clearly and had said to his wife, "The fat's in the fire now—and we'll just have to tough it out!" He had put General McClellan to work, and the small general turned to the task with a will. The North would not be so easily routed again.

A few Southern military men, such as Stonewall Jackson and Robert E. Lee, had tried to sound the alarm, but the South was euphoric. It held victory balls and wrote songs about the brave soldiers, while McClellan forged the Army of the Potomac into a formidable fighting force. Watching all of this, General Stonewall Jackson said bitterly, "It would have been better if we'd lost at Bull Run, for the South is overconfident."

Now as Paul looked around those gathered at his family's table, he drew a deep breath. He had long ago, even while in England, decided that he would not fight for "the Cause." It was becoming quite evident that such a decision was going to make life painful indeed. Still, he knew no way to explain— even to his parents and family—why he could not join in the rush to the colors.

He noted that both of the older DeSpains were staring at him, and he knew they typified what the world might become: outspoken, certain of the rightness of their cause, and shocked by and intolerant of any who did not have the good sense to agree with them. Luci, he noted, was less shocked, but still there was disappointment in her face.

She'll do a little more shopping around for a husband now, Paul thought wryly. *And he'd better be wearing a uniform and be dedicated to killing Yankees!*

It was Marie who took over the conversation, changing the subject at once. "Mother, that was a delightful meal," she said with a dimpled smile. "But I do believe it is time we moved into the parlor. I know Paul has some wonderful tintypes to show us, and I've barely been able to contain my excitement during the meal! I can't wait to see what the women in Europe are wearing!" She rose, giving the others no choice but to follow her out of the dining room into the parlor, where they spent the rest of the evening looking at the tintypes Paul had brought from France. The tension lessened, and even Austin seemed to forget that Paul was not going to wear Confederate gray.

Later, when their guests were gone, Paul found himself alone with Marie. He went to her, hugged her with affection, and said, "You're a smart girl, sister mine." The edges of his lips pulled upward in a slight smile. "I think they'd have had me shot for cowardice if you hadn't led them off to look at pictures."

Marie reached up and brushed a lock of his hair back from where it had fallen over his brow. She was a merry girl, but her face was serious as she said, "Paul, are you sure—"

"About not grabbing up a gun and killing off the Yankees?"

"It's not like that," Marie said quietly. "You can't make fun of what's going on. Look at how many of our men are already in the army. Even cousin Clay. . .and he doesn't even believe in the Cause!"

A gloomy light darkened Paul's eyes, and he nodded. "I know, Marie. And I'm not making fun of Clay—or of anybody else. They feel it's what they've got to do. But I just don't see any sense in it."

Marie took his hand and held it. She and Paul had been very

close once. She studied his hand, admiring the long, tapering fingers, which were so strong and flexible. Thinking of how it had been years ago, she looked up at him, saying, "You know, Paul, when I was a little girl, I thought you were the greatest person in the whole world. You—you weren't like my friends' brothers. Most of them didn't have any time for kid sisters. But you always did, didn't you?"

Paul nodded. "Yes, I did. You were such a curious little thing—always underfoot. No matter if you got stepped on or hurt, you never cried. I thought that was fine! And you're just the same now." A sudden bitterness swept over him, and he lowered his eyes. "Those were good days, but we can't go back to them."

"No, but we can have something else," Marie urged at once. She had said little to Paul since his return, but now she burst out, "Oh, Paul! What's *wrong* with you? You used to have such joy—but now you seem so—so *jaded*! Can't you tell me what it is?"

Paul Bristol stood there looking down into his sister's face. He wanted to tell her how the years had passed so quickly and about the changes that had taken place inside of him. He tried, saying almost hoarsely, "Marie, I remember when we were kids, we always looked forward to something. Maybe nothing much. . .like a coon hunt—remember how we loved that?"

"I remember!"

"And when we grew up. . .or when I did, anyway, I looked

23

forward to great things. But there was one thing in particular that I always knew: I was going to be an artist! Not just any artist, either. A great one! Even when people doubted me...even when Father made it clear painting just wasn't a manly thing to do. . .even then, I knew I was going to be a great artist." A bitter laugh broke from his lips, and he shook his head almost fiercely. "Well, that's not going to happen. I'm *not* going to be a great artist, Marie."

"Maybe you will—"

"No, I found that much out, at least, while I was in Europe. Artists are pretty rare around here, but they're thick as fleas over in France and Italy and England." Paul's voice dropped to a whisper. "I. . .I gave it all I had—" He broke off, and his face contorted. "All I had! And it's not enough!"

Marie ached for him. She longed to put her arms around him, to comfort him and to tell him it would be all right. She did say quietly, "We all have our disappointments, Paul. Look at Mother. She wants a strong husband, but she'll probably never have one."

Paul stared at his sister, surprised. This was the first time she'd ever put into words what both of them knew. The silence ran on, and finally Paul said, "I know, but she's got this place. She's got you and Austin. It may not be all she hoped for—but it's *something*!"

They stood there, shocked at what had exploded from a seemingly simple conversation. Marie yearned for some sort of wisdom but could find no comfort to offer her brother. Finally she asked, "What will you do?"

"Do?" Paul summoned a smile, and there was a mocking light in his eyes as he said, "Why, I guess I'll make the best of things. Do something about the war. Don't know what, but a man can't live in the South unless he proves he's a real patriot. I've sponged off Father and Mother for thirty-one years. Seems only fair that a rich man like Clarence DeSpain should have to take over for the next thirty."

"Don't talk like that, Paul!"

But Paul Bristol's jaw was set in a hard line. "I'll throw all of my paints and brushes away—get that nonsense out of my head. Marry Luci, of course. Have to give her father *something* for his money, don't I?"

Finally he stopped, and his eyes narrowed. "You know, sister, I might just enlist after all. It'd be a lot easier to take a bullet in the brain than to put up with such an empty life for the next thirty years!"

He wheeled, and as he left the room, Marie shook her head, saying, "Oh, Paul—!" But he was gone, leaving her with a dark sense of foreboding. She saw nothing hopeful in the future for her older brother, and grief for him had a sharp tooth that cut like a razor as he left the room.

CHAPTER 2

COLD STEEL OR HOT LEAD?

The artistic side of Paul Bristol always responded to Gracefield, the home of the Rocklins. He pulled Queenie up sharply, holding the fiery mare in a firm grip, admiring the long sweeping drive lined with massive oaks that led to the house. In the spring, those oaks formed a leafy canopy. Now, however, they were bare—a ruined choir loft where few birds sang. But even the black, naked limbs lifted to the bleak sky had an austere beauty, looking symmetrical and somehow mournful.

"Come on, Queenie! Stop your fussing!"

The sleek black mare snorted and pawed the earth, then tried to unseat her rider with a lurching sideways motion. Bristol was taken unaware and, for one moment, was in danger of losing his seat—but he recovered quickly, a grin breaking across his face, and brought the mare up short. "You contrary female! Why don't you settle down and behave yourself?" But as he spurred the mare down the driveway, a thought flickered through his mind: *What about you, Mr. Bristol? You're the one who needs settling down, not Queenie!*

Shaking his shoulders as if to clear his mind of the unwelcome thought, Bristol pulled the mare down to a walk, turning his attention to the house that Noah Rocklin had built for his bride many years ago. A simple two-story house, Gracefield was given an impressive air by the white Corinthian columns across the front and on both sides. A balcony, set off by an ornate iron grill that was painted gleaming white, enclosed the house; tall, wide windows with blue shutters broke the gleaming white clapboard. The steeply pitched roof, which ran up to a center point, got a glance of approval from Bristol. He admired the three gables on each side, recalling how effective they were at giving light and air to the attic rooms. The high-rising chimneys, which were capped with curving covers of brick, released columns of white smoke that rose like incense on the morning air.

Bristol pulled Queenie up, came to the ground with an easy motion, and tossed the reins to a grinning black servant. "Highboy, you rascal! How are you?"

Highboy, a tall, strongly built man of thirty-eight, grinned and nodded. "Mist' Paul, you sho' been gone a long time!"

Bristol fished in his pocket, came out with a fistful of change. Handing it to Highboy, he said, "Happy birthday, Highboy."

"Why, thank you, suh!" Pocketing the money adroitly, Highboy lowered his voice and said, "Marse Paul...?"

"Yes? What is it?"

"Well, suh, when you marries up wif Miss Luci, me and Lutie would make some mighty nice house servants." Highboy's warm brown eyes smiled, and he said, "Iffen you could buy us and our chilluns, we sho' would do a good job, Marse Paul."

Bristol was flattered and amused. "Miss Luci and I aren't engaged, Highboy."

"Oh no, suh!" Highboy said instantly. "But when you *is* married up wif her, I wants you to think 'bout Lutie and me." Feeling the impact of Bristol's gaze, the black man hesitated, then said quietly, "We thinks a heap of our folks here, Marse Paul, but things ain't so easy these days."

Instantly Paul thought of what he had heard about Clay Rocklin's difficulty with his wife, Ellen, and asked, "Is Miss Ellen giving you problems, Highboy?"

But the servant was too well versed in the tenuous and fragile ties that bound slave and owner together to answer that question directly. He looked steadily at Bristol, saying only, "We be mighty happy if you buy us, Marse Paul. You knows how much we bof thinks of you."

"I'll think about it, Highboy," Bristol said with a nod. He was very fond of Highboy, for it was he who had taught Paul much of what he knew about horses. In fact, some of Bristol's best memories were tied in with the times he had spent at the stables with Highboy. "If I don't see Lutie, be sure to tell her I've missed her."

As Highboy led Queenie away, Bristol was troubled about what he had heard, for he admired his cousin Clay Rocklin.

As he went up the broad steps, he thought of Clay's tragic life, remembering how he'd lost out in his courtship of the woman he loved, Melanie Benton, who married Clay's cousin Gideon. On the rebound, Clay had married Melanie's cousin, Ellen, but their marriage had been stormy from the beginning.

It must have been a pretty bad marriage, Bristol reflected as he reached the top of the stairs. *Bad enough for Clay to abandon her and the children for years.*

The enormous white door opened, and Zander, the tall butler and manservant of Thomas Rocklin, greeted him. "Come in, Marse Paul. Lemme take yo' coat and gloves."

"You're looking well, Zander." Paul smiled, yielding the items. "How's Dorrie?"

"We both fine, suh." He hung the coat carefully on one of the brass hooks set in the wall of the spacious foyer. "Mistuh Thomas, he ain't well. I worried about him." The intelligent eyes of the butler studied Paul for a moment, and then a smile spread on the man's dark face. "My, my! You done been all over the world, Mistuh Paul! I bet yo' ma and pa glad to see you back. An' Miss Luci, too, I 'spec'?"

Paul Bristol returned the smile. "Well, it's nice to be back where everyone knows my business, Zander. Saves me a lot of thinking about what to do." He had almost forgotten how efficient and tightly knit was the system that existed in the South. The slaves knew practically everything about their owners, for the house servants picked up the details and passed them along to the field hands. Paul had been amused at how vitally interested the English were in the activities of the Royal Family, but now as he looked at Zander, he suddenly realized that nothing that the Rocklins or the Bristols or the Franklins did was hidden from the eyes of these black pieces of property.

Pieces of property. . . The thought drew Paul's attention to Zander, and he studied the handsome features of the coal-black face thoughtfully. Though he could think of those thousands of faceless slaves all over the South as "property," he had always had problems thinking of the slaves he himself knew in that fashion. Zander and Highboy and the other black men and women who had been part of his world—how could they be "property"?

His mare, Queenie, she was property. How could anyone believe that this tall man who had given a life of faithful service to Thomas and Susanna Rocklin was of no more consequence than a horse? Paul shrugged his thoughts off impatiently. This was the question that was tearing the United States apart, and he wasn't going to answer it by himself. Even so, a rebellious streak ran through him, for—no matter how Southern he might be—he refused to believe that Zander was the same in kind as a dumb beast.

"The family, dey expectin' you, Mistuh Paul," Zander prodded. "Dey havin' breakfus' in de fambly dinin' room."

"All right, Zander." He paused and took out some bills, peeled two of them off, and handed them to the butler. "Christmas gift, a little early." He smiled.

Zander stared at the bills, his eyes opening wide. "Why,

dat's a mighty fine gif', Mistuh Paul!"

"I've missed three or four Christmases. And that's some of that new Confederate money." Bristol smiled. "Better spend it while it's still good."

"Yas, *suh*!"

Bristol moved out of the foyer and, as he passed the broad stairway that divided the lower sections of the house, thought of how Gracefield seemed to have been constructed for the purpose of holding formal balls. Fully half of the space on the first floor was designated for that purpose. Even now the maids were decorating the enormous ballroom for the ball that was to take place that evening. Turning to his left, Paul moved down the wide hallway and heard the sound of voices. He followed the sound through a large doorway into the small dining room, where he found the Rocklins gathered around the table.

"Paul!" Susanna Rocklin was sitting beside her husband, Thomas. As Thomas looked up, an expression of genuine pleasure crossed Susanna's face. "You did come after all! Come and sit beside me." At the age of sixty, Susanna was a most attractive woman. She had long been a favorite aunt of Paul's. He went to her at once, bent over, and kissed her cheek, saying, "You'd better keep an eye on this woman at the ball, Uncle Thomas. Some handsome devil will run off with her!"

"Good! Let him pay her bills!" Thomas Rocklin smiled faintly at Susanna, but the smile faded quickly. "Sit down, boy, sit down!"

He looks very bad, Paul thought. *There's a shadow on him, just as Mother said.* But he hid his reaction and began to pile his plate high with the battered eggs and sausage that Susanna handed him. Looking across the table, he nodded to Ellen, saying, "How are you, Ellen?" He had met his cousin Clay's wife only once, when the family had gathered earlier in the month at Lindwood for a photo session. She had been anything but pleasant then.

"I'm not well," Ellen snapped waspishly.

Paul did his best to keep his voice soothing as he answered her. "I'm sorry to hear that." He hadn't spoken to Clay at any length since his return from Europe, and he asked, "Didn't Mother tell me that Clay came home on leave?"

Ellen's brown eyes seemed to harden, and her lips tightened. "He's on leave, but he's never here. You'd think a man would want to be home with his wife and family after being in the war, wouldn't you?" Her voice rose shrilly, and she gripped the arms of the chair until her knuckles turned white. "But no, he's got *better* things to do!" She glared around the room, challenging them all. When no one spoke, she turned her bitter eyes back on Paul. "If you want to see Clay, you'll have to go over to where he stays, with that white trash Yancy bunch!"

Paul felt the oppressive silence that had fallen on the room, and a quick glance at Ellen's children showed him the pained embarrassment that both of them felt. Rena, at fifteen, was a sensitive young girl, and she dropped her head at once, her cheeks red. David masked his feelings better, for at nearly twenty he was more able to do such things. Though his features were almost a copy of his brother Dent's, David was the most thoughtful and steadiest of Clay Rocklin's children. He said quietly, "My father is in a venture with Buford Yancy, Paul. He thinks it's unwise to plant cotton, so he and Buford are going to plant corn and feed pigs out."

Paul nodded. "I'd say that's smart. We can't eat cotton, and neither can the army. Are you going to do the same, Uncle Thomas?"

But Ellen was not interested in pigs and cotton. She glared at David, saying bitterly, "Clay's not over there to talk about growing corn, and you well know it, David! He's there chasing after Melora Yancy!"

"Oh, don't be silly, Ellen!" Susanna Rocklin held her head high, and temper flared in her fine eyes. She was furious that her daughter-in-law would say such a thing, especially in front of Rena! "If you can't speak more properly, I'll be glad to have your meals served in your room."

The suddenness of Susanna's attack brought a dead silence into the room. Ellen gasped and pushed her chair back from the table. "I see what I'm to be treated like!" she panted, her face contorted with anger. "You're all against me!"

David rose at once, took hold of Ellen's arm, and led her away from the table. "Come along, Mother. We'll finish our coffee in your room."

When the pair disappeared, Susanna looked across at Rena, saying, "Don't mind your mother, dear. She's upset."

"Yes, Grandma."

Paul saw the stricken expression on the girl's face. "I brought you a present, Rena," he said quickly. "I meant to give it to you for Christmas, but it didn't get here in time. You still like to draw and paint?"

"Oh yes!"

"Well, if you'll go find Highboy and have him take the package out of my saddlebags, you'll find something you'll like—lots of brushes and paint and pencils."

Rena forgot her humiliation, her eyes lighting up. "Oh, will you give me a lesson, Paul?"

"Sure I will!"

Rena ran out at once, and Thomas said heavily, "That was kind of you, Paul." Rocklin had been a handsome man in his youth, but sickness had drained him of much of his vitality. He had been, Paul sensed, as humiliated by Ellen's behavior as the rest of them but was too tired to do more than say, "You'll have to excuse Ellen, Paul. I sometimes wonder if the events in her life haven't disturbed her emotionally."

"Yes, sir, that can happen." Paul felt uneasy, for the history of Ellen Rocklin was not only tragic, but sordid. She had been an immoral woman for years—behavior that had only seemed to grow worse when Clay rejected her. Even now, Paul had noted that she had the look of a loose woman about her.

Paul shook his head slightly. He had heard how Clay had returned just in time to save Gracefield from falling into the hands of creditors, but he had also heard that Clay was in love with Melora Yancy. Everyone in the Rocklin and Bristol clans knew that Ellen Rocklin didn't want Clay—hated him, in fact, and made no secret of it—and yet she was filled with a blind, unreasonable jealousy over Melora Yancy. As a result, Ellen did all she could to make Clay's life miserable, which greatly affected the rest of the family, as well.

Thomas took a drink of his coffee, then asked suddenly, "So you're giving away your paints and brushes, are you? That mean you're through with that sort of thing?"

"I suppose so, Uncle Thomas." Paul shrugged. "I'm just not good enough at it." He saw the look on his uncle's face and smiled. "I suppose you're thinking you could have told me that ten years ago, aren't you?"

Thomas brushed his thin hand across his lips, attempting to hide the smile that came there, but gave it up. "Well, it's a rather unmanly sort of way to spend your life, as I told you once."

"Nonsense, Tom!" Susanna snapped impatiently. "I wish *one* of our young men would do something besides grow cotton and fight duels and hunt!"

"Susanna!" Thomas Rocklin gasped, shocked by this heresy. "What a thing to say! I only hope that now that Paul's got this art business out of his system, he'll settle down and—and—"

"And marry Luci DeSpain and live happily ever after? Is that it, Uncle Thomas?"

Thomas thought of his son Clay, trapped in a loveless marriage, fighting for a cause he didn't believe in. "There are worse things, nephew," he said gently, and the pain in his eyes made Paul look away.

"Well, sir," Paul said quietly, "if I can't paint, I guess I can do that. Provided, of course, that this war doesn't bring the whole thing down around our heads." He thought of the split in their own family. . .on the South were Clay and Dent and the Franklin men—Brad and Grant. . .and then he thought of Mason Rocklin, Thomas's younger brother, who was an officer in the Union army. *We'll all be killing each other soon*, he thought. Suddenly the hopelessness of it all descended on him, and he rose, saying, "Well, it's a good time for a ball. Did you two plan it so I could court Luci DeSpain?"

Susanna smiled at him. "No, but that's what balls are for."

"Just be careful about how you talk about the war, Paul," Thomas spoke up. "You're not joining the army, and that's bad enough at this time, but if you say the wrong thing, you'll have half the young fireballs in the room offering to trade shots with you!"

"I'll be careful, Uncle Thomas. The last thing I want is a duel!"

Luci DeSpain had never looked lovelier than she did that evening. She came into the room wearing a pale blue crinoline dress, which almost matched the color of her eyes, and which set off her figure in a spectacular fashion. The young men swarmed her at once.

Paul was standing with Clay Rocklin and Brad Franklin, who was married to Clay's only sister, Amy. Franklin was a major in the Richmond Grays, and he cut a fine figure as he stood there in his uniform. Clay was not wearing his uniform but looked very handsome in a brown wool suit.

"You'd better not let those young fellows have too much of a head start, Paul," Clay teased Bristol. Sipping the cider that Zander was passing around, his eyes went over the room. When Paul asked him about the army rather hesitantly, he shrugged and spoke mostly of his sons Dent and Lowell, and of Brad's son Grant.

"The Richmond Grays is one of the finest companies around," Clay said proudly, "and I like to think that's because of our sons' involvement." Brad Franklin smiled and nodded in agreement. Their sons were among the most respected soldiers in the Richmond Grays, a company filled mostly with young aristocrats from the area.

Just then Amy Franklin came up and laid her hand on her husband's arm. Amy, the only daughter of Thomas Rocklin, was not really a beautiful woman, but she made people think she was. She was tall and dark like her father, and her fine dark eyes were her best feature.

"Excuse me, gentlemen," she said, "but I need to steal the major away. I so seldom get the chance to dance with him, and I'm not letting this opportunity pass me by."

Clay and Paul laughed at the look on Franklin's face, but Brad quickly recovered. "If you'll excuse me, gentlemen," he said, "I never refuse the request of a beautiful woman." And with that he swept Amy out onto the dance floor.

Paul watched them for a few moments; then he and Clay began talking again about the war. Paul had read what the papers had to say, but he was more interested in Clay Rocklin's views. He had heard so much about the man and discovered that his cousin was very different from the man he remembered. The two of them had been well acquainted, of course, and Paul remembered Clay as a wild young man, given to fits of temper and moodiness. But the man who stood beside him was as solid an individual as Paul had ever met. Clay was one of the "Black Rocklins," with raven hair and dark eyes. He was a big man, six feet two, and heavier than Paul remembered. There was an air of authority about him, and Paul had heard his father say, "Clay enlisted as a private, but he'll be an officer before this war is over. He's got whatever it is that makes men obey and follow."

Paul sensed that power as the two of them stood there talking, and once again he felt a queer sort of kinship with his cousin. Perhaps, he thought, it was because both of them had been aliens, wandering far from their homes. Clay had left in disgrace, had even become a slave trader, but eventually left that sordid profession in disgust. Paul had been away from the South for years, trying to find some sort of meaning for his life. Now the two of them seemed to be thrown together, and Paul was curious about Clay's views on the war.

"Do you think the South will actually win this war, Clay?"

he asked. As Clay spoke, he discovered his cousin held little real hope for final victory in the South. He spoke of the huge armies of the North and how the smaller population of the South would soon be depleted. He soberly reflected on the might of Northern factories, one of which was owned by their uncle Stephen Rocklin.

"The only hope the South has," Clay concluded finally, "is that the North will get tired of the struggle. There's a peace party now in the North, and if we can hurt their armies badly enough and quickly enough, they might be able to bring enough pressure so that Lincoln will have to cave in."

Paul shook his head. "Well, I'd like to see the thing over at once. It's a bad war, and I think the South will suffer for it!"

They had not noticed that several young men had come to stand close, listening to their conversation. And it was one of these who took exception to Paul's remark. "If you like the North so much, why don't you go live there?" the man demanded roughly.

Paul blinked in surprise, becoming aware of the small group. He turned to find a tall, bulky man, who was dressed in a black suit, glaring at him. He had to think to come up with the fellow's name, but finally succeeded. Leighton Huger. . .and he was, Paul remembered, one of Luci's suitors.

Paul frowned. "Why, I didn't mean—"

"You've got a fine right to talk, Bristol!" Huger broke in, his eyes hot with anger. "Go on back and play with your little paintbrushes in France! I've heard those artists over there are womanish enough for a fellow like you!"

"Now, Leighton," Clay Rocklin said at once, "let's not have any trouble."

"Not with you, sir," Huger said at once. "We all know where you stand. You and your sons are a fine example to Virginia, but I have no patience with a coward who runs away and lets his native state fight to the death while he draws pretty little pictures!"

There was more to Huger's anger than the matter of politics, Paul understood at once. *He figures to show me up in front of Luci,* was the thought that came to him. But he was determined not to let that happen. "Look, Huger, I'm sorry if my remark offended you. I love the South and wouldn't do anything—"

"Love the South!" Leighton Huger's florid face glowed with anger. "You insult the Cause, then stand there and say you love our Confederacy?"

"I didn't say I loved the Confederacy," Paul snapped, aware that the quarrel had attracted the attention of many, most of whom had turned to stare. "I said I loved the South!" But he knew it was hopeless, and when Huger grew abusive, he shrugged. "This is no place for talk like this. Not for a gentleman."

That was when Huger lifted his hand and slapped Paul in the face. A gasp went around the room, and Paul saw that Luci's eyes were gleaming with some emotion that he'd never seen in them before. But he didn't have the time to figure out what she was thinking—he had to deal with the situation at hand. Huger had left him no choice, not unless he wanted to leave Virginia. The code of his people was strong, and any man of his class who refused to stand up to such an offensive act as Huger's was forever branded.

"Shall it be cold steel or hot lead, Mr. Huger?" he inquired.

"You must choose, sir!"

"Very well. My man will call on you."

Paul left the room at once, furious and disgusted. He turned when he heard his name called. "Paul, let me be your friend in this matter." Clay had come to stand in front of him, his face creased with concern.

"That's generous of you, Clay." Paul nodded. He shook his head sadly. "What a stupid thing! Two grown men trying to kill each other over a harmless remark! Well, make the arrangements, Clay. And pray that we both miss!"

The duel took place at dawn, just as the sun reddened the sky. One of Huger's friends, a heavy young man who was so nervous he could hardly speak, stood with Clay as the two men examined the weapons—a fine set of dueling pistols that had belonged to Noah Rocklin. Clay loaded them carefully, then offered the pair of them to Huger. He took one indifferently, then watched as Paul Bristol took the other. Paul noticed that Huger's face was pale and that he had nothing to say.

He's about as scared as I am, Paul thought suddenly. As Clay gave them the instructions and he moved into position, he realized that he *was* afraid. He had never faced death, and the idea that in a few seconds his brain might be suddenly shut down and his heart stilled brought fear. Not of the pain that a bullet might bring, but of what might follow. He was not a godly man, but he had seen true faith in his own family, in a fighting man like Clay Rocklin.

He recalled the words from Shakespeare's play *Hamlet*, that it was not the fear of death itself that caused alarm, but "in that sleep of death, what dreams may come?" As he held the pistol at the ready and began to pace off the distance while Clay counted clearly, he was sad that he might leave the good things of earth—and fearful of what might come after death.

He heard the final count, whirled, and lowered his piece until it pointed at Huger. He pulled the trigger at once and heard Huger's pistol go off at almost the same instant.

And nothing happened!

He stood there, swaying slightly, and saw that Huger was doing the same. A great relief swept over him, and then Clay said, "Now your honor has been satisfied, and there will be no more action. The two of you should shake hands."

And then it was over, the two parties leaving the little mound as if they were guilty of some crime. When they were out of hearing of the other party, Paul stopped and pulled out his handkerchief. He mopped his brow, then stared at Clay. "I might as well tell you, Clay, I was scared spitless!"

"Sensible." Clay nodded. Then he said, "Makes a fellow think about what his life means, doesn't it, Paul? Seems like we don't really think about it much until it looks like we're going to lose it."

They moved down the path, and when they mounted their horses, Paul remarked a little critically, "It didn't seem to bother you much that I might get killed."

"Didn't bother me at all," Clay said cheerfully. "Because I knew that was impossible."

Paul looked at him in surprise. "How could you know we'd both miss?"

"Because I loaded the pistols."

Paul pulled Queenie up sharply and stared at his cousin. A light dawned, and he exclaimed, "You did something to those pistols, Clay!"

"Sure I did," Clay agreed. "Didn't want to see either you or Huger get killed. Be a waste."

"What did you load the pistols with?"

"I had Dorrie bake me some little pieces of bread, nice and round—just the size of pistol balls. Matter of fact, they *looked* exactly like the balls that were in Grandfather's set." Humor twinkled in Clay's eyes, and he said, "Had to be real careful that I got the right ones when I loaded the pistols."

For a moment, anger rose in Paul, and his face turned hard. Then a strange thing happened. He thought of how solemn he and Huger had been. . .and how it must have looked to Clay. . . . His lips began to twitch, and he suddenly grinned. "You scoundrel!" he cried. "I ought to shoot you with a real bullet!"

And then he began to laugh, and Clay joined him. Soon they both were roaring, and finally he gasped, "I can't—help thinking, Clay—how pompous—we were! And then we shot each other—with *toast*!"

"Don't tell anyone, not ever, Paul!" Clay warned, merriment still dancing in his eyes. "It would humiliate Huger."

"Huger!" Paul demanded. "What about *me*?"

"You've got more sense," Clay remarked. "Let's go get some hot chocolate. This foolishness has frozen me to the marrow!"

CHAPTER 3

AN OFFER FROM THE PRESIDENT

*W*hen the Southern Confederacy chose Jefferson Davis as president, the choice polarized the newborn nation.

Half of the Southern people were disappointed, for the new chief magistrate was an austere man, not given to gestures designed to please the multitude (as were others who had sought the office). To this segment, Davis seemed a cold, unbending man who lacked warmth and charm.

But the other half of the population saw in Davis the noblest aristocrat whom the South had yet produced. As a senator from Mississippi, he had skillfully led that body in a masterful fashion; as a hero of the Mexican War, he had the military mind necessary to lead a nation at war.

To Varina Davis, his beautiful young wife, he was a man capable of gentleness and fervent love, but she was well aware that this side of her husband's nature was not easily seen by those who viewed him only as a soldier or a statesman. Mrs.

Davis was small, dark, and very beautiful, and she felt that she had been selected by destiny to rule over the newborn nation. She was a vibrant woman, vivacious and witty, who saw far more clearly than her husband that the Confederacy was not one in spirit. How could it be, when they were fighting for states' rights and, by definition, that meant that the various elements of the Confederacy were at least as loyal to their native states as to the Confederacy itself? Already this had become a problem, for the governor of South Carolina refused to surrender the huge supplies gathered by that state to troops from other areas!

Varina Davis had one friend with whom she shared almost everything—a confidante in whom she put complete trust. It was to this beloved friend, Mary Chesnut, that the president's wife turned for assurance one bright and sunny day in early December.

"Mary," Varina said as the two of them sat knitting socks for the soldiers, "did you read what the *Examiner* wrote about President Davis this week?"

Mary Boykin Chesnut was originally from South Carolina. However, she had become a leader of Richmond society since coming to live there. Though not a beautiful woman, she had the sort of attractive manners that drew admirers from both sexes. Her dark hair was parted in the center and drawn back to form a bun, and her eyes were dark and penetrating.

"It wasn't as bad as what the Charleston *Mercury* said," Mrs. Chesnut remarked.

"It was frightful!" Mrs. Davis jabbed at the yarn spitefully, then tossed the unfinished task aside. She had made many speeches urging the women of Richmond to do their best for their boys in gray, but so far as Mary Chesnut knew, the president's wife had finished only four pair of socks since the war had started. Varina got up and paced the floor nervously, speaking of the unfair criticism her husband had received from the press. She had some justification for her anger at the criticism, for many felt that the South should be attacking the Northern forces, not sitting around basking in the glory of one battle won.

Finally Mrs. Chesnut tactfully changed the subject. "Has your husband been getting along with General Johnston better?"

"Oh my, no!" Mrs. Davis said emphatically. "That gentleman is as touchy as a man without a skin!"

"Well, Johnston feels that he was passed over when the president chose other men above him."

"He must accept my husband's estimate of the situation. After all, the president knows more about military matters than any of the generals. He told me that he would rather have been chosen general of the army than president."

This was true, and it was a fact that was destined to cause grave problems for the Confederacy. Jefferson Davis *did* see himself as an expert in military matters, which hindered him from ever completely trusting his generals to do the wise thing. He developed a habit of voiding the plans of campaigns, which only irritated and shocked Generals Beauregard and Joseph E. Johnston. Unfortunately, neither general ever seemed to learn that Jefferson Davis had a large ego that demanded constant attention. Johnston especially was so proud himself that he never bothered to placate the president. He considered himself the best military mind in the South and spent much time expounding on this publicly.

Mrs. Chesnut spoke about the feud between General Johnston and the president, adding, "Your husband prefers Albert Sidney Johnston, I believe."

"Yes! He says that he has one *real* general, at least."

"I wonder how General Lee feels about this," Mrs. Chesnut mused. "He never says a negative word about anything."

"Oh, my husband thinks there's no man like General Lee! But he can't spare him for active duty. Lee is such a thoughtful man, isn't he? He takes a great load from my poor husband's shoulders, but because of that, we could on no account allow him to go into the field."

Mary longed to reply that it was a terrible waste to keep one of the ablest generals in Richmond cooped up just to soothe President Davis's nerves, but she was wise enough to say only, "I suppose Lee's chance will come."

Ten minutes later the door opened and President Davis entered. His rather haggard features lit up at the sight of his wife, and he went to her at once, touching her shoulder and murmuring a few words. Then he turned to say, "Well, Mary, how is the sock situation in the Southern Confederacy? I'll venture you knit them in your sleep!" The president was fond of Mary and had great confidence in her husband, Colonel

James Chesnut—so much so that he had sent him on the all-important mission of settling the surrender of Fort Sumter. The president sat down and, for half an hour, talked about books with Mrs. Chesnut, his face relaxing as he put aside the heavy weight of office.

Eventually, though, the conversation turned to the war, as all conversations ultimately did in Richmond. It was the president who brought up the subject of the power of the press. "That fellow Horace Greeley does us more harm than the Yankee Army," he snapped. "He's a fool, but people listen to him. The peace party might be fairly effective if the newspapers would stop hammering at the people to go to war!"

"Well, some of our own newspapers do us more harm than good," Mrs. Davis said. "I don't see why you put up with the lies they tell about you."

"I put up with it, my dear," Davis said with a trace of a smile, "because I'm the president and not the king. I hardly have the power to behead those who disagree with me."

"I wish you did!" Varina Davis snapped. "You could start with the editor of the *Mercury*. Getting rid of him would be something to be proud of!"

"Yes, I daresay you're right, but I can't call the man out and fight a duel with him." Davis had a lean, almost shrunken face, with deep-set eyes and a thin, ascetic mouth. He had been a most able senator, but he had not and never would master the art of choosing capable men and then letting them have full authority. He was in poor health, which may well have lain at the root of many of his poor decisions. But Davis was astute, and he well understood that hard, difficult days lay ahead for the South, despite the fact that since the first battle, both the North and the South had pulled back and experienced only minor engagements in Kentucky and Tennessee.

"You know," the president said, watching the two women thoughtfully. "I've been thinking of a plan to make our people more aware of the war." He laced his long fingers together, adding, "The Yankees are sending artists to the battles. They make sketches of the battle scenes, which the newspapers print. I think we must do something like that."

"Why, that's a splendid idea!" his wife exclaimed, her dark eyes glowing. "Think of how wonderful it would be if people could actually see pictures of our noble troops being led into battle!"

As the president and his wife spoke of the advantages of the use of drawing, Mary Chesnut was getting another idea. When the pair seemed to have agreed that something should be done, she said, "Mr. President, wouldn't it be possible to send someone to take actual pictures of the battles?"

Davis blinked in surprise, then exclaimed, "Why, I've seen some of those, Mary! Some fellow named Brady took one of those camera contraptions to Bull Run. Actually got daguerreotypes of the Washington crowd on their way back to Washington!" Davis rose at once and began pacing the floor, his face alight with excitement. "Yes, that would be just the thing! This fellow Brady. . .I met him once. He's got a studio in New

York. Does wonderful work! I think he's taken a daguerreotype of all the living presidents. I've seen the one he made of Old Hickory. Marvelous!"

Mrs. Chesnut was pleased that her suggestion had taken hold so quickly. When the president began to ask, "Now let's see, where do we find a man who could do such a thing? Most of those fellows are in New York and Washington—," she broke in quietly:

"I have a suggestion, Mr. President."

Jefferson Davis came to sit beside her, and Mrs. Chesnut said, "There is a young man named Paul Bristol. . ."

❧

"And this is Mr. Paul Bristol, the young man I was telling you about, Mr. President." Mary Chesnut smiled. "Mr. Bristol, President Jefferson Davis."

Bristol took the lean hand the president offered, saying, "It's a great pleasure, Mr. President."

"I'm happy to meet you, Mr. Bristol," Davis said with a smile. "I suppose you're wondering about being summoned here on such short notice?"

"Well. . ." Paul hesitated, not certain how to answer. When a messenger had brought the brief note from President Davis, he had been perplexed—and a little apprehensive. His father had been the same. "I wonder if he's heard about that affair you and Huger had?" Claude Bristol asked nervously when Paul showed him the note.

"Perhaps so," Paul had answered. "But I don't think it's about that. If Jefferson Davis summoned everyone who had doubts about the government, he wouldn't have time for anything else."

Paul had thought about the strangeness of it for two days, and when he'd finally entered the Chesnut home, where the note had instructed him to appear, he'd simply given up. *I guess he can't have me shot,* he thought as he entered the house and surrendered his hat and coat to the servant. *I can always tell him that Huger and I used toast instead of real bullets!*

When he met the president, he saw at once that he was not in trouble, for Davis was smiling warmly. "Here, sit down and let's let these ladies wait on us." Davis sat down on a horsehide chair, waving toward a matching chair that faced him. "Coffee, Mr. Bristol? Oh, I forgot, there isn't any. The Yankee blockade is getting to be a real inconvenience. But we do have some wine, don't we, Mrs. Chesnut?"

"Yes, we do, Mr. President." While Mrs. Chesnut moved to a large sideboard and poured two glasses of wine, the president spoke in an animated fashion about England, and Paul, at Davis's request, gave his opinion of the Confederacy's chances of recognition.

Finally Davis took the wine glass and proposed a toast: "To the South—may her future be as glorious as her past!" He drank his wine, then smiled as he saw that Paul had joined him. "You concur with that toast, I take it, Mr. Bristol?"

"Why, of course, Mr. President!"

Davis rarely smiled, but when he did, it changed his entire appearance, making him look much younger. Now as he considered Paul, his eyes had a definite glow of humor. "I'm happy that your little affair with Mr. Huger ended so pleasantly. Our country needs young men such as you." For one awful moment, Paul was afraid that Clay had betrayed him, that the president knew about the trick with the bullets and was about to laugh at him! But he relaxed when the president nodded and continued firmly, "You are both young men of courage. It would indeed have been a tragedy for the Cause to have lost either of you. But no more duels, I take it?"

"Oh no, sir!"

Davis sat there studying Paul carefully. He had heard this young man's history from Mrs. Chesnut and had planned out how to approach him. "Mr. Bristol, you are a little out of step with most young men of your age," he said finally. "I suppose that is because you are an artist and most men of art seem to be out of step with this world, at least to some extent. Of course, you've been in Europe, Mrs. Chesnut informs me, for the past few years, and that means you haven't been in the center of the storm as have the rest of us."

Bristol saw that a response was expected and said, "Why, that's about the way it is, Mr. President. I feel like an old man when I see these young fellows twenty years old getting ready for the war."

"Yes, I can imagine. You are—what? Thirty years old?"

"Thirty-one, sir."

"Well, that's young from *my* point of view," Davis said with a nod. "But war is a young man's affair." A sadness touched his deep-set eyes, and he said quietly, "We'll see boys and old men in uniform before it's over." He shrugged his shoulders, then seemed to grow more businesslike. "Mrs. Chesnut tells me you've had some experience with making pictures. . .with daguerreotypes? I'd like to hear about that, if you don't mind, Mr. Bristol."

Bewildered, but willing enough, Paul spoke of his days in Paris, where he'd studied under Louis-Jacques-Mandé Daguerre, inventor of the daguerreotype. "I was taking some drawing lessons from one of his students, and he invited me to go for a visit to Daguerre's studio. Well, it was quite a show, Mr. President!" Paul spoke excitedly, unaware that Mrs. Davis and Mrs. Chesnut had come to sit close by. "He's such a fine man! So unselfish—Monsieur Daguerre, I mean. Why, he *gave* the secret of his process to the world when it would have made him a millionaire!"

"I didn't know that," the president said, impressed. "And did you master the process?"

"Oh, I wouldn't say that," Paul protested. "I learned a great deal from my friend: how to take the pictures, how to develop them, how to use the equipment. . .that sort of thing." Paul had been thinking rapidly and came to a conclusion. "Are you thinking of some sort of unit to photograph the battles, Mr. President?"

Davis nodded. "That's exactly right, Mr. Bristol. What do you think of the idea?"

Paul said thoughtfully, "It could be a two-edged sword, Mr. President."

Davis was surprised. "How do you mean?"

"You were in the Mexican War. Imagine if there had been pictures of the American dead. What effect would that have had on the country's support of the war?"

Davis grew thoughtful. "I see that I haven't thought this thing out thoroughly. That *would* be a problem. Of course. . .if the people saw pictures of the Yankee dead only. . . ?"

For the next hour the president, Paul, and the two women spoke of the project. Finally Davis asked, "Mr. Bristol, would you be willing to undertake such a task?"

Paul had expected this but said honestly, "It would be a great challenge, sir, but I must tell you that there are men in the South who are much better qualified than I am."

His manner pleased Davis, who nodded briskly. "There will be room for them if this turns out well." He hesitated, then said, "This cannot be a military unit. I will have my secretary work out the details of financing the equipment, salary, and so forth. Are you free to begin at once?"

"Yes, sir."

"Fine!" The president rose, saying, "Oh, one more thing, Mr. Bristol. In view of the rather controversial nature of this thing, I would prefer that you send all of your plates to my office."

"I understand." Paul smiled. He knew that the selection of pictures for release would be made by the president and his wife, which didn't disturb him. After a few more moments, he had received his instructions from the president, and Mrs. Chesnut showed him to the door.

"I know this was your idea, Mrs. Chesnut," he said. "I'm sure you know it will make things a great deal easier on me."

Mary Boykin Chesnut did indeed know a great deal about Paul Bristol. Some of it came from Clay's daughter-in-law, Raimey, who was married to Dent. She was the daughter of one of the leading citizens of Richmond and so had known Mrs. Chesnut for some time. They often discussed each other's families.

"I hope this won't interfere with your other obligations, Mr. Bristol...such as Miss Luci DeSpain?" When Paul stared at her in amazement, Mrs. Chesnut laughed, saying, "I'm an incurable romantic, Mr. Bristol, like most of my sex. But I daresay you can manage an engagement *and* a new profession at the same time."

Paul said, "I'll bring my camera by and take your picture."

"Don't waste your time with old married women." Mrs. Chesnut smiled, then revealed her vanity by saying, "Well, bring your camera, Mr. Bristol, but give me notice so I can get my hair fixed!"

Later that same day, at suppertime, Paul gave his news to his family. "I'm going to work for the government," he announced when Marie kept after him about his interview with the president. He told the story, and their reactions were amusing. Marie began at once to clamor for a picture of herself.

His father and Austin were obviously relieved. *Now they have a good explanation for people who wonder why I'm not in uniform,* Paul thought. His mother, he saw, was not as happy over his new career as he'd expected.

"Does this mean you won't paint anymore?" she asked quietly.

"Just for my own pleasure—and yours," he said, putting his arm around her. "The camera does it better than I ever could."

"No, I don't think so. It's so—*mechanical*!"

"I don't think so...not altogether," Paul said pensively. "That fellow Brady, he's got a knack of getting the—the *quality* of a person in his photographs. I saw the photograph he made of Jenny Lind. Even if you didn't know who she was, you'd *like* the woman who smiles out at you. And that's what I'm going to do, Mother. I'm going to catch the essence of what I photograph."

"But—I thought President Davis wanted you to take pictures of battles, Paul!"

"Battles are men, and one picture of one man with his eyes dazed with the horror of war...that's more effective than a picture of a thousand men marching in neat little ranks."

Marianne Bristol reached up and put her hand on Paul's cheek. "I'm afraid President Davis may have trouble with you!"

Paul kissed her, then laughed. "Well, it's his turn! I've given you and Father trouble for the first half of my life; now let President Jefferson Davis have a taste of it!"

CHAPTER 4

THE ADVENTURE BEGINS

New York was colder than Virginia, as Paul quickly discovered. December snow was still hard-packed on Broadway. The footing was precarious, and as Bristol disembarked from his carriage, his feet slid out from under him. He sprawled on the ground, and the cabby peered at him, grinned, and said, "Careful, gov'ner! Street's a bit slippery!"

Paul heaved himself upright, cast a baleful look at the man, and said, "Thanks for the warning." He paid his fare, taking some consolation in withholding the extra dollar he'd planned to give the driver for bringing him from the railway station. The cabby, in turn, tossed Bristol's suitcase down deliberately so that it hit the frozen sidewalk with a loud thumping noise. "Yer welcome, gov'ner!" He nodded disdainfully and touched the horse with his whip.

Picking up the suitcase, Bristol turned to face the building and was disconcerted. He had told the cabby to take him to

Brady's Photographic Gallery, but he found himself standing in front of Thomson's Saloon. Then he lifted his gaze and saw that the three upper floors were labeled BRADY'S DAGUERREOTYPE GALLERY. In the glass window resided some specimens of Brady's fine daguerreotype work.

After climbing the stairs to the second floor, the first thing Paul saw was two large folded doors made of glazed glass etched with figures of flowers. Passing through them, he found himself in a reception room at least twenty-four feet wide and forty feet long. The floors were carpeted in a deep rose, and velvet drapes embroidered with gold threads hung to the floor. The ceiling was frescoed, and in the center was suspended a glittering glass chandelier from which prismatic drops sparkled like stars. Imported curtains with intricate needlework decorated the windows, and the way the deep rich wood of the furnishings imprisoned the glow of the chandelier immediately told Paul that the furniture was rosewood. A large reception desk was to his left, and the walls were covered with portraits of great men and women—American leaders, living and dead, who had sat for Brady and for history.

"Would it be possible to see Mr. Brady?" Paul inquired of a slender man wearing steel-rimmed glasses who was seated at the desk.

The man looked up from the ledger he was examining and smiled. "Why, I think so. It's uncommonly slack just now. He's up on the top floor. You can go up those stairs."

"Thank you."

Bristol climbed the stairs and found himself in a large room where sunlight poured through skylights covered with mesh. Several men were gathered around a stove—drinking coffee, it seemed—and one of them spotted Paul. Leaving the group, he came forward to ask, "May I help you, sir?"

"My name is Paul Bristol. I'm looking for Mr. Brady."

"I'm Mathew Brady."

Paul was surprised, for Brady was small and not at all impressive. He had sharp features, a pair of weak-looking eyes, and a mass of curly black hair. He wore a plain black suit covered with a white apron.

Paul had come to New York after discovering that the equipment and supplies he needed could only be purchased there. It had occurred to him on the train that he might get some sound advice on new techniques from some of the New York photographers, and he'd come to Brady's studio, not really expecting to get in to see the man. He knew Brady was very busy and tried at once to engage the smaller man's interest.

"I'm just back from France, Mr. Brady," he said quickly. "I was a pupil of Monsieur Daguerre."

He had chosen his introduction well. Brady's face lit up at once, and he said, "Ah! We must talk, Mr. Bristol. Yes, indeed. Come to my office."

For the next thirty minutes, Paul was rather hard put: Mathew Brady knew his trade and was vitally interested in any new developments in the world of photography. Though Paul did all he could to make his brief time under Daguerre seem much longer, he soon was out of his depth as Brady fired questions at him concerning techniques.

"Mr. Brady!" Bristol said at last, holding up his hands. "I must confess, I am not a professional photographer. Only a beginner."

Brady was disappointed. "Oh. I was hoping you might be interested in joining my staff." He saw that the young man was astonished at his proposal and laughed. "Well now, let me explain. I have a dream, Mr. Bristol. I want to photograph this war we're in. . . ." Paul listened as Brady went on to speak of how he'd gone right to the top, to General McClellan and President Lincoln. "Both have sat for me, of course, and they agreed that it would be a good idea. General McClellan even suggested that he would like photographs of enemy installations if such a thing were possible."

Bristol made a note of that in case it was something that President Davis might find interesting! But he said only, "A tremendous undertaking, Mr. Brady. But you're the obvious choice for the job. Of course, you'll be needing a great deal of extra help, covering the entire war."

"Yes, which is why I was hoping you'd come with us."

Paul took a deep breath, then said carefully, "Actually, Mr. Brady, I intend to photograph the coming battles myself, but from. . .a different point of view than the one you propose."

Brady's eyes narrowed. "Where did you say you were from, Mr. Bristol?"

"Virginia."

Brady's expression changed, and suddenly a smile touched

his lips. "I believe I understand." He studied the young man, and Paul thought, *He's going to turn me in for a spy!*

But Brady had no such intention. "Well, sir, as a Union man, I must be for my country, but as an artist, I must be happy that the conflict will be covered from, as you say, a 'different point of view.' What can I do for you?"

"I know you're very busy, but if you could have one of your assistants fill me in on new techniques and give me some advice about where to buy equipment and supplies—"

"Of course! The latter is easy enough. Go to Anthony's Supply House. It's on Broadway. Tell him I sent you and that I'd appreciate it if he gave you professional rates."

"Very kind of you, sir!"

Brady looked across the room. "James, come here, please." When a young man with a bushy crop of whiskers came to say, "Sir?" Brady nodded. "This is Mr. Bristol. James Tinney is my best assistant. James, take Mr. Bristol on a very thorough tour. Explain our new processes. Be very polite, for he's going to do some fine things with our battle scenes."

"Really, sir?"

"Yes, indeed!" Brady's eyes gleamed with humor. "He's going to photograph them from. . .a different point of view." Then Brady put out his hand, saying, "If you will, send me some of your plates, Mr. Bristol. I'd like to see things from your perspective!"

"If I am able, I'll certainly do that, sir. And thank you very much!"

James Tinney proved to be a gift from heaven to Paul Bristol.

He was one of those people who loved to *explain* things, and for the next three days he kept Bristol at his side. There was no aspect of the art that he failed to demonstrate or to permit his pupil to try. Thus Paul was able to do the actual work while Tinney looked on and gave instruction and encouragement. Of course, everything in Brady's was of superior quality. On one floor was the plate cleaning room and the electrotype room, and on another a spare operational room and chemical room.

Paul used what little spare time he had at Anthony's Supply House, laying in an enormous inventory of chemicals. In addition, he purchased a fine camera, complete with extra parts. *It's not like I can run down to the corner store and buy this material,* he consoled himself as the costs soared. *Whatever I use, I have to get right now!*

One week later—though Paul felt more as though he'd been in New York for months—he took the train for Richmond. He traveled in the boxcar to make sure no careless brakeman treated his precious cases roughly. As the train rattled and clicked along, Bristol smiled as he thought of his last visit to Anthony's Supply House. When the clerk had presented the bill, a terrible temptation came to Bristol. He longed to say, "Will it be all right if I pay for this in Confederate money?" But he stifled that urge and paid in gold, the money having been advanced by President Davis's secretary.

Now I've got something to work with, Paul thought as the train rushed toward the heart of the Confederacy. *All I need is time to learn, some good help—and lots of luck!*

CHAPTER 5

A MOST UNUSUAL ASSISTANT

Paul Bristol's first month back home was hectic. Richmond had been a relatively small town a year earlier, but when it was decided to move the capitol of the Confederacy from Montgomery to Richmond, the city had mushroomed! Paul sought in vain for a place, almost any sort of place, to store his equipment and chemicals. But there was no place, or so it seemed. Desperate, he went to the president's office, but Davis was off on one of his periodic trips to view military units and fortifications. The secretary could not suggest anything, and finally Paul hired a wagon and hauled his camera and supplies to Hartsworth, where he commandeered a part of a barn for his studio.

But that was just the beginning. He had to build a lightproof room and places to store his equipment. Not being much of a carpenter, he would have been in trouble if his father and brother had not come to his aid. Not that they did much of the actual *work*, of course, but they put the hands to work. If it had been planting time, neither of them would have thought of taking the men out of the fields, but in January there was little field work to do.

It took a few weeks, and when the last board was nailed in place, Claude said, "Well, I think we've done a fine job! I certainly hope President Davis appreciates it!"

"Well, I don't know about the president, Father, but *I* appreciate it!" Paul smiled warmly and clapped his father on the shoulder. "You and I and Austin, we make a pretty good team, don't we?"

Claude Bristol turned suddenly to stare at Paul. The pressure of his son's hand on his shoulder gave him a queer feeling. It was, he realized, the first time he could remember Paul touching him since he was a boy. He nodded slowly, then said, "Remember how we used to go fishing at the river when you were just a little boy?"

"Of course I remember."

"Those. . .those were fine days, weren't they, Paul?" There was a sudden loneliness in his father's eyes that caught Paul off guard. He had not been close to his father for years, and it came as a revelation to him to discover that somehow his father *needed* him. He kept his hand in place, and the two of them stood very still. "Yes, Father, they were good days. Very good days. I've never forgotten them."

Then the moment was broken as Austin came running up to ask Paul when the picture taking would start. "I'll need about fifty pictures to keep the girls happy," he said with a nod, at which both Paul and his father laughed and told him to go soak his head.

"What's next?" Claude asked, looking around at the cases of supplies neatly stacked on shelves.

"Learn how to take pictures."

"Why, I thought you already knew how to do that!"

"It'll be a little different, what I plan to do. It's one thing to get a picture in a studio, but I can't imagine how to handle it in a wagon with cannon fire exploding all around."

Claude was startled. "I—I guess this photography thing is going to be a little different from what I had thought. Anything I can do to help?"

"You've done a lot, Father." Paul smiled. "Next thing is a What-Is-It wagon."

"A *what* kind of wagon?"

"That's what the soldiers called Brady's wagon at Bull Run. It's got to be tight as a jug, part of it has to be lightproof, and it's got to have shelves specially built to hold supplies in place so they won't bounce around or leak."

"Have you ever *seen* one of these contraptions?" Claude demanded.

"No. . .but as soon as we build it, we'll both have seen one!"

"All right. What else?"

"Got to hire an assistant. This isn't going to be a one-man job. Takes one man to make the exposures, and another man to get the plates ready for the camera and develop the exposed plates."

"Better put an ad in the paper."

"Already did that. There won't be too many applicants, though. Not many unemployed daguerreoists running around Richmond, would you say, Father?"

"Not only would I not say it; I can't even *pronounce* it." Claude grinned. "But if any applicants show up, I'll send them on to you."

❧

The What-Is-It wagon was finished a week later, but not a single applicant had appeared. "What'll you do if you can't hire anyone?" Marie asked Paul at breakfast.

"Do without," he grunted. He was growing thin, and the twenty-hour days he'd been putting in were cutting his nerves raw. He'd simply ignored everyone's pleas that he slow down, for he felt that he had to get his technique perfected. Now he looked at his sister with bloodshot eyes and tried to smile. "I'm going to make a run. Don't open the door to the wagon, okay?"

When he left, Marie said, "Mother, he's not going to hold up. He's so tired he's almost falling down. Why don't you make him stop?"

Marianne smiled at her daughter. "The last time I 'made' Paul do something was when he was twelve years old." She looked thoughtfully out the window, catching sight of her son as he trudged toward the barn. "He was always this way—anything he did, he did it with all the strength he had."

The barn was warm, and Paul had mastered the technique of developing the plates in high temperatures. But he knew that battles would be fought in the snow, so he pulled the wagon outside and let the cold air bring the temperature down. Then he got back inside, closed the curtain, and began to work awkwardly. He was so tired that as he waited for the time to lapse between steps, he found himself dozing off. His fingers grew stiff and numb with cold, and he dropped a bottle of vile-smelling hypo, the fumes filling the room and making him feel sick.

Then, just when he was involved in the last step, the curtain behind him suddenly opened! Paul yelped, "What the devil—!" He came out of the dark area and stopped abruptly, blinded by the sun. Squinting, he saw a figure standing before him, but he could only wait until his eyes grew accustomed to the light to see who it was.

"Don't you know better than to open the curtain in a darkroom?" he yelled. "Who are you, anyway?"

"My name is Frankie Aimes. I came to apply for the job as assistant photographer."

Paul had opened his mouth to berate the intruder, but changed his mind at once. At last he might get some help!

"Well. . ." Bristol squinted hard but could see only a blurred shape. "Let's go inside where it's warm and talk about it." He walked toward the barn, asking, "Do you have any experience?"

"Yes, I do."

Paul opened the door and marched into the barn. "Shut the blasted door," he commanded. "It's cold out there this—," and then he halted and his jaw dropped.

"Why, you're a. . .a girl!"

"Yes. The ad didn't specify anything about gender."

Paul had heard of people being speechless but had always considered it to be a figure of speech. Now he knew it was not. He stood there, his mouth open, and simply could not think of a single thing to say. Anger suddenly built up in him—the result of too much work, too little sleep, and the dashing of his hope that he'd found some help.

"I can't use a female," he said in disgust. "Never thought about one asking for the job. Sorry you made the trip for nothing," he added grudgingly. "I'll see you get a ride back to town if you don't have a way."

"I want the job, Mr. Bristol. I can do the work, and it doesn't seem that the job has been filled yet."

Paul glared at the girl, trying to keep a hold on his temper. She was a strange-looking sight. For one thing, she was wearing men's clothing—which was shocking to him, to say the least. She wore a pair of loose-fitting black trousers, and a pair of boots peeped out from under the cuffs. A thick red-and-black wool coat covered her upper body, and a black felt hat with a broad brim came down over her brow. She might have passed for a young man, but her face—though stronger than most women's—was clearly feminine. Fair skin with a very faint line of freckles across a short nose complemented her green eyes,

69

which were large and wide set, and her thick eyelashes could only belong to a woman. Her hair, what showed from under the hat, seemed to be auburn and curly.

She endured his inspection silently, then held out her hands so suddenly that he blinked. "Feel the palms," she said quietly.

Paul took one of her hands and was startled when she squeezed his hand so hard that he flinched. "Those are calluses," she said. "I'm as strong as lots of men, Mr. Bristol." With that, she pulled her hand back abruptly and waited.

Paul had to smile at her methods. "I'm not looking for field hands, Miss. . . What's your name again? Frankie Aimes? Well, I'm impressed with your strength, but I need a little more than that in an assistant."

"I learned photography from Mr. Mathew Brady," the girl said suddenly, and when she saw the surprise in his face, her lips curved slightly in a smile. "I have a letter of introduction from Mr. Brady," she said, holding it out. As Paul took the letter and glanced over it, Frankie said, "I'll be glad to show you what I can do."

Paul snapped a question at her. "What is collodion?"

"Collodion is a mixture of bromide and iodide of potassium, or ammonia, or cadmium."

"What's it used for?"

"Copper plates are coated with it to make them ready to receive the image."

Paul shot out question after question and was highly surprised to discover that the blasted girl knew as much about photography as *he* did! Finally he shook his head. "Well, you *know* enough, Miss Aimes. But I still can't use you."

"I have another letter for you, Mr. Bristol."

Paul took the second letter, glanced at the signature, and gave the girl a startled glance. "You know my cousin—Gideon Rocklin?"

"Yes, sir. I worked for him, nursing his son Tyler when he was shot."

Paul read the brief letter, which simply stated that Frankie Aimes, who had been very helpful to the Rocklin family, wanted very much to have a career in photography. One sentence said, *"Miss Aimes is not involved in politics and takes no sides in this war. I believe you feel the same way, Paul, so if you could help her, I would appreciate it."*

Still, Bristol was not convinced. "It just wouldn't work," he said harshly, shoving the letter back at her. "Sorry you went to all the trouble for nothing."

Every young woman he knew would have turned and fled at such abrupt and ill-mannered treatment. It was what he expected, but the girl stood there patiently, saying, "You need an assistant who's able to help with the picture-taking process. And you'll be going to the battlefields, so you need someone who's able to rough it, to camp out and sleep on the ground and do without hot food and sleep."

"Well, that's right, but—"

"I don't mean to be proud, Mr. Bristol, but I reckon I can do those things better than. . ."

Paul stared at her, then finished her sentence. "Better than I can? Is that what you mean?"

The girl faltered slightly at his angry tone, then pulled her head up. "I didn't mean to say that, but I have lived outdoors all my life, and you haven't, have you, Mr. Bristol?" She glanced at Paul's hands, and he knew that she was reminding him that his own hands were smooth and uncalloused.

Once again he felt his anger rising; only this time it was because he suspected the girl was *right*. "Makes no difference," he snapped. "An unmarried man and an unmarried woman can't go all over the country in a wagon alone." A thought came to him, and he asked, "You're not married, are you?"

"No, I'm not."

Paul was irritated at the girl and asked angrily, "Don't you have a family? All I need is for your father to catch up with me and wave a shotgun in my face for ruining his daughter."

"You...don't have to worry about that, Mr. Bristol. Nobody's going to come looking for me."

For the first time, Paul caught a sense of fragility, of femininity, in the girl. She was so abrupt and strongly made that it was only a hint, but he dropped his abusive manner. "Miss Aimes, I just can't do it. It...it wouldn't look proper."

"You wouldn't harm me, would you, Mr. Bristol? And you wouldn't ask me to do anything that's wrong, would you?"

Her directness caught him off guard. He flushed but said, "No! Of course not!"

"Then you're afraid of what people would say about us?"

"Well, not exactly *afraid*." Paul was growing very uncomfortable, and he turned away abruptly. "Have some coffee," he said to take the strain from the moment. "I keep it on the stove all the time." He poured two cups and added, "It's the last of the real coffee."

She took the coffee in both her hands, and his gentler manner caused her to smile at him. His eyebrows rose, for it was a surprisingly attractive smile. She sipped the coffee, and he was pleased that she didn't rattle on. *At least she can endure silence, which is more than I can say about most women.* He looked at her again. *But what will people say? What will Luci say?*

Then he gave an angry snort. *What business is it of theirs? As long as the girl does her work?* Standing suddenly, he said, "Miss Aimes, I think this might be a disaster. I can't be responsible for you. I intend to take this wagon as close to battle lines as I can drive it, and a shell doesn't know the difference between an enemy soldier and a mere photographer. Either of us could be killed or maimed."

"I know that."

Paul was suddenly impressed with her coolness. "Well, I might mention that you'll be right in the middle of thousands of soldiers. Not all of them are gentlemen. They'll try to force themselves on you."

"I know. But they won't have any luck."

Bristol smiled. He admired courage above all things, and the girl seemed to have plenty of that! As for her being a woman, well, Bristol had been subjected to beautiful women for years.

And as he looked at Frankie Aimes in her rumpled clothing, he thought, *Well, the one thing I won't have to worry about is falling in love with her! She's too peculiar for my tastes.*

"All right, I'll give you a try," he said suddenly. "If you can do the work, you get the job."

Again the smile crossed her face, and this time it reached her green eyes. "I'll do my best to please you, Mr. Bristol."

And so it was that Frankie Aimes came to be Paul Bristol's assistant. But only after several minor wars, all over the same thing: *"Paul! You can't do it! Not a woman!"*

Two specific responses surprised him: His mother was dead set against it, while Luci laughed at the thing.

"Mother, don't you like the girl?" Paul asked when Marianne begged him to abandon the idea.

"Yes. I do like her," she said. Frankie had spent almost a week at Hartsworth, and Marianne had taken pains to get to know her. Now a slight frown crossed Marianne's face, and she said, "But you're not as strong as you think you are where women are concerned, my boy. You could fall in love with her—or worse, get involved with her *without* that. Then you'd either have to cast her off or marry her."

"Mother, please! Don't be…well, *ridiculous* is the word. She's how old? Seventeen or eighteen? And I'm thirty-one. Besides, have you taken a look at her? She's really not my type."

"Oh? And men are never attracted to women younger than they are?" Marianne loved this tall son of hers and said earnestly, "It will be a lonely, dangerous job. You two will be cut off from the world, you know. And when you're tired and weak and lonely, she'll be right there. Your 'type' or not, Paul, she is still a woman. And you are still a man. Don't do it!"

His mother's warning almost changed Paul's mind, but there was literally no one else to fill the position. *Besides,* Paul thought ruefully, *she's my mother. It's her job to worry about me!*

When he told Luci about his new assistant, she had stared at him, her lips growing tight. "A woman? You're going to take a woman with you?"

It was rough sledding, but when Paul took Luci to the barn and introduced her to Frankie Aimes, all was well. Frankie had just come out of the What-Is-It wagon and was dripping with sweat and smelling of chemicals. She was wearing the oldest clothing she had, which was tattered and baggy. She had on a pair of steel spectacles, which she wore for close work at times—and she looked terrible.

Luci greeted her; then when she and Paul were alone, she laughed at her fears. "What a ragamuffin! Paul, I was jealous, but I see how foolish I was. But can you stand her? She's such...such a mess!"

"She can develop plates." Paul smiled, relieved. "That's all she has to do. Looking good isn't a job requirement."

Luci leaned against him and whispered, "You asked me to marry you last month, Paul. Do you still want me?"

"Yes!" He kissed her, and when she stepped back, she gave him an arch smile. "There, think of *that* while you're out taking your old pictures!"

When Luci left, Paul went back and helped Frankie clean up.

"Are you going to marry her, Mr. Bristol?" she asked, watching him carefully.

"Yes, I am."

Frankie lifted her green eyes and gave him a sudden smile. "She's so beautiful. I hope you'll be very happy."

"Got to take lots of pictures first." Paul stood quietly, thinking of the days to come. "We'll leave tomorrow. There's a battle shaping up west of here. I think I'd like to have a try then to see what we can do."

"I'm ready," Frankie said, then thought again of Luci. "She sure is beautiful."

"Yes, she is, Frankie. Well, let's get loaded. We'll get away at first light."

"All right, Mr. Bristol."

PART TWO
The Vivandier—January 1861

CHAPTER 6

A WOMAN GROWN

The first morning of 1861 came on the heels of a heavy snow that almost buried Flint, Michigan. All night long, flakes as large as quarters swirled out of the sky, covering the towns and the countryside with a thick white blanket of pristine snow.

Frankie Aimes forced open the front door of her house, shoving back the deep mound of snow piled against its base and stepping outside. She blinked at the brilliance of the landscape before her. Shutting the door quickly, she stood for one moment, taking delight in the smooth, unbroken expanse of white, glittering with diamondlike flashes. The rawness of the brown earth was clothed with a flawless layer of white, which looked like a blanket of cotton. Even the trees with their bare, naked arms had become graceful, sweeping forms under the white mantle.

"Well. . .this won't get the milking done." The young woman spoke aloud—a habit she had formed while working alone in the fields or hunting in the woods. She stepped into the eighteen-inch blanket of snow, sank at once to her knees in the fluffy drift, then forged her way across the yard to the barn. The air was biting cold, which brought a rosy flush to her cheeks.

She loved the cold weather! As she opened the barn door, having to clear the snow away in front of one of the doors first, she thought of how she might go fishing later in the day. She had learned long ago how to cut a hole through the ice covering the nearby pond and drop in her line, complete with a bait custom-designed to tantalize the fish below. "Fresh-caught fish for dinner," she said with a smile. "Now that's something to look forward to."

All five of the cows looked up as she entered the barn, and soon she was engaged in milking. Leaning her cheek against a silky rump, she smiled at Blaze, the black-and-white cat who took station a few feet away. "Want some breakfast?" She sent a stream of the frothy milk at him, and he took it in greedily, not minding the spatters that covered his face and front. Frankie laughed as the cat at once began taking a bath. "If you don't start cleaning up on the rats out here, I'm going to trade you in for a terrier who'll do the job," she threatened. But Blaze, as cats are wont to do, ignored her totally and went on licking his fur.

When the milking was finished, Frankie fed the horses, pigs, and chickens, then took a pail of the warm milk back to the house.

"Morning, Tim," she said, greeting the young man who was

standing in front of the cookstove warming his hands. "Want some nice warm milk while I fix breakfast?"

"I guess so." Timothy Aimes, the only boy in the family, at the age of twenty was only three years older than Frankie. However, he looked much older. He was below medium height, and something in his face reflected that a childhood sickness had almost killed him. He had fragile features, with soft brown eyes and a vulnerable mouth. "You sit down and let me cook this morning," he said.

Frankie poured a glass of milk into a cup, then moved to hand it to her brother with a fond smile. "All right, you can spoil me. I'll read the paper out loud to you."

Tim grinned as he began collecting the eggs and bacon from the larder. "Good. We've only read it about ten times up until now." Still, he listened raptly as she read aloud from the editorial on the front page. His movements were slow, and his hands were thin and frail, not at all like the strong, rounded arms and firm hands of the girl who read the paper.

When he put the bowl of eggs and the platter of bacon on the table and poured the coffee into two mugs, he said, "Let's eat, Frankie. Those girls are going to sleep all day."

"They always do when Pa's away." She bowed her head while Tim asked the blessing, then plunged into her food with gusto, talking about the story in the paper. "Looks like there's going to be a war, doesn't it, Tim."

"I guess so." Tim picked at his food, shoving it around with a fork. "Looks as though 1861 is going to be a pretty bad year for this country. President Buchanan's never been a strong leader, and now he's a lame duck. He's so out of touch with things, it's pitiful, Frankie."

"What does that mean, Tim, all that about Fort Sumter?"

"When South Carolina seceded from the Union, she claimed all the Union forts in her territory. One of those was Fort Sumter. Now a Union officer, Major Anderson, has moved his troops into the fort. The hotheads in South Carolina consider that an act of aggression, so if the new president tries to send help or supplies to Anderson, they'll fire on them. And if that happens, the North will have to shoot back. . .and we'll be in the middle of a war."

Frankie and Tim sat at the table talking until the younger girls got up. This brother and sister were very close, partly because of their ages. Sarah and Jane, ages ten and twelve, were cut off from Frankie and Tim by a generation gap—but there was more than that to account for the elder siblings' closeness. There was their father, Silas Aimes. He had wanted a large family and longed for boys to help with the farm. His wife had been a happy woman, attractive with auburn hair and green eyes, and when their first child had been a son, Silas had been happy, assured that Tim would be the first boy of many to come.

But Silas's dream had died. The first deathblow came when Tim was stricken with some sort of fever that the doctors could neither name nor cure. Though the boy lived, he would never be strong. Sadly, he was an especially bright lad, which meant it didn't take long for him to realize he was a disappointment to his father. As a result, though his mother did her best to make up for his father's disdain, Tim gave up on his own hopes and dreams.

The final blow to Silas Aimes's dream came when Leah, his wife, presented him with three more children—all girls. With each new daughter, Silas grew more taciturn and bitter.

Like Tim, Frankie was quite bright and observant. She had grasped at a very early age the fact that her father was not happy with her. Confused and troubled, she labored to understand why this was. When she finally understood that it was because she was not a boy, it almost broke her heart. She was a loving, affectionate child, and as long as her mother had lived, there was some outlet. But Leah Aimes had died when Sarah was born, thus leaving a terrible void in the lives of both Frankie and Tim—another factor that drew them closer together.

As the years had passed, a pattern established itself, without being planned or discussed, in the Aimes household. Frankie, because she was hearty and strong, began to do the heavy work of the farm, while Tim had no choice but to take over the running of the household. By the time Frankie was fourteen, she could plow a furrow as straight as her father. By the time she was sixteen, she could put in a full day sawing wood or breaking new ground.

Of course, the reversal of roles between Tim and Frankie had some hidden costs. Tim grew more dependent and less decisive, and Frankie's assumption of a male's role went deeper than just doing a man's work. She entered puberty and passed through it without gaining any of the feminine graces or insights that come to girls with mothers. Frankie lived far out in the country, worked hard at all times, and passed from being a girl to being a woman—in form, but not in spirit.

Tim had seen some of this as he watched his sister grow, and now as he sat there watching her, he said suddenly, "Are you going to go to the dance over at Henderson in two weeks?"

Had he asked her if she were going to China, Frankie could not have been more surprised. "Why, I can't do that, Tim!"

"Why not? You need to have some fun once in a while." A bitterness touched his lips, and he added, "You sure don't get any around here!"

Frankie, for all that she was three years younger than her brother, had a strong maternal instinct. She got to her feet, went to the sink, set down her plate and cup, then came to stand beside him. Brushing his unkempt hair into place, she said, "I have lots of fun, Tim. This afternoon I'm going fishing on the pond."

Tim shook his head and turned to face her. "You never go to dances or do any of the things young girls do. How are you going to ever find a husband, Frankie? You've got to think ahead. Someday you've got to get married and have a home and children of your own."

Tim's words disturbed Frankie, and she threw up a defensive shield. Laughing lightly, she said, "I've got you, Tim. Taking care of one man is enough for me."

"It's not the same thing." Tim's thin face was haggard, and he shook his head. "*I'll* never do anything, but I want to see you have a good life, Frankie. Why, you. . .you've become little more than a hired hand around this place. Pa will work you to death if you don't get away." He cast a pleading glance at her. "Go to the dance."

Frankie spoke nervously. "I...don't have anything to wear... and I can't dance, anyway." Then her voice dropped to a whisper. "Besides, none of the young men want me, Tim."

It was the most revealing statement Frankie had ever made to her brother, and Tim wanted to put his arm around her and comfort her. Instead he said, "Frankie, you've got to make an effort. Buy a dress; learn to dance. You'd be pretty if you'd do what the other girls do. Men would notice you; I know they would."

But the years had ground something into Frankie that could not be changed by simply putting on a dress. Somewhere along the line she had packed away the dreams that most girls had and now was resigned to the fact that she always would be different. Instead of regretting her life, she took pride in her physical strength and her ability to keep up with most men. That was what fulfilled her and satisfied her, and it was enough. At least, that's what she told herself.

But no matter how content she believed she was, she could not stop the dull pain that would sometimes overwhelm her when she saw a young couple together, walking hand in hand, laughing into each other's eyes. Nor could she rid herself of the longings that would come to her unbidden—longings to be loved, cherished, and accepted as she was by one man who cared for her above all else—longings that could still keep her awake at night as tears coursed down her face and soaked into her hard pillow.

Only once had she let those longings come to the surface. With Davey Trapper. She had met him while out hunting several years ago. His surprise at finding a young girl in the woods had been evident—as had his amazement at her ability with a rifle, for she was a far better shot than he. When Davey asked her to help him learn to shoot better, she could not find a valid reason to refuse such a simple request. And so they spent the afternoon hunting together, and by the end of the day, Frankie suddenly found herself with a friend—something she had never before experienced. She was careful, however, never to mention Davey to her father. She had no doubt that he would not approve.

Frankie and Davey went hunting together often. They would meet in the woods, then go tramping through the wilderness, talking and growing ever closer. Before long, Frankie found herself thinking about Davey more and more. His quick smile and laughing eyes were a balm to her heart in all its weariness. And she grew more and more certain that here, at last, was a man who loved her despite the fact that her dress and manners were different from those of other girls.

Certain, that is, until that day in the woods when her fragile confidence came crashing down around her. The memory still brought a blush of humiliation to Frankie's cheeks whenever she let herself think of it—which she seldom did. She had worked up the courage to tell Davey her feelings, but instead of smiling and taking her hands—as she had imagined he would do—he had stared at her, dumbfounded.

And then he had started to laugh.

"Oh, Frankie, that's some joke!" he'd hooted. "You almost sound serious!" One look at her stricken face had put an abrupt end to his laughter, and his eyes had widened in shock. "You... you *are* serious," he'd said in disbelief. Desperately hurt, Frankie had only been able to stand there, fighting to keep the tears that clamored at her eyes from sliding down her cheeks. An uncomfortable silence had fallen over the two. Finally Davey tried to stammer out an apology, to explain that she was a "right capable hunter and a good pal," but that he'd never really looked at her as a woman.

They had finished their hunt—Frankie never shirked her responsibilities to her family, and they needed meat—but the usual talk and laughter were glaringly absent. . .and Frankie's one friendship died a painful death. That was the last day she ever saw Davey.

And it was the last time she had trusted her heart.

Now she smiled at her brother and said, "It's too late for me, Tim. I'll be fine the way I am."

Suddenly the girls bounded into the room, loudly demanding breakfast. They had been protected by both Frankie and Tim from the pressures that had made their lives so hard. Now, though, as Frankie looked at her young sisters, she thought, *They'll learn pretty soon that Pa has no use for girls. I wish they didn't have to!*

The cold weather was to hold on for the rest of the month, but ferment heated up the political climate in both the South and the North. It was Jefferson Davis, then a senator from Mississippi, who had broken the news to President Buchanan that Major Anderson was at Fort Sumter, adding, "And now, Mr. President, you are surrounded with blood and dishonor on all sides!"

Buchanan wanted only to keep clear of the problem of Fort Sumter, so he did nothing, waiting for Lincoln to assume the burden. On January 5, 1861, General Scott sent the *Star of the West*, a merchant vessel, with 250 troops to reinforce Major Anderson at Sumter. But on January 9 the ship was driven off by cannon fire from a South Carolina battery and had to make her way back home with the troops. All that Scott had accomplished was to pour oil on the fire. Robert Barnwell Rhett, the fire-eating editor of the Charleston *Mercury*, wrote that "powder had been burnt over the degrees of our state, and the firing on the *Star of the West* is the opening ball of the Revolution. South Carolina is honored to be the first thus to resist the Yankee tyranny. She has not hesitated to strike the first blow in the face of her insulter."

Frankie read about the struggles in the paper, how the Southern states began to coalesce, with Mississippi voting eighty-four to fifteen in favor of secession. Then on January 10, Florida joined Mississippi and South Carolina. A day later, Alabama left the Union. Other states were certain to follow.

Frankie had left to go hunting on that same morning,

hoping to bring back a deer. She rose at dawn, saddled her mare, and rode ten miles deep into the hills, where she bagged a fine six-pointer a little after noon. By the time she had loaded the buck and made her way home, the shadows were beginning to lengthen. As she rode up to the house, her father stepped outside and came to inspect the kill.

Silas Aimes was a big man, standing slightly over six feet and weighing over two hundred pounds. Years of hard work had hardened his muscles and turned his features heavy. He was only fifty, but his gray hair and lined face made him look several years older. He glanced at the deer, then at Frankie. "Get him with one shot?"

"Wasn't too hard." Frankie shrugged. "He came up twenty feet away." She started to lead the horse away from the house, saying, "I'll have time to dress him out before dark, Pa...," but then paused, for another man had stepped outside the house and walked to the edge of the porch.

Silas glanced toward the visitor, then stepped over to take the reins of Frankie's mare. "I'll do that. You go get cleaned up. Tim's got supper started." He hesitated, then added, "Mr. Buck's going to take supper with us."

"Howdy, Miss Frankie." Alvin Buck owned the farm that joined theirs—a large farm that covered over seven hundred acres, including the timber. He was forty-six years old, and a widower with five children. "You always bring back your deer, don't you, now?"

Frankie nodded. "Do my best, Mr. Buck. But I miss once

in a while." She moved up on the porch and entered the house, followed closely by her father's visitor. "Smells good, Tim," she said with a smile. "I'm starved." She went upstairs, washed in cold water, changed clothes, then ran a comb through her stubborn curls without looking in the mirror. When she went downstairs, she found the girls helping Tim with the meal.

"Sit down here and rest up, Frankie," Buck said, nodding toward the seat next to him. "I brought the latest papers along from town. Thought you might like to read up on how the war's going." Buck was a short man, no more than five feet nine inches tall, and very thick. His huge limbs filled his trousers and shirtsleeves so tightly that they looked like fat sausages. He had a round, florid face with small dark eyes and an incongruous rim of hair around his bulletlike head. He was wearing, Frankie noted, what seemed to be new clothes, but she seldom saw him dressed in anything but overalls, so she could not be sure.

She sat there growing drowsy before the open fire, listening as Alvin Buck read items from the paper and commented on them from time to time. Frankie answered in monosyllables and was almost asleep when her father came in. "Supper ready?" he asked.

"Soon as you wash up," Tim said. When this task was done, they sat down to eat, Silas at the head of the table, with Tim at the other end and Sarah and Jane at his right, which placed Frankie and Buck on his left. Most of the conversation concerned farming matters, with some speculation on what the South—and the new president—would do.

Frankie listened as the men talked, commenting mostly to Tim on how good the food was. Once she felt Alvin Buck's knee touch hers, but she moved at once, hardly noticing.

After supper Silas said, "Sarah, you and Jane do the dishes and clean up."

"Oh, I'll do that, Pa," Frankie said, but her father shook his head. "Let the younguns do it. They don't do enough work as it is."

The evening was a long one for Frankie. She sat with the others, taking little part in the talk, until, about eight o'clock, Tim set the girls at the table. "Time for your schooling," he said firmly.

"Pa, I'd better go put Julie in the barn. She might drop her calf tonight, and I don't want her to do it out in the cold," Frankie said.

"I'll just go along with you," Buck said quickly. "Got to be on my way home, but I'll help you with the cow."

Frankie looked up with surprise but said only, "Well, it's not much of a job, but come along if you want."

She put on her heavy coat, and the two of them left the house. "Won't snow again for a few days," Buck observed. "Hope we have an early spring. I'm going to break fifty acres of new ground. Need to get an early start."

A pale moon illuminated the barnyard, and Frankie had only to speak to the cow, who followed her into the barn. When she had put some feed in the box, she turned to go but found her way blocked by Buck's stocky form.

"Been a'wantin' to talk to you," he said. His small eyes were bright and eager in the lamplight, and there was something about his manner that made Frankie grow still and alert. "You know, it's been pretty hard on me and the kids, losing my wife like I did a couple of years ago," Buck went on. "Got so much land it takes all a man can do to get the crops in. 'Course, my boys are big enough to do a man's work, but Ellie's too young to keep house much, especially with the baby hardly out of diapers."

A brown rat that had sought the heat of the barn suddenly poked his head out from between two boards, and Frankie frowned. "Rats been bad this winter over here. You bothered much with 'em, Mr. Buck?"

"What? Oh, well, we keep a dog and some cats," Buck said. "Sure wish you'd call me by my first name, Frankie."

Again a slight warning went off inside the girl, and she shook her head. "Pa would thrash me if I did. He taught me to call people Mister and Missus."

"That was when you was a little girl, but you're a grown woman now, Frankie." Buck grinned suddenly and added, "And a right purty one, too!"

Frankie had never been good at handling compliments, mainly because she hadn't had much experience receiving them, so she tried to change the subject. "Well, guess I'd better get back—"

But Alvin moved closer and suddenly reached out and seized Frankie by the arm. "You're a woman, sure enough, and

90

I been thinking how wasted you are. Not married, I mean."

Panic shot through Frankie—and shame, for there was a light in Buck's small eyes that was not right. She tried to break away, but he was a powerful man, and he only laughed deep in his chest. "You ain't never had no doin's with men, have you, Frankie? Wal, that's good. . .but a man like me can teach you all you need to know!"

With that, Buck jerked Frankie into his arms and, before she could react, kissed her full on the lips. Revulsion swept over her and her skin crawled, for there was something feral about the man. With surprising force, she fought clear of his embrace.

"Don't you *ever* do that!" she spat out, furious. "I'll tell my pa!"

"Go right ahead," Buck said with a nod and a pleased expression on his face. "He won't be mad. I done talked to him. Only proper thing to do—see a gal's pa before asking her to marry."

"Marry!" Frankie shook her head and spun around to flee from the barn, dodging Buck as he reached for her again.

"You're just scared," he called after her. "Which is what a gal's supposed to be, but you'll like me better after we git hitched!"

Frankie ran to the house but could not bear to go inside and face her father, so she turned to the left and, for the next half hour, walked along a narrow trail that led to the nearby river. Anger and shame rose within her, and she wanted to scream and beat her fists against the bark of one of the huge oaks that lined the path.

When she got to the river, she walked along the bank, able to see by the moonlight, staring morosely at the glittering black water as it flowed silently along. The sibilant sound of the wave at the brink of the stream seemed to soothe her nerves, and finally she turned back to the house.

Pa won't let him come around, she thought, drawing a deep breath. *He wouldn't want to lose me.* But when she stepped inside the house, one look at her father's face told her she was wrong.

"Guess Alvin told you—about marrying up with you."

Her stomach tightened into a knot, and she struggled to keep her voice steady. "I—I can't do it, Pa!"

"I guess you will, girl." Silas's voice was hard, much the way it was when Frankie had heard him speaking to stubborn animals. She knew, all too well, that if the warning note in his voice was not enough, he would beat them.

"You've got to get married sometime, Frankie," her father said. "Only natural thing for a woman to do. And I won't have you runnin' off with some worthless boy. Now Alvin's a little older than you might like, but he's a steady man."

"Just let me stay here, Pa," Frankie pleaded. "I'll work lots harder!"

Her father continued as though she had not spoken. "And there's this we got to consider: Alvin's farm joins mine. If you marry him, one day his place will be yours. Then we'll have one of the biggest and best farms in this part of Michigan."

"I just. . .can't do it, Pa!"

Silas laid his eyes on her, and she saw with a sinking heart that there was no softness in them. "I say you will, and that's the end to it." He moved away from her, but when he got to the door leading to his bedroom, he turned to add, "Alvin's in a hurry. Guess it might as well be soon. You and him can go to town first of next week and see the justice of the peace."

Frankie had not cried in front of her father for years, but now tears ran unbidden down her cheeks as she stared at him dumbly. Some faint trace of compassion stirred inside Silas Aimes as he studied the girl, then said, "Well, it won't be so bad, Frankie. You'll get used to it."

Then he turned and left her alone—more alone than she'd ever been in her entire life.

CHAPTER 7

THE RUNAWAY

The third step from the bottom squeaked loudly, so Frankie carefully skipped it and was able to make the journey from the second floor silently. Her father was a heavy sleeper, but she took no chances. She wore wool trousers, as usual, and her heavy coat over a man's shirt. The suitcase she carried was old and patched, and it bulged at the seams, for she had stuffed into it all it would possibly hold.

The house was still, for at two in the morning everyone would be sound asleep. She herself had not slept at all, and now as she moved across the wooden floor, her nerves were frayed—so much so that when a voice spoke off to her left, she uttered a desperate cry despite herself.

"Frankie."

Whirling around, Frankie saw by the light of the single lamp that Tim was sitting in a chair by the fireplace. "Tim!" she gasped and looked upstairs suddenly, afraid that her father might have heard.

Tim got up and came to stand in front of her. "I knew you were going away."

"How did you know that?" Frankie whispered.

"Because I saw you couldn't do anything else. Every night I looked in the attic, because that's where the only suitcase we have is. It wasn't there last night, so I knew you'd be leaving."

Frankie shook her head, desperation in her eyes. "I have to go, Tim. I *have* to!"

"Sure, I know." Tim reached into his pocket and pulled something out, then held it toward the girl. "You'll need some money."

"Why, this is the money you're saving to buy that guitar you wanted, Tim!"

"I'll get it someday. Go on, take the money."

Frankie put the thin packet of bills into her pants pocket, then reached out and hugged her brother. She clung to him fiercely, and a great sadness came over her. "It'll be bad for you when I'm gone," she whispered. "You won't have anybody to talk to."

Tim stepped back, and in the yellow light, his thin face seemed even frailer than usual. "I'll miss you. Write to me, but send it to Johnson's Store. I'll pick it up there."

"And you'll write me back?"

"Sure I will. And when you get settled, I may come and visit with you." They both knew this would never happen, but the pretense made the leaving easier. "You have food for the trip?

95

You know it'll take you near all day to get to town, and you'll need something to eat on the way." She nodded, touched at his concern for her.

Tim took a deep breath, then said, "Pa will be after you, Frankie. First thing he'll do is check the trains out of Henderson."

"Oh! I hadn't thought of that!"

"The train leaves at one fifteen. On foot it will be tight. But if you take your mare, you can make it. Pa may find out you got on the train, but he won't go any further once he knows you're out of town."

"What about the horse?"

"Leave her at the blacksmith shop. Have you written a note to Pa?"

"N–no."

"Here, sit down and write it now. Tell him you're leaving and won't be back for a long time. And tell him about the mare."

Frankie wrote a brief note, saying only that she could not bear the thought of marrying someone she did not love and that she would make out on her own. She wrote about the mare, then tried to put in some sort of personal word—some fond farewell—to her father. But nothing came. Finally she signed it, then put it on the table. "Let him find it here, Tim. I don't want him to know you helped me. And try to make Sarah and Jane understand. . . . Tell them I love them!"

"Better get going," Tim said gently. He walked with her to the door, and she turned to kiss him. It was an awkward kiss, for they had not been outwardly demonstrative. "God will take care of you, Frankie," Tim said quietly. "And I want you to listen when He speaks to you."

Frankie knew that her brother was a man who believed deeply in God—he'd gotten that from their mother—and as she whispered her final good-bye, she wished with all her heart that she had some of that same faith.

Quickly she saddled the horse and tied the suitcase behind the saddle with some twine. She swung into the saddle and walked the mare out of the horse lot, holding her breath until she made the dogleg turn in the road. As the house was lost to view, her courage almost failed her. But then she thought of Alvin Buck and lifted her head. "Come on, girl, let's go!"

She kept the mare at a fast walk. She knew some of their neighbors would be starting to get up for their morning chores before too long and was grateful that she saw none of them. Not to speak to, at least. Old Mrs. Crane came out on the porch and waved at her, but Frankie merely returned the salute and moved on. The ride was long. She got to Henderson an hour before the train was due, so she had plenty of time to take the mare by the blacksmith shop, taking care to conceal the suitcase in some bushes beforehand.

The blacksmith boarded horses regularly and agreed to keep the mare until her father came for her. Frankie slipped the saddle off and rubbed the animal's velvet nose in a final gesture. She loved the mare and knew wherever she went she'd never again have one she loved so well. Then she turned and walked away, her back straight and her face stiff, not even turning when the horse whickered after her.

Retrieving her suitcase, she walked to the station, devoutly hoping that she'd encounter nobody she knew. She bought a ticket for Detroit—for no other reason than the fact that her mother had a sister who lived there, her aunt Clara. It had been years since her aunt had written. She might have moved, or even have died, but it was all that Frankie could think of to do.

The train came huffing in, blowing clouds of steam that frightened Frankie. Picking up her suitcase, she moved to the step. The conductor looked at her ticket and nodded. "Get aboard, folks," he called loudly as Frankie climbed the short steps. She turned to her left and entered the car—the first one she'd ever seen. It had two rows of wicker seats, each seat wide enough for two people, with an aisle between. There were no more than ten or twelve people seated, most of whom were reading or looking out the window. One passenger, a huge, black-bearded man, stared at Frankie curiously as she moved down the aisle and took her seat. Soon the train lurched backward, then forward. As it picked up speed, the whistle screamed, and the station seemed to move backward.

Frankie sat stiffly on the seat, watching the country flow by. Then the conductor stepped inside and came to her. "Ticket?" He took her ticket, punched it, and handed it back. He paused, his blue eyes curious. "Long ride to Detroit. We'll stop long enough at Haysville to eat. I'll make sure we don't go off and leave you if you want to buy something."

"Thank you," Frankie said gratefully, smiling. The conductor moved on, and she leaned back and relaxed. For the next hour she watched the scenery, then grew sleepy. The *click-clack* of the wheels and the heat from the coal stove at the front of the car combined to make her drowsy. Putting her head back, she closed her eyes and began to plan what she would do when she got to Detroit. She drifted off to sleep, awaking sometime later with that strange and bewildering sensation that sometimes comes upon awakening in a new place. For one sickening, frightening moment, she had no idea where she was. Her head jerked forward, and she restrained the cry that came to her lips as she remembered what she had done.

"Not far to Haysville," a man's voice said. Frankie jumped at the sound and turned to see that the big man who had watched her enter the car had stopped beside her seat. He smiled and added, "I'm hungry as a bear. Like to have something to eat?"

"No, I'm not hungry." Actually, she *was* hungry and had planned to get a sandwich, but something warned her that she must not go with this man.

"Aw, come on," he coaxed. "Nice little café there, and the train can't leave for an hour. Has to make connection with the northbound."

When Frankie shook her head, the man's eyes narrowed. He sat down suddenly in the seat across from her and studied her carefully. "Going to Detroit? So am I. Maybe we know the same people there."

Frankie ignored him, or tried to, but he was loud and kept

himself directly in front of her. Finally the conductor stuck his head in the car, crying out, "Haysville! One-hour stop. Café is half a block to your left!"

"C'mon, no sense sittin' on this train for an hour." The big man took Frankie's arm and pulled her to her feet.

At that moment a woman's voice said, "Let her go, trash!"

The big man swiveled his head to see a very small older woman, dressed in black, who had come to stand beside him. "What did you say?" he blustered.

"Are you deaf as well as ugly and stupid? I said to let that girl go."

"You'd better shut your trap, Grandma!" The big man kept his grip on Frankie's arm and leered at the woman. "Get on your broomstick and stay outta my business!"

All of the passengers were now watching the scene, and one of them stepped out of his seat. He was a tall man with a tanned face and a pair of level gray eyes. He walked down the aisle and asked in a rather gentle voice, "Can I help you ladies?"

The elderly woman nodded primly. "Yes, thank you, sir. Would you please take out that pistol I see beneath your coat and point it at this white trash?"

Frankie saw that the old woman was speaking the truth. There *was* a gun under the tall man's coat. The rough man suddenly released her arm and stood there staring at the gray-eyed stranger. He could not take his eyes off of the other man's gun and said hastily, "Now...wait a minute!"

"Shut your mouth," the tall man remarked almost pleasantly.

Then he turned to the two women, and a smile touched his thin lips. "You two ladies just go on now and have your lunch."

"Thank you, sir." The old woman nodded, pleased, the sunlight from the windows making her silver hair shine. She gave the man an open look, her bright black eyes warm and appreciative. "You're from the South, I believe?"

"Yes, ma'am. From the sovereign state of Alabama."

"Well, Alabama should be most proud of you. You have shown great honor today."

"I couldn't do any less, dear lady," the man replied with a warm smile. "As for you—," he said, then nodded at the big man, and the two of them moved off.

"Now let's get something to eat!" the woman said briskly, taking Frankie's hand, pausing only to look around at the staring passengers. Frankie suppressed a grin as the woman lifted her voice and remarked, "All right, the show's over!" at which all of the passengers left the car with alacrity. "Now," the woman said, a satisfied tone in her voice, "let's find that café."

Fifteen minutes later Frankie had discovered that Deborah Simms Satterfield was a widow, that she had been born and reared in Georgia, and that she had an insatiable curiosity. The first thing she asked when they had ordered their meal was: "Why in the world are you wearing that outlandish garb, my dear?"

Before they had returned to the car, Frankie felt that she had been drained dry. Mrs. Satterfield would have made an excellent detective, for she had gotten the entire story from her young charge, then had at once invited her to stay in her home for a few days. When Frankie had awkwardly protested, Mrs. Satterfield scoffed, "Nonsense! Of *course* you're going home with me! Why, you might be *arrested* if you walked the streets in that outfit!" Then she'd smiled and put a kinder note in her voice. "Mr. Satterfield had the poor judgment to die two years ago. I rattle around in that huge house he built for us. I have my two sisters with me, but it'll be good to have someone young to talk to." Then she nodded sharply, adding, "And I think I can find something a little more feminine than that—that—*thing* you're wearing!"

༄

During Frankie's visit with Mrs. Satterfield, she grew very fond of the old woman. She was not surprised when, after only three days, the widow asked her to live with her. But the restraint of the life in the Satterfield home was killing to the young girl, for the three widows lived in a Victorian past. The sisters, Violet and Maybelle, like Mrs. Satterfield, wore black, and all three were tied to the routine of their limited lives. There was little money and little color or excitement in the household. So Frankie gently explained that she must move on.

"I knew you'd say that." Mrs. Satterfield nodded. "This place would bore a mummy to death! If it weren't for Maybelle and Violet, I'd sell it and move back to Georgia!"

Frankie said, "That might not be a good place to be right now."

"Because of the war? Yes, you're right."

"Do you think the South can win?"

"Win? Of course they can't win!" She thumped the table with her tiny fist, her eyes bright. "Southerners have a wagonload of courage and a thimbleful of sense! And they're stubborn as mules! They'll die to the last man before they'll admit they're wrong!" And then she grew quiet, adding in a small voice, "But I wish I could go be with them when they make their stand!"

One day Frankie tried to please the three sisters by putting on a dress, one that had belonged to a daughter of Violet. But the next morning she was back to her trousers and man's shirt. "I just feel all trapped in a dress," she explained with a shrug. "I've worn men's clothes so long. Had to, what with working and hunting and riding."

"Well, you won't attract a man in that outfit," Mrs. Satterfield sniffed. "But then—you don't especially want to attract a man, do you, Frankie?"

"No."

The old woman considered her young friend but did not argue except to say, "Someday you will. Then nobody will have to beg you to put on a dress."

For a week Frankie read the ads in the papers, hoping to find some sort of work. But there was nothing for young women such as herself. She walked along the streets, thinking maybe she'd see a need she might fill, but all she knew was farming and caring for animals. It came to her that she might get on as a hired hand with a farmer, and that became her goal.

Then one morning, Mrs. Satterfield brought her a paper with an ad circled. "Why don't you look into this, Frankie?"

Taking the paper, Frankie read the following advertisement:

BOOK AGENTS WANTED IN NEW YORK STATE
L. P. Crown and Company, publishers, requires young agents to canvass for New Pictorial, Standard, Historical, and Religious Works. The company publishes a large number of most valuable books, which are very popular and of such a moral and religious influence that a good agent may safely engage in their circulation. The agents will confer a public BENEFIT and receive a FAIR COMPENSATION for their labor.

To persons of enterprise and tact this business offers an opportunity for profitable employment seldom to be met with. There is not a town in North America where a right, honest, and well-disposed person can fail selling from fifty to two hundred volumes, depending on the population.

Persons wishing to engage in the venture may apply at the Bradley Building, Room 222. References are required.

"Why, I'm not a salesman!" Frankie said at once.

"You're honest and well disposed, aren't you?" Mrs. Satterfield snapped. "That's what they want."

"But. . .they want *men!*"

"Doesn't say a word about gender. It says 'agent.' I should think that could be either a man or a woman."

Frankie read the ad again and began to grow interested. "I do love to read," she confessed. "But could I *sell* anything?"

Mrs. Satterfield smiled suddenly. "Child, you can! You just wear that rig you've got on. Why, I'll wager they've never seen anything like you in New York! They'll let you in the house just to find out what you are. And when you smile and blink those long lashes of yours, they'll buy books like they were made out of gold!"

It took a great deal of persuasion, but the next morning at nine o'clock, Frankie took a deep breath and pushed open the door to room 222 of the Bradley Building. It was a very small room that contained only one desk, four chairs, and one man.

The man was seated in front of a window, his back to the desk. He was smoking a cigar and staring out at the traffic in the street. When Frankie entered, he didn't even turn around. He just said, "Fill out the form on the desk."

Frankie looked down and saw a stack of forms and, without saying a word, sat down and filled one of them out. Her three references were Deborah, Violet, and Maybelle. Under "Business History" she wrote, "Farm work."

"I'm finished," she said. At the sound of her voice, the man swiveled around and stared at her. He was a small man, and his checked suit was crisp and businesslike. He must have been about sixty, though it was difficult to tell, for his face had a kind of ageless look to it. He had a pair of brown eyes, a small round mouth, and a large nose. "Oi! What's this?" he demanded. "I thought you was a person seeking a job."

Frankie took the advertisement out of her pocket and put it on the desk. "I am looking for a job. This one," she said, nodding.

A look of astonishment touched the man's face, and then he chuckled. "Well, now I've seen it all! You want to sell the books? No, no, no. Only young men can do that."

"Why?"

"'Why?'" Frankie's simple question caused his large eyebrows to fly up, giving him an expression of astonishment. "She asks me why?" He looked up as though carrying on a conversation with someone on the ceiling. "Because no young woman can do it, *that's* why."

"Did you ever let one try?"

The man's eyes widened for a moment; then a curious light came into them. "So what's your name, young woman?" He waited for it, then nodded. "I'm heppy to meet you, Miss Aimes. My name is Solomon Levy. And no, I didn't let no young ladies try to sell no books." He seemed interested in what he saw and asked, "Why do you want to sell my books?"

Frankie smiled, and her green eyes glinted with humor. "I want to confer a public benefit and receive a fair compensation for my labor, like it says right here," she concluded, tapping the advertisement.

Levy smiled and nodded. "You're a clever young lady. You got a husband? No? And a family, you've got? No? Ah, that's too bad." He put the cigar between his teeth and sucked on it industriously, sending billows of purple smoke toward the ceiling. He studied the patterns of the smoke, sitting still for so long that Frankie feared he had forgotten about her.

"All right," Levy said, bringing his round face to bear on her.

"All right...*what?*" Frankie asked, startled by his suddenness.

"All right, we see if you can sell my books."

"I get the job?"

"No, you get a chance to see if you can do the job," Levy corrected her. "I pay your expenses to New York. You sell the books, you get the job."

"Oh, thank you, Mr. Levy!"

"Don't thank me," he protested. "It's hard for young men, being an agent. Long hours and lots of walking."

Frankie laughed in delight. "Well, walking and long hours are my speciality. I. . .don't know too much about books, though."

"That I will teach you myself." He rummaged through some literature, then tossed some of it to her. "Go home and learn how to say all this. Practice looking sincere. Come back tomorrow and try to sell me a book."

Frankie went back to Mrs. Satterfield's house, and the old woman drilled her until nearly midnight. The next morning when Solomon Levy came to open his office, he found Frankie waiting. Smiling, he said, "You going to sell me a book?"

"Yes, sir, I sure am!" Frankie followed him inside, and when

107

he sat down, she held up a book. With a bright smile, she poured out the approach that had been written in one of the sales booklets. When she finished, she said, "Now you see, don't you, Mr. Levy, that you simply can't *afford* to do without these wonderful books! Why, a man in your position *owes* it to the community to keep up his education. . . ."

Levy took his cigar from his lips, rolled his eyes to the ceiling, and demanded, "Who is this girl? Why is she selling me these books?" Then he looked at Frankie and smiled, and it was a strangely gentle smile. "All right, I'll buy the books."

They talked about the details, how Frankie would be paid, and finally Levy grew serious. "My other agents are all young men, Miss Aimes. I must say this to you—there will be no wrongdoing."

Frankie divined his meaning at once. "Oh no, Mr. Levy!"

"I am very serious about this." Levy studied the young woman and asked, "Are you a Christian, Frankie?"

The question came as a total surprise. "N–no, I'm not."

"Well, *I* am!"

Frankie stared at him with such astonishment that Levy laughed deep in his chest. "Oh, I'm Jewish; anyone can see that! But I'm a Christian Jew." Levy spoke quietly for the next ten minutes, telling her how he'd been brought up as an orthodox Jew, then had drifted into an immoral life. He spoke of how he'd made a great deal of money, yet confessed that he'd had no joy at all. And then he told her how he'd met a man—a Christian— who, after several years, had won him to Jesus Christ.

"So I am now a Christian." Levy smiled, and Frankie could see the joy in his eyes. "My agents, however, are not. And they will try you, as young men try young women. And you must promise me now that you will be virtuous when that temptation comes."

"I'm a good girl, Mr. Levy," Frankie said quietly. "My brother is a good Christian, as was my mother before she died." Dropping her eyes, she whispered, "I hope someday I'll be a Christian, too."

Solomon Levy stared at the girl, compassion in his warm brown eyes. "You are not far from the kingdom, child," he said. "If you have troubles with the young men, or any problems at all, come to me. Will you do that?"

"Yes! I will!"

Sol Levy nodded. The night before, he had been troubled with grave reservations about hiring a young woman, but now he felt a real peace about it. *Maybe I'm put here especially for this one,* he thought. He smiled gently at Frankie. "We'll leave for New York in three days. Study the books—and ask the good Lord to be with you."

"I will, Mr. Levy."

As she left the office and stepped into the street, a strange feeling came over Frankie. *It's going to be all right!* was the thought that came, and somehow she felt that all that had just happened was somehow *right*.

For three days she worked hard, and when she left Deborah Satterfield's home, the widow hugged her and said, "Good-bye, Frankie. Don't forget to write. You can always come back here."

Frankie left Detroit that night in the company of Mr. Solomon Levy and five young men. She was well aware that she would have to prove herself to her employer—and she was equally aware that the young men would put her to the test—but she was happy. As the train pulled out of the station, its whistle screaming, Frankie said a little prayer: *God, I don't know where I'm going, but I guess You do. Don't let me disappoint Mr. Levy—and make whatever You want out of me!*

CHAPTER 8

THE VIVANDIER

S he's just a stuck-up hick, Jack! And I'm sick of hearing Old Man Levy always talking about how great she is."

The two nattily dressed young men were sitting in the lobby of the Crescent Hotel in Melton, a small town in upstate New York. The speaker, Harry Deal, glared upward toward where Sol Levy's room was located. "Those two been in their 'meeting' for over an hour." Suspicion gleamed in his pale blue eyes, and he swiveled his head to stare at his companion. "Say, Jack, I think there's something funny about them."

"The old man and Frankie?"

"That's who we're talking about, ain't it?" Harry lowered his voice and motioned upward toward the second floor. "You notice he don't never have *us* in his room for no long *private* meetings, don'cha?" A knowing grin appeared on his thick lips, which were almost hidden under a bushy mustache. "You ever wonder if them two—"

"Aw, come on, Harry!" Jack protested. "The old man's at least sixty years old! And he's been fair enough to us."

"Fair! He gives Frankie all the good territory! No wonder she's sold more books since we come to New York than any of the rest of us! Not only that, but he's always taking her out to eat and givin' her special *lessons*." Harry stared upward again and shook his head. "Something ain't right about that pair, Jack. And don't give me that sixty-year-old bit, neither! Lots of old guys go after the girlies!"

Jack Ferrago grinned suddenly at the angry face of his companion. "You know what, Harry? I think you're just sore because Frankie gave you the brush-off."

This seemed to enrage Harry, who snorted indignantly, "What you talking about? That freak give *Harry Deal* a brush-off? Not on your tintype, buster! Sure, I felt a little sorry for the kid when Levy dragged her into the firm," he added righteously. "The way she dressed in those baggy old clothes was pitiful! Nothing but a field hand, Jack, you remember! So I tried to help her out, kind of show her the ropes."

"You never went out of your way to help me or any of the rest of us guys when we first started, Harry," Jack jibed with a wicked grin. "And don't I remember that she dumped a plate of dumplings over your head once at supper? Said you were pinching her leg?"

"It was a blasted lie! I—I dropped my fork and was trying to pick it up when that crazy girl up and done that!"

"Oh sure! Any man could mistake Frankie's leg for a fork,"

Jack said with a grin. "You're just sore, Harry. The old man's square and so is the kid. She just outworks and outsells you; that's why you're always putting her down."

"You'll see, Jack," Harry growled. "I'm glad this tour is over. I'm telling the old man that I ain't working with that freak no more! It's her or me, and that's it."

"Well, it's been nice working with you, Harry," the other man said with a shrug. "Hope you get another job without too much trouble." He got to his feet and picked up his suitcase. "Come on, let's get something to eat before the train comes in."

Harry gave one last malevolent glare upward, then snatched up his own suitcase and stalked out of the lobby. His parting shot to Jack was: "Notice the old man and Frankie are staying over another night? Don't that mean something?"

"It means that Fredrickson and Johnson won't be in with their final sales until tonight, and that'll be too late for Mr. Levy and Frankie to catch a train. Now shut your face, Harry. I'm sick of your whining!"

Harry shot another angry look upward, but his gaze was off by about seventy feet. Levy's room was that far down the hall from the spot the young man had been glaring at. Inside the room, Sol was sitting at a large table that was covered with papers, humming to himself as he sorted through the pile. Periodically he would pick up a pen, dip it in an inkwell, then make an entry in a large black book that lay open. Finally he drew a line carefully and began to total the figures, totally immersed in the task.

Frankie looked up from the chair where she was reading the book Levy had given her. She started to say something but stopped and waited for him to finish. The clothes she wore now, though still men's garments, fit her better than the rough outfit she'd worn when applying for work. Her light brown wool trousers were held up by maroon suspenders, and her white cotton shirt was covered by a loose-fitting vest with small blue checks. Her hair was still clipped short but now was clean and lay in curly ringlets around her head. Her hands, though still hard from years of hard work, were clean, and her nails were neatly trimmed.

I'm sorry this job is over, she was thinking as she studied Levy's face. The past few months had been an exciting time. She remembered suddenly how she'd been petrified with fear the first time she'd stepped up to a strange house and knocked on the door to sell books. It had been in upstate New York, and she had almost turned and fled in a panic. Fortunately, the woman who answered the door was a cheerful lady of sixty, a well-to-do widow who was puzzled, then fascinated, by the young girl who stood before her in the strange garb. She'd invited Frankie in and, being a rather voluble individual, had done quite a bit of talking—enough to give Frankie time to regain her composure. Frankie smiled as she thought of how she'd run at once to find Sol Levy, crying out, "I did it! She bought the whole set, Mr. Levy!"

Frankie set her book down, then idly rose and moved to the window, which was open to let in fresh air. The day had been warm and humid, and the air in the room was almost stifling. Frankie perched on the windowsill and watched the activity in the street. The town was a small one, like all the others she'd been in since coming to New York. But she hadn't spent much time in the actual towns.

"Country people are easier to sell to," Sol had informed her at once. "And a country girl like you, why, they'll like you right off."

He had been right, Frankie had discovered. The men on the team had stuck to the towns, but Frankie had rented a horse and headed for the country lying in the hills. The people there were like those she knew, and in almost every case she could win a hearing by saying, "I've got a mare just like the one in your pasture back on the farm in Michigan." She knew farming and animals, and the rural people she met trusted her in a way they would not have trusted a man like Harry Deal.

She also discovered that she actually liked the work, and this showed in her clear green eyes, which glowed with excitement as she made her pitch. She always insisted on having the children present if possible, so that she could show them the beautiful pictures in the large Bible and the other books. She had realized at once that the children could sell more books than she ever would. Often all she did was turn the presentation over to them.

Still, she had never forced a sale, not even once. If the prospect didn't want the books, Frankie would be just as cheerful as if they had bought the entire stock. More than once she had said gently to a poor family who wanted to overbuy: "You might like to wait for a time on some of these. Why don't you just take this one and see how you like it?" Several times when a rough-handed mountain woman would handle a book, usually a Bible, with tender longing, then would hand it back with a regretful sigh, Frankie had said, "You keep the Bible, ma'am. Compliments of the publisher."

She had mentioned one of these instances to Sol, who had said, "You were right, Frankie; the publisher pays!" Frankie smiled at the recollection.

Suddenly Levy spoke up, causing Frankie to turn from where she stood. "Well now! It looks like the winner is you!"

"Winner?" she asked. "Winner of what, Mr. Levy?"

"Winner of the prize for most books sold on the New York tour," he answered with a broad grin. "Come and see." He held the book out, and Frankie leaned over his shoulder to see the columns he had totaled up. At the top of each list was the name of an agent. As she scanned the totals, Frankie took a sudden sharp breath.

"You beat them all! And in your first season!" Sol nodded, beaming at her. "I'll bet those boys will be sick when they hear about this!"

Frankie stood up, but the smile faded. "It—it really wasn't fair, Mr. Levy," she said. "The only reason I sold more than they did was because you helped me more. Besides, lots of people let me in just because I was different, you know?" She hesitated, then looked at him, her eyes wide. "Why don't you just divide the bonus up among all of us?"

Sol stared at Frankie, then nodded slowly. "If you say so. But I'll tell the other agents it was your idea." He closed the book and began to put the papers into some sort of order. As he worked, he spoke of the past few months, mostly about how well Frankie had done. Finally he stood up, saying, "Let's go eat. We got to stay over until Fredrickson and Johnson come with their final sales over in Bentonville."

"All right."

The two of them left the hotel and walked down the board walkway toward the small café where they'd eaten a few times. Several people glanced at them curiously, for they made a strange-looking pair: the short, rotund Jew dressed in a black suit with a round derby on his head and the tall, athletic, unusually dressed young woman. As they entered the café, they were greeted by the owner, Al Sharp, who said, "Got a table right here, folks. Roast beef is good tonight."

Frankie, who had never eaten in a café in her life before joining Levy's crew, had developed some taste. She had sampled some pretty bad food at different restaurants all over upper New York, and when their meal came, she waited until Sol asked a blessing, then sampled the roast beef critically. "This *is* good." She smiled. "Not like that shoe leather we had in Elmira."

Sol ate hungrily, for he was a man who loved to eat, but he could eat and talk and think at the same time, so he was aware that Frankie was not as cheerful as usual. He kept her entertained until after the dessert was out of the way; then as they sipped the strong black coffee the waitress brought, he said abruptly, "Tonight you're a little sad, Frankie. Wot's the trouble?"

"Oh. . .nothing!" Frankie looked up quickly, drawn out of her thoughts by the question.

"Now you think old Sol don't know about you? After all these months?" A fond smile touched his lips as he said, "You don't know I can read minds?"

"Oh, don't be silly!"

"Silly? I'll show you, den, what it is that's taken all your sparkle." He leaned forward and whispered, "Right now, Frankie, you are thinking: *I wonder what in the world I'll do with myself now that the job is over.*" He laughed aloud then, for the girl had blinked with astonishment, her jaw dropping. "Oi!" he cackled, pleased that he had surprised her. "Maybe I go into vaudeville."

Frankie smiled, confessing, "I guess I don't hide my feelings very well, do I? But it's been such a wonderful time that I. . .I hate to see it end!"

Levy leaned back and studied the girl. He had grown very fond of her. His own wife had died twenty years earlier, and they'd had no children. He'd lived alone, throwing himself into his work, but was actually a lonely man. Being a Jew had not helped, for there was much feeling against his race, even in America. He knew hundreds of people all over the country but was close to few of them. He stayed on the road constantly, for there was a restlessness in him that could not be content.

This young woman had been a challenge to him—and he loved challenges, this short, fat Jew! And he had won! For

Frankie had been a jewel that he had polished with loving care. The agents resented her, for he had spent much time with her, not only teaching her about the book business, but just talking. He had introduced her to a better sort of literature than she had known, and he had listened. He was a good listener, and though Frankie never said much about her past, he sensed the tragedy that had driven her alone into the world.

And he had been vaguely troubled these last weeks, as the end of the tour rushed to meet them. He had been selling books for years, but something in his profession didn't satisfy him. An idea had been slowly forming in his fertile mind, and now as he sat across from Frankie, he knew that he was going to take a bold step—one that might well be disastrous.

"I'm a little sad myself, Frankie," he said slowly.

"Why, what's the matter, Mr. Levy?" Frankie was surprised, for in the time she'd known him, the man was always cheerful. But she saw now that he was indeed not smiling in his usual fashion, and there was a sober light in his brown eyes.

"It's this terrible war," Levy answered, shaking his head. "All the killing that's going to come. . .I feel so bad about it!" He held his hands palms upward in a helpless gesture. "But what's an old Jew like me to do? I can't fight like the young men."

"Maybe it won't come, this war."

"Child, it's here already! The North is raising an enormous army, and the South is armed to the teeth! Any day now the Union army is going to move south, and when they do, there'll be war." He looked at her, then asked, "Do you have any relatives—

brothers, perhaps—who are of age to fight?"

"Only one brother, but he's almost an invalid."

"Ah, well, that may be best." Sol Levy sat there quietly, then said, "I have asked God to tell me what to do, and I think He has told me something." He smiled abruptly, seeing Frankie's shocked expression. "Oh, I'm not going crazy or hearing voices, child! But I've learned to wait on God since I've become a Christian. And now I have waited, and I know what I must do. And it concerns you, Frankie."

"Me!"

"Yes. I think God has put me in your way, to be a father to you for a time, to watch over you."

Frankie felt a warm glow as she heard this, and she whispered, "You. . .you've been the only real father I've ever known!"

"Ah. . ." Sol was pleased, and his eyes glowed as he regarded Frankie. "That makes things much easier! Now here is what I must do. I must become a sutler."

"A sutler?" Frankie asked. "What's that?"

"A person who sells supplies to the soldiers: tobacco and paper and even whiskey. But in this case, I will take many books—not to sell, but to give to the soldiers." Sol grew excited as he spoke, making gestures with his fat hands. "Books and tracts for the soldiers—all Christian books, telling about the Savior, Jesus Christ! I am not a preacher, Frankie, but I can pass along the Good News about my Lord in this way. Men who face death," he said more soberly, "they will be hungry for the gospel, and I will see that they have it!"

"But what does that have to do with me?" Frankie asked.

"Why, you will help me, child!" Sol said, his eyebrows going up. "It is why God sent you to me, I think. We will take the books and the tracts to the camps and to the hospitals."

"But, Mr. Levy. . .I'm not a Christian!"

The old man looked at her, wisdom in his warm brown eyes. "Ah, that doesn't matter—as far as the men are concerned. It's the message, not the messenger, that saves people. And I believe that your time is coming, child."

"My time?"

"Yes. Every man and every woman—every person on this planet, in fact—has a time. A time to choose for God, for His Son, Jesus. Jesus said one time, 'No man can come to me, except the Father which hath sent me draw him.' Oi! God knows how to draw a man!" Levy smiled. "If He can draw an old Jew like me, He can do the same thing for a young girl like Frankie Aimes!"

Frankie sat very still, and the old man put his hand on hers. "Will you do it, child?"

Frankie felt again the same inexplicable sense of assurance that had come to her months ago, a peace that she had never been able to explain. It washed over her now, and she smiled at the man who was watching her so anxiously.

"Yes, Mr. Levy, I'll help you."

"Good—I am so happy!" Sol beamed and patted her hand; then a thought came to him. "I have been doing a little study on this, and I find out that I will be a sutler, but you will be called something else. There is a French word used for women who sell supplies to the soldiers. I think it sounds nice."

Frankie asked curiously, "What will I be, Mr. Levy?"

"You will be a *vivandier!*"

Frankie pronounced it carefully, imitating Levy as closely as possible: "*Vee-vahn-dee-ay*? Like that?" She repeated it again, then laughed, her eyes bright and her lips curving in a delighted way. "I'm a vivandier! Oh, Sol!" she cried, using his first name for the first time. "I'm so glad we're not going to be separated!"

The old Jew nodded and whispered, "I, too, am most glad, child!"

❧

"Well, Frankie, so what do you think of Washington?"

Frankie and Sol had entered the city and driven along the main thoroughfare, which was four miles long and 160 feet wide. To get there, however, Sol had driven through Center Market—where brothels and gambling houses operated openly—and through Swampoodle, Negro Hill, and other alley domains. They had traveled along the Old City Canal, a fetid bayou filled with floating dead cats—and all kinds of putridity—and reeking with pestilential odors. Cattle, sheep, swine, and geese ran everywhere.

Now as they were leaving the city, Frankie made a face at her companion. "It stinks!"

"Yes, it does," Sol agreed. "I hope the camp will smell better." He looked back under the canvas at the heavily loaded wagon and remarked, "We'll have to get permission to set up our shop.

I hope the bribe I'll have to pay won't be too steep."

"Bribe? What's that?" Frankie asked.

"All business in government has to be paid for." Sol shrugged. "Every sutler will have to buy a license, but that's only the beginning. There'll be other palms to grease before we can do business."

"Why, that's *terrible!*"

"It's the way of the world, Frankie. If we want to help the soldiers, we'll just have to pay for the privilege."

By the time they reached the camp, a large area filled with parade grounds and acres of tents, the sun was high in the sky. The corporal who stopped them and asked for a pass listened as Sol explained their mission, then said, "You'll have to go to regimental headquarters." He gave them instructions, adding, "Ask for either Colonel Bradford or Major Rocklin."

As they drove along, they were overwhelmed at the tremendous activity in the camp. Sergeants were yelling at their squads; horses raced by with couriers; and caissons rumbled along, forcing Sol off the narrow road. Somehow they found their way to a large tent with a narrow pennant waving over it. "I guess that's it," Sol said. "Come along and we'll see about a permit."

Frankie scrambled down, and the two of them approached the large round tent. "We'd like to see the commanding officer, Corporal," Sol said to the soldier standing there.

The man peered at the two suspiciously, then shrugged. "I'll have to ask." He disappeared into the tent but came back almost at once. "Major Rocklin says you can come in."

"Thank you." Sol fished in his pocket and came out with a slender pamphlet and handed it to the soldier. "For you."

"Why—thanks!"

The pair entered the tent and were met by a tall officer with dark hair and eyes. "I'm Major Gideon Rocklin," he said. "What can I do for you?"

"We need a sutler's permit, Major," Sol said.

"I can arrange that." He moved to sit down at a portable desk, selected a single sheet of paper, and dipped a pen into an inkwell. "Your name?"

"I'm Solomon Levy, and this is Miss Frankie Aimes."

Rocklin paused and looked up with interest. His eyes rested on Frankie, and he hesitated before saying, "Miss Aimes is your. . . ?"

"She's my employee, Major." Levy added quickly that he was actually a bookseller and wanted to use his office as a sutler to distribute Christian books. He saw at once that this pleased the tall soldier. Levy continued, "I am a Jew, as you see, but a Christian, as well. And Miss Aimes has been my best agent for some time."

"I'm glad to have you in the regiment, sir. And you, too, Miss Aimes," Rocklin said. He filled out the form, then stood, handed it to Levy, and remarked, "The sutler situation is terrible. Some of them sell shoddy goods at outrageous prices to the men. I'm happy to finally meet one who'll be different."

"You are a Christian, Major?"

"Yes, indeed!" Gideon smiled. "And you'll find others." He turned his gaze on Frankie and asked, "You do know that soldiers are a rough lot, Miss Aimes?"

Frankie understood at once what the major implied. "Yes, sir. But Mr. Levy will watch out for me."

"Fine! Fine!" Then Rocklin frowned, saying, "You can set up your shop. I'll have someone take you to a proper place, but I'm afraid you won't have much time."

Sol gave the officer a keen stare. "I take it the army is moving out soon."

The major nodded soberly. "Very soon, Mr. Levy. I can't say when, of course, but don't count on more than a few days."

"We'll do what we can until then. And thank you, Major."

He walked outside with them and spoke to the soldier standing guard. "Corporal, take these two over to the west side of the camp, close to the big trees." He turned to say, "There's an evangelistic meeting tonight. You might like to attend it. A fine preacher, Rev. Steele, will be doing the preaching."

"Thank you. We'll be there, sir."

"He's my brother-in-law, so I can recommend him. Glad to have you in the regiment—both of you."

"A fine man!" Sol exclaimed as the two climbed into the wagon. "And a Christian! We'll have no problems now, will we, Frankie?"

"What about when the army leaves?" Frankie asked.

"Why, the sutlers will go along, of course. We'll stay well behind the troops, but every night we'll be able to provide supplies and tracts to the soldiers."

They set up shop under a large pin oak and at once began doing a tremendous business. Most of the soldiers wanted whiskey, which Levy had refused to stock, but there was a brisk sale of everything in the wagon, especially tobacco and paper for writing letters. Their "store" was composed of boards placed over barrels, and both of them were busy until a bugle drew the men back to their tents.

Frankie cooked a supper of ham and beans over a small fire, and the two friends ate hungrily. As they talked over the meal, Sol said, "I hope there are no Confederate spies around here." He took a swallow of the scalding coffee, adding, "Every private I talked to knows where the army's heading."

"I know." Frankie nodded. "Some place called Centerville. They all say the Confederates are waiting there. Where is that place, Sol?"

"Close to a little town. . .what was the name of it?" He tried to remember but couldn't, so he got up and came back to the fire with a map. Spreading it out, he squinted. "I can't see with these old eyes, Frankie. You look; it's close to a little river or creek. . .but I forget the name of that, too."

"Here it is—Centerville," Frankie announced, putting her finger on the map.

"So? And what about that little town and the river?"

Frankie peered closer, then looked up at Sol.

"Manassas. The town is Manassas. And the creek is called Bull Run."

CHAPTER 9

A SPECIAL PATIENT

The blue-clad Union soldiers who went out to fight at Bull Run with flowers stuck in the barrels of their muskets returned to Washington bleeding and in total disarray. The city was in a panic, expecting to be invaded by the victorious Confederate Army at any moment, and President Lincoln and his cabinet made plans to evacuate and find shelter in another site.

But the Confederates were almost as stunned by their victory as the Federals were by their defeat, and they were unable to take advantage of the Union rout. Stonewall Jackson begged to be allowed to press on to Washington but was ordered not to move. The victors returned to Richmond to receive a triumphant reception, while the shattered Union forces brought their dead and wounded by the thousands to the hospitals hastily set up in the capital.

Solomon Levy and Frankie Aimes narrowly escaped being trampled by the mob that stampeded back to Washington.

They had been moving along in a leisurely fashion a few miles behind the last of the Union troops, and when the rush for safety began—led by the congressmen and their families who'd gone out in a picnic mood to view the battle—Levy had taken one look at the wild-eyed drivers beating their horses on to greater speed and said abruptly, "Something's wrong, Frankie!"

His fears were confirmed when a stream of soldiers came stumbling along, some of them shouting, "Black Horse Cavalry!"

Levy turned the horses around at once and drove back to the capital. He hurried to the camp, and all day and all night, soldiers with dazed eyes came stumbling in. Some of them had minor wounds, and Solomon and Frankie put a bandage on the hand of a young private from Illinois. He could barely speak at first, but as they bandaged his wound and gave him plenty of cool water, he calmed down enough to tell what had happened.

"We come at them fellers with all we had," he mumbled. "But they kept on comin' at us. Just kept right on comin'." A shiver passed through him, and he whispered, "My best friend, Scotty. . .he got shot right off. Got hit in the stomach, and he was on the ground screamin' and beggin' me to help him, but the sergeant drove us on into the charge."

When he stopped, Frankie said, "Maybe he'll be brought back to the hospital."

"No, I went back. . .and he was dead. His. . .eyes were open. . . but he was dead!" Tears began to roll down his cheeks. "I didn't think it would be like that!"

The young private spoke what the entire nation thought, for

neither side had been prepared for the violence that had wiped out so many young lives. The South began to celebrate, but the North gave up overnight on the idea that the war would last only six months. General McDowell was blamed—somewhat unfairly—for the defeat, and Lincoln called on General George McClellan to pull the army together. McClellan began at once, and he had the flair and the drive to do the job. His first job was to give the army confidence, and he did exactly that. He was everywhere, riding on his big black charger, going from unit to unit, giving stirring speeches, telling the men that they were the Army of the Potomac and that they were victors and not losers. He gave them leaves and better food and marched them in stirring parades. He put order into an army that had had little, and he created hope where there had been none.

Sol Levy and Frankie would be there through all those months that the Army of the Potomac rose like a phoenix from its own ashes. And as the first of the battered, bleeding troops poured into Washington during those terrible, dark days after Bull Run, Sol said, "Frankie, this is very bad, but we've come with hope, you and I. Let's put ourselves into a different sort of battle—a battle for God!"

They did so, moving among the men, giving out books and tracts, selling their goods at prices that made no money for Levy, and giving much of them to those who had no money at all.

At first Frankie was shy and did not get more than a few feet from Sol's side. She slept in the wagon while Sol slept in a tent, and the two of them went almost every night to one of the religious services that were held at the camp. In the beginning, the soldiers merely stared at Frankie—most of them, at least. Some bolder spirits attempted to get closer only to discover that the young woman was simply not available. But what puzzled them even more than Frankie's aloofness was that she never got angry with those who tested her.

In the minds of most soldiers, even of most men, there were two kinds of women: good and bad. The good women stayed at home, kept house, and reared children. The bad women could be found in the numerous brothels and dance halls that were scattered all over Washington. The entire regiment speculated as to which exactly Frankie was—good or bad. They discussed her often—how she lived with an old man, wore men's clothing, and talked with men freely—but they could not figure her out. Finally, as the days and weeks passed, the men came to accept her for what she was: sincere, honest, good-humored, and decent.

Three weeks after Bull Run, Major Rocklin came by to speak to Sol and Frankie, and he mentioned the men's reaction to Sol's assistant. He'd been telling Levy how grateful he was for the good work the pair of them were doing, and he turned to smile at Frankie. "The men had quite a time trying to put a label on you, Miss Aimes," he said. "But I think you've shown them what you really are. Have any of them been ungentlemanly?"

"Quite a few, Major," Frankie said with a shy smile. "But they come around. I think they miss their wives and sisters."

"Of course, some of them are away from home for the first time." Gideon nodded. "I've seen you at our services, too."

"It's wonderful to be able to serve the Lord," Sol said happily. "Your brother-in-law is a fine preacher!"

"I'll tell him you said so." Rocklin gave the two of them a speculative look, then said, "I know you two work hard, but if you have a chance, I wish you'd go by and pass out some tracts, and maybe even some tobacco, to our boys in the hospital. They get pretty lonesome. I'll be happy to pay for the items—"

"No! No!" Sol protested. "It will be our privilege, Frankie's and mine. Will they let us in?"

"Let you in!" Rocklin grinned. "The question is, will they let you out! I visit as often as I can, and they practically hang on to me just to have someone to talk to!"

That afternoon Sol and Frankie loaded themselves down with tracts, tobacco, and sweets, then went into the city. They found the regimental hospital of the Washington Blues easily, for it was a huge old mansion that had been converted to house the wounded men. They also discovered that Major Rocklin had been exactly right: The men were so happy to see them that they stayed until very late.

Frankie moved from bed to bed, shyly approaching the men. She was horrified by some of the terrible wounds but managed not to show it. It was not difficult to talk to the men, for most of them were starved for someone to listen. And they were frightened. For the most part, they were very young, not much older than Frankie herself. Even if they'd ever had any inclinations about romance, they had little now. Most of them had more important things to worry about, such as gangrene, which killed as many men in the long run as were slain instantly on the battlefield.

The third young soldier she talked to revealed this almost universal fear. His name was Jimmy Seeger. He was nineteen years old—and had a stump instead of a right arm. When Frankie sat down and asked him if he needed tobacco or paper, he shook his head. "Don't smoke and can't write," he said with a faint smile. Then he looked down at his ruined arm and said bitterly, "Even if I'd ever learned how. . .I couldn't write now."

Frankie said quickly, "I'll write a letter for you, Private."

"Would you, miss?" Seeger was delighted and dictated a short, highly stilted letter to his mother. When it was written, he asked to see it. "My, look at all them words!" he breathed. Then he lay back and grew still. Frankie was not sure how to talk to him, but she did the best she could. Finally it came out. The boy was convinced that he was going to die. "Every day they come and get one of our fellers, take him out, and bury him," he said, biting his lip. "It's that there gangrene that kills 'em." He blinked his eyes and said, "It's going to finish me off, too, I reckon."

"Oh no! You mustn't say that!" Frankie began to encourage him as best she could. But when he asked, "Are you a Christian, miss?" she could only shake her head. When the boy's face fell, she felt terrible—and then she had a quick thought. "I have a friend who's a fine Christian," she said. "I'll go get him!"

Ten minutes later Frankie stood back, watching and listening as Sol Levy sat beside Jimmy Seeger. Levy spoke quietly but earnestly for some time, reading scriptures from time to time from the Bible he always carried. Some of the verses Frankie remembered faintly, for they had been favorites of her mother's. She bowed her head as the old man prayed fervently for a complete healing for the soldier, and when he was finished, she saw tears in Seeger's eyes.

But Levy was not finished, not at all. He said, "Now, my boy, you must look to God, not only to keep you from dying, but to save you from hell. And that's exactly what Jesus Christ came to do. He died for you and for this old Jew, and I don't want to go to heaven and not find you there!"

"I—I'd sure like to know I was going to heaven, sir!" Jimmy whispered. "But I ain't been very good. Matter of fact, I've done some pretty bad things."

"Good!" Sol Levy exclaimed, and when the boy's face grew shocked, he said, "You're a sinner, Jimmy? Then that makes you a friend of Jesus!"

"It does?" he asked in surprise.

"Yes, because the Bible says in Saint John 15 that Jesus is the friend of sinners. And all of us are sinners, Jimmy. It says so in Romans 3:23: 'All have sinned, and come short of the glory of God.' But it says in that same book, 'But God commendeth his love toward us, in that, while we were yet sinners, Christ died for us.' The only question is, Do you want to have the Lord Jesus Christ in your heart? Do you really want to be saved from hell and to be clean from sin?"

Jimmy swallowed hard and nodded. "Yes, sir, I sure do!" he whispered.

"Then God is ready to save you, and you are ready to be saved!" Levy said. "What do you do, my boy, when you want something from someone?"

"Why, I ask for it."

"Exactly! And in Romans chapter 10 and verse 13, the Bible says, 'For whosoever shall call upon the name of the Lord shall be saved.' And so I want to pray for you, Jimmy, and as I pray, you just ask God for what you want. Will you do that?"

"Y–yes, sir."

Frankie felt strange as she stood there, her own heart pounding. Something like fear came to her as she listened—it was as though God was right at her side. Suddenly she bowed her head and closed her eyes. She began to tremble and felt her eyes burning. She heard Jimmy pray, asking God to save him, and then she heard him say, "I done it! I asked Jesus to save me, and He done it!"

For the next few minutes, Levy spoke with the wounded boy and then rose, saying, "We'll be back to see you tomorrow, Jimmy. And we'll bring you some books that will help you in your Christian life."

"Oh—I can't read!"

Sol hesitated, then nodded. "This young lady will read some to you, won't you, Miss Aimes?" Without waiting for a reply, he turned and the two of them left the hospital. As they got into the wagon and started back to the camp, Sol was practically ecstatic. "Wasn't that wonderful, Frankie! That dear lad! And now he's saved!"

Frankie said little, for the experience had shaken her. She went to bed early and, the next afternoon, joined Sol on another visit to the hospital. They went at once to Jimmy, who greeted them with a big smile. "I been telling all my friends about how I got saved," he announced. "And I told them they could listen while Miss Aimes reads to me."

"Splendid!" Sol beamed and left at once to visit other men. Frankie felt like an impostor, but the men were all watching her, so she sat down and introduced herself. She learned their names and saw to it that they all had something from the bag of goodies she'd brought. Finally she took out the book that Sol had given her, marked at the place, and began to read. The men listened quietly, and she read for almost an hour. Then she closed the book and asked, "Would one of you like to keep the book? Then you can read it to Jimmy anytime." One of the men agreed at once, and Frankie handed it to him.

"Will you come back?" a tall, bearded man named Dowley asked. "Sure would like to get a letter written to my wife."

"Yes, I'll come tomorrow."

That was the beginning, and there was no end. For weeks and even months, Sol and Frankie spent every waking hour with the men, either at the camp or at the hospitals. And they went to more than one hospital, for Washington was filled with them. They also attended the services held in the out-of-doors, and as Frankie heard the gospel preached, she became more and more aware that there was an emptiness in her—a longing that it seemed nothing could fill.

135

And so the days went by, with the army growing ever stronger. New recruits came in to be trained in the art of war, and both North and South waited for the next alarm that would call the men in uniform to the clash of battle. It would come, they all knew. Often as Sol watched the troops drill or march by in long columns, he would shake his head sadly and say, "Some of them will not be here next year, Frankie. Oh, that they were all saved!"

"Miss Aimes, this is my son, Private Tyler Rocklin. And this is Miss Frankie Aimes, the best vivandier in the whole Union army."

Frankie had moved along the line of beds at the regimental hospital late one afternoon and had not paid any heed to the tall officer who stood beside one of the beds. But when she heard her name, she turned at once to find Major Rocklin smiling at her.

"Hello, Miss Aimes," the young soldier on the cot greeted her. "And what in the world did my father say you are?"

"Oh, just a fancy word for a lady sutler." Frankie shrugged. The young man looked very strong, but his left leg was heavily bandaged and there was an unhealthy pallor in his face. "You must have come in today, Private Rocklin," Frankie ventured.

Major Rocklin spoke up. "Yes, he came in early this morning." Frankie saw that the man was worried, although he tried not to show it. "He got damaged a little in a fracas with the Confederate cavalry."

"Shot by a cavalryman!" the wounded man groaned. "I'm disgraced!"

"Don't worry about it, son," his father said quickly. "You'll be up and around soon. Maybe you can get a crack at that bunch the next time." He tried to smile, but when he saw that the young man's face was tense and pale, he said hurriedly, "Well, your mother will be here as soon as she gets home, Tyler." He bent over and patted the younger man's uninjured leg. "I'm proud of you, son!" Then he straightened up and gave Frankie a nod, indicating that he wanted her to follow him. She did, and when they were outside in the hall, Rocklin said, "My wife's away for an overnight visit. These people are pretty busy, so I'm going to ask a favor of you."

"You want me to sit with him tonight, Major?"

A look of relief came to Rocklin's face at the offer. "I'd feel better about it if you would. Just for a while, until he goes to sleep."

"I'll be glad to, Major Rocklin," Frankie said promptly. Then she asked, "What do the doctors say?"

"Well, they don't like the looks of the wound. A shell went off, and the leg was badly damaged, especially the knee. And these wounds are tricky, as you know. Always a danger of their going bad."

"I'll be happy to help all I can. You've been very kind to Mr. Levy and me."

Rocklin nodded. "I'll come tomorrow, but I'd like someone with him tonight."

When the major left, Frankie went back and found the young man moving around uncomfortably. "Is the pain bad?" she asked.

"Bad enough!" Tyler gasped. "I never could sleep on my back, but that's the only way I can lie down now."

Frankie had had some experience with this sort of thing. The men with certain wounds could only lie in one position, and this produced such discomfort some of them almost wept. She studied the young man, then said tentatively, "I'm not a nurse, but do you think if I could prop your leg up you could lie on your side?"

He stared at her, his lips tight, then said, "It's worth a try. Don't pay any attention to me if I holler."

Frankie went to the male nurse in charge and asked for extra pillows, which he found for her. She carried them back and dropped them on the floor. "It'll probably hurt when you roll over," she said, but Tyler only nodded, so she pulled the sheet back, then put her hands under his bandaged leg. "I'll hold your leg as steady as I can...." As the young man pushed himself over, she held his leg carefully, and when he was over, she quickly put two of the pillows under the wounded limb and eased it down.

"Is that any better?" she asked, moving to the head of the bed.

"I'll say!" Tyler whispered. His face was pale, but there was a relaxed look to his mouth, and he lay there with his eyes closed for a moment, then said, "Never thought lying on my side could feel so good!"

He grew still, and Frankie leaned forward to see his face. He had gone to sleep at once, and she smiled and straightened up. Carefully she pulled the chair close to his bed and then sat there watching him sleep. For over an hour he slept, and twice she had to hold the leg to keep it from moving. The male nurse came by and saw what she was doing. "That's a good idea. First time he's slept since he's been here." He grinned at her, adding, "You'd make a good nurse, miss!"

Frankie had planned to go back to the camp with Sol, but when he came, she saw that young Rocklin's fever was going up. "Sol, do you think I might stay here with him tonight? He's in a lot of pain, and I think if I could get some cool water and cloths, I could get his fever down. It's what I did with my sisters."

"I'll see." Sol moved away, then came back at once. "We'll both stay," he said quietly. "The doctor said it was all right."

They spent most of the night working with Tyler, bathing him with cool water, keeping his leg elevated from time to time. They took turns dozing in the chair, until Sol finally left to lie down on a couch in the outer room. Frankie sat there dozing until finally morning came.

"Well. . .I didn't expect you to do this, Miss Aimes!"

Frankie came out of a half-sleep with a jolt of alarm, then looked up to see Gideon Rocklin standing over her. She got to her feet, her neck aching. "He's had a restless night."

"Hello, Dad. . . ." Tyler was awake and looked very weak.

"Hello, son. How do you feel?"

"Better than if my nurse hadn't been here." He told his father

139

how Frankie had found a way for him to change positions, then tried to grin. "Lots of the fellows here didn't get such good care. Guess it pays to have your father running the show."

Rocklin turned to Frankie, saying, "Go get some rest, Miss Aimes. I appreciate all you've done."

Frankie smiled tiredly. "I hope you get better today, Private," she said, and then she went to find Sol.

He was asleep on the couch and got up slowly, his old bones aching. "How's the boy doing?" he asked, trying to straighten his neck.

"Not very well, I'm afraid," Frankie said. "I think his leg is hurt pretty bad."

The two of them rode back to camp, and soon business was under full steam. It was a long day, made even more so by the nearly sleepless night they both had experienced. Sol gave up and went to bed at noon, so Frankie had to manage the sutler business by herself. That evening, Major Rocklin came by to give them a report.

"How's your boy, Major?" Sol asked at once.

"Not doing well, I'm afraid." Rocklin's face looked craggy, and he shook his head in a discouraging motion. "He's had a fever, and the leg hurts all the time."

"I'm sorry, but we will pray that God will do a healing work," Sol said quietly.

"I appreciate that. Just wanted to stop and tell you how grateful I am to you two. It means a great deal to me and to his mother."

"Is your wife back, Major?" Frankie asked.

"Yes, but she's not too well herself. There's an epidemic going around, and I hope she's not got that." He straightened his broad shoulders, saying, "Thanks again for taking care of him."

"He's worried," Frankie said after the major walked away. "He's afraid his son might get gangrene and lose the leg—or die."

"You can't blame him." Sol nodded. "We'll have to go back and see the young fellow."

They did go back the next day and found that the patient was little improved. He tried to smile, but the fever was eating away at him, and his leg was very painful. He tried to talk but was obviously very ill.

Frankie went back to the camp depressed, and all the next day she thought about the young soldier. She was still thinking about him when Major Rocklin rode up and dismounted. "Is Tyler any better, Major?"

"Not really. Doesn't seem to be able to get any strength." Rocklin stood there, a strong figure in his blue uniform, and seemed unable to speak.

"What is it, Major Rocklin?" Frankie asked.

"I've been talking to the doctors—to my family doctor, too. He came out and took a look at Tyler. They all say the same thing—that he might be better off at home."

"Are you taking him there?"

"Well, we want to, but my wife is not well. She just can't seem to shake off that thing that's got her down. But I've *got* to see that my boy gets every chance. So—"He took a deep breath and asked, "Would you come to my house in town and take care of him, Miss Aimes?"

"Why, I'm no nurse!"

"You're enough of a nurse for us," Rocklin said. "Tyler told me how much you helped him. If you could come, just until I can find somebody else. . ."

Frankie stood there watching his face, and then she said, "I'll come if Mr. Levy says I can."

"Good! I believe he'll be agreeable." They went at once to find Sol, who immediately gave his consent.

"Go along, Frankie!" He nodded, and at Major Rocklin's urging, Frankie got her clothes. "Can you ride a horse to the hospital?" he asked.

"Can I ride? It's what I do best!" Frankie said with a smile. The two of them rode to the hospital, where Major Rocklin made arrangements to have Tyler brought out to the ambulance. A private drove the black vehicle to the Rocklin home, and he and the major carried the patient inside on a stretcher.

"Take care of him, Frankie," the major said quietly when they had Tyler in bed. "My wife is asleep, so the house is yours."

He left then, and Frankie moved to stand close to Tyler. He woke up out of the drugged sleep. His eyes were cloudy as he focused on her.

"Where am I?" he muttered thickly.

"Home," Frankie whispered.

CHAPTER 10

FRANKIE LOSES A FRIEND

*F*rankie met Major Rocklin's wife the next day when she took her breakfast into the large bedroom. She knocked on the door and, when a faint reply came, pushed it open and entered. She found Melanie Rocklin in bed, her face pale. "Oh, you must be Miss Aimes," Melanie said at once.

"Yes, ma'am." Frankie nodded. "Major Rocklin said you've been poorly, so I thought I'd fix you a little something to eat."

Melanie smiled, and as pale and wan as she was, Frankie thought she was one of the most beautiful women she'd ever seen. "Oh, don't get up, Mrs. Rocklin," she protested when the woman started to sit up. "I put it on a tray so you could have breakfast in bed." Before the sick woman could protest, Frankie had placed the bed tray in position, saying, "I just made some light food, an egg and toast. And tea is always good when you don't feel well."

"Oh, this is so nice, Miss Aimes!" Melanie said. "I *am* a

little hungry this morning."

"Just call me Frankie, Mrs. Rocklin." Frankie nodded. "When you finish, I'll help you into that nice overstuffed chair and change the sheets on your bed."

"That will be nice," Melanie said. She buttered a piece of toast, then put some strawberry jam on it, asking, "How is Tyler this morning?"

"Well, he had some fever, but I got it down about midnight. His leg seemed to be hurting pretty badly, so I gave him some of the medicine the doctor sent from the hospital. Then he slept pretty well."

"I feel so terrible." Melanie shook her head. "He needs me, and here I am wallowing around in bed!"

"You'll be better soon; then you can take care of him." Frankie moved around the room, picking up clothing. "I'll wash these things, Mrs. Rocklin."

"Oh, we have a woman who does the laundry," Melanie protested. "Just put it by the back door." She smiled and added, "I daresay you have more than enough to do already, my dear." She took a sip of the hot tea and smiled. "My, that tastes wonderful. Now come and sit down for a while, Frankie. My husband has told me a little about you and Mr. Levy, but you know how men are! They give you headlines, but we women want the fine print, don't we? Now tell me how you got to be a lady sutler."

When Major Rocklin hurried up the front steps and entered

the house that evening, he had a concerned look on his face. His duties had required all his time that day, and though he'd let none of his concern show on his face, he was very worried about Tyler. He'd waited anxiously until he could finally get away from the camp, then mounted his horse and ridden home.

"How is Tyler?" he demanded as Frankie came out of the kitchen to meet him. "Did the doctor come by?"

Frankie was wearing a pair of light gray trousers and a pale yellow shirt. Her auburn hair ringed her face, and she looked very competent. "He's better, a little bit, Major. The doctor came this afternoon. He changed the dressing and showed me how to do it, too."

"What did he say, Frankie?" Rocklin shot the question at her.

"He said if we can keep the fever down and keep the wound clean and see that Tyler eats, the chances are good for a full recovery." Frankie nodded emphatically. "He's a good doctor, isn't he? You can tell he tells the truth."

"Yes, he is." Rocklin took a deep breath as much of the concern that had been plaguing him melted away. He smiled ruefully at Frankie. "My apologies, Frankie, for sounding so brusque when I came in. Things were infernally busy today, and all I could think of was Tyler and the fact that I couldn't be home. . .and what I would do if I came home to the news that. . .that he—" His voice broke, and Frankie was deeply touched by the man's evident love for his son.

What would it be like to have a father who loved you so much? she wondered.

"Well. . ." Rocklin recovered his voice. "Thank God for the good news! Now how are you getting on, and how is Mrs. Rocklin?"

Frankie smiled reassuringly. "She's pretty weak, but she ate this morning, and a little tonight. I think she must be over the worst of her illness. I expect she'd like to see you." Frankie added, with a twinkle in her eye, "She's the prettiest lady—and so *nice!*"

Gideon laughed, saying, "Well, *I* think so, Frankie."

He turned at once toward the bedroom he shared with his wife, and Frankie went to the kitchen, where she got a basin of hot water and some towels. Then she went to Tyler's room, announcing at once, "Your father just came in. Let me fix you up a little so you won't scare him to death."

"Do I look that bad, Frankie?" Tyler managed a small grin. "It'll take more than a nurse to pretty me up!" Frankie picked up a comb and brush and began to smooth his black hair. When she caught a snag, he yelped, "Hey! That hurts!"

"Oh, don't be such a baby!" Frankie said. "Tomorrow I'm going to wash your hair and cut it, too. You're woolly as a bear."

"How would you know how woolly a bear is?" Tyler growled.

"I've killed four of them," Frankie shot back.

"Aw, you never did that!"

Frankie smiled, pausing to concentrate on her task. Tyler's matted hair was hard to manage, so she began to hold to the thick locks with one hand, pulling the comb through with the other. "Sure I did," she finally responded. "And I faced down another one that just about got me." As she worked on Tyler, getting him cleaned up, she told the story of how she'd met a female grizzly bent on guarding her pair of cubs—and how she'd nearly been their lunch. It made an exciting story, and Tyler listened with intense interest.

"I've never even *seen* a grizzly bear, Frankie," he observed, "let alone had to face one down. You must be pretty good with a gun."

"Had to be," she said, smiling. "When there's a family to feed and you've got only so much money for powder, you can't afford to miss." She stepped back, studying her handiwork with some degree of approval. "That'll do until I can wash it," she announced. "Now let me have that nightshirt."

Tyler flushed, his square face showing some embarrassment. He began to struggle to pull the garment off, but Frankie saw his face grow tense with pain as the movement strained his wounded leg.

"Hold on, Tyler." She pulled a sheet over his lower body, then stepped forward, saying, "Let me help you with that." She was very strong, Tyler saw right off as she moved him easily into a sitting position and eased the nightshirt off. He pulled the sheet up, saying, "A sick man shouldn't worry about modesty, I guess."

Frankie grinned at him. "Don't worry about it, Private. I've taken care of a sick brother most of my life. You won't shock me.

Now why don't you wash while I get you a fresh nightshirt."

When Gideon entered the room five minutes later, he found Tyler looking much better than he had the previous night. His freshly combed hair and clean clothing vastly improved his appearance. His eyes were clearer, too, which was a good sign. "Why, you look fit to soldier!" Gideon remarked with a smile and moved over to sit down next to the bed. Frankie was gathering up the towels and the basin, and he asked, "He been a good patient, Frankie?"

"Contrary as a mule," she shot back. "You tell him if he doesn't shave himself, I'm going to do it for him!"

Rocklin laughed, and as the girl left, he turned back to his son. "If I were you, I'd mind that girl. She's liable to do what she says."

"Where'd you find her?" Tyler asked. "She sure is a funny sort of girl."

Rocklin gave a brief history, telling what little he knew of Frankie, and ended by saying, "I think she's had a pretty hard time, Tyler. Pretty tough to live like she does." He shrugged his shoulders, adding, "You know how soldiers are as far as women are concerned. I was pretty skeptical at first whether she'd be a help or a problem. Some of these women who call themselves sutlers are no better than camp followers. But this one is a fine girl, maybe because of Sol Levy."

Tyler sat there listening and finally said, "Well, she's a strong young woman. Handles me like I was stuffed with feathers! And did you know she's killed four bears and outwitted a mama grizzly bent on protecting her cubs?"

Gideon laughed, exclaiming, "No, but it doesn't surprise me." He sat there talking with Tyler, and finally the boy expressed a fear that had been in him.

"I. . .worry some about this leg, Dad," he said, looking down at the bandages.

"Dr. Smith said you're doing well."

"You know how quickly these things can go bad," Tyler said slowly. He was a blocky young man, built much like his grandfather. His dark brown eyes usually danced with devilment, but now they were filled with apprehension. "And if the knee is torn up too bad, I–I'll be a cripple."

"The doctors were pretty sure that wouldn't happen," Gideon said quickly, wanting to give Tyler some assurance. What he didn't mention was that all of the doctors had agreed that, even at best, the knee would heal slowly—which meant Tyler would be out of the army. He smiled at his son. "First, we've got to get this wound healed up. Then you can begin exercising that leg a little at a time. It'll take awhile, but I'm thanking God that you didn't lose the leg and that you weren't killed."

"Sure, Dad," Tyler agreed with a nod. "I am, too. But it's going to be hard lying here with nothing to do."

"Coax Frankie to entertain you." Gideon smiled. "She's very good with the men in the hospital."

"She can't stay here forever, though."

Gideon had no answer for that, for he felt that he had already asked too much of the girl. Later, however, when he sought out

Frankie, who was cleaning up the kitchen, he cautiously began to explore the possibility of keeping her on.

"I know Mr. Levy must need you, Frankie," he said. "You two stay busy all the time."

"He told me to stay as long as you needed me, Major Rocklin," Frankie answered. She looked up from the sink, and the amber glow from the light overhead brought a reddish glint to her short curly hair. She had, Rocklin noticed, strong, square hands.

"I've got to hire someone to take care of Tyler for a while, and my wife needs looking after, too. I know it's asking a great deal, but you've done so well that I'd like to keep you on." He mentioned a salary, then added, "It would be doing us all a great service if you could stay here for a time."

"Why, I'll be happy to stay, Major," Frankie said. "Personally, I think I'm better at plowing behind a mule than I am at housework, but I'll do my best. I'll stay as long as Sol says it's all right."

"Fine!" Rocklin said, greatly relieved. He got to his feet at once. "That's a great relief to me, and to my wife, too. I'll just go tell her that you'll be staying on. I'll let you break the news to Tyler."

When Frankie told Tyler that she'd agreed to stay, he looked as relieved as his father had. "I'm glad to hear that! Hate to go to all the trouble of breaking a new nurse in!"

Frankie sniffed, saying, "I'm not going to put up with your bossy ways, Private Rocklin. Now I'm going to try to get you cleaned up." A humorous light touched her green eyes, and she added, "I entered a pig in the contest at the county fair once. Got him cleaned up fine enough to win first place, too."

Tyler stared at her. "I'm not a pig!"

"I should say not! You're not in as good a shape as my pig was! You certainly won't win first place! But I'll do the best I can. Person has to use whatever's at hand."

She left the room, and Tyler called out as she passed through the door, "Hey, I can always go back to the hospital, where I'll get a little respect!" When the door closed behind her, he chuckled and ran his hand through his hair. "I am a pretty sorry sight, I guess," he muttered. Then he raked his fingernails across his jaw, thinking, *Guess a shave wouldn't hurt, either. . . .*

In the weeks that followed, Gideon Rocklin offered fervent thanks that God had sent Miss Frankie Aimes his way. Melanie seemed to improve for a time, but then a setback that even Dr. Smith could not explain laid her low, keeping her bedfast for many days. As for Tyler, his progress was erratic at best. His leg healed very slowly, and sudden fevers would assail him, leaving him weak and pale.

During the trying days of his family's illnesses, Gideon was forced to spend long hours at camp, working with the Army of the Potomac, which was composed of still-shattered men in desperate need of confidence in themselves or their cause. General George McClellan worked at putting the army back together night and day, and he had sent for Gideon early on. The two men had spent a pleasant half hour reminiscing about their days in service in the Mexican War. It amazed Gideon that the general remembered him, but McClellan was a remarkable man in many ways. Primarily he was a man of organization, able to pull loose threads together. As their talk had drawn to a close, he had said, "Major, I'm depending on you to pull your regiment into a strong unit. The president wants to strike at the enemy as soon as possible, and I propose to do exactly that!"

"General Scott believes we must first control the Mississippi and the coast—that we must strangle the South."

McClellan had waved his hand airily. "Oh, I admire General Scott, of course, but his plan would take far too long. We must strike the South where it lives: Richmond."

"Well, it will take a strong army, General McClellan. We'll be on their ground, and our supply lines will be very long. You know Jeb Stuart and what he can do."

But McClellan would acknowledge no danger of failure, and Rocklin had committed himself to getting the regiment up to full strength. Throwing himself into that task forced him to rely greatly on Frankie to care for his family, which she did with great efficiency.

Sol Levy came often, visiting with Tyler and keeping Frankie posted on his activities. He came at odd times, sometimes early in the morning, and once in a while in the evenings. Late one afternoon in October, Frankie answered a knock at the door and found the old man standing there. He looked very tired, and, startled, Frankie pulled him inside, scolding him for going around in such cold weather without a heavier coat.

"Can't have you getting sick," she fussed, making him sit down and pull his soaked shoes off beside the wood cookstove. She fixed him a hot meal of eggs, ham, and biscuits and molasses. Finally she sat down and drank coffee with him.

He ate slowly, and Frankie watched him, a worried frown creasing her brow. She noted that he had lost weight, and his eyes seemed sunken back more deeply into his skull. He appeared to be in good spirits, but he spoke far more slowly than was his habit, and he looked exhausted.

"Tell me about the boy," he said, sipping his coffee as Frankie gave him the details of Tyler's recovery. Sol listened and nodded. "He will be all right. I have prayed much for him. Now I will tell you about the work. . . ."

He spoke with pride of how many thousands of tracts and books he had passed on to the soldiers, and Frankie understood that his work as a sutler meant nothing to him. He was very proud of how he'd learned to speak with the men about their soul, though he laughed ruefully as he added, "Some of them get offended, but I think even they know I love them." He leaned forward, resting his arms on the table, saying with wonder, "I *do* love them, Frankie! And that's a miracle, because until I found Jesus, I never really loved anyone except myself."

"I can't believe that, Sol." Frankie put her hand on his and squeezed it. "You've shown such love to me!"

"Only because God put it there." Levy lifted his faded eyes

153

and studied the face of the young woman. He wanted to say so much more to her, to warn her that life was short and every day without God was not only dangerous but a tragic loss. But he had learned when to speak and when to keep quiet, so he only smiled at her, saying, "You will find out someday, daughter, that the thing most people call 'love' isn't really love at all. Only the love that flows from God through us…only *that* love is real and lasts forever."

He left shortly afterward, and when Frankie went in to give Tyler his medicine, he saw at once that she was not as cheerful as usual. "What's the matter, Frankie?" he asked. "All this nursing getting you down?"

"Oh no," she sighed. "It's just that I worry about my friend, Mr. Levy." She poured the dark brown medicine from a bottle into a spoon, then said to him as he opened his mouth, "You're just like a baby bird opening his mouth for a worm!"

Tyler made a terrible face, then grinned. "I'd just as soon eat worms as that stuff!" He shifted in his bed, then said, "Sit down and talk to me, Frankie. I'm so tired of myself I could scream." When she was seated, he said, "Tell me about yourself. I've told you everything I ever did in my whole life, but I don't know anything about you."

Frankie began to speak of Sol Levy and how he'd come to her at a time in her life when she desperately needed somebody. The room was quiet, and without intending to, she spoke about her past and her family. She even told Tyler how much her father had wanted sons, and how her brother, Timothy, had been a disappointment to him. She shared stories of her childhood days, talking of hunting, fishing, and riding—unwittingly painting a poignant picture of a young girl learning to work and play like a boy.

Tyler listened quietly, thinking as Frankie spoke: *Poor girl! Why, she never had a childhood! That old reprobate of a father ought to be horsewhipped, and I wouldn't mind taking on the job!* He began to understand why Frankie wore men's clothing and seemed somewhat mannish in her ways. *She's got to learn to be a woman,* he decided. *Can't go through life wearing britches and acting like a man.*

He tried to touch on this when she was finished and got up to leave. "Frankie, haven't you ever wanted to buy a frilly dress and go to dances?"

Frankie gave him an odd look but merely said, "I guess I'm too old for all that, Tyler. I'll just have to be what I am." She left the room, and the young man lay there, growing drowsy from the effects of the medicine Frankie had given him. He tried to think of some way he could help but could come up with nothing. Just before he dropped off, he gave an impatient snort and mumbled, "Well, blast it! What can I do?"

Melanie Rocklin recovered from her setback as rapidly as she had come down with it—within three days she was up and about. She was so happy to be able to take care of Tyler and do her work that Gideon and Dr. Smith took her to task for

155

overdoing it, but Melanie was a woman who hated inactivity.

"God has healed me, and He doesn't intend for me to stay in that bed and be waited on," she told them with a bright smile. "It's His present to me, and I intend to enjoy it!"

Before long, she had decided that nothing would do but to have a party to celebrate her recovery—and Tyler's, as well, for by the middle of November, he had passed through the crisis. Dr. Smith gave his opinion to the family that the wounds were healed. "No chance of gangrene now," he said, smiling.

Gideon and Melanie rejoiced, and Tyler was relieved. "What about this knee, Dr. Smith?" he asked. "Can I start using it?"

"Yes, but have a little sense, young man. The knee is one of the most complicated and fragile mechanisms of your body. It needs a slow period of light exercise, plus rest. Miss Aimes, I'm going to give you the exercises our young friend should do and trust you to run herd on him." A smile touched the doctor's thin lips. "And you'd best go cut yourself a switch to use on this young fellow if he gets too ambitious."

"I think Mrs. Rocklin will have to use the switch," Frankie said. "I've got to get back to work."

"Oh?" Dr. Smith lifted his eyebrows. "Well, I want to tell you what a fine job you've done, Miss Frankie. I'm sure the Rocklins will miss you. They've all told me how fond they've become of you, so don't be surprised if they object to your leaving."

They did protest, Tyler most of all. He moaned, "I'm spoiled, Frankie! Mother won't bring me hot chocolate every night like you do!"

But Frankie only shook her head when both Gideon and Melanie asked her to stay on. "You don't really need me now, and I'm worried about Mr. Levy. He hasn't been well this winter."

"No, he hasn't," Gideon agreed. "You ought to make him take time off and rest up."

"Just what I'm going to do!"

When Gideon took Frankie back to camp, he spoke of his gratitude. "Money won't pay for what you did, Frankie," he said. "Don't know how we'd have made it without you." He paid her a bonus, but it was his words and the knowledge of a job well done that pleased Frankie the most. She shook the major's hand and gave him a warm smile, then went in search of Sol.

When she finally found him, Frankie was shocked at the sight of her friend. He was in his tent, too weak to get out of bed. "Sol! How long have you been sick?" she demanded.

"Oh, I've just been a little under the weather," he whispered. "Be all right soon, now that you're here."

"You're not staying in this tent another day!" Frankie announced. "You're going into the hospital!"

Frankie marched into regimental headquarters and asked to see the major. He came out immediately and asked, "What's wrong? Is it Mr. Levy?"

"Yes, sir. He's real sick. He's got to be cared for, and I was wondering if you could get him a bed in the hospital here. That way I could take care of him and still keep the store open."

"Why, of course!" Rocklin nodded. "It may bend regulations a little, but I think the army owes that man a great deal. Sergeant, go with this young lady. Get an ambulance and take Mr. Levy to the hospital. I'll give you a note for Major Turner. See to it that Miss Aimes here gets whatever she needs to take care of Mr. Levy." He turned back to Frankie. "Don't worry, Frankie. We'll see that he gets good care. Come and see me if you need anything at all."

"Thank you, Major!"

Sol Levy found himself helpless in the hands of his employee. He tried to protest, but by noon he was in a bed, all washed and shaved, with an army doctor poking at him. Major Turner, the chief surgeon, was a muscular man of fifty with a thick mane of white hair. He was a rough sort, but said in a straightforward fashion, "Mr. Levy, you're old enough that you should have come in sooner, but I think we'll be able to fix you up."

But when he spoke to Frankie alone, there was a somber look on his face. "He's a pretty sick man, Miss Frankie. His age is against him, of course, and he's pretty frail."

"But. . .he'll be all right, won't he, Doctor?"

Turner hesitated. "I never make guarantees. Been wrong too many times. We'll do our best, but. . .well, if he gets pneumonia—"

Frankie was frightened by Major Turner's warning. She began at once spending much time with Sol, taking only as much time selling merchandise to the men as was necessary. For two days Sol seemed to hold his own, but Frankie noticed on the third day that he was having trouble breathing. When Major Turner came through, she asked him to look at Sol, and he complied. He was cheerful enough while speaking to Sol but took Frankie outside at once. "It's not good, I'm afraid," he said slowly. "His lungs are filling with fluid."

"Pneumonia?" Frankie whispered.

"I'm afraid it is."

"Can't you do *anything*?"

Turner gave the girl a compassionate look. "There's not much we doctors can do: set a bone, stitch up a cut. Most of the time it's the body that does the healing." The surgeon knew a little about the young woman who stood before him, her face filled with fear, for Major Rocklin had told him some of her story. He hesitated, then said, "I'll be honest with you, Miss Frankie. He doesn't have much of a chance."

"He's going to die?"

"We all have to do that eventually." Turner hated this part of his job, but he was a fine doctor and knew he had to be honest: Levy would die unless a miracle took place. He himself was not a Christian, so he could only say, "He's a fine man. He's done a lot for the men. But if he has any family close by, you'd better tell them to come at once."

Frankie knew then that the doctor had given up hope, and when he left, she had to fight back the terrible grief that swept over her. She waited until she could smile, then went back to sit beside Sol. He was asleep, but he woke up later and peered at her. As sick as he was, he saw at once that she was disturbed and knew what was troubling her.

"The doctors can only do so much, daughter," he whispered.

His voice was weak, and it rattled in his chest. He lifted his hand, and she grabbed it blindly. It was so thin it felt like a bird's claw, all bones and skin.

Sol lay quietly all afternoon, and when he drifted off to sleep, Frankie went outside. She was standing in the cold, tears running down her face, not even noticing that the men who passed were watching her. She tried to pray, but nothing came. Finally she went back inside.

Sol slept fitfully for most of the night, but at dawn he roused up. His eyes were clear, and he once again reached for Frankie's hand. Nodding, he smiled at her, saying, "I don't want you to grieve over me, Frankie. Will you promise me that?"

Frankie could not speak. She shook her head, then dropped to her knees, throwing her arms around the old man's frail form. "I—I can't help it!" she moaned. "You've done so much for me, and I never did anything for you!"

"Ah, you are wrong! Very wrong!" Sol seemed to grow stronger, and he pulled her tearstained face up so that he could see her eyes. "God gave you to this old man for a daughter, just for a little while." He touched her cheek, and his eyes traced her face. "I must go now. . .to my Savior. But I don't have to go alone, for you are here with me."

They held on to one another, and for a while Sol Levy spoke quietly. He told her again how he had been so happy since finding Jesus. Then he seemed to fade away.

Frankie was alarmed and begged, "Don't go! Sol, please! Don't leave me!"

But Sol smiled—an easy, gentle smile. "It's only. . .for a little while. . .daughter. You will find Jesus. God has told me that! Praise His name forever!"

Five minutes later he opened his eyes and whispered, "You have been. . .a blessing. . .my daughter."

Thus saying, he took one shallow breath, and then Solomon Levy went to join the God of his fathers.

CHAPTER 11

A TASTE OF BLACKMAIL

By early December Tyler was walking with crutches—and driving his mother crazy.

"Gideon," Melanie finally said one night when her husband was home for one of his rare weekend leaves, "what are we going to do about Tyler?" She was sitting on the side of her bed, brushing her long blond hair as he undressed.

"Do about him?" Gideon asked, throwing a puzzled glance toward her. "Why, he's improving faster than any of us thought he might." He pulled a flannel nightshirt over his head and turned the lamp wick down, then quickly got under the covers.

Melanie had only enough time to put her comb down before the light was dimmed, but as she turned to slip under the covers, she persisted. "Oh, he's well enough physically, but you know how active he's always been. Gid, he's read every book in the house, and he follows me around all day long." Gideon's arms went around her, and she felt as always when he embraced her. . .like a young girl. She had heard of women who endured the intimacies of marriage with distaste, but she had never been able to understand how that could be. She loved Gideon's caresses, but now she drew back, saying, "Tyler misses Frankie a lot. She was such good company for him. He can't go back in the army for a long time, can he?"

Gideon was stroking Melanie's long hair, not thinking so much of his son as he was of how nice his wife smelled and how soft, yet firm, she was. "Hmm? Oh—no, not for quite a while, Mellie. That knee's got to have lots of rest."

Melanie reached out and imprisoned his hand, which was tracing the smoothness of her neck. Holding it tightly, she said, "We simply must find something for Tyler to do, or he'll go crazy. And drive the rest of us crazy right along with him! Maybe he could go to work at your father's factory."

Gideon smiled tenderly. "I'll talk to him about it," he assured her, holding her small hands in his big ones. His eyes regarded her warmly, and the love Melanie saw reflected in their depths touched her so deeply she felt a wave of emotion wash over her. How good God had been to let them come together!

"You know," Gid went on, his voice soft, a crooked smile on his face, "I'll be gone for quite a while when the army moves against Richmond. Sure hate to think of all the handsome chaps who'll be left to guard Washington. . . . Maybe I'd better hire some sort of duenna to keep an eye on you."

"You idiot!" she laughed and moved against him.

Only three days later, Tyler left the house for the first time since being brought there by the ambulance. He had Amos hitch up the family carriage and help him make his way down the sidewalk, which was icy and dangerous.

"Miz Rocklin gonna skin bof of us!" the tall black man complained as he hoisted the young man into the closed vehicle. He leaned in and arranged a blanket around Tyler's knees, grumbling steadily. "Fust time you cotches her gone, you gits dis crazy idea to go rummaging around. It ain't right! No, it ain't!"

Tyler grinned at the man, saying, "I won't tell if you won't, Amos. Now let's get going!" He sat back, enjoying the cold air, which was refreshing after the long weeks in the confines of the house. All around him the trees were heavy with ice and glittered like diamonds as the breeze shook them. Christmas was two weeks away, and he saw signs of the coming holiday in a few decorations already appearing in windows and on the fronts of houses lining the streets.

He moved his knee carefully, noting that it was less painful than it had been two days ago when Dr. Smith had tested it. *"Stay off it for another week. Then we'll see,"* he'd said. But Tyler had endured being cooped up in the house for as long as he could. When his mother had left to go to the church and roll bandages for the troops, he knew that he was going to have a holiday, even if it killed him. Amos had argued and fussed, but

Tyler had bribed him with a gold coin, and now as the carriage rolled along, Tyler's eyes drank in all that was around him with a new appreciation. Life seemed fairer than ever.

Tyler had never been sick before, and the long convalescence had been hard on him. As long as Frankie had been there to read to him, to play chess and checkers, or just to talk, it had been bearable. But after she left, he had been thrown back on his own resources, and he had to admit that he had found himself a poor companion.

He sat back, enjoying the ride, and when the carriage turned off the main road toward the camp, he grew eager. Sitting up, he took in the long rows of tents that made up the camp. "Take me to the Washington Blues' regimental headquarters, Amos," he called out. The servant knew that place well, having brought his mistress there often. When they reached the area, Tyler called out, "Over there, where those wagons are." When the carriage stopped, he threw the blanket back and carefully let himself out of the coach.

Amos said sharply, "Now will you wait jes' a minute till I can get there!" He reached up and helped Tyler down, then fished his crutches out. "Now where at you goin'?" he huffed when Tyler started out.

"Not too far," he answered. "You can come along, but if I nod at you, I want you to skedaddle!"

Amos stared at his young master, frowned, and shook his head. "You up to somethin', Mistuh Tyler! I kin tell!"

Tyler only laughed at him and swung himself across the

frozen ground toward an open area where three large canvas-covered wagons were set up about twenty feet apart, each with an adjacent tent. Tyler called out, and a man stuck his head out of the flap of one of the tents, asking, "Want to buy something, soldier?"

"Looking for Frankie Aimes."

"Last tent down."

"Thanks." Tyler swung along, calling out when he got close to the third tent, "Hi! Any vivandiers in there?"

At once the flap opened and Frankie emerged. Her face lit up when she saw who was calling, and she ran to meet him. "Tyler! What in the world are you doing way out here?" She was wearing a pair of blue wool trousers with a shirt to match, and on her head was perched a blue forage cap. Her eyes were brighter than he remembered, and her hair redder.

"You look different," he said, grinning. "First time I've ever seen you in uniform."

"Come in where it's warm," Frankie said. "You, too, Amos." She ducked inside the tent, and soon the three of them were drinking scalding coffee that she'd brewed on the small woodstove that warmed the tent. She gave them both some pie and plied Tyler with questions.

After the pie, Tyler sent a subtle signal to Amos, who rose from the wooden box he was sitting on and said, "I gonna look around for my friend Washington. He one of de cooks fo' Major Gideon."

As soon as the black man left, Tyler said quietly, "I was

sorry to hear about Mr. Levy, Frankie. He was a fine man, and I know losing him was hard on you."

Frankie dropped her eyes, fingered a button on her shirt, then looked up at him. "It's still hard, Tyler. He was so kind to me!" She gave her head a shake and, pulling her shoulders together, came up with a small smile. "I'll see him again—that's the last thing he said to me, Tyler." Then she began to ask him how he was doing, and Tyler knew she wasn't ready to talk about her loss any further. He gave her his report on his knee, told her about his mother and his relatives, and regaled her with the antics of the cat, Lothar, who had been a favorite with Frankie.

He also told her about the Southern branch of the Rocklin family, for Frankie had grown very interested in them during her stay with Tyler's family. After telling her about his uncle Clay and his family, he asked, "Did I ever tell you about my uncle Paul?" When Frankie shook her head, Tyler said, "I only met him once, but he's really something. Artist type, studied in Europe. Came back all against the Rebellion."

"Don't guess his family likes that much, do they?"

"No, it's been pretty tough on them, but he fell for a Southern belle, and he's gone to work for the government, taking pictures of the battles." Tyler shook his head, a thoughtful look in his brown eyes. "That's a funny way to fight a war—taking pictures."

"Will he marry the girl?"

"Oh, I don't know, Frankie." Tyler shrugged. "I suppose so. Her family has money, and she's supposed to be a raving beauty.

Now tell me about your family."

Frankie pulled out some letters from Timothy and notes from her sisters and read parts of them to Tyler. When she finished, he asked hesitantly, "Nothing from your father?"

"No. I...I don't think there'll be anything." Frankie changed the subject, and for the next hour the two drank coffee and finished off the pie. Just as the last slice was disappearing, a voice called out, "Any wayward soldiers in there with you, Miss Aimes?"

"It's my father!" Tyler said and got to his feet, grabbing his crutches. He followed Frankie outside and saw his father with another man, a civilian. Amos eyed Tyler from a position at the wagon.

"You scoundrel!" Tyler called out to the servant. "Why, you're nothing but a—a—"

"He did his duty," Major Rocklin cut in with a grin. "Told me he wasn't taking any punishment from your mother over this trip."

Tyler looked crestfallen but faced his father, setting his jaw firmly. "I *had* to get out of the house," he said. "I need the exercise."

"Nice how you came straight to see your father." Gideon tried to sound severe, but Tyler could see the smile that threatened to break out on his father's face.

"I was coming to see you before I left," he said lamely.

Gideon did smile then, and he shook his head indulgently. He glanced at the man standing beside him. "Mr. Pinkerton, this is my son, Private Tyler Rocklin. And this is Miss Frankie Aimes, one of our fine sutlers. Tyler, Frankie, meet Mr. Allan Pinkerton."

"The detective?" Tyler asked, giving the man a startled look. He offered his hand. "An honor to meet you, sir!"

Though only of medium height, Pinkerton was powerfully built. He had a round, pleasant face and brown hair. His searching blue-gray eyes took in the young man, then shifted to Frankie. "Pleasure to meet both of you," he said.

Tyler had read a story about the famous detective in the newspaper and had been impressed by it. Pinkerton had been a police officer before opening his own detective agency, and he had been called on by General McClellan to put his talents at the service of the government. So far, he had been instrumental in capturing several spies—including the most famous of all, Rose O'Neal Greenhow.

"I'm sending you home, Tyler," Major Rocklin said firmly. "Your mother would skin me alive if I didn't. And since Mr. Pinkerton has to go back to town, you can give him a lift."

"Why, of course!"

Tyler said a hasty good-bye to Frankie, adding urgently, "I came to invite you to our Christmas party. Mother says if you don't come, she'll have Father arrest you and put you in the stockade. It's on the twenty-fourth."

"I'd like that," Frankie said, smiling.

Pinkerton walked with Tyler to the wagon, and when he saw the black man start to get down from the driver's seat to help young Rocklin on, he said, "I'll do it." With surprising strength for a small man, he almost lifted Tyler into the coach, then got in himself. Leaning out the window, he said, "I'll be back next Wednesday, Major. I'd appreciate it if you'd have your estimates ready."

"I'll have them." Rocklin nodded. "See you tomorrow, son."

As the coach pulled away and turned around for the trip back to the city, Pinkerton pulled out a cigar, bit the end of it off, and lit it. "Your father is very proud of you, sir." He smiled at Tyler as the smoke ascended. "And I know you're proud of him."

Tyler shrugged. "He's a good man—and a fine soldier, but it looks like I'm out of it. The war will be over before this knee heals up."

"Wouldn't be too sure of that," Pinkerton replied. "Anyway, there are other things you can do while you're waiting. They need men to run the War Department. Your father could get you into something along that line."

"I'd be bored to tears!"

Pinkerton studied the young man, a critical light in his eyes. "You like adventure, eh? Well, most young men do."

"Not very likely to have any, not with this knee."

Pinkerton said nothing more about Tyler's prospects but began to tell of a case he'd worked on once. When he got out in downtown Washington, he said, "Don't get discouraged, Private. Something will turn up. Let me know if I can help."

Tyler was quiet and thoughtful on the rest of the drive home.

The next day he asked his father about Pinkerton's business with the army.

"Well, it's not to be talked about," his father said, "but he's organized a Secret Service. General McClellan has great confidence in him. As I understand it, Pinkerton will handle the spies and their reports."

Tyler's face had grown serious as he listened. "He's a pretty smart man—and tough, too. I could see that."

"He's got to be," Gideon replied. "He's got a tough job!"

By December 24, Tyler had exchanged his crutches for a cane. When he admitted Frankie at the door early that evening, she noted the change at once. "Oh, you're walking so much better, Tyler!" she exclaimed.

"Yes, and ready to get better still!" He smiled, surveying the young woman who was smiling at him. He was not surprised that Frankie had arrived for the party wearing her usual garb instead of a dress. He'd told her the occasion would be informal, but he knew any other young woman would have come dressed to the teeth. Still, he had to admit that she looked very well. With a grin, he said, "Come on in. We've got to sample the eggnog."

The party was not large; it was small enough for all the guests to assemble in the large parlor. Frankie had met most of those present: Tyler's grandparents, Stephen and Ruth Rocklin, and Tyler's younger brothers, Robert and Frank, she had met several times while taking care of Tyler. She'd met Major Rocklin's sister, Laura, and had heard her husband, Amos Steele, preach many times. One of their sons, Clinton, she hadn't met before, and their two other sons were not able to be there.

"And this is my daughter, Deborah, Miss Aimes. And this is Private Noel Kojak, her fiancé." Laura Steele smiled as she introduced the couple to Frankie, adding, "We're very fortunate to have Noel here for Christmas."

"Tyler told me about how you helped him escape from a Confederate hospital, Miss Steele," Frankie said. "I couldn't have done a thing like that!"

Deborah Steele was a beautiful young woman, and Frankie noted that she had as much poise as any man. "I think you could, Miss Aimes," she said, smiling. "Uncle Gideon has been telling us how you jumped in and took care of Tyler. I think you must be very resourceful."

Noel said, "I only hope your future husband has better sense than to get himself put in a Confederate hospital under guard." Frankie considered the young soldier. He was not handsome, but his steady gray eyes and regular features gave him a pleasant appearance. He looked rather shyly at Frankie, adding, "I'm glad you're here tonight, Miss Aimes. We're all grateful for the way you helped Tyler and Mrs. Rocklin."

"Watch out, Frankie!" Tyler had come to stand beside Frankie, his eyes gleaming with humor. "That fellow is deceiving! He's a writer, you know, and if you're not careful, he'll put you in one of his stories!"

They stood there chatting, and Frankie slowly relaxed. She had been rather terrified of coming, for she knew her manners were rough. But Tyler stayed beside her, making it easy for her. He sat next to her while they talked and made it a point at dinner to sit at the big table at her right.

The meal was stupendous: turkey, dressing, ham, vegetables, baked breads, apple pie, all cooked exquisitely. Frankie soon was able to relax and eat without worrying too much over her manners. She listened as the talk and laughter flowed around the table, deciding that this was a happy family—totally unlike her own.

Amos Steele glanced at her at one point during the meal and said, "I know how much you miss Sol Levy, Miss Aimes. The rest of us feel his loss, too. He was wonderful with the men! I think he must have won at least fifty of them to the Lord!" His words brought a warmth to Frankie, and she was pleased when Major Rocklin joined in the conversation, speaking of the work her friend had done.

After the meal, there was a little ceremony in the parlor. Gideon read the Christmas story from the Bible, and Rev. Steele spoke briefly about the meaning of the birth of Jesus. Then everyone bowed their heads while one of the family members prayed.

It was over about ten o'clock, and Tyler limped out to the carriage with Frankie. When she was bundled up inside, he looked at her, saying with some hesitation, "I'm glad you came, Frankie. My family took you in...I could tell. I mean the others, of course, the Steeles and Noel. My parents already think you're very special."

"It was wonderful," Frankie said, a smile lighting her face. "I won't forget it." Then she said, "Good night, Tyler!" and the coach pulled off.

Tyler stood there staring after the carriage as it disappeared. He frowned and muttered aloud, "Have I done the right thing?" He shook his head doubtfully, then took a deep breath.

"It'll be all right," he said with a nod. "She'll see how it is. . . ." Then, with another shake of his head, he limped back inside.

"I suppose you're wondering why I wanted to see you, Miss Aimes?"

Frankie was sitting nervously on one of the three straight-backed chairs in the office to which a corporal had led her. He'd given her a message from Major Rocklin, which said briefly, "Mr. Allan Pinkerton would like to talk to you. The corporal who brings this note will take you to his office."

Frankie looked at the detective, nodded, and waited for his answer.

"Well, I suppose you know what it is that I do?" Pinkerton was standing beside a window and gave her a sudden smile. "Nobody is supposed to know about the Secret Service. And, of course, everybody *does*. You've heard of it, I would suppose?"

"Why, yes, sir." Frankie nodded. "The men talk about you a lot."

"Ah, well, there it is!" Pinkerton frowned and came to stand beside the pine desk. "Impossible to keep a thing this large a secret. Quite impossible." He pulled out a cigar, lit it, and, when it was drawing to his satisfaction, looked at her keenly. "Miss Aimes, I need your help."

Surprise showed clearly on Frankie's face. At once she shook her head. "Why, I can't think what I could do for a man like you!"

"No? Let me tell you, then. The war is stepping up, Miss Aimes, and soon there is going to be a great battle. The North has to move an enormous amount of supplies and a great many troops to the South. Now the South doesn't really have to move much. It's their home ground, and they know it like a man knows his own backyard. When the attack comes, our generals and our officers will be at a great disadvantage. They won't know the territory, and they won't know the strength of the enemy."

He paused for a long moment, then said evenly, "My job is to see that General McClellan *does* know those things. And I'll use anything or anyone I can to help our army achieve a victory."

Frankie saw that the small man was entirely serious, but she was totally bewildered. "But. . .Mr. Pinkerton, I've never even *been* in the South! I couldn't help—"

Pinkerton interrupted her, saying, "You are a great friend of Private Tyler Rocklin, Miss Aimes?"

"Why. . .yes."

"Well, he came to me recently with a very interesting

proposal. A proposal that requires your help if it is to succeed." Pinkerton drew on his cigar, then suddenly sat down in the chair behind the desk. "He said that he has a relative who has just contracted to take pictures of upcoming battles for the Confederate government. I think he's mentioned this to you?"

"Yes. Paul Bristol is his name, isn't it?"

"That's the man. Private Rocklin has been thinking about a plan involving this situation. Though his days as a soldier are over—for a time, at least—Rocklin wants to serve his country."

"What does he want to do?"

"He wants you to go to Richmond and work for this man Bristol." Pinkerton was watching the young woman's face carefully and saw a flicker come to her green eyes. "Yes, you will be an agent working for the government of the United States." He grew excited then, adding, "It's *perfect*! Photographers go everywhere, and both sides leave them alone. Our Mathew Brady has proven this. So you will travel as an assistant to Bristol, and you will collect information, which you will pass on to Tyler Rocklin."

"To *Tyler*?"

"Oh yes! He will be there in Virginia, too. Under cover, of course. He wants to help our cause, and he was certain that you'd want to do the same."

Frankie shook her head. "I—I couldn't do it, Mr. Pinkerton. I couldn't be a spy!"

The next fifteen minutes were among the worst that

Frankie had ever known. She tried desperately to convince the man across from her that she could not do what he asked, but he refused to give in. Finally she grew angry. "I won't do it!" she cried, rising out of her chair.

She had reached the door when Pinkerton said calmly, "That's very unfortunate. It's going to be hard on your brother, Timothy."

Frankie whirled and stared at Pinkerton. "What does my brother have to do with this?"

"Haven't you heard about the new conscription act?"

"What's that?"

"A new law, Miss Aimes. Able-bodied men will be con-scripted, that is, taken into the army. We need more soldiers, and we aren't getting enough volunteers. Congress just passed the act, and your brother is the right age."

Frankie stared at Pinkerton. "Tim can't be a soldier! He's been sick all his life! Forcing him to be a soldier would probably kill him!"

Pinkerton's blue-gray eyes were cold. "Be that as it may, I believe he'll be conscripted, Miss Aimes. Unless, of course, you agree to help your country. If you volunteered, I believe I have enough influence to get your brother exempted."

Frankie had never felt such rage as washed over her at that moment, but with a jolt she realized it was hopeless. Everything in her hated the idea of being a spy, but the thought of poor Timothy being thrown into the rough life of a soldier. . . *He wouldn't live a week!* she thought desperately.

"Well, Miss Aimes? Which will it be? You or your brother?"

Squaring her shoulders and lifting her chin, Frankie gave Pinkerton a level look. "I'll do it. . .what you say." Her voice was even and cold. "But it won't work. I don't know a thing about taking pictures. And Bristol would never hire a girl, anyway."

Pinkerton smiled. "Oh, I think we can handle those two problems. Mathew Brady has agreed to train you in the science of taking pictures. And Tyler has told me how much Major Rocklin appreciates your kindness to him. He'll tell his father that you want a job and ask him to write his cousin Paul a letter of recommendation concerning one Frankie Aimes, aspiring photographer."

Frankie shook her head, feeling as though she was drowning. "But. . .I'm from the North! He won't hire a Yankee!"

"Ah, another excellent point. Which is exactly why the letter will state that you have no political affiliations, that all you want to do is take pictures. It will suffice, believe me!"

Then Allan Pinkerton smiled, his eyes shining. "Welcome to the Secret Service, Miss Aimes!"

CHAPTER 12

FRANKIE LEARNS A TRADE

*A*llan Pinkerton was two men, Frankie quickly decided. He was capable of crushing anyone who stood in his way, and yet he could show great kindness to those who cooperated with him. Frankie tried to put this in a letter to Timothy but was hampered by knowing that she must not say too much. It occurred to her that Pinkerton might have her letters intercepted, so she said nothing at all about becoming an agent for the Federal Secret Service.

> *Dear Timothy,*
>
> *I'm writing to tell you that I will not be working as a sutler for the army any longer. Since Mr. Levy died, I have not been able to do as well, so I have decided to accept a new job. I am being trained by Mr. Mathew Brady to make pictures, and when I am ready, I will travel over the country taking all sorts of pictures.*

I was so nervous when I first went to Brady's gallery, because he is a famous man. But he was so nice to me that I quickly felt at ease. He showed me all over the studio—which is very large!—and introduced me to all of his employees. One of them, a young man named James Tinney, will train me since Mr. Brady is too busy to take much time for lowly pupils!

It may be that I will have to leave here suddenly to begin the work, so don't be worried if my letters don't come as often. I'll write when I can and will keep on sending money for the girls. You can write me in care of Brady's studio in New York for now.

Love, Frankie

She put the letter inside an envelope, sealed it with wax, then addressed it. She glanced around the small room that Pinkerton had found for her, thinking, *It won't take me long to become a liar in this job!* The reality of what was happening to her was far different from what she had stated to Timothy. Pinkerton had taken the reins firmly in hand, giving her little to say about anything. He had found a room for her and assigned her to one of his chief agents: a tall man named Nick Biddle, who spent considerable time with both Frankie and Tyler.

With a sigh, Frankie rose from the small table, slipped into her heavy coat, and left the room. As she made her way down Broadway, she thought of how difficult it had been for her to adjust to Tyler after her meeting with Pinkerton. He had arrived at her tent the day after the meeting and was enthusiastic, to say the least. His eyes had been glowing, and although his leg still gave him problems, he could not keep still. He had spoken with excitement of all that they might do, finally saying, "I can't be a soldier, Frankie, but I can do this, and it might mean more to my country than being a private!"

He had been so eager, his face so filled with the desire to serve! But Frankie was still fighting the anger she'd felt at the pressure put on her by Pinkerton. She had assumed that Tyler was somehow involved in Pinkerton's threat against Timothy— how else could Pinkerton have known she even *had* a brother except from Tyler?

But as Tyler had spoken, she'd studied him carefully, and her certainty began to ebb. *Maybe he didn't have anything to do with it,* she thought and finally decided to test him. Cautiously she said, "It'll be hard for me to be so far away from my family, especially Timothy." Tyler had nodded and voiced his regret. Then Frankie had said casually, "I've been worried about the new conscription law, Tyler."

Tyler had stared at her with blank surprise. "Why, you're not thinking about your brother, are you? I thought he was an invalid."

"Oh, he is, but he's able to be out of bed and to work around the house. What if they just take him and put him in the army?"

"Frankie, there's no danger of that," Tyler had responded at once. "I've talked to my father about it, and he says they're only going to take able-bodied men.'"

As he had rushed to explain the way the law worked, Frankie realized he was concerned for her, that he didn't want her worrying about her brother. There was such an innocence and honesty in Tyler's broad face that relief had washed over Frankie as she decided, *He doesn't know about Pinkerton's threat!*

Now as Frankie entered Brady's Daguerreotype Gallery, she felt again that sense of relief. It would have been very difficult to work with Tyler feeling the resentment she'd felt earlier. She was still bitter at being forced to do something she didn't agree with, but at least she knew that Tyler was in no way responsible.

James Tinney met her as she entered the laboratory, smiling as he said, "Good morning, Miss Aimes. Ready for another lesson?"

"Yes, Mr. Tinney."

"Oh, call me James," the young man said. "Come along. I think you're ready for something new."

As Tinney led Frankie to a large table covered with photographic equipment, she wondered how much he knew about her mission. Brady knew, for Pinkerton had spoken of it when introducing Frankie to the photographer. "This young lady," he'd said, "will be working for the Secret Service on the other side of the line, Mr. Brady. She'll need to know a great deal about taking pictures." Brady, an ardent patriot, had found the plan fascinating and had pledged to do everything he could to help.

Frankie was certain that neither Tinney nor any of the other employees had any idea of her real task. As far as they were concerned, she was just a young woman who had somehow gotten Mr. Brady to agree to teach her the skills of photography.

Tinney turned, and his bushy beard fascinated Frankie. It covered his entire lower face so that only his ruddy lips appeared. *I wonder if he keeps that brush just to cover a weak chin?* she wondered, but decided that the young man felt the whiskers made him look older. He was no more than twenty, Brady had confided in her, and yet he was one of his best men.

"Now you've learned quite a bit about working with daguerreotypes—and I must say you've picked the elements up very quickly!—but I want to show you something this morning that's going to make all that outdated before you know it!"

"You mean daguerreotypes won't be used any longer?"

"Oh, they'll be around for a while." Tinney shrugged, looked around cautiously, then added in a lower voice, "Mr. Brady got his start with daguerreotypes, so he clings to them. But the future of photography lies in wet plates."

"Wet plates?" Frankie asked in a puzzled tone. "Sounds like dishes being washed!"

Tinney laughed and went on to explain, which he loved to do! "Back in 1851, Miss Frankie, photography took a giant step forward. An English sculptor named Frederick Scott Archer came up with a new method of preserving an image. You know what collodion is? A sticky liquid made by dissolving nitrated cotton in a mixture of alcohol and ether. It's used as an agent to make the light-sensitive image adhere to a glass plate."

As Tinney spoke, showing Frankie various elements of the process, she concentrated on every word, knowing that the success of Pinkerton's scheme depended on her ability to perform.

"You see," Tinney concluded, "the ether and alcohol evaporate quickly, leaving behind a smooth, transparent film on the glass. This glass is sensitized by dipping it into a bath of silver nitrate solution. The sensitivity is lost when the plate dries. Then all you do is develop it in a solution of ferrous sulfate with acetic acid. Then you simply 'fix' the image by dipping it into a solution of potassium cyanide."

Frankie asked, "And you make a picture from the plate?"

"As many as you like!" Tinney beamed. "That's the great advantage of the wet-plate process, Miss Frankie. You can make an unlimited number of prints from a wet plate."

"So the daguerreotype is doomed?"

"Oh, don't let Mr. Brady hear you say that!" Tinney burst out quickly. Then he added in a low tone, "But you're right. You see, Miss Frankie, photography a few years ago was just a fascinating new art. Now it's big business." A sly smile came to his red lips as he added, "Men like P. T. Barnum use huge pictures to catch attention, and if Brady makes a large print, why, Guerney makes them larger, and then Lawrence tops them both! But Mr. Brady topped them all," he added. "He made hanging portraits of Morse, Field, and Franklin on a transparency measuring fifty by twenty-five feet, lighted by six hundred candles, just outside the gallery last summer!"

"He photographs lots of important people, doesn't he?"

"Oh my word, you've no idea! But you'll see some of them before you finish our training."

Tinney's words were prophetic, for three days later Brady's gallery had a distinguished client—indeed, the *most* distinguished visitor it was possible to have!

"Look, Miss Frankie!" Tinney whispered excitedly. "It's the president!"

They were on the second floor, where portraits were made, for Tinney had decided that his pupil needed some training in the taking of formal portraits. Frankie watched as Mr. Brady entered, accompanied by a major and President Abraham Lincoln. She had seen many pictures of Lincoln, but seeing him in person was quite a different matter! Expecting to be asked to leave, she saw Mr. Brady's eyes fall on her, and at once he leaned forward and whispered something to the president. Lincoln nodded, then turned to look at Frankie. He said something to Brady, who at once called out, "Miss Aimes, come here, please."

Frankie was so nervous as she approached the men that she was afraid she'd trip over her own feet. When she stood in front of the president, he smiled suddenly, saying, "I'm most grateful for your help in serving the Union, Miss Aimes. Mr. Pinkerton has told me all about it." He put his hand out suddenly, and when Frankie took it, Lincoln said, "It's a difficult and dangerous task, and I pray that you'll be kept safe."

"Th–thank you, Mr. President!" Frankie whispered. She looked up into Lincoln's face and thought, *How sad his eyes are—and how kind!* His hand was so large that her own was lost in it, and she knew that she'd never forget the moment. Not ever.

Then Brady gently ended the scene by saying, "Now, Mr. President, I'd like to get a full-length portrait."

Frankie moved away, but as she came to stand beside Tinney, she could still hear their conversation. "I'm six feet four," the president said, and a smile touched his full lips as he added dryly, "I saw a picture not long ago of a landscape. It had been made in several segments and pasted together. Guess you can use that method on me."

"Not necessary at all, Mr. President," Brady assured him. He began adjusting the camera, and Lincoln, at his signal, asked, "Shall I hold my arms like this?"

"Just be natural, sir."

Lincoln smiled again, humor in his deep-set eyes. "Just what I wanted to avoid," he remarked. As Brady hovered around, he said, "Major Flowers, there was a fine custom-built sawmill in my home county in Illinois. The owner was very proud of it. One day a farmer brought in a big walnut log, and while the owner was cutting it, there was a tremendous crash. Somebody had driven an iron spike into that tree, and the wood had grown over it. Well, the owner began investigating the cause of the accident, and the farmer came over and demanded, 'You ain't spoiled my plank, have you?' The owner yelled, 'Blast your plank! Look what it's done to my mill!'"

Lincoln winked at the officer, adding, "Mr. Brady's worried about the picture, but he ought to be worried about what I might do to his camera!" Brady and the officer laughed, and Lincoln kept up a lively conversation until the sitting was over and Brady came back with the plates.

"Which one do you like the best, Mr. President?" Brady asked.

Lincoln stared at them, then shook his head. "They look as alike as three peas," he remarked. "I will leave the choice to you, sir." He picked up his coat and put it on, then placed his tall stovepipe hat atop his head. As he left the room, he had to pass close to Frankie, and seeing her, he halted abruptly. "My best wishes to you, Miss Aimes," he said gently, and there was a kind look on his homely face.

After he left, Tinney stared at Frankie. "I didn't know you were so important," he said.

Tiny tips of gold came to the hard buds of the trees as spring broke the iron grip that winter had held on the land. Snow melted, creating rivers that ran across brown fields that had seemed dead but were beginning to put up tender shoots of emerald.

The Army of the Potomac—tired of drills and the long, monotonous months of winter—emerged as a first-rate fighting force, molded and inspired by "Little Mac," as the soldiers affectionately called General McClellan. He had managed somehow to wipe away the shameful memories of their flight from Bull Run, and now they were poised, aimed at the South, and ready to march—a quarter of a million men organized into army corps, divisions, brigades, and regiments, with artillery, cavalry, engineers, a signal corps, and a transportation unit of wagon trains. All the while, Allan Pinkerton had driven the intelligence corps hard, gathering information about the enemy's operations and intentions.

Frankie said good-bye to Mathew Brady late one afternoon, and the photographer seemed anxious. He took her hand in both of his, saying, "Now, my dear Miss Aimes, you must be very careful. Very careful indeed." His kind brown eyes glowed, and he tried to make a joke out of the danger he was well aware that the young woman was about to plunge into. "Mr. Tinney and I have spent too much time teaching you my art to see it go to waste, so you come back to us safe and in good health."

"I will, Mr. Brady," Frankie replied. "I won't ever forget these days."

She left on that note and later in the day met with Allan Pinkerton and Tyler at the detective's office. Pinkerton spoke rapidly, stressing the need for accurate information about troop movements. Once he pounded his fist into his palm, saying emphatically, "General McClellan depends utterly on my information. And I will depend on you two and others like you. Don't fail me!"

Tyler spoke up, excitement in his voice and eyes. "Don't worry, sir; we'll get the best reports in the whole service for you!"

Pinkerton liked the young man, and the young woman, as well. He had regretted having to force the girl into service, but planned to make it up to her. "Fine! Fine!" he said, nodding. "Now I don't think it wise to keep anything in writing. If nothing's on paper, there's no way you can be convicted if you're captured. Miss Aimes, keep all the figures in your head. You have a fine memory, a fact that Mr. Brady has commented on often. Give the figures to Tyler verbally, and he'll give them to his contact the same way."

Tyler said thoughtfully, "I'm not sure that's wise, Mr. Pinkerton. Every time something gets told, there's a chance for error. I think it would be better if Frankie and I worked up some sort of a code—something that looks innocent but can be interpreted by you. That way the figures wouldn't get changed by repetition."

Pinkerton stared hard at the young man. "Well, that would be much better from *my* standpoint, but more dangerous for you."

"Oh, Frankie and I can come up with something, can't we, Frankie?"

Frankie had been thinking as the two men spoke. "I think we might do it by an order for photographic supplies," she said slowly. "We could give each army unit a chemical name."

"I don't understand," Pinkerton said.

"Well, let's say we agree that potassium stands for a regiment. If I put down on an order blank 'three pounds of potassium,' that will mean three regiments."

"Why, that would be absolutely safe!" Pinkerton exclaimed. "And how would you indicate where these regiments are?"

"How about if we give the latitude and longitude as an order number? Three pounds of potassium, number 2459, would mean three regiments at where the 24 and 59 lines cross on a map."

Pinkerton clapped enthusiastically. "That will do it! And since Rocklin here will be posing as a traveling peddler, no one would ever suspect a simple order form of holding a message! Miss Aimes, I take my hat off to you!"

They spent an hour working out the code, and when it was time to part, Pinkerton detained Frankie as Tyler left to get the wagon. He seemed upset and embarrassed, and finally he said, "Well, Miss Aimes, I have been unfair to you." He smiled briefly at the young woman's look of surprise. "Everyone says I'm too busy with my job to understand the needs of people, but I'd like to think that there's another side of me. I *do* care about people, and I care about you. I forced you into this job, and it's too late to back out now. But I'll make you a promise. You do this one job for me, and when it's over, you're free to go your way."

"And my brother?"

Pinkerton shook his head. "He won't ever be conscripted, Miss Aimes. I bluffed you on that one. So even if you walked away from this job right now, your brother is safe." He watched the young woman's face, knowing he had just left himself

190

vulnerable—a thing he did not do often. For one moment he feared she was about to call his hand, but he was wrong.

"I'll go with Tyler," Frankie said at last. "I can't let him down. But it makes a difference, what you just said, Mr. Pinkerton. I—I think better of you now."

Pinkerton was a hard man, but he showed a rare flush of pleasure as he took the young woman's hand. "I'm glad you do, Frankie. I. . .have worried about you, for this is a dangerous mission. God bless you and bring you back safely."

Frankie left Pinkerton's office and walked rapidly to where Tyler was seated on the wagon. He was to drive her to the railroad station, then drive the wagon south to Virginia. It was Sol Levy's wagon, or had been, but he had left it to Frankie. Pinkerton had come up with the idea of sending Tyler into the South posing as a peddler, but thought it best for Frankie to take the train. *The two of you must not be seen together any more than necessary,* " he had warned them.

Now it was time for the mission to begin, and as Frankie rode along, she felt that there was something unreal about it all. She said as much to Tyler, who agreed. "It's like something out of a dime novel," he said, nodding, his face serious. "But it'll be real enough when we get to Virginia."

They spoke of the arrangements for meeting until they got close to the station, and then Frankie said, "I'll walk from here on, Tyler. There'll be Southerners on the train, and we don't need to be seen together."

When he pulled the horses up, he suddenly reached out and

put his arm around her waist. Frankie was so startled that she could not speak.

"I'm sorry I got you into this, Frankie," Tyler said slowly. "Now that we're almost into it, I see how unfair I was, dragging you into a dangerous thing like this. I should have done it alone."

Frankie was very nervous, acutely aware of his arm around her. "It—it's all right," she said quickly. "I was against it at first, but it's something we have to do."

Tyler didn't respond. He was too startled to do so, for he had been made aware of a strange fact. He was so accustomed to thinking of Frankie as a good companion, or a nurse, or a fellow conspirator, that the feel of her slim waist beneath his hand somehow shocked him. Looking into her face, he saw nothing masculine at all in the wide green eyes, the smooth skin, and the clean sweep of her jaw. He sat there, suddenly aware that this was not a fellow soldier, but a young and lovely woman. He stared at her, noticing for the first time how well shaped and somehow enticing her lips were. . .and, without thinking, he pulled her close and kissed her.

For one moment he was intoxicated by the feel of his lips against hers, the warmth of her breath on his face—and then he was shoved away almost frantically. Caught off guard, he scrambled to avoid falling from the wagon seat. He looked at Frankie, confused, and was startled by the desperate look in her eyes.

"Don't you *ever* do that to me!" she whispered hotly, then

jumped to the ground, snatched her suitcase from the seat, and whirled to leave. She paused long enough to say shortly, "I'll get word to you when there's a report," and then she was gone, striding up the street toward the station. Indignation showed clearly in the set of her stiff back, and Tyler knew he had made a sad mistake.

"Well, old boy," he said aloud, "you certainly know how to turn on the charm, don't you?" He jiggled the reins, and the horses moved forward. As he headed for the outskirts of Washington, he thought about what had just happened. He was a little shocked at himself, wondering at first what could have possessed him to kiss Frankie, and then wondering why he'd never considered doing so before.

He realized that he'd always had a sense, despite the masculine clothing and manners, that Frankie Aimes was a tender and warm woman—and he was suddenly aware that this very fact somehow frightened her. She did all she could to give the image of being strong and capable, someone who didn't need anyone else. And yet. . .Tyler knew better. He'd seen her with Sol Levy, and with his family, and with himself.

He addressed the horses, saying, "Well, boys, I guess I've discovered a secret already—only this is Frankie's secret. Funny thing is, I'm not even sure she knows she has it. See, she doesn't want a man—or, more to the point, she doesn't *want* to want a man. She doesn't want to open herself up to anyone, or seem like she needs anyone to take care of her—that's for sure. Guess that's why she dresses like a man and tries to act like one, so we'll just leave her alone." He mused on that, then finally shook his head.

"Too bad trappings don't make a bit of difference. Like it or not, Frankie Aimes is very definitely a woman. But it doesn't seem too likely she'll ever let that part of herself out!"

PART THREE

The Impostor—March 1862

CHAPTER 13

A STRANGE PAIR

From his earliest days, Claude Bristol was better at gambling than he was at raising cotton. He had appeared in Richmond from nowhere, and with the help of an aristocratic charm—and a rather small mare that could travel a quarter of a mile faster than any other horse in the county—he had successfully established himself in the second level of Virginia aristocracy.

Not the first level. That, of course, belonged to the Lees, the Randolphs, the Hugers, and a dozen other families. Still, Bristol was a handsome man, and his French ancestry had provided him with enough wile and sense to obtain Hartsworth—a fine plantation—and with enough romance to sweep Marianne Rocklin off her feet for the first and the last time in her life.

Marianne had always had much good sense and, as a rule, fine judgment. It was quite unfortunate, then, that in this one instance she failed to see that the young Frenchman who had won her heart was much better as a suitor than he would ever be as a husband. Her parents, on the other hand, had not been so deceived and had taken every opportunity to warn their daughter against the man. But Marianne was possessed of the one trait that identified a Rocklin faster than lightning: mule-headed stubbornness. And so she stuck to her guns, went against the wishes of her parents, and married the young man. And she lived to regret it.

Even so, it was a silent regret. If there was one thing that Marianne was not, it was a whiner. Her father, the late Noah Rocklin, had brought her up with the firm rule that people had to live with their errors. More than once she had heard him remark, "Whining about matters that we ourselves have helped to create. . .well, that simply is not the act of a lady or a gentleman."

Now, at the age of fifty-two, the mistress of Hartsworth had managed to overcome the disappointment of having chosen a weak man. She had Hartsworth, she had three children who had not yet disgraced the family—though Paul had been a sore trial—and she had God. Most of all she had God. Long ago she had given her heart to serve Him, and she had found His love to be sufficient, even when her marriage had demonstrated a sad lack of either love or fidelity.

On a blustery Sunday in March of 1862, Marianne rose early, went about her work, then got into the carriage with her daughter, Marie, and drove to church. They went alone, for Claude never attended, and Austin, the youngest son, was sporadic in his churchgoing.

They arrived late but entered and took their places—the same pew that the child Marianne had sat on when she had attended with her parents. The church was cold despite the two woodstoves that burned, for most of the heat ascended to the top of the high-pitched ceiling. Looking upward, Marianne thought as she always did, *I wish I could sit up there. At least my feet would stay warm!*

She listened critically to the minister, Rev. Dan Parks, and as they left the church, she took his hand, saying, "Your theology was sound today, Brother Parks."

Dan Parks was a sturdy young man who had made his share of mistakes since coming to pastor the church, but he had a quiet wit. And it gleamed in his eyes as he nodded, saying, "I've got just enough theology to be dangerous, Mrs. Bristol. But I always feel safe with you sitting out there in the congregation."

"Safe?"

"Yes. I have the absolute certainty that if I fall into error in one of my sermons, you'll leap to your feet and demand that the service be dismissed until the pastor has time to clear his doctrine up a little!"

Marianne liked Rev. Parks very much. She and her sister-in-law, Susanna, the wife of her brother Thomas, had been responsible for keeping Parks in the church when his impolitic pronouncements moved the leaders to decide to run him off. Now she said, "The Bible says, 'Let your women keep silence in the churches,' Brother Parks." Her dark blue eyes gleamed with humor as she asked, "Do you think I would go against the scripture?"

Parks shook his head. "I never try to think about what a woman will do, because I'm always wrong. But I do think you'd find a scripture to back you up if you had to."

"It *was* a good message," Marianne said warmly. "You are one of the few ministers I know who hears from God. Too many get their sermons from other men. It's good to know that my pastor has an audience with the Almighty!"

Later, as Marianne and her daughter rode home, Marie spoke of her cousin Clay Rocklin with some hesitation.

"And they say cousin Clay is in love with Melora Yancy. That's not right, is it, Mama?"

Marianne defended her nephew instantly. "I brought you up better than to listen to gossip, Marie. Clay has had a hard life, and he did great wrong to his family. But if ever a man tried to make up for his mistakes, it was Clay Rocklin. As for Melora, well, she is a fine girl. All the talk about the two of them comes from a bunch of gossips who've got tongues long enough that they could sit in the parlor and lick the skillet in the kitchen! If there is anything I cannot abide, it is people who try to make their own pitiful lives seem better by gossiping about others. The good Lord gave us enough to concentrate on in our own lives, so for heaven's sake, let's leave other people's lives alone!"

Marie was surprised at her mother's sudden outburst. "Why, *I* don't believe there's anything wrong between Clay and Melora,

Mama!" She sat there quietly, thinking suddenly of her parents. She was a bright girl and for years had known that they were not happy. It had broken her heart when she had first discovered that her father was a weak man who was unfaithful and prone to the sins of the flesh. If anyone had a right to complain or gossip, it was Marianne Bristol, but Marie had never heard her mother speak a word of criticism about her father. She shook her head slightly, wishing that things could have been better for her mother. Then she asked, "What do you think about Paul, Mama? When will he and his assistant start for the front?"

"Didn't you know? They're leaving tomorrow."

Marie looked surprised. "Paul didn't tell me he was going."

"He's been working very hard. I suppose he just forgot to mention it."

"Is he going to the Valley where Jackson is fighting?"

"No, that's too far. He said this first trip would be sort of a trial run. He has to try out his camera and What-Is-It wagon under actual conditions."

They were within sight of the Big House now, and Marie suddenly said, "Look, there's Paul now, Mama. Let's go see what he's doing."

"No, he's busy. You can see him when he comes in to eat dinner."

"Mama...," Marie asked tentatively, "don't you think there's something...funny about that girl he hired?"

Marianne looked at her daughter at once. "What's funny about her?"

"Oh, Mama!" Marie said, tossing her head. "Everyone is talking about it." She saw her mother winding up to deliver another sermon on gossiping and held up her hand quickly. "Now don't start preaching at me again! And you might as well get used to people talking about Paul and Frankie, because they're going to do it!"

Marianne didn't speak until she pulled up in front of the tall white house. Then she said, "I suppose so. She *is* a strange young woman, Marie, but Paul said he didn't have any choice. Come on, now," she said abruptly, "we're going to be late with dinner."

Blossom, the cook and second-in-command to Marianne Bristol, already had the meal cooked, however, so all that the mistress of Hartsworth had to do was summon the pair working outside. Claude Bristol and Austin were in the library arguing about horses when Marianne called them to the dining room. When the four of them sat down, Claude asked, "What about Paul and his young woman? Aren't they going to eat?"

Even as he spoke, they heard the front door close, and Austin called, "Better hurry up, you two. You know how mad Blossom gets when people are late for her meals."

Paul sat down across from Austin, and Frankie took the seat next to him, opposite Marie. He smiled at his mother, saying, "Not a long grace, Mother. Frankie and I have a long way to go."

They all bowed their heads, and right on the heels of the "Amen" from Marianne, Claude asked, "You're not starting at this time of day? It'll be dark in a few hours."

"We're only going to the camps outside Richmond, Father," Paul replied. "From what I've heard, they've really started to throw up some stout works."

"The soldiers don't like it—all the digging," Austin said. He stuffed a biscuit into his mouth.

Paul slathered a flaky biscuit with yellow butter, tasted it, then called out, "Blossom, these biscuits are *good*!" He waited until Blossom's voice came faintly: "Yassuh, Mistuh Paul!" Then he responded to Austin's comment. "When the Yankees get here, those fortifications will come in handy."

"Oh, nonsense!" Austin retorted. "The Yankees will never get to Richmond!" He began to explain in a dogmatic fashion how impossible it was for a Yankee army to whip the Confederate Army, informing everyone that any Southern soldier could whip six Yankees. Austin was a husky man of thirty and was very strong. And he was, much like his older brother, the despair of the mothers with marriageable daughters in the vicinity. He had been engaged twice but somehow had never made it to the altar. He was faithful in doing his work at Hartsworth but was more interested in hunting and social life in Richmond than anything else.

Finally Marianne asked, "Didn't my nephew say that you were some sort of sutler at one time, Miss Aimes?"

"Yes, Mrs. Bristol. I worked for a man named Sol Levy." Frankie spoke carefully, hoping no one noticed how tense she was. Knowing there were weak spots in her story, she explained vaguely, "After he died, I didn't have anything to do, but I'd always been interested in photography. I was quite fortunate that Mr. Brady took me on. Then when I heard from Major Rocklin what Mr. Paul was doing, I asked him to help me get a job here."

"But don't you feel a little out of place?" Claude asked, not unkindly. "I mean, *I'd* feel that way if I were in the North."

"I—don't really feel strongly about the war," Frankie said, uncomfortably aware that they all were watching her. "I don't care for slavery myself, but I think the South has a right to run its own business." It was the answer that she and Tyler had decided was best, and she breathed a sigh of relief when she saw by the reactions around the table that it was a success.

"Why, that's the way many Southerners feel. General Lee, for one," Marie said with a nod.

"What did you think of the Yankee Army, Miss Aimes?" Marianne asked. "Everybody in the South seems to think since we whipped them at Bull Run, it'll be easy to do it again."

Frankie shook her head. "I don't know much about that, Mrs. Bristol. I just worked for Mr. Levy. We sold tobacco and supplies to the soldiers and passed out tracts and Bibles. But there's a lot of them. Soldiers, I mean. After Bull Run, they were pretty well whipped and discouraged, but I guess General McClellan has pulled them together."

"They won't give up," Paul said with certainty. "This is not going to be a short war."

After the meal was over, Paul looked at his family. "Well,

we'll be leaving for Richmond. I think we'll be back pretty soon. We'll take lots of wet plates, then bring them all back and try to figure out what we did wrong."

After the good-byes were said and Frankie and Paul had taken their leave, the other members of the family sat at the table discussing the pair. Marianne listened more than she spoke, but as she saw the black, hearselike wagon roll out from the barn and head down the road to Richmond, she thought, *What a strange pair! But Paul's always been on the outside of what most consider normal, somehow. He never quite fit in anywhere. And now he's hooked up with this girl, who doesn't fit either.*

"I hope they don't get too close to the bullets and shells," Claude murmured.

But his wife said, "There are some things more dangerous than minié balls and cannons, I think."

❧

"Wish we had Blossom here to do the cooking," Paul said regretfully. He dumped the armload of dead branches he'd gathered from the woods on the ground and then began feeding them into the fire. "I hope you can cook better than I can, Frankie," he said with a shrug. "Otherwise we're in big trouble."

Frankie had pulled the cooking gear out of the compartment reserved for groceries and utensils and was cutting strips of beef from a large chunk of meat. She looked up and smiled, saying, "I like to cook, Mr. Bristol. Especially over a campfire."

Bristol sat down and watched her, noting how efficiently

she worked. He had been so involved with the details of photography that he had thought little of such mundane things as food, but as the smell of hot coffee and cooking meat came to him, he said, "I'm glad you got the food. I'm hungry as a bear. Can I help?"

"Not with the cooking. That's my job."

Bristol grinned. "I won't argue with that." He leaned back against a tree, soaking up the warmth of the fire. It had been an easy day—easier than many would be, he knew, for he was soft and out of shape. The little fire made a beacon under the heavy timber, and he was pleased with the feeling of security. Soon he drifted off to sleep, coming awake with a start when Frankie said, "Come and get it!"

"What!" Bristol jerked up and pushed his hat back, confused for a moment, then relaxed against the tree. He reached out to take the plate Frankie handed him, sniffing appreciatively. It was piled high with fried potatoes, roast beef with gravy, and biscuits. He ate hungrily, asking only, "How'd you make the gravy?"

"Oh, I brought it from the house in a jar. The biscuits are Blossom's, but I'll make some fresh ones tomorrow. I brought my sourdough starter."

"You're sure a fine cook, Frankie!"

She put her plate down and filled a mug with coffee, handed it to Bristol, then poured one for herself. "Wait until you taste my black bug soup," she said, nodding.

"Your *what* kind of soup?"

"Black bug," Frankie said, a glint of humor in her eyes. "I cut up the cooked beef, add vegetables and spices, then put it over the fire to simmer."

"What about the black bugs?" Bristol demanded.

"Oh, every once in a while a big black bug dives into it. Makes kind of a sizzle. But they make the stew tasty."

"You keep a lid on the pot, you hear me?" Paul ordered. "I'm not eating any bugs!"

"Why, I heard that people in France eat snails. Did you eat any while you were over there?"

"Well, yes, but—"

Frankie said emphatically, "I'd rather eat a bug than one of those slimy old snails anytime!"

Bristol grinned at her across the fire. "I guess it all depends on how you're brought up." He finished his meal and sat back, taking a sip of the coffee. He grimaced slightly, for real coffee was no longer available, thanks to the blockades. The "coffee" Paul drank was actually a brew made from roasted and ground acorns. Still, it was hot and black.

An owl was hooting deep in the woods, and he listened carefully. "Always thought that was a sad sound, the hoot of an owl."

Frankie nodded but said nothing. The silence ran on, and Bristol watched her, noting that she seemed totally aware of her surroundings. The flames made a flickering yellow play on her smooth face, throwing her features into stark relief. Her eyes were dark and shadowed, but her cheekbones seemed high and sculpted, as though cut out of some sort of smooth stone. She had a calmness about her that most women lacked. . .and Paul suddenly realized he was puzzled by her—had been from the first. Now he wondered how the experiment would turn out. For that was what this trip was, though he had not told her so. It was a test to see how she would do. If it went badly, he would just let her go. And he had been convinced that was exactly what would happen.

Now, however, as she sat quietly, listening to the sibilant whisper of the wind and letting her eyes go from point to point seeking some movement in the darkness of the woods, he was not so sure. She was certainly efficient, not only in photography, but in the business of driving the wagon and setting up camp. Besides, it would be a relief to have a good cook, for he hated the job.

Still, he was uncertain. There were too many factors involved that could not be planned, and the possibility of subjecting a woman to some of them made him frown in displeasure. He stirred, pulled his coat collar up, and said, "Cold tonight. I hope it warms up tomorrow." It was not what he had planned to say, and he was irritated with himself. *If it was a man here with me,* he thought with some frustration, *I wouldn't have to manufacture conversation.*

He asked in an offhand tone, "Do you like the South?"

Frankie had her mug half lifted to her lips. She paused and looked across the fire. "Oh, it's all right. I guess the summers will be hotter than I'm used to."

"I mean the people, not the weather."

"I like your family." A glow came to Frankie's cheeks, and she added, "You're lucky, having a family like that!"

Paul moved uneasily. He let the silence run on, then shrugged. "Well, they're not so lucky to have me."

"Don't say that!"

He looked up sharply, surprised at the force in her words. "Why not?" he demanded. "It's true enough. I haven't brought them any happiness."

"That's not true. Your mother loves you very much, and so do the others."

"My mother would love Judas Iscariot," Bristol replied with a shrug. "But yes, they do love me. Even so, I think it's the kind of love families have for an outcast child. . .more pity than real love." He saw the slight negative motion she made with her head and asked, "You don't believe that?"

"No, I think love doesn't have anything to do with what a person *does*. It's what he *is* that matters."

"That's an interesting theory, but it doesn't really hold true. Just look around you, Frankie. You see people all the time practically screaming about how they love each other, but most of the time it doesn't last. A man loses his teeth and his hair, and suddenly the woman wonders what has happened to the fine-looking chap she fell in love with."

Frankie was not ready for such a debate, but something in her denied what Bristol was saying. She'd had almost no experience with the kind of love she'd referred to, neither had she read a great deal about such things. . . . Still, she was filled with some sort of strange certainty that real love had to be more than Bristol made out.

"In the hospital in Washington, Mr. Levy and I used to go take gifts to the soldiers who'd been wounded. Some of them were in terrible shape. . .just awful!" The memory brought a sudden tension into the girl's smooth lips. She halted as the owl called again, then continued speaking. "One of the patients was a young sergeant. . .only eighteen years old. He'd lost both hands and one eye, and his face was terribly scarred. He. . .showed me his wedding picture. It had been taken only a month before he left for the army."

Frankie picked up a stick and began poking at the glowing coals, her eyes half closed as she sat looking in the fire. "He was so afraid! He told me lots of times he wished he'd been killed instead of all cut up. He loved his wife so much, and he was afraid she'd turn from him. He'd been such a handsome fellow! I—I was afraid, too," she whispered. "But she came into the hospital one afternoon. I was there and I saw it!" Frankie's eyes glistened, and she smiled tremulously. "She was such a pretty girl. . .and she went right up to him and kissed his cheek, then kissed his stumps—"

Her voice cracked with emotion, and she paused for a moment, then looked at Paul, meeting his eyes with confidence as she continued: "When he started to say how he wasn't the same man she'd married, she smiled at him and kissed him again. And she said, 'I didn't marry your hands, Bobby; I married *you*!'"

Bristol had listened to her carefully, and now he said quietly, "That's a wonderful story, Frankie."

She saw the doubt in his eyes. "But you don't think most people are like that, do you, Mr. Bristol?"

Paul met her eyes and was forced to tell the truth. "I'm glad you believe people are good, Frankie. I hope you always do, but I'm too old and have seen too much, I guess, to think like that."

Frankie wanted to argue with him but saw that it was no use. They sat watching the fire in silence for a while, until Bristol turned the talk to technical matters. Finally he got to his feet, saying, "I guess we can go to bed. We'll have a long day tomorrow." He hesitated, then said, "Sure you want the tent? Be more snug in the wagon." The matter of sleeping arrangements had troubled him, but Frankie had been quite practical: "If you'll get me a little tent," she'd said, "I'll make out fine. And we can fix you a nice bed in the wagon. It's the way Mr. Levy and I did it."

"No, I like sleeping in a tent. I'll clean the dishes, then turn in."

Bristol nodded, then climbed into the wagon. He pulled off his boots, then shucked off his shirt and breeches. The air was sharp, but he burrowed under the warm blankets and dropped off to sleep at once.

After cleaning the dishes and mugs, then scrubbing the frying pan, Frankie sat in front of the dying fire. She thought of her family and wished she could see them. Even her father.

How long would it be before she saw them again? Then her thoughts turned to Tyler and to the kiss he'd given her. A disturbed wrinkle creased her brow. She liked Tyler very much, but something in his kiss had made her uneasy, and she could not get it out of her mind.

The future was as uncertain as the wind, and though she did not fear the dangers of battle, an uneasiness began to fill her. She had come on this mission first because she'd had no choice, but even when an opportunity to avoid it came, somehow she had persisted.

What am I doing here? she wondered, not for the first time. She looked up and saw the stars glinting far overhead like a handful of diamonds scattered by a mighty hand. She thought of Sol Levy and wished she could have his warm voice to encourage her—but that voice was stilled forever, and the thought saddened her.

Finally she banked the fire and went into the tent. She removed her boots, took off her clothing, and slipped into a heavy nightshirt, one that had belonged to Sol. Then she wrapped herself in the heavy wool blankets and drifted off to sleep.

The last sound she heard was the owl hooting, calling mournfully from somewhere deep in the dark woods.

CHAPTER 14

BLOSSOM'S WARNING

*T*his place looks like it's been hit by an earthquake!"

Frankie took a moment to adjust the legs of the tripod holding the bulky camera before answering. It was high noon, and they had waited for maximum light conditions so they could record a series of trenches faced by odd-looking devices made of large saplings. The saplings were sharpened on the tips and bound together at the center with all the points radiating outward. Carefully Frankie opened the lens, counted off twenty seconds, then closed the lens. Only then did she answer.

"It's not very pretty, is it?"

Paul shook his head, studying the miles of ditches with raw dirt piled high and wooden palisades pointing outward away from the city. He felt depressed. "Looks pretty grubby, and it's going to get worse."

Frankie removed the plates from the camera and moved to the What-Is-It wagon. Mounting the low step they had built on the rear, she lifted the black curtain and disappeared inside. Paul watched the cloth stir as she went through the process of developing and fixing the plates. When she emerged, he went on. Scowling at the trenches, he said, "I don't think pictures of holes in the ground are what President Davis had in mind to inspire the Confederacy. He wants a cavalry charge with sabers flashing in the sun and guidons snapping in the breeze."

"Well, he won't get *that*!" Frankie wiped her hands carefully on a towel and came to stand beside the camera again. "To get a really good picture, we have to have the subject remain absolutely still for as long as twenty seconds. Be hard to get a charging regiment of the Black Horse Cavalry led by Jeb Stuart to be still that long, wouldn't it?"

Paul grinned suddenly, struck by her droll observation. He had discovered that despite her rather reserved manner, she had a pixieish wit. He had even suspected her of laughing at him at times behind her solemn greenish eyes, though he could not prove it. "No, I suppose not," he said, still grinning. "But we're going to have to get *somebody* to stand still. Got to have more than piles of dirt and sharpened sticks to show."

A cloud passed over Frankie's face as a thought came to her. "We'll have subjects who'll be still enough," she said evenly.

At first Bristol didn't understand her, and then it came to him. "The dead? Well, it'll have to be Federal dead. I can't imagine the president approving pictures of dead Confederate soldiers." He gave a characteristic shrug, then said, "Let's pack up and head for home. I'm tired, and I know you are, too."

"Don't go home on my account, Mr. Bristol," Frankie said quickly. "I feel fine."

Bristol gave her a sour look. "Wait until you're old like I am; then you'll see how it is."

"You're not old!" Frankie spoke without thought and at once was embarrassed. To cover her confusion, she said, "I'd like to stay in Richmond for a couple of days. Would that be all right?"

"I guess so. Someone from Hartsworth comes into town pretty often. They can bring you back."

They loaded the wagon, and as they passed through town, Paul stopped in front of the Spotswood Hotel. "Payday," he announced, taking some cash out of his pocket. Handing it to her, he said, "This is a pretty rough place, you know. Lots of soldiers come here. You sure you'll be all right?"

Frankie smiled as she took the money and stuck it in her pocket. "I'll be fine. And I'll hitch a ride back to Hartsworth with someone." A shy smile touched her lips. "It's been a good time, Mr. Bristol."

Paul slapped her on the shoulder as he would have done with a youthful male companion, smiled, and said, "You've been a great help. Couldn't have done it without you." He noted that she drew away from his touch, and this made him frown slightly. But he just said, "See you at home, Frankie. Have a good time."

She watched him drive away, then turned at once and went to the café across the street. After a quick meal of greasy pork

213

and boiled potatoes, she left the café, asking the owner about a livery stable. Following his directions, she walked down the street for three blocks, turned right, and saw a sign that said SIMMONS LIVERY STABLE. A short, bulky man came at once to her, saying, "I'm Harvey Simmons. C'n I help you?"

"I want to rent a horse for two days."

"Well, I ain't got a gentle horse, miss," Simmons said, shaking his head. He had a pair of quick, dark eyes and was taking her in carefully. *A born gossip,* Frankie thought. *He'll remember me, so I'd better be careful.*

"Oh, I can ride a spirited horse."

"Can you, now? Well, in that case I can accommodate you." He scratched his cheek, which sported a three-day growth of iron-gray stubble. "Don't mean to be nosy, but is they anybody in town who can vouch for you? Can't let a stranger ride out with a valuable animal. No offense, miss."

"None taken. I'm Frankie Aimes, Mr. Paul Bristol's assistant."

The words changed the man at once. "Sho' now, miss, that's good enough. Come along and I'll put a saddle on for you." As Simmons saddled the horse—a roan mare with long legs and a nervous disposition—he talked constantly, trying to find out as much about his customer as he possibly could.

Frankie said only enough to satisfy a fraction of Simmons's avid curiosity. Then when the mare was ready, she stepped into the saddle and rode out, keeping a tight rein on the prancing horse.

"So. . .that's the female ever'body's been buzzin' about!"

Simmons said aloud. "Blast my eyes, but she's a daisy! Wearin' pants and riding astride like a man!" His beady little eyes grew sharp, and he nodded with a knowing expression. "Runnin' around all over the country alone with a man! Well, she ain't no better'n she should be, I'd say!" He was the type of man who always told what he knew, and when he knew nothing, he invented his own facts. He left the station, spotted two men leaning against the wall of a dry goods store, and called out, "Hey, Ed! You and Jim, let's go have one. I gotta tell you 'bout my new customer. . . ."

Frankie was aware that Simmons would give good coverage of her visit, but there was nothing she could do about it. Rather than worry, she concentrated on enjoying the mare. Once it was settled between them who was going to decide on the pace and the route, they got along very well.

It was a sparkling day, with winter pushed back by the warm winds of spring. The sky was a blue parchment, with puffs of cotton clouds, and the birds were back, their tiny chorus of song filling the air.

As she rode, Frankie realized that she was tired, more so than she'd wanted to admit to Bristol. But the fresh, crisp air drove the lethargy away as she rode at a steady trot that ate up the miles. Two hours later she arrived in Lake City, the small town she and Tyler had settled on as a rendezvous point. It was composed of one street, which ran parallel to the bank of a fine little lake that shimmered in the late afternoon sunlight. A few people were strolling along the walks in front of the shops and stores, but nobody paid more than casual attention to Frankie.

She was afraid that Tyler might be out scouting, then spotted the familiar wagon in front of what seemed to be a combination hotel and café. She noticed a sign on the side of the wagon that read MILLER'S ROLLING MERCANTILE. BARGAINS IN SOFT AND HARD GOODS! JAMES MILLER, OWNER. She dismounted stiffly, tied the mare firmly to the hitching post, then stepped up on the walk and glanced at the sign over the door: ELITE HOTEL. Stepping inside, she saw a desk, behind which were room keys hung on hooks mounted on the wall. To her left a door opened into the restaurant, and, moving inside, she caught the attention of a thin man wearing a white apron. He came toward her, eyeing her clothing suspiciously before saying, "What can I do for you?"

"I need a room and something to eat," Frankie said.

The man seemed undecided, and Frankie had no idea of how to ask any differently. She was pretty sure he was trying to figure out exactly what sort of girl she was—and having little success. *People want to put folks in boxes,* she thought. *They figure if I'm a good woman, I wouldn't be wearing pants. That's what he's worrying about.*

Then the man shrugged. "Be three dollars for the room," he said. "Supper's in an hour."

He walked to the desk, turned a book around, and read her writing as she signed it. He plucked a key off the hook, saying, "Number 112, right up those stairs."

Frankie picked up her small bag and, as she mounted the

stairs, felt his eyes follow her. It gave her a queer feeling. She was accustomed to men staring at her—and women, too, for that matter—but this was different. She had a quick vision of herself in a courtroom of officers, with the man saying as he testified, *"Why, yes, I know her. Name's Frankie Aimes. Stayed in my place one night. I thought she looked suspicious, but didn't have no idea she was a spy."*

Frankie walked down the hall, opened the door to her room, then stepped in and threw her bag on the bed. Locking the door decisively, she took off her clothes and washed as well as she could using the basin on the washstand. Then she dressed in clean trousers and a white cotton shirt and combed her hair out. As she worked on it, she sat at the window and watched the street below. There was no sign of Tyler, so she decided that he was in his room in this very hotel.

She put the brush away, then lay down on the bed to rest before supper. But she misjudged her fatigue and awoke with a start in a dark room. Quickly she came off the bed, lit a lamp, and pulled the small pocket watch out. "Seven thirty!" she exclaimed and hurried out, locking the room carefully as she left. Descending the stairs, she had to step aside to let two rough-looking men pass. They gave her bold looks, and one said, "Why, hello, sweetheart!" She paid them no heed, ignoring the crude remarks and laughter that followed her as she came to the first floor and entered the café.

She saw Tyler at once, sitting at a table with another man, but never looked in his direction. When she took a table, a young woman came to say, "We got beef and chicken, potatoes, and apple pie."

"I'll have the chicken and potatoes." Frankie sat with her back to Tyler and his companion, but she could hear them talking. There were only four other customers in the café, and slowly the tension left her. Tyler was telling his companion how he'd been doing well in the country. "People are short of everything since the blockade," Frankie heard him say. When the man he sat with asked if he ever had any trouble bringing his merchandise through the Union lines, he laughed, saying, "Oh, I have to pay a little *tax* on my stores, but then I make it back twice over."

Frankie rose and returned to her room, knowing that Tyler had seen her. Thirty minutes later, she heard a faint tapping at her door.

"Frankie, it's good to see you!" Tyler exclaimed when she let him in. His eyes gleamed with excitement. He was wearing a plaid, rather outlandish suit, and she noticed that he was using his cane less than before. "Any trouble getting away?" he asked at once.

"No. I have to be back tomorrow, though." Frankie found that she was very glad to see him and said, "Sit down and tell me everything." She perched on the bed while Tyler sat in the single chair. He told her how simple it had been to get through on the road leading to Virginia. "I got stopped by Union and Rebel soldiers, but they weren't hard to satisfy. I made them presents of tobacco, and they waved me right on. I guess they figure a peddler doesn't have any country." He brushed his hair back from his forehead in a familiar gesture, then said, "Now you talk. How did Paul take having a girl come to ask for a job?"

Frankie recounted her meeting with Bristol, ending with, "He didn't want me, Tyler, but the letter from your father changed his mind. Does it bother you, deceiving your father about me?"

"Well...yes, to be honest, it does. But Dad would understand. I'd like to tell him, but we can't let anybody in on this."

"I—I feel mean about it." Frankie bit her lower lip, and when she lifted her eyes to meet his, he saw that she was troubled. "They all trust me...all the Bristols. And I'm nothing but a spy."

"Aw, don't think about it like that," Tyler said quickly. "We're soldiers, even though we don't wear uniforms. When I carried a rifle, I did it because I wanted to see the Union preserved. What I'm doing now is for the same reason."

Frankie was tempted to tell him how Pinkerton had forced her to agree to serve, for she was certain that Tyler knew nothing about it. But that was over now, so she said only, "I suppose you're right, but it hurts to think I'm betraying people who've been so good to me."

Tyler saw that there was nothing he could do to change her feelings, but he was not at all certain he wanted to. There was something touching about her as she sat there, a kind of grief pulling the gladness from her eyes. He chose to take her thoughts away from that aspect of their service by saying, "Well, what have you got for Pinkerton?"

"Jackson has gone to the Valley, which everyone knows," Frankie said. "But Paul and I have been taking pictures of the area around Richmond, and I think the officers need to know how hard it will be to get inside. The whole army is digging trenches. . . ."

They talked together for an hour, and finally Tyler said, "You're right, Frankie. I'll get word back to Pinkerton at once. But I don't think I need to put anything in writing."

"When will the attack come, Tyler?"

"I don't know. Father told me the president and General McClellan don't agree. Dad is on General Scott's staff—and though everyone knows Scott is out and McClellan is in, everything still goes through the old man. Dad says that the president wants to attack by land, right down the Valley. But McClellan wants to move the army by water."

"Who will decide?"

"Oh, Lincoln will have to give way to Little Mac." Tyler shrugged. "Can't have the president making military decisions like that, can you? No general worth his stuff would stand for it."

"I don't know about that," Frankie mused. "I think Mr. Lincoln would do whatever he thought he had to do to win this war."

"He's still new at his job. Let's hope Little Mac lives up to his boast to win the war quickly. If he does, the war will be over in a few weeks and we can all go home." He leaned forward to study Frankie, asking curiously, "What will you do then, Frankie...when the war is over?"

"Oh, I don't know. Sell books, I guess."

"Why, you can't do that the rest of your life! You'll get married someday."

His statement somehow fractured the warm intimacy of the moment. Frankie at once got to her feet, saying, "I'm played out, Tyler. Where will we meet when I have something else to pass on?"

Tyler rose, leaning on his cane. "Can't we talk a little longer?" he asked, disappointed. "It may be quite awhile before we get another chance."

Frankie wouldn't meet his eyes. "Not tonight. I'm too tired."

Tyler knew he had to leave, so they agreed on methods of contact. "Send a letter to John Smith here in Lake City, General Delivery," he said. "Mention that you've seen an old friend of mine, and name the time and place. I'll be there whenever you say. You know, like 'I saw Olan Richards at the Crescent Hotel last Thursday at noon.' I'll be there the next Thursday at twelve o'clock."

"All right."

For a moment he hesitated, then said, "Last time we parted, you got pretty mad at me." When Frankie only nodded, he continued, "You know, it seems to me that a young woman would be more likely to get mad if a young fellow *doesn't* try to get a kiss."

Frankie shook her head abruptly. "I—I don't want to think of you like that, Tyler. You're my friend. That's what I want. . .for us to be good friends and nothing more." She saw an argument coming and stepped to the door. Opening it, she looked outside and said, "Quick, now, you'd better go before someone sees you!"

Tyler gave up and stepped outside. "Be careful, Frankie," he whispered. "If you get found out, try to get away and meet me here. I'll get you back to the Union lines."

"All right—you be careful, too, Tyler."

The door closed, and Frankie leaned against it. *Why did he have to bring up that kiss?* she thought resentfully. *I just want a friend, that's all. I don't need anything else from Tyler. . .or from anyone.* For a fleeting moment, she saw the image of Paul Bristol's face. . .but pushed it away fiercely.

Still, she knew the matter with Tyler was not settled, and the thought of future confrontations disturbed her. She went to bed at once but tossed for some time before she went to sleep. The next morning she rose at dawn and was on the road back to Richmond as the sun fired the tops of the trees.

"You left your young woman in Richmond, Paul?" Luci DeSpain had come to Hartsworth for the purpose of bringing Clay Rocklin's daughter for a visit. At least, that was her stated purpose. The two women had arrived a few hours before Paul Bristol drove in, and he and Luci had come to sit in the parlor after supper.

"She's not *my* young woman, Luci," Paul said with just a

trifle more force than was required.

Luci knew she was looking well. She'd chosen her dress carefully, aware that the beautiful green silk with white lace at the bodice gave her a delicate air. Her jade earrings caught the light as her head moved, and her lips were lightly rouged. "Well, I certainly hope not!" she said, smiling playfully. "But you needn't get so defensive. It was just a figure of speech."

Paul drank the last of the wine from his glass, then shrugged. "I'd guess that there have been worse figures of speech about the crazy Paul Bristol and his female helper."

Luci put her hand on his arm, urging him to look at her. "There *has* been some talk, of course. It's inevitable, you know, when a man travels all over the countryside alone with a young woman. People *do* notice."

"Do you resent Frankie?"

Luci DeSpain was far too clever to give a direct answer to such a question. If she said yes, she would be recognizing the girl as a threat. So she shook her head quickly, saying, "Of course not! But I *do* worry about you. Such talk isn't good for your reputation."

Paul grinned unexpectedly. "I haven't had any of that for quite a few years, Luci." He got to his feet, saying, "I'm so tired I can barely keep my eyes open. Photography is hard work."

"Tell me all about what you did," Luci commanded. She leaned back, making sure to sit in such a way that her figure showed to best advantage, and listened as Paul related the events of the past week. She cared little about the details of the work

223

itself, but was highly interested in the accommodations.

"You mean you weren't able to get hotel rooms in the city?" she asked.

"Oh, I suppose we could have this time," Paul admitted. "But when it's really time to take pictures, there won't be anything around like hotels. The battles will be in the woods somewhere, and I'll want to be as close to the front as I can."

"You like comfort as well as any man I ever saw," Luci said with a nod. "Your idea of roughing it has always been staying in the Empire Suite at the Spotswood Hotel!"

"You've got that right." Paul smiled ruefully. "Never saw much fun in sleeping outside and trying to cook over a smoky fire in the drizzling rain. But at least the winter's over. All I'll have to worry about is being eaten alive by mosquitoes."

"You could have taken a cot, couldn't you?" Luci asked idly.

"No room in the wagon for that. But I had a pretty good bed fixed up inside." He understood suddenly where Luci was headed and added casually, "We carry a tent for Frankie. Just a small one, but it keeps the rain off." He was amused at how Luci refused to ask questions about Frankie, but finally said, "Frankie worked out all right. She learned her trade well from Brady. And she's a better woodsman than I am. And a *lot* better cook!"

Luci noted the admiring tone in Paul's voice and the light in his eyes as he discussed his assistant. A flash of irritation shot through her, but she quelled it when he got to his feet, then reached down and pulled her from the couch.

Paul smiled at her, breathing in the scent of lilac that surrounded her. He put his arms around her, and she swayed toward him willingly and looked up, her lips parted. When he lowered his head, she met his kiss, pressing against him. He savored the taste of her yielding lips for a long moment. He had known women—too many of them—and there was a hunger in Luci that matched his own. And that startled him at times.

Finally it was Bristol who stepped back. "You're sweet, Luci!"

She smiled. *Let his little assistant match that!* she thought, but said only, "Am I, Paul?"

"You know you are." He shook his head. "Women always know how to stir a man," he acknowledged with a smile, reaching up to touch her face gently. "Good night, my dear. I'll see you at breakfast."

Luci watched as he left the room, a slight frown on her face. Paul had said all the right things about his little assistant, and yet. . .there was something in the way he spoke of Frankie, and in the look on his face, that set off warning bells in Luci's head.

She frowned. Perhaps she should find out more about this girl. . . .

❧

Paul slept late the next morning, soaking up the comfort of the feather bed. Finally, around eleven, he went down and found only Blossom in the kitchen. "I'm hungry!" he announced.

"If you gonna sleep all day, you kin wait another hour fo' dinner!" was the only response he got. Blossom ruled the kitchen with an iron hand, and Paul knew it. He got a biscuit from the pie safe, sat down, and nibbled appreciatively. "Miss Aimes and I missed your cooking," he said as he chewed. "Your biscuits are the best in Virginia!"

Blossom was not much over five feet tall, but she weighed enough to be six feet. She was not fat, just strong and firm. Now she laid a baleful eye on Paul and shook her head. "Nevuh you mind 'bout how good my biscuits is! You ain't gettin' no breakfus, so you might as well git!"

Bristol laughed out loud. "And people say I'm able to handle women! I never could get anything by you, could I, Blossom? Even when I was a little boy, you always saw right through me. Better than my parents."

"Dey wuz nevuh able to see whut a rascal you wuz." Blossom nodded. She was well over sixty, but only a few strands of her dark hair had gone gray, and her eyes were as sharp as when Paul was a child. "Yo' daddy spoilt you, das whut he done! Yo' mama and me, we bof tried to tell 'im you needed a stick, but dat man wouldn't listen!"

"I always came to you when I was in trouble, didn't I?"

Blossom's eyes softened. "Yas, Mistuh Paul, you did do that." A faint longing came into her eyes, and she said, "I wisht you wuz a little boy again. I can't help you now."

Paul came to put his arm around her. "Yes, you can, Blossom. I always knew I could come to you. And I still do." He squeezed her firm shoulders, then said, "Even if I've made too big a mess of my life for you to do anything about it now."

"But de Lawd kin do somethin'!" Blossom nodded vigorously. "I prayed fo' God to keep you the mornin' you come into the world, and I ain't missed a day since!" She gave Paul a direct look, adding, "And I gonna see the good Lawd answer all them prayers!"

Paul was greatly moved. This was a part of Hartsworth that he had missed. With an affectionate smile he said, "When Miss Luci and I get married, why don't you come and take care of me, Blossom?"

She gave him an enigmatic stare, then shook her head. "Go on with you. Dat young woman done come back; go see dat she comes and eats dinner."

"Miss Frankie? She's back?" He walked to the window and stared at the stable containing the lab and saw a thin spiral of smoke rising from the chimney. He turned to ask, "Blossom, what do you think of her?"

"She ain't proud, like some I could name," Blossom muttered. "Doan know whut fo' she wear men's clothes, though. Doan she nevuh put on a dress?"

"I don't think so."

Blossom stood there silently, kneading the dough. Finally she looked up and said, "Wal, men's clothes or not, dat gal is quality, Marse Paul."

Bristol knew this was the highest compliment the slave ever paid a white person. "I don't know what to make of her," he admitted frankly. "She works as hard as any man and never complains. But sometimes...sometimes it's almost like a scared little girl is looking at me from behind her eyes." He shook his head. "What in the world will become of her, Blossom?"

"You watch yo'self, Marse Paul," Blossom warned quietly. "You knows women, but dis heah gal, she different. Doan you be foolin' with her!"

Bristol flushed, the direct words of the old woman stirring memories he would prefer to forget. "Don't worry," he said quickly. "She's safe enough from me. I never think of her as a woman at all, just as a helper." He flushed as Blossom held her steady gaze on him. "Well...almost never, anyway."

Blossom studied the man, and all the affection that had built up for him since she had first held him as a baby welled up within her. She had seen him throw his life away, and it had hurt her as much as if one of her own had gone to ruin. It was one of those strange instances of love that slaves sometimes had for their masters that no abolitionist was capable of understanding. She longed to hold him, to protect him as she had done when he'd come to her as a child with his hurts, but he was past that sort of help.

Finally she did something she hadn't done for years. Wiping her hands on her apron, she came to him and took his hand, holding it tenderly between her own. Looking up into his face, she whispered, "Dis gal is jes' a baby, Marse Paul. If you cause any hurt to her, you won't nevuh be no man again!"

Paul had learned long ago of the deep wisdom this woman

seemed to have within her. His eyes searched her face intently; then he said soberly, "All right, Blossom. I'll remember what you say."

He left the kitchen and made his way to the laboratory. When he found Frankie mixing chemicals, he greeted her casually, "Hello. I see you got back." She looked at him, a light coming to her eyes and a quick smile crossing her face, a smile that somehow had such a vulnerable quality that Paul knew he would never be around Frankie Aimes again without hearing Blossom's soft voice: *"If you cause any hurt to her, you won't nevuh be no man again!"*

CHAPTER 15

"WHAT IS A WOMAN, ANYWAY?"

*O*ne thought, above all others, occupied the minds of those in the South. Nothing, not even the war, could stir as much excitement as this single realization: Spring was here!

Descendants of the Civil War–era Rocklins and Bristols would never be able to experience—or even grasp—the importance of this fact in the lives of their ancestors. Plantations such as Gracefield and Hartsworth were miniature empires, part and parcel of a feudal society that was no less rigid than that of the Middle Ages in Europe. At the tip of the social pyramid were the wealthy planters, such as Wade Hampton and the Lees. Below these aristocrats was a layer of professional men, such as lawyers and doctors. Next came the shopkeepers and owners of small businesses. Beneath them were the poor whites.

Yet all of this society rested on that which made up the bottom of the pyramid: black slaves—owners of nothing, not even their own bodies.

Later Americans, except for a few *isolatoes* who fled the cities and towns to disappear into the wilderness, would have no sense of the isolation of the plantation. The roads leading from town to town became quagmires during the winters, making travel at best unpleasant and difficult, at worst, virtually impossible. Cut off from the large cities and even the towns, the plantation of the antebellum South was an island surrounded, not by water, but by wilderness.

So it was with Hartsworth, which was a microcosm: a small world in itself that mirrored the larger world outside. The inhabitants of this world grew their own food, mined their own salt, grew their own cotton and wool—out of which they made their own clothing, constructed their houses from their own timber, and for the most part made their own tools.

Perhaps it was due to such isolation, especially in the dreary winters when even a trip to town was a major expedition, that spring came as a gift from heaven each year. For with spring the roads would grow firm; the biting weather would grow warm and gentle.

And the parties could begin!

Marie Bristol had cornered her father in February, when icicles still hung like daggers from the eaves of the house and the biting wind reddened the nose of anyone who stepped outside.

"Daddy, I want to start getting ready for a ball."

Bristol had stared at Marie blankly, then had laughed. "Well, of course, why not? The temperature's twenty below and a buggy

231

goes up to the hubs in frozen mud. Why not have a ball?"

"Oh, not now!" Marie had assured him. "But I want us to have the very *first* ball in the county this year."

Her father had agreed, but not before he teased his daughter about her unmarried state at the ancient age of twenty-five. "I guess we'd better do just that if you're going to snare Bates Streeter. After all," he had said with a shrug, "got to get you off my hands somehow!"

Marie had made a face at him, for they both knew she had had several good offers already. "I'll take care of the party arrangements, Daddy," she had said. "All you have to do is pay for it!"

Bristol hadn't given it another thought—until he came into the house after a two-day visit to Richmond and found the house swarming with activity. He dodged past several of the male slaves who were moving furniture, craned his neck to see over a group of the female house servants, and finally caught sight of his wife and daughter.

"What's going on?" he demanded, coming up to stand beside them.

"Why, we're getting ready for the ball, Daddy," Marie said. "You didn't forget, did you? And I've got to have some money to get some new decorations."

Bristol shook his head. "Haven't you heard there's a war on?"

"Oh, Daddy, don't be obstinate! The ball is *for* the soldiers." Marie didn't wink at her mother, but Bristol had the feeling that she was laughing at him. However, since he was himself addicted to parties and balls, he protested only enough to save face. "Well, I suppose we'll have to go through with it, but I'm keeping a close eye on the expenses!"

Luci arrived the following day, bringing with her Rena Rocklin, the fifteen-year-old daughter of Clay and Ellen Rocklin.

"Clay begged me to bring Rena over for a visit," she explained to Paul. "Poor child needs to have *some* social life, doesn't she?" She had found Paul at the Big House and had pulled him aside to explain her mission. She was wearing a light green dress with a short yellow jacket and looked very pretty. She glanced toward Rena, who was being entertained by Marie, then added, "I thought it would be nice for her to spend some time away from Gracefield."

"Is Ellen giving her a hard time?" Paul asked, then held up his hand. "Never mind; you don't even need to answer that. Ellen gives everyone a hard time from what I hear."

"She *is* difficult," Luci said, shrugging. "But then, we mustn't be too hard on her. It must be quite an adjustment for her to have to live at Gracefield now and not have the money to be independent."

"Some of that 'independence' was ill used anyway," Paul said dryly. "But there's no profit talking about that. I always liked Clay, and Marie and Mother both say that Rena is a fine girl."

"Oh, she is," Luci agreed, then asked abruptly, "How's your little friend getting along? Miss Frankie, I mean."

"Why, well enough, I suppose."

"I've decided to help the poor thing," Luci said.

"Help her?" Paul was puzzled. "Help her how, Luci?"

"Oh, Paul!" Luci said with a shake of her head. "I declare, you men are all blind as bats! You apparently can't see what a *mess* the poor girl is!"

"She seems to be fairly happy."

"Happy? How could she be happy when she doesn't know the first thing about being a lady?" Luci nodded, and there was a light in her eyes that Bristol couldn't quite identify. "I'm going to take the poor girl in hand and teach her how to be a woman, which she evidently hasn't ever learned. But don't worry your head about it; I'll take care of everything."

Paul was inexplicably disturbed about this idea of Luci's, but she shooed him away, saying, "Now don't you dare run off taking your old pictures before the ball. You'll be the handsomest man there, and I want to show you off."

"You make me sound like some kind of a cute puppy or a fuzzy kitten," he objected. "But don't worry; we won't go to the field. Not unless we get word a battle's started." He looked at Rena. "I want Rena to meet Frankie. Let me take her down there; then you and I can have some time together."

Five minutes later he was saying, "Frankie, you've heard about my cousin Clay Rocklin, I believe. This is his daughter, Rena. And, Rena, this is my assistant, Miss Frankie Aimes."

Frankie smiled at once, for she had indeed heard a great deal about the girl's father. "I'm glad to meet you, Rena. Did you come for the ball?"

"Yes, Miss Aimes."

"Oh, you can't call me that!" Frankie said at once. "I'm not all that much older than you are. Just call me Frankie." The girl, she saw, was very pretty but terribly shy. "Why don't you let me make your picture, Rena?" she asked quickly. "Then you can watch me develop. We can make a nice copy for your parents, and that would be a nice present."

A shy smile broke over Rena's lips, and she said, "Oh, that would be fun!"

"Fine!" Paul said. "Make a good picture of her, Frankie. But that shouldn't be too hard, since you have such a lovely subject." He smiled, and there was a gentleness in his features as he moved to place his hand on Rena's shoulder. "We may enter it in a contest, especially if beautiful young ladies are candidates. And I'll bet we win!"

Rena flushed with pleasure, and when Paul had turned and left, she shook her head, saying, "I couldn't win a contest, but it was nice of him to say so."

Frankie cocked her head and studied the girl. "Well now, when I was working in Mathew Brady's studio in New York, Miss Jenny Lind came in one day for a picture. She's a beautiful woman, but she doesn't have your coloring, Rena. Too bad we can't make a color photograph."

"You really saw her? Jenny Lind?"

"Sure did," she said with a grin. "And lots of other famous people. They all come to Mr. Brady. Come on and we'll take some pictures, and I'll tell you about some of them."

Two hours later, the two young women were holding a tintype, peering at it in delight. "Oh, I don't look that good!" Rena protested, fascinated by the image that looked back at her.

"The camera can lie, Rena," Frankie admitted. "We can take out some wrinkles and warts, when it's needed. But that wasn't necessary on this one." She was delighted with the portrait; it was truly fine. She'd managed to catch Rena with her lips slightly parted and her eyes open wide with wonder. The picture reflected the innocence and freshness of the girl, and more than any other picture she'd made, Frankie prized this one.

"My father will like it so much!" Rena breathed. "He's been after me to have a likeness made for a long time."

Frankie noticed that the girl didn't mention her mother, but said only, "Let's find a silver frame and make it into a birthday gift. When's your father's birthday?" When Rena informed her it was in September, she laughed, saying, "That's close enough!"

From that moment Rena was never far from Frankie's side. She was starved for the company of young people, being the "baby" at Gracefield, and Frankie was not "grown-up" in her ways. The young girl determined to stay overnight to be sure she didn't miss any of the excitement. Though several overnight guests were coming to stay for the ball, and the house would be crowded, Rena managed to get a small attic room for herself and Frankie.

Frankie enjoyed the girl. She had not been around young people since leaving her sisters, and somehow there was a vulnerable quality in Rena that gave Frankie a protective feeling.

She took Rena riding across the fields and rabbit hunting in the woods. Once Frankie said to Paul, "Rena seems lonesome, Mr. Bristol. I know I'm taking up too much time with her—"

"Don't worry about that, Frankie," Paul broke in reassuringly. "Spend all the time with her you can." He hesitated, then added, "She's in a pretty bad spot. I guess you know the story of her parents?"

"A little. Rena never mentions her mother, but she talks about her father all the time. She's lost since he joined the army."

"Clay doesn't really believe in the Cause any more than I do. I think he believes in his family. And he knows that no matter how the war comes out, he's got to throw himself into the thing to keep his family unified."

They were sitting on a pair of boxes in the laboratory, and as they got up and started for the house, Bristol said, "By the way, Miss Luci said she wanted to get to know you better. I think that would be a good idea."

Frankie glanced at him quickly. Luci had made several overtures to her, but somehow she'd not been able to respond. There was something about her that Frankie just didn't trust. "She's—been very nice," she said quickly. "I guess we're so different, I feel ugly and awkward around her."

"You shouldn't feel that way," Paul insisted. "Why, you're graceful as a deer!" Frankie looked at him in surprise, and their eyes met and locked for a moment. A sudden warmth filled Paul as he looked into those green eyes—a warmth that shook him deeply. With an impatient gesture, he turned away.

"Luci wants to help you, so give her a chance, all right?" he said brusquely.

"If you say so, Mr. Bristol," Frankie said tonelessly.

Paul whirled to face her, started to say something, then turned again and stalked out of the barn. Frankie watched him go, confused and hurt by his abrupt behavior—and disturbed by the look she had seen, for just a fraction of a second, in his dark eyes.

❦

Later that afternoon, Luci came to Frankie, who was teaching Rena how to make a horsehair rope. "What are you two up to?" she asked. When Frankie confessed what they were making, Luci laughed. "My stars! What a thing to do!"

"It's fun, Luci," Rena said quickly. "They're lots more flexible than the other kind."

"I'm sure they are, dear," Luci said dryly. "But what about the ball tomorrow? I'll bet neither one of you has given a thought to what you're going to wear."

"I'm not sure Papa will let me come," Rena said.

"Nonsense! He will if you ask him properly. When I was younger than you, I could get anything I wanted out of my father!"

"How'd you do it?" Rena asked curiously.

"Oh, I'd sit on his lap and stroke his hair and tell him how handsome he was." Luci smiled placidly. "Men aren't hard to handle if you know the right things to say and do."

Rena grimaced. "I don't think that would work on my father. What I do is just ask him, and he either says yes or no."

"Well, you let me talk to him, honey," Luci said easily. "And I'll bet we can find you a dress that'll be just right." She turned to Frankie. "And what about you, Miss Frankie? What sort of dress will you be wearing?"

Frankie sensed that the girl was well aware that she had no dress but said at once, "I don't own a dress, but that doesn't matter because I'm not going to the ball."

"Oh dear, that is too bad!" Luci shook her head. "Didn't Paul ask you to go? He told me he thought you ought to attend."

Frankie looked at the woman, startled. "He said that?"

"Oh yes. I think he'd be very disappointed if you didn't come. Of course, as he said, he can't *force* you to come, even if you are his employee...."

Frankie was caught off guard. "I–I'd want to do whatever Mr. Bristol wanted."

Luci watched her with interest, noting the flush that was tinting Frankie's smooth cheeks. She forced herself to smile. "Of course, I *knew* you'd agree when the matter was presented to you in the right way. Now about a dress—let me see...." She looked carefully at Frankie, then nodded. "I think I have one that will look just fine on you. About the shoes, we may have to see. My foot is so small, you see? Well, we'll worry about that after we get the dress fitted. Now I think I'd better take you and Rena to Richmond with me. I've still got a few things to pick up. We'll get one of the slaves to drive us in—"

"Oh, I can drive us," Frankie offered. "You want to go today?"

"Yes, we'd better. Come along, then, and I'll talk to Rena's father and get a buggy to go in."

When they entered the house, Luci led the way into the parlor, where they found the master and mistress of Hartsworth with Rena's parents, Clay and Ellen Rocklin, who had just arrived. When Frankie was introduced, she was shocked by the resemblance that Clay bore to his cousin Gideon. He was taller and thinner, and much better looking, but the Rocklin lines were clearly evident. Looking at Clay, Frankie could well believe he was the handsomest of all the Rocklins. He stood up to greet her and, at six feet two inches, looked lean and fit. He had olive skin, raven hair, and piercing black eyes. His features were classic: straight nose, wide mouth, deep-set eyes under black brows, and a cleft in his determined chin.

"So you are the young woman who saved young Tyler's life?" he remarked at once, smiling down on Frankie. "I received a long letter from my cousin Gideon and his wife, Melanie. Gid warned if I didn't treat you right that he would come to Virginia himself and give me a thrashing."

"Oh," Frankie exclaimed, embarrassed and pleased at the same time. "I didn't do all that much for Tyler, Mr. Rocklin!"

"That's not what the boy's mother said," Clay contradicted. "According to Melanie's version, you not only saved Tyler's life, but her life, as well."

"Odd that Melanie didn't write and tell *me* about all this," a cold, cynical voice broke in. Frankie turned to face the woman standing there, who gave her a rather condescending smile. "Since no one is going to introduce us, I'll do the honors myself, Miss Aimes. I am Ellen Rocklin."

"I'm sorry, Ellen," Clay said evenly. "I was so pleased to meet Tyler's nurse that I forgot my manners."

"I'm sure your old *friend* told you everything." Ellen Rocklin had a strong face, one that had been attractive but now was heavily lined, showing signs of her less-than-respectable lifestyle. She had been one of those women—lush and full-bodied—whom men are drawn to. Now she had become somewhat overweight. She was wearing a dress that would have fit her well when she weighed less, but which only served now to make her look like a sausage in a tight skin. Her eyes were sharp and predatory; her lips sensuous and a little cruel, and painted with too much rouge.

Frankie had heard about Ellen Rocklin, and looking at the face of the woman, she now believed that much, if not all, of it was true. Still, she smiled and said, "I'm glad to know you both. Major Rocklin thinks so much of you. Of all the family, as a matter of fact."

"Major Rocklin will shoot my husband dead if he comes on him in battle," Ellen said and seemed to savor the thought. "*That's* how much that Yankee thinks of us!"

"Well, Ellen, I guess we don't need to talk about the war," Clay said quickly. "What about that ball? You have a dress picked out, Rena?"

Luci laughed at the expression on Rena's face. "See? I told

241

you your father would want to show you off! Now you get some money from him, and I'll take you and Miss Aimes to town right now."

"A sergeant in the Confederate Army makes sixteen dollars a month," Clay said with a grin. "Can you get a dress for that?" But he pulled some money from his pocket, handed it to Rena, and said, "Get a pretty one, now."

"I will, Father!" Rena promised, hugging him, a look of pure joy on her face.

"Can I get you anything from Richmond, Mrs. Rocklin?" Luci asked politely.

"Me? What in the world could I possibly need? Nobody is going to pay any attention to an old woman at a ball!"

The harshness of her words silenced the group for a moment. Then Clay looked at Luci and smiled wearily. "Thank you for your offer, Luci. But you three had better get going to town before it gets much later." Luci gladly led the young women off at once.

"Come to my room, Clay," Ellen snapped. She said no more, letting Clay make the proper remarks. But as soon as he had reached the room, she turned on him, saying, "You love it, don't you? Getting letters from your precious Melanie!"

"Oh, for pity's sake, Ellen," Clay said wearily. "I've only got a few days' leave. Let's not spoil it by—"

"And maybe you think I don't know how you sneaked around and went to see your white-trash girlfriend yesterday?" Ellen's fury rolled over her face. "Make you proud of yourself,

Clay Rocklin? Leaving your lawful wife to go be with that hussy?"

Clay stood there as her curses and vile flow of language rolled over him. He had learned that there was no reasoning with Ellen. Time only seemed to have sharpened her tongue, and she lashed him now with all the poison of her tormented mind.

She's not responsible, Clay kept reminding himself as she raved on and on. *She's a sick woman, in mind and spirit. She needs kindness, not anger and bitterness.*

Finally Ellen screamed, "Go on! Get out! Go to her, that whey-faced Melora! Oh God, if I had a gun, I'd kill her! And you, too, Clay!"

He left the room, aware that though he had faced bullets in battle, none of them had made his hands tremble and his knees grow weak as this scene had. He left the house, going like a sickened animal into the deep woods to seek healing. Only by prayer could he survive the virulent attacks that Ellen threw at him. He knew that if it had not been for God's grace, he would have lost the battle and fled Ellen long ago. But he had run away from his responsibilities once before, deserting his family, and had paid dearly for it. Now he knew, as he cried out to God for patience and wisdom, that he would never do it again, not even if Ellen crucified him!

❧

"Luci is nice, isn't she, Frankie?" Rena's young voice was filled with admiration. The two girls were sharing an ancient cherrywood bed in the attic, and they were both tired after a long day. Luci had dragged them into every store in Richmond, or so it had seemed to Frankie.

"Yes, she sure is," Frankie answered, keeping her voice level. She had been filled with doubts about the ball from the first and now was even more frightened at the thought of going. "I wish I didn't have to go to that old party!"

"Not go!" Rena was aghast. "But why not?"

After a moment's pause, Frankie began to tell Rena about her background. She knew the girl had been wondering about her, and she wanted her to understand. Finally she said, "I'm just not good at things like that—things like dancing and flirting. I'm good at hunting and shooting and farming."

Rena had indeed been puzzled by Frankie but had said nothing. Now that the older girl had brought the matter up, she felt it was all right to ask, "Frankie, aren't you ever going to get married?"

"No."

"But—what else *is* there for a woman?" Rena asked.

"Well, what is a woman, anyway?" Frankie's voice was low, but Rena caught the tone: anger and bewilderment. Old memories surged over Frankie—and old fears. "I just want to be myself, that's all! Why do I need anyone else, man or woman?"

Rena was silent, feeling very sorry for the older girl. She had not had a happy childhood and had seen firsthand the tragedy of a marriage where there was no love. For as long as Rena could remember, her mother had been careless, paying little heed to her children. And Rena had learned that her mother had been bad, too, though she never mentioned it to a soul. Then when her father had returned after abandoning them all, the girl had longed to see a real marriage between her parents, to have what other children had: a father and a mother who loved each other.

But that had not happened. At first Rena had blamed her father. She'd hated him for leaving them. . .for leaving her when she was only a baby. But in the short time since he'd returned, she had learned to love him as she did few others. And she knew her father would have made things right with her mother if he could have, if her mother would let him. Rena sighed. If anyone should lose faith in love, it was she. . .but she was still convinced, despite the failures she'd grown up with, that there *was* love in the world.

"A woman needs a husband, Frankie," she whispered. "And a man needs a wife. That's the way the Bible says it ought to be."

Frankie could not argue with Rena, but neither could she erase the images of Davey laughing at her and Alvin Buck leering at her. She forced her fears deep down and said, "I know, Rena. I'm just scared of making a fool of myself at the ball. Don't pay any attention to me. Now you're going to look *beautiful* in that dress of yours!"

❧

The next day was a torment for Frankie. All day long the carriages rolled up to the front door of the house and guests disembarked from them, disappearing into the house. The sounds of music began early, and it was Paul who came to find her still in the laboratory. He was dressed in a fine black suit with a ruffled white shirt and looked totally handsome, but there was a worried frown on his face as he said with agitation, "Frankie, you've got to get ready! Luci's looked everywhere for you!"

Frankie swallowed and said, "Mr. Bristol, I—I don't want to go."

"Not go? Of course you're going, Frankie!" Bristol had convinced himself that for her own good, the young woman had to be made to act like a lady. Now he smiled and tried to ease her fears. "You'll have a fine time. Come along; I'm looking forward to having a dance with you."

Frankie was paralyzed at the thought but allowed him to lead her to the house. "Now you go to the side entrance. Luci's waiting for you, to help you with your hair and dress. Go on, now!"

Frankie moved obediently and, when she got to Luci's room, was at once pounced on. "Where have you *been*?" Luci scolded her. "We only have twenty minutes. Now get those awful clothes off!"

Frankie undressed, her mind blank with terror. She put on the undergarments Luci had laid out, then stood like a statue while Luci pulled first the petticoats over her head, then the dress. "Now sit down and let me fix your hair," she ordered.

Twenty minutes later, Luci stepped back, cocked her head,

and said, "All right, you look fine. Now for some makeup."

"Oh, I don't want—" But Frankie's protests were overwhelmed by Luci's firm voice.

"Of course you do!" she said with a smile that somehow didn't quite reach her eyes. "You want to look your very best for Mr. Bristol. . .and the others, don't you?"

Frankie sat there, confused, and Luci took the opportunity to attend to business—all the while noting with irritation how just the mention of pleasing Paul Bristol could sway the girl.

Finally Luci stepped back, a satisfied expression on her face. "Now I'm going to finish dressing. You'd better wait here, Frankie. Let me go down first, and when you hear the musicians playing 'Dixie,' you come right down, all right?"

Frankie frowned, but Luci didn't even give her a chance to object. "All right," she finally said to Luci's back as she left the room.

Luci examined herself in the mirror, a smile of pure satisfaction crossing her face. Her dress was a stunning pink that complemented both her coloring and her figure. "Let's see you resist this, Mr. Bristol," she said with a low chuckle and then went downstairs. At the bottom of the stairs, she was met by Paul.

"You look beautiful, Luci!" he said, his eyes bright with admiration.

"Do you really think so?" Luci said, a well-practiced note of uncertainty in her voice. "I'm glad, Paul. I want to be beautiful for you!"

Her hand on his arm, they entered the room, moving

around and stopping to speak to their friends. Whenever they paused beside someone, Luci would pull one of the young women aside, careful not to catch Paul's attention as she did so and whisper in the girl's ear. The reaction was almost universal: an exclamation something like, "Not *really*, Luci!" and then a giggle of delight. With that, the girl would move on to do her own whispering.

Finally, after twenty minutes, Paul looked around the room. "Where's Frankie? I've been looking for her."

"Oh, she insisted on doing her own dressing and makeup," Luci said with a note of regret in her voice. "I'm sure she'll be down when she's ready. Now come dance with me."

Across the room Clay and Ellen were watching the dancing couples. Ellen was wearing a new dress, which was pretty but much too youthful for her. She commented on the dancers acidly, bitterness dripping from her words. Finally Clay got relief by saying, "Look, there's Rena!" He rose from his chair and went to meet his daughter.

"Look at you!" he said with pride in his fine eyes. "Not a baby anymore, but a beautiful young woman!"

Rena was wearing a lovely blue taffeta dress that was trimmed with white. Her hair was arranged in beautiful curls, with little wisps dancing around her face, and her eyes were like stars as she said, "Oh, Daddy! I feel so—so—!"

"And you look the same way," Clay laughed. "Come on! Let's see if those expensive dancing lessons I paid for were worth it."

Paul watched the two glide across the floor to a waltz tune. "They look nice, don't they?" he said to Luci, and she nodded.

"Clay's very handsome. What a shame he's tied to that woman!"

Just then the waltz ended, and someone cried, "Let's have 'Dixie'!"

The lively strains of the song began, and as it played on, Paul heard someone giggle and say, "Oh my! Look at that!"

Curious, he turned just in time to see Frankie enter the room—and he wanted to run to her and hustle her out of sight!

"Great day!" he exclaimed before he could stop himself. "Luci. . .she looks. . .*hideous!*"

Almost choking on a giggle, Luci quickly laid a sympathetic hand on Paul's sleeve. "I tried to get her to let me help, but she insisted on doing it all herself." Luci put just the right amount of regret in her voice, but a light of triumph glowed in her eyes. Oh, this was perfect! She had planned this moment from the time she had tried to get Paul to send the girl away and he had refused. *Now let him see what a pitiful thing she is!* she thought, and she looked around to see that almost everyone in the room was staring at the girl.

Frankie had not even looked at herself in the mirror. She had followed Paul's instructions and trusted Luci, so she had no idea of the picture she presented. The dress that Luci had given her was too large for her and was a terrible shade of purple that made Frankie's clear skin look almost gray. The effect was terrible, and the makeup was worse. Luci had painted Frankie's face with layers of rouge, giving her the appearance of a woman of the streets. Her beautiful hair had been pulled back into a tight bun that made her face tight, and the huge cheap imitation gems that hung from her ears made her look like a clown.

When she first entered the room, Frankie had been paralyzed with fear. She had stopped abruptly, searching the room desperately for Paul's face. . .and then became aware that people were staring at her.

And then. . .then she heard the laughter, the giggling of the women and the guffaws of the men. Heat rushed to her face, and a shocked, sick feeling hit her and washed over her in waves.

They're—laughing at me! The thought came like a bolt of lightning, and she suddenly began to tremble. Her eyes swept the room, but she did not see the looks of compassion in the eyes of Clay Rocklin or of Rena. What she did see, with sudden focus, was the wretched look on Paul Bristol's face. She did not know, sadly, that it stemmed out of his miserable disappointment on her behalf. Instead, she interpreted it as shame *because* of her. Paul was ashamed of her!

As the laughter grew louder, Frankie suddenly uttered a cry of pain, then whirled and ran out of the room. She reached the outside door, opened it, then ran into the night. The moon was clear, throwing silver beams over the fields and trees, but the distraught girl didn't see the beauty of it all. She heard someone calling her name, but the shame that filled her like agony drove her to run faster. She reached a grove of pecan trees, standing tall like sentinels in the silvery night, and fell at the foot of one of them. Her breath was coming in short gasps, and as she pressed her face against the rough bark, hot tears ran down her cheeks.

She began to shake violently. And then the sobs came, racking her body in hard waves. Sobs that released the pain, grief, and shame that she had kept buried inside since the first moment she had realized she was not what her father wanted… or what Davey wanted…or what Paul wanted. Slowly she sank down to the ground as the tears that she had had under control since she was a little girl fell onto the earth.

A tall, rangy hound came from the house, his nose quivering. He advanced to within ten feet of the weeping girl, studied her curiously—then opined that it was not hound-dog business by returning to continue his nap under the porch.

CHAPTER 16

ROAD TO SHILOH

Paul got up an hour before dawn, dressed, and went downstairs. Hearing a sound in the kitchen, he entered and found his mother standing at the cookstove pouring a cup of coffee. She turned to him, said, "Good morning," and then picked up the heavy coffeepot. "I'll fix you some breakfast."

"Don't want any. Just coffee." As he sat down, she brought the mug of coffee and sat down across from him. Taking a cautious sip, he watched with bleary eyes as his mother drank her coffee but said nothing. Still, he figured she noticed how unsteady his hands were. That, combined with his glum expression and bloodshot eyes, would be enough to tell her he had had too much to drink at the ball.

Indeed, Marianne was aware of all those things, just as she had been aware of Frankie last night when she entered the ballroom, and aware of the laughter. Now she fixed Paul with an intent stare and said, "Paul, what in the world possessed you to let Frankie come to the ball in such a terrible state?"

"Now, Mother, don't you start on me!" Paul's voice was tense, and he glared at her angrily. "It wasn't my fault. All Luci and I wanted to do was to help the ridiculous girl."

"Oh, I see," Marianne said, raising her eyebrows. *Well, I'd be willing to bet that the only help Luci gave that poor child was to dress her up in that awful rig and paint her like a clown,* she thought. Marianne was well aware that Luci did not like Paul having Frankie around. Now she was fairly certain young Miss DeSpain had chosen this way to humiliate a woman she perceived as some kind of threat.

Marianne took another sip of coffee, longing to point out the obvious to her son, but she knew better. She had learned long ago about dealing with Paul. He was, for all his outward polish, extremely sensitive—especially to criticism from her. So she sipped her coffee and let the moment go. . .for now.

Paul himself had been so disturbed by the incident at the ball that he had slept very badly. His mother's silence now only increased his desire to justify himself. He set his coffee cup down with a bang and said, "I should have been more careful! But Luci said Frankie wouldn't let her help with the dress and getting ready. Who would have thought she'd make such a mess out of it?"

"Well. . .from what I've heard of Frankie's life, she hasn't had the chance to learn the things other girls pick up, Paul. Actually, if anyone is to blame, it's me. I should have made sure I was there to help her."

Paul got up and paced the floor nervously. "I had a blazing row with Luci after it happened. I ran outside to find Frankie, to try to talk to her." He gave a frustrated snort. "Couldn't find a trace of her anywhere. It was like she up and disappeared! When I came back to the house, Luci lit into me for leaving the party. I was pretty shaken up, so I just got mad and walked out."

"A lot of people noticed that you were gone," Marianne said. "I'm sorry the party was spoiled."

"I don't care about the stupid ball, Mother," Paul said forcefully. He stopped and put his hands on a chair, leaning on it. "I'm worried what this has done to Frankie!" At his mother's surprised expression, he hurried to explain. "I mean, it's going to be hard to work with that girl now. I wouldn't be surprised if she packed up and left. Matter of fact, she may have done it already!"

"No, I checked last night. She came in after everyone else was in bed." Marianne shook her head. "She's pretty tough, Paul."

"Well—that was a brutal thing last night," he muttered. "I wanted to take a whip to the whole bunch of jackals. How they could treat her that way. . ." His voice trailed off, and he straightened up. "I'm going to work. When Frankie gets up, will you talk to her?"

"You're the one to do that, son."

He stared at her, certain there was some special meaning behind her words and trying to understand it. With a sigh, he finally said, "Yes, I suppose you're right." He walked to the door but turned and gave her a grimace. "Do you think you'll ever get me raised, Mother?"

Marianne rose and went to him, laying her hand tenderly against his cheek. "Oh yes. God gave Blossom and me a promise about you the day you were born. Your time will come, Paul. I'm sure of it."

He stood there looking down at his mother, thinking of all the years he had caused her pain and grief. "How do you do it?" he murmured. "All these years, and you never give up!"

"Love is like that, son," Marianne said quietly. "It never changes, and it never gives up. When I get upset with you and want to give up, I remember that God has never given up on me! And then I know that it will be all right."

"Frankie said something like that once. I told her I didn't believe it. But. . .when I think about how you've never thrown me off, it makes me think both of you are right." He suddenly leaned down and kissed her cheek, then left the kitchen. Stumbling through the darkness, he went at once to the laboratory, built a fire, and threw himself into his work.

❧

When Frankie opened her eyes that morning, she prayed the night before had been a dream. But she knew in her heart it had not.

She had crept into the attic room after one o'clock, relieved to find that Rena was not there. She'd stayed in the woods for hours after running away from the party, coming in only after all the carriages had left and the lights in the house had gone out. Stripping off the hateful dress, she had thrown it with disgust to the floor, then washed her face with soap and cold water until every trace of rouge was gone. A powerful desire to run away had come over her, and she had had to struggle to force herself to put on a nightshirt and crawl into the bed.

She had been exhausted, weak from weeping, and emotionally drained. Even so, sleep had evaded her as time and again she relived that terrible moment when the whole assembly had turned to stare at her—and laughed! Burying her face in the pillow, she had willed herself to think of something else, with no success.

For what had seemed like hours, she struggled as anger rose like a burning flood in her. *It was her! Luci! She did it on purpose. I hate her!* She had been angry before, plenty of times, but never in her life had she known she possessed the depth of fury that had risen in her at that realization. Tossing in the feather bed, she'd wanted to scream out, to beat the floor with her fists. Strangely enough, though, there was no anger in her toward Paul Bristol. After all, he had been the one who insisted she attend the ball. He had been the one she'd been trying to please. . . .

No, it was all Luci's fault. Paul wanted me at the ball. He didn't have anything to do with humiliating me! In fact, she'd felt almost certain that it had been his voice calling her name repeatedly as she lay in the pecan grove.

Tormented again and again by the memory of the event,

she had thought she was going insane. Then, finally, relief had come—but in a most unexpected form. She had been lying on her back, fists clenched so tightly that they ached, tears of mortification trickling down her cheeks, when she suddenly thought of Sol Levy. She remembered asking him once how he stood the jeers and taunts that came from some who hated Jews. He had given her a gentle smile, then said, *"Frankie, that's their problem, not mine. I can't do anything about the way they feel, but I can let Jesus Christ do something about my feelings!"*

Until that moment, Frankie had not understood that statement, but as she lay there, she realized a little of what the old man had meant. She was no more able to control her feelings than a ship could control its movement when tossed by a fierce storm. If help came—if she ever would be able to rid herself of the bitter hatred that had settled in her heart for Luci DeSpain—it would not be her doing. God would have to do it! Knowing this, she had tried to pray and finally had drifted off to sleep.

Now as she awakened in the darkness, she felt the anger and shame of the night before rising in her. With a sound of disgust, she threw back her covers, rose, and dressed. Better to be up and busy than lying in a bed letting such things build up. She put on a pair of gray wool trousers and a warm shirt with blue checks, then pulled on warm wool socks and short boots. The act of putting on her own clothes gave her a good feeling, and she left the room and moved down the stairs. But as she walked down the hall toward the outer door, Marianne Bristol came out the kitchen door and spoke to her.

"I've got some biscuits made," she said. "Come on and help me eat them."

Frankie didn't want to talk to anyone but could not refuse. Soon the two were at the table, eating and drinking coffee. Marianne spoke of the new calf that had come, of the war, of spring...but she said nothing of the events of the past evening.

Frankie slowly relaxed and managed to eat a little. Smiling at Paul's mother, she said, "I think we'll be leaving pretty soon, Mrs. Bristol. I guess your son told you about it?"

"No, he didn't. Where will you be going?"

"Well, Mr. Bristol says that since General Grant's taken Fort Donelson, he's sure to push on south. General Albert Sidney Johnston's waiting for him, and there's going to be a big battle somewhere around in Tennessee."

"There's going to be a battle here, from what Clay says," Marianne said. "All our spies say that McClellan's on his way to attack Richmond."

"Yes, ma'am, that's what everyone says. I don't see what Mr. Bristol wants to go running to Tennessee for, but I reckon that's what he'll do."

The two women sat there talking about the war, and finally Frankie felt secure enough to speak of the party. "I—I'm sorry I made such a mess of things last night, Mrs. Bristol."

Marianne saw that the girl's fists were white as she clenched them around her coffee mug, and she longed to comfort her. "It was terrible for you, Frankie," she said. "Nothing is worse than being humiliated, is it? I'd rather be deathly sick for a month than to be terribly embarrassed. Once when I was a little younger than you, I was in a wedding. Oh, I was so proud! Mama got me a new outfit, and it was beautiful! All pink taffeta!"

"What happened?" Frankie asked when the woman stopped speaking, her eyes thoughtful as the memory came.

"Oh, it was frightful! I had on a pair of pantaloons that came down to my ankles and just peeped out from under my skirt. It was my job to walk down the staircase, carrying flowers. The bride was to come right behind me, of course. Well, I practiced walking down that staircase for *weeks*! And when I heard the music and started down in front of the bride, it was the most exciting and proudest moment of my life!" Marianne's eyes glowed as she spoke, and her lips curved in a smile.

"But I hadn't taken two steps when the string holding up those pantaloons came untied. I felt them slipping down, but it was too late! They went down around my ankles, and I went flying, head over heels! My head hit every stair, I think, and all the guests got a good view of my new underclothes!"

"How awful!"

"Oh, it was, my dear." Marianne nodded. "As I went somersaulting down those stairs, I prayed that I'd die, but no such luck. I hit the last step and sprawled out with my face up, and all I could see was Mary Jane Jennings, the bride. She was up at the top of the stairs, and she was crying! I didn't blame her, of course. Here was the moment she'd lived for all her life, ruined!"

"Oh, Mrs. Bristol!" Frankie whispered, tears glinting in her green eyes. "What did you do?"

"Do? Well, I got up, and I was crying, of course. All I wanted to do was get away from there. I started running, blind from my tears, but I didn't get far! My father came down the stairs quick as a flash. He caught me, hugged me, and whispered in my ear, 'Daughter, you'll take harder falls than this one in the years to come. But you're the daughter of Noah Rocklin! So you're going to go back up those stairs, and you're going to come down them like a queen!'"

"Oh, how wonderful!" Frankie's eyes grew large, and she asked, "Did you do it?"

"Do it? Of course I did! I *am* the daughter of Noah Rocklin." Marianne nodded emphatically. "My father looked around at the guests and said, 'We'll have a thirty-minute intermission right now. Go get something to drink, and when you come back here, be ready to see my daughter float down those blasted stairs like an angel!'"

"What a wonderful story! How you must have loved your father!"

"I still do," Marianne said quietly. Her eyes were misty as she added, "Christians never say good-bye, Frankie! My father and I will be seeing each other again soon, no matter what happens." She sipped her coffee, and her voice grew soft. She knew that a traumatic experience such as Frankie had gone through could leave very painful emotional scars on a young woman. And she had the feeling that this particular young woman didn't need any more scars! She prayed for wisdom, then said, "I'm sorry you had to go through that embarrassing business about the dress last night."

Frankie flushed, the color rising to her clear cheeks. She raised a hand to one burning cheek—a gesture that made her seem even younger than she was—then said, "I. . .shouldn't have gone."

Frankie was sitting on a pine deacon's bench made by one of the slaves. At her words, Marianne rose and moved around the table. Sitting down beside the young woman, she put her arm around her and looked into her eyes. "I wish my father were here," she said. "He'd say, 'Frankie, you've had a nasty fall, but I want you to get up and run at the problem. Don't let it control you! You're young and strong and have a great life ahead of you. Just don't you quit!'" Marianne saw the tears rise to the girl's clear eyes and, without planning to, put her other arm around Frankie and drew her close.

Frankie fell against Paul's mother. She had thought that she was cried out, but Marianne's kindness, and the motherly feel of her arms holding her close, was more than the girl could take. She clung to Marianne, burying her face on her breast, and let the tears flow yet again. A broad maternal smile came to the lips of the older woman, and she held the girl, rocking her back and forth as she would have done with a small child.

Finally Frankie drew back, saying, "Oh, Mrs. Bristol, I'm so sorry! I'm not usually such a crybaby."

"Tears have to be shed," Marianne said. "They turn bitter

if you don't get rid of them. Nothing like a good cry to clean a woman out."

The two women sat there at the table for a long time, Frankie speaking of herself more freely than she ever had to any other person. Marianne Bristol was a good listener, and when the girl finished, she said, "You'll forget last night. Or maybe you won't. . .but soon it will be like an old scar, like this one on my hand. I cut myself when I was twelve years old. When it happened, it hurt dreadfully, but it doesn't hurt a bit now. Last night will be like that, my dear, if you let God do a little healing."

"I–I'll try, Mrs. Bristol."

"Why don't you call me Marianne? I'd like that very much."

"All right." Frankie rose and pulled a handkerchief from her pocket. She dabbed at her eyes and managed to come up with a smile. "I never really knew my mother," she said. "But if I had, I'm sure this is what it would have been like."

"I'd be so proud if you'd think of me in that way, Frankie!"

The two smiled warmly at each other; then Frankie turned and left. *If I could only be like her,* she thought as she went to the laboratory. Then a darker thought came: *If she knew I was a spy, I wonder if she'd be so kind.* She could not bear the thought of hurting Marianne, so she tried to push the thought away.

When she entered the lab, Paul looked up, and a strange light came to his eyes. He set the flask of amber liquid he'd been holding down on a table and came to her. "I'm sorry about last night," he said at once, taking her hands in his. His eyes looked tired, and his hair was rumpled. "I had a terrible fight with Luci about it. Where'd you go when you ran out? I looked everywhere for you!"

"I just wanted to be alone, Mr. Bristol," she said, acutely aware of the strength of his hands around hers. "And it's all right. I. . .was pretty hurt, but your mother. . .she helped me a lot just now."

"She's good at that," Paul said, suddenly aware that he felt as awkward as he could ever remember feeling. Frankie always seemed so sturdy and confident, yet as she stood before him now she seemed to be almost fragile. He wanted to hug her, to hold and comfort her. *Just like I would Marie,* he told himself, ignoring the small voice that called him a liar. But he knew Frankie would not stand for such action from him, so he just said, "Well, next time we'll do it better." A smile touched his lips, and he added, "Tell you what, next time I'll take on the job of getting you ready. It'll be like. . .well, like you were my daughter."

Frankie looked at him, startled and not at all pleased. "No!" she exclaimed, then when he looked at her in surprise, went on, "You're—you're too young to be my father!"

"Well, maybe an older brother," Bristol corrected, taken aback by her adamant assertion. Then, not wanting to drag the moment on, he said, "I've decided to leave for Tennessee."

"You mean right away?"

"Day after tomorrow," he said, nodding. "Grant's not going

to wait long. He's got the men and the arms to fight, and that man's a fighter! I hear General Johnston's begging Davis for every man he can spare, but with McClellan coming toward Richmond, there just aren't any extra troops. I figure we'll have to hurry to get to Tennessee before the thing starts."

"All right. We'll need some more supplies, Mr. Bristol."

A frown came to Paul's face. "Look, you can't go on calling me that. It makes me sound…old—" He broke off for a moment at the unpleasant realization that he *was* old compared to Frankie, then pushed that thought away. "Everyone calls my father Mr. Bristol," he finished offhandedly. "Can't have you confusing them by calling me the same thing. My name is Paul."

"All right—Paul." The use of his first name gave Frankie a queer sensation, and she smiled shyly. "It sounds funny when I call you that. Like calling President Davis 'Jeff.'"

Bristol laughed, saying, "Better not try that if you ever meet him, Frankie. He's pretty formal."

"Oh, I wouldn't do that. When I met President Lincoln, I didn't call him 'Abe.'" She saw him staring at her, astonishment on his face. "Didn't I ever tell you? He came to have Mr. Brady take his picture. I got to meet him, though. He has the hugest hands, Paul!" He noted with pleasure how easily his name came to her. "And the kindest eyes!"

"Not like what we see in the Richmond papers? A gorilla ready to kill us all?"

"Oh no! He's so. . .so very sad! He told funny stories and made everyone laugh, but his heart is breaking. I could tell."

Bristol thought about her words, then shook his head. "It's all so crazy. A man like that—and I'm supposed to hate him. And there's Clay and Dent and the Franklins—Brad, Grant, and Vince. . .most of our family's men from the South going to fight Gideon and Tyler and our own kin whose only fault is that they live in the North." A gloom came to him, and he shook it off, saying, "It's more than I can figure out. So I guess it's good that all I have to do is take pictures. Let's make a list of everything we need, Frankie. We'll have to load the wagon up to the sideboards!"

With that, they got to work, each one reflecting on what a pleasure it was to work with—to *be* with—the other. . .and then each one chastising him- or herself for having such unbusinesslike thoughts!

The sun was shining when Paul and Frankie left Virginia—a bright yellow April sun that poured its warmth over the land. They had left early, having said all their good-byes the evening before. All day they traveled west, making good time on the dry roads. They made camp very late, off the road beside a small stream. By the time Paul had unharnessed the team, set them out to graze, and put up the tent, Frankie had built a fire and was cooking supper. "Sit down, Paul," she said cheerfully. "Supper's almost ready."

Bristol lay down, propping himself up on his elbow, watching her as she took the bacon out of the pan and began frying eggs. "Made good time today," he said. "Hope the weather holds up." They chatted comfortably until she had finished cooking; then the two of them ate hungrily. Paul shoveled the eggs down, saying, "I've decided to head for the Tennessee River as soon as we're out of Virginia. I think we can get the wagon on a flat-bottomed barge. Unless the river's low, we can go through Chattanooga. The river cuts south for a bit, but we can ride it all the way back up to Shiloh in Tennessee, provided it doesn't get too dangerous."

"You mean we might run into Federal troops?"

"Sure. When Forts Donelson and Henry were taken, that gave the Yankees control of the Cumberland and the Tennessee. We'll have to get off the barge somewhere south of the Mississippi border and find the Confederate Army."

When they had finished the bacon and eggs, Frankie said, "Got a surprise for you." She rose and went to the wagon, then came back with a flat box. "Your mother said these were your favorite."

Bristol took the box, opened it, then looked up with pleasure. "Fried apple pies!" He fished one of the small pies out, took a huge bite, and mumbled, "Delicious! Did Mother make them?"

"No, I did, but she showed me how."

Paul had been lifting the pie to his mouth but paused and looked at her suspiciously. "You say *you* made these pies? I don't believe it! Nobody ever made them this good, except Blossom and Mother!"

"They're easy to make," Frankie said, pleasure filling her. She watched him for a moment, then arched an eyebrow. "Are you going to eat them all?"

"Oh! Here—," Paul said sheepishly, handing her the box. Then a devilish grin broke out on his face. "You can't have more than two or three, though," he warned. "You'll find I'm totally selfish—and even belligerent—when it comes to fried apple pie."

Never one to ignore a challenge, Frankie grinned at him impishly. "Is that so?" she asked casually, reaching out. "Well then, I guess I'd better just. . ."—she grasped the box—*"take what I can!"* She jumped up and ran for the wagon. In a flash, Paul was after her, and she screamed in laughter when he grabbed her from behind, lifting her from the ground. With a tug, he got the box away from her, then stood there, holding the box high with one hand and using his free arm to pin Frankie against his side. She struggled briefly, then gave it up, weak from laughter.

"You win, you big bully!" she said, looking up at him, and then her breath caught in her throat. Paul was staring at her as though he had never seen her before—or as though he were seeing her for the first time. Her eyes widened at the expression on his face, and for one panic-filled moment she thought he was going to kiss her.

Exactly what he had planned to do would remain a mystery, though, for it was at that precise moment that one of the pies chose to slip from the box and fall, landing squarely on Paul's head.

"Oh!" Frankie exclaimed, then could not help herself—she dissolved into laughter.

"What the—!" Paul yelled in surprise, letting her go. Then he, too, began to laugh as pie crust and filling slipped down his forehead. Still laughing, they returned to the campfire, and Paul went down to the stream to clean up. By the time he returned, Frankie had another pot of coffee brewed.

They sat there eating the pies—Paul ate four, Frankie one—and then drank coffee in thick mugs. The wind moved overhead, causing a dance in the branches of the water oaks they sat under. Now and then the rumble of a wagon from the road came to them, or the tattoo of a galloping horse—but it all seemed far away.

Paul found himself watching Frankie, admiring her skills and efficiency—and the way the firelight glowed on her face. "You like this, don't you, Frankie?" he asked, smiling. "Camping out, I mean."

"Well, I guess I've spent about as much time sleeping outside as I have inside. Yes, I like it. I miss hunting most, I guess. Did I ever tell you about my dogs?"

"No. Coon hounds?" He listened as she spoke with affection of her dogs. He was tired, but warm and comfortable, and now and then he nibbled at a pie. When she ceased speaking, he said, "Look at the sky. . . . I never saw such stars!"

"I love it when the stars glitter like this." Frankie put her cup down on the ground and lay on her back, throwing her arms up over her head, studying the sky. The sudden movement threw her graceful figure into prominence—and the curves of her body startled Bristol. The feelings that had surged through him when he'd held her close during their pie struggle returned with a vengeance, and he thought at once of Blossom's warning. He looked away hastily and said, "Guess I'll go to bed. Long trip tomorrow, and I'm sore from sitting down so long."

"Good night, Paul," she said, still staring at the stars.

He stood up and started for the wagon, then turned to ask, "Frankie, you're all right, aren't you? I mean. . .you're not thinking about the ball anymore?"

"I'm fine." Frankie rolled over on her side, rested her cheek on her hand, and smiled at him. Her teeth were very white, and her curly hair framed her face. "Don't think about it anymore. I should never have gone. From now on, I'll hunt coons and run around with whiskery photographers."

Paul was relieved. The girl seemed to have gotten over the dreadful scene. "I'll shave in the morning," he said. "Good night, Frankie."

For the next few days they drove the horses at as fast a rate as they dared. They camped out, grateful for the fine weather conditions. As the days passed, they grew more comfortable with each other—though Paul was careful to avoid any real physical contact with Frankie—and by the time they reached the Tennessee River, they were so acquainted with each other's ways that they could sit for hours without speaking, neither one needing to make useless talk.

They managed to find passage on a flat-bottomed scow,

and Paul paid the fare with gold instead of Confederate money, which pleased the captain of the small craft, a short, chunky man named Lomax. Paul watched as Lomax's men loaded the wagon and then unharnessed the team. There was a small store close by, so he walked with Frankie to buy feed for the animals. When they returned, Lomax grunted, "I'm ready if you folks are."

The scow moved slowly down the river, but they traveled at night and so made good time. Since the scow had no accommodation for passengers, Paul gave Frankie orders to sleep in the wagon while he bunked underneath in his blankets. Lomax turned out to be addicted to poker and would not rest until he got Bristol into a game. The result was that Paul won their fare back and probably would have won the barge, as well, but he refused to play any more.

Lomax was sullen for the rest of the trip. When they got to the Mississippi border, he said, "This is far as I go. The Yankees are upriver." So they unloaded their wagon and team and headed out on land.

That night they stopped at a farmhouse, and the farmer agreed to let them camp on his property. "Better not be headin' north," he warned them. "Army is there, over at Corinth, I heard. And the Yankees got more soldiers than a hound dog's got fleas, so they say." He peered at the two carefully. "Be you Yankees or Confederates?" he asked suddenly.

"Confederate," Paul said at once. "We've got to find General Johnston's army right away."

"Well, you kin sleep out in the pasture, and in the mornin'

you'd better skedaddle down the road to Corinth. You won't have no trouble findin' the army, I don't reckon."

They slept until four in the morning, had a cold breakfast, and by dawn were on their way to Corinth. At three that afternoon, they were stopped by a patrol of Confederate cavalry. The lieutenant, a stripling of no more than nineteen, looked at their papers—especially the one signed by President Davis—and grinned. "Come to take pictures of the Bluebellies gettin' whipped? Come on, I'll take you to headquarters. Got enough generals there to stock a store."

He wheeled his horse, and Paul whipped the horses up to follow. "Well, this is the place, Frankie. Are you scared?"

"No. We'll be all right. Your mother's praying for us, didn't you know?"

Bristol grinned at her. "Well now, how did I forget a thing like that?" He laughed softly, shook his head, then cried out, "Git up, you lazy mules. We got some pictures to take!"

CHAPTER 17

A SMALL CASUALTY

The old adage "Too many cooks spoil the broth" found firm proof of its truth at Corinth, Mississippi, in early April of 1862. A revised version could read, "Too many commanders spoil the battle."

General Albert Sidney Johnston was the supreme commander of the Army of Mississippi in the West, but he had received too much help from General Beauregard, the hero of Bull Run. Beauregard considered himself a military genius and had carved the army into four corps, each with two or more divisions. The officers he appointed as corps commanders were distinguished men, though not necessarily in the military field. Brigadier General John C. Breckinridge, who headed a corps of 7,200, had been vice president of the United States under Buchanan...but he had never led troops in battle. Major General Leonidas Polk was outstanding as an Episcopal bishop, but lacked the experience to make full use of his West Point training as he commanded a 9,400-man corps. Major General William J. Hardee, whose corps had 6,700 men, was a capable officer and tactician who had served as commander of cadets at West Point.

The fourth commander was a puzzling figure. Major General Braxton Bragg, Johnston's adjutant and commander of the Second Corps, which boasted 16,200 men, was a West Pointer who had served with distinction in the Mexican War. Bragg was forceful in the extreme, highly confident—and deeply flawed. His foul temper, belligerence, and chronic inflexibility had become legend in both armies. Grant liked to tell a joke about the time Bragg did temporary duty as both company commander and quartermaster. As company commander, he demanded certain supplies; as quartermaster, he refused. He continued an angry exchange of memorandums to himself in these two roles and finally referred the matter to his post commander. That officer cried, "My God, Mr. Bragg, you have quarreled with every officer in the army, and now you are quarreling with yourself!"

On the evening of April 2, word arrived in Corinth from General Beauregard that the Confederate Army must strike their foes. "Now is the moment to advance and strike the enemy at Pittsburg Landing."

The whole thing was a matter of numbers, as General Albert Sidney Johnston well knew. Grant was advancing with 30,000 men, approximately the same number as Johnston commanded. However, another Union force—the Army of the

Ohio under Major General Don Carlos Buell—was marching from Nashville to join Grant with fifty thousand men. Once the two were united, the Confederates would be outnumbered two to one.

Johnston devised a simple plan of attack: The Confederate Army would move ahead in a simple order of advance in compact columns. But once again, Beauregard gave too much help. He concocted a more difficult scheme, suitable only for experienced units, in which three corps would attack in three successive lines, each spread across a three-mile front.

The weakness of Beauregard's plan was made apparent even as the troops tried to march to Pittsburg Landing, where Grant was camped. Merely managing the heavy traffic on the two roads to Pittsburg Landing required an intricate march pattern for infantry, cavalry, artillery, and supply wagons. The roads converged seven miles from the landing at a crossroads known as Mickey's, so called after a house that stood there. The army was to rendezvous at Mickey's, then move up and form battle lines.

Hardee was late, so there could be no attack on the fourth. Late on that night a cold rain began to fall. It came down in torrents all night. The roads turned to mud, guns and wagons sank to their hubs, units became separated, commands intermixed.

Noon passed on the fifth, and still the army was tangled in a hopeless morass. Johnston looked at his watch and exclaimed, "This is perfectly puerile! This is not war!" Finally the way was cleared, the tangle somewhat resolved, and the attack was postponed another day—to Sunday, April 6.

Now forty thousand Confederates were poised within two miles of the Federal camps. To have any chance at all of taking the enemy by surprise, the troops would have to hold strict silence. But the raw young soldiers popped away at deer in the woods and whooped and fired their muskets to see if their powder was dry. Bugles sounded, drums rolled, and men yelled. Officers frantically went about trying to hush the men, but to no avail.

Beauregard was noted for his mercurial mood changes. That night in a meeting of the staff officers, he cried in desperation, "Now they will be entrenched to the eyes! We must call off the attack and return to Corinth!"

General Albert Sidney Johnston listened calmly to the nervous Beauregard, then said, "Gentlemen, we shall attack at daylight tomorrow. I would fight them if they were a million."

Meanwhile, the Federal Army had plentiful evidence of the enemy but had chosen to discount it. General Grant, the conqueror of Donelson and Henry, seemed to have fallen into some sort of depression. He remained in Tennessee at Crump's Landing, and his enemies would later say he went to Savannah every evening to get drunk. On Saturday, the day before the battle began, he telegraphed a message to his commanding officer, stating: "I have scarcely the faintest idea of an attack being made upon us, but will be prepared should such a thing take place." Later that afternoon, he said to a group of his officers, "There will be no fight here at Pittsburg Landing. We will have to go to Corinth where the Rebels are fortified."

General Sherman, left in charge at Pittsburg Landing by Grant, was no more discerning than his commander. When told that the Confederates were massing less than two miles away, he scoffed, "Oh, tut, tut! You militia officers get scared too easily!"

On the night of April 5, the stage was set for a massive Southern victory. The Confederates were poised to throw a tremendous attack against Union troops that had not even bothered to dig entrenchments or put out pickets. If the Confederates carried the day—as it seemed they surely would—the entire face of the war would be changed.

❧

"Take one fer my gal back in Alabama!"

"Hey, missy, how about gettin' a picture of *me*? These ugly warthogs will shore break yore camera!"

Bristol and Frankie had no lack of subjects for their pictures on the afternoon of the fifth. The raw troops, most of them dressed in homespun and carrying whatever weapons they had brought from their homes, crowded around, curious as a band of raccoons. Most of them were amazed to find a young woman working with the photographer and were not shy about offering to show her the camp. They were respectful enough, though, and wanted only to be included in the pictures that Paul and Frankie were taking.

The two photographers had arrived in Corinth late the night before and had caught up with the army that morning.

Both of them were shocked and a little dazed at the confusion they encountered. There seemed to be no order, and despite the still-soggy ground, there was an almost festive air about the entire affair. Some soldiers were singing songs; others cooked over small fires as they laughed and told jokes.

"They act like they're going to a church social," Paul said to Frankie as they set up their camera at the edge of the encampment. "The battle must have been called off. Nobody as lighthearted as these fellows could be facing death tomorrow!"

Frankie shook her head. "I talked with one of the sergeants, Paul. He told me the battle will start at dawn for sure." She gazed around at the men who were seemingly as happy as larks. "I've seen men come back from battle—but they weren't like this. I don't understand it."

"This is the chance of a lifetime, Frankie!" Paul's dark eyes glowed with excitement. "We'll get as many shots as we can of these young fellows now. . .catch the happy-go-lucky atmosphere in camp. Smiling faces, happy grins—men playing ball like that bunch over there. It's never been done before."

Frankie looked around and saw at once what Paul meant. The two went to work, taking picture after picture of the youthful soldiers. Then they turned their camera on soldiers who weren't so youthful, and both noticed that these older men were more serious. Frankie asked one of the men, a grizzled veteran of Bull Run, about the lighthearted spirits of the men. "Well, miss, it's usually like that. Most of them are scared green but dassn't admit it in front of their friends. Wait until they've seen the elephant. Then you'll see some faces that have looked at hell. This time tomorrow, you'll be hard put to find a smilin' face."

Finally the light grew too dim for taking pictures, and the weary photographers cleaned up their equipment and made their small fire. They ate a little but found they were too keyed up for much appetite. Afterward they sat close to the fire, watching the other fires that dotted the landscape like the red eyes of demons.

"I'm pretty scared, Paul," Frankie confessed.

He smiled grimly, his white teeth gleaming against his mustache. "So am I," he said. "And we won't even be running straight into the guns of those fellows over there. I'll tell you something, Frankie—I don't think I could do it."

"Yes, you could. You'd do it if you had to, just like Clay and Dent."

"Sure about that, are you?"

"Yes."

"Glad that one of us is," he said, his eyes dark and uncertain.

They spoke quietly, speaking almost in whispers as if someone might be eavesdropping. Finally Frankie laughed. "Why are we whispering? Those Yankees can't hear us two miles away!"

Paul joined in, laughing at their foolishness. Then he grew serious, his eyes intent on Frankie's face. "When the battle starts, you stay back of the lines."

"I'll stay as far back as this wagon stays!" she retorted, a stubborn set to her jaw.

"You'll do what I tell you to do!" Paul said, suddenly angry.

Frankie crossed her arms over her chest and stuck out her chin. "As long as you don't tell me to do something silly, like not do my job." Nerves on edge, Bristol got to his feet. Frankie stood at once to face him, breaking in before he could speak. "You wouldn't tell a man to stay back, would you?"

"That's not the point, Frankie—!"

"Yes, it is!" she hissed, her voice low and angry. "I hired on to do a job, and right now that job means staying with you and with this wagon! I'm as good as any man at taking pictures."

"That's not the problem, and you know it!" Bristol argued hotly. He bit back his next words and deliberately forced himself to calm down. Looking into her mutinous face, he said, "You may not like it, Frankie, but the fact is that you're a woman. You can put on breeches and chew tobacco or do anything else to make yourself think you're a man. . .but that's your problem, not mine. My problem is that you *are* a woman, and I'm not going to let you get killed!"

"You could be killed, too! It's not like the bullets will know the difference between a man or a woman. We knew it would be dangerous before we came, and now you're trying to change the rules!"

Frustrated, Paul put his hands on his hips and leaned forward until his face almost touched Frankie's. "I'm not going to argue about it," he said through gritted teeth. "You're *not* going to stay with the wagon, and that's final."

"Are you going to tie me to a tree?" Frankie challenged. "Because that's what you'll have to do, Paul!" Her eyes were enormous as they reflected the light of the flickering fire and shot as many sparks as the burning wood, making her look fierce—and incredibly attractive.

For a moment Paul was taken aback. His eyes blinked, and he stared at her in surprise. *I'll bet she has no idea how beautiful she is,* he thought irrelevantly. He took in the set expression of her full lips, the tense attitude of her trim figure—and, with a sigh, gave it up. "Frankie," he groaned, "be reasonable! How could I ever forgive myself if something happened to you?"

Frankie saw that he was weakening, and her face and voice softened. "It wouldn't be your fault. We're both doing a job. If I get killed, you're no more responsible than a general is if one of his soldiers gets killed." He shook his head in disagreement, and she stepped forward and put her hand on his arm. Looking up, she pleaded, "Paul, don't worry about me! You just take care of yourself. If. . .if you were killed, I'd be—" She broke off, as though suddenly aware that she was saying something she shouldn't. She saw that he was staring at her with an expression of surprise. She dropped her hand hastily and stepped back. "Well," she finished lamely, "I'd be grieved. After all, you've been a good boss. But we still have to do our jobs. Both of us."

Bristol was not happy, but he had no choice. *Never should have brought her in the first place,* he thought. But he said, "Well, I hope Mother is praying for us."

Frankie's face broke into a smile. "She is, Paul! I know she is." Then she turned back to the fire. "Let's have more coffee. And are there any of those fried pies left?"

"Just one. I'll split it with you."

"My, you *are* getting generous!" Frankie's smile widened. She was glad that the argument was over, and as the two sat down side by side, she poured the coffee while Paul dug the surviving apple pie out of the battered box. "Wish you were a dozen," he said, eyeing it mournfully. Carefully he broke it in two, then handed one half to Frankie. He stared at his, then shook his head. "The last one," he muttered. "When it's gone, there'll be no more."

"Oh, I'll cook you a wagonload of the things when we get back to Hartsworth!"

"Will you? Promise?"

"Promise," Frankie said with a laugh. She nibbled at her morsel of pie, watching as Paul wolfed his down. When he had finished and was licking his fingers carefully, she reached out and handed her half to him. "Here, eat mine. I don't like them as much as you do."

His eyes lit up. "Really? I told you, I have no generosity or honor about fried pies." He took her pie, ate it, and licked the crumbs from his hands. Frankie shook her head, smiling indulgently.

They sat there for a while, listening to the fire crackle, and then a man from one of the fires began singing in a fine tenor voice.

When the daylight fades on the tented field
And the campfire cheerfully burns,
Then the soldier's thought like a carrier dove
To his own loved home returns.
Like a carrier dove, a carrier dove,
And gleams beyond the foam,
So a light springs up in the soldier's heart
As he thinks of the girls at home.

Now the silver rays of the setting sun
Through the lofty sycamores creep,
And the fires burn low and the sentries watch
O'er the armed host asleep,
The sentries watch, the sentries watch,
Till morning gilds the dome—
And the rattling drums shall the sleepers rouse
From the dreams of the girls at home.

The voice faded, and Frankie looked at Paul, who was watching the fire with hooded eyes.

"I guess you're thinking of Luci, aren't you?" she asked flatly, then rose and walked to the tent without another word, closing the flap behind her.

Paul watched her leave, startled. He had been thinking of the battle the next day and so could only stare at the tent in confusion. *Now what in blazes was that all about?* he wondered, then went to his bunk and lay down.

In the days that followed the battle of Shiloh, Paul learned a lot about the details of the fight. One of his military friends pointed out that the battle was neatly divided into two periods, with the Confederates winning on the first day, April 6, and the Union winning on the second day. To help Paul understand what had happened, the man drew two maps showing the movements of those days.

Paul's friend used small black rectangles to show the Union corps, white ones for the Confederates. It was all very easy and simple to follow as drawn on those two maps. On the map for the first day, Paul could almost see the driving Confederates as they stormed toward the startled Union troops, and how Johnston's corps commanders drove the bewildered Federals almost into the Tennessee River. Only darkness had saved the Federal Army that day. . .that, and a spot of ground that came to be called the "Hornet's Nest," where a small force of Union troops stopped the Rebel drive dead in its tracks. Looking at the map, Paul noted the peach orchard on the flank of the Hornet's Nest, where General Albert Johnston had led a furious bayonet assault on the Union stronghold—and was killed.

Paul glanced at the map that illustrated the fighting of the second day. It was simple enough to trace the change of fortune in the battle. Grant had returned to his army just in time to shore it up, and when the Federal Army had pushed ahead, the Confederates had to retreat back to Corinth.

But those bits of paper that told so much after the fact meant nothing *during* the battle—not to the soldiers who fought, and not to Paul and Frankie. For as the battle raged back and forth, most of the untested troops knew only their own little fragment of the huge battleground. Men fought and died, and their blood incarnadined the pond near the Hornet's Nest—a pond that came to be called the "Bloody Pond."

Paul kept as close as he could to the fighting, and some of his best pictures were of wounded men staggering away from the furnace of battle, their eyes wide with fear, their mouths open as though they could not get enough air.

All day Bristol and Frankie worked, taking picture after picture—many of which were ruined when they had to move the wagon over rough ground and some of the glass plates were smashed. At noon they pulled the wagon under some trees. A field hospital was set up a hundred yards away, and Paul's face was grim as he said, "We'll get some pictures here." He asked the surgeon's permission—which he gave with a grim nod—and for two hours he and Frankie labored. Often one or both of them would cringe when the air filled with the screams of the wounded, the sound of the surgeon's saw grating on bone, and the cries for water or for a mother or sweetheart.

Paul photographed the pile of amputated legs and arms behind the surgeon's tent, then vomited until he was weak. He was glad that Frankie was in the wagon, developing plates, for he would have hated for her to see the carnage—or to see him showing such weakness.

Finally, blessedly, night came, and the armies lay panting, exhausted and waiting for morning. Paul and Frankie were too worn out to build a fire and could not have eaten if they had.

"It'll be bad tomorrow," Bristol said quietly. They were sitting in front of the wagon, watching the flash of distant cannon and waiting for the reports. "One of the staff officers said that Buell has joined with Grant. They'll outnumber our boys two to one. We'll have to be ready to move back at the first sign of a rout."

Frankie only nodded, staring into the darkness wearily, wondering if she would ever be able to forget the things she had seen that day.

At dawn they rose, and Paul managed to get what he considered the most powerful pictures of all. He drove forward to where a Union charge had penetrated the Confederate lines and found dead men strewed over a field. They lay in eloquent positions, as though they had fallen from a high place, their arms often raised, frozen in an unwitting attitude of prayer. Some of the soldiers had fallen with their muskets in their hands, and often a dead Federal would be found in the embrace of an equally dead Confederate—frozen in a fight that ended the world for both of them.

Paul took the shots, and by the time Frankie had developed them, they grew aware that something was wrong. Paul frowned, watching the action around them intently. "We're being driven back!" he shouted suddenly, galvanized into action. "Get in the wagon!"

They mounted the seat and Bristol reversed the wagon, but it was too late. Figures in blue were breaking out of the woods, coming toward them, and the musket fire rose to a crescendo. It sounded to Frankie like a giant breaking thousands of small sticks. She clung to the seat as Bristol whipped the horses into a gallop, and they were almost clear when she felt something strike her in the back. She thought it was a branch from a tree, but then the pain hit her. Startled, unbelieving, she looked down to see a hole high in her shirt front and blood staining the fabric the most brilliant crimson she'd ever seen.

She tried to speak, but there was no air—someone seemed to be cutting it off. As she slid to the floor, she heard Paul cry out, but he sounded as though he were far away instead of beside her on the seat.

"Frankie!"

Then the floor of the wagon rose up and hit her on the forehead, and she slipped into a cold, black hole that closed around her.

❧

By the time Paul got the team stopped and pulled Frankie up to a sitting position, he saw that the Union attack had been halted by a countercharge of Confederate cavalry. Frantically he jumped to the ground, pulled Frankie's limp form from the seat, and carried her to the shade of an oak tree. The horses were bucking, so he had to lay her gently down, then run for them. He grabbed their reins, tied them to a sapling, then dashed back to Frankie. His heart grew sick as he saw that the entire front of her shirt was soaked with blood. His first thought was to get her to a doctor; then he realized that might take too long. She could well bleed to death.

He knelt beside her, ripped the buttons off her shirt, and pulled it away to view the small hole high over her right breast. Pulling her forward, he saw that the bullet had entered her back and so had gone completely through. He was no doctor, but he knew that it was good that the bullet had gone clear through her flesh. And he saw that it had passed through very high, angling upward. "Don't think it hit a lung!" he said with a gust of relief.

Paul laid her gently back against the tree, his heart pounding. She had lost so much blood. . . . He at once ripped off his cotton shirt and used part of it to make two bandages, then tore the rest into strips. He placed the pads over the wounds and tied them in place, then looked around. A grim expression crossed his face. Sooner or later the Federals would come.

"Got to get her out of here!" he muttered. Knowing he had no choice, he picked her up and carried her to the wagon. It was difficult, but he managed to get into the wagon and put her into the bunk he slept in. He tied her fast so that she could not fall out, then jumped out and untied the team. Leaping to the seat, he drove away from the battlefield and half an hour later was on the road that was already filling up with wounded men staggering back toward Corinth.

The sounds of the battle came to him, muted by distance,

but an hour later they were very faint. He stopped the wagon twice to go back and check on the wounded girl. She was pale and unconscious, but he noted with relief that the bleeding seemed to be stopped.

Finally he found a small stream that crossed the road, and he turned the team to follow it. The ground was level, and soon he was out of sight of the main road. He pulled up under some chestnut trees, jumped down, tied the horses, and got Frankie out of the wagon.

As he was laying her down, her eyes opened. "How do you feel, Frankie?" Paul asked, trying to keep his voice calm.

A weak smile crossed her face. "Not—very good. . . ," she whispered, then closed her eyes and was unconscious again. Paul was filled with fear, for he thought she was either dead or dying. He leaped to the wagon, pulled blankets out, and made a bed. As he gently placed her on it, she stirred and licked her lips, which he saw were very dry. He got a cup, then scooped some of the water from the creek and tasted it. It was cool and sweet. Going to sit beside her, he lifted her head and held the cup to her lips.

Frankie's eyelids fluttered, and she began to drink. When she was through, she whispered, "That was so good!"

All that afternoon and into the night, Bristol nursed the wounded girl. As he removed the blood-soaked bandages and replaced them with fresh dressing, he found himself praying— something he hadn't done since he was a small boy. All night long he kept close watch, and he felt his heart tighten when

Frankie developed a fever. Her skin grew so hot that he was alarmed, and finally he resorted to the remedy his mother had used on him when he was a child. He got a bucket of cool creek water and soaked a sheet in it. Then he carried Frankie to the wagon and removed her heavy boots and clothing. When he placed the wet sheet over her fevered body, she began to shiver and opened her eyes.

"What's wrong with me, Paul?" she whispered, delirium and fear in her eyes.

"Hush, now." His voice was low and soothing, his eyes gentle. "You've been wounded and have a fever, but you'll be all right." He saw her eyes focus on him, and as he watched, he saw the fear leave. His throat tightened painfully at her trust in him, and it was a few moments before he could speak. "I'll take care of you, Frankie," he vowed. "And remember, Mother's praying for you."

It took two hours, but by dawn the fever was broken. Exhausted, Paul pulled a blanket over Frankie and went and slumped down on a box beside her. She was sleeping a normal sleep, and he lay down on the bare wood of the wagon floor and dropped off to sleep as if he'd been drugged.

"Paul?"

At the sound of Frankie's voice, he awoke instantly and got stiffly to his feet. Leaning over her, he asked, "How do you feel?"

"Can I have some water, please?"

Paul got some fresh water and watched as she drank it. She gave him the cup back, and he frowned at how frail she looked. Dark circles gave her green eyes a sunken look, and she winced with pain when she moved. She reached up and touched the bandage on her chest, then let her hand fall. "I feel better. Last night I was burning up, wasn't I?"

"Yes. The fever was pretty high." He reached out and pushed her hair back from her forehead. "You gave me a pretty bad scare, Frankie. But you'll be all right now. I think we'll move away from here—if you can stand the ride. Federals probably will be headed this way pretty soon, and I'd hate to see us wind up in a Yankee prison."

Frankie closed her eyes, then said, "Yes, let's go."

Paul got out of the back of the wagon, then climbed into the seat. He drove steadily all morning, stopping often to check Frankie's condition and give her plenty of water. He made some soup at noon and was pleased that it seemed to do her good. Encouraged, he ate ravenously. That night he camped just outside a small town, and Frankie asked if she could go outside. "It's so stuffy in here. Let me sleep on the ground."

He fixed her a bed beneath the wagon, put her in it, then made a fire and heated more soup. She ate some and drank a lot of water. "I can't seem to get enough," she said, giving him the cup.

"It's that way with a wound, so I hear." He cleaned the dishes, then went to feed the horses. Coming back, he sat down close to her, saying, "I want to get you home, but it's a long way.

We'll have to take it easy. I'll send a wire to my folks and tell them we're all right but won't be home for a while. Want me to send anyone a wire?"

"No, there's no need for that," she said but wouldn't meet Paul's eyes. She seemed preoccupied, though not depressed or in great pain.

"Are you all right, Frankie?" he asked, concerned.

She looked up at him, and he saw by the flickering firelight that her face was relaxed. "Yes, I'm all right. But something happened to me." She was propped up in a sitting position, back braced against one of the wheels, and she reached up and brushed her hair away from her face. "Last night when the fever was so high, I kept having a dream."

"A bad dream?"

She smiled then and shook her head. "No, a good one. I dreamed about Sol Levy. It wasn't like any dream I've ever had, Paul. You didn't know him, but he was the most wonderful man!" She spoke quietly, telling Paul about the man who had done so much for her. Then she said in a voice of wonder, "I heard him talk to so many soldiers about becoming Christians. It was all he cared about, really, to see men get saved. And when my fever was so high I thought I was going to burn up, I seemed to see him and to hear him talking."

"What did he say?" Paul asked, leaning forward with intense interest.

"He said, 'It's time for you, daughter.' He always called me that, and he always said that the time would come for me to be saved. I never believed it, though. Not until I had the dream."

Paul watched her curiously. Her face had a restful look to it, despite the strain of the sickness. She seemed somehow—different. He could not put his finger on it, but felt it had something to do with the wall that she'd kept around herself ever since he'd known her. It had been an almost palpable barrier, so that no matter how she smiled, he'd never felt close to her. Now that barrier was gone, and he wondered at the change in her.

"Sol said it was time for me to call on God," she continued. "To ask Jesus to save me." She closed her eyes, thinking about it, then opened them and smiled. "And I did. It wasn't hard, not like I always thought it would be. I just sort of. . .gave up. I was so tired and sick, and there was nothing I could do. So I asked God to forgive me in the name of Jesus, and as soon as I did that, Paul, I knew I wasn't going to die." She looked at him then, and her eyes seemed to glow. "And ever since then, I. . .I've had this wonderful peace! It's like I'm free, somehow. . .and I'm not afraid anymore."

"Afraid? Of whom?"

"Of myself, of who and what I am. . .and of. . .others. . ." Her voice trailed off wearily. She wanted to go on, to explain to him that the Lord had come in and taken away her deepest fear—the fear of loving, and being loved by, a man—but she was just too tired. *Later. . .*, she thought. *I'll tell him later.*

Paul stared at her, not able to speak for a moment. Something had happened to the girl, no question about that. *Probably just the strain.* But he could not shake off the feeling that it went much deeper than that. Finally he said, "I'm glad for you, Frankie. And my mother will be very glad, indeed."

He could see from her face how weary she was, so he made her lie down. As she dropped off to sleep, she reached up toward him. When he took her hand, she held it to her cheek and closed her eyes. "Don't leave me, Paul," she muttered with a sigh.

For a long time he sat there holding her hand, studying her face, and wondering what would happen to her. She was so different. Finally he laid her hand under her blanket, then went to roll up in his own blankets. He was bone tired, but thought of the past two days, his mind so hazy he could hardly piece the events together. It was a long way to Virginia, but they would make it. They would get home, back to his mother and father, back to Marie, back to...

Luci DeSpain. Paul frowned. Luci would be there, of course, waiting to talk about their wedding. But he would have to see to Frankie, too—make sure she'd be taken care of. And he'd have to give the pictures to the War Department, to the president. And he'd have to decide what he was going to do next. Suddenly the future seemed to rise up, with a thousand tasks ready to press down on him. He closed his eyes, and finally sleep came. He forgot the bloody battlefield and dreamed of Hartsworth...and a woman with laughing green eyes.

The darkness closed in on the two sleepers, and the stars looked down, glittering like jewels. The woods were silent, and except for the sound of the small stream, a holy quietness fell over the little glade.

293

PART FOUR

The Awakening—May 1862

CHAPTER 18

A WOMAN'S JEALOUSY

*L*uci DeSpain arrived at Hartsworth just after one o'clock in the afternoon. She had heard from her father that Paul Bristol had returned from Tennessee and at once had rousted out one of the slaves to drive her to the Bristol plantation. When she arrived, she was met at the front door by one of the maids, who said, "Miz Bristol up takin' care of Miss Frankie, in de blue room."

Luci ascended the stairs and knocked at the door. When Marianne's voice called out, "Come in," she stepped inside. There she saw Paul's young assistant sitting on a straight-backed chair with Marianne standing beside her, a bandage in her hand.

"Why, Luci," Marianne said with obvious surprise. "Paul's gone to your place to see you."

Luci had been angry since hearing that Bristol was back—he had not come to her at once. Now she swallowed the bitter words that had been rising to her lips and managed to smile.

"Oh, I guess I missed him," she said lamely. Then she stared at the young woman sitting on the chair. "I hope you're better, Miss Aimes. Paul wrote me about your wound."

Frankie looked up at Marianne with a smile. "I'm fine, Miss DeSpain," she said easily. "My nurse won't let me do much, though."

Luci had expected the girl to look pale and washed out, but there was no sign of sickness in the rosy cheeks and clear eyes she saw before her. Frankie was wearing a petticoat, and the wound high up on her chest was clearly healing well.

"She's a healthy girl," Marianne said with a smile, noting Luci's stare at the small puckered wound. "And Paul's a good nurse. He drove back from Shiloh very slowly and was careful to change the bandages. Look, the scar on the back is even smaller than the one in front."

Luci came to peer at the wound on Frankie's back, which was, indeed, healing well. "I didn't know Paul was a nurse," she remarked. "I suppose the doctors took good care of you?"

"Oh, they didn't have time for a little thing like this," Frankie said at once. "Men were dying everywhere. Paul had to do it all." Her face glowed, and she smiled at Paul's mother. "He said once all he did was try to think of what you would do, and then try to do the same."

Marianne laughed, then said, "Well, let me see about this." She studied the wound. "I think we'd better keep a light bandage on for a day or two." Skillfully she secured the bandages, wrapping a thin strip of cotton cloth over the girl's shoulder, then around her chest. "If that bullet had been much lower," she remarked, "it would have hit the lung. But the worst evidence you'll have now are two small scars, front and back." She stepped back and said without thinking, "But they'll only show with ball gowns and party dresses that are cut low—"

All three women were aware of the sudden silence, and all three were thinking of the last party dress Frankie had worn. Luci flushed, but it was Frankie who eased the moment. "Oh, I don't go to many parties," she said, "but when I do, I'll put one of those beauty marks on the scar."

The stiffness went out of the atmosphere, and Luci said quickly, "Well, I'm glad to see you're recovering so well." She hesitated, then asked, "I imagine you've had enough of battlefields. You won't go back with Paul when he leaves for another assignment, will you?"

Frankie looked at the girl, aware that the question was not as simple as it seemed—and her eyes widened with sudden comprehension. Luci DeSpain was jealous! Though Frankie was far from adept in the manners of courtship—she had never taken any interest in such things—she was very quick at reading people. Now she saw the slight tension at the corners of Luci's lips and the resentful glint in her eyes. . .and was disturbed. She didn't want to make trouble for Paul.

Choosing her words carefully, Frankie said, "Oh, I don't think we'll be leaving, Miss DeSpain. McClellan's on his way here. Paul says we can get all the pictures of battles right around Richmond."

"I'm glad to hear that," Luci said. Then she looked at Marianne. "I'll wait for Paul if I may. I assume he'll come back here when he finds out I'm not at home."

"Of course, Luci. Would you like to sit down and visit with Frankie for a while?" There was a mischievous streak in Marianne that sometimes surfaced. She well knew that Luci would rather do *anything* other than sit and talk with this young woman, but she just couldn't keep herself from asking.

To Luci's credit, she did manage to keep a pleasant smile on her face as she said quickly, "Oh no! I'd just be in the way. I'll just go get Blossom to fix me some tea."

Luci turned, and as she left the room, Frankie rose and picked up the blue robe that Marianne had provided for her. Slipping into it, she said, "I can't get over it. . .how different I feel about Luci now." She moved carefully as she fastened the buttons, her eyes thoughtful. "After the ball, I hated her worse than I ever hated anybody, I think. But now that's all gone."

"It may come back," Marianne warned. "You've let Jesus Christ come into your heart, Frankie, but there are some difficult times ahead." She smiled pensively, adding, "I thought when I became a Christian that I'd never have any problems with anger or bitterness, but I soon found out differently." Her eyes twinkled as she looked at the younger woman. "If a person likes chocolate cake *before* they're saved, they'll like chocolate cake *after* they're saved."

Frankie frowned. "But—I don't hate her like I did!"

"No, and that's a sign that God is doing a work in your

297

heart. But if you find one day that some of that ugly feeling has crept back, don't panic. You're like a baby, Frankie. We all are when we first come into the kingdom. And every day you'll be growing, learning how to please and worship God. But I've seen so many who slipped back into bad feelings or habits after they were saved, and they thought they'd lost God. The truth is, we don't lose God when we fail, no more than we lose our parents because we fail them."

Frankie looked up quickly at that. "You're thinking about Paul, aren't you?"

"Yes, I always think about him."

"He was so gentle with me, like I was a baby. I was just about as helpless as one! I tried to get him to drive faster, but he said it might hurt me." She looked out the window, the memory putting a thoughtful expression into her eyes. "I couldn't even hold my head up to drink, Marianne. He had to do it. I've never been sick, and. . .it shamed me, somehow. But he did everything so kindly that I didn't mind after a while."

"Paul's always prided himself on being a man's man," Marianne said. "But he's always had a tender heart. Oh, he tries to cover it up—he's like my father in that. Why, I remember a time when Paul was a boy, oh, no more than seven or eight, I think. One of his dogs died, and he tried to keep the tears back, but I saw them. When he knew I'd seen, he grew very gruff. 'Got something in my eye!' he said." She smiled tenderly. "But I knew better."

"Men don't cry, do they?"

"Not often, and it's not good that they don't!" Marianne sniffed, and a disdainful look swept over her face. "Look at the Bible. King David cried, and Prince Jonathan, and they were the two greatest soldiers of Israel. If they can cry, I can't see why our men should be ashamed to do so. I suppose it all comes from our English blood. . .keep a stiff upper lip, never let anyone see you show emotion. . .what nonsense!"

"Well, I showed plenty of emotion when I got shot and while I was sick. I guess Paul thinks I'm a crybaby. And I wouldn't blame him."

Marianne gave her a level look. "He thinks you're quite a woman. He told me that most women would have gone to pieces if they had to go through what you did, but you bore it all with calm and courage."

A flush came to Frankie's cheeks, and she said, "Miss DeSpain doesn't like it, my going around the country with Paul. She doesn't think it looks right." She turned to Marianne, her lips drawn tight. "Do you think it's wrong?"

"No!" Marianne wanted to say more but held the words back. After a few moments, she said, "I only hope she doesn't start in on Paul again. He's polite and likes to let her have her way, but Luci will soon find out something about Paul Bristol. When he *does* set his foot down, he can make the heavens ring!"

❧

Marianne's hope that Luci would not speak of her displeasure about Frankie to Paul was to go unfulfilled.

When Paul came into the house an hour later, she went to him at once, and he put his arms around her and kissed her. She held him tightly, saying, "Oh, Paul, I've been worried sick!"

He kissed her again, then teased her, "I'm fine, but I figure it only does a woman good to worry about her man. Now come on down to the laboratory. I'll show you some of the plates."

Ten minutes later the two of them were studying the plates. Paul had laid them out on a table, and at once Luci exclaimed, "Oh, how clear these are!"

"I had to throw quite a few away, but we got a pretty good selection." He watched her as she picked up the plates to study them closely. She was a beautiful girl, well able to stir a man's blood. . .but Paul was hesitant to broach the subject he knew she most wanted to discuss: their wedding.

"Oh—how awful!" Paul looked at her, startled from his thoughts by her dismayed exclamation. She was staring at the picture of the pile of arms and legs outside the surgeon's tent. It had been one of the clearest plates of all—so clear that a wedding ring was plainly visible on one of the hands.

The sight of it brought back the memory of the men's screams, and he repressed a shudder. "Awful, isn't it?"

Turning to face him, Luci put the print down, saying, "Why in the world did you take a picture of *that*?"

"It was there, Luci," he said with a shrug. "A product of this war. People need to know what it's costing us."

Luci was horrified. "President Davis didn't send you to get pictures like this, Paul! He wanted you to take pictures that would make people feel *good* about the war, make them support it!"

"Well, we got some of those, too. Here, look at these." Paul showed her the pictures that he and Frankie had made the night before the battle. "See how happy they are? Smiling and laughing—" He broke off, his voice growing hard. "Now a lot of them are in shallow graves. . .or in hospitals, missing arms and legs."

"You can't show these awful things to President Davis!" Luci cried. "He knows what war is like. He's *been* a soldier. He needs someone to help him pull the people together. Do you think these. . .these *things* will make men want to fight, or women want to send their husbands and sweethearts to war?"

Paul refused to argue, for he'd known that the pictures showing the reality of war—the raw horrors—would not be accepted by many people. "Well, I'm just the photographer, Luci. Someone else will decide which pictures to release."

Luci looked at him quickly, then felt pleased, for it seemed she had won the argument. She took his arm as the two of them walked out of the lab. The sun was warm, and Paul said, "Let's go down to the pond and see the ducks." They took the well-worn path across the pasture, arriving at a large pond surrounded by tall pines. It was cool in the shade, and Paul said, "Look, there they are! I was afraid the turtles might have gotten them."

Luci was delighted with the flotilla of yellow ducklings that came toward them at once. "Oh, how darling!" she cried. "I love baby animals!"

They watched the ducks for a time; then Luci turned to Paul, a shadow crossing her face. "I heard about Ellen Rocklin's accident, Paul. How terrible for her, to be crippled for life! Have you spoken to Clay since the shooting?" Paul shook his head, recalling his father's explanation about the "accident" that had brought Ellen to her present state. *"She was seeing this fellow Simon Duvall,"* he had said, his eyes showing his disapproval. *"And there was a shooting. Duvall's bullet wasn't meant for Ellen, but it hit her in the back. The doctors said it was too close to the spine to get it out. So she lived, but she'll never walk again."*

It was Paul's sister who had given him the rest of the story. *"Everybody said Clay would leave Ellen when she was paralyzed, but I knew he wouldn't. He was converted, you know, and even though he loves Melora Yancy, he'll stay with Ellen, as awful as she treats him, as long as she lives!"*

Now he looked at Luci, who was the picture of grace and health, and felt pity for Ellen and the life she faced.

"No," he said, "I haven't spoken to either of them. But I know this has not been an easy time for either Clay or Ellen."

Luci watched Paul's face, noting the emotions that crossed his handsome features, then stepped toward him, saying, "I've been lonely without you, Paul. You won't be going away again, will you? Not soon, anyway."

"No. The battle will be here around Richmond." He studied the ducks as they turned upside down, then added, "It may be the South's last battle."

"Oh, Paul, don't talk like that! We can't lose!" Luci, like many

Southerners, had a blind spot about the war. They simply refused to consider the possibility of losing. To talk to them about the North's superior numbers or the South's pitiful factory system was a waste of time. *"One Confederate can whip five Yankees!"* Paul had heard it over and over, with only a slight variation. Sometimes it was *ten* Yankees.

"Luci, if we do lose, life won't be the same around here," he said. "And even if we win, I don't have anything to offer you. I can't claim any part of Hartsworth. Austin and Marie, they've stayed and worked for the place while I was out making smears on canvas."

Luci shook her head. "Your mother doesn't think like that. She told me the plantation would be divided equally between her three children."

"I wouldn't take it," Paul said adamantly. "And you ought to think about this seriously, Luci. You're used to fine things, and I don't think I'll ever be able to provide that for you."

Luci insisted that she would share whatever he had, but Paul knew that she had no idea what it meant to do without. *I don't either,* he thought cynically. *Never made a dollar in my life on my own.*

Luci waved away his words but then asked cautiously, "Paul, you won't be taking Frankie along with you, will you?" At his look of surprise, she spoke more quickly. "I mean, well, surely she's not able to do much, is she? With her wound and all?"

"She'll be all right." Paul shook his head, saying, "I was just about crazy with worry for a while, Luci! If she'd died, it would have been my fault."

"Nonsense!" Luci snapped. "You didn't *force* her to go!"

"No, but she was in my care." Taking a deep breath, he shook his head, still not over the anguish he'd felt when he realized she'd been shot. "It was bad, Luci, very bad! No doctor, and Frankie shot all the way through."

Luci stared at him, her lips tight. "You must be a pretty good nurse. I didn't know you were so expert in bullet wounds."

Paul didn't see the hard light in Luci's eyes. "I didn't know it, either. I've doctored a few dogs and horses that were injured, but that's a little different from nursing a young woman with a bullet wound."

Luci thought suddenly of Frankie Aimes's rounded, smooth shoulders, and a streak of jealousy ran along her nerves. "It's a good thing she's not a modest person," she said, a hard edge in her tone.

"Modest?" Paul was bewildered. "What does that mean?"

"I think it's obvious, Paul." Luci shrugged. "I was there this afternoon while your mother was changing the bandage. Don't try to tell me she was fully dressed when you changed her bandages!"

Bristol could not believe what he was hearing. "Why, I don't think I ever thought about it, Luci. She was so sick, and I was so frantic, it never occurred to me—" He broke off, frowning. "Frankie's about as modest as a woman can be."

"How can you say that?" she demanded hotly. "Why, the girl has done nothing but hang around men, Paul! She says so herself, doesn't she? No woman could stay around soldiers as she's done without losing her delicacy."

Bristol stared at Luci, his eyes narrowing. "Don't you trust me, Luci?"

"Would you trust me if I was running around the country with a young man, alone and subjected to all sorts of—temptations?"

"Yes, I'd trust you," he said, his voice growing hard. "I don't know much about love, but isn't marriage built on trust? Don't the man and woman vow to be faithful to each other? Well, I'm asking you to be faithful, to have faith in me. Because if you don't, then we might as well know that now."

Afraid she had gone too far, Luci put on her most winning smile and reached up to touch Paul's cheek. "Oh, let's not quarrel, dear! You don't think I could be *jealous* of that poor thing, do you?" She laughed. "I might be jealous if you ran around the country alone with Violet Cunningham, but not poor Frankie." She pulled his head down and kissed him, then stood back, smiling. "Now Mrs. Davis has asked me to come for a tea at her house tomorrow. The president will be there, and General Lee. You can ask them to let you take their pictures."

"Yes, that would be a good time," Paul agreed. He seemed to forget all about the argument, but it was only a temporary lull in the battle for Luci. As she smiled and clung to him, she made an inner vow that Paul Bristol had made his last tour with Frankie Aimes!

CHAPTER 19

ELLEN'S REVENGE

*W*ant to go see some hogs, daughter?"

"Hogs?" Rena looked up from her book to her father, who had come into his small house. He had moved into it when he had returned from his wanderings, choosing not to move into the Big House with Ellen. It was a small summerhouse, old and weathered, but he'd fixed it up with cast-off furniture and bookshelves. Rena, who loved books, spent more time at the summerhouse than she did at home—which irritated Ellen a great deal.

"Yes, hogs. . .bacon on the hoof. Want to see some?" Clay grinned at Rena's puzzled look and explained, "Buford sent word that our first crop of young pigs is about ready to sell. Wants me to come and look at them."

"You don't know anything about hogs, Daddy!"

Clay grinned. "I sure don't, but they're going to be worth a lot more than bales of cotton left sitting on the wharf. Well, do you want to come or not?"

"Yes!" Rena said at once. When she went outside, she saw that her father had saddled her little mare along with his own horse. She gave him a sideways glance. "Pretty sure I'd go with you, weren't you?"

"I know you could never resist a ride with a good-looking man."

"My, you *are* conceited!" Rena sniffed but privately agreed. She thought that her father was the best-looking man in Virginia, or anywhere else, for that matter. She loved him with a single-minded devotion.

Clay knew this about his daughter, and he was as proud of that fact as of anything on earth. As he watched her ride beside him, he thought, *She's growing up so fast! Soon she'll be thinking of marriage, and I'll lose her.* The thought saddened him, but he snapped out of it. *Better to enjoy today than fear tomorrow!* He listened, smiling as she told him about one of the stories she was writing.

They followed the main road for five miles, then turned off and made their way along a dusty road that wound through first-growth timber. It was cool under the shade of the big trees, and Clay felt a peace that was rare for him. Even so, he was worried about his boys and said so. "Dent will be going back on active duty pretty soon," he said. "And Lowell will be in action. We all will, I guess."

"Daddy, I'm afraid," Rena said. She turned to him, and for one moment he was startled. She looked very much as Ellen had years ago, when he had first met her. Rena had the same dark eyes and brown hair. *But she's not like Ellen,* he thought with relief. *She's like Mother and Grandmother.*

"We all are, I guess, Rena. Not for ourselves so much as for others." As they rode along, he tried to cheer her up and succeeded. He had the power to give her assurance, and it troubled him to think that when he was gone back on duty— very soon, now—she would be left pretty well on her own. David was still home, and his mother. But Rena could not confide in either of them. Clay thought of all the men who had to leave children and wives, and he knew that all over the country men were worrying about sons and daughters. That was one of the high costs of war.

They reached the Yancy cabin before noon, and as the youngsters came running out to meet them, Clay said, "I hope you remember their names. I get some of them mixed up." Then Melora came out to meet him, and he found himself—as always when first seeing her—a little stunned.

Melora Yancy was as tall and slender as a mountain spruce, or she seemed to be. She had green eyes and the blackest hair possible and was one of those people who never seemed to age. It was difficult for those meeting her for the first time to believe that she was twenty-seven instead of nineteen or twenty.

"Hello, Mister Clay," she said, a smile on her wide lips. She glanced at Rena and winked. "You know, of all the times your father's come here, I can't remember once when it wasn't mealtime."

"I'm no fool." Clay grinned. "Where's Buford?"

"Out with those pesky pigs," Melora said tartly. "I believe he thinks more of them than he does of his children."

"Oh, not really, Melora?" Rena stared. She admired Melora tremendously, wanting to be and look like her more than anyone else in the world.

"Well, I got a bad cold last week," Melora said, smiling impishly, "and Pa never even noticed. But you let one of those blasted swine so much as cough, and he'll be down there quick as a shot pouring medicine down its throat!" Glancing at the children, who had ringed the two visitors, she said, "Rose, you and Martha watch that corn bread so it doesn't burn. I'm going to take Mister Clay and Rena to see those beautiful animals." She ignored the cry of protest, saying, "You can all see Mister Clay at dinner. Come along, Rena. I want to hear about your new stories."

The three made their way along the trail leading away from the house, Clay walking behind the two women. He watched Melora, noting how much—and how little—she had changed since he'd first met her when she was a child. Then she had been a small girl he was kind to, whom he bought books for...someone who believed in him. Then when he'd come back to try to pick up the threads of his life, he'd been startled to discover that the little girl was gone, replaced in that mysterious way of nature by a startlingly beautiful young woman.

Before long, they knew they loved each other, but he was a married man, in name and under the law. The fact that his wife made life as difficult for him as possible was not a factor, for his goal was to honor God in his role as a father and husband, and as a son to his parents. That meant staying with and caring for his wife, despite the anger and bitterness that constantly spilled out of her. It meant that he could not make promises to Melora, except that he would continue to be her friend, as he always had been. He had tried to get her to marry Jeremiah Irons, a pastor whom both Clay and Melora had counted a dear friend, but Irons had died in the war. Clay frowned, troubled. *Lord, I don't understand. Wouldn't it have been better if Jeremiah had lived? He would have made Melora a good husband. . . .* He shook his head, praying that God would care for the woman who walked in front of him.

Before long they heard the grunting and shrill yelps of the pigs and soon arrived at the hog pens. Buford Yancy saw the three walking out of the woods and came at once to offer his hand to Clay. "Make you feel proud to own such a mess of fine hogs, Clay?" Yancy, a widower in his early fifties, was six feet tall and lean as a lizard. He had greenish eyes and tow-colored hair and was strong and agile in the way of mountain men. He looked at Clay Rocklin, approval and admiration evident in his eyes. "Glad you made it back. How are my boys, Bob and Lonnie?"

"Best soldiers in the regiment, except for Lowell, of course!"

Yancy spit an amber stream of tobacco juice to one side, then grinned and waved at the hogs. "There they be. Ain't they purty?"

Clay looked doubtfully at the pigs, then shook his head. "I guess so, Yancy. I'm not much of an authority on pigs. We going to sell them?"

"Not right off. I saved enough grain to feed 'em out for another month. By that time I figure we won't have no trouble sellin' 'em in Richmond."

"You're right about that, Buford." Clay nodded. "But we give the Richmond Grays first shot. Bob and Lonnie and the rest of the boys would sure like some good ham and bacon this winter."

Buford showed them the finer points of the hogs; then they all went back to the cabin for dinner. As they sat down at the table, Clay looked around and smiled. "I remember the first time I ever sat down at this table." He looked at Melora, who was going around the table pouring buttermilk into cups and glasses. "It was the first time I got to sit up and eat after Irons brought me here when I was so sick. Bet you don't remember what I ate, Melora."

"Mush and some dumplings."

Clay stared at her. "How in blazes can you remember that? You weren't more than seven or eight."

"I was six," Melora said, then sat down beside her father. "Mister Clay, please ask the blessing." She waited until he was through, then said to Rena, "Your father gave me my first book. I still have it, along with all the others."

The meal was fine, and afterward Clay talked for an hour with Buford, mostly about plans for next year's crop of corn and pigs. Melora enlisted Rena's help in cleaning up, and finally it was time for the Rocklins to go. Clay had only a moment alone with Melora while the children ganged up around Rena, begging her to come back and bring more books and candy.

"I miss Jeremiah," Clay said simply. "I think he was the best man I ever knew."

"I think we all loved him. He was so kind!"

Clay hesitated, then said, "I wish he had lived, Melora. I would like to see you with your own family, your own home."

She smiled. "I know, Clay. But I can't help but wonder if I could have made him happy. Jeremiah knew I was fond of him, but he also knew he could never have all of me." Her green eyes met his squarely. "He knew I loved you."

Clay nodded. She spoke so directly, so honestly! "I wish things were different, Melora."

"I know that. It's all right, Clay. God knows our hearts, and He will help us to do what is right."

And then Rena was there, and the two mounted and left the homestead. Rena talked most of the way home, explaining how she was going to get some new books and take them to Melora and the children.

Clay said little until they pulled up and dismounted. "Let's go see how your grandfather is," he suggested.

They found Thomas Rocklin out in the scuppernong arbor watching a flock of sparrows fight over the crumbs he threw them. "When a man's good for nothing but feeding a bunch of dumb birds, it's pretty bad, isn't it, Clay?"

"How do you feel today?"

"Well—I feel more like I do now than I did before I felt like this." Thomas laughed at the puzzled expression on Rena's face. "Figure that out, girl." He looked bad to Clay—his face was pale and his tall frame shrunken. Clay knew his father had a bad stomach, and the doctors could find no definite cause. Now Thomas smiled up at his son. "Sit down and tell me the news. When do you have to go back to the regiment?"

"In four days," Clay said. "Let me tell you about my pigs. . . ." In the midst of his story, the sound of wheels on the bricks came to them. Clay paused briefly, glancing up to see his wife, Ellen, in her wheelchair. Clay nodded at her, said hello, then kept on with his story.

Ellen sat there listening and then, to the shock of the three across from her, cried out, "I knew you'd been to see that woman! I knew it! And to take your own daughter with you on your nasty business!"

Clay and Thomas stood up, both of them trying to speak.

"Ellen, it was just a visit—," Clay began, but Ellen flew into a rage, cursing him.

"Rena," Clay said sharply, "go to the house. Your mother's not well."

Rena, who had turned quite pale, ran at once to the house. As she fled, she heard her mother screaming obscenities and her father asking her to listen to reason. She ran upstairs and threw herself on the bed, burying her face in a pillow. She began to weep, her body torn with great sobs. After a time, she heard her door open and looked up quickly to see her grandmother, who came to her at once.

Susanna Rocklin sat on the edge of the bed and took the girl into her arms, holding her tightly, stroking her hair. "I wish you hadn't heard that, Rena."

"I hate her!" Rena sobbed. "She's so mean to Daddy!"

"You must not hate her, child. She's all mixed up inside. Has been for a long time. I know it's hard, but you must not let hate get a hold on you. That would only hurt you. . .and none of us—not your grandfather, nor I, nor your father—could stand that!" Susanna waited until the girl's sobs ceased, then held her at arm's length. "Ellen is a difficult person, Rena, but she is your mother. Promise me you'll let Jesus love her through you. It's the only way any of us can love those who misuse us."

Rena wiped the tears that still streamed down her cheeks. "How can I do that, Grandmother?"

"I'll try to tell you. . . ." And the two sat there, the older woman speaking quietly, Rena listening intently.

Outside in the grape arbor, Thomas shook his head, grateful that Ellen had finally wheeled herself off. "I'm proud of you, son," he said, looking at Clay. "Not many men would hang around and take the kind of punishment that woman hands out." Thomas reached out to do something he couldn't have done at one time, something that only the grace of God in his life and in Clay's life made possible: He put his arm around Clay's shoulder and said, "You're a fine son to me. I couldn't have had better!"

Inside, Ellen sat in her room, watching the two men from her window. Her mind was filled with rage, and she muttered, "That woman—she won't have him! I'll see to that!" She wheeled herself around, got some paper from her desk, and began scribbling furiously. When the letter was finished, she put it into an envelope, sealed it carefully with wax, then made her way to the front porch.

A tall young black was working on the yard, and he looked up when he heard his named called. Dropping his spade, he went to the porch and removed his hat. "Yas, Miz Rocklin?"

"Highboy, take this letter into Richmond. Take it to the Crescent Hotel and give it to the man at the desk." She handed him a coin. "That's for you, but this is nobody's business but mine, you understand?"

"Yas, Miz Rocklin. I do it right now, but you hafta tell Miz Susanna why I didn't finish—"

"Go on! Take one of the saddle horses!"

Ellen watched as the tall slave hurried to the stable, then came out five minutes later. She kept her eyes on him until he disappeared, then smiled cruelly.

"We'll see about Miss Melora Yancy!" There was a wild light in her eyes, and she talked to herself as she wheeled away, muttering and laughing in a disturbing way.

CHAPTER 20

A DANGEROUS ASSIGNMENT

*T*he letter came in an innocent-looking envelope, addressed simply to Miss Frankie Aimes, Hartsworth, Richmond, Virginia.

As soon as Paul handed it to her, saying, "Letter for you, Frankie," a stab of fear shot through her.

She took the envelope and remarked casually, "Wonder who it could be from?" She broke the wax seal, pulled out a single sheet of paper, and read it quickly:

My dear niece,

I have just come from your home, and my brother informed me that you are now in Virginia working as a photographer. Needless to say, this came as quite a surprise to me. As you know, I have been in England for the last eighteen months, traveling extensively, so I did not get the news that you had left home.

I will be passing through Lake City, a small town

316

in Virginia, on May 20. Unfortunately I cannot spare
the time to get to Hartsworth, or even to meet you in
Richmond. If, however, you could come to Lake City, we
could have a short visit, and I would like that very much.
We have been out of touch, and if we could have just a
brief time together, we could get caught up on all the news.
I will be staying at the Elite Hotel and hope that you can
find the time to come.

    Oh yes, my friend Allan will be with me, and he asks me
to give you his encouragement to come. He remembers you
with affection, and I know you would like to see him again.

Your loving uncle,

James Miller

"My friend Allan," Frankie thought quickly. *That's Allan
Pinkerton. I'll have to go!*

She looked up at Paul, who was reading a letter of his own.
"It's from my Uncle James," she said. "My father's brother. He's
going to be passing through Lake City, and he'd like for me to
come and see him."

"Lake City? Well, that's not far. When will he be there?"

"On the twentieth. That's the day after tomorrow."

Paul was interested, for Frankie had never spoken of her
family. "Would you like to go?"

"Oh yes. I've always liked Uncle James. He's a businessman
and travels a lot, but it would be nice, if you can spare me."

Bristol shrugged. "I'm not sure it'd be good for you to ride a

317

horse that far. Might not be good for that wound. I'll drive you over in the big carriage."

"Oh no!" Frankie spoke impulsively. "I can drive a buggy."

Bristol was surprised at her adamant refusal. "I don't mind, Frankie."

"I know, but. . ." She thought desperately, then blurted out, "I—I don't think Miss Luci would like it." She saw Paul's jaw harden and knew that he was going to be stubborn. "And she's right, I think," she said quickly. "It's one thing for us to travel together to get pictures, but this is personal. I think it would be better for me to go alone."

Paul seemed about to argue; then he sighed. "You're right, of course. I'll have one of the stable hands drive you. Or, if you insist, you can go alone if you're sure you're up to it."

"Oh, I'd enjoy the drive, Paul!" Relief ran through Frankie, and she said lightly, "Look, I can hold my arm up now so easy!" She held up her right hand triumphantly. "See? It's almost as good as new."

Bristol was pleased. "Just do me a favor and don't ever get shot again, Frankie. It's too hard on an old man's nerves." He smiled at her. "I'll pay your salary before we leave, and maybe toss in a bonus for a job well done."

"Oh, don't do that!" Frankie protested. She was wearing a pair of beechnut-dyed men's trousers and a long-sleeved cotton shirt partly covered by a brown vest buttoned halfway up. Bristol noticed that she'd gained back the weight she had lost while recovering from her wound, and from the color in her cheeks, no one would have suspected that she had been ill.

She felt his eyes on her and reddened slightly, saying, "Well, I'll only be gone overnight."

"When you get back, we'll go to Richmond. My parents have been invited to some sort of party at Colonel Chesnut's. They want you to go with us."

"That would be nice, Paul. I'll look forward to it."

All that afternoon and through most of the night, Frankie thought about the summons from Tyler. When she finally left early on the morning of the twentieth, it was with a mixture of relief and apprehension. She drove the team easily, glad to discover that her wound was no problem. She was also glad to discover that Marianne had been right when she had assured her the scars were small and would grow less noticeable with the passage of time.

Frankie stopped twice for a drink of cool water, then at noon pulled over under the shade of some large hickory trees beside a small creek. She watered the horses and ate the lunch that Blossom had packed for her—sandwiches, boiled eggs, and sweet rolls. The food made her drowsy, and when she leaned back against one of the huge trunks and closed her eyes, the humming of bees and the warm air put her to sleep. Waking with a start, she looked at the sun, noting with relief that she hadn't slept too long.

Guess I'm not fully recovered yet, she thought, stretching and yawning. *Can't remember the last time I had to take naps in the middle of the day!*

Shadows were growing long as she pulled into Lake City. She put the buggy up at the livery stable, instructing the stubby hostler to grain the horses well. She was glad that the streets were mostly unoccupied and the stores were closing up—no one would be around to notice or remember her. But when she entered the hotel lobby, she found the same thin man who'd rented her a room before behind the desk.

He watched with interest as she came up to the desk. "Hello. Back again, I see."

"Yes. I need a room just for tonight."

"Take 216," he said, and as Frankie signed her name, she was struck with apprehension. *It's bad that he remembers me. We should have used another place,* she thought. But she took the small suitcase she'd packed and went to the room, which was a carbon copy of the last one she'd had, right down to the bed, dresser, and one straight chair. It took only a few moments to unpack her things and place them in the drawer of the shaky dresser. She removed her vest and shirt and sluiced away the dust from the road, then put them back on. There was nothing to do for the next hour but sit in the chair beside the window and watch the street below.

Finally it was time for the meeting, so she lit the lamp, turned it down low, and left the room. The restaurant was fairly busy, but there was no sign of Tyler or Pinkerton. Frankie smiled when she spotted a large hand-printed sign over the back wall next to the kitchen door: IF YOU DON'T LIKE OUR GRUB, DON'T EAT HERE! She moved to a table, and when the

320

waitress said, "We got buffalo fish and pork chops," she chose the fish. The wait for her food was long, and she was tempted to ask if they had to go to the lake and catch the fish, but she refrained. No sense in saying something that the waitress probably would remember her for.

She drank buttermilk while she waited, watching the patrons carefully. None of them looked like spies. . .but then she shook her head. *How would I know what a spy looks like?*

Finally her meal came, and though the fish was greasy, it was flaky and crisp. Taking a bite, she found she was very hungry and so finished all on her plate, including some turnip greens that had been added. The waitress came to ask if she wanted some blackberry pie, and she sampled that, too, along with something that was called "coffee" but was actually made from ground and roasted acorns. Still, it was hot and black, and glancing back at the sign, Frankie smiled and drank half of the bitter liquid.

Finally she rose and paid the bill, then left the restaurant. She had thought Tyler and Pinkerton would be there by now. For a woman, there was nothing at all to do in town to pass time—not for a young unescorted single woman, anyway. A man could go into one of the three bars to drink and gamble, but Frankie knew that if she even walked down the street, she would be noticed—just what she didn't want. So with a sigh she mounted the stairs and entered her room. Turning up the lamp, she pulled the chair close to it and began to read the Bible that Sol Levy had given her.

The evening was warm, and there was little breeze coming through the open window—although mosquitoes and flies had no trouble finding their way in. Frankie ignored the pests, reading steadily. She was fascinated by the Bible, amazed at how it spoke to her. Before and after her conversion, she had tried to read the scripture but had given up in despair. It wasn't until Marianne had taught her how to begin, and she'd become caught up in the gospels—especially the Gospel of John—that she'd found she could enjoy reading the Bible.

"The Spirit of God will teach you, Frankie," Marianne had said. *"You couldn't understand the Bible before you were saved because only those who are born of the Spirit can understand and accept what is written there. Those who are lost have nothing in them to help them understand, but when you were saved, God put His Spirit in you. And the Spirit acts as a kind of interpreter for us. Pray as you read, and you'll find that God will speak to you and help you understand His words."*

That had happened, and as Frankie read on, she was made more and more aware that the Christian life was basically knowing Jesus. Other things were important, but the joy in her came from the absolute certainty that somehow Jesus Christ was *in* her. She never heard voices, but there was a strong sense that she was not alone—and that was a wonderful thing!

Finally she grew sleepy and put the Bible down, then stretched out on the bed and drifted off to sleep. She came awake instantly when a faint knocking came at her door. Coming off the bed, she went to the door. "Who is it?"

"Your uncle James."

Frankie unlocked the door, and at once Tyler stepped inside. He was wearing the same suit she'd seen him wear before, and he still carried the cane, though he seemed not to need it. The yellow lamplight fell on him, and he was smiling. "I'm glad to see you, Frankie," he said quietly.

Frankie answered his smile and put her hand out. When he took it eagerly, she said, "I'm glad to see you, too, Tyler. Come and sit down." She saw that his limp was very slight as he moved. "You're walking better all the time."

"Oh yes, but not enough to march with a full pack." He sat down on the chair, and she came to sit on the bed. "Now how are you? Does the wound trouble you?"

"No, it's almost well. If it had been a little lower, I don't think I'd be here."

"I was worried sick when I didn't hear from you for so long!" Tyler blurted out. "When I got your letter, of course, you were out of danger, but it made me feel so helpless, knowing you'd been through that and all I'd done was sit around here! I almost came to Hartsworth to see how you were."

"That would have been a mistake."

"Sure, but when a fellow's not thinking straight, he's apt to make mistakes." He studied her carefully, then nodded his approval. "You look good. Now tell me all about it."

Frankie told the story. When she finished, Tyler said, "Sounds like Paul Bristol is a handy sort of fellow to have around, especially when you get shot." He asked with a rather casual air, "How do you two get along?"

"Why, well enough, I suppose."

Tyler shifted a little, seeming to hunt for words. "Well, he's kind of a different man than most of the Rocklins, I guess. He always seemed caught up in things the rest of us didn't really understand, his art and all. We always wondered why he never joined the war or married."

"He's engaged to a young woman now. Luci DeSpain."

"Is that right? I hadn't heard that it was official. What's she like?"

"Very rich and beautiful."

Tyler grinned suddenly. "Better than marrying a girl who's poor and ugly!"

"You idiot!" Frankie laughed. She found herself very much at ease with Tyler, and for half an hour they talked, mostly about Tyler's family. Finally he said, "Well, I guess you were pretty shocked to get my letter."

"Yes. Especially the part about Pinkerton being here. Where is he?"

"Actually, he's not coming." Tyler shrugged. "It would be pretty dangerous, of course. But an agent came this morning with a set of instructions straight from him. Right now he's with McClellan and the Army of the Potomac."

"What does he want us to do?"

"If you'll turn your back, I'll fish it out and read it to you. I'm carrying it under my clothes."

Frankie turned her head away, amused. As he struggled to

get the packet from beneath his shirt, she said, "You weren't so modest when I was nursing you."

"I didn't have any choice. Ah, here it is." She turned back to him and saw him pulling a paper from an oilcloth pouch. He began to read, and Frankie listened to the message carefully. It outlined a highly complicated plan that called for the two of them to gather detailed information on the location and strength of Confederate troops and to pass it along to couriers. There were signs and countersigns and all sorts of precautions involved, and Frankie lost track of most of it. When Tyler finished, he replaced the paper in the pouch, saying, "Sounds like he wants more than we can deliver."

"It's so *complicated*, Tyler!" Frankie protested. "If just one part of it goes wrong, the whole thing will break down."

"I know it," Tyler answered gloomily. "This kind of thing is an obsession with Pinkerton, I think. He gets too clever and thinks that if a plan is complicated enough, it'll confuse the Rebels. Trouble is, this thing is so blasted complicated that it confuses *me!*" He sighed heavily, then added, "Well, what do you think?"

Frankie sat there trying to think, but she was aware that her heart was not in any of this. From the first she had agreed to help Tyler, but now that she had met the Bristols and the Rocklins of Virginia, she felt a sharp twinge of guilt at the thought of her task. Heavily she said, "I wish it were over, Tyler. I—I can't help thinking of how fine the Bristols are, and the Rocklins, too." She saw him prepare to argue, but she was familiar with all the arguments, so she spoke up quickly. "Oh, I'll do it, if it can be done."

Tyler was relieved and began speaking rapidly. "Here's what's happening. McClellan got slowed up at Yorktown, Virginia. Joe Johnston fooled him pretty bad—made him think he had about five times as many troops as he really had. But now McClellan is headed for Richmond." He frowned, shaking his head. "The trouble is, Stonewall Jackson is somewhere in the Shenandoah Valley. There are three Federal armies there under Shields, Banks, and Fremont, so they should be able to handle him, but McClellan is counting on the three Federal armies to help take Richmond."

"Why, one army couldn't beat *three*, could it, Tyler?"

"Well, they *shouldn't*, but Jackson is a fox! Anyway, McClellan is headed up the peninsula for Richmond. Now, the Rebels know he's coming, and they'll throw every man they have into the battle to stop him. What we have to do is pinpoint *where* Joe Johnston puts his forces. If McClellan knows that, he'll win. Now, I know Pinkerton's got some agents there, but none of them will be as free to move around as you."

Frankie remembered the reports that Paul had given her of his sessions with the president and some of his advisers. "I'm not so sure that we'll be going to the battle, Tyler. The president didn't like some of the pictures we made—of the dead and wounded. And the advisers were dead set against letting Paul go back."

"But—if you can't move around, our whole operation is busted."

Secretly Frankie hoped Paul *would* be taken off the job, but felt there was little real chance of that. For all the advisers' complaints and objections, President Davis still seemed in favor of the photographs. "Well, I'll do what I can. But you can bet on one thing: McClellan may not know where the Rebels are, but they'll sure know where *he* is!"

"Sure! Every farmer and hunter in the country will be feeding the Union position to General Johnston. That's why we need to get McClellan the information he needs. Without it, he'll be fighting blind."

"Tyler, how will I get the information to you? I can't get away to come here."

"No, you can't. That's why I'm coming to Richmond."

"You can't do that!" Frankie blinked with surprise, then shook her head. "They'll be watching strangers like a hawk, Tyler; you know that."

"I won't have anything in writing." Tyler's eyes were bright, as if he welcomed the danger—as indeed he did! He felt that he had failed by not being in the active service, and throwing himself into a dangerous mission helped him to feel better. It was foolish, but it was the way he felt.

Now he laughed at the expression on Frankie's face. "Think of it this way: If a fellow's born to be hanged, he'll never get drowned, will he?"

Frankie shook her head, a dread rising in her. "It's too

dangerous. Nobody will be watching me, but you can bet that the minute you start moving around, you'll get stopped. Last week they caught a spy in Richmond. They searched him and didn't find a thing, until one of the officers made him take off his shoes. He had secret papers for the Union there. They. . . they hung him from a lamppost!" She shivered and pleaded with him. "We'll have to think of a better way."

But argue as she would, Tyler would not budge. Finally he said, "Look, this isn't as dangerous as charging the Rebs with a bayonet. We won't put anything in writing unless we have to, and we'll do it in the order forms, like we discussed with Pinkerton."

Frankie sat there, unhappy and afraid. "I'm thinking of your mother and your father," she said quietly. "If something happened to you—"

"Sure, I know, Frankie, but I've got to do it." He leaned over and took her hand, and when she lifted her head, he smiled. "I like it when you worry about me."

Frankie bit her lip, then said quietly, "I do worry about you."

Her hand was warm in his, and he held it tighter. "I feel very strongly about you, Frankie. I guess I owe my life to you and Sol Levy. Makes me feel that somehow we were meant to be a part of each other's lives." He stood up, and when she rose, he kept his grip. "Now don't jump out of your skin," he said in a cautious, serious tone, "but I'm going to give you a very mild, innocent little kiss."

Frankie smiled, amused at his careful manner. "Well, stop

talking and do it, then."

Tyler stared at her, speechless, then leaned forward and kissed her lightly. Shaking his head, he marveled, "What happened to the girl who almost took my head off last time I tried that?"

Frankie moved away from him to look out the window. The yellow lanterns that dotted the night glowed like fireflies, and she watched as a young man and woman walked along the plank walk, holding hands.

She turned back to face Tyler, a brightness in her eyes and a look of expectancy on her lips as she said, "I didn't tell you all that happened at Shiloh. Sit down, and let me tell you the best thing of all!"

Tyler sat down, and for the next fifteen minutes Frankie told him of her new discovery—how she'd found a new peace and freedom and joy. She spoke simply, with no trace of the slight pride that new converts sometimes manifest. When she spoke of Jesus, he noticed it was with the same sort of happiness and contentment she might have used in talking about any dear friend.

She smiled at him now. "Ever since that moment, I've been. . .oh, I don't know how to say it." She looked down at her hands, thinking how best to explain. Finally she shook her head. "It can't be said in words, I guess. But all my life I've felt alone and cut off, somehow. Now I feel like I'm—complete."

Tyler considered her, his broad face filled with something like envy. He'd seen this in his parents and in the Steeles enough to know that it was real. "But. . .what does becoming a Christian have to do with kissing?"

Frankie flushed. "I. . .think all my life, Tyler, I've been trying to be something I wasn't. I told you how my father wanted boys and never had them, except for one son who wasn't what he wanted? Well, I guess I tried to be the boy he really wanted. And I guess I became afraid to let anyone in, to trust anyone to see who I really am. Especially any man." Her face clouded for a moment. "Seemed like anytime I tried to care about a man, or to let them know how I was feeling, deep inside. . .I just got hurt. But now"—she looked at him, and the light in her eyes was wonderful—"since I met the Lord, I don't feel the same." She thought about it, then said, "Marianne helped me a lot with it. She says—"

When she broke off, Tyler demanded, "What did she say?"

"Oh, it was nothing." Frankie flushed and then smiled shyly. "She just said that the first time she saw me, she knew there was a—a beautiful woman inside, trying to get out."

"Well, she was right!" Tyler said and reached for her, his eyes bright.

Frankie put her hands out, laughing. "None of that now, Tyler Rocklin! I still need time to get used to this change in me, and you're just going to have to behave yourself until I do." She picked up his cane, handed it to him, then pushed him toward the door. "Now where will I contact you in Richmond?"

He allowed her to hustle him out, turning to give her a grin. "Look for me at a little hotel named the Arlington. One of the agents said nobody would be paying much attention to it. Pretty bad place, I guess, but you can send for me there. I'll still be James Miller."

"I'll get word to you as soon as I have something, Tyler. Now you go on—"

He paused and took her hand for a moment, then lifted it to his lips. He pressed a gentle kiss against it, then closed her fingers around the warm spot he'd left in her palm. His eyes twinkled at her as he said, "There! You can just keep that safe until you let me give you a real one." His smile grew serious then, and he added, "And you can keep yourself safe, too." With that, he was on his way.

She stood for a moment, a thoughtful look on her face, then sighed. She realized that she had allowed Tyler to think that she was more interested in him than was the case. *He's such a fine man,* she thought. *But there won't ever be anything between us but friendship. I'll have to be careful. . .no more kisses. And somehow I'll have to make sure he knows what my real feelings are. It would be terrible to hurt him!*

Frankie closed the door slowly, then walked to the mirror and stared at her face. She pulled off her vest, turned sideways, and fluffed out her curly hair. Then she suddenly laughed at herself, saying aloud, "You're just a farm girl, at best, Frankie Aimes! Put on all the dresses you like; you're still rough cut and more tomboy than girl." She suddenly thought of Luci DeSpain's delicate beauty, then looked at the reflection of her own rough hands and strong limbs—and for no reason that she could discern, a heaviness came over her. "You may be a woman," she said, meeting the eyes of her reflection, "but you'll never be a beauty." She turned from the mirror in disgust.

Later, after she had put on her nightshirt and was in bed, reading, she happened on a scripture that seemed to leap out at her, as many of them had been doing lately. She read it aloud slowly: " 'Behold, thou art fair, my love; behold, thou art fair; thou hast doves' eyes.' "

The words were from a book in the Bible she'd never read before: Song of Solomon. *What a strange thing to say in the Bible!* she thought as she read the next few verses.

> Behold, thou art fair, my beloved, yea, pleasant: also
> our bed is green. . . .I am the rose of Sharon, and the
> lily of the valleys.

"Oh, that's nice!" she whispered, and then she read the next line and could not believe what she was reading:

> As the lily among thorns, so is my love among the
> daughters.

Frankie blinked, and her hands trembled so that she could not see the print. *"As the lily among thorns. . . ,"* she thought. *Not one of the thorns, like I've always thought I was, but a lily among thorns!* She had no idea what the theological meaning was, but the words charmed her: *As the lily among thorns. . .the rose of Sharon. . .thou art fair.*

For a long time she read, confused but entranced by the rich imagery of the language. It was like nothing she'd ever read, and the sensuous quality of some of the lines brought a flush to her cheeks.

Why, it's like a love letter! she thought. Many of the passages spoke of physical love, while others seemed to be more about spiritual love. She read avidly, and remembering how Marianne had instructed her to ask God to help her understand His Word, she did just that.

Finally her eyes grew tired, and she read one final passage from chapter 5. It seemed to be a question asked by a group of young women.

What is thy beloved more than another beloved,
O thou fairest among women? what is thy beloved more
than another beloved, that thou dost so charge us?

Frankie thought about the question, wondering who the beloved of the young woman was. Then she read the young woman's answer to the question.

My beloved is white and ruddy, the chiefest among ten
thousand.

His head is as the most fine gold, his locks are bushy,
and black as a raven.

His eyes are as the eyes of doves by the rivers of waters, washed with milk, and fitly set.

His cheeks are as a bed of spices, as sweet flowers: his lips like lilies, dropping sweet smelling myrrh.

His hands are as gold rings set with the beryl: his belly is as bright ivory overlaid with sapphires.

His legs are as pillars of marble, set upon sockets of fine gold: his countenance is as Lebanon, excellent as the cedars.

Frankie was caught up in the description. Though she wasn't at all certain of the meaning, she was filled with wonder at the magnificence of the language. Suddenly the image of a strong face flitted through her mind. Quickly she shut her eyes and tried to force it away. . .but it remained there, blue eyes glowing warmly. She started to close the Bible, but before she did, her eyes fell on the last verse: "His mouth is most sweet: yea, he is altogether lovely. This is my beloved, and this is my friend, O daughters of Jerusalem!"

Abruptly she shut the Bible and blew out the lamp. But even as she lay in the bed with her eyes shut tight, the face she'd seen lingered. . .and she seemed to hear a voice she knew well, saying softly, "Behold, you are fair, my love."

CHAPTER 21

NO MERCY

As McClellan probed forward with his army of more than one hundred thousand men, every Southern eye was turned toward the blue-clad host. Clay Rocklin and his two sons, Lowell and Dent, returned to their unit, the Richmond Grays. There they were placed in the first of the three lines of troops that ringed Richmond. General Joseph Johnston and President Davis for once agreed on tactics, and they bled the other areas dry, shifting every available man to the Richmond theater.

The entire country was rampant with rumors, and at Gracefield, the Rocklins were more on edge than most. The men had left with their regiment; and Paul and Frankie were gone, as well, having been given new assignments by President Davis—assignments that sent them ever closer to the front lines. As though that wasn't enough to worry about, another problem had grown so severe that neither Thomas nor Susanna knew what to do.

Ever since Ellen had been sentenced to a wheelchair, she had grown more and more acrimonious and difficult. She demanded attention, flying into fits of weeping when she didn't get her way or fits of rage when she was crossed. During Clay's leave, she had done all she could to make life terrible for him. After he returned to the front, she poured out her bitterness on anyone who had the misfortune to come near her.

The slaves dreaded her, for she cursed them and even struck them when they came within reach. But they had the advantage of living in their cabins in the slave quarters rather than in the Big House. In that place, there was no escape from the woman's mindless rages.

David, Denton's twin brother, was far more easygoing than his twin and could put up with Ellen's impossible demands with a patience that astonished Thomas, David's grandfather. One day, when Ellen had cursed David and struck at him wildly, he merely said, "Mother, I'll take you for a ride after a while."

Later, when David had come to sit with his grandfather in the grape arbor, Thomas said, "David, Dent would have gone crazy if he'd had to put up with your mother. Yet you never seem to lose your temper with her."

David considered the remark, then said, "Mother's the most miserable person I know, Grandfather. She's cooped up in a helpless body. Seems to me that would be terrible for anyone, but it's worse for her because she has no resources, no good things to concentrate on. She doesn't like her husband or her family, but what's worse is she doesn't like herself. I think that's why she's done the things she has. She's always felt inferior, and I guess she always sought out the kind of company that matched that bad opinion she had of herself."

Thomas stared at his tall grandson, something akin to awe in his eyes. "You think deeper than the rest of us, David," he said. "Most Rocklin men shoot from the hip, usually without thinking, but you're always looking and watching and thinking about things. And you're right about your mother, but I'm afraid to think of what's going to happen if she doesn't accept her situation."

"She probably won't. If it were Grandmother, it would be one thing, because Grandmother has God. But Mother has only herself, and she hates herself. I figure that's why she's always screaming at everyone. She hates what she's been, and she's helpless to do anything about it. So when she screams at me or hits me, I know it's all really meant for herself. And if it helps her to feel better for a while, well, I can handle it." He lowered his voice, casting a look at Rena, who was in the yard playing with Buck, her huge, formidable deerhound. "Mother is the type who could take her own life, you know."

Thomas started, then, after a moment, nodded slowly. "Yes, I think she could. Her mind's getting worse, isn't it?"

"Every day she slips a little." David's face grew sad. "If she doesn't find peace, she'll lose her mind completely, I'm afraid."

"She was happy for a while after you fixed the buggy for her." The buggy had been Ellen's one diversion. David had taken an old rig and had a carpenter work on it, fixing it so that Ellen could be placed into it. Then David had found an old horse incapable of more than a fast walk to hitch to it, and given the rig to Ellen. It took a strong man to pick her up from her chair and place her in the cut-down seat, but once there, she could take short drives alone.

"Yes, but it didn't last long, did it? Now Mother says the rides just remind her of all she's lost."

As the two sat there talking quietly, Ellen was in her room. Located on the first floor, the room had been the master bedroom, used by Thomas and Susanna until Ellen's accident. When they had given it up and moved upstairs, Ellen had not so much as said a word of thanks. She simply complained constantly about things she didn't like about the room. Now she wheeled herself to the window and glared balefully at the two men and Rena.

"They're talking about me. . .I know them!" she muttered angrily. For a short time she watched, then had to move, to do something. David's analysis—*"She has no resources"*—had been highly accurate. Ellen had never been a reader. If she had loved books as her daughter, Rena, did, she might have been able to use them to fight off the terrible boredom that crushed her. Nor did she sew or quilt or do any of the fine needlework that most Southern women took pride in. She had no interest in the plantation, either. Gracefield was a source of income to her, a place where she could go when she got tired of Richmond society. But she knew nothing about the operation of the place—and could not have cared less that this was the case.

This, then, was the root of the problem: Ellen Rocklin had nothing to do. If Susanna had been put in the wheelchair, she would have run Gracefield from it. She would have been busy with her family, her home, her Bible, her church—being confined to a wheelchair would have been an irritation, but no more than that. But Ellen was basically an empty woman who had filled that emptiness with the wrong things—men and alcohol—and now that those fillers were no longer available, the days became a torment. She roamed the house and the grounds, restless as a caged animal, ready to strike at anyone who came close to her.

Turning from the window, she shoved herself across the room and pulled open a drawer in the cherry dresser. The drawer was stuffed with papers and mementos, which she yanked out, scattering them over the floor. Rummaging through the drawer, she found a single piece of gray paper with a few words scrawled in a rough hand: *Will meet you Wednesday in the arbor at midnight. Don't have nobody with you!!*

There was no signature, and Ellen stared at it fixedly, then tore the paper to shreds and tossed the fragments into the drawer. Wheeling around, she left the room and, passing one of the maids, snapped waspishly, "Bessie! Go clean up my room! It looks like a pigsty!"

She spent the day moving over the grounds on the brick paths, going to the kitchen to complain about the food. Dinner passed, then supper, and the house grew quiet as the family went to bed about nine o'clock. Ellen's nerves grew tighter as she waited impatiently for midnight. At eleven thirty she left her room, moving across the pine floor slowly. The family bedrooms were all upstairs, so there was little danger of waking anyone. However, sometimes the house servants were on the lower floor. Of course, they usually were in bed by now.

That seemed to be the case, for Ellen saw no one as she carefully opened the kitchen door and wheeled herself outside. She left the house and wheeled herself as quietly as possible toward the scuppernong arbor. The wheels of her chair clattered on the brick, and once she stopped, holding her breath, thinking that she had heard something. But as she listened, the only sounds around her were the chirping of crickets and the hoarse cry of a bullfrog from the pond.

Though the arbor was next to the house, no one could see inside the thick covering of vines, nor could they hear a conversation. It was for this reason that she had sent a message to Clyde Donner to meet her at this spot. She pulled inside the arbor, stopped, and waited.

Thoughts ran through her mind, sometimes flashing and sharp, sometimes random and without logical pattern. She was aware that she was not thinking in normal patterns and, in rare moments of lucidity, feared she was losing her mind. But this was not a lucid moment. Rather, as she sat in the warm darkness, she thought of Melora Yancy—and hatred washed over her like a red tide. There had been a time when she had believed Clay and Melora had done nothing wrong, but lately a fixation had come to her.... She'd been having dreams in which

Clay left her and went to the younger woman.

Of course, Ellen no longer felt any love for her husband—if, indeed, she ever had. She had known when they were married that young Clay was in love with Melanie Benton, who was now married to Gideon, Clay's cousin. Ellen knew Clay had married her only because she had tricked him into it, yet she laid the blame for the unhappiness of her marriage at Melanie's feet. The years had passed, and Clay had long since resolved his feelings for Melanie. . .but now there was Melora. And when Ellen thought back to the past, the acid of old memories bringing aching bitterness, she often could not distinguish between Melanie's face and Melora's. In her mind, they had become one. And all of her hatred was focused on that mixed image of the two women she believed wanted to steal her husband from her.

Ellen shivered. She knew time had become vague and indistinct to her, that she often wandered in her mind between the past and the present—and it frightened her greatly. Sometimes she wept in terror, tears running down her cheeks, and wondered how she had come to such a terrible fate. Now, though, as she sat there in the darkness, there were no tears, for the thought of Clay and Melora filled her poor twisted soul, leaving room for nothing but a cold fury.

The sound of a horse coming down the road startled her from her bitter thoughts. The animal stopped, and there was a long silence; then she heard faint footfalls and a hoarse whisper. "Anybody here?"

"Come into the arbor, Clyde," Ellen whispered urgently. A sense of exultation came to her. He was here! Now she could do it! "Don't worry; everybody's in bed. Come closer so I can see you."

She peered at the short, stubby figure of the man who advanced. He wore a black hat low on his forehead, but the moonlight was bright enough for her to recognize him. Donner was a gambler who was not good at his trade and so had turned to robbery—and worse—to offset his losses. He had a lantern jaw and a pair of smallish blue eyes. Ellen had known him for a long time—for a brief time they had even been lovers—then Donner had been sent to jail for theft. This was the first she had seen him since he had gotten out of prison.

A crafty man, Donner looked around, alert as any animal. "Don't like to come like this, Ellen," he said. "What you want?" He holstered a revolver he'd been holding at the ready and came closer. "You must be hard up to send for me!"

Ellen had always been able to handle Donner by playing on his addiction to lust, but that was before her accident. Now she knew her only tool was money. She narrowed her eyes and spoke softly. "Clyde, I want somebody hurt—bad."

Donner's pale eyes glinted with a sly expression. "That mean you want 'em dead?"

"Yes!" Ellen almost choked on the word, then forced herself to smile. "You're a sharp fellow. I always said that."

"No, you always said I wasn't very bright," Donner answered. "Who you want shot? Your husband?"

Ellen's head snapped back. "Clay? Of course not!"

Donner shrugged, his mouth holding a slack smile. "When a woman loses her man, she usually wants him killed."

"Who says I've lost him?" Ellen's eyes glinted with a wild expression, and she grasped the arms of her chair, her back arching in a vain effort to rise.

"Well, you ain't no good to him no more, are you? Man wants a good, strong woman, not a cripple."

Blinding lights seemed to go off inside Ellen's head, and a sharp metallic taste came to her mouth. What went through her mind were not thoughts—they were not orderly enough for that—but waves of hatred so strong they seemed to scald the inside of her skull. But for all that, she still retained enough craftiness not to lash out at Donner. He was her only hope of getting at Melora, and she would take no chances on alienating him. She waited until the storm inside her head subsided, then said, "That's none of your business, Clyde. Clay's a man, and men are weak. No, I want you to kill the woman who's trying to take him from me."

"Sure, the Yancy woman." Donner grinned when he saw Ellen flinch, then shrugged his heavy shoulders. "No secret 'bout that, I reckon. Especially as you told it all over Richmond 'fore you got shot."

Ellen closed her lips firmly for a moment, then took a deep breath. "All right, it's her. I'll give you two hundred dollars to kill her."

"Two hundred dollars?" Donner gave her an insulted look,

GILBERT MORRIS

then turned to go. When she called out to him, he stopped and faced her impatiently. "In the first place, I ain't killin' no woman. I got my standards, Ellen, and unless I *got* to do it, I ain't shootin' no female! And in the second place, even if I was to do the job, it'd cost a lot more than two hundred dollars!"

"I'll give you more!" Ellen whispered. "Five hundred!"

"You ain't *got* five hundred," Donner snapped. "This place is having a hard time like all the other cotton plantations. They're all mortgaged to the hilt. You couldn't raise five hundred dollars hard money to save your life! And Rocklin ain't lettin' you handle no money, is he, now?" Donner sneered at the woman, enjoying himself. Watching her squirm was little enough revenge for the many times she had taunted and humiliated him—and for the way she'd refused to see him after he got out of prison.

He grinned at her, sharklike in the pale moonlight. "Look, honey, you had your good times; now let that husband of yours have his! So long!" And then he was gone, having disappeared into the darkness.

Ellen sat there, struck dumb with the rebuff. For a long time she stayed in the arbor, her mind rolling with images that flashed and seemed to go on endlessly. Finally she lifted her head and blinked several times. "I don't need you, Clyde! I don't need anybody!" she whispered.

Her journey back into the house was uneventful, but instead of turning to go to her room, she turned the opposite direction. The double doors that led into the study gave her a problem, but she managed to open them. Moonlight fell through the tall windows on the east of the room, and she slowly rolled to the huge rolltop desk where Thomas Rocklin did his work. Carefully she opened a lower drawer, reached down, and pulled out the pistol that lay inside. She put the gun in her lap, fingering it almost lovingly, then closed the drawer and left the room.

When she was safely inside her bedroom, she moved to turn up the lamp on the table, then examined the weapon. It was not a large gun—much smaller than the .44 that Clay kept. Thomas had bought it for use against prowlers and had tried to teach Susanna to use it, but to no avail. "I'll trust the good Lord and not a pistol!" Susanna had said firmly.

Ellen knew little about guns, but she could see that the chambers in the cylinder were loaded. She pulled the hammer back and spun the cylinder as she had seen Thomas do, then put both hands on the handle and aimed the gun at a picture of Jefferson Davis on the wall. She squeezed the trigger very slightly, felt it move, and released it at once.

A strange smile came to her lips, and she rolled her chair to the dresser. The right drawer, which she kept locked, was stuffed with old letters. Once when she had raged at the servants, accusing them of spying on her and picking at her things, David had installed the lock himself, removing it from an old chest in the attic. She carefully unlocked the drawer, moved the letters to the front, then put the gun down and covered it with the letters. Locking the drawer, she moved to the table and picked up a piece of paper and a goose-quill pen. Dipping the pen into the inkwell, she began to write slowly:

Miss Yancy,

*You will be shocked to receive this letter from me,
I'm sure. We have not been friends, of course. In fact, I
must confess that I have hated you for years. Undoubtedly
you have heard of my misfortune. I am confined to a
wheelchair, and will be for the rest of my life. When one is
in this condition, there is a lot of time to think, and I have
been thinking about my husband a great deal.*

*He assures me that there is nothing more than
friendship between you two. I have found that hard to
believe, but I would like to trust Clay. He is all I have left
now, and if I could really know that he is faithful, I could
bear my infirmity much better.*

*I need to hear the truth from you. My mind is not clear
on many things, but you are, from what others tell me, an
honest woman. If I could only talk to you, I'm sure I could
look into your eyes and see the truth! It would mean so
much to me.*

*I do not think it would be wise for you to come to
Gracefield. And I can't come to your house. I am able,
however, to drive a buggy. I have no right to ask this, and
you will probably refuse, but if I drove out toward your
place some afternoon, could you give me just a few minutes?
I am sending this letter by a trusted slave, one who will tell
nothing. If you would see me, give him the message, and
I will be on the old plank road by the deserted sawmill at
dusk tomorrow. You know the spot. It is close to Gracefield*

and far from your home, I am afraid, but I cannot make long journeys. Just tell the slave that the answer is yes if you will come, and please burn this letter!

Please come!
Ellen Rocklin

When she had signed her name, she sprinkled fine sand over the letter, sifted it, then dropped the sand into a wastebasket. She put the letter into an envelope, heated a small cylinder of red wax, and carefully sealed the flap. Then she sat back in her chair, trembling.

It was done.

She went to bed, managing the transfer from chair to bed with difficulty, then waited for sleep. *I'll give Highboy ten dollars to take the letter, and I'll tell him he'll be sold down the river if he ever tells anyone about it.*

❧

The sun looked weak and tired as it dropped over the top of the hill, pale and obscure from its labor of heating the earth—or so it seemed to Melora as she rode along the abandoned plank road. She had thought of little else but Ellen Rocklin's letter since receiving it. She had been startled when a tall black man had stepped out from behind a tree as she was on her way to the hog pen.

"Miz Rocklin, she said give you dis and not let nobody see me," he had said.

Melora had read the letter quickly and knew that she had no choice. "Tell Mrs. Rocklin the answer is yes," she said. The tall slave had nodded, then disappeared at once into the woods.

Over and over Melora had read the letter but had said nothing to her father. Today, acting as casual as she could manage, she had said, "I'm going to the store, Pa. I'll be a little late coming back, so don't worry."

Buford was accustomed to Melora's wanderings and said only, "Bring back some blackstrap, daughter. We ate the last yesterday."

Dressed in men's overalls so that she could ride astride, Melora had made it a point to go to Hardee's Store and pick up some blackstrap. Then she had headed north. Now as her mare trotted toward the spot Ellen had named, Melora thought of the strangeness of what she was doing. In the last few months, she and Rena had grown close. The young girl had often shared facts about her mother with Melora, and she well knew that Ellen was not only physically infirm but failing in her mind.

She's a pitiful thing, Melora thought as she turned off the main road. For the rest of the journey, she tried to think of some way to speak to Ellen so that her innocence—and Clay's—would be evident.

The old plank road had once been used for passage to a sawmill, but the mill had been abandoned for years, so only hunters and fishermen used it any longer. The surrounding terrain was rough, broken by deep little valleys and sharply rising ridges. The road snaked around the high places, skirting abrupt drop-offs, and as Melora rounded a sharp bend, she saw in the fading light a woman seated in a small buggy. The rig was on a narrow road—so narrow that there was only room enough for the buggy. To the left was the steep wall of a bluff. To the right, a sharp drop-off. It would take careful driving to thread the dangerous spot.

As Melora rode up, she was greeted at once.

"So you did come!" A smile appeared on Ellen's lips.

"I told your slave I'd be here." Melora slipped off the horse and dropped the reins. The horse was trained to stand and made no move as Melora went to stand beneath Ellen.

"I'm glad you asked me to come, Mrs. Rocklin," Melora said quietly. "I've wanted to talk to you for a long time."

"And I've wanted to see you, too." Ellen's smile appeared to be fixed on her lips. She had slept not at all since receiving Melora's reply, and now she had a headache, fierce and raging— the kind that often came when her mind grew too active. "Did you tell anyone you were coming to meet me?"

"No. I didn't think it was necessary."

"Ah, good! Well now, tell me about you and Clay." The pain in Ellen's head came sharply, causing her eyes to blink, but her pleasure at finding the woman before her made her endure it. "Tell me there's nothing between you!"

"We have been good friends for many years," Melora began, trying to speak as clearly as she could. She was troubled by the expression on Ellen's face, the fixed smile and the wide-staring eyes with the bright glitter. However, she spoke clearly and without hurry. She felt a great pity for Ellen, knowing that the woman had nothing to sustain her in her great trial. She thought of Rena and Clay and prayed that somehow her words would be able to persuade Ellen that she had nothing to be jealous about.

Finally, when she had spoken as well as she could, she concluded, "Your husband is an honorable man, Mrs. Rocklin. Even if I wanted to take him, he'd never leave you."

Ellen had listened, saying nothing. Now she nodded and whispered, "You're very beautiful, Melanie. . . . You always were."

Startled, Melora looked at the woman. "I'm Melora, Mrs. Rocklin."

And then Ellen laughed, a wild, crazy laugh that seemed to resound around them.

She's insane! Melora thought with a jolt.

"Oh, you don't need to lie, Melanie," Ellen said with a nod. And then she lifted the revolver, which she'd been holding on her lap. She smiled at the look of shock on the young woman's face. "I've wanted to kill you for years," she said almost pleasantly. "Ever since you took Clay away from me."

Melora knew she was in terrible danger but allowed no fear to show in her face. "Mrs. Rocklin, you're not well. Put the gun down. . . . I'll take you home."

"Take me home? Oh, you're clever! And they'll lock me up in the crazy house in Richmond?" Again the wild laugh, and then the smile faded and the glitter in Ellen Rocklin's eyes grew brilliant as she began to scream. "You'll never have him! He's mine, do you hear! You can't take him—!"

She lifted the revolver and fired.

Melora felt a burning sensation on the left side of her neck as the bullet grazed her, but had no time to do more than throw up her hand in a futile gesture. Ellen's horse, startled by the sudden explosion, suddenly reared, which threw the crippled woman back against the seat. As she fell, she pulled the trigger again, but this time the bullet struck the horse a raking blow on the side of her rump. Instantly the mare went wild, uttering a shrill scream and lunging forward, blind with fear.

The buggy flew into the rocky side of the bluff and then careened wildly toward the other side of the road. Melora spun around in time to see the buggy wheels drop off the sheer edge and hear Ellen's scream: "Oh my God! No!" Then the buggy flipped over, and Melora watched with horror as Ellen was thrown from the buggy into the sharp outcroppings of stone. She hit on her neck and shoulders and then went rolling down the bluff, legs flopping loosely.

Melora ran to the edge, scrambled over the side, and plunged down the jagged edges until she came to the limp body. Ellen was lying on her face, motionless. When Melora rolled her over, she saw no terrible wounds. Ellen's face was bruised, and blood oozed from a slight cut on her left temple, and she was unconscious. Melora checked to be sure the woman was breathing, then gently laid her back down and climbed up the slope. The buggy was gone, pulled away from the edge and dragged around the bend by the crazed mare, but Melora's horse was standing nearby, his eyes fixed on her.

Got to get help! I can't carry Ellen back up the slope!

Melora started to run toward her horse, then spotted the revolver lying near the edge of the cliff. She picked it up, stuck it in the pocket of her overalls, then mounted quickly and drove the roan at a hard run. She kept the pace up until she arrived at the road that led to Gracefield. By the time she pulled up in front of the mansion, the horse was white with lather. Melora fell off the mare, stumbled, and saw David come running out of the house.

"Melora!" he cried out, coming to her at once. "What happened?" His eyes widened when he saw the blood on her neck, which had soaked into the neckline of her dress. "You're bleeding!" he said in concern.

Melora shook her head. "It's just a scratch," she gasped. "But your mother...sh–she's had a terrible accident!"

Thomas and Susanna had come out of the house, and they listened with grim expressions as Melora went on. "She was on the plank road. . . . She asked me to meet her there." She hesitated slightly, then said hurriedly, "The buggy went off a cliff. I'm afraid she's badly hurt."

At once David wheeled and began yelling orders. "Highboy! Hitch up the light wagon! Lucy, bring some blankets from the house! And tell Chester to ride like the devil to get Doc Slavins!"

Melora stood there, a tragic light in her eyes, and although no one asked, she knew she had to share what had happened. Susanna ordered the slaves to bring water and salve for Melora's neck as Melora briefly told David and his grandparents about the note and the meeting—not mentioning the gun until David had run to ready a buggy.

Thomas watched grimly as Susanna quickly cleaned and bandaged the place where Ellen's bullet had grazed Melora's neck. Melora told them the rest of the story as quickly as she could, then said, "I'll go back with David. I don't think anyone except you two needs to know that she tried to shoot me." She pulled the gun out of her pocket and handed it to Thomas. "She didn't know what she was doing."

Thomas looked at the weapon. "She must have taken it from my desk." He shook his head. "But you're right, my dear. Nothing to be gained by telling Clay or any of the children."

Ten minutes later Melora was on the seat of the wagon, with David beside her and two strong field hands following on mules. "She wanted to talk to me alone, David. She was so determined! The...horse bolted, and when the buggy went over, she was thrown clear."

David gave the young woman a strange look, and she knew that he was not sure of her story. But he did say, "She's a very confused woman, Melora. And she's had a lot of trouble."

Ellen was alive when the men brought her back up the slope. Melora rode in the back with her, cradling the injured woman's head while David drove as carefully as he could over the rough road. When they got back to the house, all was ready, and Ellen was put in her own bed. She remained unconscious through it all, even when Dr. Slavins came and examined her.

"How is she, Doctor?" David asked when Slavins came out into the hall.

"I can't say. She's in some sort of coma." He studied David's face and decided to add, "I'm afraid she's in poor shape, David. Her condition was bad enough before this incident. And. . .she may never wake up. But on the other hand, we mustn't give up hope."

David dropped his head, unable to respond. After a few moments of silence, he lifted his eyes. "Thank you, Doctor. I'll send for Dad right away."

"Might be best. And have Lowell and Dent come, too, if possible."

Melora would not stay—she feared it would distress Ellen greatly should she awaken and find her there—so Thomas sent her home in a carriage. As she left, he said painfully, "You're a generous woman, Miss Yancy. God bless you for what you tried to do."

Melora could do no more than nod. All the way home she thought about the poor broken woman who lay like a stone in the deep feather bed at Gracefield. . .and could only cry out silently, *Oh God! Help her!*

CHAPTER 22

BEFORE THE BATTLE

General George McClellan glared across the table at the short form of Allan Pinkerton, anger in his stern eyes.

"You've failed in your assignment, Mr. Pinkerton," McClellan stated bluntly. "You inform me that the rebels have over 150,000 troops, but you can't tell me *where* they are. I can't blindly commit this army to a battle!"

Allan Pinkerton clamped down his lips on the short cigar between his teeth. His nerves were on edge, but he kept them under firm control. "My agents are doing their best, General, but two things are against them. First, the security in Rebel territory around Richmond is very tight—so tight that I've lost four of my most trusted men, all hanged as spies. Second, the troops are being shifted around so fast that information that was good yesterday is worthless today."

McClellan took a deep breath, then shook his head. "I know it's difficult, but I've *got* to have at least a general idea of where

Johnston's troops are concentrated. Can't you go yourself?"

"Yes, I intend to. Our best agents haven't reported in. I'm going to go find them myself. They're right on the inside, General, and if they haven't been caught, they should have all we need to know. I'll leave now, and if things go well, I should be back within three days with the information you need to make the attack."

"Make it as fast as you can, Mr. Pinkerton," McClellan said, a worried look on his drawn face. "I've got my forces split in two parts by the Chickahominy River, one corps on the north bank, the other four to the south. If the Rebels attack before I can pull the army together, we'll be in serious trouble."

He said a brief good-bye to Pinkerton, then returned to a study of his map. He was a careful, patient man and knew how to train and move an army, but something had gone wrong with his plan. Three things, in fact.

First, McDowell's corps, which had been promised to him, had been kept in Washington. Stonewall Jackson's spectacular success in the Valley, where he had defeated three Federal armies, had so alarmed Lincoln that he had kept McDowell's troops to protect the capital. And although McClellan didn't know it, Jackson's small army was even now back at Richmond under Lee's command.

The second disadvantage that McClellan faced was the fact that General Joseph Johnston had been wounded at the Battle of Fair Oaks, and General Robert E. Lee was now in command of the army. If McClellan had known what this actually meant, he would have gone back to Washington at once, for Lee was the most aggressive general in the war, on either side. Johnston was great at retreat, but Lee had the fighting instinct that only a few great generals have had. That, combined with the man's knowledge of tactics, made him the most dangerous opponent the North ever faced.

The third obstacle was the weather. The rains had come with a vengeance, taking out bridges, flooding the bottomlands, and sweeping away the corduroy roads. The entire country was a bog, and the two parts of McClellan's armies were helplessly separated by a sea of mud. The longer he stared at the map, the more worried the general grew. Finally he said aloud, "If Pinkerton doesn't get me the position of the Rebel Army, we will be defeated!"

Even as General McClellan was studying his maps and trying desperately to make some sort of a plan, General Robert E. Lee was meeting with his staff with much the same intention. The difference was that Lee had accurate information on the position of the Union army. Initially he had gotten tips from farmers who had ridden in daily to give information about troop movements. He had followed this up by sending General Jeb Stuart on a scouting mission. Stuart, a brigadier at twenty-nine, was square-built, of average height, and had china blue eyes, a bushy cinnamon beard, and flamboyant tastes in clothing. Generally, he wore thigh-high boots, a yellow sash, elbow-length gauntlets, a red-lined cape, and a soft hat with the brim pinned up on one side by a gold star supporting a foot-long ostrich plume. In addition, he had a strong thirst for exploits.

When Lee ordered Stuart to scout the location of the Federals, the flashy general had taken his twelve hundred cavalrymen and, in three days, had ridden around McClellan's entire Federal Army. He had returned to a hero's reception, having lost only one man—and having brought back 170 prisoners, along with three hundred horses and mules. But more important than prisoners or mules was the information Stuart brought back, which pinpointed McClellan's army. He drew the enemy's locations out on a map, then handed it to General Lee, saying, "There it is, sir, Little Mac and his Bluebellies!"

Lee studied the map carefully, knowing that he would have to act soon. There was no way he could use his small force of fewer than eighty thousand men to drive one hundred thousand well-entrenched soldiers away from Richmond. He had but two choices: to retreat, thus abandoning Richmond, or to strike before his opponent got rolling. But he saw at once that he would have to take a tremendous gamble: He would have to pull most of his army away from the larger Union corps, leaving only a small force south of the Chickahominy to stand against the Federals. Then he would strike Major General Fitz John Porter's corps on the flank beyond the Chickahominy. This would enable him to seize McClellan's base at the White House.

Once the Union commander was cut off from his supplies, he would be obliged to come out and fight on the ground of Lee's choosing.

So it was that at almost the same moment as McClellan was looking at his maps, General Robert E. Lee was presenting his own map to four men who would fight the battle. All four were young men, though they disguised the fact with beards. James Longstreet was the oldest at forty-one; Ambrose Powell (A. P.) Hill, at thirty-six, was the youngest. Daniel Harvey (D. H.) Hill was forty, and Stonewall Jackson thirty-eight. Twenty or so years earlier, all had attended West Point.

Now they gathered around a table, bending over to study the map, listening as Lee explained what had to be done. "Here is the plan, gentlemen," Lee said as he traced the part each would play in the battle:

"As you can see, I am leaving only Generals Magruder and Huger to hold McClellan's main force in place. General Jackson, you will bring your men down from the north, keeping General Stuart's cavalry on your left flank. The rest of you will cross the Chickahominy in sequence: General A. P. Hill first, then General D. H. Hill, and then you, General Longstreet. You will sweep the left bank of the river, clearing Porter's troops as far as New Bridge, where you will cross the river and strike the main Federal force from the rear."

The council broke up about nightfall, and the four generals went to their headquarters. Each of them had about the same thought: *If we can push Porter out of the way and hit McClellan from the rear, the Federals will run like rabbits for Washington— just as they did at Bull Run!*

Thus two mighty armies faced each other, each well aware that the next few days might bring an end to the Civil War. If McClellan could use his superior force to overwhelm Robert E. Lee's thin gray line and take Richmond, the South would be lost. But if Lee's plan worked and the armies of the North were whipped as they had been at Bull Run, McClellan would take them back to Washington—and the powerful Peace Party might well be able to force the president and Congress to simply let the South go its own way.

An air of destiny hovered over the rain-soaked fields outside of Richmond. Fate was about to move, to turn the course of the nation. The events of the next few days would determine the course of what some called the "War of Secession" and others called the "War of the Rebellion."

While mighty hosts were gathering for the onslaught of battle and the nation was holding its breath over the future of the entire country, life went on pretty much as always in the lives of common people. War and destiny, powerful as they might be, did not set aside everyday living.

War, with all its banners flying, might shake the earth with a mighty thunder of guns, but it did not feed the pigs and chickens. The earth still had to be broken for planting; weeds still waited to be chopped out of the rows of cotton. Work went on, and love went on. Robert E. Lee and George McClellan might grow weary studying maps, but to Tabitha, the slave woman bringing her first baby into the world in a small cabin at Gracefield, all the armies meant nothing. Her world was no larger than the pain that tore her apart as she lay writhing on the rope bed, aided by Susanna Rocklin and one of the black midwives.

Likewise, the blacksmith, Box, paid no heed to the wild rumors that the Yankees might come across the fields of Gracefield at any moment. At the age of seventy-one, he cared little for such things. Let the Yankees free black people; he would keep right on making horseshoes for Thomas Rocklin. Ten thousand men might die that day in battle, but for Box, that was not reality. For him, reality was the ten-pound sledge he lifted, and the shoe he was making for the mare, and the hot sparks that flew as he dropped the hammer against the iron. The mare was real; the horseshoe was tangible. And so he beat the red-hot metal skillfully, his world no larger than the curving piece of iron on the anvil.

As for those who lived inside the Big House at Gracefield, they found themselves feeling strangely out of place. They had grown up inside the big mansion, but childhood days seemed eons away now—memories that slipped in from time to time, flashing images of activities and gatherings. Memories summoned on this day by Ellen Rocklin, though she was silent and still in her bed.

By some miracle, despite the impending battle, Clay, Denton, and Lowell had all managed to get emergency leave. Colonel

James Benton, who was Melanie's father, Gideon Rocklin's father-in-law, and Ellen Rocklin's uncle, had received the message about Ellen from David. Benton had then called Lieutenant Dent Rocklin into his tent at once, saying, "Denton, your mother has had an accident. I think it's serious."

Dent Rocklin's good looks had been spoiled by the slash of a saber at Bull Run. One side of his face was as handsome as that of any man in the South, but the other side was marred by a scar that ran down his cheek, drawing one eye down in a seemingly sinister expression and marking the flesh with an angry, deep trench. But those who knew Dent Rocklin knew that his marred appearance was a poor reflection of the man, for he was good and honorable and did all he could to serve his country and his God.

Upon hearing of his mother's accident, Dent had stared at his commanding officer, listening as the older man gave what information he had. "You know we'll be fighting very soon," Benton said, compassion in his eyes. "But I think we have a few days, perhaps a week. Get your father and Lowell and go home. I've made out passes for all three of you."

Dent took the slips of paper. "Thank you, Colonel. This is handsome of you. We'll leave at once, and we'll be back as soon as. . .we find out something." He had left the tent and gone to find his father drilling some recruits. Drawing him off, he said quietly, "Mother's had an accident. You and Lowell and I are leaving as soon as I can get three horses."

The three of them had ridden their horses almost into the

ground on a flying trip to Gracefield. They had arrived at dusk and were greeted by Thomas, whose face was pale with fatigue. "Glad you all got here," he said, embracing each one.

"How is she?" Clay demanded as soon as they were in the foyer.

"Very bad. Come into the parlor and I'll tell you about it. Susanna is with her now, taking care of her needs. When she comes out, you can go in."

Thomas had explained the accident carefully, leaving out only the matter of the gun. He noted that when Melora's name was mentioned, Clay's eyes sprung wide, and the two boys showed surprise. He ended by saying, "The horse got spooked, Melora said, and Ellen lost control. She was thrown down a steep slope, and Melora rode here and got David at once. He brought Ellen home, but she hasn't come out of the coma."

At that moment Susanna came into the room. She embraced Clay at once, then her two grandsons. "You can come in now," she said quietly. She led the way, and when the men were inside the room, the three of them stared down at the woman in the bed.

"She. . .doesn't look bad," Dent whispered. "I was afraid. . . ."

When he halted his speech, Susanna spoke up. "Dr. Slavins can't find any bones broken, and she wasn't cut up much by the fall." She hesitated slightly. "What he fears is that somehow the bullet that they couldn't get out got pushed closer to the spine."

"She hasn't spoken at all?" Clay asked.

"Not a word, son. And she hasn't moved a muscle. I. . .think what Dr. Slavins fears is that she's completely paralyzed."

The three tall men stood around the bed, helplessly looking down at the wife and mother who had given none of them happiness—and yet the sight of her still, white face made each man forget the misery she had brought to him. Finally they turned and left the room, going back to the parlor. Rena came to throw herself in Clay's arms, her eyes swollen with weeping. She clung to him fiercely for a few moments, then moved away, whispering, "I'm glad you're here, Daddy!"

And so the long vigil began. Servants crept by, whispering. Meals were set out that no one wanted. Dr. Slavins came and went, unable to give them the reassurance they craved. Short conversations would start, only to quickly break off. And long silences stretched on while the family sat around, silences interrupted only when someone would rise and go outside to walk aimlessly around the grounds.

The next morning the Bristols and Franklins came, along with other friends and close neighbors. Rachel and Amy Franklin and Marianne and Claude Bristol gave what comfort they could, which was woefully little. Finally Claude said to his brother-in-law, "Thomas, we've got to go to Richmond. I hate to leave you alone at a time like this—"

"Go on, Claude," Thomas said at once. "Ellen may live for a few days or a month, or she may survive, after all. You can't wait around here all that time. Now what's going on in Richmond?"

Bristol shrugged, a cynical look coming into his face. "A

fancy dress ball—if you can believe it. With the world about to fall around our ears, we're going to a dance!" He shook his head, then spoke in a lower tone. "We're only going because of Frankie. You know what happened to her at the last ball—coming out in that horrible dress and everyone laughing at her! Well, Marianne's determined to set that right. We're going to buy the girl a fine gown and get her hair all fixed, you know." He shrugged, saying, "Just between you and me, Tom, Marianne is convinced it was Luci DeSpain who engineered the whole mess last time, and she's going to see to it that Frankie gets another chance if it costs every dime we've got. I swear, my wife has latched onto that girl like she's some long-lost daughter just returned to her."

Thomas nodded. "Well, women do get the strangest notions sometimes, and we sure don't do ourselves a service by fighting them. Now you go on. I'll let you know if there's any change." He said good-bye to Bristol, then went to speak with his wife. When he informed her of the Bristols' mission, he was surprised at her reaction.

"Good!" she snapped, her eyes sharp. "Paul Bristol is blind as a bat! That DeSpain girl will make him miserable!"

"Why, I didn't know you felt like that, Susanna!" Thomas stared at her, then came up with a smile. "I guess I'm pretty blind about things like that myself." He suddenly put his arm around her, and a flash of the charm that had been his as a young man appeared. "I still remember when you were eighteen at the ball in Atlanta. You were the prettiest thing I'd ever seen!"

He kissed her cheek and smiled. "You still are!"

"Oh, Tom!" Tears appeared in Susanna's eyes at the rare gesture, and the two of them clung together for a moment, thinking of the days long gone.

❧

Early one evening, Paul pulled the wagon up in front of the Spotswood Hotel and for a moment sat there, so weary he dreaded the simple task of getting to the ground. He and Frankie had not stopped working for days except to camp.

Just before they had left on this assignment, Paul had agreed to meet his parents at the hotel so his mother could help Frankie get ready for the Richmond Ball. "I'm not leaving anything to chance this time," Marianne had told her son.

Now, glancing across the seat, he saw that Frankie was sound asleep, utterly exhausted. Reaching out, he gave her shoulder a slight shake. "Wake up. It's time to go to bed."

Frankie jerked as she came out of sleep, then looked around wildly. Then she saw the hotel and gave Paul a tired smile. "I must have dozed off."

"For two hours, but I don't blame you. I'd have gone to sleep myself if I hadn't had to drive the wagon." He nodded toward the hotel. "You go on in. My parents ought to be there, but even if they've gone out, they'll have gotten a room. Better take your things."

Frankie scrambled into the interior of the wagon, threw some clothes into her old carpetbag, then emerged and climbed to the ground. "What about you?"

"I'm going to store these plates somewhere." He scratched his whiskery cheeks. "Then I'll get a bath and a shave."

"Will we be going back to take more pictures tomorrow?"

"No, not unless the battle starts." He hesitated. "I'm supposed to take Luci to a couple of things—a dress ball and a party at the Chesnuts to start with." He kicked the brake off, looking thoughtful for a moment. Then he seemed to shake his thoughts off and smiled down at her. "Go take some rest, Frankie. You deserve it!"

Frankie watched as he drove down the street; then she turned and entered the hotel. She felt more conspicuous than usual—the Spotswood was the most elegant hotel in Richmond, and her dirty, wrinkled clothing made her a draw for every eye. Trying to ignore the stares of those around her, she walked up to the desk. "Are Mr. and Mrs. Bristol here?"

The clerk, a short man with slick black hair and a fussy manner, turned to stare at her. "Why. . .ah, yes, I believe they are. May I. . .ah, help you?"

"Which room?" Frankie demanded, too exhausted to get angry at his condescending tone.

"Ah. . .I believe the Bristols are in 306." He looked at a card, then back at her. "Are you. . .ah, Miss Frankie Aimes?"

"Yes."

"Then you're in. . .ah. . .room 308."

Frankie took the key, stared at the clerk, muttered, "Ah. . . thank you very much," then turned and marched up the stairs.

She went first to the Bristols' room, but no one answered her knock. So she went to room 308, opened the door, stepped inside—and froze in a stunned silence. She stared at the room with awe, for she'd never seen such ornate furnishings and decor! She closed the door, then moved around, touching the fine cherry furniture carefully. As she fingered the fine sheets on the bed, fatigue hit her heavily. She took off her clothes, washed her face, then put on a nightshirt and fell into the bed, going to sleep at once.

She awoke when an insistent knock came at her door. Groggy with sleep, she grabbed at the old cotton robe she sometimes wore, then went to open the door. "Oh, Marianne!" she exclaimed. "Come on in. I was asleep."

Marianne gave Frankie a hug, then said, "I wanted to let you sleep. That son of mine has worn you out!" She stood there smiling at the young woman. "We saw him a few hours ago, and he told us what a hard time the two of you have had. He was worried about you, Frankie."

"Oh, I'm all right. Just a little tired."

"Well, if you think you're tired now, wait until *I* get through with you! Taking pictures may be tiring, but it's nothing compared to shopping, I can tell you! Now first we get some hot water up here to give you a bath, and then we're off."

"What are you talking about?" Frankie asked with bewilderment, still fuzzy from lack of sleep. But Marianne just took her in hand to such an extent that she didn't really *have* to think a great deal.

Before long, maids came to the room carrying copper teakettles filled with scalding water. Frankie was ordered into the bathtub; then she was scrubbed and soaped. Next she was fluffed and powdered to within an inch of her life and practically wedged into a dress and a pair of lightweight ladies' shoes. When she finally stood, her hair brushed and combed, for Marianne's inspection, she complained, "You're treating me like a big doll!"

The older woman came to take the girl's shoulders in her hands, gripping them gently. "I haven't had a daughter to dress for a ball since Marie was very young. And I want you to be the most beautiful girl at the ball. We are going to do it, aren't we?"

Nonplussed, Frankie stared at Marianne. Then a smile lit up her face. "I read a verse in the Bible that said, 'You are fair.' It. . . it made me feel so odd! Like. . .like a woman, Marianne!"

"Good!" Marianne nodded. "Now let's go get the most beautiful girl at the ball ready to turn Richmond upside down!"

CHAPTER 23

ACT OF FORGIVENESS

*C*lay had been sitting beside Ellen for two hours, staring out the window at the setting sun and at the slow-moving slaves who were cutting the green grass around the huge trees. From time to time the sound of their liquid voices drifted to him. Buck, Rena's huge dog, broke into a crescendo of barking as he chased a gray squirrel up a tree. *That dog has tried to catch a million squirrels—and never caught one. You'd think he'd learn!*

Rocklin closed his eyes, which were reddened from lack of sleep, and at once began to drift off. Soft sounds came to him from the rest of the house, and that, added to the heat of the room, caused him to nod off. He sat there dozing until a slight sound inside the room brought him awake.

His eyes flew open, and a quick glance outside told him it was late, for stars dotted the dark sky. With a sigh, he looked down: Ellen's eyelids were fluttering, and her lips were moving slightly.

Clay came out of the chair, caught her limp hand, and whispered, "Ellen! Ellen! Can you hear me?"

At first there was no response—in fact, he began to wonder if she had moved at all. Then slowly her eyes came open, and he cried out again. "Ellen! It's me, Clay." He leaned closer, noting that her eyes were clear but somewhat confused. "Can you hear me, Ellen?"

He held his breath, waiting—and then her lips moved! It was only a faint movement, and he put his ear next to her lips and strained to hear. Nothing. . .and yet, *something*! Clay said, "Try to say my name if you can hear me, Ellen."

Indistinctly he heard her speak, and it seemed to him that she whispered, "Clay!"

Clay lifted his head and began to speak to her as gently and reassuringly as he could. "Ellen, you had an accident." As he spoke, he watched her eyes and was certain she was understanding him. Finally he said, "Can you move at all? Can you move these fingers?" He lifted her hand and stared at the fingers, but there was no movement that he could discern. He held on to her hand, nodded, and smiled. "Don't worry; it'll come back." He reached out and touched her face, whispering, "I won't leave you, Ellen."

He sat there for a long time, watching her closely and speaking from time to time. Though he was encouraged by her ability to communicate, her deathly pallor and dull eyes filled him with a sense of foreboding. It would not be long.

Finally he laid her hand down, saying, "I'll go get the boys—," but he paused, for her eyelids were blinking rapidly, as if she wanted to speak. He bent closer, asking, "What is it, Ellen? What can I get you?" He stood there helplessly, then said, "I'm going to name some things. When I name what you want, blink twice. Blink twice now if you understand."

Her eyelids blinked twice, and Clay said, "Do you want water? No? Food?" He named the things that came to his mind, none of which she wanted. Finally he asked, "Is it someone you want to see? Yes!" He smiled encouragingly, then began to name the family: "Denton? David? Lowell?" but none of these brought a response. Finally he shook his head, saying, "I'll go down the alphabet. When I get to the first letter of the person's name, blink twice. Now, *A*, *B*, *C*. . ." And so it went with no response until he reached *M*. She blinked twice.

"*M*? Let me see, is it Marianne? No? Well, is it Mattie?" He named everyone he could think of, but the eyes remained still. "I can't think of anyone else—let me get Mother—"

But Ellen's eyes blinked furiously, and so he stopped. "You don't want me to go? Well, let me—" Clay halted abruptly, then looked at Ellen, surprise on his face. "Is it Melora?" At once Ellen's eyes blinked, and he could only stare at her. To be sure, he said, "You want to see Melora?" Her eyes closed twice, slowly and deliberately. "All right, I'll ride and get her. I'll go tell the boys." He hesitated, then leaned over and kissed her cheek.

It was the first caress he'd given her in years, and he felt strange. When he lifted his head, he saw two tears tracing their way down her pale cheeks. Taking out his handkerchief, he wiped them away, whispering, "It'll be all right, Ellen." Then he left the room, calling as soon he was outside: "Dent! David! Lowell!" When they came, he told them rapidly what had happened, adding, "She wants to see Melora. I'm going to get her. Go in with your mother, but remember that she can't do much, just blink once for no and twice for yes. Don't let her be alone, boys."

And then he was gone, running hard down the hall and out the door.

⟡

Clay pulled the buggy up in front of the Yancy cabin, leaped off the seat, and went to bang on the door. It was after midnight, and Yancy's voice came roughly: "Who's there? Stand away!"

"Buford! It's me, Clay Rocklin. Open the door!"

Yancy pulled the door open, his face registering his surprise and concern. "What's wrong, Clay?" Even as he spoke, Melora came into the room tying the belt of a robe. Clay looked at the two.

"It's Ellen. I think she's dying—and she's calling for you, Melora."

"I'll get dressed," she said at once and left the room.

"I'll need to change horses, Buford," Clay said, and hurriedly the two men left the cabin. By the time they had switched teams, Melora was ready and got into the buggy.

"I'll have her back when I can, Buford," Clay said, leaping into the seat beside Melora and whipping up the team.

Yancy waved as they left and yelled, "Hope she's better, Clay.

Don't spare them horses!"

As the buggy bounced along at top speed, Clay told Melora of Ellen's condition. "I don't think she can live long," he concluded.

"We must pray," Melora said, and they both did so, silently, all the way back to Gracefield. When they arrived, Clay jumped down, ran around, and reached up to pluck Melora up and set her on the ground. He held her arm as they hurried up the steps, where the door was opened by his father. "How is she?" Clay asked.

"No better, I'm afraid. She keeps dropping off into some sort of coma. You'd better hurry—"

Clay and Melora went at once to Ellen's room, where they found Marianne and Clay's children. As he approached the bed, Clay heard his mother say, "Come, let's give them some time alone." He was vaguely aware of their departure as he bent over, saying, "Ellen." When her eyes opened slowly, he said, "Here's Melora."

Melora came at once to the other side of the bed and took Ellen's hand. "Mrs. Rocklin, can I do anything for you?" She watched as the sick woman's eyes seemed to strain and her lips moved slightly. Melora leaned close, her ear almost touching Ellen's lips. The sick woman was making some sound, trying to talk, but it was vague and indistinct. But Melora finally made out the word.

" 'Forgive'? Is that it, Mrs. Rocklin?" Ellen blinked twice. "You want me to forgive you?" Melora again received the sign.

"Oh yes!" she whispered. "I forgive you with all my heart!" She saw Ellen's lips try to move again, leaned close to listen, and thought she understood. "I forgive you everything, Mrs. Rocklin, not just for what happened at the mill, but for all the things in the past. I can forgive you because God has given me a special love for you!"

Ellen was listening, they saw, and at Melora's words, tears gathered in the woman's eyes. Clay gently wiped them away, and Ellen fixed her eyes on him.

"She wants you to forgive her, I think," Melora whispered.

Clay had long ago gotten all bitterness against his wife out of the way—or so he had thought. But now as she looked at him, he realized that he had not been complete in his forgiveness. He bent his head, took her hand, and held it firmly. He put his hand on her cheek and said, "I forgive you, Ellen—for everything. But you must forgive me, too. I treated you and the children terribly. I forgive you. Can you forgive me?"

As Clay and Melora watched, the eyes that had for so long been filled with hate and bitterness grew soft. She blinked twice, and Clay said thickly, "Thank you, Ellen!"

He and Melora sat beside the dying woman, both aware that she was passing from the world. After a few moments, Melora said, "Mrs. Rocklin, I've forgiven you, and so has your husband, but you need the forgiveness that comes from heaven. May I tell you how to get forgiveness from God?"

Clay watched as Melora sat there, her face filled with compassion, speaking of the love of God for sinners. She spoke softly yet with certainty of Jesus—how He had come to save sinners, how He loved all who had sinned and had paid on the cross for their sins. Ellen's eyes were fixed on the young woman, and time and again Clay had to wipe away the tears that ran down his wife's pale cheeks.

Finally Melora said, "I know you can't speak, Mrs. Rocklin, but God knows your heart. I feel He is speaking to your heart now. Jesus wants to come in and make you pure. Would you like for Him to do that?"

Clay hadn't realized he was holding his breath until Ellen blinked twice, and then he let out a sigh of great gladness.

Melora smiled brightly. "Oh, Mrs. Rocklin! I knew you would! Let me pray with you, and as I pray, you pray, too. The words aren't as important as people might think. Jesus died to save you, and He's been waiting for years to hear you call on Him! Now let's ask Him to save you."

As Clay bowed his head and prayed for his wife, his cheeks were damp with tears. Neither he nor Melora could pray eloquently, but both pleaded with God to hear Ellen. When Clay finally opened his eyes, he saw a look in his wife's eyes that he had never seen before. For the first time in her life, Ellen Rocklin's eyes glowed with peace.

Melora began to praise God, for it was clear a miracle had taken place. She and Clay sat with the dying woman for a long time, and finally they rose and called the family. When the others had gathered in the room, Clay told them of Ellen's coming into the kingdom, and there was great rejoicing, for Ellen had been the last member of the family to become a Christian.

Ellen died at sunrise, surrounded by her family. Just as the first rays of the crimson sun broke through the window and fell on her face, she opened her eyes. She looked at Clay, then shifted her gaze from face to face: Denton, David, Lowell, Rena, Susanna, and Thomas. And then Melora.

Clay leaned forward to brush his wife's hair back from her forehead. "Are you happy, Ellen?"

She looked at him, blinked twice, and then looked toward the sunrise. She seemed to watch the golden bars of light that fell across the room, lighting the faces around her. Then, slowly, she looked again at each face, ending with Clay. He took her in his arms, held her gently. She watched him with eyes that suddenly were filled with love.

Then her eyes closed. . .her breast rose and fell. . .and it was over.

Carefully Clay laid his wife's still form back on the bed and arranged her hair around her forehead. Then he rose and went to his children. "Your mother has gone to be with the Lord."

Melora moved across the room, pausing at the doorway to cast one glance at the family surrounding the bed, embracing each other. Rena's face was pressed against her father's chest, and Clay's sons held him from each side. As Thomas and Susanna moved to be included, Melora left the room. Closing the door, she went outside and looked at the rising sun, tears coming to her eyes as she stood under the sky.

She had never felt so alone. She was a strong woman, but

now she felt weak. How long she stood there, fighting back the awful loneliness, she never knew. But then she felt a hand on her shoulder, a hard but gentle hand—and peace came to her, the loneliness fleeing as she turned.

CHAPTER 24

FRANKIE'S DRESS

Once again Paul Bristol practically turned Richmond upside down seeking a place to store his precious wet plates, but to no avail. Richmond was crowded to the walls, and there was no room anywhere to store the plates safely. Finally in despair Paul drove to Hartsworth and put them carefully in his laboratory. Exhausted, he went to his room and fell into bed, sleeping that night and half the next day. When he managed to pull himself out of bed, he remembered the ball in Richmond. Groaning, he stumbled to the washbasin, shaved, then dug out his best suit and put it on.

When he arrived at the DeSpain home, Luci gave him a cold greeting. "You missed the party last night at the Chesnuts," she said, turning her cheek to take his kiss.

"I'm sorry, Luci," Paul muttered. "But I wouldn't have been good company. Frankie and I haven't slept a full night for two weeks. I believe we've taken a picture of every soldier in the

Army of Northern Virginia, and of every ditch and fortification in this state!" He was tired and irritable, and when Luci only frowned, he said shortly, "If you don't want to go to the ball, I'll understand."

"Not go!" she exclaimed in astonishment. "What in the world are you talking about, Paul? We've *got* to go to the ball!"

"Well, let's do it, then," he said brusquely, and they left the house and rode along the streets of Richmond. They arrived at the Auction Hall, where the ball was to be held, and they had to wait while gowned ladies and handsomely dressed gentlemen disembarked from carriages and entered the brightly lit structure.

Once inside, they found themselves greeted by friends of Luci, most of whom Paul had met briefly but didn't really know. Luci had grown up in Richmond at the top of the social ladder and was swarmed by a group of young people at once. Glancing around, Paul noted that most of the young men wore gray uniforms. He felt as out of place as a sparrow at a convention of peacocks.

Luci made the situation no better by apologizing over and over for Paul, explaining that he was doing important work and couldn't serve in the army. Once, when she made this explanation to a captain of artillery, Paul said in exasperation, "I'm too old and decrepit to be a soldier, Luci, and the captain doesn't give a bean why I'm not in uniform—do you, Captain?"

The young man was too embarrassed to answer. Luci, on the other hand, was furious—and had plenty to say. When she got Paul alone, she rounded on him and said between clenched teeth, "I don't understand you, Paul; I declare, I don't! You've got to tell people *something*! People look down on every man who isn't in uniform!"

"Well, let them look down, Luci," Paul said wearily. "I'm not going to be wearing a uniform, so we'll just have to live with their looks. But stop apologizing for me, will you?"

They moved to the dance floor and danced the first dance in stony silence. Then Paul surrendered her to a tall young lieutenant named Dale Phillips. "Luci and I are old beaux, you know, Mr. Bristol," Phillips warned him lightly. "I fell in love with her when I was sixteen years old. Better keep an eye on me—I might give you trouble."

Paul liked the young man's direct approach. "All's fair in love and war, Lieutenant," he said with a smile. "If you tamper with her affection, it'll be pistols for two and whiskey for one!" But Phillips could tell by his tone of voice that he wasn't serious, though Luci frowned at her fiancé's seemingly light manner.

Paul turned and made his way to the edge of the dance floor, then heard his name being called. Turning, he saw his mother motioning to him. Going to her, he said, "I heard about Ellen's accident when I got home. How is she?"

"Not well." Marianne frowned. "Claude and I wanted to stay with Tom and Susanna, but we'd agreed to come to this ball. We'll go there after we leave here tonight."

"I'll go by Gracefield, too." Paul looked around the room. "Where's Father. . .and Frankie?"

"Claude's talking with some of the officers in the dining

room. I don't think Frankie's come down yet."

Paul frowned. "I hope you got a decent dress for her, Mother." The thought of the last ball came to him, and he shook his head, adding, "And maybe you could keep her from putting on too much makeup."

"Oh, I think the dress will do," Marianne said offhandedly, a twinkle in her eyes. "Why don't you meet her when she comes in so she doesn't have to face the room alone?"

"All right." He looked out over the dance floor to where Luci was gliding across the floor, smiling up into the lieutenant's face. "Luci is happy now," he said without expression. "She doesn't have to feel embarrassed anymore by being with a man who isn't in uniform."

"Isn't that the Phillips boy?" Marianne asked suddenly. "He was engaged to Luci once—or almost engaged—I forget which. But everyone was sure they'd wind up together. He comes from a very wealthy family."

Paul watched the pair for a moment, then shook his head. "Maybe I can get a job as a doorman or something. If a uniform is what she wants, I guess I ought to get one for her."

"Don't be silly! People love one another for what they are, not for what they wear!"

"I suppose." The dance ended, and Paul started to move toward Luci, but before he made two steps, she was claimed by a blond major of the cavalry. Paul gave his mother a caustic smile. "Can't compete with the glamour of the cavalry." He moved away and went at once to the dining room, where a group of men were seated around a table, talking and smoking cigars. Paul took a seat beside his father, listening as the men discussed the only subject of importance: when the fighting would begin, and whether or not Lee could win over McClellan's numbers.

Quickly he grew tired of the talk and whispered, "I'd better go check on Luci."

The room was brightly lit by the chandeliers, and the dance floor was a colorful mosaic of red, green, and yellow dresses glittering under the lights. The men's red and yellow sashes made a brilliant counterpoint to the women's outfits, giving the whole room a festive air.

As Paul entered, he saw that Luci was dancing with Phillips. He waited to feel some jealousy. . .but none came. As he moved through the crowd, he was thoughtful and even puzzled about that. *Shouldn't I care that she's dancing with an old flame? When I was twenty, I'd have called a fellow out for just talking too long with a woman I wanted, but now. . .I don't even care.*

He found a place against the wall and was leaning against it when his mother came to him. "Paul, you've got to do something about Frankie!"

He came away from the wall with a start, looking around the room quickly. "Frankie? What's wrong with her?"

"She's afraid to come into the ballroom. I guess the memory of the last time was too much for her."

Paul didn't even hesitate—a fact that Marianne noted with a barely concealed smile. "Where is she?" he asked firmly. "I'll go get her."

"She's sitting outside in one of those little alcoves. Go out through that door over there, and you'll see a pair of french doors that lead to sort of a tiny garden. Go talk to her, Paul, but for heaven's sake, don't be rough!"

"Rough? What's that supposed to mean?" Paul asked in astonishment.

Marianne put her hand on her son's cheek and held it there. "You always think of her as a sort of tough young hooligan because of the way she's been. But she doesn't need firm handling tonight. She's out there alone and terrified, and she needs a man to treat her gently and to tell her she's attractive. Will you do that, son?"

"Why, certainly, Mother! I must say, you make me out to be quite an insensitive character!" With a sniff he turned and made his way through the crowd, passing outside the main ballroom and entering an empty gallery. He spotted the french doors at once, and as he moved toward them, he thought of his mother's admonition. Setting his jaw, he resolved to do his best with the girl. *We've gotten to be good friends—ought not to be too hard*, he concluded as he stepped outside. His eyes were accustomed to the glare of the lights, and for a moment he stood there, unable to see.

"Frankie?" He spoke quietly. "Are you out here?"

"Yes."

Paul turned to his right and saw her standing beside a large white pillar. He stepped closer, but she stood in the shadow of the pillar, so that all he could see was a shadowy image. "I came to get you," he said quickly. "Let's go inside."

"No. I'm not going in there."

Frankie had been delighted with her time with Marianne Bristol. The two of them had visited every shop in Richmond, or so it seemed. Frankie saw how much it pleased the older woman to look at the dresses, and though she herself was not convinced that she could be made into any sort of beauty, she had enjoyed the shopping. But that afternoon as Marianne had helped her get ready for the ball, her newfound confidence had begun to wane. By the time the music was beginning and she was dressed, she wanted nothing so much as to turn and flee the whole thing!

Still, she had managed to come from the hotel with the Bristols, but the moment she had stepped out of the carriage, she had felt a blind panic. With a muffled excuse, she had escaped to the ladies' dressing room. Marianne had found her there and coaxed her as far as the gallery—but that was when Frankie's courage failed. She had dodged out the french doors, telling Marianne, "You go on. I'm going to stay here!"

Now as Paul stood before her, tall and handsome in his dark suit, his shirt's pure white ruffles gleaming in the moonlight that flooded the garden, she felt herself trembling.

Paul stepped closer and took her arm. "You can't stay out here," he said lightly. "Come on, now, let me see your new dress."

"I don't want to!"

At the stubborn tone of her voice, Paul wanted to pull her out of the shadows, but he remembered his mother's warning to treat her gently. He stood there, trying to think of a way to win her confidence, but nothing came. Finally he said, "Well, I'll tell you what, Frankie, I'm not having a very good time inside, myself."

"You're not?"

"No. Luci only likes to dance with men in uniform, which leaves me out."

"She—she shouldn't do that!"

"Oh, I guess I can see why she'd like the young fellows in their bright new buttons and sashes. A girl likes romance, doesn't she?"

"You look fine! You're romantic enough for—" She suddenly broke off.

Paul laughed. "For what? For you, Frankie? Well, I'm glad to hear that, because I've got an idea." He looked around at the flagstone terrace, which was illuminated by the silver rays of the moon and the amber beams of light that came through the french doors. Then he looked back at her, smiling in a winning way. "This is going to be *our* dance floor, just yours and mine." He looked very young to Frankie at that moment, and she caught her breath when he held his hands out to her. "I think that's a waltz, isn't it? Will you join me, Miss Aimes?"

Bristol looked so fine, and there was such a kind expression on his face, that the fear that had frozen Frankie began to leave. If he had pressured her, she would have resisted, run away. But he just stood there, smiling that gentle smile and holding his hands out to her.

Frankie took a quick breath and then put her hands in his. His fingers closed around hers with a gentle yet firm pressure. He held them, seeming to enjoy the simple act. She felt the strength that was in him, and for once took pleasure in the knowledge that she was weaker. She stood there in the shadows for a long moment, the music floating on the warm air. . .and then she stepped into the gleaming moonlight.

Paul took one look, and his face changed abruptly.

Frankie saw the change at once and shook her head, fighting to hold back the tears of mortification that sprang to her eyes. "You don't like the dress, do you?" she asked softly. She tried to pull her hands away, but he held her fast, his eyes wide as he studied her. He had hoped for some sort of *acceptable* dress— one that would not embarrass the girl—and for some sort of hairstyle and makeup that would not subject her to ridicule. But what stood before him was far more than any of that. What stood before him was an absolute vision.

The dress was a light blue—with just enough green to catch the emerald of Frankie's eyes—and trimmed with silver. Its simple lines fitted Frankie snugly at the waist and bosom, then fell to her feet in graceful folds, setting off but not flaunting her trim figure. For a moment, Paul stared at her wordlessly, finding it impossible to reconcile the youthful and womanly curves he now saw with the girl in baggy clothes to which he'd grown accustomed.

Her hair was arranged in curls that framed her square face, and even in the poor light, he could see the reddish tint that gave such life to her tresses. Somehow the short hair seemed very feminine, for the curls were delicate and moved lightly as she turned her head.

And her face looked so—so *different!* Paul took in the wide eyes and the long, thick lashes that lent the girl an air of mystery. Her cheeks were smooth, and though she had always had a beautiful complexion, now he admired the alabaster sheen of the fine skin on her face and neck. He would not have known her lips, either, for they were soft and full—as though she were waiting to be kissed.

Waiting to be—! Paul drew in his breath sharply, startled by the thought, then suddenly noticed that Frankie was trembling. He met her eyes and was shocked to see tears there. With a sinking heart he realized he hadn't responded to her question. He spoke quickly, with a throat that had inexplicably gone dry, making his words hoarse. "Frankie, I—I don't know what to say!"

"It's all right, Paul," she answered huskily. "You don't have to—"

But he broke in as though she hadn't spoken, his voice hushed with wonder. "You look absolutely beautiful!" She lifted her head abruptly, her eyes filled with surprise, and he quickly went on. "I expected you to look presentable enough, of course. I knew Mother would see to that...but I never thought to find you so changed!"

"Changed, Paul?"

"Why, didn't you look in the mirror?" Paul demanded. "And

it's not just the dress, Frankie—it's *everything!*"

Frankie's lips trembled, and she stared at him, trying hard to believe what she was hearing. "If you like me—the way I look… then I don't care what the others think," she whispered.

As if from far off, Paul noticed the music was playing. He smiled down into her eyes. "Our dance?"

Frankie felt him gently pull her into his embrace, and timidly she put her hand on his shoulder. The touch of his hand on her back sent a strange sensation through her as he began to move to the sounds of the waltz. She found herself following him, and as they went around the flagstone terrace, wheeling and turning, she was suddenly aware of what it meant to follow a man's lead. Somehow she *knew* exactly what he would do next, where he would step, which way he would turn. It came to her through the touch of his hand on her back, perhaps, or maybe in the way he held her hand in a tight clasp. No matter how it happened, Frankie Aimes found herself sweeping across the terrace effortlessly and with a grace she had not known was in her, held secure in the arms of Paul Bristol.

As for Bristol, he was speechless. The woman he held in his arms…this could *not* be the same boyish figure he'd seen every day for weeks! And yet it was! He had known many women, but none had the innocence and youthful beauty of this one. Perhaps it was the faint trace of awkwardness that set her apart, for the women he'd known had been polished—too much so. Or maybe it was the scent that Frankie wore, a faint fragrance that filled his senses and that somehow made the girl seem even more fragile and feminine.

Fragile! He'd always thought of Frankie as tough, but now he realized that what he'd been seeing was only the image she'd chosen to show the world. She was innocent and vulnerable, and that realization brought a warm rush of sudden protectiveness to him. She seemed very young, and as he looked into her eyes, he found himself feeling younger, too.

Around and around they went, until the music finally stopped. Slowly, almost regretfully, they came to a halt. Paul bowed and she curtsied. Then Paul said with a wicked grin, "I believe the next dance is mine?" he asked.

"Let me look at my program, sir," Frankie responded pertly. She took the small card that Marianne had given her, looked down at the blank lines, pursed her lips—*A most delightful habit, indeed!* Paul thought—and said, "I do think I can spare just *one* dance, Mr. Bristol!"

They danced the next three dances. But Paul eventually realized he could keep her away no longer and said, "Should we go inside? Give the young fellows a shot at the prettiest girl at the ball?"

When she only shook her head and said, "No, please—let's stay out here!" a great gladness filled him, and he swept her back into his arms.

They danced several more times, and finally a very slow set began. "Time for a rest, Miss Aimes," Paul said. He drew her close, and they moved slowly around the terrace. The music was soft, and as they moved in rhythm to its beat, Frankie slowly moved closer—not purposely, but in a natural manner. Paul was acutely conscious of the firm curves of her body as they moved. If it had been any other young woman, he would have known that he was being teased on purpose, but as he looked down into Frankie's face, he saw that the smile on her face was contented and innocent—almost as though she were unaware of her partner.

They moved more slowly as the music died. With a sigh, she looked up and said, "The dance is over—," but broke off as their eyes met. There was a still moment that caught at both of them. Paul knew in that moment that he had never seen anything lovelier than Frankie's face and nothing had ever filled him with such a sense of wonder as her wide and trusting eyes. Slowly he pulled her closer. "My mother told me to do something, Frankie."

"What was it?"

"She said, 'Be gentle with Frankie, and tell her she's the most beautiful girl at the ball.'" His arms tightened around her, and she rested her cheek against his chest, looking up at him. His eyes roamed her face, and he whispered, "You *are* beautiful, Frankie!" And then, without haste, he lowered his head and put his lips on hers.

Frankie could have moved her head aside, but she did not. When his lips touched hers, she waited to feel the fear and disgust that had filled her when Alvin Buck had kissed her— but this time, she felt only a sense of trust. . .and joy. Paul's arms drew her tighter, and she surrendered to his embrace, for the first time in her life knowing the richness of womanhood without shame.

As for Bristol, he found that there was a gentleness in him that he had never felt for any woman. Frankie was soft and yielding, her lips fresh and innocent. He wanted to go on holding her, to never let her out of his arms or his life, for she stirred him as no woman ever had.

At last he pulled his head back and said huskily, "Frankie, you are the sweetest young woman in the world—"

At that moment the french doors swung open, and Luci DeSpain's voice snapped across the terrace. "Well, Paul, are you quite finished?"

Frankie stepped back, her face flushed, and Paul said hurriedly, "Now, Luci, don't be upset—," but that was as far as he got.

Luci could have borne it if Paul had been chasing any other girl—any girl, at least, of *class*. But her voice was icy as she cut him off. "Paul, I've seen this coming for some time. Well, you've got what you want now, so I won't stand in your way. Here!" She pulled off the ring he'd given her and thrust it at him, then turned and stalked away, her back straight.

Paul stared at the ring, then looked up at Frankie. He saw the humiliation on her face and said quickly, "This isn't your doing, Frankie. It's been coming for some time. Don't let it upset you."

But it had upset her, and she whispered, "Will you take me to the hotel?"

"Of course. Let me tell my parents and get your coat."

It was a difficult ride, for Paul was aware of how hurt the young woman was. She kept her face averted, refusing to speak. When they got to the hotel, he started to get out, but she said, "Please. . .don't come in. I—just want to be alone."

"Frankie—"

"Please! I–I'll see you in the morning, if you want."

"Well, all right, but tomorrow things will look better."

"Good night, Paul," she murmured and ran into the hotel without looking back. She unlocked her door and stepped inside, then closed it and threw herself on the bed and wept, muffling her sobs by pressing her face into the covers. She didn't know how long she lay there, but after some time she sat up and held her arms across her breasts. Catching her reflection in the mirror on the wall opposite the bed, she noted with disgust that her hair was in disarray and her eyes were red and swollen.

But that was not the worst of it. Somehow. . .she felt ashamed, but did not know why. Could it be that her feelings when Paul had kissed her were shameful? Had she been wrong to kiss him back? She had no experience in such things—only the few kisses Tyler had given her, and they didn't compare in any way to what she had shared with Paul—so she just sat there until a dullness set in. Listlessly she undressed, throwing the dress across a chair with revulsion. A fine nightgown lay across the bed—a gift from Marianne—but she reached out for her familiar old nightshirt and pulled it on. Then she put out the light, slipped under the covers, and lay there in the darkness.

Images of Paul came again and again. She remembered each step of every dance, and she remembered the laughter and the sight of his face. How young he had looked tonight! And how happy! She closed her eyes and could feel his arms around her and his lips against hers—and then all broke into disarray when she remembered Luci bursting into the little world that she had found so wonderful.

Finally she dozed off, but her sleep was fitful and filled with restless dreams. When a sharp knock sounded on her door, she sat bolt upright. The knock came again, followed by two more.

Tyler! That knock was the sign they had agreed on! She came out of the bed, slipped into her robe, and opened the door. Her friend stood there wearing an old black coat and a shapeless hat that she'd never seen before. His face was pale, his mouth a mere slit.

"Tyler! What is it?" she whispered.

He stepped into the room, saying in terse tones, "Get dressed, Frankie! Quickly!"

She saw that he was tense as a wire and said, "Turn your back." While she dressed in her old clothing, she asked, "What's happened?"

"They're onto me—and you, too, I think."

"Tyler! How could they be?"

"A double agent," he said grimly. He related how he'd been on the move, getting what information he could about troop locations, but he'd been betrayed by a man named Henson, a Confederate spy who had managed to get into Pinkerton's service. "I gave him the slip, but he'll have everyone in the country on the lookout for me! We've got to get back through the lines—and it's going to be tricky."

Dressed and ready, Frankie came to put her hand on his arm. "What are we going to do?"

"Pinkerton's waiting for us at a place called Miller's Crossing. It's pretty safe, if we can get to it. I've got two fast horses, and one of our agents is going to guide us through the backcountry. Are you ready?"

"No. I—have to write a letter."

"There's no time for that!"

"You go on, then!" Frankie blazed at him. "I'll get out on my own!"

Tyler stared at her; then a weary smile broke across his face. "Write your letter. I'll wait."

Frankie found a pen and paper and sat down at the small desk in the room. She wrote steadily for ten minutes, then put down the pen, folded the letter, and put it in an envelope. She wrote the name *Paul Bristol* across the front of the envelope, then put it faceup on the table. "Let me throw my things in a bag, and I'm ready."

Five nerve-wracking hours later, she and Tyler stood at dawn in a small room, facing Allan Pinkerton. They had given him the positions of the Confederate Army, and when they were finished, Pinkerton said, "Good! I'll get this to General McClellan." He half turned, then wheeled back to say with a small smile, "You two have done well. But don't show your faces in Richmond! Go back to Washington. I'll send for you when I get back."

"Not for me, Mr. Pinkerton," Frankie said, looking him in the eyes. "Remember what you promised."

Pinkerton nodded at once. "Then take with you our thanks, Frankie. You've served well." He glanced at the young man, asking sharply, "You'll see that she gets back safely?"

"Yes, sir, I will!"

Pinkerton left, and Tyler stood there, suddenly very tired. "Well, it's over. I wonder if what we did was worth it all?"

Frankie stared at him, her lips trembling. "I hope so, Tyler—but how much would that have to be to make up for betraying people who love you?"

Tyler looked at her sharply. "People who love you. . .or people you love?"

Frankie felt a blush color her cheeks, but her gaze didn't waver. Reading his answer in her eyes, Tyler looked stricken.

"But—what about *us*, Frankie?"

Her eyes softened, and she reached out to touch his arm lightly. "Tyler, I admire you so much. . .but there could never be anything more between us than friendship. There is only one man for me, Tyler—" Her voice cracked. "And I doubt he will ever want to see me again. I—I don't know what's ahead for me, but whatever it is, I'll have to face it on my own."

He started to protest, but she halted him by holding up her hand. His eyes searched her face, and the pain he saw reflected there struck him deeply. He lowered his eyes to the floor, struggling with a sense of defeat.

Frankie wanted to comfort him, but she knew instinctively that the greatest kindness she could show her friend was to walk away. She turned and left the room, not pausing as she walked down the hallway and out the door of the building. She mounted her horse and spurred it into a run, and Tyler had to hurry to mount and catch up. Behind them the rumble of distant cannon fire sounded, and the dark horizon flickered with tiny spurts of flame.

Frankie rode on, her eyes half blinded with tears. She said nothing to Tyler as they rode away from the sound of the guns, and he knew that Frankie Aimes was not the same girl who had ridden out of Washington a few months earlier.

CHAPTER 25

"YOU'RE A WOMAN!"

Always when the harvest had come, Silas Aimes had been aware that the most certain factor in the process would be Frankie and the work she did.

Now as the last August sun seemed to drag itself over the inverted gray circle of the sky, it was harvesttime. But Aimes was aware that this harvest was to be different. Unless, of course, Frankie came to herself!

He chopped wood steadily, each movement precise and machinelike, and was troubled by thought. Usually he performed routine tasks without much thought, but since Frankie had come back, he had been shaken from his routine in several ways.

Aimes didn't like changes. He'd been heard to say, "There've been a lot of changes since I was a young man, and I've been against every one of them!" His splitting maul struck the round cylinder, and the two pieces fell neatly to the ground. He picked up one, split it, and then grabbed the other.

Frankie used to do some of the wood splitting. He straightened up and turned his eyes toward the house, and a frown creased his brow. *What'd she come back for if she didn't want to work?*

And yet he knew that wasn't quite right. From the minute she'd come back three weeks ago, she had worked—but not in the old way. She'd dressed differently, acted differently. Aimes snorted. *Wears a dress all the time—spends all day cooking and working inside the house!*

He piled his arms high with the split wood, walked to the house, and entered the kitchen. Dumping the sticks inside the wood box, he turned to Frankie and the two girls who were standing over the stove. "What you three up to?"

"I'm teaching them to make candy," Frankie said. She was wearing a simple brown dress, and somehow it bothered Silas. She looked so—so *womanly* in it. He'd never thought of her as a woman, not particularly. Now the very way she held the bowl and stirred it with a wooden spoon—why, she didn't seem at all like a boy, not anymore.

"Need some more wood split," Aimes said, and he cast a watchful eye to see the effect his speech had on Frankie.

"I'll tell Monroe to do it when he comes in." Les Monroe was the teenage neighbor who had come to take up the slack that Frankie had left. Silas had assumed that he could let the boy go and save the cost of his wages now that she was home, but it hadn't turned out that way. He stared at Frankie, half tempted to tell her that she wasn't too good to split a little wood—but for some reason he decided not to. He turned and stalked out of the kitchen.

Frankie knew what was on her father's mind but had never made an issue of it. When she'd come back, she had needed the solitude of the farm. It had taken awhile, but slowly she had lost the tense look around her lips. Now she had grown more peaceful and relaxed, though she was still unwilling to speak of what she'd done while away from the farm. A fact that caused the two younger Aimes girls no end of curiosity—or frustration, for Frankie wouldn't answer even one of their constant questions.

Timothy knew her best and so asked no questions at all. Not at first. He saw that she was on edge and carefully gave her his attention when she needed it and let her alone when she required that. On her first day back, she had told him about becoming a Christian, and he'd been filled with joy and relief. He'd known the time would come for Frankie to find God, and he was grateful it had finally happened. But as for the other things that troubled her. . .well, he would just wait until she was ready to talk about it.

He knew, of course, that some great change had taken place in her. Not just because she now shunned men's work, seeking instead the work usually done by women. No, it went much deeper than that, and Timothy, for all his isolation, was very insightful. *She's met a man somewhere,* he decided very soon. *And I'd guess he let her down.*

Frankie had known they were all puzzled by her behavior but could not bear to speak of Paul or of her work for Pinkerton. She tried to block it all out of her mind, filling her days with teaching the girls the simple skills, keeping house, and reading book after book.

That worked very well during the days, but the nights were long, and nothing seemed to stop the memories from trooping in the moment she closed her eyes. Then there were the dreams—full of images of Tyler and Pinkerton…and Paul. Many mornings she rose looking more worn out than when she'd gone to bed, and she knew Timothy watched her with concern—and prayed for her constantly.

As the days passed, though, she began to grow calmer—the monotony of the life was good for her—and she slowly became more talkative.

"What's wrong with her, anyway?" Silas asked Timothy once. "She's acting mighty strange."

"I don't know about that, Pa," Timothy said, shrugging. "I think she's acting *right* for the first time."

Silas had glared at him, frustrated by what he sensed was criticism. He'd had his own thoughts of the thing and was a man who hated to admit he was wrong. "She was happy enough until she run off," he grunted. "Wisht she'd never of done it!"

Finally Silas Aimes gave up. *She ain't never gonna be no good to me except as a cook.* When he came to that conclusion, the tension that had surrounded him passed, and he found himself strangely content with his family. The food was better, the house was well kept, and the work got done outside. He was vaguely relieved, feeling that he had successfully solved a problem.

One Friday evening they were all sitting down to an early supper when they heard the sound of a horse outside. Silas looked at Timothy. "Who kin that be?" he asked, and when a knock sounded, he got up and went to the door. Opening it, he found himself facing a tall, well-dressed man who looked to be in his thirties.

"I'm looking for the Aimes place," he said.

Frankie was standing at the stove, taking out biscuits. She turned out of curiosity to see who was at the door and, at the sound of the voice, dropped the pan of biscuits. Timothy rose and picked them up, but when he started to tease Frankie, he stopped abruptly, for her face was pale and she was trembling.

Silas Aimes had turned around at the sound of the biscuit tin hitting the floor, and he, too, noted that Frankie was upset. At once he turned back to the man, his eyes narrowing. "I'm Silas Aimes," he said gruffly. "Who are you?"

Paul Bristol looked over the man's shoulder, aware that this obviously was the father of the clan. When his eyes met Frankie's startled stare, he smiled.

"Well? Answer me!" Aimes demanded. "Who are you? What've you come here for?"

Still holding Frankie's gaze, Bristol drawled, "Well, Mr. Aimes, who am I? I'm the man who's going to be your son-in-law. As for what I came for. . ." He paused, then stepped past Aimes and went right across the room to stand in front of Frankie. "I've come for you," he said quietly.

A dead silence fell on the room, and then Timothy said, "Well, I'm your future brother-in-law. My name's Timothy." He put out a thin hand and smiled. "Welcome to the family."

Paul returned the smile, immediately liking this young man.

He took Timothy's hand, then turned and said, "Mr. Aimes, I've come to ask for your daughter in marriage. I love her." He glanced at Frankie sideways, grinning. "And I think she loves me."

"Well, if you don't beat all—!" Silas Aimes burst out. "You come in here, a total stranger, and want to take my daughter? Get out!"

Paul did not seem disturbed by the old man's anger. He turned to Frankie and asked, "Will you come for a walk with me, Frankie?"

Frankie's hands were trembling, a fact she tried to hide by snatching off her apron. "Yes, but not for long!" She led the way out of the kitchen, not even noticing her blustering father, and Bristol closed the door behind them.

"Is he really gonna marry Sister?" Jane asked, her eyes large as silver dollars.

"I'd say he's a man who's used to getting his own way," Timothy answered with a grin. "Better get used to it, Pa. She's gonna rare a bit, but you can be sure she'll have him."

Outside Frankie had walked rapidly until she came to a large oak, then turned and began, indeed, to "rare" at Paul.

"You must think you're really something," she said coldly. "Marry you! Whatever gave you such an idea—"

Paul took off his hat and let it fall to the ground. When she had first disappeared, leaving only that cursed note, he'd had a bad time of it. He'd had to struggle through feelings of betrayal and anger—he'd even wanted to hunt her down and make her pay for what she'd done. A spy! He could scarcely believe it.

But since it had been there, written in her own hand, he'd had to believe it. Then, after too many sleepless nights had made him almost impossible to live with, his mother had taken him aside for a talk. It hadn't taken long for the real source of his pain to come out: He couldn't bear losing Frankie. He could live without a lot of things, but he'd discovered that he couldn't stand the thought of life without her! He knew from her note why she had worked for Pinkerton—and he knew they would need to really talk things out someday—but right now, none of that mattered. All that was important was that he loved her—and he wasn't returning home without her.

He paid no heed to her protests. He simply waited until she ran down, then said simply, "Frankie, I had to come. I've told other women I loved them, but now I know it wasn't so. I wish I'd never said those words before, because I want to say them for the first time to you."

Frankie grew very still, her eyes searching his face. He stepped forward and took her face gently between his hands. When her eyes opened very wide, he whispered, "Never be afraid of me, Frankie. I'd cut my arms off before I'd hurt you." He lowered his head and kissed first her forehead, then her cheeks. "You must know that I love you, Frankie." His breath fanned her face gently as he spoke. "And I'm not leaving here without you." She shivered and closed her eyes, and he kissed her eyelids. "So you'd better agree to marry me, because I don't think your father and I would do so well living in the same house for too long." She gave a half laugh, half sob, and he covered her mouth with his, kissing her gently. She went completely still for a few moments, then, with a soft cry, threw her arms around him and held him fiercely.

His arms went around her possessively, and he smiled as she said in a muffled voice, "I—thought I'd lost you!"

Reaching down, he lifted her face. "You're never going to lose me—never!"

"I prayed that God would help you understand, that you wouldn't hate me. . . ." Her voice trailed off.

"Well, you gave Him a pretty tough assignment, at least at first. But you and God had a pretty effective tool in my mother. She helped set me straight one day." He smiled at the memory of their conversation.

"Paul Bristol," she had finally said, *"if you don't go after that girl and bring her back, then I'll know I've raised a complete fool!"*

He looked into Frankie's eyes and went on. "She helped me see what mattered most to me, and so I came here to claim it. . . to claim you. So you might just as well marry me, Miss Aimes, because I'll be hanged if I'm going to live without you!"

Then he kissed her, letting the fierce emotions he'd been holding back spill out—and she kissed him back with equal fervor. They clung to each other, and finally Bristol said, "I'm too old for you, I haven't got any money, and have absolutely no prospects. Will you marry me?"

Laughter bubbled up in Frankie, and her eyes twinkled merrily as she cried out, "Yes!" He held her tight against his chest, and she snuggled close, feeling safe, protected, and cherished.

After a few precious moments, they started back to the cabin, but Paul kept Frankie nestled close against his side as they walked. She glanced up at him and asked about his people. "They all hate me, don't they?"

"They don't have anything to hate you for." Surprise showed on her face, and he shrugged. "Only my parents and I read your note. We didn't see any reason to tell anyone else about it. The authorities did suspect Tyler, and after talking to the hotel clerk, they believed he had an accomplice. But no one had any idea it was you. We were questioned about Tyler, seeing as we are family, but we could tell them quite honestly we didn't know what he'd been doing or where he had gone." He looked down at her, smiling tenderly. "It was wise of you not to write anything about him in your note. So nobody knows about your involvement except Mother, Father, and myself. My parents won't say anything, because they understand. . .and because they happen to love you. They know you only did what you had to. And they want you to come home."

She laughed ruefully, and her eyes were green in the sunlight. "All the spying I did—and it didn't do a bit of good! General Lee whipped the socks off Little Mac! I might as well have stayed at home!"

"I'm glad you didn't," Paul said. He stopped and drew her close again. "You and I are different from most others, my love. Neither of us believe in the war. But I do believe that when it's over, we may be able to help bring healing—to both sides."

"What will we do until then?" Frankie asked. She looked up

at him, and he smiled down at her.

"You're a woman, Frankie," Bristol said. "You'll be that, and I'll be the man who loves you." He kissed her gently. "That's good enough for me. Is it enough for you?"

With a contented sigh, Frankie leaned against him. "Oh yes, Paul, it's enough!"

OUT OF THE WHIRLWIND

Editor's Note:

The Quakers are well known for their unique speech patterns, particularly their use of *thee* in place of *you*. This is especially true among the old-line Quakers. However, as with any tradition, we found that younger generations tend to use the two terms more or less interchangeably, depending upon circumstance and audience. We have attempted to adhere to this pattern in *Out of the Whirlwind*, making the old-line Quaker characters consistent in their use of *thee*, while the younger and more prominent characters will at times replace *thee* with the more common *you*.

PART ONE

The Spinster and the Prodigal

CHAPTER 1

A GENTLEMAN CALLER—AT LAST!

March 1862

When Clyde Dortch appeared at the home of Amos Swenson with a bouquet of flowers in his hand, Swenson at once assumed that the young man had come to court his youngest daughter, Prudence. "Come in, Friend Dortch," Swenson said, stepping back. "Thee has come calling on Prudence, I take it?"

Clyde Dortch, a trim young man of twenty-eight with crisp, curly auburn hair and bright brown eyes, stepped inside, but surprised the older man by saying, "Why no, sir, I'm calling on Miss Grace."

If Dortch had announced that he had come to burn the house down, Amos Swenson could not have been more taken aback.

"Grace? Thee is calling on Grace?"

"Yes, sir," Dortch said, seeming to enjoy the older man's

411

confusion. "I should have asked your permission first, but I'm doing that right now."

Amos Swenson, at the age of sixty-nine, was broken in health but not in mind; he was still a sharp man. He knew every acre of his fine farm in detail, and his careful and judicious use of hired hands enabled him to keep it as up-to-date as any farm in Pennsylvania.

In Amos's youth, he had been a very tall man, but age and sickness had broken him down so that he was bent and stooped. His white hair was still full and thick, and his face wore the patient look of a chronically ill man. He was never sullen or resentful—he was too fine a Christian for that! Yet one could often see the pain he suffered reflected in his mild eyes. Now he fixed his light blue eyes on the young man as he quickly rearranged his thoughts.

After Amos's wife had died, he had never remarried. Thankfully, he had been gifted with enough wisdom to raise five girls, guiding three of them through courtship into successful marriages. With those three, it had not been a matter of enticing suitors, but of sorting through the numerous young men who cluttered up the house. It would be the same with his youngest daughter, Prudence, for at the age of seventeen, she was already drawing attention.

But Grace. . .ah, Grace was another proposition entirely.

Swenson became aware that Dortch was waiting for his response and said at once, "Well, come into the parlor, Friend Dortch." Turning, he led the young man into the parlor, then said, "I'll fetch Grace." He hesitated, then attempted to probe the mystery of Dortch's sudden appearance. "Is she expecting thee?"

"I don't think so, Friend Swenson." Dortch was wearing a Sunday meeting suit of brown wool, which fit him superbly. He was a fine dresser—which made some of the old-line Quakers suspicious of him. However, he managed to stay away from the more colorful items of dress and was the envy of most of the young men of his acquaintance—not to mention the young ladies. "It just came to me that I'd like to pay a call on her," Dortch added and smiled, exposing perfect white teeth. "Perhaps with the idea of seeing if she'd be receptive to my calling on a regular basis."

Swenson blinked with surprise. This was serious! Among the Friends, calling on a young woman "on a regular basis" was tantamount to an engagement! At the very least, it was a statement that a young man was prepared to advance toward the state of matrimony.

"There's a new tract from that evangelist named Finney you might like to read," Swenson said quickly. "It may take Grace a few minutes to freshen up."

"Oh, tell her not to hurry, sir!" Dortch picked up the tract and settled himself firmly on the horsehair sofa. "I'll just see what the minister has to say." He began reading the tract, but as soon as Swenson left the room, he tossed it on the table beside him, then got up and wandered around the room. Had anyone looked in upon him at that moment, they would have noted that Dortch had the air of a man who'd made up his mind to do something difficult and was set to do whatever was necessary to accomplish the task.

Swenson hurried out to the barn and found his eldest daughter forking hay out of the loft so that it fell to the floor in a great shimmering flow.

"Grace, come down!"

Grace Swenson paused and looked down at her father, who seemed strangely agitated. His hair was wild due to his running his hands through it—a sign that he was disturbed, the young woman knew. At once she tossed the hand-carved wooden fork aside and came down the ladder. She was wearing a pair of men's trousers, a plaid shirt that had been her father's, and a pair of heavy work shoes that had seen much service. It was her usual costume when she did the heavy chores outside the house, and usually her father paid no attention. Now, however, he eyed her with dismay.

"Grace, get thee inside and put on something fitting."

Grace stared at him sharply. "What's wrong, Father?"

Amos Swenson shook his head, and there was wonder and hope in his blue eyes such as Grace had not seen for some time.

"It is Clyde Dortch," he said with a trace of excitement. "He has come calling."

"Oh." Grace understood at once—or thought she did. "Well, didn't thee tell him that Prudence is visiting over with the Williamsons?"

"No, Grace, thee doesn't understand!" Suddenly Swenson took a deep breath, for a sharp pain had come to him. He had felt it before, this pain. It made him feel fragile, like hollow glass about to shatter. Generally he had come to expect it, but now it came without warning, shooting into him, leaving him feeling a sick gray emptiness within, like a hole had cut clean through his body. He looked down to hide the pain on his face from Grace, waited until he could speak firmly, then said, "It is thee he has come to call on, not Prudence."

The announcement, he saw, was almost as much a shock to his daughter as it had been to him. She stared at him uncomprehendingly for a moment, then licked her lips. "To call on me, Father?"

"Yes. Thee had better go clean up and put on a fitting dress."

Grace dropped her gaze to hide the confusion she knew must be showing on her face. As she struggled with her emotions, her father studied her with compassion and love. This daughter had always been his favorite, though he'd kept it hidden from her and from her sisters—or tried to.

She's like me, he thought, noting the tall, erect figure and the solid features. *All the others looked like Martha—but Grace is like me.* The other girls had been small and dark, like their mother. Grace alone had his height and Scandinavian ruddiness and blond hair. *It would have been better if she'd looked like the others,* he thought with a stab of regret.

Yet as he kept his gaze on her, he could not keep down the surge of pride that came to him. He'd wanted sons, of course.

When none came, he'd learned to love his daughters well enough, but it was Grace who had been most like a son—perhaps because she was so much stronger than the others, or perhaps because she seemed to have gotten that part of his blood that loved the land and the animals. While the other girls had been playing with dolls, Grace had been right at her father's heels as he plowed or fed the stock. By the time she turned thirteen, she had become the equal of almost any hired man, making up in enthusiasm for what she lacked in physical strength.

After Martha Swenson had died, during Prudence's birth, it had been Grace who'd kept the house together. *Shouldn't have let her do it*, Swenson thought suddenly. *She should have been spending that time seeing young men and that sort of thing. Instead she was taking care of the others.*

His thoughts were interrupted when she looked up and said briefly, "I'll go change clothes."

"Put on thy blue dress," her father said, a smile coming to his thin, pale lips. "I've always been partial to that one."

"All right, Father."

Grace turned, and as she left, her father said, "It would do thee no harm to use a little of that rice powder Prudence is so fond of."

But she shook her head, saying, "That would not go well with the Friends, would it, Father? A preacher decorating her face with powder?"

"It never hurt a woman to make herself look well, daughter," Swenson retorted. He had never gotten accustomed to the fact that his daughter was a Quaker preacher. He himself was a faithful Friend, but it somehow never ceased to give him some sort of shock when she stood up to preach at meeting. Shaking his head, he went back to the parlor to entertain the young man.

Grace left the barn, thinking not of her unexpected caller but of how poorly her father looked. He had failed badly since the spell he'd had the previous summer. It took all the strength he had, she knew, just to get out of bed some days. A stab of fear shot through her, and she lifted a short prayer as she crossed the barnyard and stepped into the house. *Lord, look to my father. Let him have strength for this day.*

She had developed the habit of offering short prayers as she went about her work. No one had taught her this, but she was a woman who thought much about God, and it was as natural as breathing for her to speak to Him, sharing with Him her thoughts, wishes, and fears.

Once in her room, she didn't take long to get ready for her first suitor. She washed her face and hands at the washstand, using the heavy china basin, then turned to the pegs that held her clothing. Most of her dresses were gray or black or dark brown. She frowned. They worked very well for meeting time… but were not at all what a woman would wear to please a man!

She regarded the dark blue dress her father had mentioned, the only silk dress she'd ever owned. She'd worn it only twice since her father had almost forced her to buy it on one of their rare trips to Philadelphia. Both times she had worn it to please him rather than out of vanity.

Slipping into a pair of cotton stockings and pulling a heavy, stiff petticoat over her head, she took the blue dress from the peg. For a moment she stood there, running her work-roughened fingers over the smooth material, then pulled it on. She tied the sash and picked up a comb and brush, but catching her reflection in the small oval mirror, she studied herself.

She saw reflected there a woman of twenty-six years, who was tall and strongly built. The blue dress set off her figure well, for she was not fat—simply robust and more statuesque than her sisters. While a stranger viewing her would consider her fine indeed to look at, she turned from her own reflection with a regretful shake of her head. Her ideas of feminine beauty came from her sisters, all of whom were petite and slender as their mother had been—so much so that Grace had always felt outsized and awkward when she stood beside them.

She had her father's broad, well-shaped face, with a broad mouth and large eyes. But again, she had come to believe that her features were coarse and masculine. Had she been an only child—or at least been blessed with handsome brothers instead of petite, beautiful sisters—she would not have reached the age of twenty-six without having had a suitor.

Not that Grace was homely. Far from it! But her facial structure was *strong* rather than delicate, and she was labeled plain and out of scale when weighed against the feminine prettiness of her four younger sisters. It was something that she had accepted when she was in her early teens, and others had sensed this in her. Particularly her sisters. It was not uncommon for one of these fair ladies to remark publicly, "Oh, Grace isn't interested in young men." And with the callousness of pretty young women who are told too often just how pretty they are, they spoke more freely in the privacy of the home. Such statements as "It's a good thing Grace is so taken up with religion and being a preacher, because as plain as she is, she'd have a hard time catching a good man" were painfully common.

Now as Grace examined herself in the mirror, she wondered what it would be like to have a home and a husband. For the greatest irony of her situation was that, in acting as a mother to her sisters, she had developed a maternal side to her character that none of the other girls possessed.

Maybe a little of that rice powder wouldn't hurt. The thought flashed through her mind, and for an instant she was tempted to go to Prudence's chest and take out the small china case in which her sister kept the cosmetic. But almost instantly she rebelled against the impulse, saying under her breath: "Grace Swenson, thee needs no man who has to be caught by dust on a woman's face!"

She drew the comb through her long blond hair, then tied it quickly back and left the room. As she approached the parlor, she heard Dortch talking with her father, and she stopped abruptly. Standing in the hall, she had the absurd impulse to turn and flee—to run into the barn and hide, or rush along the path beside the brook in the woods. She was a sensitive young woman, far more so than most people knew, and her lack of knowledge of men made her anxious and vulnerable in a situation such as this.

Quakers were not known for parties or dances, but they had, over the years, established a highly developed system of courtship. Since her teenage years, Grace had dreaded such things as she was about to face. The other girls had lived for the encounters with boys, it seemed to her, but she had only memories of shame and humiliation in such situations. She had grown tall during adolescence, so that the boys of her own age were shorter than she, and this made her feel like some kind of giantess. A feeling that the boys only confirmed by their avoidance of her, and the girls only made worse by their pitying glances. Gradually Grace had managed to assume the role of sponsor at such affairs, serving the food and doing the other small chores that kept her busy—and enabled her to avoid the embarrassment of sitting alone with no young man coming to talk to her.

In all her twenty-six years, no young man had ever come to call. And now that one had, she was possessed of a terror wondering what she would say to him! She had listened to the laughing talk of young couples and was certain she could never achieve such a teasing tone or such lightness of spirit.

Grace closed her eyes. *Lord, I feel so—so helpless. Help me to talk to this man!* Then, opening her eyes and clenching her teeth, she entered the parlor.

"Ah, here thee is, Miss Grace!" Dortch stood up at once, and a smile exposed his fine teeth. "Your father and I were about to get into a controversy."

"No! No!" Grace's father shook his head with alarm. "That would not do—not at all!"

Grace said, "It's good to see thee, Friend Dortch, but I think you'll find it hard to have an argument with my father." She smiled fondly at her father, adding, "He's not much for contention."

"Oh, I was only joking," Dortch said quickly. "We were just discussing this man Charles Finney and his 'new measures.'"

Swenson said quickly, "I'll leave Grace to defend Mr. Finney. She's quite taken with him." He got up, nodded, and left the room.

Dortch smiled ruefully at the woman who stood regarding him, saying, "I know better than to argue religion with a preacher, Miss Grace. And the truth is, I don't really understand what it is Finney's doing that's caused all the controversy. I wish you'd explain it to me."

Relief washed over Grace. This was something she could talk about! *Thank You, Lord!*

"Why, I'm no authority, Friend Dortch," she said. "I don't know what it is about Rev. Finney that's caused all the controversy, but I *have* studied Rev. Finney's teaching closely."

"Fine!" Dortch exclaimed. "Why don't we sit down and thee can try to explain it to a rather thickheaded layman." He indicated the narrow couch, and when Grace sat down, he joined her. Grace tried to forget that this was the couch the girls called the "Courting Couch" for obvious reasons. When two adults sat together, they were very close. She licked her lips nervously and began talking.

"Well, Mr. Finney teaches that the new birth is necessary

421

for everyone who comes into the world. . . ," Grace began, and for the next half hour she explained Finney's "new measures" and some of the controversy that they had occasioned.

Dortch listened carefully—or seemed to. He kept his eyes fixed on Grace, asking an occasional question. He was not a tall man, being of no more than average height, so that his eyes were on a level with those of the woman next to him. "So Mr. Finney says that revivals of religion are 'harvests'? Is that it?" he asked. "And you don't quite agree with that?"

Grace was beginning to have a difficult time concentrating on theology. The narrow couch worked very well as long as the occupants sat straight up and faced the front, as if they were sitting on a wagon seat. But Clyde Dortch and Grace were forced to turn slightly so that they could face each other—and in the process, Dortch's knee had come to press against Grace's knee.

The intimacy of the contact brought a slight flush to Grace's cheeks, but Dortch didn't seem to notice. As they continued to talk, however, the pressure of his knee grew more pronounced, and his right shoulder somehow began to press on her left.

Don't be a fool! Grace told herself when the thought came into her mind that she was allowing the man too much liberty. *You've got to get over this foolishness!*

Nevertheless, she said abruptly, "Friend Dortch, I baked yesterday. Would thee like some pecan pie and a glass of milk?"

"That would be fine," Dortch responded, his teeth gleaming. "The best part of our socials are your pies and cakes, Miss Grace."

The compliment caused a rosy flush to touch Grace's cheeks, and she grew flustered. "Oh, there are better cooks than I am!" she murmured, getting to her feet.

"Now that's your opinion, Miss Grace, but it's not valid," Dortch responded. "Everybody knows you're the best in the whole community at making pies."

Grace was pleased at his praise, and when he ate two thick wedges of the pecan pie, she said, "Would thee like to take some home, Friend Dortch? I still bake for six after all this time."

"That would be a treat for a lonely bachelor," Dortch said, then added with a winsome smile, "but I can think of one thing I'd like even better than the pie."

"Why, what's that, Friend Dortch?"

"That we agree to call each other by names, not titles." Dortch made a slight face, adding, "Don't you think 'Friend Dortch' sounds too formal? Couldn't it just be Clyde and Grace?"

"I—I don't see why not," Grace said slowly.

Noticing the hesitation in her voice, Dortch said quickly, "I don't want to be presumptuous or forward, Grace, but—well, the truth is, I've admired thee for a long time."

This admission drew a glance of astonishment from Grace. For some time, Clyde Dortch had been one of the most eligible bachelors in the Quaker community. His family was not prosperous, but their farm was better than average. Hiram Dortch, Clyde's father, had suffered a stroke two years earlier and was an invalid, so it was Clyde's older brother, Daniel, who was now in charge. The Dortches were good Quakers—though a little too prone to slightly radical doctrine than the more conservative element of the fellowship liked.

Still, Clyde was handsome and stood to own at least half the farm one day. He was a fine musician, too, which made him a popular addition to the social life of the community. Grace well knew that Dortch liked the company of women, but she also knew he had never singled out any one girl for special attention. She recalled he had had some trouble with a few of the other young men whose sweethearts showed too much attention to him. Grace's sister Dove had once said, *"Clyde likes women, but he likes taking them away from other men too well."*

Grace thought about that fleetingly, but his compliment silenced her concerns—though not before she had a quick flash of memory of a time when James Thomson had beaten Clyde thoroughly for trying to take Hannah Toler from him.

"I didn't know you ever thought about me," Grace said finally.

"Oh, for a long time," Dortch said quickly. Then he shrugged and grinned ruefully. "But I never said anything."

"Why not..., Clyde?" The use of his first name was difficult for Grace. "Was it so hard?"

"Oh, I think it's because you're a preacher," Clyde said thoughtfully. "That scares fellows off, you know."

"I suppose so."

"Sure it does! I mean, how's a fellow supposed to *act* when a girl is a preacher?"

Grace stared at him. "Couldn't thee act just like thee does

with other young women?"

"And if I did," Dortch asked quickly, his eyes gleaming, "what would you do?" He suddenly reached forward and took her hand, holding it tightly. "For example, it's not unusual for a fellow to hold a girl's hand like this. Do you mind, Grace?"

The suddenness of his action caught Grace off guard, and her first impulse was to jerk her hand back.

But that would prove he is right!

"Nooo. . .I don't think I mind." She spoke slowly. With great daring, she pressed his hand—then color rushed to her cheeks. She laughed awkwardly and pulled her hand back. "I'll put your pie in a covered dish," she said and got to her feet.

When Clyde left, he smiled at her, saying, "I'd like to come by some evening. Your father said he wouldn't mind."

Grace said, "Why, yes, Clyde. Why don't you come for dinner tomorrow?"

"I'll be here!" Dortch looked at her and asked, "Will you wear that blue dress?"

Grace nodded and smiled at him. "I might even put on some of Prudence's rice powder."

"Don't do that, Grace!" Dortch said quickly. "That's only for girls who need it. You have the most beautiful complexion I've ever seen!"

Grace watched as he mounted his gray mare and rode away. Slowly she made her way back to the kitchen and washed up the dishes.

I didn't make a fool of myself, she thought. *He's really very nice. . .if only he were a bit taller.* Then she scolded herself for her foolish wish.

"Did thee have a good visit with the young man?"

Grace was so preoccupied with her thoughts that her father's voice startled her. She turned quickly to face him, saying awkwardly, "Oh yes. It was nice."

"Fine-looking young man."

Something in her father's tone made Grace look at him. "Well, I asked him to come to dinner tomorrow. Is that all right, Father?"

"Of course, daughter. Be nice to have him."

Grace felt very awkward, which was unusual for her, for she and her father were great friends. "Father, I—I let him hold my hand."

Swenson smiled. "Did thee, now?"

"Yes. Do you think that was wrong?"

"No, I don't," Swenson said firmly. "I held your mother's hand before we were married."

The admission made Grace smile. She had a wry sense of humor that few ever saw, and it came out now. "Sit down and drink some milk," she ordered. "And thee can tell me how to trap a man."

"Oh, now—!"

"I can't ask anyone else, can I?" Grace poured a glass of milk and set it before him, then sat down and put her chin on her hand. Now that the ordeal was over, she was feeling light and happy. "Come now, give me some counsel. Shall I order some

French perfume from Philadelphia? Or maybe one of those dresses with a bustle on the back?"

"Daughter! Thee would get read out of the meeting!"

Grace broke into laughter at the horrified look on her father's face. "I can see myself rigged out like that! Wouldn't it be something to see, though? My going to preach in a thing like that?"

Swenson suddenly laughed with her. "Might do us good. Nobody would go to sleep, would they?" He took a sip of the milk, then shook his head and grew silent. Finally he said, "I wish thee could marry and have children." He looked at her, asking, "Has thee thought of that?"

Grace sobered at once. "When I was younger. Not for a long time."

Her confession seemed to hurt Swenson. He knew his illness was serious and that he would not live very long—though he had never mentioned this to his family. "I wish I could go back," he said heavily. "I made a mistake letting thee work so hard."

"I don't want thee to think that, Father!" Grace spoke almost sharply and went to stand behind him. Leaning over, she put her arms around him and placed her cheek next to his. "God will take care of me—and of thee."

She could feel the thinness of his frame and knew a moment of fear as the thought of losing him came to her. She held him tightly, whispering, "Don't thee mind about me! I'm choosy about my men! Until I find one as good and loving as the one right here in this chair, I'll not have him!"

Swenson's eyes filled with tears, and he reached up and held her hands. *Good Lord in heaven—keep this lamb safe as the apple of Thy eye!*

CHAPTER 2

TWO KISSES

$\mathcal{A}$mong the Quakers, affairs such as courtship move very slowly. One wag put it, "If you enjoy watching the movements of major icebergs, you'll enjoy watching the courtship of Quakers."

As for Grace, she was not at all disturbed that Clyde Dortch had little to show for the fact that he had come to take dinner with the Swensons twice a week for two months—little, that is, besides the slight bulge around his middle. She was not by nature a hasty young woman, and she was prepared to cook twice a week for ten more months before the next stage of courtship began.

Truthfully, she was enjoying the mild sensation that the courtship had stirred in the small, tranquil world of the Friends. For the first time in her life, she was aware that people were staring at her, watching with interest as she moved through the rites of passage! Always before it had been one of her sisters, though Grace had never resented their moments of glory—if a Quaker courtship could be so labeled.

The community had long ago, she realized, grown accustomed to the notion that their lady preacher would remain in single bliss, taking care of her father and serving as an aging aunt for the offspring of her sisters. It was a role that they could understand and approve. They loved ritual and the even tenor of habit, these Quakers, and Grace Swenson had been neatly identified, labeled, and consigned to a certain slot.

Now the tall young woman had astounded them all by stepping outside the classification into which they had locked her, and it set her little world—and in particular a Mrs. Lula Belle Gatz—to buzzing. One of the Friends had said of Lula Belle Gatz, "She's got a tongue long enough to sit in the living room and lick the skillet in the kitchen!" While this might have proven anatomically impossible for the lady, metaphorically, she lived up to the reputation!

Sister Gatz, in truth, had too little to do at home—her children being all grown and mostly beyond her "arrangings"—so she moved from house to house, from quilting to quilting, discussing the affairs of others. She was at heart a kindly woman—a Dorcas, who was always the first to help when trouble came. She was so assiduous in this sort of thing that folks in the community swore it was always "First Lula Belle, then the doctor, then the undertaker!" Once, when Mary Rochard sickened and died with record speed, Sister Gatz arrived *after* the doctor and the undertaker had come and gone. It grieved her so greatly that she became almost ill over her delinquency, but she found solace in rearranging the funeral plans made by the family.

When she presented herself at the front door of the Swenson home bearing a quilt as a wedding gift, both Grace and her father knew that it would be an expensive gift. And they were not mistaken, for with the quilt came a host of warnings, suggestions, and searching questions about the match.

"She's settling in for a long visit, Grace," Amos said gloomily. "I don't think I feel up to it. That woman is worse than a case of grippe!"

Grace laughed at the gloomy comparison. "Go lie down, Father. Don't come out until I come for thee," she said. In truth, she was worried about her father. He seemed to have grown weaker for the past two months, and she spent much time fixing foods he would eat.

"That might not come for a day or two," Amos sighed. "Sister Gatz is a fine woman, but gives away too much advice."

After she got her father off for his nap, Grace squared her shoulders, put a smile on her lips, and marched in to take her medicine. It proved to be a long, rather bitter dose. She sat in her rocker knitting socks as the older woman spent two hours running down a rather vivid list of dangers that a young couple could expect to begin no later than ten minutes after they were married. Sister Gatz was an angular woman, in shape as well as in mind, with a hungry-looking face set in sharp planes and a pair of piercing black eyes.

As she drew breath to begin another chapter in her remarks, she happened to glance out the window. The words shut down momentarily, and her mouth drew into a small round O. "Isn't that young Prudence with Clyde?" she demanded, turning an accusing look upon Grace.

Grace glanced up from her knitting, looked out the window, and nodded. "Yes, Sister Gatz. Prudence needed to go over to Riverton to fetch some material for my dress. Gelt's Store didn't have anything suitable."

The O of Sister Gatz's mouth drew down to form an inverted U. "I'd think thee would want to go choose thy own material, Sister Swenson."

"Oh, the new calf is due, and I'm expecting some trouble with the birthing. And Prudence has a better eye for dress material than I have."

"Humph!" Sister Gatz formed this monosyllabic expression by snorting through her long nose. It was an odd sound, but one the lady used effectively to express doubt, disgust, or displeasure. She stared out the window, observing the couple as Clyde helped Prudence out of the buggy, noting the ease with which he lifted her up and set her down. The two were laughing—a most inappropriate activity in Sister Gatz's mind, for she was always suspicious when a young man and a young woman laughed together.

"Humph!" she echoed, and when the pair came into the parlor, she carefully examined Prudence's rosy complexion and bright eyes. Then she fixed her sharp gaze on Dortch, noting the pleased look on his face. Though she dared not use a third "humph"—even she recognized this would be overly critical— she did sit straighter, and she nodded only slightly when Dortch said, "Good afternoon, Sister Gatz. Has thee had a good visit with Grace?"

"We've had an edifying time."

"Oh, Grace!" Prudence's dark blue eyes were sparkling, and she looked fresh and pretty in a simple, well-fitted tan dress. "The circus was in town! We saw an elephant, didn't we, Clyde?"

"Yes, we did." He came over and sat down in the oak rocker. He was looking handsome and dapper in a gray suit and his flat-crowned hat, which he left on his head as was the fashion of Quakers. He looked pleased and happy, and there was a satisfied look on his handsome face as he laughed. "Does thee know what I thought when I saw the beast, Grace?"

"I can't imagine."

"I thought, There is no such animal as that!"

Prudence giggled suddenly, adding, "The great beast stopped right in front of us and put his—his nose out for something to eat. It was so scary, Grace! But Clyde wasn't a bit afraid of him. He just laughed and gave the creature the last of my sandwich!"

Clyde became aware of Sister Gatz's scowl and said quickly, "I wish thee had been there, Grace. I thought we might go back tomorrow and see the circus."

"Oh, can I go?" Prudence demanded. "The sign on the side

of one of the wagons said there was an 'Ethiopian Eccentricity.' I can't imagine what that is!"

"Nothing that thee should be seeing, I'm sure, Sister Prudence!" With that phrase, Sister Gatz firmly settled the question of a trip to the circus!

Prudence glared at the woman and would have argued, but Dortch said quickly, "Prudence, why don't you show Grace the material?"

Grace put aside her knitting, and soon she and Prudence were examining the fine white silk Prudence had found—but the beautiful material pleased Sister Gatz even less than the idea of an Ethiopian Eccentricity. "I don't recall ever seeing one of our young women wearing such finery," she sniffed. Getting to her feet, she looked at Dortch, then at Prudence, and then at the glistening silk in Grace's hands.

"Humph!" she snorted. "I'll take my leave of thee."

When she was safely out of hearing, Clyde winked wickedly at the two women, then bowed in the direction of the door. "Thee could not have taken anything from me that I would be more willing to give," he said mockingly. Prudence giggled, but Grace shook her head.

"She's a very unhappy woman," Grace said.

Prudence removed her bonnet and shook her mass of dark curls in a careless manner. She had little patience with the ways of older people and said sharply, "She's too nosy and a terrible gossip." Then she dismissed the old woman from her mind. "I couldn't find any ribbon that I liked. I'm going to change, and then Clyde and I are going to Ellen Dorsey's and see if she has any."

Clyde said suddenly, "Grace, you come and we'll look at the ribbon."

Grace looked at him with a slight surprise. "Why—all right, Clyde. But Prudence will have to make the final decision." She rose and moved to get her cloak and bonnet, pausing long enough to stop and give her younger sister an affectionate pat on the shoulder. "I'll just tell Father where we're going."

"Oh, I'll stay home if thee is going," Prudence said. "It doesn't take two to pick out a ribbon!"

She spoke sharply, causing Grace to stare after her sister as she flounced out of the room without another word. But Grace was accustomed to Prudence's sudden mood changes, and she said only, "I'm ready, Clyde."

When they got to the buggy, Dortch attempted to help Grace into the wagon, but she was unaccustomed to such attention and pulled herself into the seat with a quick ease that left him standing there looking slightly foolish. Grace saw the displeasure in his eyes and thought, *I've got to learn to wait—to let him help me.*

When they pulled up in front of the dressmaker's shop, she forced herself to wait as Clyde stepped out of the buggy and came to her side. She took his hand and stepped out, smiling at him. He was a well-built man but not tall, and though he did his best to hide it from Grace, it touched his vanity that she was able to look him squarely in the eye. He forced a smile to his lips. "Let's go get some ice cream after we get the ribbon, Grace."

"All right."

They shared a pleasant time. Grace examined every ribbon that Ellen Dorsey had, but in the end could only say, "Thee and Prudence will have to decide."

"Why, thee has a good eye for color, Sister Grace," Mrs. Dorsey said a little impatiently. She was an attractive widow of thirty-five who supported her three children by her needle. She had followed the courtship of the young couple before her avidly—as had practically every other member of the community. Now as she stood there with ribbons draped over her arm, she studied the young pair, then frowned slightly as if something seemed not quite right to her. Carefully she said, "Prudence came to talk to me about the dress, but thee needs to come in so we can decide on it."

Grace agreed, but when she and Clyde left the dressmaker's shop, Mrs. Dorsey went next door at once, where she told her neighbor of the visit. Shaking her head, she said with asperity, "Sister Grace had better give more attention to this wedding. Why, her sister Prudence acts as though *she's* the one getting married!"

Blissfully unaware of the currents of speculation around her, Grace enjoyed the afternoon, especially the visit to the ice cream parlor, where she ate two helpings of ice cream. Afterward she walked along the streets of the small town with Dortch, speaking to those they passed. She remembered to let Dortch help her into the buggy, and when they got back to the farm, she said, "I've got to get supper ready, Clyde. Why doesn't thee sit and talk to Father while thee waits?"

"All right, Grace." When they reached the house, however, Amos Swenson was napping. So Clyde sat in the parlor for a time, reading a week-old paper, then grew restless. He wandered outside to stroll around the farm, admiring the sturdy stone barn and the smaller outbuildings. The stock were all sleek and healthy, the fences all tightly knit, the fields all laid out in a carefully planned design. He spoke to the two hired men, Jed Satterfield and Benny George, discussing the state of the crops and the animals. Both men, Dortch knew, were hard workers who did a good job of handling the work Swenson could no longer do himself.

Satterfield, a tall, gangling man of thirty, gave Dortch a careful look, then said, "Guess you won't be needing one of us when you and Sister Grace get married."

"Oh, there'll be plenty of work for three men, Jed," Dortch said quickly. "I've got some new ideas that'll be taking up a lot of my time, so thee and Benny can count on staying on."

As Dortch wandered away from the barn, he decided to head for the pasture to look over the cattle grazing by the creek. As he walked, a sensation of satisfaction came over him. He had been unhappy at home since his father's stroke. His older brother had little of Clyde's lighthearted approach to life. In direct contrast to Clyde, Daniel was heavy in body and mind, caring little for anything except his religion and the farm. He put in long, hard days and expected everyone else to do the same.

Clyde, however, did not hold with such a strict outlook on life, and hard feelings had developed between the two brothers. Mrs. Dortch had spoiled her younger son, and her husband had been swayed by her so that he had not curbed Clyde's careless ways. As long as Mr. Dortch had been in charge, he had let Clyde slide by with his work—but now Clyde's father was helpless, and Daniel had laid his iron hand to everything on the farm. Especially Clyde. The tension had become so intense that Daniel had finally said, "If thee wants to be a gentleman of leisure, thee will have to find another place to do it, Brother Clyde!"

Now, walking about the Swenson farm, breathing air that was fresh as wine, Clyde smiled to himself. "Indeed, Brother Daniel, thee was right," he muttered with some satisfaction as he considered what his days would hold after his marriage to Grace. He strolled along the pathway that led to the lower pasture, enjoying himself immensely. He was not a man to think much of the future, but as he walked along and counted the fat cows dotting the landscape, he thought of how pleasant it would be to escape Daniel's harsh demands. Here, things would be different! A man wouldn't have to kill himself working, not with two good hands like Benny and Jed!

He thought suddenly of Grace and shook his head in an involuntary gesture. She was a fine girl, of course—just not very exciting. *Never thought I'd wind up marrying a preacher,* he thought, a wry smile on his full lips. *She's no beauty—but she'll take care of a husband well enough.* He thought of the good food and the other advantages of being master of this fine farm and shrugged slightly. *A man can't have everything, I guess. Besides, Grace will never give me any trouble. She's too glad to get a husband for that!*

Suddenly Clyde heard his name called. He looked up to see Prudence standing beside the creek, waving at him. Immediately his mood lightened, and he hurried across the field to her. "What are you doing out here, Prudence?"

"Picking flowers." She motioned toward a basket lying on the ground beside the creek, filled with yellow, blue, and red wildflowers. She was wearing a thin white cotton dress, and the beauty of her figure startled Dortch. She caught his expression, understood it for what it was, and smiled. "Did thee have a good time in town?" she asked demurely.

Dortch shrugged carelessly. "I guess so. Grace said that thee would have to help pick out the ribbons."

"What else did thee do?"

"Oh, we got some ice cream." Dortch made a slight gesture of depreciation. "It wasn't a thrilling trip, I guess." He smiled at her, his teeth white against his skin. "Not nearly as much fun as seeing an elephant."

The memory of their visit to Riverton lit Prudence's face. "Oh, that was fun, wasn't it, Clyde! I'd give anything if we could go see the actual show!"

Prudence may not have known what an attractive picture

she made as she stood there looking up at him. She was petite, small, and well formed—and very pretty. It did something for Dortch's vanity to have her look up at him as she was, her eyes bright with excitement. It made him feel much taller, and he suddenly found himself saying, "I'd like to take thee there, Prudence—" Then he caught himself and added quickly, "But of course, that wouldn't look good."

"Oh, *pooh*! I get absolutely *sick* of having to care about what people think!"

"Prudence!"

She shook her head angrily, her curls bouncing about in a most appealing manner. "Well, I don't care if that shocks thee. Sometimes I think I'm in a jail or something. A girl can't even *smile* at a young man without those—those old *vultures* starting to gossip!" She looked up at Clyde, her lips drawn into a pout. "There! Now thee will think I'm a brazen hussy, won't thee?"

Clyde laughed suddenly. "No, I won't, because I feel exactly the same way most of the time." This was true, for Clyde's religion was not terribly deep. He was the most liberal of liberal Quakers and had often wished he was an Episcopalian so that he could have a little breathing room. As a rule, he kept this heresy to himself, but now that Prudence had spoken so frankly, he felt secure enough to agree.

"I'm not much of a Quaker, I guess," he said ruefully. "I just can't see anything wrong with having a little fun. After all, there's dancing and singing in the Bible, isn't there?"

Prudence nodded at once. "Yes, there is, but can thee imagine what Father would say if we went to a dance?" Her eyes gleamed wickedly, and she giggled. "We'd be read out of meeting!"

"Well, I don't much care." Clyde grinned. "We could have some fun—and then we could repent and get back in."

"Oh, Clyde, that's just awful!" Prudence tried to look shocked, but her amusement won out. "Come on, thee can help me pick some flowers. We'll decide what wicked thing we'll do to get put out of the meeting. . . ."

For the next hour, Clyde Dortch had one of the most enjoyable times of his life. He liked sprightly young women and had not known that this youngest Swenson girl was so lively and clever. The two of them wandered over the fields, picking flowers from time to time, but mostly talking and laughing.

By the time they got back to the creek, the sun was turning the water red with afternoon beams. They stood there admiring it until Clyde said, "I guess we'd better get to supper." Regret was heavy in his voice. He turned to the girl standing close beside him. "This has been nice, Prue. We'll have to pick flowers more often together."

Prudence stood before him and suddenly gave voice to a thought that had been lurking inside her for some time. "Clyde, you're so *different* from Grace. How will thee ever—?" When Prudence broke off uncertainly, Clyde understood what she was trying to say.

"How will Grace and I get along?"

"Well—she's so *religious*!"

"And I'm not." Dortch nodded slowly. He had thought

of this at length but had arrived at no good answers. He was honest enough to admit his faults and knew that he would be cheating Grace Swenson out of what every man should bring to a marriage—an honest love. He'd fought this battle out, however, and justified his course by telling himself that since Grace wasn't likely to get any sort of a husband other than him, he was actually doing her a service. Even so, he was realistic enough to understand that he would not be entirely happy in their relationship. He had been trying to blot this out of his mind by telling himself that it would be an *easy* life and that he would be relieved from the drudgery of work that he was now doomed to.

Now, though, as he looked down into Prudence's sweet face, he suddenly became serious. The sun in the west cast shadows on his clean-cut features, and he spoke quietly and honestly—something he hadn't done much of lately! "I'll be giving Grace something," he said quietly. "She'll have a husband—and that is something she never thought to have."

Prudence was a quick girl. She read into Dortch's words what lay beneath them. "But what about *thee*, Clyde?" With an impulsive gesture, she moved closer to him and put her hand on his arm. Looking up into his eyes, she whispered, "What will thee get?"

Dortch looked down at Prudence and said evenly, "Most people say I'm getting a good farm out of it."

But Prudence, to his relief, didn't even answer that. Her features softened, and she whispered, "Thee will be a lonesome man, Clyde." There was an air of sadness about her as she spoke. "And that's not right—because thee is a man who needs loving and fun."

As Prudence stood looking up at him with such an air of sweetness and concern, Clyde suddenly was acutely aware of her youth and beauty. He had thought of her as a pretty girl who would grow up someday. . .but now, in the silence of the evening air, as she looked up at him with her lips slightly parted, he knew that she was already a woman.

Almost without meaning to, he moved to put his arms around her and let his lips fall on hers. She was soft and yielding, and he felt the pressure of her arms around his neck. Her embrace stirred him as nothing else had ever done. And he was aware that she was stirred, as well, for she clung to him, holding him fast.

Finally she pulled away, and her voice was unsteady as she said, "Clyde—we shouldn't—!"

"No, I guess not," he said huskily.

She saw that he was half ashamed of kissing her, and it was part of Prudence's charm that she knew how to make people feel better. She gave him a dimpled smile and said in a bright voice, "Well, that's one kiss Grace won't get!"

Clyde could not refrain from smiling. "Someday you're going to keep a man hopping, Prudence. The man thee gets will never know exactly what thee is going to say or do next."

Struggling to conceal the tumult Clyde's kiss had stirred in her, she said, "It's good for a man to be teased. Keeps him on his toes." She picked up the basket of flowers, then said, "Come on, I'll race thee to the house!"

They returned just as Grace came out on the porch. "I was coming to call you two for supper." Her eyes fell on the flowers, and she smiled. "Put them in the blue vase, Prudence. They'll look nice on the table."

"Clyde helped me," Prudence said quickly. She smiled, adding, "He's a good flower picker." She left and went to look for the vase, and Clyde said quickly, "Didn't mean to stay out so long, Grace."

"Oh, I'm glad you and Prudence had some time together," Grace said at once. "She gets lonely out here sometimes. Thee'll be good company for her after we're married."

Clyde had the grace to look uncomfortable, and that night at supper he was quieter than usual. The talk came, as it always did, to the War Between the States. They were all saddened by it, for Quakers, who were opposed to all violence, were particularly grieved over a civil war.

"I don't think it will last long," Clyde remarked. "The Rebels whipped us so badly at Bull Run that people won't stand for going on with the campaign."

"I don't think that's the way it will go," Amos disagreed. "The Union was beaten in that battle, but the people want slavery outlawed. And they don't want the Union broken up by secession. No, this new president won't let it drop. It'll be a long war, I'm afraid."

Clyde prepared to leave shortly after supper. "Got to get

an early start in the morning," he said, excusing himself. Grace went with him out on the porch, where he turned and said, "It was a fine supper, Grace."

"I'm glad thee enjoyed it, Clyde."

Dortch had a sudden thought and moved closer to Grace. She looked at him with quick apprehension in her eyes—he intended to kiss her. He had done so only twice thus far, and both times had been rather perfunctory affairs.

But this time he took her in his arms and pulled her close— so that she felt the pressure of his arms and the beating of his heart beneath her palms where they rested on his chest—and the intimacy of the contact frightened her. Still, as he sought her lips, she submitted, for she knew this was part of courtship—or so she had been told. She had heard girls laughing and joking about being kissed and had never been able to join in.

Clyde's lips were hard and demanding, and something about the way his hands touched her only increased her fear. Instinctively she pushed him away, though with more force than she intended. Dortch stared at her, something in his face that she could not read.

"Forgive me, Grace," he said briefly. His tone was clipped and terse, but he tried to smile. "I'll see thee tomorrow."

As Dortch wheeled abruptly and walked to his horse, Grace clasped her hands together tightly. She opened her mouth to call out, to say something that would take the sting from her abrupt rejection, but no words came. Finally as he mounted and spurred his horse into a run, she called out.

"Clyde—!"

But he was gone, and she stood there in the warm darkness, her cheeks burning, thinking of what had happened. Tears burned at her eyes unexpectedly, and she brushed them away impatiently. She was a warmhearted young woman, and she had been sure that when this time of her life came—the time when she agreed to marry a man—she would be able to respond to her beloved's caress. But all she had felt with Dortch was fear. . . and repulsion.

There must be something wrong with me. Turning, she moved back into the house, her heart heavy and her mind troubled.

When her father saw her face, he asked quickly, "Did thee and the young man have a quarrel?"

"No, Father," she said, but there was no happiness in her face, and as she left to go to her room, Swenson watched her carefully. He knew she was more afraid of marriage than looking forward to it. Finally he shook his head, muttering, "There's no way I can help her with this thing." He moved slowly to blow out the lamp, then turned and went to his room, where he lay awake for a long time thinking of many things.

Chapter 3

Good-bye to Love

Spring had come, and the days when the sun was sharp and bright and full became more common. The sun settled westward, seeming to melt into a bed of gold flame as it touched the faraway mountains, and the air became warmer with breezes coming out of the south, smelling of pleasant weather.

Amos Swenson knew his land as well as he knew himself. He well understood that in another few months' time, winter would crouch on the rim of the horizon, ready in one day or night to come over the land, turning it black and bitter, shriveling every living thing exposed to it. But it was for this violent change of seasons that Amos loved this land—a land that was full of goodness, like a smiling and beautiful woman whose lavish warmth and generosity sprang from those same strongly primitive sources that could make her cruel.

Yet it was not just the changing of the seasons that Amos felt as the days began to lengthen. No, he knew that he himself was beginning to fade. He measured his strength carefully, grieving at times as he thought of the vigor of his youth, but he felt no fear at leaving this life behind. For him it was like stepping over from a dangerous and difficult place into a place filled with kindness and light.

His only regret was leaving his daughters.

One evening he sat on his front porch, wrapped in a light blanket against the breath of the cool night air, studying the stars. They glittered overhead like cold fire—tiny points of light that never failed to draw his interest and admiration.

Grace came out, looked down at him, then sat down in the swing. Following his gaze upward to the brightly lit heavens, she asked, "How many are there, do you suppose?"

"Someday I'll ask the good Lord to let me count them." Almost he added, "And it won't be a long wait until that day," but he caught himself, coughing slightly to cover his near slip.

Grace looked at him quickly. "It's too cool out here. Let's go in the house, Father."

"Nothing in there like that." Amos smiled, waving at the spangled heavens. " 'The heavens declare the glory of God; and the firmament sheweth his handiwork.'"

Grace looked upward again, but her mind was on her father. He was failing rapidly, and the doctor could do nothing. *Don't let yourself hope too much, Grace,"* the doctor had said quietly to her in private. *"His heart is very weak. He could go at any moment."*

A thickness came to her throat as she thought of losing her

father, and she dropped her eyes from the stars to look across the porch at him. He had been an anchor in her life ever since she was a little girl, and the thought of being alone stirred a sharp pain in her breast.

She sat there trying to turn her thoughts away from loss, and his quiet voice broke the silence. "Has thee made up thy mind about the wedding, daughter?"

"Sometime soon," Grace said evasively.

Swenson was not a persistent man, but there was an urgency in his thin voice as he said, "It would please me if thee made the date soon."

Grace looked up, startled—this was as close as her father had come to mentioning his death. Filled with confusion, she could not answer, and he added, "It would be a comfort to me, Grace, to know you were provided for."

"I don't want thee to worry about me," she said quickly. She sought some reassurance that would give him comfort and said finally, "Thee has taught me how to run this farm. It's paid for, and there's good help in Jed and Benny. I am well taken care of."

Silence seemed to fall all about them as they sat there. Grace could hear the ticking of the big clock in the hall, and even at that moment it chimed seven times—a mellow sound that faded slowly away.

"We are God's children, Grace," Amos said slowly. He'd been thinking about his departure, and now he decided that it was time to discuss it with this tall daughter of his. "We've not talked about it, but I'll not be here long." Grace made a

449

small sound, and her father got up and went to sit beside her on the swing. He took her hand and held it in both of his, saying nothing until she grew still.

"We're not like people tied to the earth, are we?" he asked. "We're pilgrims, looking for a city not built with hands. And when I leave, I'll see my dear mother and father and my brothers. And my beloved Martha. And one day, thee and thy sisters will come, and then all the others. It'll be one family, Grace—the family of God, all together! That's a thought I've clung to for years, and it's more real now than ever."

"But I'll be all alone!"

"No! No!" Amos said quickly. "Thee will have the Lord Jesus! 'I will never leave thee, nor forsake thee,' He said. Remember that?"

"Oh yes, but it's hard!"

Swenson squeezed her hand, wishing he didn't have to continue—but he was a wise man and knew that certain things had to be discussed. "Let me tell thee what must be done. . . ."

Grace sat there as he spoke of his funeral and where he wanted to be laid at rest. He mentioned that he'd seen Lawyer Simms and that all was in order. "The farm is left to thee," he said. "Thy married sisters have husbands to care for them. I can depend on thee to take care of Prudence until she marries." He hesitated slightly, then nodded. "When thee marries Clyde, that will make a difference as far as the farm is concerned."

Grace sensed some doubt in her father's voice. "How is that, Father?"

Swenson stroked his chin, considering what he must say. It was not a simple matter, and he had prayed much over it. "Clyde is not a settled man, Grace." He held up his hand quickly as if to ward off her protest. "That's not to say I'm opposed to him as thy husband. But he's not had his own place to run, has he?"

"N–no," Grace agreed haltingly. "But he's a good farmer!"

"I do not doubt this, but it is one thing to know how to plow and another to keep a place going. Think of how many times we've seen young men who couldn't manage that. Some of them were just too young, and others were just the kind who can't build."

"And you think Clyde is one such as those?"

"I think he needs time to mature. That's why I'm leaving the farm in thy name, and I'm asking thee to let it stay that way for two years. By that time, the young man will either have proven himself—or he will need more time."

Grace thought of what he was saying, then shook her head. "I don't know if Clyde will agree. Isn't the man supposed to be the head of the family? He might be shamed at such a thing."

"Pride is a dangerous thing, Grace. It's the sin through which the angels fell."

When Grace didn't respond to this, Amos added gently, "I've prayed much about this. The Lord has given me a scripture." This often occurred with Amos Swenson, and Grace had learned to trust such things. Since her youth she had seen her father wait on the Lord in times of need, meditating on the scripture until some portion of it fixed itself in his mind.

"What is the word?" she asked.

"It's a verse from the third chapter of Lamentations." Amos nodded. " 'It is good for a man that he bear the yoke in his youth.' " He sat there silently, the creaking of the swing making a faint noise, then added, "I believe it is God's will that thee should wait until Clyde proves himself before handing over the farm to him."

Grace was troubled, but it never occurred to her to dispute her father. "I'll tell him right away."

"No, that is my place," Swenson said at once. "It is but a small matter, if he will have it so." He hesitated, then asked again, "Will the wedding be soon?"

Grace nodded slowly, knowing that her father wished to see her safely married before he died.

"Yes, Father," she said quietly. "I'll speak with Clyde. It'll be very soon."

Summer came to Pennsylvania overnight, it seemed. With the wedding drawing ever nearer, this should have been a happy, exciting time for Grace. Instead it was a time of tension, for her father grew no better. He spent long hours in bed. When he did rise and make his way around the house, it was with the careful steps of the confirmed invalid. More and more, Grace stayed close to the house, leaving the outside work for Jed and Benny, not wanting to be far from her father's side.

The plans for the wedding were made, but she felt little of

the joy she had always believed such an occasion would bring her. Rather, she felt queer stirrings at the thought of what lay ahead. She had seen less of Clyde than she'd expected, for as the date of their marriage grew closer, he seemed to be more and more taken up with other things. Grace felt that she was the cause of some of this, for she had refused to go with him on more than one occasion, pleading as an excuse that she had to stay close to her father.

More than once she had suggested that he take Prudence to accompany him. After a brief resistance, he would agree. One time Prudence, who hated to miss any sort of activity, had said, "It's you who should be going with Clyde, Grace."

But Grace had smiled, saying, "I'm a better nurse than you are, Prudence. Go on and have a good time. I know it gets lonesome for you around the farm."

One of Grace's good friends, Charity Blankenship, came often to visit with her. The two women were the same age and had been close since childhood. Charity, who was married and had one child, a boy named Caleb, was a cheerful young woman. She had found great happiness in her marriage and with her lot in life.

One afternoon Charity drove her buggy up to the front door and brought her three-year-old Caleb into the kitchen. Grace put him at once on a high stool and proceeded to stuff sugar cookies into his mouth as though he were a young bird. She loved children, and as Charity rambled on about what she'd been doing, Grace listened quietly.

Finally the two women sat down at the table to hot, spicy sassafras tea. Almost at once Charity asked, "Well, how does it feel to be nearly married, Grace?"

"Oh, fine," Grace said at once.

Something in her tone drew the other woman's attention, and she laid a sharp glance on her friend. "Thee doesn't sound as happy as I'd like," she murmured. "Not having some last-minute fears, are you?"

Grace shrugged uncomfortably, then came up with a small smile. "I suppose most women do, don't they?"

"I don't know about other women. *I* didn't have any."

"You're different, Charity. You and Tom were made for each other."

Charity sipped her tea, then said carefully, "I think it's pretty common for women—and men, too—to have some doubts. It's a big thing, getting married. Aside from choosing to serve God, it's the biggest decision any of us ever make."

"That's true, isn't it? It's for the rest of our life." Grace's smooth face usually reflected a peace that most people admired, but she was agitated now. "If thee makes a mistake in marriage, there's no way to go back and erase it and start over."

"Grace, aren't you certain about Clyde? I've heard you talk about how we can know God's will so often. Don't you have any inner light on getting married?"

"I—thought so." Grace nodded. "But lately I've been wondering if it might not have been something *I* wanted instead of something God has planned." She leaned forward, shaking her head with doubt. "Father wants me to be married, and I've always leaned on him for counsel. But lately I've thought his sickness has influenced him. He wants so much to see me safe before—" She broke off abruptly. "In case something happens to him," she finished. Then she frowned and laughed shortly. "And it's sort of a last chance for me, Charity."

"You don't know that, Grace!"

"No? Hasn't thee noticed there isn't a group of young men lined up to court me? Clyde's the only one—and I can't risk missing out on marriage and having a family!"

Charity yearned to help her friend, but she didn't know what to say. Finally she gave it up, saying, "Well, I'm sure thee and Clyde will be happy."

"I'm trusting we will."

"Where's Prudence? I wanted to talk to her a little about the plans for the wedding."

"We needed some things from town, so she and Clyde rode in to get them." Almost defensively she said, "I would have gone, but Father's having a bad spell, and he seems to be comfortable only when I'm here."

"Oh, that's too bad, Grace." Charity studied her friend and seemed about to say something, then apparently changed her mind. With a sigh she said, "Well, this time next week thee will be an old married woman like me. Then you'll have a little Caleb to take care of. It'll be nice when we can get together with our children and our husbands, won't it, Grace?"

"Oh yes!" The thought brightened Grace's eyes, and she

seemed to brush away the cares that had been weighing her down. By the time Charity left, she felt much better and went to check on her father. He was asleep, but half an hour later he came into the kitchen and sat down.

"How about some fresh milk?" Grace said with a smile. She had been trying everything she could think of to get food into him, and she insisted that he eat one of her cookies and drink some milk.

He nibbled dutifully at the cookie but obviously had no appetite. "Was that someone come to visit?" he asked. His voice was rusty—as though from lack of use—and his eyes were dim with the pain that never seemed to leave him.

"Yes, Charity came by," Grace said with a nod. "She wanted to talk about the wedding plans."

Amos looked out the window, swallowed a sip of milk, then asked, "Prudence and Clyde not back yet?"

"Not yet. They had quite a few errands." Grace came to sit closer to him on the deacon's bench. "How does thee feel?"

"I can't complain."

Grace put her hand on his and whispered, "Thee never does."

The two sat there quietly, letting the old clock tick away the seconds. It was a gift they had, this ability to sit and say nothing while drawing strength from each other. It was the Quaker gift of inner peace, of silence, and as the time ran on, neither of them felt the need to say anything.

Finally Grace moved her head. "I think I hear them." Getting up, she went to the window and looked across the yard. "Yes, it's them." She watched as the wagon drew up and as Clyde jumped to the ground then moved quickly to lift Prudence to the ground. He put his hands on her sides and lifted her slight weight as though she were a child.

Too bad he'll never be able to lift me like that, Grace thought. *He can't help it if he's small, and I can't help it if I'm large.*

As she watched the two laughing together about something, Grace realized sadly that she didn't have her sister's light air and feminine mannerisms. She had thought of this before, but there was no way she could change herself. *I can't be the kind of wife Prudence would be—but I can make him good food and give him comfort in his home.*

Somehow that didn't seem like much, but it was all Grace could think of, and she forced herself to smile as the two entered the kitchen with their arms full of bundles.

"It looks like thee bought the store out." Grace smiled, helping to unload the boxes. "It took a long time."

Prudence turned to face Grace at once, saying, "It takes time to buy things for a wedding party!"

Her sister's sharp tone surprised Grace. "Why, of course, Prudence," she said at once. "I wasn't scolding."

Clyde said quickly, "It was my fault it took so long, Grace. I was hungry, so we went to the restaurant and had some pie and coffee."

"Was it as good as my pie?" Grace asked, trying to lighten the moment. Prudence had been so quick to offend lately.

"No one makes pies as good as thee, Grace," Clyde said. He went outside to get the other boxes. When he returned, he smiled at Amos. "How does thee feel, sir?"

"Oh, very well, Clyde." Amos nodded. "The Lord is good."

"Stay and have supper, Clyde," Grace said.

But Dortch seemed troubled. "No, I thank thee. I have things to do at home." He said his good-byes, then left the kitchen.

"Clyde seems upset," Amos observed. "What's the matter with him, Prudence?"

"Why, nothing that I know of, Father," Prudence said. She looked pale and tired and turned at once to go to her room, saying, "I'll come and help with supper in a bit, Grace."

There was silence for a few moments; then Amos sighed. "I'm a little worried about Prudence. She's been touchy lately." He looked over the table, which was now filled with supplies for the wedding party. "Didn't take all this when Martha and I got married. Sometimes I think it'd be better if young couples just went back to the simpler ways."

"Thee is just stingy," Grace teased him. "Thee would like to save the money thee must spend on thy daughter's wedding." She came to stand beside him and brushed a lock of lank white hair from his forehead. "Thee has certainly spent thy share on marrying daughters off!"

Swenson reached up and caught her hand. He held it gently, noting how round and strong it was, then said, "I never was so happy to see any of thy sisters married as I am to see thee married, Grace."

He could not see her face, so he missed the expression of doubt that tightened her features. "I know," she whispered. "It will be soon, Father. Then your ugly duckling will be safely married." She ignored his protests at the name she gave herself and held his head tightly to her breast in a protective gesture.

"Oh, you look beautiful, Grace!"

Charity stood back and gazed with admiration at Grace, surprised at the way the white silk wedding dress brought a pristine beauty to her friend. The dress was simple, as befitted a Quaker bride. The bodice was decorated with embroidery around the high neckline, and the only color was the silver lace that the dressmaker had added at the neck and cuffs. The skirt fell to the floor, barely touching the fine white calf slippers, and with every motion the tall woman made, it shimmered like compressed light.

Grace turned to stare into the mirror, and she gasped at the effect. "It—it's the most beautiful dress I've ever seen, Charity!"

Charity was filled with admiration. "It must be nice to be tall," she said with a sigh. "I'm so short and stubby that everything I put on makes me look like a *keg*! Thee looks like a—a *queen* or a princess!"

Grace laughed, "Oh, come now, Charity—!"

"I mean it, Grace," Charity said fervently.

She turned to look at herself again. "I—I hope Clyde likes it."

"He'd have to be *blind* not to love you in that dress," Charity said emphatically. For the next few minutes, she stayed and talked with Grace, then said, "I guess the night before a girl's wedding, there's bound to be a few butterflies in the stomach. But after tomorrow, you'll be fine."

Grace tried to smile, but after Charity left, she found her hands trembling as she removed the dress and hung it up. She put on a robe and left her room, going to the kitchen. It was late afternoon, and the sky was gray and threatening. She stood at the window, staring out at the grass and trees, which would gladly soak up the impending rain, and wished that it were all over.

A noise behind her caused Grace to turn, and she found Prudence standing in the doorway. "The dress fits fine," Grace said. "I thought you might come and help me try it on."

"I. . .meant to," Prudence said with a slight hesitation. "But I wasn't feeling too well."

"Oh? What's wrong, Prudence? Not flu coming on, I hope?"

"No, just a headache."

"Well, thee go lie down and I'll fix supper."

"No, I'm all right now," Prudence said. She looked tired, and Grace thought that the preparations for the wedding might have been too much for her. But Prudence insisted, "Go sit with Father while I fix supper."

"If you don't mind, I'd like to."

Grace found her father in the parlor reading his Bible. She sat with him until suppertime, listening as he read slowly but with enjoyment. Finally they went in to eat, and his appetite seemed somewhat better. "I'm looking forward to the wedding," he said after the meal. "Everybody in the community will be there to wish thee well."

Grace dreaded being the object of so much attention but said nothing. It was Prudence who broke the silence. "I think I'll go to bed early."

Grace went to her, put her arm around her, and said, "I've let thee do too much. After the wedding, I want thee to rest up. We can take a trip to Riverton. It'll be good for us to spend more time together."

"That would be. . .nice." Prudence held her head down, but when she looked up, both Grace and her father saw that there were tears in her eyes. She started to speak but seemed to change her mind and left abruptly.

"That's strange," Amos murmured.

"She's worn herself out," Grace said. "She needs to be around young people more."

After Grace washed the dishes, she saw that her father was very tired. "I think we all need to go to bed early," she said. When he agreed, she gave him his medicine and, when he was in bed, kissed him, saying, "Good night. Tomorrow thee will have a new son-in-law."

"And thee will be a wife."

Grace left him and went to bed at once. She was tired, but it took some time for her to go to sleep. Finally she drifted off into a fitful slumber, awakening several times during the night. She dreamed short, unhappy dreams, and when morning finally arrived, she got up more drawn and weary than she'd been when she had gone to bed.

Pulling on her robe, she moved out of her room and down the hall toward the kitchen. She went at once to the stove and built a fire, then moved to the cabinet to get coffee.

As she reached for the heavy white coffee jar, she noticed an envelope leaning against it. She blinked with surprise when she saw her name on the front of the envelope, in Prudence's handwriting. Puzzled, she opened the envelope and took out the single page inside. She began to read—and at once her face lost all color. The room seemed to tilt under her feet, and her stomach knotted up.

> *Grace,*
> *I know thee will hate me, but I can't help myself. I love Clyde, and he loves me. We are going away to be married. We have been so unhappy and could not find a way to tell thee. Take care of Father and try not to hate me too much.*
>
> *Prudence*

Grace closed her eyes and for a moment swayed slightly as the words seemed to burn into her soul. She had never fainted before but felt she must be perilously close to doing so at that moment. She became nauseated, and unconsciously crumpling the note into a ball, she walked across the room and opened the door, then stepped outside.

The fresh, cool morning air did nothing to wash away the

sickness that seemed to choke her. Her legs began to tremble, and she reached out and grasped one of the posts that held up the roof. Clinging to it until her hands ached with strain, she pressed her brow against the rounded surface and began to weep. Her body shook with great sobs, and she could not muffle the sound that disturbed the quietness of the morning.

Rip, the old sheepdog, came up to the porch and stared at the sobbing woman uneasily. He climbed the steps and timidly put his nose against Grace's hip. Startled, Grace stopped weeping and looked down. "Oh, Rip!" she cried and sank beside the dog, hugging him and holding back the tears. Rip wiggled, trying to lick her face, then put his huge paw on Grace's leg and whined sadly.

Finally Grace arose, patted the dog, then turned and walked back into the kitchen. She washed her face at the sink, dried her face, and then stood for one moment, thinking of what had to be done.

The wedding would have to be canceled—and she would have to bear the brunt of the reaction...the shame of being cast off and of having a sister who had proved to be totally untrue. She knew that from this time forward, men and women would stare after her and whisper things as she passed.

Suddenly a great bitterness began to grow within her—and at once she knew her danger. Falling on her knees, she prayed, "Oh God, forgive me for my thoughts! Let me not be a bitter woman! I pray for my sister...and—and for Clyde, too! Bless them and let me never harbor hatred for them. I forgive them...as

You forgave me when I was but a sinner. . . ."

For some time she knelt there praying, opening her heart to God in sorrow and repentance. Finally she slowly rose to her feet. Once again there were tears on her cheeks, and she carefully washed them away, then soaked her face with a cold cloth, pressing away as much as she could of the marks of strain.

I'll have to stay close to Father, she thought. *He'll blame himself for agreeing to the marriage. I'll have to make him understand that it's not his fault.*

She turned and filled the kettle, then put it on the stove and moved about the room, making preparations for breakfast, praying constantly. *It's not the end of the world,* she thought. *I have Father to take care of. I have work on the farm. I have my church—and I have Jesus.*

By the time she'd poured the scalding water into the coffeepot, then drank two cups, she was ready. She poured hot coffee into her father's mug, added milk and sugar the way he liked it, then turned toward his room. She knew he would be awake, for she always brought him his coffee at this early hour. As she carried the cup, she took some pride in the fact that her hands were steady and her face was calm.

As she came to his door and reached for the knob, she prayed one quick prayer that the news would not upset him too much. Pain shot through her again, and she leaned her head against the door, praying for strength. When at last she lifted her head, there was resolve in her eyes.

I'll never be a wife. This is the time that I say good-bye to love. From now on, I'll have God's love—and that will be far sweeter than any man's love!

Then she turned the knob and entered the room. When her father greeted her, she said, "Father, take your coffee. We have to have a talk."

CHAPTER 4

"I Won't Have a Husband"

I'm afraid he's going, Sister Grace." Dr. Wells's round face was filled with compassion, for he knew how attached Grace Swenson was to her father. He'd watched her carefully some time earlier, when she'd gone through an experience that would have devastated most young women, and had been impressed with how well she'd borne the deception of her sister and Clyde Dortch.

The doctor was not himself a man of faith—he leaned more in the direction of agnosticism—but he'd told his wife, "That oldest Swenson girl, she's got grit enough for ten men! Most girls would have been ruined by what happened to her, but Grace has kept her head up high. If I ever became any kind of a Christian, I guess I'd like to look into the Quaker brand!"

Grace was aware of Dr. Wells's scrutiny. She had grown to respect him during the last few months, for he had been kind and honest. Now she looked at him and nodded. "Is it time to call in the family, Doctor?"

"I think that would be best." He hesitated, then added, "I wish there was more that I could do, Miss Swenson. I really do."

"Thee has been so good to my father...and to me, Dr. Wells," Grace said, smiling at him warmly. "No doctor in the world could have been more attentive. But it's time for my father to go meet his God, and we must all accept that."

Wells dropped his head, stared at the floor for a long moment, then lifted his gaze to meet her honest blue eyes. "I admire your faith. Your father, he's the kind of Christian I didn't think existed. The way he's faced this illness—and is facing death—makes me think I've been a little hasty in forming my beliefs." Then, as if he was afraid he'd revealed too much, the stubby physician cleared his throat and said in a businesslike tone, "I'll stay close by for the next few days. Call me anytime."

"God bless thee, Dr. Wells." Grace showed him to the door, then moved back to the bedroom. Her father's eyes opened as she sat down beside him, and she asked, "Can I get thee something, Father?"

"Yes...call the girls."

Grace whispered, "All right. I'll send for them right away." She left the room and found the two hands splitting wood. "Father's sinking," she said at once. "We have to get the girls here."

"Aw, that's too bad, Miss Grace!" Jed Satterfield shook his head. He was very fond of Amos Swenson, and sadness came to his face. "You want me to go fetch them?"

"Thee go tell Martha and Dove. Benny, thee please take word to Sarah and. . .Prudence."

Benny and Jed exchanged a quick glance. Prudence had not been to see her father since she had left with Clyde Dortch. Word had come that they had returned and were staying at the Dortch farm. "All right, Miss Grace." Benny nodded agreement for both men. "We'll be right fast about it."

"It's good to have you both," Grace said. "I don't see how we could have gotten by without the two of you." She turned and walked quickly into the house, and the two men went to saddle up for their errands.

"If it was me," Benny said as he clapped a bridle into the mouth of a gray stallion, "I'd not have the woman on the place, sister or no!"

"Well, it *ain't* you, so jist do whut Miss Grace tells you to!" Jed Satterfield's disagreement with the shorter man was more out of habit than anything else, for truly he felt exactly the same way as Benny. He slapped a saddle on a roan mare and, as he drew the cinches tight, muttered under his breath, "Don't see how them two could have the unmitigated gall to come back after whut they done to Miss Grace!"

"What you mumbling about?" Benny demanded as he swung into the saddle.

"Nothing! Now git on your way and don't take all day about it!"

"Wasn't plannin' on no pleasure ride, thank you!" Benny George drove his heels into the sides of the stallion and shot out of the barn. He rode hard until he came to the farm belonging to Nick Sanderson, Sarah's husband. Sarah met Benny at the door, and he pulled his hat off to say haltingly, "Miss Sarah— Miss Grace sent me to tell you you'd better come quick."

"How is he, Benny?"

"Well, Miss Grace said for you to hurry up, please."

"We'll go at once."

Benny nodded, went back to his horse, and rode off toward the Dortch farm. When he came into the front yard and dismounted, Mrs. Dortch, Clyde's mother, came out of the house. "Got to see Miss Prudence, Miz Dortch," Benny said briefly.

The woman stared at him, then nodded. "I'll fetch her." She stepped into the house and went upstairs, where she found Prudence sitting listlessly beside her bed. "One of your father's hired hands just come in. Wants to see thee."

Prudence looked up quickly, fear in her eyes. "It must be my father!" She leaped up and ran down the stairs. Rushing outside, she looked up at Benny.

"Is it Father?" she whispered.

"Yes, ma'am, it is." Benny nodded without expression.

Prudence's face flushed under his accusing stare. "Did—who asked you to come for me?"

"Miss Grace." Having delivered his message, Benny turned to pull himself back into the saddle. He added curtly, "She allowed you'd better hurry." He kicked the stallion's flanks and the horse shot out, sending mud flying from his hooves.

Prudence stood watching him go, then turned and slowly

made her way back into the house. Mrs. Dortch came to ask, "Thy father is going?"

"Yes," Prudence whispered; then she hugged herself and said, "I'll go tell Clyde."

"He's working with Daniel over to the south meadow, burning stumps." Mrs. Dortch was a thin woman, worn down with the constant care of her invalid husband. She had not been unkind to Prudence when Clyde had showed up with her, tired and hungry, but there had been little she could do to shield the couple from her older son's hard ways. Daniel had allowed them to stay but insisted that they both work hard for their keep. As Prudence walked out of the house, Mrs. Dortch asked, "Do you think Clyde will go to thy place with thee?"

Prudence could only say, "It's my father—we've got to go."

She walked the mile and a quarter to the south meadow, and as she drew near, both men stopped work. "It's my father, Clyde," she said. "He's dying."

Clyde was thinner than he had been, for Daniel had driven him hard. He was wearing a pair of worn overalls, and his hands were blistered. He stared at Prudence with lackluster eyes, asking, "Did he send for us?"

"Yes. And we'd better hurry."

Clyde bit his lip nervously. His marriage had been a hard thing, for when their money had run out, there was no place to go but back to the home place. He'd worked harder than ever, with no pay and little prospect of any. He'd grown to hate his brother, Daniel, but had no options other than to continue on as he was. And if there was one thing Clyde Dortch hated, it was feeling helpless.

"Wouldn't think thee would want to go back and face them," Daniel grunted to his brother. "Best let her go and thee stay here."

Clyde glared at him, then threw down his ax. "We'll be back when we see how things are," he announced defiantly. He well knew that Daniel would begrudge him every moment he was away. The anger that rose in him gave him the impetus he needed to go back and face Grace and her father.

Daniel Dortch glared at the pair. "Better be careful. It's only my generosity puts food in your stomachs and a roof over your heads!"

"Come on, Prue," Clyde said shortly. He ignored his brother, and when they were out of earshot, he said, "I—don't feel good about going back to your place."

Prudence shook her head. "I know. But we've got to do it."

When they reached the barn, Clyde hitched up the team while Prudence went inside to gather up some clothes. She came out as he drove up, and he held the horses steady while she tossed the bag inside and climbed up to sit beside him.

"I'm ready, Clyde," she said quietly, and he spoke to the horses, sending them out of the yard at a fast clip. They rode without speaking for half an hour, and finally Prudence asked, "What will Daniel say when he finds you've taken his team and buggy?"

"I don't care *what* he says!"

"We'll—have to come back," Prudence said, shaking her head. "There's no place else for us to go."

A hot answer rose to Clyde's lips, but the bitter truth of her words silenced him. As they moved along down the rutted road, he wondered how he'd ever gotten himself into such a predicament. Truth was, he thought about little else these days, but the more he considered it, the less he understood.

I could have had an easy life, he thought bitterly. *Grace may not look like much—but that doesn't seem to matter now.* He wanted to blame Prudence, but there was enough honesty left in him to know she had not been at fault—not completely. *We were both crazy,* he concluded. *She's a pretty, lively woman, and I wanted her, just like she wanted me. But if we had it to do over—!*

When they were within sight of the house, Prudence said, "Oh, Clyde, how can we face them?"

Shaking his head, Clyde said doggedly, "They sent for us. Maybe it won't be so bad." He halted the buggy, then got down and went around to help Prudence step to the ground. They turned, and when they reached the porch, the door opened.

Grace came outside and met them, her expression calm. She walked right up to Prudence and embraced her, and Prudence gave a small cry and clung to her fiercely. Grace's lips were broad and maternal as she held the sobbing girl. She turned to meet Clyde's eyes, but he dropped his head to stare at the ground.

"I'm glad you've come," Grace said, including both of them in her welcome. "Come inside. The others should be here soon."

"How is Father?" Prudence asked as they entered the foyer.

"Very weak, I'm afraid. He's been asking for thee."

When the two women turned to go to the sick man's room, Clyde remained where he was. When Grace turned to him with an inquiring look, he said tersely, "He won't want to see me."

"Yes, he's been asking for thee, too," Grace said.

Clyde stared at her for a moment, then nodded. "All right, then, if he wants me."

When they entered the room, Amos looked up and smiled faintly. He whispered, "My children. . .come to me!" Sarah and her husband quietly left the room to give the newcomers some time alone with the dying man.

Prudence ran, weeping wildly, to fall on her knees and into the arms of her father. Swenson held her, patted her with one hand, then looked up and held out his other hand to Clyde, who took it awkwardly.

Quietly Grace returned to the kitchen. She was putting a roast in the oven when she heard the bedroom door close, and she turned to face Prudence and Clyde as they entered. Prudence's face was swollen, and Clyde looked terrible. He said hoarsely, "He. . .forgave us both, Grace." He swallowed, and his voice dropped to a whisper. "Got no right to ask, but we treated you shamefully, Grace. How thee must hate us!"

Grace went to them at once, shaking her head. "No, Clyde. I don't hate thee. It would have been easy to fall into that, but God has delivered me from it. He's given me a love for you both. Please, let us speak of it no more."

Prudence began to weep again, and Clyde's face was pale as

paste. It took some time for Grace to convince them that she harbored no malice toward them, but before too long, the pair had gained some control.

Dove and Martha arrived later, and the house grew busy with the activity of the three girls' small children. Grace thought it well that there was so much to do, for it gave Prudence no time to linger in embarrassment. Grace was certain that her sisters had talked with their husbands, for all three of Clyde's brothers-in-law said nothing of the circumstances of his marriage. There was, to be sure, some distance between the newlyweds and the others, but Grace did all she could to show affection for them. This did much to assure the others, and by evening when they sat down for dinner, Clyde and Prudence were able to join in the conversation to some extent.

Afterward, Martha helped Grace with the dishes. With the closeness that sisters share, she felt able to ask cautiously, "Thee feels no anger toward Prudence and Clyde?"

"I did, Martha, but God has taken it from me."

Martha smiled and gave Grace a sudden hug. "Only thee could forgive so completely!"

Grace shook off the praise, saying, "They've had a very hard time, Martha. Prudence is miserable, and so is Clyde."

Martha nodded. "I think living with Daniel Dortch could have that effect. He's a hard man."

The two women talked quietly, and it did Grace good to share a little of what was in her heart with her sister. Afterward, she found beds for everyone, but when they retired, she went to sit beside her father. He seemed quiet enough, but about one o'clock, Grace woke up from where she'd been dozing to find him seeming to gasp for air.

At once she knew that it was the end and ran to knock on the door of a bedroom, calling out, "Martha, Father's very bad! Get the others and come quickly!"

She ran back to her father and did what she could to relieve his discomfort. When Martha and her husband, Lige, rushed in, Grace said, "Lige, would thee send Jed for Dr. Wells?"

"Right away!"

But even as her brother-in-law rushed away, Grace knew that the doctor would be too late. By the time the others had gathered and Lige returned to report that Jed was on his way, Amos Swenson was almost gone.

"Can't we do something, Grace?" Dove whispered.

"He's in God's hands, Dove."

The room was silent except for the harsh gasping breaths of the dying man. As Grace gently wiped the clammy sweat from her father's brow, he opened his eyes and looked at her.

"Father. . .does thee know me?"

"Yes." Amos seemed to grow stronger. His eyes went around the room, and his breathing grew easier. "I've asked the Lord. . . for time to say a farewell to you—"

None of the family ever forgot the next half hour. Amos spoke to every one of them, telling how each one had blessed him in his life, assuring them all of his love for them. As he spoke to Prudence and Clyde, both were ashen-faced, but he smiled and held their hands, saying, "You two have had a bad beginning, but God is merciful. Obey Him and submit to His love, and He will keep you in His care."

Then, finally, after he had spoken to all the others, he looked at Grace. Fighting her tears, she went to him. "Come closer," he whispered, and when Grace put her head very close to his face, he laid his hands upon her head. "Thee has been the delight of my life, daughter," he whispered. "The Lord has chosen thee to serve Him in a special manner. Thee will be alone, but not alone, for the good Lord will be at thy side always. Thee will have great sorrow, but God will turn thy mourning into joy."

Hot tears filled Grace's eyes and flowed down her face, and he finally said, so faintly that only she heard his words, "Thee has been my crown and my joy on this earth, Grace. I will tell thy mother. . .how like. . .thee are. . .to her—"

He smiled faintly, drew a deep breath, and looked around the room, saying clearly, "God watch over you!" And then he closed his eyes—and how well he endured his going forth!

When Lawyer Simms read the will to the family, there were no surprises. Swenson had talked to all his daughters prior to his passing, explaining that he was dividing his cash assets equally among the four married sisters. The farm was left to Grace, and Martha spoke for all of them when she said, "It's a fair settlement. Father was wise."

After the reading of the will, Martha, Sarah, and Dove all

left with their families. Grace asked Prudence to stay and help her clean the house. As they worked, Grace drew her sister out skillfully, listening carefully as she talked about their life at the Dortch house. Prudence tried to be cheerful, but Grace knew she was miserable.

Finally, when the house was cleaned, Clyde came in to say that the buggy was hitched up. His mouth was tight, and Prudence knew he was dreading the return to his father's farm. "Can't we take our share of the money and go away, Clyde?" she asked timidly.

"I think we'd better," he said grimly.

Grace said suddenly, "I want to talk to you both. Come and sit down." She fixed coffee, and when they were seated, she said simply, "I want you to stay here."

Clyde blinked with astonishment. "Stay here? On the farm?"

"Yes." Grace nodded. "I know thee is unhappy working for thy brother, Clyde."

"That's true enough," Clyde acknowledged. He glanced at Prudence, whose eyes were suddenly alive with hope.

"Oh, Clyde, could we?"

Clyde licked his lips, seeming to struggle with a thought. Finally he said in a halting fashion, "Why, Grace, I can't deny that would be good for us, but what about for thee? People would talk."

Grace shook her head. "No, they won't talk."

Clyde said stubbornly, "Thee has a better opinion of people than I have. Why, I can hear Mrs. Gatz babbling now about how strange it is that thee would take in the people who betrayed thee—"

"We've agreed to forget that, Clyde," Grace said, breaking in. "I spoke with Father about this, and he was pleased. A bride needs her own house"—Grace smiled at Prudence—"and I would like to have you both here."

Clyde swallowed hard, then glanced at Prudence. He knew she was miserable at his father's house, as much as he was himself. With a sigh that was both from relief and apprehension, he finally said, "If thee will have us, we'll be grateful, Grace."

"Good, that's settled!" Grace nodded. "Now, Clyde, thee go tell thy people and bring thy things back."

It was a happy day for Prudence, and for the next month she radiated joy. Clyde, too, was so relieved to be out from under the iron control of Daniel that he threw himself into the work on the farm with all his might.

The three of them got along well after the strangeness of the situation wore off. Grace stayed alone much of the time, riding her mare through the solitude of the woods. Watching her, Prudence thought she seemed withdrawn. "Why is Grace so—so distant?" she finally asked Clyde.

"Got to be a little uncomfortable for her, Prue." He shrugged. "I know she's forgiven us, but she can't have *forgotten* what we did."

"I don't think she's angry with us," Prudence disagreed. "She's unhappy about something."

"Don't go pestering her, Prue," Clyde said quickly. "Likely she misses thy father. They were very close."

Clyde was right in that respect. The loss of her father had left Grace with little intimate companionship. She rode often to visit Martha, but even spending time with her sister could not fill the gap left by Amos's death. Grace was regular in her church duties, even more devoted to good works, but still everyone noticed that she was not as lively as she had been.

Then, to make matters worse, a problem arose about the management of the farm. Clyde wanted to do more than simple chores. For the first time in his life, he was ready to take hold of something, but he had nothing of his own to take hold of. Jed and Benny quickly discovered that Clyde had no authority, and both of them felt they knew the farm better than he, which was true enough. This resulted in Clyde's feeling useless and out of place.

Prudence saw Clyde's restlessness and spoke of it to Grace. "It's just that he needs some responsibility, Grace. Can't thee let him do more?"

Grace agreed to think about it, and in less than a week she came in from a long ride. She found Clyde putting up a fence and called out, "Clyde, come to the house!"

Clyde followed her, and when Prudence met them, Grace said, "I've been seeking guidance from the Lord." She smiled at Prudence. "I fear thee has noticed I've been a little distant lately. Well, my answer just came." She removed her bonnet and shook her hair loose, her blue eyes bright. "It came suddenly," she said in wonder.

"What is it, Grace?" Prudence asked.

Grace hung her bonnet on a peg, then turned to face them. "I'm leaving the farm for a while."

"Leaving here?" Prudence asked, giving Clyde a glance of surprise. "Why—where will thee go, Grace?"

"I'm going to Washington," Grace said.

"The capital?" Clyde asked. "What in the world for?"

"The papers are full of stories about the wounded soldiers," Grace said. "The hospitals are filled with them—and there are not enough nurses." When she saw the astonishment in their faces, she nodded. "I am against war—but it's God's commandment to take care of the sick and helpless. Now sit down and I'll tell you the rest. . . ."

When they had sat at the table, she went on. "Clyde, thee will be manager of the farm. Thee must make all the decisions as if it were thy farm. I may be gone for years, until the war is over, I suppose. Whatever profits come from the farm we will share equally. Does this suit thee?"

Clyde stared at Grace, wonder in his face. "Suit me? Why, I'd be a fool if such a thing didn't please me!"

The conference lasted long, and Grace was happy to see what a difference the new situation made to her sister and brother-in-law. They were ecstatic, and she was hopeful that Clyde would throw off his old careless ways and find satisfaction and fulfillment in his new responsibilities.

She herself was anxious to leave. Now that she felt she knew God's direction, she longed to be gone. "I want to leave as soon as possible," she said finally. "We'll draw up the agreement and take it to the lawyer tomorrow. Then I'll leave."

"So soon?" Prudence exclaimed in surprise.

"I must be about my Father's business." Grace smiled.

Two days later Clyde and Prudence drove her to the train station. She kissed them both, boarded, and, as the train pulled out, waved at them through the window.

As the train wound its way along the narrow gauge tracks, she felt a burden lift from her heart.

I won't have a husband, she thought, *but I'll be serving God!*

CHAPTER 5

THE RETURN OF BURKE ROCKLIN

July 1862

The black walnut of Ellen Rocklin's casket had been sanded and polished until it glowed with a rich warmth. The two oil lamps—one stationed at the head of the coffin and the other at the foot—shed their amber glow over the room, somewhat dispelling the predawn darkness.

The gleam of the yellow lamplight highlighted Clay Rocklin's face as he sat loosely in a leather-covered sofa across the room. He was a big man, darkly handsome with black hair and strong features. He wore the uniform of a sergeant in the Confederate Army.

As the silence of the house seemed to close around him, he let his dark eyes gaze at the casket, thinking of the woman who lay within. She had been his wife for over twenty years—every single one of which had been stormy. He thought of the early years of their marriage, but even those had not been happy. Ellen had known that Clay had married her while loving her cousin Melanie. This knowledge had embittered her, creating a hardness in her heart that only grew worse as the years went by—a hardness that inspired sarcasm, resentment, and criticism; a hardness that left no room for real love.

Shaking his head, Clay rose and went to stand over the casket, pain evident on the sharp planes of his face. *If I hadn't abandoned her and the children,* he thought bitterly, *she might have been different.*

Tormented by his love for Melanie, who was married to his cousin Gideon, Clay had left Ellen after only a few years of marriage. He thought of his years of wandering, of the time he spent working and living on a slave ship. Those had been bitter and hard years for him, but he knew they had been even harder on his family. While he had been running from one empty endeavor to another, Ellen had stayed at Gracefield with their children—and before long had become a promiscuous woman. When Clay had finally returned to his home and his family, he found little welcome. Now, looking at Ellen's still face, Clay admitted to himself that Ellen's lifestyle had been, at least in part, his fault. *Should have stayed here for Ellen. . .for us and for the children!*

The pain in Clay's eyes deepened at the thought of his children. They were all grown now, or almost so. Dent and David, the twins, and Lowell, their younger brother, were men. Clay and Ellen's only daughter, Rena, was on the verge of young womanhood. At the thought of Rena, Clay's stern face relaxed into smoother lines. Although the boys had not forgiven him upon his return—though he had had hopes that they would do so someday—Rena had received him almost at once. She had been so starved for love, especially for a father's love, that it had been simple to win her confidence.

Clay pulled his eyes away from the casket, thinking of his return from the years of wandering. It had been difficult, asking his family to forgive him. Dent had been the hardest of all, but now the two of them had come closer together and Clay's hopes had been realized. David and Lowell had been much readier to accept him, as had his father and mother.

But Ellen—!

Bitter memories came to Clay as he stood there in the gloomy room, memories of how Ellen had changed so greatly during his absence that he scarcely knew her when he returned. She'd become a hard woman and had lost most of her prettiness in her pursuit of pleasure. Even when Clay had become a Christian and begun to live a life of sincere faith, Ellen had not softened at all—and she'd had affair after affair since he'd returned home. Then came the accident that had made her a hopeless invalid, bound to a wheelchair....

Clay desperately tried to convince himself that he'd done all he could to make her life as comfortable as possible, but he'd been gone—serving with the Richmond Grays—most of the time. He'd known that Ellen's mind, as well as her body, had been affected by her injury, but none of them, he thought bitterly, had known how seriously her mind had warped.

"Well, we know now how bad off she was." Clay's whisper seemed very loud to his own ears. He started as though the suddenness of it might disturb someone, but the only one who could possibly have heard him would never hear again. Clay whirled and walked over to the door at the end of the large room, opened it, and stepped outside.

The summer nighttime sky was lit up by a large moon and millions of glittering stars. He took a deep breath, relieved to be out of the room, and tried to pray. Far off he heard the cry of a foxhound, shrill and clear, and subconsciously noted that the dog was on the scent.

Standing in the shadow of the overhanging balcony, he ran his eyes over the grounds of Gracefield. He'd been away from this place for so many years—and now would be away for many more, he feared. After the Confederate victory of Bull Run, some zealots had insisted that the Yankees would never come back. But they had—over one hundred thousand of them under the command of General George McClellan.

Shaking off the memories, he half turned to go back in when a movement caught his eye. It was only a shadow, but as he watched, he saw that it was a man. Clay grew alert, then relaxed. Perhaps it was one of the slaves.

But which of them would be out at three in the morning?

The figure moved across the yard, and Clay stepped out on the grass, walking to the corner of the house. Peering around, he saw the man approach the steps that led to the west entrance of Gracefield. Something about the way the intruder moved made Clay suspicious, and he moved forward quietly, his feet making no sound on the tender grass as he avoided the oyster-shell drive.

Clay had no gun, so he came up behind the figure so close

that he could grapple with him if necessary. He could see only that the man was very tall, and without warning, Clay reached out and grabbed the intruder by the arm, saying abruptly, "Who are you, and what—!"

He got no further, for the man had suddenly whirled with a catlike motion, striking out with a hard fist that caught Clay on the temple. Lights seemed to explode in Clay's head, but he managed to retain his grasp on the man's arm. He threw his arms around the man, butting him in the face with his head. The blow drew a sharp gasp of pain from his antagonist, but the man did not go down. Clay could feel his opponent's strength as they struggled, and he hung on determinedly, pinioning the man's arms until his head cleared.

When he could think straight, Clay quickly stepped back, ducked a hard right, and threw a hard left to the man's body, following it with a thundering right to his chin. The blow drove his man backward, and Clay went in at once but was caught by an unexpected blow in the mouth. Once more he tried to close with the big man.

The two of them struggled, falling into a flower bed, grunting and straining. They fought free of the bed, stood up, and suddenly the man got a good look at his adversary.

"Clay—!"

Clay stopped short and peered suspiciously at the face of the man who stood in front of him. A pale silver bar of moonlight suddenly illuminated the man's features, and Clay cried out in shock.

"Burke!" Pure astonishment ran through him, which almost immediately became anger. "Burke, what in blazes are you doing sneaking around the house? A man can get shot for that!"

Burke Rocklin glared at his older brother—then burst into laughter. "What are *you* doing, jumping a man like that? I'd have shot you for sure if I'd had a gun." He touched his forehead, then looked at his finger and said petulantly, "You've cut me up, blast you, Clay!"

Beginning to hurt from the blows he'd taken, Clay said roughly, "Come on inside."

The two men entered the house and went at once to the kitchen. Clay poured some water from a pitcher into a basin, thinking with some irritation that it was typical of Burke to arrive home after a year's absence in such a fashion. Finding a cloth, he dipped it into the water and rinsed his face, wincing from the bruise on his mouth. He washed his hands, noting that he'd scraped his right knuckles, then washed the basin and filled it with fresh water.

"Here," he grunted, handing it to his brother. "Clean up, and then we'll talk."

"All right. Is there anything to eat?"

As Burke cleaned his face, Clay prowled through the cabinets, finding some biscuits. Then he located a large bowl of pinto beans still warm inside the oven. He set a jar of milk and a glass on the table and found the remains of a raisin pie in the pie safe. As he pulled the meal together, he studied his brother surreptitiously.

Burke, at the age of thirty-two, was ten years younger than Clay. He had always looked up to Clay, but the difference in their ages—and Clay's years of absence—had kept them from being close.

Burke's the same as he always was, Clay thought as he sat down and watched him eat ravenously. *Still wild as a hawk! But he looks as good as ever.* He thought of Burke's willful temper and the many scrapes he'd gotten himself into, some of them fairly serious. Clay himself had been fairly wild as a young man, and Burke's temper and daredevil ways seemed a mirror of Clay's younger years.

He looks no older now than he did when he was twenty, Clay thought. He let his eyes run over the tall form, all six feet three inches, and saw that Burke was still wiry and strong. With a wry smile, Clay remembered how his younger brother had despaired of ever reaching six feet in height. But when he hit his late teens, Burke suddenly "shot up like a sprout dying for the light of day," as his father had put it, and soon towered over most men.

Lifting his gaze, Clay studied the lean face, so much like his own in some ways. Dark eyes, so dark that the pupils were almost invisible, could sparkle or glare from under heavy black brows. The fine features were crowned with the blackest possible thick hair—Burke had always had hair that was the envy of men and of women. Heavy and glossy black with just a slight curl, he wore it long, and now it was hanging down almost to his collar. His face, which had tended to roundness when he was younger, was now hard and lean. His high cheekbones and fine broad forehead gave him a pleasing appearance, as did his broad mouth—which was shaded by a neat mustache—and strong chin, complete with the cleft that marked most of the Rocklin men.

Clay noted the worn coat and frayed trousers and said, "You didn't come home prosperous, I take it?"

Burke bit off a chunk of biscuit, chewed it with relish, then grinned. "Nope. Haven't got a cent."

Clay was annoyed. "Fine, just what we need around here. A broken-down gentleman." His words, he saw, had no effect on Burke. But that came as no surprise, for this younger brother of his—though he adored his older brother—had paid no attention to the advice of anyone since he was fifteen years old. "What happened to the scheme you wrote about?"

"Scheme?"

"The plan that was going to make you rich," Clay said sarcastically. "The big real estate deal in Mobile."

"Oh, that!" Burke waved the half-eaten biscuit with an airy gesture. "I sold out and went to Haiti. Lots of opportunity down there."

"Oh?" Clay raised one heavy eyebrow. "And what happened in Haiti?"

Burke sopped the bean soup with the last morsel of biscuit, popped it into his mouth, then washed it down with the rest of the milk. He ignored Clay as he pulled the pie toward him, cut off a bit with the edge of his fork, and tasted it. "That's good pie," he said with a nod. "I sure have missed Dorrie's pies!" Closing his eyes, he chewed thoughtfully on the pie, swallowed it, then shrugged. "There was a fancy gambler down there named Ace Donlin. I thought I could take him. Planned to come home and build me a mansion down the road from this place."

"And—?"

A trace of disgust showed in Burke's dark eyes. "I guess Donlin will be building the mansion." He pushed the pie around with his fork, then said, "So here I am, back to sponge off the folks again." When Clay said nothing, he shoved the plate back with irritation. "Like you said, Clay, you need another useless wastrel around."

Clay eyed Burke sharply, then frowned. "You know how things are, Burke. With this war on and no market for cotton, things are pretty thin."

"I know, I know!" Burke shrugged his shoulders and then let them sag. He looked across the table, and Clay saw the corners of his lips draw up. Burke had a perverse sense of humor, sometimes aimed at his own foibles. His dark eyes gleamed, and he said, "But I have a plan, brother. A plan that will keep me from being a parasite on my beloved family."

"Have I heard this one before?" Clay grinned in spite of himself. It was difficult to stay mad at this rascal of a brother!

"No, this one is brand new, and it doesn't involve fast horses or gambling in any form."

"That'll be different!"

Burke leaned back and studied Clay carefully. "I don't know why I never thought of it before, Clay. It's so simple!" He paused for effect, then put his hands out, palms up. "I'm going to marry a rich woman!"

Clay laughed out loud. "Aren't you the man who's always run from a wedding ring as if it were a rattlesnake? I don't believe it!"

"I'm getting mellow, Clay," Burke answered, his humor fading as quickly as it had come. "Time for me to settle down. But to what?"

"I thought you got a piece of paper from the university saying you were an engineer."

"No money in that, not unless you own a big company." Burke shook his head. "I'd have to start as a junior clerk, carrying a chain for an eighteen-year-old boy!"

Clay could not believe his brother was serious about this scheme. "Got the girl picked out? No doubt you can charm some poor young thing into falling in love with you. You never had any trouble with *that*! But rich girls are likely to have parents who'd like their son-in-law to have more than the clothes on his back."

"I can charm the girl's mama—and the papa, too."

Clay stared at his brother's smooth face. "I never know when you're joking, Burke."

"I'm serious about this," Burke replied. His mouth drew tight, and he nodded adamantly. "I'll make a good husband, Clay. Got most of my foolishness behind me. And I've gotten to where I know plantations. All I need is a beautiful girl—an only child, preferably—with rather *elderly* parents. They'll be worried about what happens to their little girl when they're gone, and I'll be there to take care of her. That makes sense, doesn't it?"

"You only left one thing out, Burke. For every rich girl, there's about fifty poor young men standing in line to 'help' her manage her money."

"Competition never bothered me." Burke took another bite of the pie. "Now tell me, what's going on around here? I haven't got a letter for weeks."

"Ellen died last Thursday," Clay answered simply.

Burke blinked and stopped chewing. Quickly he swallowed the bite, then said quietly, "I'm sorry, Clay." The words seemed inadequate, and he asked, "What was it?"

Clay hesitated, not knowing how much of the tragic story of Ellen's death he should reveal. The bare truth was that Ellen, her mind affected by her physical problem, had fallen into a jealous rage, convincing herself that Clay and Melora Yancy were having an affair. Nursing the suspicion until it became a certainty in her mind, Ellen had finally sent word for Melora to meet her at an abandoned sawmill, deep in the woods. When Melora arrived, Ellen had pulled out a pistol and tried to kill her. The shot had only grazed Melora's neck, but it had startled the horse attached to Ellen's buggy, causing it to bolt. Unable to hold on to the seat, Ellen was thrown down an incline and critically injured. Melora had gone at once for help, but by the time they got Ellen back home and under a doctor's care, it was obvious that she was dying.

All this ran through Clay's mind as he faced his brother's sympathy, but he said only, "She was thrown from her buggy in an accident, Burke. She lived only a day."

Burke dropped his eyes, ashamed of his light talk. "I wish you'd told me earlier, Clay. I wouldn't have acted such a fool."

"It's all right, Burke," Clay answered reassuringly. "In a way, Ellen's better off."

"Better off?" Burke looked up with surprise in his dark eyes. "What do you mean?"

"You can imagine how miserable she'd be, confined to a wheelchair," Clay said slowly. "Now she's free from those restrictions. And just before she died, Melora was able to help her in a wonderful way—she led Ellen to faith in Jesus." Clay rubbed the bruise on his jaw absently. "I think the last hours of Ellen's life were the only ones that held any joy for her."

Not being a man of faith, Burke wanted to argue with this. But he knew his brother's stand on God, so instead he merely asked, "How are the children taking it?"

Clay thought about the question for a long moment. "Better than I expected." He shuddered, then said, "The funeral is tomorrow. Sorry to spoil your homecoming, Burke."

Burke Rocklin was not a man to show his feelings much, but now compassion was on his face. Although he had idolized his older brother, they had never been very close because of their age difference. But he knew enough about him to realize the suffering that Clay had gone through. He sat there trying to think of something fitting to say, but could not manage it.

Seeing Burke's embarrassment, Clay stood up. "Go get some sleep, Burke. We'll talk more later."

Burke mumbled a good-night, pushed back his chair, and left. Clay returned to the parlor, going to stand beside the casket. He looked down on Ellen's still, white face. Knowing that the next day would be filled with emotional turmoil and tension—as most funerals were—he reached out and touched her hair.

"Good-bye, Ellen," he whispered. "I wish I'd done better by you!"

Then he went to the chair and sat down, waiting for the sunrise.

❧

The funeral was held in the white church three miles from Gracefield. The sanctuary was filled—every pew was packed. Clay had chosen ten o'clock in the morning for the service, knowing that the church would be sweltering if it were held at the customary hour of two in the afternoon.

Clay sat silently between Dent and Rena, with Lowell and David flanking them. Many uncles and aunts were there, along with cousins. Many of the men wore Confederate uniforms, several of them officers.

Clay heard little of the sermon. He was thinking of Rena most of all. He glanced at her from time to time, noting the pallor of her cheeks. He gently took her hand when he saw she was trembling, and she grasped it hard, looking up at him for reassurance. Her eyes were brimming with tears, and Clay was glad he was there. *She's going to need a lot of love,* he thought. *And I won't be here to give it to her.* That was the way of a war.

It tore men away when they were needed most. Unlike most Southerners, Clay didn't believe in the Cause. He hated slavery with a passion, but he had chosen to stay with his state and his family rather than join the Union forces. And then his love for his sons had compelled him to join them in the Confederate Army....

He looked more than once at his father, Thomas, and saw that the sickness that had plagued him for the past two years had made an old man out of him. Thomas Rocklin had been a fine-looking man for many years, but now he was stooped, and his legs trembled as he walked. His cheeks were pallid, his hair thin and gray. Clay glanced at his mother, Susanna, thinking, *She looks more like his daughter than his wife!* His mother's auburn hair was sprinkled with silver, but she retained much of the beauty of her youth. She caught his glance, and compassion came to her eyes as she nodded slightly at him.

Finally the service ended, and the visitors were permitted to pass by the coffin before the family did, for one last glimpse of the dead woman. When all but the family were outside, Clay stood up along with the others. He waited until all had passed by, then said, "Come, children. We'll say good-bye together."

The boys went first, Dent and David, the twins, then Lowell, the youngest. Clay took Rena's arm, and the two of them came to join the boys. Clay felt Rena tremble and held her tightly. "She's happy now," he said quietly. "I thank our God that she found Jesus." Rena began to weep, and Clay felt tears of grief sting his own eyes. He knew that if Ellen had gone out to meet her God unprepared, he would have been stricken for the rest of his life.

They turned and left, going outside to the open grave just south of the church. The crowd made a circle, with the family in close. The minister read the scripture, then prayed a brief prayer... and it was over.

All except the worst part—for Clay, at least. For now was when the family must stand and receive people's condolences.

Clay stood there, his face tight, saying to each person, "Thank you—," but the faces were a blur, and he longed for it to be over.

And then it was Melora who was standing in front of him, holding one of his hands and one of Rena's. She was wearing black, and her eyes were filled with peace as she said, "God is on His throne, isn't He?" She moved forward and embraced Rena, whispering, "We must help each other now, Rena!"

"Yes!" Rena held Melora fast, clinging to her for a long moment. "Will—will I see you, Melora?" she asked as she drew back.

"Yes, Rena," Melora said. Then she extended her hand to Clay. When he took it, she said quietly, "God be with you and give you peace, Clay."

Clay nodded, his lips dry. He had loved this woman for years—as she had loved him—but they had been faithful to God and to Clay's marriage. Despite Ellen's suspicions, Clay and Melora had never been more than dear friends. "You were a blessing to Ellen, Melora," he said now. "Thank you for helping her."

Melora turned, not unaware of the glances she received from some standing nearby. She made no sign that she noticed, but she knew that she and Clay would be the target of many eyes in the future. Gossip had been rampant about them for a long time, but Melora had never shown any anger toward those who were unkind. There was a rare sweetness in her that stemmed from her desire and determination to honor her Lord. She had fallen in love with Clay Rocklin when she was a mere child. From that first affection, she had found love growing, and by the time she was a mature woman, she knew that there was no other man in the world for her. Even so, she and Clay had long ago faced up to the sad truth that they could never share more than friendship and respect. Clay had a wife, and for both of them, that settled the matter. Neither she nor Clay would dishonor their God—or their love—by breaking his wedding vows to Ellen.

Not that Melora had lacked for suitors. She was a beautiful woman, and several men had sought her company. Her most persistent suitor had been Jeremiah Irons, the fine young pastor who had joined the Confederate Army. Jeremiah had finally won Melora's consent to marry a year and a half ago—shortly before he was killed in battle. Now, at the age of twenty-seven, she was still single.

As Melora turned away, making her way to the wagon where her father, Buford, waited for her, she saw the concern in his greenish eyes. "Are you ready to go home, Melora?" he asked.

"Ready, Pa."

Melora mounted the seat beside him as her brothers and sisters scrambled into the back of the wagon. For them, Melora was more of a mother, for after the death of their real mother, she had practically raised them.

As the wagon pulled away, Burke stood off to one side, watching the drama. He had been aware for years of the hopeless love between his brother and Melora Yancy. He had beaten one man into insensibility for speaking of the pair in public, and his skill with a dueling pistol had shut the mouths of others.

Now he saw that Clay was holding his daughter, Rena, closely—but his eyes followed Melora as the wagon moved out of the churchyard.

"Too bad for Clay," Burke muttered. He respected few women. In his opinion, most were deceiving creatures without much honor who wanted husbands and would play any game to get one. But two women he did respect were his mother—and Melora Yancy.

Burke knew there *were* other women like his mother and Melora and some of his aunts, but they were few and far between—a thought that made his self-assigned duty of finding a wealthy wife less than enjoyable. He knew he would have to make concessions to assure his future, but the thought of living with a devious woman for the rest of his life—no matter how attractive her money might be—left a sour taste in his mouth. He moved to help his father into the buggy, but his thoughts were on what lay ahead for him.

Not the war; Burke was no patriot. He was not incensed

by slavery as was Clay, yet he did believe the leadership of the South had led them into a deadly war that they would lose.

As he rode back to Gracefield, he thought of the plan he'd explained to Clay and mused, *It's got to be that way, I guess. What else am I fit to do but be some kind of kept husband?* A thin feeling of self-disgust ran through him, but he clamped his lips tightly together and settled down in the carriage, thinking of what would come in the next few weeks.

CHAPTER 6

A RAPID PROMOTION

The smoke of the fighting, which would be called the Seven Days' Battles, still hung over Richmond. The campaign was made up of a series of battles fought outside the capital, and it was Robert E. Lee's genius that staved off defeat for the newborn Confederacy.

General Joseph Johnston had been in command of the Confederate forces as the Federals' Peninsular Campaign started, but had been wounded at Seven Pines, and President Jefferson Davis had appointed General Lee as commander. That would prove to be the best decision Davis ever made as president. Lee had attacked the Federals so audaciously that McClellan had been driven off and forced to retire back to the safety of Washington.

The Seven Days' Battles rocked both North and South, for neither side had been prepared for the enormous losses they would sustain. The Union forces suffered almost sixteen thousand killed, wounded, captured, or missing. The Confederates lost approximately twenty thousand men.

The Richmond Grays, in which three of the Rocklins served, were devastated by the Seven Days' Battles. When Lieutenant Dent Rocklin, along with his father and brother, went back to camp immediately following his mother's funeral, he found that half of the officers had already been killed or wounded so badly that they would be out of action for months. His own platoon had lost over 40 percent—*and the fighting was still going on!* This meant he would have to train privates to become corporals and corporals to become sergeants, as well as commandeer whatever recruits he could manage to get his hands on. Unlike the Northern adversary, the South had scant few replacements for those who fell. All Lincoln had to do was issue a call, and he would have fifty thousand new recruits to fill the Federal ranks. But when a Southern soldier died, he left a gap that, often, no one could be found to fill. So the ranks grew thin, and those who were left had to fight harder on less supplies and energy than ever before.

After the Seven Days' Battles, Richmond was like a swimmer who had exhausted himself. The city had not been invaded as McClellan (and the North) had promised, but the herculean effort expended by Lee and the army in repelling the Army of the Potomac had drained the people terribly.

The small towns just to the northeast of Richmond marked the bloody battles. Mechanicsville, Gaines' Mill, Savage's Station, Malvern Hill. . .these tiny hamlets that most people had never heard of soon became household words all over the country. Many a parent or a wife wept over one of these names as the news came that their sons and husbands slept forever in one of the obscure towns beside the Chickahominy River.

The Peace Party in the North began sounding its cry: "Stop the War," and Abraham Lincoln padded for long hours in the White House each night, his homely face furrowed with care. When his secretary of war asked him if he could keep the North to the task of defending the Union, he said, "I knew an old fellow back home in Illinois. He kept dogs, bought and sold them. But there was one old dog he never would sell. Wasn't much of a dog to look at, and I asked him once why he wouldn't sell him. 'Abe,' he said to me, 'that ol' dog ain't much to look at, and I got dogs that's faster—but that ol' dog—you can't beat him on a cold scent!' I guess I'm like that old dog; I'm not much to look at, but I know how to hold on, and that's what I'm going to do until the Union is secure!"

McClellan's army went slinking away, whipped again, as they had been at Bull Run—but it had not been their fault that they had lost. They had fought as bravely and with as much determination as the Confederates. What had whipped them was their commander's lack of will. George McClellan was a fine commander, right up until a battle came. He could train troops and whip an army into shape and give it heart better than any man in the North. And he proved that he was an expert soldier by the manner in which he conducted his retreat from Richmond: orderly and with almost no losses.

But the man lacked nerve. When it came time to send men in large numbers to their deaths, he simply could not do it. He would prove this again and again. Lincoln could have done it, but he was not a general. It wasn't until the North found a man who *could* do this—a small, nondescript man named U. S. Grant—that the North would overcome the smaller armies of the Confederacy. When Lincoln finally found Grant and put him in charge, he received complaints about the man's drinking. In response, the president said adamantly, "I can't spare this man; he *fights!*"

So the Army of the Potomac—those who didn't remain forever in Southern soil, at any rate—went home. When they arrived, there were no parades with flags flying and people cheering. All the North, it seemed, wore black arm bands in memory of high-spirited young soldiers who had marched away a few weeks earlier, shouting "On to Richmond!"—but who now would march no more.

❧

As soon as the fighting was over, Dent sought out his father. "How are you?" he asked Clay at once.

"Fine, Lieutenant," Clay said, using the formal term as he always did when they were in uniform. When Clay had joined the army to be near Lowell, he'd told his son Denton, "You'll have to be harder on Lowell and me than on any of the others. If you don't, you'll be accused of favoritism." And Dent had acted on this, giving all the hard jobs to his father and brother.

"How's Raimey?" Clay asked, aware that she hadn't been at the funeral.

A smile crossed Dent's face. He'd married Raimey Reed, a lovely girl from a wealthy family, nearly a year ago. It had been a stormy and bizarre romance, complicated by the fact that Raimey was blind. Dent had been terribly wounded in battle, his handsome face scarred by a saber, and it had been the determination of the blind girl that had led him out of self-pity into trust in God. The journey from there to love had been short, and Dent thanked God again, as he often did, for his wife and the joy they shared. He grinned at his father. "Well, Sergeant, she's doing quite well. In fact, I have news for you. You're going to be a grandfather."

"Dent!" Clay forgot the differences in rank at once. He beamed at his son, saying, "That's wonderful! I always wanted to be a fussy old grandpa!"

Dent kept smiling. "You look like a mighty spry grandpa to me, but Raimey and I are happy." He shook his head, saying, "As much as I'd like to talk about it more, the colonel wants to see you."

"Me? What does Colonel Benton want with me?"

"You'll have to ask him, Sergeant. Come along."

Clay turned and followed his son toward the large Sibley tent used by the colonel. The two entered, and Dent said to the officer, who had his back to the entrance, "Here's Sergeant Rocklin, sir."

Colonel Benton turned, and there was a smile on his face.

"Sergeant, you did a fine job in the battles!" he said with excitement. "The men looked to you for leadership, and you provided it."

Clay thought sorrowfully of the men of his company who would fight no more. After the campaign, he'd helped clear the battlefields of the dead and wounded, and it sickened him to think of it.

He shrugged. "It was all pretty hot and heavy, Colonel. I guess none of us had a lot of time to meditate on what to do." The weariness on his face was plain. The battles, right on the heels of his wife's funeral, had taken their toll.

"That's as may be," Benton said quickly. "But we're just getting started. The Yankees will be back, and we've got to get ready for them."

"Yes, sir, they'll be back," Clay agreed. "And we lost a lot of good men."

"We did indeed." The colonel nodded sadly. "And their places have to be filled." He tugged at his mustache, winked at Dent, then said, "So from now on, you'll be *Lieutenant* Rocklin, in charge of your platoon." Colonel Benton watched the stunned expression on Clay's face and let out a long laugh. "Well, I've surprised you this time, haven't I?"

Clay glanced at Dent, who was grinning broadly. "Yes, sir, you have. I never thought I'd be an officer."

Benton laughed, exposing white teeth. "When we lost Lieutenant Simms, I knew you'd be the man to take his place. Clay, you're a natural leader, and I need you badly. Tell you what, why don't you go into town, get a uniform, then take a few days off." He hesitated, then nodded. "You've had a hard time the last few days, and the new recruits won't be in until later in the week. Lieutenant, go get yourself a flashy uniform. Go home and show off; then come back." He hesitated, then said quietly, "I want your father to see you. He'll be very proud."

"Yes, I think he will, sir." Clay nodded, saluted, and left the tent.

As soon as he was gone, Dent said, "That's a relief, Colonel. The rest of us are doing the best we can, but my father—he's one of those natural soldiers. Don't know what it is, but some men can get others to follow them, and some can't."

Colonel Benton nodded absently. "Yes, I think you're right. We'd better look out, Lieutenant, or he'll be commanding both of us!"

❧

Burke had breakfast with his parents out on the veranda. He'd gotten up late, having noticed that his father seldom rose early. His mother had come to wake him. When he'd answered her knock with a muffled "Come in," she'd entered and crossed the room to open the shade.

Burke had sat up, blinded by the bright yellow beams. He peered at her, then grinned sleepily. "Mother, you didn't bring my breakfast."

"I'll bring a stick, just like I used to, if you aren't out of that bed and down to breakfast in fifteen minutes!" she responded tartly.

506

Susanna Lee Rocklin tried to look fierce, but it was a failure. Her blue-green eyes glowed as she smiled at Burke. *I can no more be angry with him now than I could when he was a little boy,* she thought. *And Lord help me, he's finer looking than ever! All his hard living hasn't coarsened him, thank God!* But she said only, "You've loafed long enough, Burke. Come to breakfast, and after I've fed you, I'll put you to work."

"All right, Mother."

His answer was so meek and so unlike him that Susanna peered at him intently. "Butter wouldn't melt in your mouth, now, would it, Burke Rocklin! What scheme are you hatching up?"

"Me? Why, nothing!"

"Humph!" Susanna snorted. "I know you! Now get dressed and come to breakfast." She hurried out of the room, going at once to the kitchen, where she found Dorrie cooking biscuits. "Make some extra, Dorrie," she said. "You know how Burke loves your biscuits."

Dorrie considered herself the mistress of Gracefield, for she had been in charge of the house for years. Tall, heavy, and of a rich chocolate complexion, she was bossy—and loyal to the Rocklins above all things except God. "Yas, I knows about dat," she grunted. She was most partial to Burke, a weakness she tried hard—but unsuccessfully—to hide. "But I got more to do den fix biscuits for dat worthless man!"

Susanna knew Dorrie well. "He's shamelessly handsome, Dorrie. No wonder women fall into his arms." She laughed, saying, "But he still loves you the best! He told me so last night."

"I guess he do!" Dorrie snorted indignantly. "Doan see none of *them* fixin' him pies and biscuits!" She slapped a pan of biscuits into the oven and wiped her hands on her apron. "Whut he gonna do now, Miss Susanna?"

Susanna shook her head. "I really don't know, Dorrie. He's not a boy any longer. He's got to find his way."

"You don't reckon he'll join the army with Marse Clay and Marse Lowell?"

"He hasn't said what he's going to do. But he doesn't have any money, so he'll have to either go to work or go into the army."

"Plenty of work round heah," Dorrie commented flatly, but both women knew it was unlikely that Burke would throw himself into the grueling work of running a plantation. Dorrie's face assumed a heavy look, and she shook her head dolefully, "Dat boy, he need a good dose of *religion*—dat's whut'll fix him up! He gots to find the Lord."

"I think that's right, Dorrie," Susanna said with a nod. The two women worked on the breakfast, and thirty minutes later, Susanna and Thomas were sitting at the table on the veranda waiting for Burke.

Thomas was pale, and Susanna knew he was in pain. "Have some milk, dear," she urged.

"Where's Burke?" Thomas demanded. "Thought he was supposed to be here and eat with us." He looked up even as he spoke, for Burke entered and sat down. "Good afternoon, Mr. Rocklin," Thomas said sarcastically. "I hope we haven't gotten you up too early?"

"Why, this is the most civilized time to have breakfast," Burke said with a cocky grin. But his eyes were serious as he asked, "How are you, sir?"

"I feel about as bad as I look! Which is saying a lot."

"Sorry to hear that." Burke had been shocked at how much his father had aged in the year he'd been gone. The illness had eaten away at him, and he'd had to work at concealing how concerned he was. He'd learned quickly that his father didn't like conversations or comments about his health, so he said, "You're looking fine, Mother—," but he broke off as Dorrie came in with a silver tray piled high with food. "Now *here's* the real woman in my life!" He got to his feet, took the tray from Dorrie and set it down, then turned to give her a huge hug. "I thought about you every day I was gone, Dorrie," he said fervently.

Dorrie fought to keep the grin from her face as she struggled to get out of his grasp. "You thought about yo' stomach, dat's whut you thought 'bout!" she muttered. "Lemme go, you hear me?"

But Burke held her tightly and, reaching into his pocket, pulled out a silver coin. Taking her hand, he pressed it into her palm. "That's for you to buy yourself a pretty with. Come and show it to me when you get it."

Dorrie grasped the coin and did her best to look harsh. She went away mumbling something about "A fool and his money is soon parted—"

"Didn't know you came home a wealthy man, Burke," Thomas said with his eyebrows lifted. "I may have to ask you for a loan."

"Certainly, sir." Burke nodded. "Just give me a few days to get my affairs in order, and I think I can accommodate you. Now let's eat this fine breakfast...."

It was a pleasant meal, for Thomas and Susanna always enjoyed Burke's company. Though Thomas often spoke to his younger son in a seemingly harsh manner, Burke and his mother both knew it was not because the father disliked the son. Rather, it seemed to be Thomas's only way of showing concern. All the years that Clay had been gone, it had been Burke, the younger son, who'd sat in his place. And he had become a support to his parents during that time. Oh, he'd been a wild young man, but he was never vicious or careless with his family. When Clay had come back, he'd left abruptly, saying only that he needed to see the world. He'd done this before, but for shorter trips. This was the longest time he'd been gone, and his parents had missed him.

Burke noted that his father picked at his food, and he saw how concerned his mother was. He was not unaware that in the early days of their marriage, Thomas Rocklin had given his wife some difficulty. He'd had a wild streak in him—a fact that made Burke smile when his father now reprimanded him for being "wild." In fact, when their sons began to behave badly, Susanna had feared for them, worried that they would find little guidance or correction in her husband. But time had cured Thomas of his vices, and he'd become more of a husband to Susanna and a father to his sons.

We've been through a lot of changes in the last few years, this family of mine, Burke thought as he watched his parents. He remembered something his mother once had told him: "Your father's always felt inferior—especially where his brother Stephen is concerned." Stephen Rocklin had moved to the North, where he'd become a successful factory owner. Thomas spoke of him from time to time, and always with an air of respect. . .and regret that he himself had not done so well. Burke pursed his lips. He could understand that feeling of regret—far too well.

The three sat there for a long time, and finally Thomas asked, "What are your plans, Burke?"

Burke answered lightly. "I think I'll become rich, healthy, and good-looking—which is better than being poor, sick, and ugly."

But his father was not to be put off. "Will you go into the army with your brother?"

Burke grew serious at once. "No, sir, I don't plan to do that."

"I didn't think you would," Thomas sighed. He believed in the Cause and was proud of the fact that one son wore the Confederate uniform. But he knew Burke was not happy with the war, for the two of them had argued about it before. "Will you stay here and help with the work?"

Burke said evasively, "I don't know, sir. I have one idea, but it's very vague. Let me have a few weeks. I'll do what I can around here while I'm waiting. Will that be all right?"

"It'll have to be, I suppose." After a pause, Thomas started to speak again, then lifted his head and narrowed his eyes. "Who is that riding up?"

"Why, I believe it's Denton!" Susanna said, noting the uniform. She got to her feet at once. "I wonder why he's come? I hope nothing's wrong with Raimey."

The three of them waited, and then they heard boots on the pine boards—but when the officer entered, all three of them spoke out with astonishment, for it was Clay, not Dent, who entered.

"Well, here I am, in all my glory!" Clay laughed at the surprise on their faces. "Don't blame you for being shocked," he said, coming over to hug his mother. "They're really scraping the bottom of the barrel this time!"

He shook hands with his father and with Burke, then sat down and began to eat, explaining his promotion.

Thomas listened avidly, and when he finally said, "I'm very proud of you, Clay! Very proud indeed!" there was a quiver in his voice and a mistiness in his eye.

Clay couldn't speak himself, for he knew too well the grief he'd brought into his father's life, and it made him very happy to do something to redeem himself.

"How long can you stay?" Susanna asked.

"Just a few days. I want to take Rena camping."

"Good. She needs you, Clay," Susanna said.

After breakfast, Burke pulled his brother aside. "Going into Richmond to start my campaign." He grinned. "Hope I do as well as you, brother."

"Burke, you're not serious about that fool notion to marry a rich girl."

"I'm as serious as a man can get," Burke insisted. He fished into his pocket, came out with a small box, and opened it up. A flash of light caught at the diamond ring inside. "Already got the engagement ring," he said fondly. "All that's left of a big bust." He put the ring away, then said, "I sold my horse yesterday to Tom McKeever. Got enough out of him for a fancy set of clothes and some courtin' money." His white teeth gleamed as he grinned widely. "I'm off, Clay. Wish me luck."

Clay shook his head sadly. "I wish you *sense*, Burke. There's no happiness in what you're trying to do."

"No sermons!" Burke punched Clay on the arm lightly. "Congratulations, General! Father is proud as punch—and so am I!" He sauntered out the door, and as Clay looked out the window to watch his brother ride out toward Richmond, there was a heaviness in him.

Headed for a big fall, he thought sadly, then turned to find Rena.

❧

Melora was swimming in the creek, enjoying the coolness of the water after the long hours she'd spent under the blazing July sun. She kept her shift on, for visitors sometimes came and hunters often crossed their land.

She floated on the surface close to the shore, watching the tiny transparent bodies of the minnows as they hung motionless in the clear water. A movement caught her eye, and she turned to see a V-shaped ripple—a water snake, she knew instantly—and got to her feet at once. It was, she saw, a harmless snake, not a moccasin, so she released her breath.

At that moment, she heard a faint cry that sounded like her name. She waded quickly to the bank and hurriedly pulled her dress over her head. "I'm over here," she called, slipping into her shoes. She thought it was Josh, her fifteen-year-old brother, coming to fetch her for supper, so she sat in the sun, drying her hair with the towel she'd brought. When she heard his footsteps, she said, "I'm almost ready, Josh." Then, when she got no answer, she turned—and saw Clay standing there.

"Mister Clay!" Jumping to her feet, she stood stock still, taking in the new uniform. *He still doesn't know how handsome he is,* she thought, but said, "Congratulations, Lieutenant Rocklin. You look very dashing."

Clay laughed with some embarrassment. Walking toward her, he asked, "How are you, Melora?"

"I'm very well." Melora studied his face and was relieved to see that the awful strain that had marked him after Ellen's death was now gone. She knew him almost as well as he knew himself, even better at times. "Come and sit down, Clay. Tell me about your promotion."

The two of them sat down, and as the water gurgled nearby, Melora picked up her comb and ran it through her hair, listening as Clay told her the story. When that was done, he told her about Burke, expressing his fears. There was nothing he kept from her, but he knew she'd never reveal a word of it.

Finally he said, "Rena told me how you'd asked her to come

and spend the day. It was good of you." Clay's face grew heavy. He picked up a flat stone and skipped it across the water. "She needs someone, Melora. She looks as though she's almost a woman, but she's still a child in many ways."

As Melora shared her insights about his daughter, Clay glanced at her and smiled, watching her as she spoke of Rena. He knew she was unaware of what a beautiful sight she was. Her height, her father's green eyes, and her mother's black hair all made a fetching combination.

They talked of Rena for a long time; then Melora put her comb down and looked at Clay.

Clay laughed as her look brought a sudden memory to him. "I remember when I was sick and stayed at your house. You fed me soup and acted so very businesslike about your patient. You must have been about six years old."

Melora nodded. "And I remember how you promised to bring me books, and how excited I was when you carried out that promise. Our whole family has grown up on those books, Clay. I read them to Toby and Martha still. And Josh and Father listen, pretending that they're not."

"Is *Pilgrim's Progress* still your favorite?"

"Yes. I love the part when Christian slays that dragon!"

Clay grew still, and his eyes clouded. "I remember when I went off to the Mexican War. I rode out here and told you I'd slay a dragon for you." He thought of all the wasted years that had followed, and pain filled his eyes. "I've made such a mess of things, Melora!"

She could not stand to see him hurt. Tossing down the comb, she rose and came to sit beside him. She took his hand and held it in both of hers. "You're not to think that!" she said fiercely. "Since you let God take over your life, you've become a wonderful father. And you were a faithful husband to Ellen. I want you to be glad for that," she said, her eyes enormous. "Most men would have abandoned her when she got so sick. But you never gave her a cross word!"

Clay studied Melora's face for a few moments, drawing strength from the feel of her soft hands. The love and respect he saw in her eyes touched him deeply, and slowly he put his arm around her and drew her close. She came trustingly. Her lips were soft and warm under his, and he could feel the beat of her heart as he held her.

Melora was not afraid, for she knew that Clay's honor was as firm as rock. As she leaned against him, savoring his taste and touch, she was reminded again that she longed for the love she would find only in this man.

Finally she drew back, her cheeks flushed and her eyes shining. She reached up to gently touch Clay's dear face, and when she spoke, her voice was not quite steady. "I'm sure Pa and the others are wondering where we've got to. They've already waited for supper so I could come swim for a bit." She got to her feet and picked up her comb and towel, glancing at Clay with a mischievous light in her eyes. "I must admit you amaze me, Mister Clay," she said, once again using the childhood name she'd given him. "In all the years I've known you, you've *never* come to our house when it wasn't mealtime!"

"I'm a slave to my stomach," he answered, laughing. He stood and took her hand, and she paused to look up at him. "Melora, you're the finest and most beautiful woman I've ever known." His voice, too, was unsteady with emotion.

Melora stared at him, then said, "Thank you, Clay." She hesitated, then went on: "You know people will still talk about us, even though Ellen is gone?"

"Let them talk!"

She smiled at his defiance but shook her head. "You and I could bear it, Clay. But what about Rena? We can't let her be hurt."

Clay groaned. "Oh, Melora, what are we to do? I love you, I want to be with you. . .but there is still so much to keep us apart. Rena is only a part of it. I've got to go back to the war, and it may be years before I return!"

"Clay, never take counsel of your fears," Melora whispered. "You've been faithful. God never forgets faith. We'll wait." She nodded firmly, and her eyes glowed with confidence. "And we'll see what God will do with us."

Clay gazed down at her, a faint smile on his lips. "All right, Melora."

Then they turned and made their way back to the house, smiling at each other when Rena came to greet them, happiness on her face.

"Oh, Daddy!" she cried, her young face lit up with excitement. "Come and see the new pigs!"

CHAPTER 7

A-COURTIN' HE WOULD GO!

*H*aving spent all his life in the high society of Virginia planters, Burke Rocklin knew the available young ladies as well as he knew the bloodlines of the state's racing horses. But he had been gone for a year, and it took a little time to be certain how the lineup had changed—who had gotten married, who were the new arrivals, and who had risen from the middle class to the top of the social world through the riches of an industrious father.

It took only one session with Loren Delchamp, an old friend, to get all that together. Delchamp, the younger son of a rich planter from Lynchburg, was one of the first men Burke encountered after making his preparations for a siege. He'd bought a new suit and a new pair of boots, then ensconced himself in a nice room at the Majestic Hotel. When he had discovered that Delchamp was in that same hotel, he had considered it a stroke of good fortune.

The two had gone to eat at the hotel restaurant to talk over old times. Delchamp, a rather slight man of Burke's age, was very glad to see him. As they ate heartily and drank their wine, he spoke freely of the past year. "The worst thing, Burke," he complained, "is that the women have gone *crazy* over uniforms! Never saw anything like it!" He tossed off a glass of wine, filled his glass, and announced with disgust, "Society is gone to Hades in a bucket! At every dance, the women practically swoon over some bumpkin who was pushing a plow before he joined up. Nowadays, unless a man's wearing brass buttons and a saber, he might as well stay home!"

"Always that way during a war." Burke nodded wisely. He sipped his wine and asked casually, "What about Annabelle Symington? She still the belle of the ball?"

"Oh my word! She married Phil Townsend right before the battle at Bull Run! Poor Phil lost a leg there, but he's set, I suppose. The Symingtons take care of him very well."

Burke crossed one name off his mental list and for the next half hour skillfully plied Delchamp. Finally he had three names that he would use to plan his campaign; then his eyes grew sharp when Loren said, "There is a new star on the firmament, Burke. Family rich as Croesus."

"Ugly as an anvil, I suppose?" Burke shrugged.

"Ugly! Not a bit of it!" Loren insisted. "Good-looking wench named Belinda King. Her father owns four or five garment factories." He drained his glass, then gave Burke a sour look. "I made a try for her, but the competition was too hot." He grinned as a thought came to him. "Now there's something that would be a challenge to your talents, Burke!"

"Always liked a challenge," Burke murmured.

"I'd like to see you win her away from that big snob she runs with." Delchamp filled his glass again, drank it down, then said, "An old friend of yours."

"Who?"

"Chad Barnes."

At the name, Burke's eyes narrowed. Barnes, the son of a wealthy planter in the next county, had courted the same girl as Burke for a time, and it had turned out to be a rather nasty business. Angry words had been spoken, and if it had not been for the intervention of friends, a duel would have been fought.

"My old friend Chad, eh?"

"That interests you, doesn't it?" Delchamp grinned at his friend. "There's a ball tomorrow night in the Armory. I could introduce you to Belinda. It might be fun for you. She's a toothsome wench—and I'd like to see Barnes get left at the post!"

"Sounds like it might be fun," Burke said as he nodded. His eyes were half hooded, and as Delchamp talked on, he thought of what might come of the thing. He despised Chad Barnes—if he could steal the girl from him, so much the better. Finally he said, "Let's take in that ball tomorrow, Loren."

Delchamp grinned and winked broadly. "I'll bet you do the scoundrel in, Burke! You could always handle women!"

Burke and Delchamp spent the evening wandering around the streets of Richmond, then went back to the Majestic. They said good night but agreed to meet at six the next evening. For a long time that night Burke lay awake thinking of his future, but it seemed rather bleak. Gracefield was not going to make any money until the war was over, not with England being blockaded from reaching Confederate ports by Federal warships. And if the Yankees won the war, *nobody* would have a dime—that much was clear to him.

Only chance I have, he thought just before falling asleep, *is to marry some girl who's got money. Then get it out of farms and plantations—out of everything here in the South. Buy land or a business in the far West, even in the North if necessary!*

He did little the next day but stay in his room and read. At six he met Loren, and the two of them had supper, then proceeded to the Armory. The place was crowded, mostly by officers, for many units were stationed in Richmond. As for the women, there were plenty! "Looks like every woman in this part of the state is here," Burke murmured to Loren as they stepped inside the huge ballroom.

"All out for a bit of fun," Delchamp said, nodding. He gazed around with satisfaction. "They've done the old place up, haven't they?"

"Yes. It's pretty plush," Burke agreed. Chandeliers threw their glittering lights over the crowd below, and the reds, greens, blues, and whites of the women's gowns added splashes of color. The brass buttons of uniforms glittered as dancers moved across the floor to the music of the excellent band. The noise was terrific, for everyone seemed to be talking at the top of their lungs.

Suddenly Delchamp nudged Burke. "There she is! Belinda

King. The one in the blue dress dancing with the major."

Burke saw her at once and was impressed. She was petite, very pretty, and blessed with long blond hair that hung down her back. At the moment she was smiling up at her partner, revealing two charming dimples. "Not bad," he said. "Let's move in so you can introduce me."

They maneuvered themselves so that when the dance was over, they were directly in the path of the pair. Loren appeared to be surprised as he said, "Oh, Miss King! How nice to see you!"

"Hello, Loren."

Belinda King and her partner would have moved on, but Loren said quickly, "I don't think you've met Burke Rocklin, have you? He's been out of town on business for some time."

Burke smiled and stepped forward. Before she could protest, he took her hand and bent over it with a graceful movement. He kissed it lightly and said in a low voice, "I'm charmed, Miss King."

Belinda King was accustomed to fine-looking men, but this man before her was exceptional. He was tall, dressed in excellent clothing, and was handsome almost to a fault. His dark eyes were somehow magnetic, and when he said, "May I have this dance, Miss King?" she found herself in his arms without quite knowing how it happened.

"Really, Mr. Rocklin," she protested mildly, "this is Lieutenant Baxter's dance."

"Well, we all have our disappointments in life." Burke smiled down at her. "I've discovered that what's bad for some is good for others. The lieutenant's misfortune is my good fortune."

He was, Belinda discovered, the best dancer she'd ever had for a partner. He made her feel as though she was floating weightlessly along and, at the same time, complimented her on her dancing skills. She was accustomed to being sought after—perhaps too accustomed, for she had grown weary of all the pretty compliments and accommodating young bucks who sought to please and win her. But as she gazed up into Burke Rocklin's eyes, she became aware that he looked down at her with a smile that was charming but somewhat removed—as though he was letting her know that while he was glad she was dancing with him, he would not have been terribly upset had she refused! Her eyes widened at the realization that here was a man with a definite streak of independence—and the challenge that this presented her drew her more than all the pretty prose others had written, paying homage to her eyes or her delicate beauty.

When the dance was over, he was halfway through a story that amused her, so she allowed him to take her to the refreshment table. Then, drinks in hand, they moved to the section of the dance floor set apart for talk.

They sat out two dances, so amused by his conversation, and the third was just beginning when they were interrupted.

"I believe this is our dance, Belinda?"

"Oh dear!" Belinda rose at once, flustered. "I'm so sorry, Chad! I forgot." She looked at the two men, then said, "Chad, this is—"

"I know Mr. Rocklin," Barnes broke in stiffly. His nod toward Burke was brief, and he held his hand out to Belinda. "Shall we dance?"

"Yes, of course." Belinda smiled at Burke. "I'll see you later, Mr. Rocklin."

"Yes, you will, Miss King!"

As Barnes swept Belinda King out onto the crowded floor, she said, "You were rude to the gentleman, Chad."

"Burke Rocklin is no gentleman, Belinda!"

"Oh? He *looks* like a gentleman."

It was at this point that Chad Barnes made his big mistake. If he had shrugged off her questions, Belinda probably would have let the matter alone, but Barnes was a demanding man, accustomed to having his own way. "Belinda," he said sternly, "he's no good! I forbid you to dance with him or to have anything to do with him!"

Demanding, Chad Barnes was. Prudent, he was not. Immediately he saw that he had made his demands at the wrong place, at the wrong time, and to the wrong woman. Belinda's face darkened with fury, and she stared at him, saying in a cold voice, "I beg your pardon, *Mister* Barnes, but I will see anyone I please! You're not my father to forbid me from doing anything!"

Quickly Chad tried to regain control of the situation. He softened his voice to sound concerned. "But—he's no good, Belinda! And you have your reputation to think of."

How many young girls have heard those words: "He's no good"? And how many have been swayed by them? Forbidden fruit always looks more delicious than the ordinary, easily available variety. Cap that with the suggestion that one's reputation could be so easily destroyed merely by association with one tall, handsome, undeniably charming man. . .

"I will thank you, sir, to tend to your own affairs," Belinda remarked stiffly as the dance came to an end. "And I will attend to mine." Her words were timed perfectly, so that she pulled away from Barnes just as the music ended, and no one around them was aware anything was amiss. No one except Barnes, Belinda. . .and Burke Rocklin, who had watched the whole thing with increasing amusement and satisfaction. He'd been almost sure Barnes would try something heavy-handed, such as forbidding the girl from seeing him. Burke smiled. If he had judged Belinda King correctly, he was certain that the one way to ensure she would pursue a man was to forbid her from being near him!

Apparently that was the case, for Belinda made it her business to dance with Burke Rocklin twice more, and when Barnes objected, she was so incensed that she agreed to go for a carriage ride with Rocklin the following afternoon.

"I don't know how you do it, Burke," Loren Delchamp sighed as the pair arrived at the Majestic after the ball. "But you never miss with a woman."

Burke knew that the campaign had just begun, but he was content with it so far. "Tell me about the girl's family, Loren," he insisted. Loren loved to talk, so for the next hour he told Burke all he knew and all he'd heard about Belinda's parents. When the two parted, Burke knew how to handle Mr. and Mrs. King.

Neither of them would welcome a penniless son-in-law, but there were ways to conceal that fact. The one thing in Burke's favor was that Cyrus King was a self-made man. He'd been a fatherless boy and had pulled himself up by his bootstraps. Now that he had money, he wanted prestige. Both he and his wife wanted a marriage for their daughter that would pull them up in the social world of Virginia.

And there was Burke's chance. The Rocklins were not the Lees or the Hugers, but they *were* high in that world. Still, other young men, such as Chad Barnes, had both a good family *and* money. Burke frowned momentarily.

My only chance is to dazzle the girl, he thought. *She's spoiled rotten, I'd suppose, and if she chooses me, she'll have me or drive her people crazy.*

He smiled as he crawled into bed. "Well then, Burke, old boy, your duty is clear. You've got to make her fall for you!"

By the end of the third week of his courtship, Burke knew that he was in danger of losing it all. He'd pursued Belinda using every trick he knew, and she was swayed by it. But he was coming perilously close to the end of his funds, and she still was not willing to choose him.

It all came down to the fact that he was not in uniform.

Burke saw at once that Belinda was caught in the war fever that held Richmond. Everything centered around the war, and any able-bodied young man not wearing a uniform was suspect.

Belinda had inquired more than once as to his plans regarding enlistment, but her comments had *assumed* that he would serve sooner or later. "Which branch do you think you'll choose, Burke?" That was her way of putting it, and Burke was too wily to say that he had no intention of serving in *any* branch! Rather, he would simply sidestep the issue.

Finally a crisis came when Chad Barnes enlisted as an officer in the cavalry. He made a splendid picture in his new uniform, and Burke could sense Belinda slipping away from him.

Got to find an answer or I'm a dead duck! he thought desperately. But though he searched for a way to gain the woman, nothing seemed to work.

He was almost ready to admit defeat on the day that he accompanied Belinda to a tea held at her parents' home. When he arrived, he saw nothing but uniforms and was filled with despair. He moved around the room with Belinda, feeling very much out of the whole thing.

Suddenly Belinda whispered, "Look, Burke! There's General Lee!"

Burke looked across the room and was favorably impressed with General Lee. A fine-looking man, Lee wore only the simplest of uniforms. Belinda drew Burke with her as she pressed closer to hear what the general was saying.

"Yes, there will be other battles, sir, but I trust we'll be able to move out and meet the enemy a little farther away from Richmond than in the last battle."

Someone asked Lee what he needed most in the way

of soldiers, and he mentioned several needs, then added thoughtfully, "It may sound strange, but in my thinking, we need engineers worse than anything else. Of course, being an engineer myself, I may be biased."

Burke was seized by a sudden thought, and he spoke up almost without thinking. "Pardon me, General Lee. My name is Burke Rocklin. I'm an engineer myself, but I wasn't aware that the need for one with my skills was so great."

At once Lee asked about his training, and after listening carefully as Burke mentioned his background, his eyes grew brighter. "Why, you could be a great help, Mr. Rocklin!" he exclaimed. "As a matter of fact, I could use you on my own staff for the next three or four months."

Instantly Burke said, "I'd count it an honor to serve under you, General Lee. Would it be possible for me to serve a short term that would give me time to prove myself?"

"Certainly, Mr. Rocklin," Lee said, nodding. He turned to the officer standing beside him. "Major Turner, would you go into this with Mr. Rocklin? I think we could brevet him as a first lieutenant for three months. By the end of that time, we'll know a little more about his place with our staff."

"Of course, General Lee."

"Thank you, General," Burke said. "I'll serve the Cause as best I can."

"No man can do more than that, Mr. Rocklin," Lee said with a smile.

Belinda was beside herself with happiness. When she got

Burke to one side, she suddenly reached up and kissed him. "Oh, I'm so proud of you, Burke! And to serve on General Lee's staff!"

"It comes as quite a shock," Burke said slowly. He'd jumped into the thing on impulse but now was wondering if he'd done the smart thing. Then he looked at Belinda beaming up at him and thought, *It's only for three months—and engineers don't fight in battles.* He held Belinda close and said, "A man needs a woman when he goes off to war, sweetheart."

"Does he, Burke?"

"Yes!" He kissed her then, and her response told him clearly that she was his. "I love you, Belinda," he whispered. "I want more than anything else to marry you. Will you have me?"

"Oh, Burke—yes! I'll marry you!" She kissed him again, then said, "Come on, we have to tell my parents!"

That evening when Burke went back to the hotel, he was an engaged man. Belinda's parents were taken aback, but agreed to an engagement. They had insisted that the couple wait until Burke's short-term service was up, and Burke had nodded solemnly. "Yes, sir, that would be wise, and I thank you for your counsel."

Loren Delchamp was filled with admiration. "By George, you pulled it off!" he exclaimed jubilantly. "I knew you could do it! Now your worries are over. Her father's got enough money to burn a wet mule!"

Loren's reaction came as no surprise to Burke. Clay's reaction, on the other hand, was not what he expected.

529

"You'll be miserable, Burke!" Clay said when Burke told him the news. "You don't love her, and she's only infatuated with you. That's not enough for a happy marriage."

"It's enough for me, Clay," Burke shot back angrily. "Mother and Father don't have any objections, so why should you?"

"They don't know why you're marrying the girl," Clay responded. "Tell them the truth and then see how they react."

Burke grew angrier, but Clay held his ground. "You're making a mistake about the marriage and about the army. I know you don't have any patriotism. You don't belong in either one!"

"I've got as much patriotism as you, brother!" Burke said at once. "You've said this war was a mistake from the first, yet here you stand, a lieutenant in the army."

"And I'll stay in the army until it's over," Clay said. "When I joined, I did so with every intention of serving to the best of my ability. You only joined to impress Belinda King. After your three months are done, you'll marry her and never serve another day."

The truth of this stung Burke, and he said angrily, "Well, you can keep out of it, Clay. I'm marrying Belinda, and that's final!"

Clay watched his brother storm away, wishing he could talk to his parents about the whole mess. But he knew he could not tell them any of this. Instead he shared it with Melora. "He's going to make the biggest mistake in his whole life," he said to her. She had come to spend the day with Rena, and Clay had taken her to one side to talk.

Melora listened quietly, then shook her head. "You can't do

any more, Clay," she said. "Burke has got his mind made up. But we must pray for him. A great deal can happen in three months. Let's join in prayer and ask God to keep Burke from going wrong."

"All right," Clay said heavily. He came up with a smile, saying, "I always bring all my troubles to you, Melora."

She reached up and touched his face gently, saying, "Who else would you take them to, Clay?"

CHAPTER 8

THE BATTLE

The first three weeks of Burke Rocklin's military career were splendid. He invested the last of his cash in a dashing uniform and escorted Belinda King to one social event after another. They became the most admired couple on the Richmond social scene, and despite the fact that Burke had never even smelled the smoke of battle, great things were predicted for him.

His military duties were not difficult. He reported each morning to headquarters, where he sat in on meetings with his commanding officer, Lieutenant Colonel Jeremy Gilmer, Lee's chief of engineers. They were a small group, and Burke found himself well able to keep up with the few tasks that came his way. Colonel Gilmer, a hard-driving man of forty, was amiable enough, but demanding. He spent some time with Burke, sounding out his ability, and seemed satisfied. "We'll have need of you in the field soon enough, Lieutenant Rocklin." He nodded. He'd kept Burke after the main meeting to go over some figures with him, and the two of them were now having coffee in the small office.

"When do you expect the action to begin, Colonel?" Burke asked. He had hopes that it might be several months, but was disappointed to hear Gilmer's reply.

"Oh, those Bluebellies haven't given up on taking Richmond," he said with a shrug. "Lincoln has gotten pretty sick of McClellan, so he's replaced him with another commander." He sipped his coffee and shook his head. "Fellow called John Pope. General Lee can't stand the man. As a matter of fact, he's the *only* man I've ever heard Lee speak against publicly."

"Why is that, I wonder?"

"Oh, the man's a braggart, and you know how modest General Lee is. Pope made a windbag of a speech to his troops when Lincoln appointed him. Said things like, 'I come to you from the West, where we have always seen the backs of our enemies, and I presume I've been sent here to teach you how to soldier.' You can imagine how *that* went over with his men! Then he told a reporter his headquarters would be in his saddle." Gilmer suddenly hooted with laughter, adding, "General Lee said the man didn't know his headquarters from his hindquarters."

Burke joined in the laughter, saying, "Man sounds like a fool."

"I hope so, Lieutenant," Gilmer said, nodding fervently. "We need every bit of help we can get, and it would be nice to have a fool in charge of the Army of the Potomac."

"Maybe they'll give up and go home," Burke mused. "They

lost a lot of men in the Seven Days'."

"So did we," Gilmer answered. "Half the houses in Richmond have wounded men in them from that battle. Can't build hospitals fast enough to take care of our own men, and we have a host of wounded Federals, as well." He drank the last of his coffee and shrugged. "I expect we'll be busy pretty soon. General Lee's plotting something. He won't let Pope come any closer to Richmond than he has to. So don't wander off too far. You may be needed pretty urgently."

"Yes, sir," Burke said with a nod. He saluted and left the office. All day he worked on maps that showed the area around Richmond; then at five o'clock he left and went to meet Belinda. The Kings lived in a large brick house on the outskirts of Richmond, and Belinda's father was at home when Burke arrived.

"Glad to see you, Burke," Cyrus King said, greeting him with a handshake. "Come in, come in, and let's have a talk while that girl of mine gets ready."

Burke followed King into an opulent library, where he was offered wine and a cigar, which he accepted. "Now tell me about what's going on in this war, my boy," the older man said, settling himself in a large chair as Burke spoke of the War Department's strategy. King listened avidly and was rather irritated when Belinda entered. "I never have any time with this young man," he grumbled. "Where are you hauling him off to now?"

"We're going to an engagement party, Father," Belinda smiled. She was wearing a beautiful dress made of pink silk with light blue ribbons on the bodice. Her fine blond hair hung down over her shoulders, and she looked very pretty indeed. "It's Mary Lou Allen and Luke Hoakly. We'll be late, I think."

"You always are," her father grumbled as she kissed him. "Come and see me sometime when we can talk longer, Burke."

"Yes, sir, I'll do that."

When they were in the carriage, Burke said thoughtfully, "I like your father very much, and your mother, as well."

"I'm glad, Burke," Belinda said with a smile. "They're very fond of you."

"Funny, I've heard so many stories about in-laws that I've always dreaded the thought of them." He put his arm around her and drew her close. "Now I'm getting the most beautiful girl in the world and a set of nice in-laws in the bargain!" He kissed her, and she clung to him. "I wish we could get married now, before I have to leave," he whispered. She was a beautiful girl, and though she was spoiled, Burke was surprised to realize that he'd become fond of her. He wanted nothing to go wrong with his plans and wished she'd agree to marry him at once.

"No, we can't do that, much as I'd like to, Burke," Belinda answered. "Three months isn't too long to wait, and it's all my parents asked of you."

"I know, but I love you so much it's hard to wait!"

Burke had told other women he loved them, but not once had it been the truth. Nor was it the truth this time. Now as the carriage moved down the streets and he held Belinda tightly in his arms, he wondered about himself. *Have I become an utter scoundrel? This girl loves me—or thinks she does. But I don't love her, probably never will love any woman.* He glanced at her and felt a sudden stab of remorse. *She'll never have to know I don't really love her. I'm a pretty good actor. Still, she's not getting much in the way of a husband. I guess some men just aren't capable of real love—and I'm one of those unlucky fellows!*

They arrived at the house, went inside, and enjoyed the party. The house was filled with young people, soldiers, and pretty girls. The only distraction was a clash Burke had with Chad Barnes. It came late in the evening, just as Burke and Belinda were preparing to leave, and it caught them both off guard.

Earlier, Barnes had come across the floor to confront the pair, and it was obvious that he was angry. He tried to conceal it, but Burke had learned enough about men to recognize the small signs. *He's spoiling for trouble*, Burke thought and was on his guard instantly.

Barnes was a big man, as tall as Burke and much heavier. He had a blunt, ruddy face and a pair of light blue eyes that dominated his face. Almost at once he began making remarks that verged on insult, but Burke was determined to ignore the man. He was rather proud of himself and said so to Belinda when he got her alone.

"Barnes is looking for trouble, but I've managed to keep my temper." He grinned at her and nodded. "I must be getting senile. When I was younger, I'd have called him out for less than he's done tonight."

"Oh, don't do that, Burke!" Belinda's eyes widened with

alarm, and she put her hand on his chest with an imploring gesture. "Don't fight with him!"

"All right, but I think we'd better leave early. I don't need to be tempted any more than I have been."

Burke managed to stay away from Barnes for the rest of the evening, and it was only when he was helping Belinda on with her coat that the trouble came. He felt a hand on his shoulder and was abruptly turned around. His temper flared when he saw that it was Barnes, and he said, "Keep your hands off me, Barnes!"

"You're touchy, aren't you, Rocklin?" Barnes's ruddy face was flushed with drink, and he sneered at Burke. "You might have Belinda fooled, but you're not fooling me!"

"Chad, you're drunk!" Belinda whispered. "Come on, Burke—"

But Barnes reached out and grabbed Burke's arm. "Think I don't know what you're up to? You're a woman chaser, Rocklin. Always were!" Barnes looked around at the faces of the guests and lifted his voice: "Why, when he was after Maureen Bailey—"

A sudden crack across the face cut off Barnes's words, and he stood there gaping with shock at Burke, who said, "You're no gentleman, Barnes. I won't have you mention a lady's name in public."

A shocked silence fell on the room, and Barnes's face drained. He touched his cheek, then said in a voice filled with fury, "My friends will call on you, Rocklin!"

Burke said clearly, "You know army regulations forbid dueling, Barnes. Your friends can save themselves the trouble."

"Coward!"

"You know my record better than that." Burke would have turned and escorted Belinda from the room, but at that moment Barnes completely lost control. He drew back his massive fist and threw a tremendous blow at Burke's head.

Burke had seen the flash of movement and drew back just in time to avoid the blow. Off balance, Barnes fell against his opponent, but Burke gave him a hard push, saying, "You're drunk, Barnes! Go home and sleep it off."

The push sent Barnes reeling back, but when he caught his balance, his eyes burned with drunken rage. "If you won't fight with a gun, you'll fight with your fists!"

Several men came at once, trying to pull Barnes away, but he shook them off. "There's no regulation about a fistfight, Rocklin. Now come outside—or are you yellow clear through?"

Burke stared at the big man and knew there was no way he was going to get out of a fight. If he refused, he'd be branded a coward by everybody in Richmond. He said tersely, "If you have to have a fight, Barnes, I'll give you one."

"Come outside!" Barnes cried out. "I'm going to open you up and let the yellow run out so everyone can see what you are!"

Burke turned to Belinda. "You know this isn't of my doing, but I'll have to fight him."

"Oh, Burke! Be careful!" Belinda cried. "He's so strong!" But Rocklin noted that her eyes were glistening with the thrill of the affair, and he knew that she was not entirely sorry to be fought over. Struggling to hide his disgust, he turned and moved away from her.

Women are all alike—wanting men to fight over them like dogs!

Barnes was waiting for him in a courtyard, the yellow light of the lanterns gleaming in his eyes. He stripped off his coat and threw it to the ground. As soon as Burke had done the same, he uttered a hoarse curse and threw himself across the flagstones.

Burke caught the full fury of the rush and was driven back against some of the men who'd made a circle around the pair. He had misjudged the speed of the big man and took several painful blows to the chest and stomach as a result. Gasping with pain, he twisted free and stepped around so that he was away from Barnes.

Got to stay away from him and wear him down, then take him out bit by bit. He's too strong for me to fight head-on!

Barnes came at him again, but this time Burke sidestepped and, as the big man stumbled, drove two hard blows to his face. The blows made a sharp, meaty sound, and a mutter went up from the circle of men. But if the blows hurt Barnes, he didn't show it. Blood ran down from the corner of his mouth and he came in more slowly, but he was still dangerous. He had big legs and arms and hulking shoulders. His eyes glittered as he followed Burke over the rough flagstones. "Stand still and fight!" he grated, then without warning threw himself forward, aiming a tremendous blow at Burke's face.

If it had landed, Burke would have had his face smashed, but he managed to parry with his left so that his opponent's fist only grazed his temple. There was nothing to do then but survive the blows that Barnes rained on him, and Burke took most of them on his forearms and his shoulders. They hurt and he knew he'd be black-and-blue, but he rode out the storm grimly, waiting his chance.

The eyes of the spectators glittered by the light of the lanterns. They were like wolves gathered in a circle to watch a fight to the death, and the same faces that had seemed so cultured in the drawing room a few moments earlier were now cruel and predatory, for the men seemed to have reverted to some ancient strain of blood that craved action and violence.

Burke was bleeding now, his face cut by the massive blows of Barnes's fists. His ribs ached, and he suspected that one of them might be cracked. Most of the men in the circle, he realized dimly, thought he was whipped. But he had forced himself to wait and watch—and now he saw what he'd been waiting for: a slowness in the big man's movements and a rasp in his breathing.

Burke waited one more second as Barnes dropped his heavy arms and gasped for breath; then he moved. He shot forward and drove a thundering right into the mouth of the winded man, driving him backward. Following him fiercely, Burke hit his enemy in the pit of the stomach with as hard a punch as he'd ever thrown. The blow struck Barnes right below that spot where the nerves are bunched, just below the rib cage—and that punch proved a disaster for the big man!

His arms dropped and his eyes glazed. Burke knew what that was like, for he'd been stopped in the same fashion. A hard blow in that spot robs a man of everything—he can't breath or move or think, but is totally helpless.

With almost any other man, Burke would have called off the fight, but he knew with Barnes that doing so could be fatal. So he moved ahead, determined to put Barnes down, which he managed to do only after striking him in the jaw repeatedly. The man sank to the flagstones, his mouth open, his arms pawing helplessly. He tried to get up, but his legs didn't seem to support him.

"That's enough—!" Burke said, grabbing for breath. "Stay away from me, Barnes, or you'll get worse!" He walked over to pick up his coat, and as he left, he felt the hands of the men on his shoulders and heard their voices congratulating him. *If Barnes had won, they'd be saying the same things to him,* he thought bitterly. He found Belinda waiting and knew she'd watched from the window. "Come on, let's go," he said almost harshly.

When they were in the carriage, she leaned toward him and touched his wounded face. "Oh, my dear, he hurt you!"

Burke let her murmur her little endearments but was aware that she was not nearly so upset as she pretended. *She knows this will be all over Richmond,* he thought wearily. *Well, let her have her little triumph. I guess she's giving me enough to make up for a few bruises!*

❧

Burke was correct in assuming that the fight would furnish delectable fare for the gossip mills of Richmond. He was disgusted

541

with himself and with Barnes, but he realized it added glitter to his "reputation" and so made no protests.

His fellow officers ragged him a little but were mostly supportive. Colonel Gilmer, however, said sourly, "Better save some of that energy for *real* fighting, Lieutenant."

"It wasn't of my choosing, sir," Burke protested.

"Well, this fight that's coming up isn't of *my* choosing," Gilmer shot back. "If you've got time to roll around in a brawl, I guess you don't have enough work to do. I'll see to it that you have."

The colonel was faithful to his word, and for the next few days Burke was forced to stay late. Belinda pouted, but Burke pointed out that it was the price he had to pay for fighting over her. Belinda found this a satisfactory reason and said, "Well, you must get free next Wednesday. We've got an invitation to dine at the Chesnuts, and President and Mrs. Davis will be there!"

Burke never made it to that engagement. He was greeted on Wednesday morning by Colonel Gilmer, who said, "Pack your gear, Lieutenant. We're moving out."

Burke stared at him blankly for one instant, then inquired, "Where will we be going, sir?"

"You'll know when we get there!" Gilmer snapped. Then he mitigated his reply. "Didn't mean to bite your head off, Rocklin, but we've got to move fast. All I can say now is that General Lee's going to meet John Pope, and we've got to do some engineering for him in a hurry!"

"Will I have time to say any farewells, Colonel?"

"We're leaving in two hours, but you'll need that time to get your gear and help us load the equipment. Write your apologies and send a runner."

Hastily Burke wrote notes to Belinda and to his parents, explaining his sudden departure. The one to Belinda he dispatched by a corporal, and the one to his parents he was able to deliver himself into Clay's hands.

He found his older brother drilling his platoon, and after calling him to one side, he said, "I've got orders to leave right away. Will you see that Father gets this note?"

Clay took the envelope but said, "I'll have to send it out, Burke. We're moving out ourselves."

"What's happening, Clay?"

"Going to whip Johnnie Pope, I guess." Clay studied his younger brother, then said thoughtfully, "We've had differences, Burke, but let's not be angry with each other now."

Burke was surprised but glad. "Sure, Clay!" He clapped his hand on Clay's shoulder, saying, "We Black Rocklins have to stick together."

"That's right." Clay smiled. "Keep your head down, you hear?"

"Can't shoot a man who's born to hang, can they, now?" Burke grinned and then left, saying only, "After this is over, we'll have some time to go hunting, okay?"

"God go with you, Burke," Clay muttered under his breath as he watched Burke's tall form march away. Then he turned to his men, calling out, "All right, men, let's sharpen those lines!"

Waco Smith came to Clay later, after drill was over, and asked, "We goin' to see the Bluebellies, Lieutenant?" Smith, a Texan who'd been with Clay at Bull Run, still carried a .44 in a holster on his hip, the same one he carried when he'd been a Texas Ranger. He was a lean man with light green eyes and sharp features. He was utterly dependable and fearless to a fault.

"I think that sums up our situation, Sergeant," Clay said with a nod. "The men ready?"

"Got to be." Waco bit off a huge bite of tobacco, tucked it into his cheek, then nodded. "You watch out for yourself, Clay," he warned, forgetting protocol for a moment. "I don't want to have to go to all the trouble of breaking in a new lieutenant."

"I'll do my best, Waco. And you show a little sense. Don't try to whip the Yankees all by yourself like you did at Malvern Hill!" Clay's eyes were moody, and he added with a sad tone, "This is going to be a long war, so take care of yourself." Waco winked at him and walked away, but both of them were aware that there was no way for a man to "take care of himself" when the bullets started flying.

The only people who have a very clear idea of what a battle is like are generals. Robert E. Lee and Stonewall Jackson understood the entire scope of what was taking place on August 29, 1862, at the Battle of Second Manassas, but infantrymen knew only their small portion of it.

Lee and Jackson planned a masterful campaign, one of the

most daring in U.S. military history. Faced with superior numbers, Lee did an astonishing thing: He divided his small army into *two smaller* armies! This violated every rule of tactics in every military history book, but Robert E. Lee was an inveterate gambler.

Acting on instinct, Lee sent Stonewall Jackson around Pope's army, while he himself stayed in place and convinced the nervous Pope that the Confederate commander had his whole force with him. It would not have worked if Lee had not had Jackson, for no other general on either side could have accomplished such a march.

When Jackson was in place, he struck Pope's forces from the rear—and the Federal commander went to pieces. He lost his head, and he lost the Battle of Second Manassas.

But all of this was unknown to most of the soldiers who fought the battle. They only were aware of their little area and fought and died for a small field, never knowing why it was so important to have the field.

Clay's company fought its way across a small creek and held a much larger Union force to a standstill. And while neither Clay nor his men knew it, their holding action had been the means for giving Jackson time to get into position to strike Pope's army. Clay lost twelve men and grieved over them as if they were his own sons. He was relieved to see that Lowell and Dent came through safely, but was worried about Burke. He knew the engineers had been sent to bridge a small river and prayed that Burke had not been hurt.

But even as Clay prayed, Burke lay unconscious. He and his fellow engineers had been caught up in an unexpected skirmish over the bridge. Two full regiments of Federals moved on the bridges, and Lee sent some of his best troops to stop the Northern troops from advancing. It had been one of those terrible battles, such as Shiloh, where ground was taken, lost, and taken again. Every man in a Confederate uniform was pressed into service, including cooks and engineers. Burke found himself lying on the ground, firing a musket at the men in the long blue lines who charged again and again.

Finally the colonel came down the line, screaming, "Get ready! We're going to drive 'em back! Get ready to charge!"

Burke's mouth was dry as he came to his feet. He had a musket with a bayonet fixed, and when the gray line moved forward, he found himself screaming with the rest. He had only one thought: to get to the line of trees where musket fire winked like evil red eyes.

But he never made it.

The Federals had gotten some artillery in place, and the shells cut the advancing Confederate line to pieces. Those who lived through the artillery fire were met by yelling Yankees who emerged from the trees in large numbers.

Burke shot one soldier, noting that he was no more than sixteen years old. He felt a pang of grief, then was suddenly trapped in a fierce melee and began clubbing with his musket as the blue-clad men rushed toward the position. He was striking furiously when a thunderous sound came from overhead, and

Burke Rocklin's world suddenly exploded into a million points of pain—and a fathomless darkness.

The shell that burst over Burke Rocklin and the men around him killed dozens of men and wounded many others. Reb and Yank lay intermingled, most of them killed instantly. The Confederates retreated, but some of them stopped beside the tangled bodies long enough to rob the dead. One of them bent over a still form and, seeing the bloody face, assumed he was dead. He looked at his own bare feet, then pulled off the injured man's boots. Then he noted the fancy gold ring—the Rocklin family ring—and tugged at it until it came off. Slipping the ring on his own finger, the man looked fearfully around, then quickly stripped the uniform from the inert body, whispering, "I can sell this back in Richmond. Be worth a heap of money!"

But the scavenger never made it to Richmond. He made it only as far as the point where a shell from one of the Union batteries caught him. It destroyed his torso, mangling his upper body and head beyond recognition. The sergeant who led the burial squad found the tattered coat of Burke Rocklin still clutched in the corpse's hand. After looking at the papers inside one of the coat pockets, he said, "We'll take this one back with us. There's a lieutenant named Rocklin in the Richmond Grays."

After the battle, Dent and Clay came to identify the body. Both of them were sick when they saw the mangled body. Clay stooped and took the ring from the dead man's finger.

"Sergeant, I want to send my brother back to Richmond. Is there a coffin available?"

"Pine one, sir."

"Put him in it. I'll see to the transportation," Dent said. He shook his head, adding, "This will just about kill the folks."

Clay didn't even have the words to answer. He turned away, sick at heart, blaming himself for not having been more of a brother to Burke.

"I'll see if the colonel will let me go home, if it's all right with you, Dent."

"Of course. I wish I could go, too."

Two days later Clay stood at his brother's graveside. The service had been simple and brief. From where he stood, Clay could see the raw earth still mounded on Ellen's grave. He stood there, tears in his eyes, and then turned away to comfort his parents, who had taken the news of Burke's death very badly.

Had he been able, Burke would have done all he could to let his family know he was not in the coffin that was lowered into the earth. But he was far from able. He was unconscious, lying on a bed in a military hospital. . .in Washington.

When he'd been found in the midst of the Union dead, the stretcher-bearers had assumed that he was a Union soldier. The Confederates commonly robbed the dead for boots and clothing, so the stretcher-bearer had said, "This one's alive, but the Rebs stripped him. Put one of them jackets on him, Maxie. If we get him to field hospital, I reckon he won't die."

The man had been correct in his reckoning. Burke Rocklin had not died. The doctors had removed the shrapnel from his neck and back, had sewed up the cuts on his face, and then had sent him in an ambulance train that was headed back to Washington. But though he was alive, he did not regain consciousness. Even when he received better care and improved physically, he lay as still as a dead man.

One of the doctors said, "Must be ruined in the head. Physically he's healing, but his mind is gone. May as well put him in Ward K."

Ward K, where Burke currently lay, was the ward for men who did nothing but stare at the walls. Like zombies, they ate and moved, but they never spoke. None of the doctors knew what to do for these men. Usually, one by one, they were eventually sent back to their homes, most of them to live the rest of their lives in attics or a spare bedroom, kept out of sight—buried, though not in the ground.

"Poor man!" One of the women who came to visit at the hospital stopped in at Ward K and looked down at Burke. Pity was in her eyes as she reached down and touched his pale, still face.

Her voice shaking with unshed tears for all she had seen, she whispered what many had thought but had not allowed themselves to say: "It would have been a mercy if he'd died. Anything is better than this!"

PART TWO

The Patient and the Nurse

CHAPTER 9

GRACE COMES TO WASHINGTON

From the time Burke fell on the battlefield, he knew nothing, which perhaps was a blessing!

The process of transporting sick and wounded men from the field of Manassas to the hospitals in Washington was as much a torture as anything that had ever taken place in the dungeon of a medieval castle. Wounded soldiers generally reached the haven only after a long delirium of agony and neglect. Most bore the gashes of canister or grape, the rent of shell splinters, or the neat hole that marked the entrance of the shattering minié ball. Frequently soldiers underwent crude amputations at the front, where field surgeons ruthlessly lopped off arms and legs, which they tossed into piles that sometimes rose man-high about the bloody operation tables.

Hungry, thirsty, and untended, the wounded at last reached a place where they were fed and washed and cared for. But the trip to Washington by road was a nightmare! While ambulances were meant to be a humane innovation, the frail two-wheeled vehicles used to transport injured soldiers tended to crack at the first strain, and their rocking motion was unbearable to suffering men. The cumbersome four-wheeled ambulances, which required four horses to pull them, were more comfortable, but for men with fresh amputations, with faces shot away, or with lead in breast or belly, being jostled, bumped, and jolted over rutted Virginia roads was excruciating.

The journey by rail was shorter, but men were closely packed on the floors, either on straw or on bare boards. Or, if they were on the flatcars, they were exposed to the blazing sun or to wind and rain.

Some of the wounded were transported by ship, but there were no lights, no figures at the rails, no stir of notice or greeting when they arrived. The injured men lay on the decks, in cabins and the saloons, or even on the stairs and gangway. Men screamed or moaned as they were unloaded, and the ghost ship then moved on to make way for another similarly loaded vessel.

By the autumn of 1862, Washington had been transformed into the vast base hospital of the Army of the Potomac. Clusters of white buildings and tents had changed the aspect of the city and its surrounding hills. Practically every construction job marked a huge new hospital. The rectangular pavilions of the new Judiciary Square Hospital replaced the old E Street Infirmary. Stanton Hospital was another modern institution, and opposite it, on Minnesota Row, the former mansions of

Douglas, Breckinridge, and Rice now constituted Douglas Hospital. Lincoln and Emory hospitals were being constructed on the plain to the east of the Capitol. Near the Smithsonian, beside the open sewer of the canal, lay the clean parallel sheds of the great Armory Square Hospital. On the distant heights, long one-story buildings, lavishly whitewashed and encircled by huts and tents, seemed to bloom like monstrous flowers in the soft Washington light.

On Independence Day of that year, the church bells had not been rung because of the suffering men who lay below them. The seizure of the churches had begun in June, and soon congregations of Union sympathizers were vying with one another in an effort to offer their buildings to the War Department. Carpets, cushions, and hymnbooks were packed away. Carpenters covered the pews with scantling, laid floors on top, and stowed pulpits and other furniture underneath. Wagonloads of furniture, drugs, and utensils were delivered, and the flag of the Union was run up as wardmasters, nurses, orderlies, cooks, and stewards arrived. Soon ambulances were stopping at the church doors, followed, last of all, by the surgeons with their knives and saws and dirty little sponges.

In the patent office, thousands of beds were installed, and at night, like some new exhibit of ghastliness, waxy faces lay in rows between the shining glass cabinets filled with curiosities, foreign presents, and models of inventions. The nurses' heels clicked on the marble floor, and over all lay the heavy smell of putrefaction and death.

A stranger wandering about the city at this time might think he could find his way by using the low, pale masses of hospitals as landmarks—but many hospitals could only be recognized upon closer inspection. Sick and wounded men lay in hotels and warehouses, in schools and seminaries, in private houses, and in the lodges of fraternal orders.

Yet when the wounded from Pope's campaign began to arrive, it was discovered all too quickly that there still was not room enough to accommodate the injured. At last the Capitol itself was temporarily requisitioned, and two thousand cots were placed in the halls of the House and Senate, in the corridors, and in the Rotunda.

Sad to say, even after the wounded reached the army hospitals, they still were miserable. The unsuitability of churches and public buildings as hospitals was evident, but renovated barracks were even worse. In addition to filthy grounds, they were dark and badly ventilated, and the administration of the hospitals left much to be desired; corrupt cooks and stewards, inexperienced nurses, and careless and incompetent surgeons were all too common.

It was into this setting of misery, pain, and death that Grace Swenson was plunged as she stepped off her train holding a small suitcase and filled with both determination and trepidation. She stood there in the center of the rushing masses of people, jostled by a host of soldiers and civilians, confused and uncertain. Making her way to the ticket counter, she asked the round-faced agent, "Please, can thee tell me how to get to the hospital?"

"Which one?"

"Why—any of them, I suppose," Grace answered. "I've come to help nurse the soldiers."

The agent peered at her intently, then scratched his balding dome. "Well, you'd better go to the War Department, I reckon. They'll put you right, miss." He motioned vaguely toward the large double doors to his left. "Get a carriage outside them doors and tell the driver to take you to the War Department."

"Thank you."

Grace followed his instructions, finding a number of cabs vying for her business. "Goin' downtown, missus?" a tall, rawboned cabbie asked, maneuvering his competitors deftly aside.

"I need to go to the War Department."

"Ah, step right in, missus! Have you there in two shakes of a duck's tail!"

Grace settled herself in the carriage, and as the cab rattled over the cobblestone streets, she stared at the city of Washington. The main thoroughfare of the city was four miles long and 160 feet wide. The Capitol, with its unfinished dome topped by a huge crane and encircled by scaffolding, blocked the straight line of Pennsylvania Avenue, which led eastward from the expanding Treasury Building and the Executive Mansion, as the White House was called.

Within minutes, a terrible odor hit her like a blow, and she finally asked the driver, "What's that awful smell?"

"Oh, that's the canal, missus." He shrugged. Glancing at the huge ditch that paralleled the road, she saw that it was a fetid bayou filled with floating dead cats and all kinds of putridity. It literally reeked with pestilential odors that nearly gagged Grace! *We do better than this in Pennsylvania,* she thought grimly.

Finally the driver pulled the taxi to a stop and nodded toward a huge building to his right. "That's the War Department, missus."

Grace descended and paid her fare, then turned and walked toward the building. Stepping inside, she found it swarming with officers of all grades. She timidly asked for the medical department, and after being sent to several wrong offices, she finally found a short major with a kindly face who listened carefully to her story.

"It's Miss Dix you'll want to see, miss."

"Miss Dix?"

"Yes, ma'am. Miss Dorothea L. Dix, to be exact." A humorous light touched the man's gray eyes, and he added quickly, "And I'd be certain to stress the word *Miss* if I were you. She's a maiden lady and doesn't like to be taken for a married woman."

"I'll be careful, Major," Grace answered. "But who *is* she exactly?"

"Her title is 'Superintendent of Women Nurses,'" he answered, leaning back in his chair. "She's rather famous in her home state of Massachusetts for her public work. She's devoted her life to aiding paupers, prisoners, and lunatics. Been able to do a lot about the terrible conditions in almshouses and jails and insane asylums. Last June she was appointed to take over the women who are coming to nurse the wounded. And she's done a fine job, too! Let me have my corporal take you to her. Her office isn't in this building."

He called a lanky corporal, instructed him to take Grace to Miss Dix's office, then wished her luck. "Thank you, Major." Grace smiled. "Thee has been very kind."

"I wish you luck, Miss Swenson, but I doubt you'll be working for Miss Dix."

Grace was startled. "But—why not?"

The major hesitated, then said, "Well, to be frank, you're just too attractive." Seeing her blink of surprise, he explained, "Miss Dix considers all persons under thirty disqualified for nursing. A friend of mine who works in her department said that an applicant must be plain almost to repulsion in dress. I think Miss Dix doesn't want attractive women because they might cause trouble with the men."

Grace was too surprised to answer for a moment, then took heart. "I'll still see her, Major. Thank thee for the warning."

She left the building, and the corporal took her to a smaller edifice where a private informed her that Miss Dix's offices were on the second floor. Climbing the stairs, she entered the office with the sign outside that read MISS DOROTHEA L. DIX, SUPERINTENDENT.

Stepping inside, she found an older woman sitting at a desk writing in a ledger. "I'd like to see Miss Dix, please," Grace said.

The woman looked up and studied her. "May I ask the nature of your business?"

"I've come to help nurse the soldiers."

The woman stared at her, then shrugged. "I'll see if Miss Dix has time to see you." She rose and disappeared into the inner office. When she came out, she said curtly, "You may go in."

"Thank you."

When Grace was inside, she closed the door and walked across the room to stand in front of the desk where a woman looked up at her. "What is your name?" she asked at once.

"Grace Swenson, Miss Dix."

Miss Dix put down her pen and stood to her feet. She was a small woman with a knot of hair that seemed too heavy for the gentle head set on a long neck. Her mouth and her chin were firm, and her blue-gray eyes were sharp. "I understand you want to join the nursing staff."

"Yes, Miss Dix."

"Why?"

The abrupt monosyllable took Grace off guard. She stared at the smaller woman and tried to explain. "I—I believe the Lord has told me to do this work," she finally said simply.

A curious light appeared in the eyes of Miss Dix. "What church do you attend?" she asked.

"I am a Friend."

"A Quaker?"

"Yes, people call us that."

Miss Dix seemed interested. She examined Grace more carefully, then said, "I don't accept young handsome women in my service, Miss Swenson. It's too distracting for the men."

Grace was prepared for this, for she had been thinking how she might answer it. "I may be young, Miss Dix, but I'm not considered handsome. I have sisters who are very attractive, so I know that I'm quite plain."

Miss Dix cocked her head to one side, caught by Grace's words. She was favorably impressed by the young woman but was careful not to let that show in her expression. "Just as well that you think so," she said quietly. She fell silent, then said, "Sit down, Miss Swenson." When they were both seated, she said, "Tell me about yourself."

Grace spoke quickly, giving Miss Dix her background. When she was finished, the older woman asked directly, "Why aren't you married?"

"I—was asked only once, Miss Dix. It didn't work out." She looked directly in the superintendent's eyes, adding, "I don't think I shall ever marry."

Miss Dix nodded, considering her words.

Though Dorothea Dix was sixty years old, there was something formidable in this fragile and consecrated woman. In a time when men were unaccustomed to having their work interfered with by women, she had come sweeping through the wards like an avenging angel and was soon detested by the medical profession. Under the pressure of her multifarious and unsystematized duties, she grew overwrought, lost her self-control, and involved herself in quarrels. Though she often was in the right, she too rarely showed the graces of tolerance and tact, which won her many opponents and few supporters.

Despite all this, she had brought cleanliness and order to the wards, which had too long been chaotic and filthy. She would stay at her post without a leave of absence throughout the entire war—small and frail but as unmovable as the Rock of Gibraltar!

"Miss Swenson," she finally said slowly. "I need nurses badly—but I screen applicants very strictly. And I may as well say that my first impulse is to refuse you."

"Oh, Miss Dix!" Grace spoke up quickly, anxiety in her eyes. "Please—give me a chance! I'm strong and willing to work. I nursed my father for years, and I know that God wants me to do this."

As the young woman spoke, Miss Dix listened carefully. In her determination to do everything herself, she had eventually buried herself in a maze of details—which was wearing her down terribly. Her authority was ill defined and conflicted with that of the surgeons, most of whom didn't approve of her or her female nurses. She feared that putting this young woman to work—who *was* attractive, despite her modesty!—could create problems in her department.

Grace, aware of Miss Dix's hesitation, finally said, "Miss Dix, I'd like to be as effective as I can, and serving under thee would be best. But if thee doesn't want me, I'll find someplace else to serve. Even if it's for only one man in a private home."

Miss Dix quickly made her decision. "Miss Swenson, I'm going to admit you to my staff on a trial basis. If you would like to come for two weeks, we'll see how it works out. At the end of that time, I'll make a final decision. That's the best I can do at this time."

"Oh, I thank thee, Miss Dix!" A radiant glow touched Grace's cheeks, and she smiled shyly. "I'll do my very best for thee and for the patients."

"I'm sure you will, Miss Swenson." Miss Dix rose and came to offer her hand. "Now I'm going to put you under our sternest supervisor, Miss Agnes Dalton." A slight smile came to her lips, and she added, "You may not last the full two weeks. Miss Dalton is a hard worker and very demanding of the nurses who serve under her. Where do you live?"

"I don't have a place, Miss Dix. I just got off the train and came straight here."

"You may have trouble finding a place. The city is packed."

"God will help me."

"I trust He will. Be at the Armory Square Hospital at seven in the morning. I'll introduce you to Miss Dalton."

"I'll be there, Miss Dix!"

Grace left the building happy, feeling as though a burden had lifted. She was going to be a nurse! As she walked along the paths, she thanked God for His provision, then turned her thoughts to finding a place to stay.

This proved to be more of a problem than she had expected, for Miss Dix had been right. Washington was packed with soldiers, government clerks, families of wounded men. Grace trudged from one rooming house to another, finding nothing.

Finally it was a cabdriver who proved to be her salvation.

He was an older man, in his late sixties with white hair and arthritic fingers—but his blue eyes were sharp, and after he had taken her to three boardinghouses, he spoke up. "Miss, it's a bad time to be looking for a room."

"Yes, I can see that." Grace looked at him suddenly, asking, "Does thee know anyplace where I might stay?"

"Well now, I know of a place. But it's not very fine."

"Oh, I'm not looking for a fine place!"

"Ah? Well now, I know of a widow woman named Mrs. Johnson. She lost her husband at Bull Run. Has two children and is havin' a hard time of it. If you'd think of sharing a room with the daughter—?"

"Oh yes, that would be fine! Could we go there now?"

"Yes, miss. My name is Ryan Callihan. And what might you be called?"

"I'm Grace Swenson, and I've just come from Pennsylvania to be a nurse."

By the time Callihan had pulled up in front of a tiny frame house on the outskirts of Washington, he'd gotten most of Grace's story. Stepping down, he tied the horses, then said, "Come along, and we'll see."

Mrs. Ida Johnson was a large woman of forty. She had dark red hair and still bore traces of an earlier beauty, but sadness had marked her. "Why, I don't know, Miss Swenson," she said slowly after the cabdriver had told her their mission. "I could use the money, but I've never had a boarder."

"I need a place very badly, Mrs. Johnson," Grace said quickly.

"I don't think I'd be here much. I suspect I'll be working long hours. And I'd be willing to pay whatever thee might ask."

"Well. . .you'd have to share a room with my daughter, Lettie."

"I'm sure we'd get along. I have four younger sisters," she said with a smile. "I get along well with young girls."

"I suppose we can try it out," Mrs. Johnson said.

"Now that's fine!" Callihan smiled. "Let me get your bag." When he brought it in, he said, "It's a long drive to the hospital. I'll be goin' into town at six ever' mornin', Miss Grace. I live right down the way. You be ready and I'll pick you up."

"God reward thee, Mr. Callihan," Grace said at once. She smiled and put out her hand. When he took it, she said, "I've heard of people who were helped by angels unawares. Thee wouldn't be one of those by any chance?"

Callihan stared at her, rather shocked. Finally a smile came to his lips, and he shook his head. "I've been called lots of things, Miss Grace, but nobody never called me an angel before!" He laughed silently, turning at the door to say, "Six sharp, Miss Grace."

"I'll be waiting, Mr. Callihan."

"Come this way and I'll show you the room, Miss Swenson." Grace followed Mrs. Johnson to the small bedroom, which contained one bed and a smattering of furniture. Mrs. Johnson left her, and she lay down for half an hour, tired from her trip and the tension. She awakened when she heard the door close. Sitting up, she saw a young girl staring at her and came to her feet. "I'm Grace Swenson. And I suppose thy name is Lettie?"

"Yes." Lettie Johnson was sixteen years old and very shy. She was not a pretty girl, but her brown hair was well cared for and her blue dress was in style.

Grace smiled gently at the girl. "Does thee mind too much, Lettie, sharing thy room with me?"

Lettie shook her head. "I don't mind," she said, then added, "I work, so I'm not here much anyway."

"Where does thee work, Lettie?"

By the time Mrs. Johnson called that supper was ready, Grace and Lettie were well acquainted. Grace's long years with younger sisters made this easy for her, and Lettie was charmed by the idea of having a nurse for a roommate.

When they went to the small dining room, Mrs. Johnson said, "Miss Swenson, this is my son, William."

Grace smiled at the ten-year-old, who had his mother's red hair and many freckles. "I'm glad to meet thee, William."

The boy stared at her curiously but only nodded. When his mother set the last bowl of food on the table and sat down, she looked nervously toward Grace. "We don't ask a blessing, but I suppose you do?"

"I'd like to." Grace smiled, then asked a simple blessing. As she began to eat hungrily, she found the food was good—well prepared and tasty—and she complimented Mrs. Johnson. "Thee is a fine cook!"

The two women began to talk about cooking, and finally William demanded, "Why do you talk funny?"

"William!" Lettie said sharply. "Don't be so impolite!"

Grace laughed aloud, saying, "It's all right, Lettie. I'm used to it." She turned to the boy, saying, "I'm what people call a Quaker, William. Our people have ways that are different. We use *thee* and *thy* because that's what the Bible uses." Grace felt it wise to give a few details about the Friends to her new acquaintances.

When she was finished, Mrs. Johnson asked, "You don't believe in war?"

"No. We feel it's wrong to kill."

"Well, it ain't wrong to kill the derned ol' Rebels!" Willie said angrily. "They killed my pa, and when I get big enough, I'm goin' to be a soldier! Then I'll show 'em!"

Mrs. Johnson said sharply, "William, be quiet!"

"Well, I am!"

The room was quiet, and Grace finally said, "I don't know much about the war. God told me to come and take care of the wounded soldiers. That's a good thing to do, doesn't thee think so, William?"

The boy watched her stubbornly. "If they're our soldiers— but not the Rebels!"

Grace was shocked at the hatred in the boy's face, but she could see that it was no time to discuss the matter. "Well, there are no wounded Rebels here."

"Oh yes, Miss Swenson," Mrs. Johnson spoke up. "There are quite a few, I understand." Bitterness touched her lips, and she said, "They killed my husband—so I don't care if they all die!"

Grace was even more distressed to see that Mrs. Johnson was filled with bitterness. *Not hard to see where William gets his terrible hatred from,* she thought. But tactfully she said, "I'll be tending our own Union soldiers." Then she changed the subject, and the meal ended pleasantly.

That night when she and Lettie went to their bedroom, Grace knew that the girl was watching her carefully. "I always read a chapter in Psalms then say a prayer at night, Lettie," she said. "Could we do it together?"

"I guess so."

Grace chose Psalm 56. When she had finished reading it out loud, she bowed her head and prayed. She felt a burden for the Johnsons and prayed for each of them by name. When she was finished, she looked up to see that there were tears on Lettie's cheeks. Grace was touched and said, "Thee must pray for me, Lettie. I am a little frightened of my new job."

Lettie gave her a startled look. "Me? I can't pray!"

"Oh, God would love for thee to pray, Lettie," Grace insisted. "He loves us all so much. Thee can just pray in thy heart. Just say, 'God, help Miss Grace be a fine nurse!'"

Lettie licked her lips and lay back on her pillow. "All right," she said finally. "I'll do it."

"Good! And I'll pray for thee, too." Grace blew out the lamp and got into bed. "Good night, Lettie. And I thank God for giving me a brand-new younger sister. Now I have five!"

Lettie lay there stiffly, for she was not an outgoing girl and this woman seemed particularly strange in her ways and talk.

But finally she whispered, "Good night, Miss Swenson."

"Just Grace. We're sisters now, Lettie and Grace."

Another silence, then. . ."Good night, Grace!"

CHAPTER 10

MYSTERIOUS PATIENT

*W*ell, Miss Dix, I suppose you've been forced to change your policy."

Brigadier General William Alexander Hammond, the surgeon general of the United States, smiled down at Miss Dix fondly. He was a big man of only thirty-four, dark and powerful. A beard and mustache covered the lower part of his heavy, intelligent face, and with his strong physique and personality, he seemed to fill every room he entered.

Miss Dix stared at him, bewildered by his remark. He'd come on one of his periodic visits, and the two of them had gone over the Armory Square Hospital thoroughly.

"Why—I don't know, sir," Miss Dix said. "Which policy have I changed?"

Hammond nodded toward the tall, strong-looking nurse who was carefully moving a patient whose legs were heavily bandaged. "Why, everyone knows you won't have good-looking young nurses." He smiled, then added, "But that young woman certainly comes in the category of good-looking."

Miss Dix flushed slightly but lifted her head in a belligerent gesture. "I haven't changed my policy at all, Dr. Hammond, but it is a foolish person who adheres blindly to a rule. Miss Swenson is an exception."

Hammond's dark eyes grew interested. "How is she exceptional?"

"She's a very serious young woman," Miss Dix said at once. "Most young women's minds are filled with thoughts of courtship and marriage, but this young lady thinks only of service." She watched the little tableau, noting how carefully the nurse eased the wounded man over to his side so that she could slide the soiled sheets out from under him, and how she spoke to him quietly the whole time. And she noted, as well, the expression on the face of the wounded man.

"Her name is Grace Swenson," Miss Dix said without taking her eyes from her young worker. "I'd like for you to meet her."

"Has she been with you long?"

"Not nearly as long as I'd like." Miss Dix's thin lips turned upward slightly in a rare smile. "Watch your behavior, General. Miss Swenson is a clergyman."

"A preacher?" Hammond's heavy brows shot upward in an involuntary fashion. "She doesn't look like any preacher I ever saw!"

"She is, though—a Quaker. Come along, General." She led the large officer to stand beside the bed, saying, "Nurse Swenson?"

The surgeon general watched as the young woman, dressed in gray except for the white bonnet on her head, helped the wounded man lie down. She was very deliberate, finishing the chore at hand before turning around to say, "Yes, Miss Dix?"

"I want you to meet someone. This is William Hammond, the surgeon general."

"I'm happy to meet thee, sir."

Hammond bowed slightly, saying, "My pleasure, Miss Swenson." He was favorably impressed with the young woman's calm demeanor. He was an astute student of people and studied faces carefully. He perceived in a glance that she was very tall, and he noted the strength in her feminine figure. He found her rather squarish face and fine complexion most pleasing to look at, and her light blue eyes held the direct stare that he was accustomed to finding only in men. Her blond hair was tied up but was obviously fine as silk, and he felt sure it would have fallen well below her waist if it were loose.

"Miss Dix tells me you're a clergyman, Miss Swenson," Hammond said. "That must be very handy when dealing with the men."

"Many of them do need spiritual healing as well as physical care," Grace said quietly. "But then, most of us need that, don't we, Doctor?"

Miss Dix had been almost intimidated by Hammond's strong personality, and it secretly pleased her to see the tall officer taken aback by Grace's straightforward manner—and by her question.

"Why—I must agree with that," Hammond stammered. He rubbed his whiskers, then said with a nod, "Yes, it is so. But do any of the men resent your preaching to them? I mean, they're a bit of a captive audience."

"Some of them are a little resentful," Grace admitted. "But I never force my beliefs on them. After all, Jesus never forced Himself on anyone, did He, Doctor?"

"I—don't believe he did," Hammond said, then hastened to add, "but I'm not a Bible scholar."

Grace gave him a slow smile. "Thee does not need to be a scholar to love God, Doctor. The only thing Jesus seeks is a hungry heart. Has thee ever felt Him knocking at thy door?"

Hammond was a tough man; he had risen to the top of his profession by sheer force of will and, as surgeon general, often found himself doing battle with Stanton, the secretary of war—a dragon who had burned many a man! So it was most disconcerting to find himself feeling almost sheepish before this young woman! Mustering his wits, he tried to bully his way out of the situation, acutely aware that Miss Dix was enjoying his discomfort. "I've not made up my mind about religion," he said gruffly. "I'm an agnostic." He caught the smile that touched the young nurse's wide lips and demanded, "What's so amusing about that, Nurse Swenson?"

Grace regarded the large man calmly—and he was somewhat put off to realize she was not in the least intimidated. "Why, it amuses me to hear thee, Doctor." She shook her head, and there was a strange mixture of gentleness and firmness in her that the general found both charming and challenging. "Thee would not say so about any other area of thy life. An agnostic says, 'I am ignorant; I don't know.' But thee would never say that of thy career, nor would thee let one of thy fellow doctors say that about his medical skill, would thee?"

"Well, no, but—"

"And we would agree that since a man's body is only here for a brief time, but his soul is forever, it can't be wise to ignore the One who made them both. So thee must seek God, Doctor, with as much eagerness and dedication as thee has sought success in thy profession."

Hammond stood before the two women silently. He wanted to lash out, to tell her to stop meddling in his private life—but somehow he could not. He had been struggling spiritually in his own life for the past year, and the young woman had put her finger on that very problem. He was a sensitive man, and though he had known many hypocrites, he had seen enough sincere Christians to make him aware that something of what they had was what he needed in his own life.

Now he said with some embarrassment, "We're keeping you from your work, Nurse Swenson."

"My work is serving God, Doctor," Grace said sweetly but with a glint of humor in her eyes. "It doesn't matter what form that takes, bandaging a wound or bearing witness of the love of Jesus to the surgeon general."

Hammond suddenly was filled with a desire to get away. "Ah, yes...well, Miss Dix, shall we move on?" When he had made his escape out of the ward, he turned abruptly, demanding, "Is she like that all the time?"

Miss Dix's smile grew broader. "She was the same with me, General. I think she'd be the same with President Lincoln."

Hammond shook his head, admiration coming into his expression. "Well, she's different from any of the other clergymen I've met. And you say she's a good nurse?"

"The finest I've had, and I've had some fine ones. She'd taken care of a sick father before she came, so she knew some things already. Not about wounds, of course, but she's very bright and catches on quickly." Miss Dix sighed and shook her head. "I wish I had a hundred like her!"

Hammond shook his heavy head. "You won't get them, I'm afraid. I don't think there *are* any more like her!" He turned, and the two of them moved through the rest of the wards. When the inspection was finished, Hammond gave his approval. "As usual, Miss Dix, you've got things in fine order. I wish the other hospitals were so well organized."

"Thank you, Dr. Hammond," Miss Dix murmured. She stood there, a small woman with an indomitable spirit, and the burly physician saw that something was troubling her. He didn't probe, but finally she said with a marked hesitation, "Dr. Hammond, I'm concerned about some of the patients."

"Oh? Which ones?"

"The men we have in Ward K. I—didn't take you to that ward, but would you come with me now?"

"Certainly."

Hammond followed the woman out of the building, across several sidewalks, and finally stepped inside another of the rectangular white structures. Glancing around curiously, the surgeon at once realized that something about this ward was very different from the others. Not that it varied in size or shape, for like the rest of the wards, it was basically a large room with two rows of beds. But the patients—!

Hammond blinked with surprise. Many of the beds were not occupied by men lying down. Rather, several patients were sitting either on the beds or in chairs, while others were walking around aimlessly. One man came over to stand five feet away, directly in front of Hammond and Miss Dix. He limped badly, but it was his face that caught the surgeon general's attention, for it seemed blank of all expression.

"How are you, Private?" Hammond asked curiously.

But the man stared at him without speaking. Hammond noted the man's long, cadaverous face, with eyes deeply sunken into their sockets. His lips were thin and pale, almost bloodless, and they twitched as he seemed to be whispering. His long fingers fumbled at the buttons on the front of his shirt, and he stared at Hammond with wide-open, unblinking eyes.

Hammond glanced at Miss Dix, then asked more loudly, "Well now, what seems to be the trouble?"

Suddenly the man's mouth opened, and a high-pitched whine emerged. It was a wordless cry that made the hair rise on the back of the physician's neck as he realized that the man was quite mad.

"Now, Roger"—Miss Dix moved forward at once, taking the man's arm and turning him around—"there's a good fellow. You just go sit down. Everything's all right."

She coaxed the man back across the room, sat him down on one of the beds, then came back to say, "He's not dangerous, poor man!"

Hammond looked around the room and understood why the chief of nurses had been hesitant to speak of this place. "These men—they're all mental cases?"

"Some of them have physical injuries," Miss Dix said, sadness in her blue-gray eyes. "But yes, their worst injuries seem to be mental. We thought it better to keep them separate from the other men. Not just for their own good, Doctor," she added quickly. "They were bad for morale."

"I can understand that," Hammond responded. He shook his head sadly, then asked, "What happens when they're well enough to be sent home?"

"Why, most of them are taken in by their people. But there are a few who are able enough to be dismissed, but they have no family. . .or their people won't have them."

"It's the asylum for them?"

The word *asylum* caused Dorothea Dix's lips to form a knifelike line, and anger sparkled in her eyes. "Yes! And you know what that's like!"

Hammond knew only too well! In most cases, an asylum was worse than many prisons. They were no more than dark holes where mentally disturbed patients were chained like wild beasts. Unwashed and uncared for, these desperate souls lived out their lives in the horror of great darkness.

"Too bad! Too bad!" Dr. Hammond shook his heavy head; then a question came to him. "I suppose the surgeons are not much help with such as these?"

"Most of them come in to care for them physically." Miss Dix shrugged. "But they don't care about their minds."

"But, Miss Dix, there isn't much they can do, is there? We know so little about this sort of problem." Hammond, a compassionate man where broken bodies were concerned, looked over the room, noting the blank faces and staring eyes. "I wouldn't know how to start with men like these!"

Miss Dix was forced to agree. "I know, sir, but we must do what we can. These men are here because they took up arms and fought to keep our Union intact. Just because their wounds are in the mind doesn't make them any less honorable than those wounded in the flesh."

"What is it you want me to do, Miss Dix?"

"Some of the surgeons want to discharge these men at once because we need the beds." Miss Dix was not a woman who begged, but now she was appealing with her whole heart. "But to do that would be a terrible injustice to these poor souls. Will you do what you can, Dr. Hammond, to let me keep this one ward for this kind of problem?"

Hammond nodded firmly. "Yes, I'll see to it." He looked over the men once more, then turned to go. When they were outside, he said, "Do any of them ever recover?"

"Oh yes, some of them."

"How do you account for it?"

"I can't, really." Miss Dix thought about his question as they walked along, and finally said, "I think all we can do is to be kind—and wait. They're locked inside some sort of grim prison. The only thing they seem to respond to is kindness."

After Miss Dix had said good-bye to Dr. Hammond, she sat at her desk for some time staring at the wall blankly. The pressures of her task were tremendous, and her nerves were strained. She thought of the men in Ward K, searching for some way to help them. It was so hopeless! So few of them ever came out of the darkness that clouded their benighted minds.

She was thankful for Dr. Hammond's willingness to help, and that made her feel a little better. Then she thought about her response to his question regarding the men's recovery: *The only thing they seem to respond to is kindness.*

Long she sat there, struggling with the problem. Then, suddenly, something came to her. She was not an impulsive woman, but the idea persisted with such force that she finally rose and moved out of her office, going to find Grace Swenson. "Nurse Swenson, come to my office, please."

Grace looked up in surprise but made no comment. She followed the superintendent through the halls, and when they were inside the small office, she took the seat Miss Dix offered her.

"I have something to ask you."

"Yes?"

Miss Dix plunged at once into the problem of the men in

Ward K and ended by saying, "It's a thankless service, I'm afraid. So few of them ever recover. But I think you could be of help to some of them."

Grace agreed instantly. "I'll do what I can, Miss Dix."

"I'm so shorthanded," Miss Dix warned. "It will have to be extra duty, I'm afraid. I'll take you off of Ward C, but it will still be more work. And you'll have to be strict with the male nurses. Some of them aren't much! They know these men can't report them, so they mistreat the patients."

"How do they do that?"

"Steal their food or the whiskey used for treatment, let them go dirty, become careless about changing dressings—there are far too many ways." Miss Dix gave the young woman a direct glance. "You can't be soft on them or your patients will suffer."

"I'll do the best I can, Miss Dix."

Pleasure came into Dorothea's thin face, and she took a deep breath. "I was hoping you would, Grace." It was the first time she'd called Grace by her given name, for she was not given to informality. "I'll see that your supervisors are informed. When would you like to begin?"

"I'll start first thing in the morning," Grace said.

Miss Dix hesitated, then said gently, "You won't be able to do much with your religious convictions, I'm afraid. They're all too far gone to understand you."

But the superintendent's words didn't seem to trouble the young woman. "God is able to minister to a troubled mind as well as to a maimed body," she said softly, then rose and left the room.

Miss Dix—who was not considered a praying woman—stared at the door, then whispered, "God be with her!"

✑

"Are you going to be nursin' *loonies*?"

It was breakfast time at the Johnson house, and Willie had listened with increasing interest as Grace spoke of her new assignment at the hospital. He blurted out his question, his eyes big as half-dollars.

"Willie, that's no way to talk!" Ida Johnson rebuked her son sharply, but there was doubt in her own expression. Turning back to face Grace, she said, "I never thought about such a thing—men losing their minds from the war."

Grace sipped her coffee thoughtfully before answering. "It's not too surprising when thee thinks about it. People go insane over less than what these men have gone through."

"Are they dangerous, Grace?" Lettie asked breathlessly.

"Oh, not at all, Lettie!" Grace spoke up quickly. "Most of them are wounded so badly they couldn't hurt anyone."

"I'd be afraid to stick my nose in the door," Mrs. Johnson announced, shaking her head. "There's something about a person losing his mind that's worse than losing an arm or a leg."

"I agree with thee, Mrs. Johnson," Grace said. "But the scripture enjoins us to comfort the feebleminded, doesn't it?" She glanced at the old clock on the mantel, then exclaimed, "I've got to hurry. Do you mind if I don't help thee with the dishes, Mrs. Johnson?"

"No, Lettie can help."

Grace grabbed her coat, put her hat on, and raced out the door just as Ryan Callihan arrived in his cab. Grace scrambled up on the seat with him, greeting him cheerfully. As he drove along, she inquired about his family. He had a grandson in the Army of the Potomac and another in the Union Navy under Farragut. When he finished his report, she spoke of her new assignment, and Callihan stared at her in astonishment. "Faith! Is it crazy men ye'll be nursin'?"

Grace was discouraged at the response from the Johnsons and from her old friend, but she shook it off. "They're God's children, and I'm thankful He's allowing me to help them."

Callihan shook his head, mystified by all of this. He had become very fond of Grace, despite her efforts to wean him from the bottle. His sharp blue eyes cut around more than once to watch her as she sat beside him, and finally when he stopped in front of Armory Square Hospital, he took her arm just as she prepared to step down.

"Lassie, you be on your guard!"

Grace patted his hand, gnarled with arthritis, and smiled fondly into his seamed face. "God will take care of me, Friend Callihan, and thee stay away from that saloon today!"

She stepped to the ground, waved at him, then turned and entered the hospital. She went at once to her locker, a wooden closet she shared with Ada Clower, and found the older woman putting on an apron. Ada was forty-two years old and built along the lines of a garden rake. She had been married twice but widowed that same number of times. Grace had heard one of Ada's patients mutter, "Her husbands must have soured to death! She'd curdle milk with that face of hers!"

But Ada was capable enough, if somewhat bitter. "I heard you wuz goin' to Ward K," she grunted as she tied her bonnet in place, giving the strings a firm yank. She peered at Grace, then shook her head. "None of the rest of us would do it. Did you know that when you told Miss Dix you'd take the job?"

"No, but it's all right, Ada. I don't mind."

"Humph!" Ada sniffed, then nodded sharply. "Ain't no picnic, waitin' on crazy men!"

Grace shook her head, saying cheerfully, "God is in Ward K, just as He's in the other wards." Turning away from the other nurse, she made her way down the hall, left the main building, and followed the raised wooden sidewalks that led to Ward K.

When she stepped inside, she stopped instantly, assaulted by the foul air. *The waste cans haven't been changed lately,* she thought, and when she moved to the first bed, she discovered that the helpless man was lying in his own filth. Anger swept through her like a fire, but she let nothing show on her face. "Now then, let's get you cleaned up," she said cheerfully.

The patient was a middle-aged man with a full crop of salt-and-pepper whiskers. He stared up at her with frightened eyes and began to flop about on the bed, crying out, "I'm all right! I'm all right!" His eyes were bright with fever, and when she touched him, she knew that it was dangerously high. Quickly she cleaned him and changed the dressing on his stomach, then put him down on the clean sheets, which she had expertly changed.

Placing her hand on his head, she stood there praying silently, and presently the wild eyes grew more calm. "I'm all right," he muttered over and over, until he finally seemed to go to sleep.

Grace left the ward at once. She prayed for a quiet spirit, but it took all the power she could summon to keep from letting her anger spill over. Going at once to the mess room, she saw Nurse Sawyer eating breakfast. Going to her, she asked directly, "Who is the night nurse in charge of Ward K?"

"Why, Jesse Ormstead," Nurse Sawyer said with surprise. She pointed at a group of the male nurses who were drinking coffee at a table near the wall. "He's the one with the brown beard."

Grace nodded, then walked to the table. The men looked up, and one of them winked at the others, saying something that made them laugh. Ignoring their behavior, Grace spoke firmly. "Jesse Ormstead, come with me."

Ormstead was a sharp-faced man with a brown scraggly beard and a pair of sharp, hard brown eyes. He looked up at Grace, leaned back indolently, then said, "Why, you must be the new nurse in Ward K, I reckon."

"That's correct."

"Well, you hustle on down to the ward," Ormstead said with a sneer in his tone. "I'll be along directly, soon as I finish this coffee." He winked at the men and settled back in his chair.

Grace's expression never altered, but she knew that if she

allowed the man to get by with his insolence, she would never be able to maintain order in the ward. She stood there watching him, and it came to her what she must do.

"I understand General McClellan is in need of fifty thousand new men for his army," she remarked pleasantly.

"Little Mac always needs men." Ormstead shrugged. "What's that got to do with me?"

Grace smiled easily. "It has this to do with thee, Jesse—" Grace's voice took on a steely edge as she pinned the man with her eyes. "Thee will be one of those men if thee does not come with me right now. I can see that thee is a sloppy man, afraid of work. But thee will work. . .or thee will go to face the Rebels!"

"Hey! Now wait just—"

"Either come with me right now and do the work you left undone, or I will go at once to Dr. William Hammond, the surgeon general. When I tell him what a poor excuse for a nurse you are, he will have thee transferred this morning to the infantry. Make up thy mind, Jesse, which it shall be."

Ormstead had always been a bully—it had served him well with other nurses—and he fell back on that now. His face grew red with anger, and he rose to his feet ominously. "I'll see you in Hades before—"

"Fine!" Grace whirled and walked purposefully away. She had no idea if she could carry out her threat, but she was hoping that Ormstead would think so.

One of the men with Ormstead whispered, "That General Hammond, he's a hard nut, Jesse! And that female looks like she means business! You'd better eat crow—and fast!"

Ormstead looked wildly after Grace, then dropped his coffee cup on the table. "Nurse!" he called out, and when she exited without a backward look, he grew pale and scurried after her.

Nurse Sawyer laughed and said to an assistant surgeon sitting across from her, "I think Ormstead's met his match! He's an arrogant fellow, and I hope Grace works him until he drops!"

Her words were almost prophetic, for after Ormstead's abject apology and promise to reform, Grace forced him to work for four hours. She saw to it that he emptied all the pails, then mopped the floor.

While he was working, she moved around the ward, meeting the patients. Some of them were badly wounded, and she spoke with them calmly, changing dressings and feeding them when the breakfast was sent in from the kitchen.

Despite her resolution to keep a warm, pleasant expression, there was something chilling about the work. It was, she recognized, the blankness in the patients' eyes that made it so. Most of the time they made no reply at all to her chatter. Some of them spoke only obscenities; others rattled off words with no meaning at all.

Grace spoke to them all the same, noting that some seemed fairly normal. But when she mentioned this to Miss Dix, who came to visit her just before noon, Miss Dix said, "Yes, some of them seem very normal—but those same men in five minutes might be raving, or they might go into that dreadful silence, just staring at the walls with poor, mad eyes."

The two women talked for fifteen minutes, and then Miss Dix asked, "Have you met John Smith yet?"

"No, I haven't. Which one is he?"

"The tall one, standing by the window."

Grace had noticed the man, for he was, to say the least, eye-catching. He was very tall, with darkly handsome features, and he seemed to have no serious wound. In fact, compared to the others in the ward, he seemed quite healthy.

"You'll be surprised when you talk to him, Nurse Swenson," Miss Dix said, watching the tall man. "He's the mystery man of our hospital."

"Mystery man?" Grace asked, her curiosity quickened.

"He's been here for nearly a month, but in all that time he's never spoken once. He had some serious wounds, but they've healed—or almost so. But the mystery is that we can't find out who he is."

"What does thee mean by that?" Grace asked, puzzled.

"Just what I said." Miss Dix shrugged. "We can't find out his name. He can't speak—or won't—and there was nothing on him to identify him when he was brought in from the battlefield."

"But surely some of his fellow soldiers—!"

"We don't know which unit he was with. The battle scattered the troops terribly, and though we've tried, nobody has been able to identify him. We gave him the name John Smith to make bookkeeping easier."

"How strange!"

"Yes, it is. But many men were taken prisoner in the battle—

or simply blown to bits. Others were buried in unmarked graves, so there are many whose identification has been lost. It's not really so surprising that we haven't been able to identify Mr. Smith as of yet."

"What will happen to him?"

"If he doesn't get better, I suppose we'll have to put him in an institution."

"The insane asylum?"

"Yes."

Grace looked again across the big room. The sunlight came in through the high windows, falling in a tapering bar across the face of the man who stood there. "What a terrible thing!" she whispered.

"War is terrible," Miss Dix said with pain in her voice and in her eyes. "Do the best you can for these men," she said, then left the room.

Grace moved about the room, stopping to speak to first one, then another, and finally came to stand beside John Smith.

"Well, Mr. Smith, you're looking very well."

For one moment she didn't think the man heard her, but then he turned and looked at her. He had the darkest eyes she'd ever seen, so black it was almost impossible to see the pupils. He regarded her carefully but said nothing, and when she saw that he was not going to speak, she said cheerfully, "Well now, my name is Nurse Swenson, Mr. Smith. I'm going to take care of you for a while."

The black eyes did not change, and finally Grace grew

uncomfortable. She had the strange feeling that somewhere behind the blank stare that this tall man laid on her was a mind screaming and clawing to get out.

Sadly, she had no idea how to set that part of him free, but as she went about her work that day, it was John Smith who occupied her thoughts the most. When she left that evening, she was still thinking of him, troubled more by his opaque black eyes than by any of the other patients.

And when she lay down beside Lettie that night, the last prayer she prayed was for life to come into those dark, suffering eyes.

CHAPTER 11

THE AWAKENING

From the first, Ward K had a special place in Grace's heart. Perhaps it was similar to the inexplicable love a mother or father has for an afflicted child born in the midst of healthy children— but however it came about, she found herself spending more and more energy and time in that ward.

Certainly it was not because she saw more progress in Ward K than in other wards. On the contrary, she saw much less! The physical cures of the patients were about the same as those in the rest of the hospital, but only rarely did she see any of the men come out of the fog that shrouded their minds.

As winter came on, with October coming in like a lion with icy breezes, she found herself paying a price for her long hours. She began to lose weight and could not sleep. Miss Dix came to notice this and asked her to have tea in her office. This was fairly common, for the superintendent liked to keep personal contact with her nurses. When Grace arrived, Miss Dix indicated one of the chairs and began to pour the tea from a brass teakettle, which was singing a merry little tune.

"Now tell me all your problems," Miss Dix said when they were sipping the tea. A thin smile touched her lips, and she shrugged. "Not that I can solve any of them—but it does one good to let them be said once in a while."

Grace returned her smile. As she waited for an answer, the older woman noticed there was a thinness in her young associate's face that had not been there in the fall, a hollowing of her cheeks and a more deep-set look about her eyes. Her color was not as good, and she seemed honed down to a thin fine edge.

"I have no complaints," Grace said. She paused and sipped the tea from her cup, then added, "Whenever I get tired or upset, I think of some of our poor patients. Those without legs or arms. It makes my problems seem so small."

"Yes, I do the same." The older woman leaned back in her chair and closed her eyes for a moment. "They keep coming in, don't they? Sometimes I think there'll never be any end to it."

The two women sat there enjoying the quiet moment. Such times were rare, for the hospital ran night and day, and new casualties kept arriving. Finally Miss Dix asked, "How are conditions in Ward K? I understand you built a fire under Jesse Ormstead."

"Does thee know everything that goes on in this hospital?" Grace asked, surprise in her tone. Then she laughed shortly and nodded. "Jesse is my heavenly sandpaper, I think. He is the most worthless man I've ever known—and that's saying a great deal! He's lazy, shiftless, dirty, and a thief."

"Why don't you let me get rid of him?"

"Oh no, don't do that." Grace looked down at her hands, studied them carefully, then looked up with a strange smile. "I think God has given me Jesse to keep me mindful of how often I've displeased Him. Just when I'm ready to hit him with a broom, I remember some of the times in my life when I must have caused God as much trouble as Jesse causes me."

"Well, that's one way of looking at it, I suppose. But if he gives you too many problems, just let me know."

Humor came to light Grace's fine eyes. "I think he's quite afraid of me," she mused. "He's convinced that I can have him put in the front lines of the army at any moment. He'll do anything in the world to escape service in the army."

Miss Dix nodded with satisfaction, pleased that Grace was able to handle her own problems. "How is our Mr. Smith?" she asked, sipping her tea. "Any sign of improvement?"

Distress came to Grace's expression, and she shook her head sadly. "I'm afraid not. His physical wounds have healed, but he still hasn't said a word."

"Too bad! Such a fine-looking man," Miss Dix said regretfully. "We still haven't been able to find out a thing about him."

"I think so much about his family," Grace murmured. "Somewhere he must have a mother and father who are grieving over him."

"Or a wife and children," Miss Dix put in; then she glanced

sharply toward Grace, thinking of why she had invited her for tea. "Grace, you're not looking well. Aren't you sleeping well?"

"Oh, I'm fine," Grace said quickly, but she flushed slightly under the scrutiny of the superintendent. "Thee must not worry about me, Miss Dix. Thee has too much of a burden as it is."

"You won't be able to help your patients at all if you fall ill," Miss Dix stated. "I've seen this before—always with my best nurses. They wear themselves out caring for their patients, and then they're flat on their backs and I'm left with no one to take their places. The better the nurse," she added thoughtfully, "the more likely this is to happen." Setting her cup down firmly, she said, "Take more time off, Grace. You can only do so much, and I think you've passed the point of good judgment."

Grace started to protest, but one look at Miss Dix and she knew that there was no use. "I'll be more careful." She nodded. "But thee must take heed of thy own advice. What would happen to the program if thee were taken ill?"

It was a thought that Dorothea Dix had pondered often, for she knew that if nurses were in short supply, there was literally no one to replace her. She held the entire structure on her frail shoulders, and if she were to leave for any length of time, the good that she had wrought in the system might well be lost.

"Both of us must be careful," she admitted, then stood up, signifying that the tea party was over.

Grace was slightly depressed by the discussion, but knew that what Miss Dix had spoken was good counsel. She knew her own body, and it was telling her to slow down. She was honest enough to admit that she worked such long hours to take her mind off of her own problems, for when she went to bed early, she would think for hours of the past—dwelling sometimes on her father until the loneliness became so painful that she could not bear it.

She thought as well of Clyde Dortch, which shamed her in some mysterious fashion. She felt a guilt over such thoughts and prayed much to not have hard feelings toward her sister and brother-in-law. Still, despite her efforts to bury the bitterness of the past, she would find herself thinking harsh and vengeful thoughts—some of which shocked her. *Oh God—don't let me have this bitterness!* she would silently cry, and for a time things would be better.

But losing Clyde had cut her deeper than she supposed. This revelation came when she discovered that she was fantasizing over what might have been. Without purposing it, she would construct a dream of herself as Clyde's wife, with a family of children. She was the heroine of these dreams, and they always ended the same—and when she snapped out of it, she would be flooded with a new wave of bitterness toward Clyde and Prudence. Then she would have to begin wearily to seek forgiveness from God for such thoughts.

As she walked down the hall toward Ward K, Grace thought about her future. Though it didn't seem like it now, someday the war would be over. *What will I do then? Where can I go?* These thoughts depressed her, and she attempted to shake them off. *No sense letting my mood bring the men down,* she thought, and as she entered, she shook off her blackness and began to go from bed to bed, examining the dressings and giving words of encouragement.

One of the patients, Aaron Bent, a tall, fierce-eyed man from Michigan, had showed some promise. He had spells of such deep depression that he seemed to die inside, but they faded away and he could have passed for normal during these periods. Now he was sitting at one of the tables used for writing and playing games, staring at a sheet of paper.

"Writing your family, Aaron?" Grace asked as she came to stand by him.

"I reckon." Bent looked up at her and shook his head. "I ain't much on my letters, Miss Grace."

"Would you like me to look at it for thee?"

"Sure would." Bent handed her the letter, then sat back and studied her as Grace read what he had written.

Alf sed he heard that you and hardy was a runing to gether all the time and he thot he wod gust quit having any thing more to doo with you for he thot it was no more yuse. I think you made a bad chois to turn off as nise a feler as Alf dyer and let that orney, thevin, drunkerd, card-playing Hardy Simons come to sea you. He aint nothin but a theef and a lopyeard, pigen toed helon. He is too orney for the devil. I will Shute him as shore as i sea him.

The letter was signed, "All my love, Aaron," which almost

brought a smile to Grace's lips. Ignoring the terrible spelling, she asked with a straight face, "I take it thee doesn't care for Hardy Simons?"

"No, I hate his guts," the soldier said with a shake of his head. "He's a dead man if he don't leave my sister alone."

"But—" Grace struggled to find something to say, but nothing seemed appropriate. "Perhaps your sister loves him."

Aaron Bent gave Grace a hard, unbelieving stare. "Ain't no sister of mine goin' to marry up with a no-account skunk like that! She kin just find some other man to love."

"But, Aaron, a woman can't—she can't just switch off love!"

"Why can't she?"

Though Grace felt she was getting in over her head, she tried valiantly to explain. "Well, when we love somebody, we can't just *stop* loving them, can we—even if they're not what they should be? What if God stopped loving us just because we didn't behave right?"

Aaron shook his head firmly. "God never told nobody to be stupid."

That comment caused Grace to stare at the tall man speechlessly, and he nodded firmly. "Shore He didn't. And any woman who marries up with Hardy Simons is gonna have a terrible life. He'll drink and steal and lie and beat her, and she'll have to raise all the kids by herself. So only a stupid woman would ask fer thet kind of life, ain't it so?"

Grace found her face glowing slightly with a blush. She said, "I—I can't answer that, Aaron."

Bent's lean face was serious, and he nodded emphatically. "Don't you be marryin' up with no trash, Miss Grace," he said firmly. A thought came to him, and he added, "I'd marry up with you myself, but I already got me a woman."

"That's. . .nice of thee, Aaron." Grace summoned a smile. "I know thy woman will be glad to have thee home again. And thee has improved so much, it won't be long now."

Bent looked down at the floor, his face growing sad. "I'm most afraid to go home. When these fits take me, I ain't fit to live with my family."

Grace suddenly felt the Holy Ghost move on her heart, more powerfully than she had ever felt it before!

"Speak the Word to him—and he will be made whole."

The message came as plainly as if it had been painted on a huge sign, and a joy filled Grace, for she knew that God was about to do something for the man who sat beside her.

"Aaron," she said quietly, "God wants to take your fears away. . . ."

Twenty minutes later, Aaron Bent called on God, asked for salvation, and was filled with the Holy Ghost and with peace. He had sat there listening as Grace had read to him from the scriptures, then had told him how God had given her peace. When she'd given Aaron the gospel and asked him to pray, he'd said at once, "I need God, Miss Grace!" He'd bowed his head and, with tears running down his face, had called on God as simply as a little child.

Finally he lifted his head, his eyes wide with wonder, and

exclaimed, "Miss Grace. . .it's all gone! All that heavy weight I been carrying! It's just gone!"

"Thank God!" Grace was weeping, too, and she noticed that a few of the patients were watching and listening avidly. Glancing around, she saw that the tall soldier who'd never spoken was leaning against the wall, watching them. Grace smiled at him, but there was no change in the stolid countenance. She turned back to Aaron and rejoiced with him. Finally she said, "Now, Aaron, let me ask thee to do something."

"Yes, Miss Grace?"

"Tell people what God has done for thee," Grace said. "Follow Jesus. Learn to love Him more. I will teach thee to pray and to read the Bible, but thee is a new creature, and it will help thee to tell people."

"Why, shore I will!" Bent exploded. He glanced around the room and said, "Some of these pore fellas can't understand much, but I'll shore tell 'em what God's done for me!"

He rose at once, saying, "Hey, Cyrus, lemme tell you what jest happened."

Grace sat at the table, unable to contain her tears. This was the first real breakthrough in Ward K, and her heart overflowed with thanks to God. Doubt had come to her many times, and the devil had whispered to her that all her efforts were in vain. Now she knew that wasn't true, and the power of the gospel was at work all around her!

Getting to her feet, she wiped the tears from her face and moved around the room, speaking to the men—and the blank looks on most of their faces didn't discourage her at all! When she came to John Smith, she smiled brightly, saying, "John, you're going to be set free! Jesus Christ is able, and I'm going to pray harder than ever for you!"

She left the ward, going at once to share her good news with Miss Dix and others. Some would doubt and scoff, but Grace was strong in the power of the Lord and cared not one pin what they thought or said! Had she not seen today the power of God displayed in her ward? And what God could do once, He could do again!

❧

The stove made popping noises as the wood burned. There were two stoves, one close to where he stood and another like it down at the other end of the room.

Everything was white and clean. Two rows of beds ran the length of the room, their heads touching the walls. Some of the beds were empty, but others held men who wore white shirts of some kind and lay still.

Looking down he saw that he was wearing a dark blue shirt. He wondered why he wasn't wearing a white shirt like the men in the beds. His pants were light blue, and he had on black boots.

Something was warm in his hands, and he looked down. He stared at the brown cup filled with hot black liquid, not understanding what it was.

Then a voice came to him, and he was suddenly afraid. He

didn't know why, though, and that made the fear worse. He looked at the table to his right and saw a man wearing the same kind of clothing he had on. He was a small man with bushy hair and wide-staring eyes. He was looking up at the ceiling and saying in a shrill whisper, "George Washington, George Washington, George Washington—!"

The staring eyes turned in his direction, and he wanted to run out of the room—but what would be there waiting for him? He looked around, and the sight of a nearby blank-faced man walking slowly back and forth and wringing his hands brought more fear.

It was better in the dark—there were no blank-faced men there. He closed his eyes, trying to go back into the warm darkness where there was nothing to frighten him. The darkness began to close in, and he felt himself slipping back. It was like a huge pool that was creeping up his body, and he knew that it would cover his chest, then his head—and there would be nothing then but the void....

But he wrenched his eyelids open with a physical effort, for he suddenly remembered that there were terrible things in the darkness, too! He couldn't remember them clearly, but shadows and phantoms danced across his brain, and he began to tremble.

A noise came to him, and he looked to his left where one of the men dressed in blue was squatting on the floor and flapping his arms like a chicken. He was making odd noises and advancing steadily. Again he wanted to run, but that would have meant leaving the room.

He closed his eyes and heard something hit the floor.

"Hey, Smith, you spilled your coffee!"

He opened his eyes to find a man standing in front of him. The man was small, but his eyes were filled with anger.

"I got more to do than clean up your mess!" The man pulled a rag from his pocket and tossed it at him. "Wipe that up! What'd you do that for?"

"I don't know."

The man's jaw sagged, and his eyes flew open wide. He grunted sharply, then reached out and grabbed the patient's arm. "Hey—what'd you say?"

"I—don't know—"

Jesse Ormstead could not believe his ears. His mouth clicked shut, and he whispered, "You all right, Smith?"

"Yes, I'm all right."

Ormstead dropped Smith's arm, wheeled, and dashed out of the room.

Smith began to be afraid again. *I did something wrong,* he thought, and he closed his eyes, trying to slip back into the darkness. His hands trembled, and he discovered he held the rag the man had given him. He stared at the pool of black liquid at his feet, then stooped down. He mopped it up, then stood up, the cup and rag in his hand, wondering helplessly what to do with them.

He heard a man's voice arguing loudly and looked down the room to see the man who'd given him the rag come in with a woman behind him.

"You'll see!" Jesse Ormstead was saying as he burst through the door. "He talked just as plain as you or me! Come on and I'll show you!"

Grace had been in the next ward when Ormstead had come bursting in, speaking so excitedly that she'd had to ask twice what he was babbling about. When she understood, she whirled and followed the orderly, her mind reeling with what she'd heard.

"Now, come on, Smith," Ormstead coaxed. "Say something!"

His relentless demand frightened Smith, who looked down at the cup in his hand in confusion.

"Let me try, Jesse." Grace moved forward and took the cup and rag from the man's loose grasp. When he looked up at her, she saw the fear in his eyes. Quietly she said, "Don't be afraid, John. Nobody's going to hurt you." Encouraged by the way he looked at her, she said, "I'm Nurse Swenson. Do you know me?"

Nurse Swenson? Yes, I know her. . . . She takes care of me—

"Yes, I. . .I know you."

"See? Didn't I tell you?" Jesse Ormstead crowed. He looked around at the men who were watching as if he'd done something wonderful. "See, he can talk good as me!"

Grace wanted to get Smith away from the other patients. "Jesse, you stay here. I'm going to take the patient to see Miss Dix."

Ormstead grew sullen. "It wuz me who made him talk. You tell her that!"

"I'll tell her, Jesse." Grace smiled at Smith, saying, "Come along with me, will you, John?"

She turned, and Smith followed her obediently. He glanced at the man who'd been saying "George Washington" and at the man who'd been scrambling across the floor toward him, and he was glad to be leaving.

As soon as they were outside, Grace put her hand lightly on the patient's arm, saying, "I want you to meet a very nice lady, John." She hesitated, then asked, "Are you afraid?"

He turned his eyes toward her. "Yes," he whispered quietly.

"You mustn't be afraid," Grace said, tightening her grip. "I won't leave you alone."

"All right."

Grace nodded, and the two made their way to the main building and, by a stroke of good fortune, found Miss Dix in and able to see them. When they entered the office, Grace saw surprise cross Miss Dix's face. "What's this, Nurse Swenson?" she demanded, rising to her feet.

"I wanted you to meet John Smith," Grace said, her face slightly pale.

Miss Dix stared at the tall man, then at Grace. "What is it?" she asked carefully.

"John, this is Miss Dix."

Miss Dix blinked, then at a nod from Grace said, a little breathlessly, "How are you, John?"

Smith looked quickly at Grace for assurance, then nodded. "I'm all right. . .Miss Dix."

Dorothea Dix gasped; then a smile spread across her face.

"I can see you are!" She motioned at the chairs, saying, "Sit down, both of you." She came to stand in front of her desk and look down at them. Carefully she said, "It's good to see you so much better, John. You've been very sick."

Both women were watching the patient intently. He seemed to be in a daze, and when he spoke, it was in a slightly husky whisper, as though his voice was rusty from disuse.

"What's wrong with me?"

At the sight of the tall, strong man sitting there, looking so lost and helpless, a wave of pity rushed through Grace. Tears stung her eyes, and without thinking, she leaned over and put her hand over his, which were tightly clenched. "You've been injured, John. Do you remember anything about it?"

The broad brow creased with effort, but finally Smith shook his head. "No, nurse."

Miss Dix said quickly, "Well, it'll come back to you, I'm sure—" She broke off suddenly as something occurred to her. "You should know, though, that we weren't able to discover your real name. So we just called you John Smith. Perhaps you can tell us your real name now."

The two women waited, and when the man said nothing, they exchanged glances. "Just your name?" Grace said encouragingly.

But John Smith had closed his eyes and dropped his head. His hands were clenched so tightly together that the veins stood out like cords. He began to tremble, and Grace at once said, "John, don't worry about it! Don't be afraid!"

"But—I can't remember!" The dark eyes opened, and fear

pooled in them as he cried out, "I can't remember my name!" He suddenly grasped Grace's hand, his iron grip hurting her. "Why don't I know who I am? What's *wrong* with me?"

Grace ignored the pain in her hand, saying very quietly, "Thee needs time, John. It'll be all right. Thee *will* remember. I promise you."

Smith stared at her, then slowly nodded and relaxed his grip. He slumped in his chair, seemingly exhausted.

Miss Dix's eyes narrowed, and she said quickly, "Nurse Swenson, why don't you take John for a walk. I'll have Nurse Miller take over your duties for a while."

Grace caught her meaning at once and nodded. "I think that would be nice. Come along, John. We'll get you a warm coat and we can go for a walk outside."

"All right." The tall man rose obediently and followed Grace out of the room.

Miss Dix stood at the window, thinking hard. Finally she saw the pair come out of a side door. They were both wearing blue coats, and the dark hair of the tall man made a striking contrast with the blond locks of the woman. Miss Dix watched them as they walked slowly along and disappeared around the corner.

Dorothea Dix did not sit down for a long time, but gazed out at the rows of white buildings, thinking of what she had just seen. Finally she took a deep breath, then said aloud, "Well, we need a miracle once in a while around here!"

Then she sat down at her desk and began writing in a small, cramped script.

CHAPTER 12

"THEE HAS A MAN OF THY OWN!"

*W*inter swept over Washington suddenly, bringing freezing rain, sleet, and driving snow, and the city struggled to free itself from the mountains of snow that were dumped on it from leaden skies. Nobody except the vendors of firewood and the excited children enjoyed it after the first fluffy drifts were transformed into sheets of ice.

On the second day of November, Grace was sitting in a large oak rocking chair, knitting gray yarn into a large sock and watching the snow fall in slanting lines out of a buttermilk sky. Beside her in another rocker, his long legs stretched out, John Smith gazed through half-shut eyes at the large flakes, which were building a crystal mound on the outside of the window.

"This is nice, isn't it, John?"

"Yes, it is."

Grace was accustomed to her companion's brief answers. For the past two weeks, she had spent a large part of every day with

603

him, robbing other patients of her service. She had the implied consent of Miss Dix, who had said at the beginning of all this, "He needs you right now more than the others do, Grace. He has a chance to recover, but somebody must stay with him and lead him out of the darkness."

Grace had taken Miss Dix at her word, and not a day had passed but that she had spent hours with the mostly silent patient. Some of the other nurses had complained, as well as one or two of the patients, but Grace chose to ignore them. She was engrossed with the man known to her as John Smith—and it was more than a casual interest. She believed in what the Quakers called the Inner Light—a divine guidance, a word from God giving directions for living.

She had tried once to explain this part of her life to Lettie Johnson but had made no headway at all. Lettie had listened carefully but had finally demanded, "But if it's all in your head, Grace, how do you know it's not just what *you* are thinking?"

Grace had been unable to answer Lettie's question, for that *was* a problem. Sometimes her own thoughts were so intermingled with the things God was speaking that she made mistakes. But this time, in the matter of John Smith, she knew as surely as she knew she was alive that God was using her to minister to his beclouded mind.

She had to restrain herself, however, for the temptation was strong to push him, to *force* him to remember his past. Early in their time together, she had learned that this was counterproductive, for the more she attempted to pressure him, the more confused he grew until he withdrew into complete silence.

Now as they sat together on the small enclosed porch that looked out on the front of Armory Square Hospital, she spoke infrequently, and he sometimes offered a comment of his own. This in itself was progress, for two weeks earlier, he would sit for hours without volunteering a word.

Now Grace looked out the window at the snow. "It reminds me of home. In Pennsylvania, where I grew up, we have deep snows like this. Sometimes we go for rides in my father's sleigh. I always liked that so much." Her eyes grew dreamy, and she stopped knitting as she went on in her quiet voice. "Riding in a sleigh is so *different* from riding in a wagon. Thee just glides over the snow, and there's no bumping. . .just a hissing sound. Thee can hear the bells jingling and the sound of the horses' hooves plopping into the snow."

Smith turned to look at her, then shook his head. "That sounds like fun. I've never done anything like that—at least I don't think so."

Never ridden in a sleigh? Where could thee have come from where thee has never gone for a sleigh ride? Grace wanted to pursue this but feared that if she did, he'd grow moody and silent. Instead she merely said, "Well, maybe thee can visit my home and I'll take thee for thy first sleigh ride."

John Smith's lean face was smooth, and he nodded with some eagerness. "I'd like that, Miss Grace." He hesitated, then shook his head. "But I doubt it'll ever happen."

"Oh, perhaps it will," Grace said quickly. She started to speak, but a sudden fit of coughing overcame her. Her body was racked by the harsh spasm, and Smith watched her with some alarm.

"I don't like the sound of that cough," he said uneasily.

"Oh, it's just a cough, John."

But he leaned forward and looked into her face closely. "I don't think so. You've had it for almost a week. It's the same kind of cough that Davie and Sim and Dexter had."

Those three had developed a fever, which then went into pneumonia, and when Grace saw the concern on John's lean face, she knew he was unhappy. It was a good sign—and a bad one, she had come to understand. It was good that he'd come to trust her, but not so good in that he'd become dependent on her.

"Now thee mustn't worry about me, John," she said with a smile, overcoming the need to cough by a monumental effort. "I'm well enough."

He was not satisfied and turned to look out the window at the white landscape. It was this sudden tendency to turn his mind inward that troubled Grace, for she knew it was not good for him. She felt weak and tired, and she longed to go home to bed—but somehow she felt that she could not leave him.

She went to the mess hall with him for dinner, and while she ate almost nothing, she was glad to see that he ate well. She watched him, studying his face while he gave his attention to his food. He had a strong jaw, determined and a little pugnacious, and the deep-set eyes glowed with intelligence. His mouth was a wide slash, and his long English nose gave him a slight aristocratic air. His raven black hair had a slight curl and was long enough to curl up over his coat collar; the black eyebrows formed a shelf over dark eyes.

He is good-looking, Grace thought, *but he has no idea of such a thing.*

He turned suddenly and met her eyes, and she felt her face redden as she dropped her gaze. "You haven't eaten two bites, Miss Grace," he said. "You have to eat."

"I had a snack earlier." Grace evaded his eyes, then said, "Thee has a good appetite, John. I think you've gained five pounds the last few weeks."

"I'm fit enough."

Grace glanced at him quickly, for there was a note in his tone that she recognized: a nonchalance that hid despair and depression. "Are you finished?" she asked. When he nodded, the two of them left and made their way back to the porch. "It's chilly out here," Grace said, "but let's sit and talk for a while before I go home."

He threw himself into a chair, and there was tightness in his lips as he stared out at the night sky. "You'd better go now," he muttered. "Not much fun talking to a man who has nothing to say."

"Oh, don't speak like that!" He really *was* despondent. Grace set herself to cheer him up. "You know how much I enjoy talking with you." She glanced out the window at the glittering stars that had come out. "Look, the sky's cleared," she said. "Maybe it won't snow any more."

"Maybe not."

Ignoring his short reply, she leaned forward, peered out the window, and exclaimed, "Look at that star, John! It's so bright! I wonder which one it is?"

Glancing at the skies, Smith said, "That's Sirius, the Dog Star."

"Really? I don't know the names of any stars. I don't think most people do."

His answer had been casual, but he suddenly straightened his back and looked at Grace, his brows raised. "I can name most of those out there. I wonder how I came to know them."

A slight thrill ran through Grace, but she suppressed it, saying with a tone of mild interest, "Maybe thee was a sailor, John. They know the stars, don't they?"

He considered that, then shook his head. "No, I wasn't a sailor."

"No?"

"No. I don't know the names of the sails on ships. A sailor would know all those, wouldn't he?"

"Yes, I suppose so." She shivered in the cold. "People of all sorts study the stars."

"You mean like astrologers?" The thought caused him to smile. "Maybe I can tell your fortune or whatever it is they do."

"No, that's nonsense, John."

"Is it, now?" He turned to her, interest making his eyes glow.

"I seem to think that people guide their lives by the stars."

"Some do, but they're foolish." Grace thought for a moment, then said, "God made the stars, just as He made us. We're to learn about ourselves from God's Word, not from the stars."

Smith's lips tensed, and he said, "You read the Bible all the time, Grace. Is there anything in there about me? Will it tell me who I am?"

"In a way, yes, it will." Grace spoke very carefully, for he had never shown any interest in the spiritual side of his life. "All of us need to know three things, John, about ourselves."

"What three things?" he asked, his curiosity aroused.

"All of us need to know where we came from, who we really are, and where we're going."

"I need that second one, at least," Smith said, irony in his voice. "I'd settle for that—just to know who I am."

"No, it wouldn't be enough, John." Grace shook her head. "The world is full of people who can give thee their names, but they don't really know who they are."

"I don't understand."

"They just live without God, as the animals do—and that's not enough."

He studied her face, intrigued by the smooth lines of her cheek. "Guess I don't understand any of it. I don't know where I came from, I don't know who I am, and I sure don't know where I'm going!"

Grace felt sympathy for him rising within her and reached out to touch his hand. "Neither do millions of people, John.

And the false religions of the world have no answer. Only the Christian knows his beginning, for Christianity has the only answer. 'In the beginning God created the heaven and the earth.' And He made man, so that's where you came from. And only the Christian knows where he is going. The other religions say when man dies, he becomes less than a human, but Jesus said He Himself would come back and that He would take us to live in a place prepared for us. That's the answer to the third question."

"Which leaves number two," Smith said evenly. "Who am I? Does Jesus answer that?"

"Yes, He does, John. Just before He died for our sins, He prayed, 'And now I am no more in the world, but these are in the world, and I come to thee. Holy Father, keep through thine own name those whom thou hast given me, that they may be one, as we are.' Isn't that marvelous, John? Jesus, the Son of God, prayed that we may be so joined to Him that throughout all eternity we'll be *one* with Him and the Father!"

Smith stared at the young woman, noting the light in her eyes and the joy in her face. But he finally shook his head, saying, "It's too much for me to take in, Grace. All I want to know is my *name!*"

Grace knew he was in despair, and quickly she said, "Don't let fear come to thee! God will help thee."

She sat there for fifteen minutes, then rose, saying, "I must go home, John—" But she had risen too rapidly, and a wave of dizziness caused her to weave.

"Miss Grace!" Smith reached out and steadied her. "What's wrong?"

Grace was so overcome with dizziness that she clung to him. He put his arms around her, and she yielded to his strength. Finally she drew back, laughing ruefully, "I just got a little giddy, John. I'm fine now."

"You shouldn't go all the way home in the dark and in this weather!"

"I'll be all right," Grace insisted and forced herself to smile. "I'll see thee in the morning."

She left the hospital, but when she finally got into a cab, she was feeling much worse. She began to cough, and her chest was racked with pain. She stumbled out of the cab, paid her fare, and, by the time she got into bed, was aware that she had a fever.

I can't be sick, she thought, but her head whirled. She began to sweat, and sometime later she awakened Lettie, who got up at once. "You're shaking, Grace!" she said in alarm. "I'll get Mama."

Grace protested, but Lettie was gone. She returned with Mrs. Johnson, who took one look and shook her head. "It's the ague," she announced. "I've got some medicine left over from when I had it last month."

"I can't be sick!" Grace protested feverishly. "I've got to be at the hospital at seven in the morning."

"No, you have not! You'll be down a week, if not longer. I'll have Dr. McGuire come in tomorrow, but he'll not be telling me anything about the ague!"

And the next day it was as Ida Johnson had so firmly said: Dr. McGuire came, announced that Grace had the ague, prescribed the medicine that Mrs. Johnson had already started pouring down her patient's throat, and commanded her to stay in bed until she'd had no fever for twenty-four hours.

Grace's protests made no dent at all in Mrs. Johnson. She was kept in bed for five days despite her protests. She did persuade Lettie to carry a letter to Miss Dix, and she got one in return that was brief and to the point: *Stay in bed until you get well. You won't help matters by returning to duty too soon. I hope your recovery is swift.*

The days dragged by interminably for Grace. She knew there was no alternative but to rest, yet she fretted and longed for the day when she could get out of the house. For the first two days, she almost drove Mrs. Johnson to distraction with her pleas to be allowed to get up, but that stopped abruptly when her landlady finally asked her impatiently, "Aren't you Quakers supposed to be patient? I always heard you'd go to church and sit around waiting for hours for God to speak. Is that right?"

"Well yes, it is—"

"Then why don't you *act* like a Quaker?" Mrs. Johnson demanded. "You've got to stay in this house for a week. Why do you have to keep fretting and fussing and driving me crazy? I wish you'd show a little of that famous Quaker patience with *me!*"

The admonition struck home, and Grace lay quietly in bed from that time on. She became so docile that her landlady said with amazement, "I declare, I wish Lettie and Willie would pay as much attention to me as you do, Grace!"

And so time moved slowly, but Grace had learned her lesson. She began to practice the art of silence. Which meant that she lay in bed, thinking of God, praying, and asking God to make His will known to her. As she did so, peace washed over her. It was a strange sort of peace, for she had no idea what would happen in the future, but she realized she didn't need to know. She only needed to know the One who was in control.

Finally the day came when she went for twenty-four hours without a trace of fever, and the next morning she got up and dressed. She was too weak to do anything more that day and the next, but on the following morning, she dressed and put on her heavy coat, and Ryan Callihan took her to the hospital. He'd been to see her twice while she was ill, and now he protested vehemently that she had no business getting out so soon.

But Grace only smiled, saying, "I'm well, Ryan. God will take care of me."

"That's as may be," the old man retorted as he pulled up in front of the hospital. "But I'm staying here to take you home, and no arguments."

"I won't stay long this morning, Ryan," Grace said. "Only an hour, perhaps."

"I'll be waitin' fer ye," he said grimly. He leaped down and helped her to the ground. She needed his help, for she was weaker than she had thought. Finally he left her inside the door, saying, "Remember, I'll be waitin' right outside."

"Yes, I'll remember."

Grace went at once to Miss Dix's office and was greeted many times as she made her way down the halls. Miss Dix stared at her with surprise, then rose to come and greet her. "You're so thin!" she exclaimed. "And what in the world are you doing here? You'll have a relapse, Grace! You should know better!"

Grace took the chair she was offered, saying rather breathlessly, "Don't scold me, Miss Dix!" She smiled and pleaded, "I just couldn't stay away any longer."

Miss Dix stood rigidly before the young woman. "You're in no condition to work," she announced. "Look at you, trembling like a reed!"

"I'll be better soon!"

"Yes, in about a month." Miss Dix nodded. "You're on a thirty-day leave as of this day. Go home and do nothing but eat and sleep. You were falling down with overwork, and this sickness has hit you hard." And then her voice softened, and she smiled. "I must be hard with you now, my dear, for your own good."

Grace pleaded, but Miss Dix was adamant. At the end of fifteen minutes, the superintendent said, "I'll call a cab for you."

"No, I have one waiting. But please, I must visit a little."

"Well, make it a *very* little. Then go home to bed!"

Grace agreed and left Miss Dix's office. She was very tired but went at once to Ward K. She had thought about all the patients, but it was John Smith who'd been foremost in her prayers. As she entered, she saw him standing with his shoulder against the wall. He looked tired, and there was defeat in the sagging shoulders.

She greeted all the men, then came to him. She was exhausted by now and spoke with an effort. "Hello, John."

"Hello." He stared at her, then shook his head, "You look weak. Why are you out in weather like this?"

"I—wanted to see thee, John."

He stared at her, then said somewhat bitterly, "Well, it's a good thing you came this morning."

She knew then that something was wrong. "What's the matter?"

"You don't know?"

"No. What is it?"

"I'm leaving here today."

"Leaving?" Grace tried to think but was so weary she could make nothing out of it. "Where is thee going?"

"To the devil, I suppose!" The answer came sharply from tense lips, but Smith saw how it hurt her and shook his head, saying in a gentler tone, "Sorry. Didn't mean to speak that way."

"Why is thee leaving?" Grace asked quietly.

"I've been asked to leave." He shrugged. "They say they need the space, and I'm able enough physically."

"But—where will thee go? I'll speak to Miss Dix—"

"No need of that. She was the one who told me I'd have to leave. It's not her choice," Smith said. "She told me she fought for me, but she has her superiors, and the order is for all able-bodied men to be discharged at once."

Grace stood there, filled with confusion. She was very tired, and her head ached, but even at that moment, she was aware that all this was not unknown to God. She whispered, "John, help me sit down. . .just for a little while."

He blinked with surprise, then shrugged. "Not much privacy around here."

"Take me to the porch, the one in front."

"All right."

He took her arm and was shocked at how weak she was. He walked slowly, and finally they reached the small enclosed porch. "Nobody here," he announced, "but it's cold as the North Pole."

"Just let me sit down. . . ."

John helped her into one of the rockers, then stood to one side where he could watch her. She was very pale and thin, and when she closed her eyes, he saw that her eyes had grown sunken, giving her a distinctly unhealthy appearance. She put her head back, and he saw that her skin was very pale; she had lost the bloom of health that had always seemed so much a part of her.

As he watched her, he thought of how he missed her. The other men had missed her, too, but only as a source of physical care. He had not needed that, but he'd desperately needed that other thing she'd brought: the lively presence that had meant hope to him. . .the only hope he'd had.

Now he watched her. Though her eyes were closed, he was aware she was not asleep. Her lips were moving slightly, and he knew that she was in a realm of which he was totally ignorant. Despite the strength of her face, there was a gentleness and a fragility such as he had not encountered in his new world.

Finally her eyelids fluttered, and then she was looking at him. Something about her expression was so changed that he stared at her, wondering what was in her mind.

"John, has thee been signed out?"

"Oh yes. They just wanted to keep me here to feed me at noon."

Grace nodded slowly. "Get thy kit together." When he stared at her uncomprehendingly, she smiled. "Thee is going with me. God has told me so."

John Smith was rocked by this as he had been by nothing since coming out of the coma. "God told you to do this?"

"Yes," Grace said firmly. "Now pack thy things."

Smith stared at her, wanting to argue, but the strength of her gaze was such that he could not. "I'm already packed up," he said with a shrug. "They gave me ten dollars and told me to pack this morning after breakfast."

"Go now and get thy things."

He left at once, and Grace sat in the rocker, staring out the window. The snow had turned to ice, and it reflected glints of light as the sun struck it. When John returned, Grace rose, and he took her arm. They left the balcony, and he led her through the corridor to the front door. When they stepped outside, Ryan Callihan spotted them at once. He spoke to the horses, and when he pulled the cab up, he said, "Put her inside, soldier. I'll see her safe home."

"He's going with us, Ryan," Grace said. She looked up at

the long step and tried to get in, but could not. Suddenly strong arms lifted her and she was lightly placed inside as easily as if she'd been a baby. She gasped and had one fleeting thought: *Clyde Dortch never would have been able to do such a thing!*

Then John was inside the coach, and she heard Ryan say, "Hup, Babe—Butch!" and the cab jerked forward.

John Smith looked out the window, watching as the low buildings of Armory Square Hospital were left behind.

Turning to her, he asked, "Where are we going?"

Grace took a deep breath and moved to meet his gaze. A smile touched her lips then, and she said, "Pennsylvania, John—to my home."

The steel-clad hooves of the team clicked against the icy streets, making a sharp sound in the stillness of the early morning air. The forms of ice-capped buildings flashed by, but though Grace was looking out the window, she saw none of them. She was thinking of Pennsylvania. And of the man beside her.

A smile curved her lips, and she thought, *Well, Grace Swenson, thee has a man of thy own. Now see what thee will do with him!*

CHAPTER 13

A SLEIGH RIDE

*C*lyde Dortch was not in a happy mood. He snapped at Prudence as she set his breakfast out, and she blinked with resentment. "What's the matter with you, honey?" she asked petulantly. "Thee has been as touchy as a hornet lately."

Dortch scowled at her as he cut his fried eggs with the edge of his fork. He speared a large segment of one, stuffed it into his mouth, and chewed it. "I don't like it, Prue," he said after swallowing. "Why'd she have to bring that fellow home?"

"Why, he's been sick, Clyde," Prudence answered. "He didn't have anyplace to go when the hospital turned him out— not with him not knowing who his family is or anything."

Dortch glared at her as if she had lost her mind. "Does thee believe that fairy tale?" he demanded. "I don't. He's a bummer looking for a place where he won't have to work."

Prudence had just started to sip her coffee, but his statement caused her to pause with the cup half lifted. "Thee doesn't really think that!"

"I'm not a fool—and that's what I'd be if I swallowed his cock-and-bull story. There's nothing wrong with him. He's strong as a workhorse." He chewed viciously on a piece of bacon, swallowed, then pointed at Prudence with his fork, punctuating each word with a jab. "Mark my words, he'll wind up marrying her, and we'll be out on our ear, Prudence!"

This had never occurred to Prudence, and the shock such a thought caused her ran over her face. She was not a thoughtful young woman. Since coming back home, she had been happy with her new husband and her new life. Now she grew frightened, for Clyde's face was dark with anger, and what he had said shook her.

"Grace would never do that to us," she whispered.

"No? Maybe *she* wouldn't," Dortch retorted, "but Smith would, in a second!"

Silence fell on the room as the two of them thought of what might lie ahead. Dortch was shaken, for he had fallen into the easy life of the farm at once. With two hired hands to do the work, he was freed from most of it. There was enough money for his needs, he had a handsome wife, and the future looked rosy.

Now all that was being threatened, and he had become an angry man since the arrival of his sister-in-law and her tall, silent guest. He had kept a smiling face when the pair were around, going to great trouble to welcome Grace back home, but his first glimpse of John Smith had set off a warning inside him. Being the kind of man he was—one who knew how to manipulate women—he suspected all other men of the same sort of behavior. As soon as Grace had introduced Smith, Dortch had thought, *He's after the farm! He'll marry Grace, and even if he lets us stay, I'll wind up doing all the work while he sits around and eats the cream!*

Dortch had not changed his mind since that first moment. Rather, he had fallen into a moody state, though he'd been careful not to show it to Grace. He'd had two weeks to think about it and had watched the pair carefully. Now he shook his head, an angry light in his brown eyes as he said, "We've got to do something about it, Prue."

"Do something? What can we do?" Prudence was upset, for she felt that her husband was a shrewd man, and if he was concerned, then something surely was afoot. "It's Grace's farm. . . . Oh, I don't see how Pa could give it to her and leave me out in the cold!"

Dortch didn't point out that their own reckless behavior might have had something to do with that. Instead he said, "We've got to get her to see the truth about that fellow Smith."

"She won't listen to us."

"Maybe not, but she listens to other people—like Jacob Wirt, for example." Wirt was an elderly man, a Quaker minister who had been Amos Swenson's best friend. He was in his eighties now, but Grace loved and revered him as she did no other man, now that her father was gone. "We'll have to let Wirt know that Grace is about to be foolish."

Prudence nodded slowly. "If anyone could do it, he'd be the one. Grace dotes on the old man." She thought of it and asked finally, "But he's a sharp one, no matter if he is old. How will we get him on our side?"

"I'm going to see him today," Dortch said at once. "I've been thinking about it, how to get the old man to talk to Grace." Dortch was a scheming man and had indeed been carefully plotting his move. "What I'll do is go see him, and I'll tell him we're worried about Grace. I'll say, 'She's been very sick, and this man has taken up with her. You know Grace, how kind she is, and he's taking advantage of her, so Prudence and I think you should have a talk with her.' That's what I'll say, and I'll bet he'll do it. He's always been jealous of Grace, like she was his only chick!"

Prudence nodded thoughtfully. "It ought to work, but I don't know." Her eyes narrowed, and she shook her head. "That man is so handsome! Grace is still mad, if you ask me, because you took me instead of her. Now she's got a chance at a big, fine-looking man like that—"

Always sensitive to any reference to his lack of height, Dortch snapped angrily, "We'll see about that! I'll just cut that fellow down to size!" He rose and yanked his coat and hat from the rack, starting for the door.

"Clyde, you haven't finished your breakfast!"

"Save it for that 'big handsome man' upstairs!" Dortch left the room, slamming the door so hard the glass rattled. He saddled his horse quickly, then left the farm, spurring the stallion into a dead run.

❧

"John, let's have that sleigh ride thee never had. It's going to be a fine evening for it."

John paused in the act of hefting an ax and looked at Grace. She was sitting on a sawbuck watching him split wood, and he thought how much change two weeks of rest and good food had made in her appearance. When they'd arrived at the farm, he'd had to carry her into the house, she'd been so exhausted by the long train ride. He'd been afraid she might have a relapse, but getting home had seemed to infuse new life into her. She had gotten up the next day, eaten the food that Prudence cooked, and talked animatedly. The following day she had sat on the porch, watching the hands put up a new fence. From that time on she had improved rapidly, so that now as he glanced at her, he was amazed at how well she looked.

She was wearing a dark blue wool dress, with a pair of sturdy black boots peeping out from underneath the skirt. A wine-colored scarf was knotted around her throat, and a blue-and-white wool knitted cap perched on her head. Her fine blond hair escaped, blowing with the slight breeze, and he was glad to see the rich color in her face and the liveliness in her sparkling blue eyes.

Suddenly he was aware that he was staring at her, and he quickly turned his attention to the wood. "I'd like a sleigh ride," he said, then set a round section of the beech upright. Lifting the ax, he brought it down with a sharp, hard blow that divided the wood neatly in two. He split the two halves into quarters and then tossed the sections on the top of a pile almost as high as his belt.

"Thee splits wood better than any man I ever saw," Grace remarked. "It looks so easy when you do it!"

"I must have had a lot of practice," he remarked. He smiled at her, his teeth very white against his dark skin. "Maybe I worked in a wood yard."

Grace smiled, glad that he had reached the point where he could talk about his cloudy past without becoming depressed and moody. "I don't think so. Thee doesn't look like a woodcutter."

"Oh?" he asked, lifting one eyebrow quizzically. "What do I look like? A lawyer?"

"No, not a lawyer." Grace's tone was light, and she shook her head, adding, "Thee looks too honest for that."

"You don't like lawyers? First time I ever heard you speak against anyone."

"They're caught in a devious trade," Grace said quickly. "Besides, thee is too—" She broke off, suddenly embarrassed.

"I'm too what?" he demanded.

Grace had been about to say, "Thee is too fine-looking to be a lawyer," but changed it to "Thee is too much an outdoorsman to be a lawyer." Color tinged her cheeks at the statement she'd almost made, but as she watched him place another section of beech upright, she thought, *He is fine-looking. More than any man I've ever seen.*

He was wearing the same light blue trousers he'd worn in

the hospital, and the exercise had caused him to take off the heavy woolen coat, which had belonged to her father. John's coal black hair glistened as the red rays of the afternoon sun touched it, and the powerful muscles of his back, arms, and chest were clearly defined through the thin cotton shirt he wore. He split the log, tossed the sections on the pile, then grinned at her.

"I'm tired of this. Let's go look at the new colt."

"All right."

"Not too tired?"

"Oh no!" Grace rose quickly, and the two of them left the backyard, following a path that led down to the barn. As they walked along, he remarked, "You're much better. I was worried about you."

Grace was pleased with his remark. "Good. I've worried about thee enough, John. It's only fair thee should worry a little about me."

He glanced at her, liking it that she was able to tease him. Still he said, "I really was worried. You were pretty weak."

She thought of how he'd had to carry her off the train like a child and put her into the buggy he'd rented for the trip to the farm. He had taken care of her all the way on that trip. It had been the first time she'd been so zealously cared for, and the memory of it had stayed with her. "I'd never have made that trip without thy care, John."

Her remark brought color to his cheeks. "Well, maybe I was just looking out for myself," he muttered. "I didn't have any other place to go."

"No, that wasn't it." Grace spoke firmly, shaking her head slightly. She dropped her hand to pet the massive head of Rip, the shaggy sheepdog, who nuzzled her. "Get away, Rip," she protested. She walked along silently, then said, "Thee is a very kind man."

Her praise disturbed him. He shook his head, saying, "Don't know about that, Grace. I am a very grateful one, though."

She glanced at him quickly and felt sure he'd been waiting for this chance to speak with her. "I'm grateful that God has let me help thee, John."

"You have helped me, Grace," he said slowly. He had thought about this for days, and now in the quietness of the afternoon, he spoke out what had been building in his mind. "I've never told you, but the first time I began to wake up was when you prayed for Aaron Bent."

"I never knew that!"

"It was like a faint echo, I guess you might say." Smith tried to find words, then shook his head. "It's hard to say how it was, Grace. The best I can put it is that it was like I was locked in a black box with no light and no sound. And then I heard this voice. Your voice, and you were praying for Aaron."

"Thee didn't show it."

"No, but it was the beginning. After that, I began to be aware of things. Mostly of you."

As they reached the corral, the leggy colt lifted his head from underneath his mother to stare at them. Smith called out, "Come here, little fellow." As the colt staggered across the rough ground, he added, "It was you praying for me and reading the Bible for me that brought me out of that darkness."

Grace watched as the colt reached a spot five feet away and stared at them, wild-eyed and ready to bolt. "I didn't think thee heard me."

Smith reached into his pocket and came out with a lump of brown sugar. He held it out, and the colt advanced nervously. He licked the sugar, tentatively at first, then with greater pleasure. When it was gone, John reached out to touch his head. The colt snorted, leaped back, and bolted in a wild stagger back to his mother.

"I heard you, Grace." He wiped his hand on the top rail, then turned to her. "And then when you came to the hospital, still sick, I was about as low as a man can get." Shaking his head, he said slowly, "If you hadn't come when you did..."

When he didn't finish, Grace said gently, "I think God knew we needed each other, John."

They stood there watching the colt, laughing at his antics. John gave Grace some sugar, and she enticed the foal to come to her, enjoying the rough texture of his tongue on her palm.

Finally he said, "Better not do too much. I still want to go on that sleigh ride."

"So do I!"

After supper that night, John went to hitch the team to the sled, and Prudence, still thinking of what Clyde had said, tried to talk with her sister. "Thee doesn't know much about him, does thee, Grace?"

"He doesn't know much about himself."

"Fellow like that, why, he might be anything," Clyde spoke up. "No telling what kind of man he is. Could be a bank robber."

"No, he's not that," Grace said instantly; then, seeing the two glance at her, she defended her statement. "He's not that sort at all."

Prudence remarked innocently, "I've wondered about his wife and children."

Grace was startled. "How does thee know he's married?"

"A fine-looking man like that?" Prudence snorted. "Of course he's married!"

"Even if he isn't," Clyde added, "he could never marry any woman as he is. He could never be sure—nor the woman, either—that he wasn't committing bigamy." He was watching Grace's face and saw that his remark had troubled her. He said, "I saw Jacob Wirt today, Grace. He wants to see you."

"I've missed him," Grace said, glad to have the subject changed. "I'll go see him this week." She heard the sound of the horses outside and got up to put on her coat. "There's John with the sleigh."

"Don't stay out too long, Grace," Prudence called as Grace left the room. "It's too cold out there for you."

But Grace only waved and left the house. She climbed into the leather seat, and John said, "Better pull that blanket over your feet. It's sharp out tonight."

When he had seen to wrapping her carefully in the blanket, he spoke to the horses, and they stepped out at once. As they left the yard and turned toward the open country that lay east of the farm, he said, "You were right, Grace. This is much different than a buggy ride!"

A huge silver moon shed its beams over the snow, which gave back a glistening reflection. The sleigh traveled easily over the hard-packed crystals, making a sibilant sound. There was no rocking, and John said, "It's almost like flying, isn't it?"

"Yes. I've always loved it. My father took us all for rides like this, almost every night. He loved it, too."

They spoke quietly as John drove the horses at a slow trot, and finally they reached the small lake that glittered under the pale moonlight. Stopping the horses, he tied the reins and leaned back to admire the view. "So quiet! I didn't know a place could be so quiet!"

Grace swept her eyes over the view. "I've missed this."

They sat quietly, letting the stillness sink into their spirits. Perhaps it was this silence that finally prompted John to say, "I didn't want to say anything until I was sure, but things are coming to me, to my mind."

"You're beginning to remember your past?" she asked at once.

"Well, not exactly—"

She saw his hesitancy, then asked, "Can thee tell me what it's like?"

He pushed his hat back, then said slowly, "It's like being in a large room with all sorts of objects. I see them and know what they're for, but I don't know what they have to do with me." He frowned, for he felt he was doing a bad job of explaining. He shook his head and remained silent.

"Does thee remember anything for certain?"

"Faces." He nodded. "All kinds of faces. People I don't know but who seem to know me. And sometimes it's. . .well, like *scenes* in a play. I seem to be in the play, and I'm doing things. Simple things, usually, like eating a meal with someone. Sometimes doing something that I don't understand, but with people I ought to know—and don't."

A great sympathy welled up in Grace. She turned to him and put her hands on his, unconscious that she'd done so. "It'll come back, John," she whispered. "God will help thee!"

He sat there, and it was a few moments before he began to respond to her. They talked quietly, watching the moonlight on the snow and the lake. The air was still but cold, and when Grace began to shiver, he said, "You're getting cold! I should have brought another blanket!"

"When we came here when I was a child, we all huddled under the blankets together," she recalled with a smile.

"Well, I guess we can do that." John pulled the blanket over them, then put his arm around her shoulders and drew her close. It gave Grace a peculiar feeling, being held close this way, but John had done it so naturally that she moved against him without restraint.

"That better?"

"Yes, it is."

They sat there huddled together under the blanket, sharing

their warmth. Suddenly he said, "I just remembered something—a line of poetry, I think."

"What is it?"

" 'Two are better than one, because they have a good reward for their labour,' " he quoted. "Don't know what that is."

"It's from the Bible, John, from the fourth chapter of Ecclesiastes." She could feel the warmth of his arm on her shoulder, and she whispered, "I'm glad thee told me that!"

He turned to face her, blinking with surprise. "I remember more of it," he said and spoke again. " 'For if they fall, the one will lift up his fellow: but woe to him that is alone when he falleth; for he hath not another to help him up.' "

"That's such a beautiful verse!" Grace whispered, gazing out at the lake. "I've always loved it so."

John smiled and went on. " 'Again, if two lie together, then they have heat: but how can one be warm alone?' "

Grace smiled and looked up at him. They were very close, closer than either of them had realized. He could feel the firmness of her shoulders under his arm, and the curves of her body pressed against his side. Her eyes were enormous under the light of the moon, and the rich curve of her lips made her suddenly very lovely.

She was looking up at him, and without intending to do so, he lowered his head, letting his lips fall on hers. She didn't move, and the softness of her lips was sweet under his. He had no thought; all was impulse, and he let his lips linger on hers, savoring the moment.

Grace was shocked, but there was something in her that had longed for such gentleness. John was not demanding, and the caress brought her some sort of fulfillment deep within, a fulfillment she had not even been aware she needed.

She had always been a lonely child—and an even lonelier young woman. Now as John held her firmly, she was only conscious that somehow this was something she had longed for—and it was sweeter than she ever could have imagined.

Then she pulled back, and when John saw tears glistening in her eyes, he was stricken. "Grace—!" he whispered. "I'm sorry!"

She put her hand on his lips. "No, thee must not be sorry," she said. "It was my fault."

"I—I've just been so lonely, Grace," he said after a long silence. He moved away from her. "I wouldn't hurt you for anything in the world." And then he tried to smile as he gave his only excuse. "You looked so beautiful, so lovely, I. . .I just couldn't help it!"

His words were like ointment to her spirit. Grace had heard so many other young women telling what their lovers had said, yet she had been forced to remain silent—for there were no lovers speaking to her. Now she had felt the caress of a man's lips and heard his tender words—and she was happy.

"We're both lonely, John," she said quietly. "I think we're entitled to one mistake."

Mistake. The word stung, though he did his best not to show it. He knew he and Grace could never be more than friends, not while he had no memory of his life before the hospital. Yet as he gazed down at her in the moonlight, he suddenly realized that his feelings for this strong, devout, beautiful woman went much deeper than mere friendship. But if she considered their kiss a mistake, then it would be best for him to keep his feelings to himself. She had done so much for him, he didn't want to impose on her tender heart with protestations of a love she did not want.

He nodded, then took the reins and spoke to the horses. They rode back and soon were talking easily. But when he lifted her out of the sleigh, they both knew that something was different. They could never be the same again, for the kiss and the moment had stirred things deep within both of them—things that would not easily be forgotten.

CHAPTER 14

AN UNEXPECTED VISITOR

At the same time that Grace Swenson was engaged in her own private battle to redeem the soldier she knew as John Smith from his bondage, the war rolled on. After Lee and Jackson had wrecked John Pope at Second Manassas, President Lincoln was in despair, thanks to the military genius of Robert E. Lee.

Four classic victories—the Seven Days', Second Manassas, Fredericksburg, and Chancellorsville—all confirmed Lee as the most gifted general of the American Civil War. He was the greatest living war asset of the Confederacy. No other general in that conflict, and few others in military history, ever displayed such a wide-ranging talent for making bricks without straw. When it came to turning retreat into advance, vulnerability into sudden dazzling promise, Robert E. Lee stood alone.

Under Lee's hand, the Army of Northern Virginia became a master weapon, one that marched into military legend with its commander. Never in the darkest days of the war did Lee even once lose the personal devotion of his army's rank and file.

This, then, was the adversary whom Lincoln faced, and the president was hard put to find a general to stand against Lee. After the debacle of Second Manassas, he put McClellan in charge again, for though the small commander had no killer instinct, he was the best general alive at putting heart into defeated men and getting them whipped into shape for another campaign. He met the defeated troops of General Pope and molded the broken Army of the Potomac into a fine striking force.

Unfortunately, Lincoln did not replace McClellan with a fighting general. He had one, though he did not realize it: one Ulysses S. Grant, who in the end would be the hammer that would bring down the Confederacy. But Grant was fighting at Vicksburg right then, and Lincoln thought he had no choice but to let McClellan lead the Army of the Potomac. Even if he *had* tried to replace McClellan, it would have caused a rebellion, for the troops admired Little Mac to a fault.

So it was that when Lee led the tattered Army of Northern Virginia into Maryland, it was McClellan he faced at Antietam. McClellan outnumbered his adversary by something like two to one and should have steamrollered Lee's thin ranks. But Little Mac once again failed to send his men into the fury of battle. Instead of ordering an overall assault, he sent men in by small units, thus giving Lee time to shift his divisions from spot to spot on that bloody field, stemming the Union tide.

Nothing reveals Lee's superiority over McClellan more than the fact that the Union commander had in his hand that which should have guaranteed Lee's destruction. For on September 13, two Federal soldiers from Indiana found some cigars wrapped in paper on the site of Lee's encampment—a paper that proved to be a missing copy of Special Order 191, which gave Lee's exact movements!

And even with *this* advantage, McClellan could not achieve a decisive win!

When the battle took place on Wednesday, September 17, McClellan failed miserably. The battle was bitter, and it cost the lives of more men than any other day of the war—12,500 Union soldiers and 13,000 Confederates killed or wounded.

Amazingly, after the battle, McClellan still had a chance to destroy the Confederate forces, for Lee's battered army was helpless. But Little Mac was so dominated by fear of Robert E. Lee that he let the Army of Northern Virginia slip away, taking its wounded. As a result, although the North won the battle at Antietam, it lost an invaluable opportunity for possibly speeding the end of the entire conflict.

Still, Antietam was enough of a success to accomplish one thing. Lincoln had been waiting for a Union victory to take a far-reaching step: to proclaim all slaves in the country free men. This he did by means of the Emancipation Proclamation.

Even so, Lincoln was through with McClellan. The absolute final straw for the exasperated president came the day after the battle, when McClellan refused to obey a direct order from

Lincoln to attack Lee. In early November 1862, McClellan was relieved of his command, and Major General Ambrose E. Burnside took over the Army of the Potomac.

In one way this was a desperate move on the part of Abraham Lincoln, but the president had reason to be desperate. The North was ready to quit—at least many of its citizens were. Even after the battle of Antietam, the Confederacy had sound reasons for optimism. The South was united in its goal: to keep the unprincipled and wholly ruthless foe at bay. There was no such unifying emotion in the North, where feelings were split over the war. The Peace Party was booming its drums, and it seemed likely that England would declare its support of the Confederacy.

Truthfully, the North was worn down with war-weariness. Twice in the eighteen months since Sumter, the Union had succumbed to the siren call "On to Richmond!" Both attempts had been defeated in battle. Now the road to Richmond was blocked again by Lee's army, which, if not fought there, would invade the North again under its daring commander.

So the president appointed Burnside, who would begin a new Union assault against the South—and the appointment sent echoes through the entire North, changing the destinies of countless thousands.

Throw a stone into a quiet lake, and its ripples move in circles evenly out to the edges of the shore. But if you drop two stones, the ripples intersect into a more complicated pattern. Throw in a handful of sand, and all is confusion. The stone of

Burnside's appointment was merely one factor in a series of days that further complicated the war, but it was the factor that sent a ripple that carried all the way to a small farm in Pennsylvania where Burke Rocklin, known as John Smith, had just begun his painful climb out of the black pit of amnesia. Slowly he seemed to be gaining ground, so that he felt he could see faint glimmers of light and hope.

Then came the ripple that threw all into confusion—and it came in the form of Colonel Harold Drecker. A man with a vision, Drecker was a moderately successful manufacturer of furniture who lived, not for his tables and chairs, but for a dream of military glory. At the age of forty-three, he had seen his chance for this glory and after Antietam had begun to raise a regiment. He had mortgaged his factory to the hilt, left his brother-in-law to run it, and started out to form the Merton Blue Devils. He had bought the flashiest uniform money could purchase, a sword with a golden handle, and a fine warhorse. Spending his money lavishly on bounties, he had managed to fill the ranks of his company to about 50 percent strength. When enlistments had dropped off, he had used every means at his command to get his men.

One of these methods was to call back to active duty soldiers who had not served out their enlistments for one reason or another. Some of the soldiers Drecker sought out were those who had been mustered out before their time had expired—others were those who had been wounded but had since recovered.

It was almost an accident that Colonel Drecker got one particular name—one of his lieutenants had the brilliant idea of going through the list of wounded men who had been released from the hospital. Among these was the name of one John Smith.

"He's able-bodied, Colonel," the young lieutenant said as he went over the list with Drecker. "But I couldn't find out his rank or his former outfit."

Drecker said instantly, "We'll have him, Lieutenant Little! Where is he?"

"Apparently living on a farm not far from here, over by Rogers."

"Ah! I'll be in Rogers next week for a rally." Drecker beamed. "I'll stop by and bring the fellow back with me."

Lieutenant Bob Little was dubious. He had never served in the army; his current rank he held by virtue of being the nephew of Colonel Drecker. He was a slight young man with a smooth face and a pair of mild blue eyes. "Don't know about that, sir," he protested. "Do you have the authority to bring men like that back into service?"

"Yes, indeed, from Secretary Stanton himself! I'll get him, Bob; don't worry! You can have him in your company if he looks like a good one."

And so it was that chance and happenstance sent Colonel Harold Drecker to Grace Swenson's small Pennsylvania farm. Of such small things life is constructed, and no man is able to know or explain why these things happen—or fail to happen!

As December approached, it seemed it would reverse the biting cold blasts of November and bring relief to Pennsylvania. With each passing day, snow began to melt slowly under the sun's rays, and by contrast the breeze seemed to grow almost warm and balmy.

Though Grace was as strong as she'd ever been, she had requested—and received—permission from Miss Dix to extend her stay for another month. Miss Dix had not asked the reason, for she had read all she needed to know in Grace's letter. *Come back when you can give your full heart to the work,* she had written, and Grace had been quick to tell John that she was not going back until spring.

As for himself, John was happy. He was fully recovered physically and spent his days working on the farm and his evenings inside the snug house, reading or talking to Grace. He had become fascinated by the Bible and asked endless questions of her. Many of them she could not answer, so the two of them had gone three times for study with Jacob Wirt. The old scholar had welcomed them, and Grace knew that he was examining John Smith carefully. She trusted Wirt implicitly and waited impatiently for his judgment of the young man.

It came one evening when another guest had taken John upstairs to show him some samples of fine early furniture. Wirt leaned back and put his wise old eyes on Grace. "Well, thee isn't asking me what I think of the young man?"

"Oh, thee knows I want so much for thee to like him!"

"Why?"

"Because. . .the Lord is doing a work in him—and He is using me as part of it."

"Ah? Thee sees him as a convert? Thee is a holy young woman!" Grace knew Wirt was laughing at her, and she blushed visibly—which only drew a broad smile from Wirt. "Has thee noticed he is a handsome fellow?" he inquired.

"Why, I believe most would say so."

"Most? What does thee say, Grace? And let thy answer be yea or nay."

Grace met Wirt's eyes and nodded. "Yes, he is handsome."

"He seems very strong."

"He—is very strong." The flush on her cheeks and neck grew richer, for she thought, *What if he asks me how I know John is strong?*

"Ah. And he is intelligent, very much so." Wirt studied the girl, thinking back over the years he had known her—all her life, actually. He had grieved over her aborted marriage, for he had told an intimate friend that of all the young women in their community, Grace Swenson was likely to make the best wife. But he knew he had to make himself plain to Grace, so he said, "What is his view of God? He listens much but says little."

"I think he is a seeker, Jacob."

"I sense that in him." Wirt grew silent, his sharp chin settling on his thin chest.

Finally Grace grew impatient. "What does thee think of him?"

Wirt lifted his eyes. "He is outside of my experience, Grace—as he is outside of thine. We have no way of knowing what sort of man he really is. He's like a babe, with no past— and yet he *does* have a past, one that I cannot help but believe will one day catch up with him." He paused, then added gently, "Thee knows all these things. Be careful, my daughter. I think thee could be in grave danger."

Grace understood the old man's gentle warning perfectly and was aware that she would get no approval from him. But she was shocked at his next statement. "Thy brother-in-law thinks John Smith is a deceiver. He asked me to warn you to have nothing to do with him."

Grace was indignant. "He had no right to come to thee!"

Wirt smiled and shrugged his shoulders. "He is afraid for himself and his wife."

Grace fell silent. She was painfully aware of the resentment in Clyde and Prudence, but she refused to speak of it, even to Wirt. Still, she knew the old man wanted some reassurance from her, and she gave it. Reaching out, she took his hand in hers, smiled, and nodded. "I will be as wise as possible. Thee must pray much for me. I am a trouble to thee, Jacob."

"Never! Thee is the apple of my eye!"

On the way back to the farm, Grace noticed that John was unusually quiet. When they entered the house, he said, "Before you go to bed, I want to show you something, Grace." Reaching into his inner coat pocket, he drew out an envelope and handed it to her. "This came yesterday," he said evenly.

Grace took the envelope with a puzzled look, took out the single sheet of paper, and scanned it. It was written in a woman's hand and was very brief:

My dear Mr. Smith:

I have just returned from a visit with Miss Dorothea Dix, superintendent of nurses at the Armory Square Hospital. My purpose was to try and find my husband, Matthew. He has been missing since the second battle of Bull Run. I have made every inquiry, including many with the Confederate war prisons, all to no avail.

Miss Dix related your history, and I write this letter to inquire if your memory has returned. If it has, you will of course be restored to your people. If you are still suffering from a loss of memory, I will simply give you a description of my husband. He is tall, several inches over six feet, and on the lean side. He has black hair and dark eyes. He is thirty-five years of age.

My two sons and my daughter I have not told of this possibility. I write with little hope, but if this fits your description and you would like to meet me, I can be reached at the address at the bottom of this letter.

Mrs. Leota Richards

Something caused a constriction to grip Grace's throat, and

she swallowed hard before she looked up to say, "Does thee think she may be right?"

"No way to tell." John's face was tense, and he shook his head with a negative expression. "I fit the description pretty well, but so must a thousand other men."

"What will thee do?"

"Already done it," John answered. "I wrote back, saying I'd meet her."

"Oh." Grace felt a pang of disappointment, for she had assumed that he'd talk it over with her before acting on it. Then she said quickly, "Yes, thee must see her."

"I knew you'd think so." His brow suddenly wrinkled, and a strange look came into his eyes. "What if I am her husband? With three children I can't even remember? And there must be other family—parents, brothers—"

"Thee must not worry," Grace said at once. "God will give you the truth of it."

"I guess Mrs. Richards will do that," John said tightly. He suddenly took her hands, saying, "I'm always trouble for you, aren't I, Grace?"

"How could you be trouble?" she protested. The warmth and strength of his hands made her nervous. Withdrawing her own hands, she said, "Go to bed. Read the Gospel of John. It's God's best prescription for a troubled heart."

But the gospel, for once, failed to calm her own spirits. She read for a long time, but when she put the Bible down and blew out the lamp, sleep would not come. The letter had shaken her world, and she tossed for what seemed like a long time. Finally she drifted off, but slept only fitfully.

Three days later an answer came. Grace herself picked it up from the post office, and it lay like lead in her purse all the way back to the farm. She found John splitting rails for a fence, and as soon as he saw her face, he asked, "What's wrong?"

"Thee has an answer from. . .the woman who wrote."

He put the maul down, took the envelope, and stared at it. Then he looked up and said wistfully, "I'd like to burn this without opening it."

"No, thee must not do that."

"I suppose not." He opened the envelope, ran his eyes over the page, then looked up. "She's coming here, Grace."

That surprised Grace. "Here? I thought she'd ask thee to come to her."

He handed her the letter. "Her family lives in Gettysburg. She'll take the train there, then come here."

"When—when will she come?" Grace asked.

"Next week." John folded the paper and put it in his pocket. He stared down at the ground steadily, then expelled his breath. "For some reason this scares me. You'd think I'd be happy as a lark, wouldn't you?"

"It's a very difficult thing." Grace shook her head, adding, "Anyone would be nervous, I think." She tried to smile, saying, "Just think, thee may be with thy family soon."

But he was gloomy and only shook his head. "Guess I'd better finish splitting these rails."

It didn't take long for Clyde to notice how quiet the tall man had become. He finally asked Grace, "What's wrong with him? He's not getting mental, is he? Going crazy?"

"Of course not, Clyde. He just has a heavy load."

The following day, that load grew much heavier.

John had gone into the woods to chop firewood, and when he returned, he found he had a visitor.

"This is John Smith," Grace said as he entered the house. "And this is Colonel Harold Drecker, John."

"Glad to see you, Mr. Smith," the officer smiled. "Or is it *Private* Smith?"

John stared at the man. Drecker was wearing a spotless uniform of light blue trousers and a long dark blue coat with two rows of polished brass buttons. Shoulder-strap insignia bore the eagles that marked his rank. A high-crowned hat with the right brim pinned up and sporting a black ostrich feather lay on the floor next to his chair. A gilt-handled saber dangled from his left side.

"What can I do for you, Colonel?" John asked.

Colonel Drecker smiled heartily. "Why, I've come to do something for you, Smith!" He spoke quickly, like a salesman, and had a habit of stabbing the air with his forefinger for emphasis. He did so now as he continued. "I'm planning to field the most distinguished regiment in the Army of the Potomac! I suppose you've heard that General Burnside has been placed in charge?"

"Yes, I've read that in the paper."

"Well, sir, I've known the general for a long time, and he's been most enthusiastic about my efforts. In fact, he's promised me that the Merton Blue Devils—that's what my regiment is named—will be at the forefront of the fighting!" Drecker beamed with pleasure, and for the next fifteen minutes he spoke rapidly about what a glorious future lay ahead for the fortunate soldiers who would be under his command. They would, he asserted boldly, whip Bobby Lee and Stonewall Jackson, then march straight into Richmond!

"The only thing I fear is that Burnside will do the job before the Blue Devils can get into action!"

"I doubt you have to worry about that, Colonel," John said dryly. "But what brings you to see me?"

"Why, I thought I'd made myself plain," Drecker said with surprise. "I'm filling the places still available in the ranks of the Blue Devils, and you're being given a chance to join with me in driving the Rebels back to Richmond."

His proposal caught both his listeners off guard. Grace said, "Mr. Smith was invalided out on a medical discharge, Colonel."

But Drecker had thought that out. "Not really, Miss Swenson. His record shows that he was wounded and sent to Armory Square Hospital, and the record there clearly indicates that his wounds were healed and that he was discharged with a clean bill of health."

"But did thee not know of his—mental problems?"

"Oh, there was a note, I believe," Drecker muttered with

a shrug, then said with energy, "but we must not give in to our fears. Many men break under the strain of battle, but they recover." He put his rather close-set brown eyes on the tall man, examined him critically, then nodded. "You seem very fit, Smith. How do you feel?"

"I'm all right, Colonel." There was no point, John saw at once, in arguing with this man.

"Of course you are!"

"But I have some—personal problems that I have to take care of, so I'm afraid I won't be going with your regiment."

Colonel Drecker lost his smile, and a hard glint appeared in his eyes. He was no longer the amiable recruiter. "You misunderstand me, Smith," he snapped harshly. "You *are* going with my regiment." He pulled a paper from his pocket, extended it, and continued as John read it: "You are not being enlisted, for you are already a soldier of the Union Army. That paper will inform you of your status—that you and the others named there are under my command. And you will notice that it's signed by Secretary Stanton himself!"

John read the order, then slowly handed it back to the officer. "I have no choice, it seems."

Drecker, now that he had his man, grew congenial again. "Oh, you'll have time to get your business done," he said with a nod, slipping the paper back into his pocket. "The regiment is forming now. I want you to take a week, Smith. Report to my headquarters on the first of December." He turned, picked up his hat, and placed it firmly on his head. "Good to have you in my regiment, my boy! I'll see you in a week."

Drecker left the house, and when the sound of his horse's rapid hoofbeats faded, Grace stared at John speechlessly. He caught her eyes, then shrugged. "Well, I don't have to worry about my future, do I? At least not until the war's over."

"Oh, John!" Grace whispered. "There must be something we can do."

"I don't think there is. If I don't go, I could be shot for desertion. I know that much about the army." Seeing the stricken expression on her face, he grew gentler, stepping closer to her and reaching down to take her hand. "Don't let this give you trouble," he said. "I'm just one man. All over the country men are being scooped up to fight this war."

Grace felt the pressure of his hand and could think of no reply. The two of them stood there, touching—and yet so far apart! Finally he said heavily, "You've done all you can for me, and I'll always be grateful." That sounded heavy and pompous to him, and he found a smile. "Why, I'd never have known what a sleigh ride is like if it hadn't been for you!"

"I—I was hoping. . ." Her voice trailed off.

He waited for her to finish, but she turned her head away. "Tell you what, Grace," he said quickly. "Let's have a fine week! Go fishing through the ice, go for a sleigh ride every night—oh, do all the things we've done together."

"All right, John," Grace answered, and she forced herself to smile. "We'll have the best week we ever had!"

CHAPTER 15

"A WIFE OUGHT TO KNOW"

air skies and mild weather blessed the land that week—John's last week on the farm. The old men and women could not remember a milder winter, and people were beginning to wonder if they would have a white Christmas. Grace and John spent the early part of the week driving the sleigh all over the county. She took him to every spot that had been a pleasure for her, and in the evenings they walked under the bright moon or spent the time in the parlor together.

It was a quiet time, a time when they both stored up memories. They didn't speak of the future, almost as though they'd made a covenant to ignore it.

On Sunday they went to meeting, and again John was impressed with the Quaker style of worship. "Whatever kind of church I went to," he told Grace once, "it wasn't like this one. I know that!"

"I think there are many ways of worshipping God, John,"

650

she'd said quietly. "The name on the sign outside the meeting place isn't as important as the condition of our hearts."

On that last Sunday, it had been Grace among the ministers who'd risen after a long time of waiting for a word. Her face was still, though somewhat pale, and as she spoke, a light seemed to flow out of her eyes. She spoke of the love of God, and her simple words moved John tremendously. After the service, while they were on the way back to the farm, he said, "I wish I knew God like you do, Grace."

"Thee must find thy own way, John," she answered at once. "But God longs for your heart. He made thee to have fellowship with Him, and thee will never be complete until thee is safe in His arms."

He sat quietly, holding the reins loosely, a puzzled look on his face. "That's a strange way to put it," he said finally. "I thought it was we who were seeking God."

"No man or woman seeks God by nature. We're too wicked for that. But God has been seeking His people ever since they fell. In the Garden He called Adam after the Fall, and He's been calling us all to come home ever since."

He stole a look at her face, wondering at the glow of joy that suffused it. He shook his head, saying, "I don't think everyone has your capacity for love, Grace. Nobody that I know has."

She parted her lips to protest but then saw that he was looking downcast. "Thee must not give up, John. If thy heart is willing, God will find you."

They spoke no more along those lines, and that night she

651

read from the parts of the Bible that stressed God's call for man to repent. He listened carefully and asked questions. When it was time to retire, he said, "Whatever happens after this week, Grace, I can't ever say that I haven't heard the gospel, can I?" His eyes grew sober, and he spoke of what they had been avoiding all week. "We'll know something after tomorrow, I guess."

"Don't take counsel of your fears, John." She knew he had been dreading the arrival of the woman who might hold the key to his past. "We will pray, and God will give us the truth."

He studied her, then nodded. "Guess I'll have to go on your faith until I get some of my own."

Grace lifted her smile to him. "That's part of what being a Christian really is, John. Learning to take from others that which we lack."

Grace never knew how much John slept that night, but she didn't sleep a wink. When they met at the breakfast table, she noted that his eyes were red-rimmed and his features stiff with fatigue. He had shaven closely and put on his best coat, but he only picked at his food.

Clyde and Prudence were already at the table when John sat down. Neither of those two knew about the crisis, for by common consent Grace and John had agreed to keep it from them. Clyde noted John's nervousness, though, and commented, "What's wrong, John? Lost your appetite?"

"Oh, not very hungry, I guess."

Grace ate little, as well, and after the meal she excused herself. John had informed her that he intended to go to town alone and meet the woman. She had agreed, knowing that it would not be wise to let Clyde and Prudence meet her.

But at nine o'clock, a knock at her bedroom door interrupted her as she was reading her Bible. She closed her Bible and went to the door. There stood John, looking rather sheepish.

"Grace, would you go to town with me?" he asked abruptly.

"Why. . .I suppose so, John. Is thee ready now?"

"Yes, let's go."

Grace put on her heavy coat and bonnet, then went down and got into the buggy with him. She drew up a blanket— thinking suddenly of the time she'd shared it with him on their sleigh ride. When he saw she was settled, he said, "Hup!" The matched grays lunged forward, and soon they were on the road leading to town.

After a period of awkward silence, John laughed aloud, rather ruefully, saying, "I guess you think I'm the world's worst coward."

"Why—!"

"Oh, don't mind saying it, Grace," he said, turning to face her, and she saw that he was embarrassed. "Well, I'll tell you right out, I'd rather be thrown into a den of rattlesnakes than meet this woman!"

"But, John—why?"

He struggled with his thoughts, then shrugged helplessly. "Hard to say." He studied the landscape, letting the horses find their own pace. There was a fineness in his face that Grace had always admired. It was more than just handsome features; it was a clean decency that she appreciated and respected.

He turned and met her eyes, then smiled. "Crazy, isn't it? I've been crying like a baby for weeks, wanting to know who I am. And now that the chance has come. . .I'm trembling!"

"Perhaps the sight of one you—of one you love—" Grace stumbled over the phrase, then recovered. "Well, it might make thee remember."

He shook his head doubtfully. "It's possible, I guess. I've been seeing more faces, sometimes in dreams, sometimes in my mind when I'm awake. I'm sure they're people I must have known. One of them came to me last night. It was a woman, and she was beautiful—older than you are, Grace, but with the same kind of gentleness."

"What did she look like, John?"

"She had auburn hair, with some gray in it. And the most striking eyes I've ever seen," he marveled. "If I were a painter, I could paint her picture!"

"Maybe thy mother?"

"Could be. I wish I knew. The thing is, these things are coming back more often—and a lot clearer. If I just had *time*—!"

Grace longed to help him but could find no words. Finally she asked, "Why did thee want me to come with thee, John? You aren't really so afraid to meet a mere woman."

He grinned wryly. "Oh, I don't know. . .just for company, I guess." He fell silent, then added, "I needed you. That's all I can say, Grace."

His simple words warmed her, and she thought, *If I never*

have more than this—I can hold it and remember it all my life!

Aloud she asked, "Does thee want me there when she comes?"

"Yes!"

"She may find it strange."

"We'll tell her you're my keeper," he said, grinning. "Maybe she'll think I'm a lunatic out of the asylum for a little break. That should send her back in a hurry. She won't want a madman for a husband."

Grace saw that he was speaking lightly to cover the apprehension inside and helped him by joining in the frivolous talk.

They got to town an hour before the train was due, and John drove to the town's only hotel and reserved a room. When the clerk asked what name, he hesitated, then said, "Mrs. Leota Richards."

"Very well, sir."

When he had signed the register, John led Grace out of the lobby and they went to a café. He ordered coffee for himself and cocoa for Grace. They sat there for half an hour, speaking about everything in the world but the matter that had brought them to town. Finally he rose abruptly. "Let's walk around, Grace."

"All right."

They walked back and forth, looking in the windows of the few stores along the street, and finally the sound of a distant whistle drew their attention.

"There it is!" he said, expelling his breath. "Let's go get it over with."

They walked toward the station, then stood on the platform until the engine pulled alongside, gusting great clouds of steam. The brakes ground until the train stopped, and then the conductor stepped down and began to assist people to make the long step to the ground.

There were only six passengers who got off, and of those, only one seemed to be the one they sought.

"I think that must be her, John," Grace said, nodding toward a woman who had stopped and was looking around.

John nodded, set his jaw, and said, "Come along, Grace." He took her arm so tightly that it hurt, and the two of them approached the woman. She was short and rather heavy—not really fat, but full figured. She turned to them instantly, and Grace saw that she was not particularly attractive. She had a pair of sharp black eyes and a narrow nose that gave her a predatory look. Her lips were firm but were set in a closemouthed expression.

"Mrs. Leota Richards?"

"Yes." The woman said no more, though both Grace and John expected her to show some sort of emotion. She studied the pair before her and then said, "Is there a place for me to stay?"

"Why—yes," John said hastily. "Which is your bag? I've taken a room for you at the hotel."

"The black one."

John took the bag and nodded toward the buildings that marked the town. "It's this way." He realized suddenly that the woman was staring at Grace and said hastily, "This is Miss Grace Swenson. She was one of the nurses at the hospital who took care of me."

"I see. And do you live here, Miss Swenson?"

"No, I live on a farm about ten miles from town, Mrs. Richards." Grace felt the gaze of the woman's piercing eyes and added quickly, "When John had to leave the hospital, he had no place to go, so he came to stay with my family."

"Very kind of you."

An awkward silence fell, and after a few steps, John asked inanely, "Did—did you have a good trip?"

"Yes. It was very comfortable."

Grace saw that John's brow was covered with perspiration despite the cool air and knew that he was somewhat desperate. *He expected the woman to identify him at once—and she says nothing! What kind of a woman can she be?*

Somehow they got to the hotel, Grace filling the silence with small talk about the weather. But when they finally reached the woman's room, John asked, "Can we talk?"

"Certainly. Come inside." Mrs. Richards stepped into the room but gave Grace a forbidding look. "If you don't mind, Miss Swenson, I'd like to speak privately."

"Why, of course!"

John gave her a rather desperate glance but nodded. "Wait in the restaurant, Grace."

Grace nodded, and when the door shut, John turned to face the woman. She was pulling off her coat calmly. "It's rather cold in this room, isn't it?"

Ignoring her remark, he demanded, "Well—?"

But she forestalled his demand, saying, "Sit down, please. I want to hear your story."

John hesitated, then surrendered. He sat down and began to speak. The woman listened to him, not taking her eyes from his face. He could not tell one thing about what was going on inside her heart, for she let nothing show in her features.

Finally he finished, saying, "So I have no idea of my past, none at all."

"You don't recognize me?"

"N–no, I don't!"

She sat quietly in her chair, then said evenly, "Your name is Matthew Richards. You're my husband."

A great emptiness suddenly swept through John, and he felt as powerless to speak as if he'd been struck in the pit of his stomach. She watched his face grow pale, then asked, "Don't you remember me at all, Matt?"

"I. . .don't think so."

Mrs. Richards studied him carefully. "It's a strange thing. It must be terrible for you." She began to speak, telling him of his family and of his past. After a time she rose and came to stand beside him. "We'll be very patient, Matt," she said. Then she asked, "Do you need to go back to the place you've been living, or can we catch the next train home?"

He licked his lips, then shook his head. "I don't know. I'm confused." He felt short of breath and somehow was terribly afraid, more so than he'd been since he'd come back from the darkness that had swallowed him.

Suddenly he knew that he *had* to get away! Just for a few minutes! "Look, I'll leave you here to rest up," he babbled desperately. "I—I need some time alone. You understand." He made a dive at the door and left her, saying, "I'll be back soon!"

He stumbled down the stairs and found Grace seated in the lobby. "Come on!" he cried hoarsely. "Let's get out of here!"

Grace rose at once, and the two of them left the hotel. He said, "Get in the buggy," then helped her in and climbed into the seat beside her. He whipped the horses up, and they snorted at that unexpected treatment, bolting forward and splashing mud on a large man, who turned and cursed them roundly as they went flying down the street.

When they were clear of the town, John let the horses run until they slowed of their own will. He sat there, his face pale, saying nothing. Grace remained silent.

The bustle of the town faded, and soon they were plodding along the muddy road, surrounded by the quietness of the countryside. The trees were naked and bare, and the raw earth of plowed fields peeped through breaks in the snow.

On and on they drove, and Grace thought, *It's a good thing I'm a Quaker and accustomed to silence! It must have been dreadful for him!*

Finally he took a deep breath and turned to her. "Sorry to act like this, Grace," he muttered. "I just had to get away for a few minutes."

"It's all right," Grace murmured. "What did she tell thee, John?"

"She says I'm Matthew Richards, her husband."

Grace had been prepared for this, for she had sensed that he would not have reacted so violently had the woman said otherwise—and yet she was stunned by the pain that shot through her to hear him say the words. "Tell me about it, John," she said, forcing her voice to be steady and calm.

He spoke quickly but jerkily as he recounted the meeting, ending by saying moodily, "She's absolutely certain I'm her husband."

Grace had listened carefully, but somehow she was troubled. "John, I need some time to pray."

"Why, of course!" John was surprised but said no more. He allowed the horses to pick their way down the muddy road for half an hour, sitting silently beside Grace as she sought the Lord. Then she turned and said firmly, "Go back to the hotel."

"What?"

"Go back to the hotel."

He stared at her, then nodded. "I guess I've got to face up to this thing."

"God has given me a word."

"What?" Confusion caused him to blink. He had heard the expression several times among the Quakers but had never understood it. "What does that mean?"

"It means that God has spoken to me."

"About me, and about—her?"

"Yes. Turn the buggy around."

He stared at her, then shrugged. "All right, Grace."

She said nothing as they made their return trip, and he was too depressed to make conversation. When they got back to the hotel, she said, "Let's go to her room."

He tied the horses, and the two of them climbed the stairs. When he tapped on the door, it opened almost at once. Mrs. Richards had a half smile on her face, but it died when she saw Grace.

Grace stepped inside, practically forcing herself past the woman. John stepped in after her, and the woman closed the door and turned to face them.

Grace met the woman's gaze squarely and spoke with quiet confidence. "Mrs. Richards, I do not think this man is thy husband!"

John's mouth dropped open, and he took a sharp breath. He was watching the woman's face and saw quick anger come to her sharp eyes.

"Are you telling me I don't know my own husband?" Mrs. Richards demanded shrilly.

"I think thee does know thy *own* husband, but thee is deceiving this man. He is not thy husband."

"Get out of here! Matthew, get this woman out of my room!"

"I'd sort of like to hear what she has to say," John remarked. He turned to Grace and studied her carefully. "What makes you so sure I'm not married to her?"

Grace didn't answer his question. Instead she faced the woman and said evenly, "How long does thee say this man has been thy husband?"

"Twelve years!"

"And how many children has thee had by him?"

"Three! Do you think I could make a mistake about a man I've been married to for that long?"

"If thee will answer one simple question, I will admit he is thy husband."

Mrs. Richards glared at Grace suspiciously. "What question?"

"The purple birthmark on thy husband's side—is it shaped like an egg or like a cat's paw?"

A dead silence fell on the room. Mrs. Richards stared at Grace, then at the man beside her. Defiantly she said, "Like a cat's paw!"

John's face broke out in a broad smile, and he said, "Well, it's been nice to meet you, Mrs. Richards. You can catch the next train to Gettysburg at six this evening." He put his hat on and took Grace's arm firmly.

He paused long enough to speak to Mrs. Richards. "The birthmark is shaped like a star, and it's on my back, not my side."

Mrs. Richard's face had lost all color. She glared at Grace, then hissed, "You'd know all about that, wouldn't you? I knew you were after him from the minute I set eyes on you!" She began to curse them both as they walked from the room, and they could hear her as they marched down the stairs.

He helped her into the buggy, barely pausing as he took up

the reins and slapped the horses into action. When they were safely out of town, John turned and took her hands in one of his. "Grace, how did you know? And why in the world did she ever come and make such a claim?"

"I suspected when we met her," Grace said quietly. "No woman who loved her husband could be so cool when she saw him after thinking he might be dead. Either she was lying, or she had never loved thee."

Relief showed in his face, and he laughed out loud. "Who could help loving me?" he demanded. "And why did she try such a crazy thing?"

"I think she took a chance that thee would never remember anything. She wants a husband so badly that she did all this to get one."

He abruptly threw his arms around her and hugged her. "Oh, Grace! I feel like I've been let out of jail!"

She lay crushed against his chest, unable to keep the grin from her own features. Finally she pushed him away and admonished him with a tremulous smile, "Don't be so conceited."

But he didn't release her immediately. He kept his arms around her for one moment longer, then let her go. "My good angel, Grace," he whispered gently. Then he said quietly, "I knew that woman wasn't my wife."

"Really, John? How did thee know that?"

He reached out and stroked her cheek. "Because," he said slowly, "I didn't feel about her. . .as I do about you."

Swift color filled Grace's face, and her heart constricted

painfully. Could he possibly mean. . . ? "Thee—thee shouldn't speak so!" Her voice was unsteady and breathless.

John Smith shook his head, pulled the horses to a stop, and dropped the reins. Reaching out, he put his arms around her and drew her close. Grace's eyes grew alarmed, and she cried out, "John—!"

But he ignored her protest. His eyes were fixed on her face and filled with a tender determination. "I love thee, Grace Swenson!" he whispered, then pulled her into his embrace, kissing her thoroughly.

His touch stirred impulses in Grace that she hadn't known were within her, and she felt as though her heart would burst with the joy that swept through her at his words. A small part of her mind scolded her, telling her she should push him away... but she ignored it blissfully.

Finally he released her, but he held her gaze, letting her see for herself the intensity of his love for her. He reached up to touch her face gently, and when he spoke, his voice was strong and deep. "I don't know who I am or where I'm going, but I know one thing full well. And that is that I love thee, Grace. For now, that is enough."

❧

Three days later, Grace stood beside John at the depot. The conductor called out, "All aboard!" and he turned and held her in a tight embrace.

"John—!" she whispered, holding him fiercely.

He kissed her, then said, "Don't forget, I love thee!" He had said it that way often the past three days, which had stirred both happiness and sorrow in her. Happiness that they had discovered such a wondrous love; sadness that they both knew the future was blank and they could make no plans.

But now as he tore himself from her and climbed the steps of the train, she felt a pang of loneliness such as she'd never known. As the train lurched and left the station, she caught a glimpse of his face and waved.

He loves me! she thought, and as she turned and walked away, she bit her lips to keep them steady. *I love thee, too—and I'll never love another!*

As she climbed into the buggy and started her homeward journey, the train whistle sounded—a lonesome, haunting wail that echoed plaintively on the stillness of the air.

665

CHAPTER 16

INTO THE VALLEY OF DEATH

The battle of Fredericksburg should never have been fought.

The Army of the Potomac was shoved into the suicidal attempt by a man who had endeavored to refuse the command of the army and who had to be directly *ordered* to assume that post by the president.

Major General Ambrose E. Burnside was a man with incredible whiskers, who moved from disaster to disaster with an uncomprehending and wholly unimaginative dignity. He had wooed a Kentucky girl and taken her to the altar, only to be flabbergasted when she returned a firm *no* to the officiating minister's climactic question. (The same girl later became engaged to an Ohio lawyer who had heard about Burnside's experience. When the wedding date arrived, this man displayed to her a revolver and a marriage license, telling her that she could choose one or the other. This time she went through with the ceremony.)

Burnside quickly won the admiration of the soldiers, for he showed a great concern for their well-being, always poking his nose into mess shacks, sampling the food, and checking on supplies. In a way, this revealed his tragic flaw, for he needed to be studying strategy and tactics in order to meet Robert E. Lee, not tasting soup!

The first plan he made was sound, and his first move caught Lee by surprise. He did not advance directly on Lee, as that general expected, but headed southeast, arriving on the Rappahannock River, just across from Fredericksburg. This left Lee out of position, with half his army at Culpepper and the other half under Jackson in the Shenandoah Valley.

For two precious days, the road to Richmond lay wide open to the Federal Army—the first and last time this happened during the Civil War!

Sadly, the pontoon bridges that Burnside had ordered from the War Department did not arrive on time, so the unique chance passed. Burnside's army waited on the north bank of the Rappahannock, looking across the river to the heights above Fredericksburg as they gradually filled with the infantry and artillery of Lee's frantically redeployed army.

Burnside had ample heavy artillery to keep the Confederates from securing the line of the south bank, but he failed to use it. His pontoon bridges had to be built under fire, and Union blood was shed by this tragic oversight. On December 11, after three wasted weeks had given Lee time to lodge the Army of Northern Virginia, the situation was hopeless for the Northern troops.

On December 10 a woman crept down to the bank of the Rappahannock and called across to the gray pickets that the Yankees had drawn a large issue of cooked rations—always a sign that action was at hand.

That night a party was given by the officers of a New England regiment in a riverside hut. Some twenty men who had no illusions about the kind of reception they were going to get when they crossed the river met to sing songs and drink whiskey punch. The hut rocked with cheers and the glasses went bottoms up, and later as they marched up to the river, they heard the high soft voice of a contraband camp servant lifted in the song "Jordan Water, Rise over Me."

The next day, the engineers put the pontoon bridge across the river, but only at a high price. Confederate sharpshooters, taking refuge in the buildings of Fredericksburg, picked them off as easily as if they were shooting squirrels. Burnside finally ordered the town destroyed by artillery, after which he sent infantry across by boat to drive the sharpshooters back.

The fight was rough while it lasted. The Twentieth Massachusetts Regiment lost ninety-seven officers and men in gaining fifty yards. In the end the town was secured, and men remembered afterward that a strange golden dusk lay upon the plain and the surrounding hills, as if a belated Indian summer evening had come bewildered out of peacetime autumn into wartime winter. A newspaper correspondent wrote: "Towering between us and the western sky, which was still showing its faded scarlet lining, was the huge somber pillar of grimy smoke that marked the burning of Fredericksburg. Ascending to a vast height, it bore away northward shaped like a plume bowed in the wind."

When darkness was complete, Lee ordered Jackson to bring his two nearest divisions to Longstreet's support. He was pleased, though he could not quite believe that *any* general would attack him in his present position! He thought of the position of the Union Army and of his own position—the strongest he had ever held in his military career. He called for a light, and when an aide brought a lantern, he studied the map on which he had placed the positions of both armies.

The Confederate Army, seventy-eight thousand men, was in a formidable line on the high ground west of the Fredericksburg plain. The ground was only forty or fifty feet above the plain, but that made it exactly right—high enough to offer an impregnable defensive line, but not high enough to scare the Federals and keep them from attacking. Directly west of the town rose a ridge called Marye's Heights. To the north, slightly higher hills slanted off to the river. To the south, the high ground pulled farther and father away from the river.

Lee studied the map and thought about the men who would lead: For the Union it would be Major William B. Franklin leading the left wing and General Joe Hooker leading the right wing; for the Confederacy, General Longstreet would defend the left and Stonewall Jackson the right.

Lee smiled, put up his map, and went to bed. *The South never had to worry less about a battle than this one,* he thought happily.

The next morning Lee and Longstreet stood looking down on the snow-pocked plain where the blue host was massing. The two men made a contrast indeed. Lee was tall and handsome, with a short-clipped iron-gray beard. Beneath the brim of a sand-colored planter's hat, his quick brown eyes had a youthfulness that disguised the fact that he would be fifty-six years old in one month.

His companion was a burly, shaggy man, six feet tall and of Dutch extraction. Except for Lee himself, no commander in the Confederate Army was more admired and loved by his men. This was based on their knowledge of his concern for their well-being in and out of combat. They called him Old Pete and sometimes the Dutchman.

The two men looked up as the third-ranking member of the army triumvirate came riding up. It was Jackson, but a Jackson quite unlike the Stonewall they were accustomed to. No officer in the army paid less heed to his dress than Stonewall Jackson. But now, gone were the mangy cadet cap and the homespun uniform worn threadbare. Instead he wore a new cap bound with gold braid and had more braid looped on the cuffs and sleeves of a brand-new uniform.

One of the men called out, "Lookee thar, Old Jack will be afraid for his clothes and will not get down to work."

Jackson got off his horse, muttering that the uniform was "a gift of my friend Stuart," and asked permission to attack.

Lee smiled, for Jackson seldom asked for anything else. "No, General Jackson. Let those people wear themselves out on our guns."

Old Pete baited him, saying, "Jackson, don't all those multitudes of Federals frighten you?"

Jackson glared at Longstreet. "We shall see very soon whether I shall not frighten *them!*"

Longstreet winked at Lee. "But what are you going to *do* with all those Yankees, Jackson?"

"Sir, we will give them the bayonet," Jackson snapped and turned and rode away.

Lee studied the masses of blue soldiers below and said, "I am afraid they will break your line, General."

Longstreet shook his head. "General, if you put every man now on the other side of the Potomac in that field to approach me over that same line, and give me plenty of ammunition, I will kill them before they reach my line!"

Lee looked down the lines at muskets that bristled from a sunken road that wandered the length of the heights, then studied the heavy artillery aimed at the open plain that the Federals would have to cross.

"I believe you are right, General Longstreet," he remarked quietly.

❧

One of the blue dots of color that made up the army that Lee looked down on was the coat worn by John Smith.

He had been mustered in only three days earlier. No one had inquired into his ability. He had been issued a musket and uniform and rushed by train along with the other members of the Merton Blue Devils to join Franklin's division, which was drawn up for battle on the banks of the Rappahannock.

Now as he looked up at the heights bristling with guns, a cold feeling gripped him. The lieutenant of his company, a young man named Robert Little, was staring at those same guns. Little swallowed hard, then said, "Cheer up, men! We won't have any trouble gettin' in!"

A burly private glared at the lieutenant and snarled resentfully, "Getting in? Them Rebs *want* us to get in. It's getting *out* that won't be so easy!"

Colonel Drecker came striding up, his face pale but filled with excitement. "Don't worry, men!" he called out. "We'll be going in soon!"

The Merton Blue Devils were held as reserves, however, and all day long they watched as masses of men marched into the fury of battle. When the order to charge came to each of the other regiments, the soldiers would surge forward—but none of them even got close to the wall of fire that belched from the guns of the defenders. Every attack "broke in blood"—failing because the men were too badly shot up to press on—and the Federals fell back, leaving the stretch of open ground thick-strewn with corpses and writhing men whose cries could be heard above the clatter of musketry.

Sunset did not slow the tempo of the fighting. A fifth major assault on Marye's Heights had been repulsed, and from be-hind the sunken wall, the Confederates taunted the warmly clad Federals coming toward them in a tangle-footed huddle, "Come on, Bluebelly! Bring them boots and blankets! Bring 'em hyar!" And they did bring them, up to within fifty yards of the flame-stitched wall. There the forward edge of the charge was frayed and broken, the survivors crawling or running to regain the protection of lower ground.

At three o'clock Colonel Drecker came to say, "All right, men, fix bayonets! We will advance!"

John looked at the man next to him and said grimly, "That's a foolish order! Not a man of ours has gotten closer than fifty yards to the Rebel lines all day!"

Then the call came, and the Blue Devils moved forward. John kept in rank as they crossed the low ground, and soon men began to fall.

"Come on, men!" Drecker screamed, waving his sword. "Your colonel will lead you!" He plunged forward, heading straight for the sunken road where bodies from five previous charges covered the ground. Shells began to burst in their ranks, blowing men to bits. One man not ten yards in front of Smith fell, his leg all but severed. Three men jumped to pick him up, but Drecker was there, screaming, "Forward! Leave him there!"

By the time they had reached the top of the incline and faced the concentrated fire of the Confederates, half of the regiment had been either killed or wounded. The slaughter continued, but Drecker plunged ahead. He turned and screamed, "Come on!

Follow me! We'll show—!"

A shell removed his head neatly, and his body slowly toppled to the ground.

The brigade stopped at once, but they were pinned down. To go back, Smith saw, was as dangerous as to go on. He threw himself into a shallow depression and dug deeper with his bayonet. Others were doing the same, and when darkness fell, he lay down and waited for morning. He thought about crawling back to his own lines, but sharpshooters were firing at everything that moved. He saw four men cut down as they tried to make it back, and finally he gave up.

He lay there, his legs twitching and his mouth as dry as dust. At last the need for water drove him to crawl five yards to get the canteen of a dead private. He tipped the canteen back and drank thirstily.

Crawling back to his hole, he huddled down, facing the enemy line. For hours he lay there, until he finally drifted off into a fitful slumber. He was awakened abruptly by a sharp pain in his shoulder. At once he came awake, reaching for his musket—but saw that it was held by a ragged Confederate who was grinning at him.

"End of the war for you, Bluebelly," the Rebel said with a nod. "Now you shuck out of them nice boots and that warm coat. You kin have mine if you want."

The wolf-lean Confederate held a .44 aimed directly at his heart, so Smith said, "I guess you got the best of the argument, Reb." He removed his boots and coat, sat down as ordered, then put on the poor bits of leather the soldier had been wearing and slipped into the thin coat. He shivered as he got to his feet, and his captor nodded, "Nice boots you Yankees bring us. I 'preciate it. Now get going!"

As John plodded along toward the enemy lines, he knew the war was over for him. The wind cut through him like a knife, and he was exhausted by the time he'd been quick-marched five miles back of the lines and placed with a large group of captured Federals.

The lieutenant in charge formed them in lines and said, "I don't reckon you fellers will be killin' any more Southern boys now, will you?"

"Where'll we be held?" one of the captives asked.

"Libby Prison." The lieutenant looked at them with pity. "You'll be wishing you got killed before you've been there long! Now march!"

As Smith slogged along the road, his feet began to freeze. The bits of leather fell off, and soon his raw feet were leaving bloodstains in the mud. The cold seemed to get worse, touching his lungs with a tongue of fire when he inhaled. He reached the point when he could go no farther and was about to fall when the command came to halt.

"You men lie down. In the morning you'll be fed; then you'll march to the station. From there you'll be took to Richmond, to Libby Prison."

John no longer cared. He took the vile-smelling blanket from a private who was handing them out, wrapped it around himself, and fell to the ground. His last thought before he slipped away was of Grace, and he prayed simply, *Lord, let me see her again!*

Three days later he was a prisoner in Libby Prison.

He also had pneumonia, which he had developed from being exposed to the icy roads of Virginia and from lying on an open flatcar in freezing weather for two days.

When he was carried into Libby Prison, he was barely conscious enough to feel the rough hands of the soldiers who carried him, but he heard the voice of the doctor well enough when he said, "Another pneumonia case? Well, he'll die in a week, like the rest of them."

But the patient was too far gone to care. It didn't seem to matter very much, so he slipped away, welcomed once again into a stark black hole that closed around him silently.

PART THREE

The Prisoner and the Bride

CHAPTER 17

CAPTAIN CLAY FINDS A MAN

"Melora, come and see!"

Melora Yancy looked up from the rough-backed hogs, who were grunting and squealing as she tossed ears of corn into the trough. Her seventeen-year-old sister, Rose, was running toward her, hair flying. The girl didn't wait to reach Melora but cried out, "It's Mister Clay, Melora—he's comin' in a funny-looking wagon!"

At once Melora tossed the rest of the corn into the pen, then threw the basket aside and ran lightly to meet her sister. Her face had paled slightly, but she said nothing, listening as Rose urged her to hurry. When they came out of the grove, Melora saw at once the closed wagon Clay was driving.

He saw her and lifted his hand in a wave. Melora's father, Buford Yancy, appeared in the doorway, had his look, then came to stand beside the two girls. Josh, Martha, and Toby were standing back shyly, watching as Clay pulled the wagon to a halt in front of the cabin.

"Hello," Clay said. He jumped down and tied the team to a slick hitching post. Turning, he faced them, and Melora's heart skipped a beat, for he was not smiling.

"Is one of the boys kilt, Clay?" Buford asked carefully. He was a tall man with green eyes and was remarkably active for his age.

"No!" Clay said quickly. "Bob took a bullet in his leg, but it's not bad."

Melora released her breath. With brothers in the Confederate Army, all of their family lived under a shadow of constant dread. "Bring him inside, Clay," she said. "Rose, go fix a bed for him."

Clay stepped to the back of the ambulance, saying, "He did fine, Buford, real fine!" Opening the canvas flap, he found eighteen-year-old Bob Yancy propping himself up, and he gave him a hand. "Easy there," he cautioned.

Bob blinked owlishly in the bright noon sunlight, then grinned sheepishly at his father. "Didn't duck fast like you told me to, Pa," he said cheerfully. He put his leg down, and the pain drew a grimace from him.

Clay nodded at Buford. "Get his other side. That leg's pretty tender."

The two men picked young Yancy up, ignoring his protests that he wasn't a baby. They carried him inside and put him on a cot beside a window; then as the two women hustled around fixing a quick meal, Clay sat back and let the wounded man tell his story. Clay deliberately kept his eyes off Melora, though only with an effort. He was intensely aware of her presence, and when she came to put a plate of stew and glass of milk before him, he looked up at her, saying, "You're looking well."

Melora nodded but studied his face. "You look tired."

"He ort to be!" Bob Yancy spoke up. He was enjoying being the center of attention. The younger children had drawn as close to him as possible, their eyes wide with worshipful adoration. Bob waved a chicken leg and grinned. "Ain't none of you noticed nothing about him?"

Only then did Melora notice the bars on Clay's shoulders. "Why, Clay—!" she exclaimed. "You're a captain!"

Clay shrugged disdainfully. "It's just a brevet promotion," he said.

"Whut's thet, Clay?" Buford demanded.

"It means he does the job of a captain but only draws a lieutenant's pay," Bob said, grinning. Then he gave Clay a look of admiration. "When them Yankees came boiling across the river right at us, we got caught with one shoe off," he explained. "Captain Simon of G Company, he went down at the first volley, and Major Franklin, he hollered, 'Clay, you're promoted to captain!'"

"Well, when Captain Simon was wounded, Colonel Benton promoted me to take his place. Wasn't very smart of the colonel," Clay broke in. "Some of the other men have more seniority."

"Aw, everybody in the regiment knows you're the best soldier in the bunch, Clay—I mean, *Captain Rocklin!*" Bob ate his meal and made light of his own wound. He talked with animation, and the rest of the family—including his father—listened intently.

Clay got up and helped Melora with the dishes, then said, "I'd better feed and water the horses."

"I'll help you." Melora took off her apron, and the two went outside. Clay unhitched the horses and took them to the corral, saying, "We'll let them roll a little after they eat." He fed them from a sack of grain he'd brought, then turned them out. He turned to her, smiled, and said, "Let's go look at your pigs."

She smiled, too, for he always teased her about the hogs the Yancys were raising. He slanted a grin at her. "I'll bet you've got some favorites, haven't you?"

"Now don't scold me, Mister Clay!" she retorted, laughing, and led him to the hog pen, pointing out the different animals' beauty. Actually it had been Clay who had persuaded Buford to raise corn and feed out hogs instead of raising cotton. *We can't eat cotton, Buford,*" he'd said bluntly. *"It won't be worth a dollar a bale next year, with the blockade cutting us off from England—but bacon will be sky high!"*

After looking at the hogs, they walked along the edge of the woods beside the small stream until they came at last to a large pool, where they stopped and looked at the rippling water.

It was in these peaceful surroundings that he began to talk about the battle, and she listened quietly. Finally she asked, "Are you all right, Clay?"

He turned to look at her and was struck by the picture she made. Her hair fell over her shoulders, framing her face. Her eyes shone emerald green, and her clear complexion gave her face an almost translucent appearance. Clay thought her the loveliest woman he had ever seen, and he rested his gaze on her, knowing that she was asking about more than his reaction to the battle.

"You mean about losing Ellen?" he asked quietly. He had always been honest with her, and now he was no different. "I feel bad about it, Melora," he said quietly, his eyes moody and tinged with sadness. "I should have been able to help her more."

"You mustn't feel like that, Clay!" Melora spoke firmly. "You stayed with her and were faithful to her for years, and that was more than any other man would have done. And at the last, she found God." She reached out to lay a gentle hand on his arm. "Let her go, Clay," she said quietly.

He studied her countenance, then slowly nodded. "I'll have to learn, I guess. I made such a mess of the first part of my life, maybe I'm afraid of doing it again."

Melora took his hand and led him along the stream, and there was nothing artful or seductive in her gesture. She was, he thought, not the kind of woman to practice such things. He was constantly amazed that she was as guileless and sweet as she had been the first time he'd met her, when she was but a child.

They walked for an hour, talking of small things; then he said, "I've got to get back, Melora. I just didn't want Bob in the hospital. He'll be out of action for quite a while, and he'll be happier here."

"Is your regiment leaving again right away?"

Clay shook his head. "I doubt it. We whipped the Yankees so badly they'll do what they always do: run back to Washington and lick their wounds. Lincoln will probably get McClellan to pull them into shape."

"And then what?" Melora asked quietly.

"Then they'll hit us again." A weariness came to Clay's shoulders, and he shook his head sadly. "There's so *many* of them! They lost twelve thousand men at Fredericksburg, but there's ten times that many in the North ready to fill the ranks." He shook his head in a hopeless gesture. "But who's going to fill Bob's shoes? Nobody! We'll be stretched a little thinner, and we'll have to fight harder." He paused for a moment, seemingly deep in thought. Melora didn't push him. Finally he went on quietly: "But there will be an end to all of this, Melora. The South doesn't have a chance unless the Peace Party in the North gets its way and calls off the war."

They returned to the corral, and Clay hitched up the horses. "I'll be back to see Bob," he said with a smile. "Which means, I guess, that I'll be back to see you."

"I'll be here, Clay," she whispered. He held her eyes for a brief moment, then nodded and went into the house to say his good-byes. Within minutes he was climbing back into the seat of the wagon and driving out of the yard. Melora stood and watched him go, sending up a prayer for his safety.

By late afternoon Clay arrived at the camp where the Richmond

Grays were stationed. He turned the ambulance over to a teamster at the quartermaster's stables, then made his way to headquarters.

Only about half of the regiment had returned to Richmond, the rest being left on the Rappahannock to keep an eye on Burnside's beaten army. Clay worked with the headquarters staff on reports for two hours, then said, "I'm going to the hospital to see Captain Dewitt, Sergeant. You can finish these reports, I think."

He made his way into Richmond, where he found his old friend Captain Taylor Dewitt in Chimborazo Hospital—and in a bad humor!

"Clay! You've got to get me out of this place!" Taylor protested at once. He'd been hit in the side and in the neck by bursting fragments from a shell and was sitting in bed, his thin, handsome face twisted with displeasure.

One of the nurses, a tall, angular woman, turned from her position three beds away and came to stand over the patient. "You are worse than any child, Captain!" she snapped. "Now if you don't lie down and rest, I have ways of handling you!"

Dewitt blustered but did as the nurse said. When she left, he grumbled and complained, but Clay was relieved. "I'm glad to see you're all right, Taylor. When I saw you go down, it made me—" Clay broke off and shook his head, thinking of the moment. "It's one thing to think about death, but it's something else to see your friends go down."

Dewitt nodded slowly. "Yes, and we lost some fine friends on this one, Clay. You'll have to write some letters to their people—and you'll have to train some new men. . . ."

For half an hour the two friends talked; then Clay rose. "I've got to go. Anything I can get you?"

"Send me some cigars. Good ones."

Clay left the hospital and returned to the camp. For the next week he was buried in work, for Colonel Benton, who knew he was going to be gone most of the time, had told him, "Clay, you'll just have to fill in. Make all the decisions you can, and hold off the rest until I get back."

It was late on Monday afternoon when Clay looked up from the drill field where he was helping train new recruits and saw a buggy pull up bearing a short civilian.

"Clay—!" The man waved, and Clay recognized the Rocklin family physician, Dr. Kermit Maxwell.

Clay said, "Take over, Lieutenant," and walked quickly to the buggy. At once he asked, "Is someone sick, Dr. Maxwell?"

"No. Can you get loose for the rest of the day?"

Clay blinked at the suddenness of the request. "Why. . .I think so. What's wrong?"

"Get yourself loose," Maxwell grunted. He was a short, heavy man of eighty-two, with a round red face and a pair of sharp blue eyes. He had no bedside manner to speak of, but had been setting bones, birthing babies, and patching up Rocklins for nearly sixty years. In addition, he was a stubborn man, Clay knew, and when he saw that he'd get no more information, he called the lieutenant over, gave him instructions, then got into the buggy.

They left the camp, and Clay waited for Maxwell to explain his abrupt actions, but Maxwell talked about the war and then filled Clay in on what had been happening in Richmond. The doctor seemed to know everyone and was a careful judge of people, so his commentary was rough and colorful.

Clay asked about his father, and Maxwell shook his head. "I wish I could give you better news, Clay, but your father is in bad shape. I've done all I know. You might want to send him to one of the big hospitals."

"No, he'd hate that." Clay shook his head. He said no more, but it brought a heaviness to him, for he'd learned to love his father. It had taken years, but he'd won his father's love and respect in the fullest measure. Now, he knew, he didn't have much time to spend with Thomas—and the war took most of it away.

Maxwell drove through the city to the James River, pulling up the team in front of Libby Prison. He got down, then said to Clay, "It's pretty hard to find a doctor who'll treat the Yankee prisoners. I've been helping out some." He spat an amber stream of tobacco juice that splattered on bricks, then grunted, "Come along."

Clay was mystified, but he followed the doctor without comment. Originally, Libby Prison had been the warehouse of Libby and Sons ship chandlers, so it was situated on the James River at the corner of Twentieth and Cary streets. It was a large four-story building that was used primarily for housing injured Union officers.

Once they were inside, Maxwell muttered, "You boys shot up so many Bluebellies, there's no place to put them. We had to put some enlisted men in here with the officers."

"Back again, Dr. Maxwell?" A smallish sergeant with a wiry mustache greeted the two men with surprise but made no objection when Maxwell mentioned he wanted to make the rounds again. "Guess it's okay." He nodded and led them to a large room packed with beds so close that there was hardly room to walk.

Maxwell was greeted by several of the patients and stopped to look at a few. He was a gruff old fellow, but Clay noted how the Yankee prisoners followed him with their eyes. He kept close to the doctor, puzzled but saying little. One of the prisoners blinked at him, then whispered, "You just wait, Captain! We'll be back."

Clay smiled and reached into his pocket. He'd put a sack of candy there, a present for the niece of one of his sergeants. "I guess you will, soldier. Here, have a treat from the Richmond Grays."

The soldier was surprised but took the sack. "That'll go pretty good, Captain." He smiled. "Thankee!"

Clay moved to where Maxwell was standing, bent over a still form. As he approached, the bulky physician suddenly moved aside and motioned for Clay to look.

The light was dim, and Clay, after giving Maxwell a quizzical glance, stepped to the cot and bent over the man. The patient had his face turned away and Clay could tell little, but then

Maxwell reached down and turned the man's head so that the light from the barred window across the room fell full on the lean face.

Clay sucked in his breath, gasping audibly. He blinked and leaned closer, studying the still features, then turned to face Maxwell, his face gone pale.

"Burke!" he whispered. "It's Burke!"

Maxwell demanded, "Are you sure, Clay?"

"Sure? You think I don't know my own brother!"

"Come on, let's get out of here."

"But—!"

"I said let's go!"

Clay grew angry and would have argued, but Maxwell gripped his arm, whispering, "Come on, you blasted fool!" And Clay suddenly understood his urgency. He nodded, not speaking until they were outside.

When they were in the buggy, Maxwell said, "I wanted you to see him without knowing who he was."

Clay was staring at the grimy old building, trying to shake off the confusion that had sent his mind reeling. "He's alive! Alive, Doc!"

"Yes—and wearing a Union uniform!" Maxwell said sharply. "It's a touchy thing, Clay. If he is Burke, he'll be shot for desertion." He studied the face of his companion, then shrugged. "Let's get out of here. We've got to figure something out."

"How sick is he?" Clay asked after they had driven a few blocks without speaking.

"Very bad," Maxwell grunted. "If he doesn't get better care, he's not going to make it."

"We've got to get him out!"

"Yes, but *how?*"

They drove along the streets of Richmond for an hour, then went inside a café, where they got a table by the back wall. Clay drank tea and Maxwell drank beer as they went over and over the thing.

"We've got to hear Burke's side of it," Clay said at last. "There's got to be an answer. And we've got to get him out of that place before he dies."

"The warden's name is D. K. Templeton, and he's a tough one," Maxwell said. "He's not going to let anybody out of Libby. We've got to find somebody with clout, Clay!"

Clay blinked abruptly, a thought forming in his mind. He was a systematic thinker and said nothing for a few minutes. The talk from the other patrons hummed softly as he sat there loosely; then he stirred his shoulders. "You're right, Doc. We'll have to have someone on our side with influence, and I think I know just the man."

Maxwell stared fixedly at Clay, then muttered, "He'd better be someone with clout. Is this man a good friend of yours?"

"No," Clay said thoughtfully, "he isn't. But I've got a friend who's a good friend of his *best* friend."

Maxwell was skeptical by nature and a cynic by reason of a long life of observing the failures of human beings. He gulped down the last swallow of his beer, wiped his mouth, and muttered heavily, "I wouldn't bet a dime on it, Clay, but if it's the best you've got—why, have at it!"

❧

Jefferson Davis was the president of the Confederate States of America, but he was a husband, as well. Despite the power of one office, he was as vulnerable as most men are when their wives decide that something must take place.

Davis, sitting in his study at his home, knew at once that his wife, Varina, was plotting something. As soon as she had entered the room accompanied by her little friend, Mrs. Raimey Rocklin, the signs were obvious. His wife was a beautiful woman and a romantic, Davis well knew. She had been captivated by Raimey, whose beauty was not in the least marred by the fact that she was blind. And when the dashing Dent Rocklin had begun to pursue the girl, Varina Davis had been thrilled. Truth be told, the Rocklin-Reed courtship seemed to have captured the imagination of all of Richmond—but no one seemed more pleased when they had finally married than the first lady of the Confederacy.

Davis himself was fond of Raimey and was fascinated by her courage and ability. He found a slight smile crossing his austere features as he watched the two women coming toward him. "Well, what are you two plotting? Last week you talked me into having a charity ball for the widows of our Confederacy. What now?"

"Sit down, dear," Varina Davis said. "I want you to hear what

Mrs. Rocklin has to say, and I know you'll help her."

Davis sighed but sat down. "All right, Mrs. Rocklin, what is this terrible problem?"

But if he was not serious at first, he became so very quickly. He was besieged by requests for leniency, and as soon as Raimey had laid the matter of Burke Rocklin before him, he knew he must be very careful indeed!

He studied the beautiful face of the blind young woman, his mind darting to and fro, in fine lawyer fashion. Finally he said, "Let me see if I understand this matter. This Federal captive is your husband's uncle? And the brother of Captain Clay Rocklin of the Richmond Grays? And he was believed to have been killed in action at Second Manassas? But—how could that be?"

Raimey said quickly, "My father-in-law, Captain Rocklin, identified the body, but only by a ring on the dead man's finger because he was—too mutilated to be identified by his face."

"And now this man everyone thought was dead turns up as a prisoner wearing a Union uniform. That's a serious offense, Mrs. Rocklin. If he really *is* Burke Rocklin, it would mean his death."

"Oh, we know that, sir," Raimey said quickly. "But we believe there must be some explanation. All we want is to give him the chance to defend himself."

"Every man must have that chance, of course."

"I *knew* you'd agree!" Varina Davis beamed at her husband, who stared at her with a confused look. Mrs. Davis lifted her eyebrows. "You do understand, sir, that the man is dying?"

"Well, that's unfortunate, but—"

"Surely you must see that we can't let him die like this? He must be nursed back to health so that he may clear his name!"

"I'm sure the doctors will do their best."

"No, sir, I know you will want to do more than that." Mrs. Davis smiled fondly at her husband. "What I would like to see is for you to parole this man into the custody of his people."

Davis thought quickly. "That would be Mr. Thomas Rocklin, I believe."

"Yes, solid supporters of your administration!" Varina smiled. This made a difference as she had known it would, and she quickly stepped up her attack. "There's no danger of the man escaping. He's completely helpless. After he recovers, a thorough investigation can be made, of course. I know you, my dear, and I know you are too compassionate a president to sacrifice one of our brave men or let him die unjustly accused."

Ten minutes later Raimey stepped outside, where she was greeted by Clay. "Well," he demanded, "did you get it?"

"Yes!" Raimey held out the slip of paper, and Clay threw his arms around her and lifted her off her feet.

"What a woman!" he cried, and he hugged her hard.

"Careful!" Raimey laughed. "Don't hug me too tightly." He released his grip at once, and she grasped his hand. "Does the prospect of being a grandfather make you feel old?"

"It makes me feel wonderful!" he answered. Raimey nodded fondly, and they moved to his carriage, talking excitedly of what had just happened.

He took her home, and when she asked what his plan was, he shook his head. "I'm taking Burke home in the morning."

"Your parents. . .how will you tell them?"

"I'll tell them that God has given Burke back to us, and we'll have to pray that we find the truth so that we can keep him!"

*

The next day at one o'clock in the afternoon, Clay pulled up in front of the Big House, sweating from nerves. He'd had no trouble getting Burke released—not with the name of Jefferson Davis on the order! But all the way home, as he'd driven the same ambulance he'd used to deliver Bob Yancy to his family, he'd been praying for a way to break the news to his parents.

His father was in poor condition, and a sudden shock could be—well, it could be serious. As for his mother, she was the stronger of the two, but this was such a shocking thing!

Finally he gave the matter to God, and when he stepped down from the seat of the ambulance, he greeted the handsome black man who came to meet him, saying, "Highboy, I'm going to speak to my parents. Hold that team right there until I get back. Don't let anybody go inside the wagon."

"Yas, Marse Clay!"

Clay found his parents in the parlor, his father reading and his mother sewing. They were very surprised, and Thomas asked at once, "Have you bad news, son?"

"No, Father," Clay said, thinking that it was the same reception he'd gotten at the Yancys. "It's good news, but you must be very calm."

"What is it, Clay?"

Clay studied his mother carefully, thankful for her strength. He said slowly, "You both know that mistakes are made in battles and afterwards. That sometimes men are reported killed. . .and later they turn up alive."

Thomas and Susanna stared at him in disbelief. Thomas looked very frail, and now he licked his dry lips. "Son—?"

"Is it Burke?" Susanna asked when her husband could not finish.

"Yes. He's alive." He came to them as they rose to their feet, their eyes filled with amazement. "Wait, there's more."

They listened as he related carefully how Burke had been found and warned them, "He's very ill and may die. We've got to be ready for that. And even if he lives, he's under a cloud of suspicion. He'll have to have a trial and prove his innocence."

Susanna listened to Clay, and then she went to her husband. Putting her arms around him, she whispered, "God has given our son back, Tom!"

Clay looked apprehensively at his father and was amazed to see a strength in Thomas Rocklin's face that he had never seen there before. He had been a weak man in his youth, but now he said firmly, "God didn't send my son back to die, Susanna. He'll live! I believe it with all my heart!"

The three of them held each other, and then Thomas drew back. "Go bring your brother in, Clay." When Clay quickly left the room, Thomas turned to his wife. "Susanna, I've not been a strong man in the past, but I swear to you—I'll die before I let our boy go!"

Susanna Rocklin had waited for this moment for years! Now she moved to her husband, folded her arms around him, and whispered, "I'm so proud of you, Tom!"

They kissed, stood silent for a brief moment, then moved out to see the son they had given up for dead.

CHAPTER 18

"I REMEMBER YOU!"

For three days Burke lingered between life and death in the master bedroom at Gracefield. Sometimes he would throw himself wildly about on the bed and had to be restrained. In his delirium he cried out, but usually his nurses could make little of his incoherent babblings.

At other times he would sink into a coma, his lank body so still that the only sign of life was a faint, ragged breathing. More than once Thomas and Susanna came to peer at his sallow face, fearing that he had slipped away.

Strangely enough, it was Thomas who never lost faith. For years it had been Susanna who had been the strength of Gracefield, but during those long hours and days when their son lay gasping for breath, it was the father who stood against the grim specter of death that lurked in the room.

Dorrie, the brown slave who had ruled Gracefield with her mistress for years, spoke of this to her husband. Zander, at the

695

age of sixty-two, looked the same as he did when he'd become the body servant of Thomas Rocklin years earlier—except that he was now white-haired and slightly overweight. On this day he had come into the kitchen to sit down on a high stool beside his wife, who was making biscuits.

"I'se scared Marse Burke ain't goin' ta make it," he muttered, shaking his head sadly.

Dorrie glared at him, snapping, "Whut you know 'bout it? You started doctorin' folks?"

Her remark angered Zander. He pushed his lips out in a mulish, angry fashion, snapping, "I knows what I knows, don't I? And I tells you dis, woman, if Marse Thomas don't watch out, he's goin' ta kill his ownself takin' care of that boy!"

His remark caught at Dorrie, bringing a thoughtful look into her brown eyes. She picked up a rolling pin and began flattening the lump of dough thoughtfully. She rolled it out, picked up an empty jar, and began cutting circles in the mass. When Zander reached over, picked up a fragment of the remains, and stuffed it into his mouth, she said out of habit, "Leave that alone." After a moment, she sat down beside Zander and said slowly, "It's de first time dat man's ever showed backbone, ain't it, now?"

Zander chewed thoughtfully on a mouthful of dough, reached for another, then nodded. "Reckon so." A look of pride came to his eyes, and he said softly, "Marse Thomas—he's got to be a right good man in his last days. Miz Susanna, she's plumb proud of him fo' de first time."

Dorrie said in a low tone, "If he kill himself takin' care of dat boy...well, there's worse ways fo' a man to die."

They sat together, these two who had no interest in the war—at least not in its political implications. Abraham Lincoln could issue a dozen papers declaring them free, but they were so bound to the Rocklins that they would die before abandoning them. It was true that there was much cruelty in slavery, but the love and devotion shared between these slaves and the Rocklins went beyond institutions, and as they thought of their future, they never once thought of anything but being part of the house of Rocklin.

Nearby in the sick man's room, the subjects of their conversation were sitting quietly, watching Burke's pale face.

"His fever's gone down," Susanna said. She stood beside her son, her hand resting lightly on his broad forehead. Her eyes dwelt on the wan features; then she looked across at her husband.

"Thomas, go get some rest," she begged. "You have to save your strength."

Thomas was slumped on a small sofa, watching the pair. His flesh had fallen away from his bones, made slack by the sickness that had come to him months ago. Only traces of his good looks remained now, and his once-proud eyes had faded and were sunken into cavernous sockets. His hands were skeleton thin and trembled where they lay loosely clasped in his lap.

But a light came to brighten his eyes, and he shook his head. "I'm all right, Susanna. But you need to get some sleep."

Susanna went to him, sat down beside him, and took his

hand. "I'll go presently," she said quietly.

Her gesture pleased him, and he turned to examine her. He was so weak that his voice was a mere whisper as he said, "You're still the best-looking woman I know."

Tears came to her eyes, and she blinked them away. "You must want something, paying compliments like that! What is it now?"

He smiled at her, then looked back at Burke. "He's better. He's going to make it."

"Yes. God is good."

They sat together, closer in spirit, they both knew, than they had been since their youth. The future looked grim indeed, for the war cast its gloom over the entire land. But Susanna was thankful, for she knew that her husband had become a man she could be proud of—something many women never had! They spoke softly, letting the long silences run on, content to be together, and each of them prayed for this broken son and for the other members of their family.

Once after a long silence, Thomas turned to face her, and she saw tears in his eyes. He was not a crying man, she knew, and she whispered, "What is it, Tom?"

"I feel that we're going to see God do a mighty work with Burke," he said, nodding. "Just now, Susanna, God dropped that into my spirit. It was as if He said, 'You will see this son redeemed.'" Wonder was on his face, for it was the first time he'd ever had such a thing happen. "Can it be God speaking to an old reprobate like me, Susanna?"

"You are God's own child, Tom," she said at once, and a great love rushed inside her spirit, so that she reached for him and pulled his head close to her breast so that he could not see her tears. "I'm so proud of you, my dear!" she whispered.

❧

Susanna was alone with Burke when he regained consciousness. She had finally persuaded Thomas to go to his room and rest, and she had gone for a quick meal, which Dorrie had prepared.

"Lemme sit wif him," Dorrie urged. "You done wore yo'self out."

Susanna smiled tiredly but shook her head. "No, you've got everything else to take care of, Dorrie. I'll be fine." She patted Dorrie's shoulder fondly, then returned to the sick man's side.

Her bones ached from the long vigil, but after she checked Burke, she curled up on the narrow couch that occupied space along the wall. Her eyelids drooped, and for five minutes she fought sleep but soon succumbed.

She awoke with a start and sat up. Her muscles were so stiff that she knew she'd been asleep for some time—but something had awakened her. . . . She looked at Burke, alarm running along her nerves. Standing quickly, she went to him at once. Picking up a cloth, she dipped it into the basin of water on the nightstand, wrung it out, then began to clean his face.

As soon as the cloth touched his face, his eyes opened, and Susanna cried out, "Burke!" When he stared at her unblinkingly, she placed her hand on his cheek, pleading, "Do you know me, son?"

Burke's eyes were clear, but she could see only a faint response. He tried to speak, but only a croak emerged. "Water—!"

Susanna quickly poured cool water from the pitcher into a glass, then helped him raise his head. As she placed the water to his lips, he gulped thirstily, bumping the glass in his eagerness so that the water ran down onto his chest.

"Careful," Susanna said. "Drink more slowly." She held his head until he'd finished the glass, then nodded. "You can have more soon." Replacing the glass, she bent over him with a tremulous smile. "You've been very sick," she said. "How do you feel?"

Burke blinked at her, then began to struggle into a sitting position. She helped him, placing a pillow behind his back. He licked his lips, then nodded. "I feel better, but I'm so thirsty."

Susanna filled the glass and handed it to him. "You've had pneumonia, Burke. And a very high fever."

He took the glass and drank it more slowly. "That tastes good," he whispered. He handed the glass back, and the act seemed to have tired him. He rested his head on the pillow for a moment, closing his eyes.

Susanna asked, "Will you be all right for a minute? I want to get Tom."

His brow wrinkled, but he nodded and she left the room. She went to her bedroom and awakened Thomas. He blinked as she told him the good news; then he got out of bed hurriedly.

Pulling on an old robe and a pair of slippers, he accompanied her down the stairs. When he entered the room where Burke sat upright against the pillows, his eyes brightened and he went at once to the bedside.

"Burke, my son," he said, his voice husky with emotion, "I was never so happy!" He bent over and put his arms around Burke, holding him close, then drew back and cleared his throat. "Now—," he said, striving for a normal voice. "Do you feel like talking?"

Burke was confused. He had only vague memories of the past, dreams mixing with some sort of foggy reality. He felt terribly weak, and the two people who stood looking down at him made his confusion worse.

"I—guess so," he muttered. Looking around the room, he saw nothing that looked familiar. "Where am I?" he asked.

"You're home, Burke. You're at Gracefield." Susanna had been watching Burke's eyes, and the vacant expression troubled her. She said quickly, "You've been so sick it's confused you."

Thomas nodded. "You don't need to talk much, son, but just tell us where you've been. We thought you were killed at Manassas." His son's dark eyes turned to gaze at him, and the expression in them somehow filled him with apprehension. "What is it, Burke? What's happened to you?"

Burke felt as though his head was spinning, and he tried desperately to find some sense in what they were saying. He looked at Thomas silently, then shook his head. "I—I can't remember this place." He licked his lips, then added, "I know

I should remember you—but it's all out of focus."

"You—you don't remember me?" Thomas stammered. He turned to exchange glances with Susanna, then shook his head. This was much worse than he had thought. He said quickly, "You're just tired, Burke. And a high fever like you've had, why, it can mess up a man's mind."

"Your father's right, son," Susanna said, nodding gently. "You'll feel better soon."

Your father!

Burke blinked as he took in the words. He stared at the two older people, and then a memory came to him—or an image, at least. He stared at the woman and remembered telling someone how clearly he'd seen her in some kind of a dream. She was the same, and he tried to pull his thoughts together.

"I. . .remember you!" he said to Susanna. "But. . .I've been in a hospital for a long time."

"A hospital?" Thomas asked, his brow wrinkling as he tried to piece this all together. "Where was this, Burke?"

Burke—that's my name!

"Why, in Washington," he said slowly. And as he lay there, memories came of that time. "I was hurt—but I got well."

"You were in a prison?" Thomas probed.

"No, it was a hospital," Burke answered. He stared hard at the man, then knew he had to tell them the truth. "My wounds healed, but my mind wasn't right. I couldn't remember who I was. Not even my name." He shook his head, adding, "You say I'm your son, but I can't remember you."

A silence fell on the room, and Burke felt sorry for both of them. He was very tired, his eyelids heavy. "I wish—," he said fuzzily, "that I could remember—"

He drifted off, his head falling to one side. Susanna at once laid him down in the bed, then stood staring down at him. "I never heard of such a thing, Tom," she said slowly. "But it explains some things."

"I guess he was mistaken for one of the Yankee soldiers," Thomas said slowly. "And the man we buried—he got hold of Burke's ring before he was killed." He looked down at the pallid face on the pillow. "We've got our son back, Susanna—but not all of him." He shook his thin shoulders in a gesture of determination, then took her hand, saying, "God is in this. We'll not doubt, and one day we'll have all of him!"

Burke slept soundly for nearly twenty-four hours. It was a healthy sleep, and he awoke with his mind free from the dark specters of doubt and confusion. Bright sunlight flooded through the window across the room, falling in golden pools on the polished heartpine flooring, and for one fleeting moment he thought, *I've seen this room. . . . I've been in it before now!*

The door opened and a woman entered, her eyes meeting his at once. Again the memory he'd had of her touched his mind, then eluded him.

"You're feeling much better, aren't you?" she said, coming to put her hand on his brow. "No fever at all and your eyes are clear."

She poured him a drink of water, then when he had finished it, asked, "Are you hungry?"

The question stirred violent hunger pangs, and he blurted out, "I'm starved!"

Susanna laughed at his vehemence. "I'll go fix your breakfast."

"I want to get up," Burke announced.

"Well, it'll be good for you." She produced a robe from the armoire, along with a pair of shoes. Throwing the cover back, she held the robe as he pushed his arms through, then pulled a chair from the wall so that it faced the window. She guided him into it and urged him to sit down, then slipped a pair of house shoes on his feet. "Now you sit right there until I get back with your breakfast," she commanded.

"I'm weak as dishwater!" he countered. "Don't guess I'll get up and run around the room."

After she left, he sat there staring out the window. Snow covered the broad grounds, reflecting the sun with bright crystal glints. He studied the wide, sweeping circular drive and the huge oaks that lined it and knew he'd seen it before. It was not a fully formed memory, but a thrill came as he realized that he knew exactly what the outside of the house looked like, though he was inside.

"Looks like I've come home," he mused aloud. He thought of the couple, of their obvious love for him, and shook his head. "I've got little to bring to them. Mostly just a shell."

But when the woman came back with a tray, he covered this feeling as he ate. "You don't need to be a glutton, Burke,"

Susanna admonished him. "You need lots of small meals, not a lot all at once."

He nodded, then ate more slowly. When he was finished with the eggs, he spread blackberry jam on one of the thick biscuits and ate it in small bites. Then he drank the hot black coffee, sipping it slowly.

"My name is Burke," he said. "Burke what?"

"Rocklin," Susanna said quietly. "You have a fine family. Your father's name is Thomas, and I'm Susanna."

Burke sat in the warm sunbeams, listening as she gave him the details of his own identity. As she spoke, faint memories tugged at his mind, some of them stronger than others. She was a beautiful woman, he realized, and very strong. Finally she smiled, saying, "Well, that's who you are, son. Do you remember any of it?"

Burke hesitated, then asked, "My father, he's not well, is he?"

"No, Burke. He started failing about a year ago."

"What is it?"

"His heart." Susanna's lips grew tight, and she dropped her eyes for a moment, staring at her hands. Then she lifted them, saying, "I must tell you something, Burke. Your coming home has done more for him than I can tell you. He's been. . .noble!"

Burke could not think of how to answer. "I feel so strange," he said with a shrug. "Like an impostor, I guess." The sound of the door opening came to him, and he turned to see Thomas enter. "Come in, sir," he said at once. "Sit down and help me finish these biscuits."

Thomas came across the room, moving slowly with a sick man's gait. His eyes searched Burke's face, and what he saw brightened his own countenance. "Ah, you're much better," he said with satisfaction. "I think you're out of danger."

Burke waited until his father seated himself in a chair that Susanna moved from the wall, then said at once, "I want to tell you all I can remember about what's happened to me." He began from the time he came out of the coma in Armory Square Hospital, and the older people sat with their eyes riveted on his face. He spoke for a long time, leaving out little of the story. Finally he paused, took a deep breath, then shrugged his shoulders. "Before I was put in the army, I was starting to remember things. I think if I'd been able to stay on the farm with Grace, my memory would have come back in time."

"You owe that young woman a great deal, don't you, Burke?" Susanna asked.

"Just about everything, I guess." A thought came to him, and he blinked. "I've got to let her know I'm alive!"

Thomas said slowly, "That might not be wise. . .not right now."

"Why not, sir?"

"Son, you're out of a Confederate prison on temporary release." Burke listened with shock as his father spoke of the terms of his release. "You'll have to defend yourself as soon as you're able," Thomas said. "I think when the authorities hear the full story, they'll understand. But you were wearing a Yankee uniform, so it might be best if you didn't contact the young woman until this thing is cleared up."

Burke's face was a study in bafflement. "So I could be shot for treason? That's what it amounts to?"

"Oh, it won't come to that, my boy! We have the ear of the president, you see."

"Jefferson Davis."

"Yes, of course! He agreed to your release when one of your relatives went to Mrs. Davis with your story."

Burke listened incredulously as Thomas told him the machinations that had gotten him out of Libby Prison, but when his father finished, he shook his head, doubt clouding his eyes. "I don't think the president will be too sympathetic to a Confederate soldier who fought against the South in the Union Army."

Thomas tried to put the best face on Burke's chances, but later when he and Susanna were alone, he was less optimistic. "Burke's got a point," he admitted. "We've got to get on this thing right now. When will Clay be here?"

"He's so busy, Thomas, with the new men and the training. Do you think we should send for him?"

"No." Thomas gave her an adamant look, then said, "I'll go see the president."

"You're not able—!" she began to protest, but a look from her husband silenced her. She had never seen such determination in his eyes.

"Susanna," he said, his voice stronger than it had been in weeks, "I'll get my son out of this trouble even if I have to die for it!"

The city of Richmond was a microcosm of the larger world. The new nation had not learned very well how to forge cannons or produce gunpowder, but it had a system of gossip equal to that of any nation.

The story of Burke Rocklin was too good to be kept secret, and it was not long before everyone who was anyone had some version of it.

Thomas Rocklin got his first warning that getting Burke set free from the charges against him would not be simple when he spoke to Davis's secretary. "The president is very busy, sir," he was told. "Perhaps you should put your request in writing. Or perhaps you should go through a member of the military staff?"

Thomas did both, but neither accomplished much. He found Clay, and the two of them discovered that while Varina Davis had great influence over her husband, the president was listening to others, as well. They finally talked to a member of Davis's cabinet, who said, "Don't use my name, if you please, but I think it fair to tell you that the president is under pressure to see that your son is charged with desertion. You'd better start looking for a good lawyer."

The strain had worn Thomas down, and when they left the office, Clay said, "Sir, you *must* go home!" His father looked ghastly, thin, and sallow, and he insisted on taking him home to Gracefield—which Thomas finally agreed to only when Clay promised he would persist in trying to see the president.

One tangible result of the talk about Burke Rocklin was a visit paid to Gracefield by one Belinda King. She had been on a visit to Lynchburg and had received the news by means of a letter from Chad Barnes. He had pursued her with determination since the "death" of Burke Rocklin, and Chad lost no time in letting her know what had happened. In a short letter, he had written:

> You will hear it soon enough, and I would rather you would hear it from me. The man we buried was not Burke Rocklin. He is alive and at Gracefield.

When Belinda read this information, her eyes grew large, and she scanned the rest of the short letter avidly. Barnes related how the president himself had paroled Burke, but there was cynicism in his written remarks concerning Burke's loss of memory:

> The story is that he lost his memory and didn't even know he was in the Confederate Army. Not only that, but he joined the Union Army and fought against our brave fellows at Fredericksburg. Well, I find that a little hard to swallow! There will be a trial or a hearing of some sort, of course. I know you will want to return at once. When you return, I will take you to see Burke myself. What this will do to what we have been feeling I am not sure. It will not

*change my feelings, but you are very romantic. I warn you
now, Belinda, I am convinced that Burke Rocklin is an
opportunist. He set out to marry you for your money, and it
is my belief that somehow when he was captured, he sold out
his country to avoid being sent to a prisoner-of-war camp.*

Belinda *was* romantic. She knew full well that the trial of
Burke Rocklin would be a sensational affair, and she longed to
be there. She packed at once and sent a wire to Barnes, and he
was there when she stepped off the train.

He kissed her, held her hard, then let her go. "Belinda, I'm
going to fight for you. I warn you now, I'll do all I can to prove
that Burke Rocklin isn't worthy of you."

This was an exciting statement to Belinda. To have two
attractive men fighting for her hand—and in full view of
Richmond—was thrilling. She put her hand on Barnes's broad
chest and whispered, "I want to do the right thing, Chad."

He studied her, then smiled. "You will, Belinda. Now let's
go see the famous man who's fought in both the blue and the
gray!"

CHAPTER 19

TWO VISITORS FOR BURKE

*T*he terrible casualties suffered by the Union Army at Fredericksburg sent shock waves throughout the North. The Peace Party stepped up its efforts to allow the South to go its own way. President Lincoln knew that they were a formidable power and feared that all the blood shed by the Union would be for nothing. It took all the moral force Lincoln possessed to keep the North from giving up, and in one sense, the winter of 1862 marked the high tide of the Confederacy.

Burnside, agonizing over his losses, withdrew the Army of the Potomac to the north bank of the Rappahannock, still determined to keep the initiative and exploit his impressive numerical superiority over Lee. But all were agreed: Burnside had to go. By January of 1863, his attempt to move upstream and cross the upper Rappahannock behind Lee's left flank foundered in liquid mud, so Burnside told Lincoln either he must have a new staff or Lincoln had to accept his resignation.

Lincoln found that the leadership of the ill-starred Army of the Potomac was only one of his problems, for the Union was suffering setbacks in other areas.

On the Mississippi, Sherman's first drive on Vicksburg had been stopped in its tracks on December 29 at Chickasaw Bluff. At Chickasaw Bluff, Lieutenant General John Pemberton, commanding the Vicksburg sector, drove back Sherman, who suffered more than seventeen hundred casualties. Hard-riding Confederate cavalry had captured Grant's supply base at Holly Springs a week earlier, and Grant withdrew to build up a new base at Milliken's Bend, twenty miles north of Vicksburg and on the wrong bank of the river—the west bank.

And so, by the New Year of 1863, it was clear that there would be no more runaway Union victories on the Mississippi and that the campaign against Vicksburg would be long and hard. Even so, despite pressure from those who believed Grant's drinking was a serious liability, Lincoln refused point-blank to replace him. "I can't spare this man," was his terse comment. "*He* fights."

The news was equally dismaying from central Tennessee. On December 26, Rosecrans marched out of Nashville to attack the Army of Tennessee under General Bragg at Murfreesboro and drive on to Chattanooga, 125 miles to the southeast. But on December 31, 1862, Bragg struck first, staging an uncanny replay of Shiloh by unleashing a storming attack on Rosecrans. As at Shiloh, the attacking Confederates bent the tortured Union Army into a horseshoe before its desperate resistance took effect. Repeated Confederate assaults only increased the toll in casualties without winning the battle.

The cost of Murfreesboro was proportionately worse than that of Fredericksburg, as terrible as that had been! Rosecrans, with an army far smaller than Burnside's, lost the same number of men: thirteen thousand. True, Bragg had lost ten thousand and could not find replacements, but the North reeled under the shock of such losses. Bragg was forced to withdraw, and Lincoln claimed a Union victory, but it was a hollow claim.

And so it was that, with the Union war machine stopped dead in its tracks in Tennessee and on the Mississippi, Lincoln shrank from the prospect of choosing a new commander for the Army of the Potomac. Finally forced to do so, he made one of the most extraordinary appointments in modern military history.

To "Fighting Joe Hooker," the most outspoken of Burnside's critics, Lincoln wrote a devastating letter of rebuke—and at the same time appointed Hooker to command the army! Lincoln poured scorn on Hooker's assertions that both the army and the government needed a dictator. "Only those generals who gain successes can set up dictators," wrote Lincoln. And he ended, "Beware of rashness, but with energy and sleepless vigilance go forward and give us victories."

Lincoln had made a poor choice, indeed, as the future would prove. Hooker was a good organizer and made some reforms, but he was far better at blustering than he was at fighting. "My plans are perfect," he announced grandly. "May God have mercy on General Lee, for I will have none!"

And so the two armies and the two nations fell back and waited as 1863 was born. An unusually foul North Virginia winter enforced a virtual two months' truce, and both North and South prepared for the bloodbath that spring would bring.

As ever, the North had all the material advantages, and Hooker made admirable use of them. By the last week of April of the New Year, he would build up the Army of the Potomac to a greater-than-ever strength of 130,000 and proclaim that it was "the finest army on the planet!"

Lee would be less sanguine. In February he would send Longstreet's corps to the lower James River to cover Union forces, and by the end of April Longstreet would still not return to join Lee. Thus Lee would have barely sixty thousand effectives to hold Hooker.

Even so, the South was accustomed to long odds. Lee and Jackson had taken on all that the North could throw at them and had sent them running back to Washington. That winter in Richmond, prices were high—but so were the hopes of the Confederacy. Rumors were flying that England would recognize the new nation soon, and it seemed likely that the Peace Party in the North would bring such pressure on Lincoln that he would be forced to let the South go its own way.

This resurgence of optimism might have been good for the Southern Confederacy, but it made things difficult for Burke Rocklin.

He had recovered from his physical ailments almost at once.

He sat up for three days, eating the heaping meals brought to him by his mother and by Dorrie and sleeping long hours. During his waking hours, his mother sat with him, reading to him and speaking of his past. She did so easily and naturally, and whether it was her constant bringing before him the details of the past, or simply the natural restorative powers of nature, was not clear, but he found himself remembering many things.

The beginning of this recovery came one afternoon when Susanna was musing about an event that took place when Burke had been six years old. It was a simple story about how Burke and Clay had gotten into trouble. As she spoke, Burke listened almost carelessly, until suddenly he was struck by a memory so clear that he exclaimed, "I remember that! Clay was sixteen and I was only six! He took me with him over to the Huger place!"

Susanna blinked with surprise. "You remember that? You were only six years old!"

"I remember it all," Burke said, his eyes wide. "Clay got drunk with Charlie and Devoe Huger. They took me with them when they went into a saloon in Richmond, and Father came in like a storm and hauled us both home. He gave Clay a whipping, and I thought he was going to start on me. But he said, 'It's not your fault, Burke,' and I wanted to cry I was so relieved!"

"Burke, that's wonderful! Thank God!"

Burke looked at her, his eyes filled with wonder. "That's what Grace would say," he said finally. "She always said God would give me back my past."

"She sounds like a fine girl," Susanna said quietly. "You think of her a great deal, don't you?"

"Yes." Burke nodded. "She filled my whole world, Mother. I didn't have a past, and she was there to fill my present."

"I'd love to meet her, son."

Burke brought his mind back to the present. "You're not likely to, I guess," he said slowly. "Looks like I'm headed for the gallows." He shook his head in a disgusted manner and summoned up a smile. "I hate a man who feels sorry for himself!" he exclaimed. He drew his lips together into a firm line, adding, "I've got a lot to be thankful for. I could have been killed at Fredericksburg, or crippled."

They sat there quietly, and then Burke reached over and took his mother's hand. "I've got a fine family," he said. "I used to wonder what it would be like if I got my memory back and found things so bad I couldn't stand it. But I found you and Father— and that's miracle enough for me!"

Susanna felt suddenly that she had her son back—all of him. She lifted her arms and put them around Burke's neck. "Tell your father that, Burke," she whispered.

"I will." He held his mother, then drew back, shaking his head. "He doesn't need the trouble I've brought him. When he comes home, you've got to keep him here."

Susanna shook her head. "No, Burke. Your father has had great fears about himself—he's always felt that his brother Stephen was far above him—but now he's shown his family, and himself, that he's a great man. I pray for him every day, but if he dies, he'll die happy, knowing that his family respects and admires him."

Burke had suspected some of this and nodded slowly. "When he comes back, I'll make it plain how much *I* admire him." He smiled and said, "Now tell me some more about what a wonderful child I was, perfect in all my ways!" He sat back, listening as she began to speak, and the following day when his father came home, he made it a point to express his thanks. Thomas was exhausted, but when Burke spoke, his eyes grew bright. Finally he held out his thin hand and clasped his son's hand, saying huskily, "It makes me feel so good to hear you say these things, Burke!"

"I mean it, sir!"

Thomas sat slumped in his chair, racked with pain but warmed by the knowledge that he had won the approval of his sons. "You know, Burke," he said slowly, "I've spent a great deal of time grieving over my youth. I've wasted most of my life."

"Oh, don't say that!"

"It's true enough. I had everything that most men long for and never have: money, position, a good wife. And I didn't know how blessed I was." He lifted his gaze, adding with a smile, "But God has restored to me the years that the locusts had eaten."

Burke looked puzzled. "What's that, sir?"

"It's from the Old Testament, from the book of Joel. God's people disobeyed Him, as I remember it, and He sent terrible judgments on them. One of them was a plague of locusts that devoured their crops and brought a famine on the land."

"I seem to remember Grace saying something about that."

"Well, it was terrible, but God said to them, If you'll turn back to Me, 'I will restore to you the years that the locust hath eaten.'"

"How could God do that?" Burke frowned. "When time is gone, it's gone, isn't it?"

Thomas suddenly felt that Burke was a man who was searching after God—and it thrilled him. Clay had been a wild young man, but now he was a fervent Christian. Now Thomas was filled with a longing to see his other son find peace with God, and he wished that Susanna were present to help. But he prayed quickly for the right words and said, "Not always, son. Oh, the time itself is gone. Time doesn't stay for any man, does it? But God can change things so that the past doesn't control us. Don't you think so?"

"Well, I don't know," Burke said slowly. "If a man gets drunk and sleeps on the railroad track and gets his leg cut off, he'll never have that leg again."

"True enough," Thomas said, nodding. "We have to live with the results of what we do. But when a man gives himself to God, the Lord can fill his life with something new and better. I think that's what the verse means. God was promising to give his people something *better* than what they had." He hesitated, then shook his head. "I'm doing a poor job of explaining," he said.

"No, I can see what you mean." Burke leaned forward, his dark eyes intent. "I've pretty well wasted my life," he stated.

"Mother's been telling me about myself. She's always kind, but I can tell I don't have much to be proud of."

"Neither did your brother," Thomas countered. "Not for many years. He ran out on his family, and no one had a good word for him. He even became a slave trader. But since he became a Christian, God has given him something wonderful, and I know He's going to reward him even more for his faithfulness."

Burke shook his head. "Your sons. . .we haven't been much pleasure to you, sir."

Thomas said at once, "I'm not a prophet, Burke, but God's given me an assurance that both my sons will be men of honor and will bring honor to the name of Rocklin."

Burke was filled with doubt. Shaking his head, he said, "Be hard to do that if I'm hanged as a traitor."

"That will never happen, Burke! I'll fight it to my last breath!"

"That's what you mustn't do," Burke said quickly. "You've done all you can, Father."

"No, I haven't." Thomas shook his head, his eyes alive in his pallid face. "When the truth is known, we'll have justice; you'll see!"

Burke saw that his father was tired, and he insisted that he go lie down. "We'll have lots of time to talk later," he said gently. He smiled, then told him how the memory of his trip to the Hugers had come to him. "You can tell me how you took a strap to Clay instead of me!"

Thomas laughed, and when Susanna came into the room

an hour later, she was pleased to find them laughing. Later, however, when she and Thomas were alone in their room, he lay down on the bed, fatigue lining his face. "I'm afraid Burke's in for a bad time," he said slowly.

Susanna came over and sat down on the bed beside him. A lock of his hair fell over his forehead, and she pushed it back. His hair was gray, and she suddenly thought of how black and glossy it had been the day they'd been married. *Like Burke's is now,* she thought. "It'll be all right, Tom," she said.

He lay still, his eyes closed, and she could see the tiny veins etched on his eyelids. "It's this war that's turned everything upside down. Everyone is either a sheep or a goat, Susanna. And I can see it in the faces of people—that they think Burke's one of the goats." Bitterness crept into his tone as he added, "Anyone who doesn't believe in the Cause is the enemy."

"That's how it was with Clay," Susanna answered. "He doesn't believe in this war, and if he hadn't joined the army in spite of that, he'd have been pulled apart."

"Yes, but Burke's in worse condition than Clay was. He was wearing a Yankee uniform, and that's the end of it for lots of people. They haven't been around like we have to see what poor shape he's in."

"He's getting better every day."

"Yes, and that's going to make people say, 'See? There never was anything wrong with him in the first place!'" He opened his eyes and said, "I'm going to retain Gaines DeQuincy. He's the best lawyer in the South—and the most expensive. But we can't take any risks with this thing."

"But isn't he in the army?"

"Yes, and that's why I want him. He's a genuine patriot, and if this thing comes to a trial, it'll be a military court. Won't hurt to have a certified supporter of the Confederacy defending Burke. I'll write him tomorrow."

*

"I feel so strange, Chad!"

Belinda King had bought a new dress for her trip to Gracefield, a light blue gown that matched her eyes perfectly. Now she touched her new hat nervously, asking, "Do I look all right?"

"Beautiful, as usual." Chad Barnes was amused at Belinda, thinking how typical it was that she thought of her looks even on such an occasion. They had had dinner the evening before, after he'd picked her up at the station. It was only now, as they were turning into the driveway that led to the Big House at Gracefield, that the blond girl showed any sign of nervousness. *As long as she's dressed in the latest style,* Barnes thought with a cynical amusement, *she can face anything.*

Aloud he said, "Are you sure you want to see him?"

"Why, of course I want to see him, Chad!" Belinda turned to Barnes with amazement in her eyes. "After all, we *were* engaged to be married."

"You'll never marry Burke, Belinda," Barnes said firmly. "You were never in love with him, anyway."

"You're just jealous, Chad!"

"I *was* at the time," Barnes admitted. "But not now."

"You don't think I could still be interested in Burke?"

They had reached the curving driveway, and Barnes slowed the horses to a walk. The trees lining the drive were black and bare, stripped of their leaves, and the icy breath of a new cold wave bit at Chad's face. "No, I don't think you are," he said slowly.

"I'm fickle—is that it?"

Barnes was a blunt man but knew better than to allow Belinda to know he thought exactly that. He'd figured this conversation was coming and knew exactly what to say. He smiled to himself. *I can handle this girl. She's filled her head with romantic notions, but once we're married, I can change that.*

"No, I don't think you're fickle, honey," he said softly. "I think you've grown up. All beautiful girls like to flirt. It was natural enough for you to like seeing Burke and me make fools of ourselves fighting over you. But I think I've seen something in you these last few weeks. You've grown up to be a mature woman and can see now that I'm the man for you."

Belinda was accustomed to hearing compliments on her beauty, but the idea that she was now a mature woman—that tickled her vanity. "Well. . . ," she said slowly, "we *have* grown close, Chad."

"Yes, and it's unthinkable what you'd have to go through if you married Burke. I couldn't bear to see you dragged through the mess that's coming." He didn't miss the fleeting expression of fear in her eyes, and he struck hard. "Burke's going to go down, I'm afraid." He shrugged. "He's a good fellow, but he's dug his own grave."

"You don't think he's a traitor, do you, Chad?"

Barnes hesitated, then said, "Yes, I do, Belinda. And it hurts me. Burke and I. . .well, we've had our differences, but I don't like to see any of my friends turn out like this."

"I—I can't believe Burke would do such a thing!"

"Well, you may be right," Barnes said, shrugging. "I hope you are. But even if Burke didn't sell out, he'll never be able to live in this country."

"What do you mean?"

Barnes stopped the horses but said before getting out, "Just that, Belinda. Even if Burke is declared innocent, he'll never be admitted to the homes of the people of the South." He drew her gaze, then added, "You'd be in exile, Belinda, if you married Burke. He'll have to leave the country, and I'd hate to see you cut off from your family and friends." He saw that the thought horrified her and knew he'd said enough for now.

He leaped to the ground, helped Belinda down, and handed the lines to a slave, who led the carriage away; then the two of them went up the steps. They were met at the door by Susanna.

"Come in," she said. "I saw you drive up."

The older woman's clear, direct gaze disturbed Belinda for some reason. Burke's mother had never been anything but courteous to her, but something in Susanna Rocklin's stately bearing made her uneasy. She said in a rather flustered manner, "I know I should have written you, Mrs. Rocklin, but after Burke—"

"It's all right, Belinda." Susanna turned to Barnes, saying, "How are you, Major Barnes?"

Now it was Barnes's turn to feel uncomfortable, and he felt totally out of place as he answered, "We shouldn't be intruding on you, Mrs. Rocklin, but Belinda and I wanted to see Burke."

"Yes, I came as soon as I got word he'd come back," Belinda said quickly. "But if he's too sick to see us. . . ?"

"He's feeling much better," Susanna said. "He's in the study now, reading. I'll take you to him."

"Is he—that is, does he remember *anything*?" Belinda asked as they followed Susanna down the hall.

"It's very selective. It's as though his memory is waking up a little at a time. Every day he remembers more, but don't be shocked if he doesn't remember you at first."

Susanna opened the large walnut door, then, stepping inside, said, "Burke, you have visitors."

Burke got up from his chair at once and laid the book he was reading on the table. He stared at the two visitors, then nodded. "Hello, Belinda."

Belinda's face glowed with surprise. "You remember me?"

"Well, not really," Burke said quickly. "Mother's told me so much about you, and there's a picture of you in my room."

Belinda looked slightly crushed at his explanation, and it was Barnes who asked, "Do you remember me, Burke?"

Burke stared at the big man carefully, noting the hostility in the stiff features. "No, I'm afraid not." He paused, then added, "But I probably will. When I meet somebody from my past, it seems to trigger something. I think about them, and usually it sorts itself out."

"You all sit down," Susanna said, "and I'll fix some tea."

"Do you mind if I walk around the grounds while you do that, Mrs. Rocklin?" Barnes asked instantly. He laid a level gaze on Burke, saying in a mocking tone, "I wouldn't want to overburden our patient with too many old 'memories.'"

Susanna stared at him, then nodded. "Perhaps that would be best, Major." She left the room at once, followed by Barnes, who turned to give a cynical smile to Belinda.

Burke watched him close the door, then turned to face Belinda. "Obviously the major thinks I'm a fraud," he remarked.

"Oh no, he's just—just careful," Belinda said quickly. She was rather confused, for the man who stood before her was greatly changed from the Burke she'd last seen. Then he had been strong and in uniform, but now he was pale and thin and wore a simple pair of brown trousers and a heavy wool shirt.

Catching her glance, Burke smiled slightly. He'd picked up enough from his parents and others to have some idea of what kind of a girl this was. Dorrie had sniffed, *"Dat little ol' gal you wuz gonna marry, she's 'bout as empty-headed as de ol' peacock dat runs round heah!"*

"This must be difficult for you, Miss King," Burke said. "But I want to make it easy on you. Won't you sit down?"

"Thank you, Burke," Belinda said quickly. When she was seated, she laughed with embarrassment. "It is hard, isn't it? Not just on me, but even more so on you. Here's a perfectly strange female come to demand that you take up where you left off."

Burke had to admire her straightforward admission. "Let's be honest with each other, Belinda—may I call you that? Well, put your mind at rest. I've got my hands too full of trouble right now to think of anything but saving my neck. I don't think it would be wise for us to build on what was in the past."

This caught Belinda totally by surprise—and hurt her feelings! It was one thing for *her* to break off an engagement, but quite different for someone else to do it! Her eyes brightened with anger, and she flared out, "You just throw me out for all Richmond to laugh at—is that it?"

Burke blinked in surprise at the attack but shook his head quickly. "I thought it would be unfair of me to make any demands on you, Belinda. When I asked you to marry me, things were very different. I don't think it would be best for you to be caught up in my trouble."

"Oh, I see," Belinda said more calmly. Then she nodded, saying, "That's very noble of you, Burke. Perhaps it might be best. But what will I say? People are already asking about us."

"Tell them that you've decided we acted too hastily, and the engagement is off."

"Well, if you think it's best, I suppose I'll have to do it," Belinda said, secretly relieved, for this was not the romantic, dashing Confederate officer she'd agreed to marry.

"Now, Burke," she said, "tell me everything."

When Barnes came in thirty minutes later, he was taken aback by Belinda's greeting. "Chad, Burke and I have agreed that our engagement was a mistake."

Prepared to fight for Belinda, Barnes was nonplussed and could only stammer, "Well—I think that's best for both of you."

"I thought you might find it convenient," Burke said dryly. He was well aware from what his parents had told him that Chad Barnes had been vindictive after the engagement was announced.

Barnes stiffened, and his voice took on a hard edge. "I don't care for what you're suggesting, Burke."

"You want to marry Belinda. From what I've been told, you always have. Now I'm out of the way, so you can pursue her with a good conscience."

Chad Barnes disliked being handed the girl as if she were a prize. He knew that the world would say exactly what Burke Rocklin had just put into words, but it angered him. Rashly he said, "I want to warn you, Burke, I don't think for one moment you're telling the truth. In fact, I think you're a turncoat and a coward!"

Burke stared at Barnes but did not raise his voice. "I suppose this is where I slap your face and we meet at dawn with pistols?" He smiled and shook his head. "I won't act a fool, even if you do. However, I do think you'd better leave this house." He turned to Belinda, saying, "I regret to have to speak this way in front of you," and then he turned and left the room.

"Come on," Barnes snarled in disgust. "Let's get out of here!"

Belinda was practically towed out of the house, and as soon

as they were in the carriage and headed toward the main road, she protested. "Why are you acting like this, Chad? I think Burke was very nice to see we weren't for each other."

But Barnes spoke furiously. "He handed you over to me as if you were a cheap prize he didn't want! I won't take his cavalier attitude, Belinda—and I'd think you'd be insulted!"

Belinda fell silent but finally asked, "You're not going to fight a duel with him, are you, Chad?"

"No. He's a coward. But I'm going to make it my business to see that he doesn't get by with this trick he's trying to pull."

"What will you do?"

Barnes struck the horses with the buggy whip and took a perverse pleasure as they leaped forward into a run. "I'm going to see that he hangs for treason, Belinda," he said, and there was a smile of satisfaction on his heavy mouth as he thought of the thing. "Mr. Burke Rocklin's always been a little brash—but a rope necktie will take that out of him!"

Chapter 20

Desperate Journey

*L*ook at that, Pat," Cotter said, nodding toward the small group of passengers who had descended and were being met by relatives. "What do you make of those two?"

Pat Grissom was a tall, stooped man of fifty who spent most of his time playing checkers with Cotter. He picked up a few dollars transporting freight and sometimes a passenger or two. He looked up from the checkerboard, stared out the window at the two men his friend had indicated, then shook his head. "Never seen 'em before."

Cotter shot his friend a disgusted look, then put his sharp black eyes back on the old man and the Negro, who was collecting his bags. "Might be a fare for you, Pat," he grunted. "But we better be careful. That darkie might be a runaway slave."

"Not likely," Grissom observed. "He wouldn't be traveling by train, would he? He'd be sent along by the Underground Railroad. But I better check it out," he muttered. "I'm a deputy

729

sheriff, you know." In the small town where he lived, the office was mostly ceremonial, but Grissom took it seriously. He watched with narrowed eyes as the tall man in the heavy coat came slowly across the brick pavement to enter the small ticket office.

"Yes, sir. Can I help you?" Grissom said brightly. He noted that the man was not young, and it was obvious that he was not in good health. Grissom noted the pain-dulled eyes and the slow, tentative movements such as only men who are very tired or sick use.

"Yes, sir." The old man nodded. "Can you direct me to a family named Swenson?"

"Why, you must mean the Amos Swenson place, I reckon," Grissom said with nod. A small alarm went off in his head, and he thought, *Got to have something to do with Sister Grace and that soldier she nursed. Always knew no good would come of that!*

"Yes, that's the name. Is it far?"

Cotter noted that the man had a Southern accent. He looked quickly at the black man, noting that he was well dressed and healthy. "It ain't in town, sir," Cotter said. "You'll need a buggy to get out there. I don't believe I caught your name? You're not related to the Swensons, I don't reckon?"

The old man hesitated, aware of the station agent's burning curiosity, then shrugged. "My name is Rocklin, and I'm no relation to the Swensons. Could you tell me where I might rent a rig?"

"Why, I reckon you're in luck, Mr. Rocklin." Cotter nodded

toward the man seated at the table. "Pat here can take you out to the Swenson place, couldn't you, Pat?"

Grissom nodded. "Guess I ain't got nothing else in the way," he grunted. "Can take you in the spring wagon—but I got a two-seat carriage that rides better. Fare will be ten dollars, though. Takes half a day of my time."

"Can we start now?"

Grissom eyed the black man, then turned to ask, "He goin', too?"

"Yes."

"All right. I got the carriage outside."

"Is there a place I can get a quick meal in town?"

"Oh sure," Cotter said, nodding. "See that sign, the little one next to the feed store? That's Ma Stevens's place. She'll feed you real good. Tell her I sent you—Al Cotter."

"Thank you, sir." Thomas turned to Zander, saying, "Put the luggage in the carriage, Zander. I'll bring you something to eat."

"Yas, Marse Rocklin."

Cotter watched as Rocklin moved slowly down the street and disappeared into the café. He saw that the black man had put two pieces of luggage into the carriage and had seated himself on one of the bales of cotton by the wayside. A thought came to him, and he filled a coffee cup with black coffee and added sugar and cream. Moving outside, he came to where the black man sat and extended it. "Have some coffee. Makes a man thirsty, them long train rides."

"Thank you, sah." Zander took the cup, sipped it, then smiled with approval. "Dat's mighty fine coffee, sah," he remarked.

"Your name is Zander, is it?" Cotter said, leaning against the bale. "Well, Zander, how's your trip been?"

"Oh, fine, sah! Mighty fine!"

"Come far, have you?"

"Well, sah, pretty far—and yet not so far, either."

For the next ten minutes Cotter tried with scant success to pry information out of Zander. But all he received were generalities. *Either this darkie is a fool or he's plenty sharp!* Cotter concluded.

"Your master, he's not too well, is he? Kind of strange he'd be making a hard trip all the way from the South to Pennsylvania, ain't it?" When Zander allowed it was, Cotter asked directly, "Well, I guess you was a slave for quite a while, wasn't you? How's it feel to be free?"

"Free? I belongs to Marse Rocklin," Zander said.

"Ain't you heard, man? President Lincoln freed you. He put it all in a paper. It's called the Emancipation Proclamation. You don't belong to nobody!" Leaning closer to Zander, Cotter said confidentially, "I know you don't want to go back South and be a slave. Maybe I can help you get away from Rocklin." He had no idea how he would do this, but thought it best to test the Negro.

But Zander gave the white man a direct look. "I ain't studyin' no paper, sah. I been wif Marse Rocklin all my life, me and my wife and our chilluns. He been good to us, and I reckon as how

I gonna die a Rocklin!"

Cotter stared at the dignified Negro in disbelief. He had read the horror stories of slavery and could not believe that there was another side to it—but though he tried his best, he could not shake Zander's adamant statement that he'd die a Rocklin.

Disgusted, Cotter left Zander and presently saw Rocklin come down the street and give a sack to the slave. "Stubborn ol' slave!" Cotter grunted to Grissom. "Ain't got a lick of sense!" Then he added, "Try to find out what Rocklin's going out to the Swenson place for, Pat."

But Grissom, though he tried valiantly, could not discover anything of this nature. All the way to the Swenson farm, he asked questions, most of which the tall man beside him on the wagon ignored. Finally, in desperation, he asked, "You know the Swensons well, do you?"

The old man did not answer for a long time, so long that Grissom thought he'd chosen to ignore his question. But finally he said, "We have a mutual friend. What is the name of that tree, may I ask?"

It was a rebuff that even a man such as Pat Grissom could not ignore, and he drove the rest of the way in sullen silence.

Grace broke the skim of ice that had formed in the basin, washed her face, then dressed in a pair of heavy wool trousers and a red flannel shirt that had belonged to her father. She put on two pair of wool socks and a pair of thick-soled leather boots, then moved to the kitchen. Clyde and Prudence slept as late as possible—especially in the winter months—so she rekindled the fire in the cookstove, made a quick breakfast, then slipped into a heavy sheepskin coat, pulled on a broad-brimmed hat, and left the house.

Since both of the hands were gone for two weeks, Grace had taken over their chores. She went to the barn, milked the cows, then, after taking the frothy buckets of milk to the house, fed the rest of the stock. Clyde had made a halfhearted offer to rise early and do these chores, but Grace had said, "I like to get up early. You and Prudence might as well sleep."

After the chores were done, she picked up her rifle and made her way across the pasture toward the woods. It was so cold that her lips and eyelids were stiff, but she didn't mind. She loved the cold weather. A large rabbit, startled by her passing, leaped up and made a wild run for the thicket, his feet making a thumping sound on the frozen ground. Grace threw up her rifle and tacked him as he zigzagged frantically, then lowered it. She could have shot him easily, but they'd had plenty of rabbit meat lately.

Entering the deep woods, she made her way along the trail, alert and aware of her surroundings. She loved the woods and knew that she would be miserable in town. The pattern of her life had been tied to the rhythms of the sun, the clouds, the seasons. In towns, men and women organized their lives by clocks, but Grace was always aware of the faint urgings of nature, just as animals are. She always knew when it was time to plant, not by something she'd read in a book, but because some combination of weather and the skies and the earth told her so.

Coming to a frozen brook, she broke the ice, stooped, and dipped the icy water with her hand. It was so cold it hurt her teeth, but she liked the taste of it better than the water that came from the well. Blowing on her hand, she proceeded to a spot she often frequented. A stand of huge oaks stood sentinel over the small brook, and in the summers she came to yank the plump bream and bluegills from a deep pool formed by an S-shaped crook in the stream. Now the stream was frozen, and as Grace leaned back against a massive oak, she wondered about the fish, what they did in winter. *How do they eat cut off from the bugs and life by the ice?* They were still there, she knew, for she'd caught them by breaking the ice and fishing for them with bits of meat.

A quietness lay over the woods, and Grace soaked it up. Overhead the sky was silver-gray, and she knew snow would be falling very soon. The thought of snow reminded her suddenly of her rides in the sleigh with John Smith—and a shadow came over her face.

He had come into her life suddenly—and had disappeared without warning. She had gone to the post office day after day, yearning for a word from him, but finally had understood that nothing was coming. She had said nothing to Clyde or Prudence, and when others had asked of the tall man who'd filled so much of her life, she'd merely said she'd had no word from him.

She'd grown more silent, had become a recluse in the days that followed. More and more she threw herself into the open, leaving the house early and staying out until dark. After supper, she'd fallen into the habit of going to her room, reading her Bible for long hours, then going to bed for a restless night's sleep.

Jacob Wirt had seen her restlessness. "You are not happy, are you, Grace? Ah, well, God knows our hearts. If the young man is for you, God will bring him back."

But Grace's spirit, which had been filled with the joy of an awakening love, grew still and sad. She sought God, but the heavens were brass, and finally she knew the anguish that comes with a lost love.

Now as she stood braced against the oak, she was attacked by a wave of bitterness. "God, why did Thee let him touch my life if Thee meant to take him away?"

Her words startled a doe that had come up on Grace's left, and as the animal leaped into the air, Grace instinctively threw up her rifle. The bead was right on the deer's heart, and all she had to do was pull the trigger. She tracked the beautiful, flowing motion of the fleeing deer but did not fire. Finally as the deer disappeared into the depths of the forest, she lowered the rifle and turned.

For two hours she tramped the cold woods, then returned to the farm. Prudence met her as she came into the kitchen, saying impatiently, "Grace, where has thee been? Thee was supposed to go look at the cattle Old Man Potter wants to sell."

"Oh, I forgot," Grace said.

"Well, Clyde went to look at them," Prudence said with a shrug. "We talked about you last night. . . . What's the matter, Grace?" She gave her sister a strange look, then shook her head. "Thee has got to forget about that man. He's not coming back."

"I know," Grace said quietly. "I'll ride over and see the cattle."

She went to her room and changed her rough clothing for a dress, then stood for a while brushing her hair. Finally she put the brush down and left her bedroom. She had no desire to go look at the cattle and made up her mind to tell Prudence so. When she did, Prudence brightened up. "Well, if thee is not going, Grace, I'll go and meet Clyde."

"And go into town later, I suppose?" Grace ventured, then smiled. "You go on, Prudence. Tell Clyde to make the decision about the cattle. He's got a good eye for stock. I'll hitch the team to the light buggy."

Prudence lost no time in shedding her apron. She rushed off to change and, when she came down, gave Grace a hug. "Now don't wait up for us. We may be late."

"All right. I'll keep something on the stove in case you are hungry."

After Prudence drove away, Grace listlessly performed the household chores. Finally she went into the parlor and sat down. Looking around the room, she saw a hundred reminders of her father, and loneliness came to her. Her thoughts returned to the days she'd spent at Armory Square Hospital, but that brought to her mind the letters she'd received from Miss Dix, asking her to return to duty.

I'll have to write her. It's not fair to let her think I'm coming back. She had tried to force herself to return but somehow could not face up to it. Now she tried again to analyze what it was that seemed to loom before her like a wall when she thought of returning to Washington. *Is it that I can't stand to be reminded of John? No, because I'm constantly reminded of him right here. What is it, then?* Something came to her mind, and she brushed it aside, but it came again persistently. *Can God be keeping me here for some purpose? What on earth could it be? I'm no good to myself or anyone else—not the way I am!*

She got up and was about to leave the room when she glanced out the window and saw a two-seated carriage emerge from the trees that blanketed the main road. *Why, that's Grissom's carriage,* she thought. *He has no reason to come here.*

But the carriage turned into their drive, and Grace hurried out to the front porch. Grissom pulled the carriage to a halt, touched the brim of his hat, and said, "Howdy, Miss Grace."

"Hello, Pat," Grace responded. "Cold drive from town."

"Yes, right sharp." He turned to the figure huddled beside him, saying, "Mister Rocklin, we're here."

Grace saw the man beside Grissom lean forward and say something quietly, and Grissom turned to say, "Miss Grace, Mr. Rocklin wants me to wait. Kin I put the team in the barn and grain 'em, let 'em warm up 'fore I start back?"

738

"Of course, Pat." Then she smiled and said, "Then come inside and warm yourself up, too." She watched as a tall black man stepped out of the backseat and helped Grissom's passenger to the ground. The two of them made their way to the steps, and the passenger took off his hat, revealing a crop of gray hair and a face gray with fatigue. He seemed to be studying Grace's face for a few moments; then he spoke in a low voice.

"My name is Rocklin, Thomas Rocklin. You are Miss Grace Swenson?"

"Yes." Grace saw that the man was trembling and said quickly, "Come in, please. It's very cold."

She held the door open as the black man helped Rocklin up the steps. "Come right in, both of you." As soon as they were inside, she said, "Come into the kitchen. It's warm there, and there's coffee on."

"I want to tell you, Miss Swenson—," Rocklin began, but she interrupted at once.

"Come and thaw out, sir. It's a cold ride from town." She supervised the thing easily, drawing out a chair, seeing that the old man was comfortable, then smiling at the black man. "What is thy name?" she asked.

"Why, it's Zander, ma'am."

"Zander, thee looks cold. Come and stand by the stove while I get something hot to thaw thee out."

Grace quickly poured two cups of coffee, lacing them with sugar and thick cream. "Drink this, and I'll heat some soup."

As the woman busied herself with the food, Thomas

exchanged glances with Zander, and they both nodded. The gleam in Zander's eyes was a mark of approval, and Thomas relaxed in the chair, soaking up the heat from the stove. He sipped the scalding coffee, almost burning his lips, and when the young woman set two bowls of steaming soup and a roll of fresh bread before him, he realized how hungry he was.

"Would thee ask the blessing on the food, Mr. Rocklin?" Grace asked.

"Why, I certainly will." Thomas nodded. He did so briefly, then said, "Zander, sit down and eat your soup."

Zander looked scandalized. He had never sat at a table in his life with white people. But his master muttered, "Don't be a fool. Sit and eat."

"Yas, suh, Marse Thomas," he said and sat down, eating carefully, keeping his eyes down.

The door opened, and Grissom entered, gratefully taking the steaming cup of coffee that Grace held out to him. He seated himself in a chair, and Thomas noted how he seemed not fully removed from the group, his eyes and ears taking in everything in the room.

Thomas ate most of the bowl of soup, saying nothing. The food warmed him, brightening his eyes and reviving him. He had had a bad time on the trip from town but now felt stronger. The young woman had sipped coffee, speaking casually of how bad the winter had been and the trouble it had caused with the stock. She was, Thomas realized, skilled at putting people at their ease, and he understood that she kept up her speaking to avoid a painful silence.

She's a smart young woman, he thought with approval. *Not many women would have that much tact.*

Finally he was finished, and she said, "Now let's go to the parlor. It's more comfortable there."

Rocklin cast his eyes at Grissom and nodded. *She knows I've come to talk—and that I want some privacy.* "Thank you for the meal," he said. "It was delicious."

He followed her down a short hall, and when they were in a small room with bookcases on one wall, she said, "Take that chair, Mr. Rocklin." While he sat down with a sigh of comfort, she put two small logs on the fire, then came to sit across from him.

Rocklin said, "I must apologize for thrusting myself on you, Miss Swenson. I asked the driver to wait because I wasn't sure if I'd be staying."

"Thee is welcome, sir."

"I—hope I will be more welcome, Miss Swenson, when you know my reason for coming." The fire snapped, and a spark rose and fell on the stone hearth. Rocklin had tried to anticipate this moment, to plan what he would say—but now that it had come, he found himself in difficulty. "I don't know how to put this to you," he said finally.

"Perhaps I can help thee," Grace said. Her face seemed to be rather pale, Rocklin noticed, and her lips trembled slightly. He was surprised, for she had been so placid until this moment. She hesitated, then asked, "Is it about thy son, Mr. Rocklin?"

Grace had fed the men, curious as to the nature of the visit, but it was not until the old man sat down in the chair that the answer came to her: *He's John's father!* Something about the planes of the older man's face, the way he held himself—and the way it was an echo of how John had sat in that very chair—brought the truth to her.

Thomas stared at her in shock, then nodded. "You're very quick, Miss Grace!"

"He is much like thee," Grace said simply.

"They say so."

Grace licked her lips, then spoke almost in a whisper. "Is he alive, Mr. Rocklin?"

"Oh yes!" Thomas rapped out at once. "Yes, indeed! I—I guess my visit does seem like a portent of doom."

Grace took a deep breath, her hand on her breast. "I'm very glad," she said simply.

"He's alive but in terrible trouble. That's why I've come to you."

"Tell me," Grace said quickly, leaning forward. And for the next twenty minutes, she sat still, asking no questions as Rocklin explained how his son had come to be in a Union hospital. He paused to say, "He's spoken of you so much, Miss Grace, that I almost feel I know you."

"But if his memory is back, how can there be trouble?" Grace asked.

Thomas hesitated, then said, "He was captured by Confederate troops, and he was wearing the uniform of a Union soldier. Do you know what that means?"

Grace grasped it at once. "He's suspected of being a traitor?"

"Exactly! And if things don't change, he'll be hanged."

Grace stared at him. "But—he didn't *know* he was a Confederate soldier. And he was *forced* to join the Union Army." She spoke rapidly, explaining how Colonel Drecker had given him no choice at all.

Thomas listened carefully, then nodded. "That's exactly what Burke told us."

Grace hesitated slightly. "His name is...Burke?"

"Yes."

Grace stood up abruptly and began to pace the floor. Her knees were weak, and she clasped her hands tightly together to control the trembling that had come to them. She had always been a calm woman, but this had shaken her, and she had to wait and pray until peace came to her. Finally she came to stand before Thomas. "Thee is not a well man, Mr. Rocklin. Why did thee not send someone else to tell me about...about Burke?"

Thomas said simply, "I don't have long to live, Miss Grace. And many of my family and friends told me I was a fool to make such a desperate journey in my condition." He shook his head, but there was a brightness in his dark eyes and a note of triumph in his voice as he added, "I've failed my family so much, but if I could do this *one* thing—if I could save Burke—why, I'd feel my life was not in vain!"

Grace suddenly knew that God was in the room. There was no change in what she saw with her eyes or what she heard.

Yet she *knew* that she was being dealt with by the Spirit of the Lord.

"What does thee want me to do, Mr. Rocklin?"

"I want you to come to Richmond with me. Our lawyer says that we have to have records from the Union hospital where Burke was treated, records that bear out what he claims about losing his memory. And he wants you to testify. If we can get those records, and if you will come and testify, Burke has a chance. If not, he will be convicted. And he will die."

Suddenly Grace understood why she had felt unable to go back to Washington. God had been keeping her here so she might do all she could to save Burke!

"I'll go with thee," she said quietly.

Thomas whispered, "Thank God!" He took her hand, kissed it, then asked, "Grace, do you love my son?"

Grace nodded. "Yes, I love him. I'll always love him."

"And I love him, too," the man said, tears glistening in his eyes.

The two sat there in the quiet room, speaking of what must be done, and as they spoke, a great joy came to Grace. *He's alive—and I can help him!* she thought.

The next morning, three passengers boarded the southbound train, and it was Al Cotter who summed up the feeling of the town: "Well, Pat, that'll be the last we see of Sister Grace! She's gone to Richmond, and there ain't no good can ever come out of a thing like that!"

CHAPTER 21

THE VERDICT

$\mathcal{G}$aines Franklin DeQuincy chewed slowly on the stub of his cigar as he stared out the window at the long icicles that hung along the eaves of the courthouse. The icicles glittered like diamonds in the morning sunlight, but the lawyer felt there was something sinister and ominous in their pristine beauty. He rolled the cigar around in his catfish-shaped mouth, thinking, *Pretty enough, but they look like knives. One of them could pierce a man to the heart.*

DeQuincy was a startling combination of cynic and romantic. He kept the romantic side of his nature carefully hidden, however, so that his friends—and his enemies—would have been startled to discover any trace of it in his makeup.

Pretty as a picture, those icicles. But it's a cold sort of beauty—like some women I've known. A bitter memory lifted like a specter out of his past and threw a fleeting shadow across his mind, and he abruptly tossed his cigar into the brass spittoon with an angry gesture.

He wheeled away from the window, turning to face Clay Rocklin and Mrs. Susanna Rocklin, wishing he'd never allowed himself to get involved with Burke Rocklin's trial. He'd accepted the case only after a persistent pleading on the part of Thomas Rocklin. And he'd warned Rocklin plainly, *"I'm not a miracle worker, Mr. Rocklin. Chances are fifty to one against acquittal."*

Now DeQuincy knew that the two in front of him were expecting exactly that—some sort of legal legerdemain—to set Burke Rocklin free.

Susanna's eyes were fixed on DeQuincy. It was the third day of the court-martial, and no visitors were permitted except as witnesses. She'd studied the lawyer each day and had been un-impressed by his appearance. DeQuincy was less than average height and not at all impressive. He wore a scruffy brown beard that covered the lower part of his face, and the only noticeable facet of his appearance was a pair of sharp brown eyes that missed nothing. His uniform was wrinkled, and traces of his breakfast were evident on the lapels of his coat. He spoke in a rather bored tone of voice, and Susanna had no way of knowing that in a courtroom he could lift that voice into a bellow that would rattle the rafters!

"You're not optimistic, are you, Major DeQuincy?" she asked.

The lawyer shot her a sudden glance. "No, Mrs. Rocklin. I am not." He pulled a fresh cigar from his pocket, bit off the end, and spit it into the cuspidor. Pulling out a match, he struck it on the surface of the desk, leaving a fresh scarred track on the walnut surface. He got the cigar going, sending clouds of lavender smoke into the air, then tossed the match on the floor. Only then did he put his sharp eyes on the two of them, saying, "It's not a case any lawyer would be hopeful about."

Clay was wearing a fresh uniform and looked very distinguished. "What's going on, Major?" He shook his broad shoulders in a gesture of impatience. "Are the officers prejudiced against my brother?"

"Why, certainly!" DeQuincy stared at Clay as if he had said something rather stupid. "Didn't you know they would be?"

"I thought a prisoner was supposed to get a fair trial." His lips drew together into an angry line. "It can't be very fair if the jury's already made up its mind!"

DeQuincy's crooked lips twisted into a wry grin. "Captain Rocklin, you don't spend a lot of time in courtrooms, do you?"

"No, I don't!"

"Well, if you did, you'd know that ninety-nine juries out of a hundred have their minds made up about their vote before they're even picked. And in this case, that fact is all but guaranteed."

"Why is that, Major?" Susanna asked quietly.

DeQuincy removed the cigar from his lips, examined it, then replaced it. "Because your son was wearing a Federal uniform." He shrugged. "No matter what other facts may be involved, they're sure about *that* fact, and nothing's going to get it out of their minds."

"I see." Susanna sat there quietly, and DeQuincy admired

her calmness. He'd never seen a woman who had her strength, and he wished he had better hopes to offer her.

"Don't give up," he grunted. "It's never over until the verdict is in."

"When will that be, Major?"

DeQuincy looked down at the fresh scar on the desk thoughtfully. Tracing it with his forefinger, he said, "I think tomorrow."

"So soon?" Clay blinked in surprise. "But they haven't heard our witnesses."

"No, but they're officers, and they don't have the freedom of civilians," DeQuincy stated. "They can be pulled out at any moment and sent to the Western theater or to some other spot. I've done all I know to slow things down, but I'm guessing they'll end it tomorrow." He looked up as a sergeant opened the door and informed him that the court-martial was about to resume. "Now you two will have to keep your temper," he warned. "Some of the members of the court are antagonistic. Don't let them make you mad. That's what they want. No matter what happens, just tell the truth as calmly as you can."

Grabbing his briefcase, he left, slamming the door behind him.

Clay stared moodily at the door, then shook his head. "He's not my idea of a great lawyer."

Susanna shook her head. "He doesn't look like much, but he's a fighter, Clay. That's what we need for Burke."

Clay nodded slowly. "That's what father said." He noted

the lines of fatigue on his mother's face and put his hand on her arm. "Hard to believe when everything's going against you, isn't it?"

"Anyone can believe when things are right," Susanna said. "Faith is for when things are all wrong." She smiled slightly, adding, "I've been thinking of Abraham. Remember how his one dream in life was to have a son? And then when he had Isaac, God told him to take the boy and sacrifice him?"

"Pretty stiff test, wasn't it?"

"Yes. All he ever wanted, and God told him to let it go." Susanna's eyes grew somber, and she fell silent. The two of them sat there as time passed, and finally she whispered, "I wonder where your father is."

Clay knew her thoughts, for he had been wondering the same thing. It had occurred to him that his father might have fallen ill on the way to Pennsylvania—that he might be lying unconscious somewhere and would never bring the woman to testify.

"I don't know, Mother, but he's doing his best. I know that!"

They sat there in the small room, helpless and totally cut off from what was happening down the hall. Their hopes were in the scrubby hands of Gaines DeQuincy—insofar as human help was concerned—and they both felt, as they sat facing their fears, that those hands seemed to be very unlikely security.

DeQuincy stared at the officers seated at the long table. They were the enemy! He always thought of the jury as the enemy, even more so than the prosecuting attorney.

"You know the prosecuting attorney is going to go for your throat," he often told young lawyers. "You can handle that. But the jury, they're the ones who can send your man to the gallows! So you fight them—but you smile and never treat them rough. Find out who's on your side and who's out to kill your man. Then you work on them!"

He stared at the five officers, then glanced down at the single page in front of him. He always drew up a chart showing the jury. In this case it was very simple. He had put the members of the court-martial into two categories: friends and enemies. Next to each of the names, he had written a description and some comments:

FRIENDS

Captain Maynard Wells. Age 25. Good combat record. Sense of humor. Listens to everything. Hard— but fair. Will vote to acquit if he has a chance.

Lieutenant Powell Carleton. Age 21. Feels out of place with senior officers. Afraid to ask questions because of his youth. (Smile at him often, give him confidence!) Seems meek, but will not kill my man unless he has to. Will acquit if evidence gives him a chance.

ENEMIES

Major Carl Lentz. Age 50. Lost an arm at Malvern Hill. Hates Yankees. Would be fair in most circumstances, but he will never be able to forget the charges against Rocklin. At best, a "maybe."

Major D. L. Patterson. Age 62. Too old for a combat officer. Has his commission as reward for political favors. Not a bad man, but a political animal. Will not *dare* set Rocklin free for fear people will say he's not a thorough patriot. Will vote to kill my man, no matter *what* I do or what evidence is produced! Will vote guilty.

Colonel Ransome Hill. Age 55. Never saw a finer looking man—except for General Lee! Tremendous field commander. Will make general sooner or later. But has lost his only two sons in the war, one at Seven Pines and one at Fredericksburg. Lives for nothing but to kill Yankees. He is fair enough as ranking officer of the court, but his eyes are cold when he looks at Burke Rocklin. Will vote guilty.

DeQuincy ran his eyes over the list. *Three to two—at best!* he thought.

"Not very good odds, eh, Major?" Burke Rocklin murmured.

DeQuincy turned, startled, to find his client staring at the sheet. He quickly wadded it up, saying, "Just a game I play, Burke. Doesn't mean a thing."

And then he looked up as Colonel Hill said, "The court will hear Captain Clay Rocklin."

When Clay entered, he turned and gave Burke an encouraging smile, then took the oath in a firm voice and sat down.

"Captain Rocklin," Colonel Hill said promptly, "please tell this court how you identified the body that was buried under the name of Burke Rocklin."

DeQuincy had heard the story several times and saw that the captain made a good impression on the two younger members of the court. When he was finished, Major Patterson demanded, "How could you have made such an error, Captain? After all, it was, supposedly, the body of your only brother!"

"Sir, the man I identified was practically destroyed from the waist up," Clay said evenly, staring at the major. "But he was wearing my brother's uniform, and he had my brother's ring on his finger."

Captain Wells, the young captain, asked with some sympathy, "Captain, did anyone else identify the body?"

"Yes, sir, my son Denton, an officer in the Army of Northern Virginia."

Score one for the home team! DeQuincy said to himself with satisfaction. *We've got Captain Wells on our side for sure. Now—give it to them again, Captain Rocklin!*

"Now, Captain Rocklin," Major Lentz piped up. His face was red, and he had the air of a drinking man. "You found your brother in Libby Prison, I believe. What was his condition?"

"Very poor," Clay said instantly. "He seemed unlikely to live."

"Are you a physician, Captain?" This from the prosecuting attorney, a lean captain of thirty named George Willing.

"No, sir," Clay said evenly. "I am not, but Kermit Maxwell

is. I believe he's already been before this court?"

The question brought a flush to Willing's cheeks. He had tried hard to shake Maxwell's testimony, to prove that Burke Rocklin had been faking his illness. But the old man had stopped him with a withering look and a few acid words. Willing said quickly, "Just answer the question, Captain!"

"No, sir, I'm not a physician."

The court asked Clay many questions, mostly concerning the matter of the defendant's loss of memory. Clay answered briefly and was not afraid to admit that it was a difficult thing to describe.

The youngest member of the court, Lieutenant Powell Carleton, finally asked, "Captain, you were convinced that the defendant was telling the truth. What made you so certain?"

Clay gave the young man a thin smile. "Two things. One, my brother was *never* an actor. If he was putting on an act, he'd changed completely. And secondly, I tried him out."

"Tried him out?" Colonel Lentz asked. He leaned forward, about to put his elbows on the table, then realized that one sleeve was empty. He sat back a little embarrassed, asking, "How did you do that?"

"I'd mention things that never happened as if they *had* happened," Clay said at once. "I'd say, 'We lost that gray stallion you liked so much,' when there'd been no stallion. He *never* remembered those things. And sometimes I'd drop things he ought never to have forgotten, and he almost always remembered them."

"What sort of things, Captain Rocklin?" Lentz demanded.

"My brother could always name the presidents of the United States with the dates they served. I'd say, 'Now when was it that Madison was in office?' and he'd always know. Once when I did that, he stared at me and asked, 'How did I know that?'"

Lentz was intrigued by this, and for some time drew Clay out. Finally he nodded, saying, "Thank you, Captain," and leaned back.

George Willing knew that he'd lost points and set out to prove that such things meant nothing. Finally Clay was dismissed, and DeQuincy whispered, "*That* didn't hurt us any!"

"Send in Mrs. Susanna Rocklin," Colonel Hill said, and they all rose when Susanna came in. She took the oath in a quiet voice, then sat down.

"Mrs. Rocklin, please tell the court of the 'recovery' of the defendant." The slight difference of tone on the word *recovery* was noticeable to everyone in the room. It was almost tangible evidence that the colonel did not accept that "recovery" as real.

Susanna heard the tone and understood it very well, but let nothing show in her face. She spoke quietly for ten minutes, then waited for the challenge she was certain would come.

And so it did, from the prosecuting attorney. "Mrs. Rocklin, you love your son, don't you?"

"Yes, I do."

"Of course." Captain Willing nodded. "And I'm sure that we all honor you for it. You'd be an unnatural mother if you didn't!"

"He's out to get her," DeQuincy whispered to Burke.

"Can't you stop him?" Burke demanded.

"Stop him?" DeQuincy turned his sharp black eyes on Burke with amazement. "Bless you, no! I hope he chops her to ribbons!" When he saw the look of indignation that leaped into Burke's eyes, he grabbed Burke's arm, saying, "He's a hothead, and he's not learned that you don't attack a woman in court—especially not the mother of a soldier in the Army of Northern Virginia! Let him go! He'll be more help to us than ten witnesses."

For the next twenty minutes, Captain Willing questioned Susanna over and over again about the details of what he termed "the alleged recovery." At one point he grew so abusive that Colonel Hill looked at the defense lawyer in disgust, asking, "Major DeQuincy, don't you object to the fashion in which Captain Willing is treating your witness?"

"No, sir," DeQuincy said smoothly. "The captain has no facts, so he's doing all he knows how—he's abusing a helpless woman." DeQuincy enjoyed the sudden reddening of his opponent's face, adding, "I'm sure the *gentlemen* on the court understand what Captain Willing is doing."

Willing was filled with wrath. "Mrs. Rocklin, you love your son, and you would do *anything* to save his life. Isn't that true?" he shouted.

"No, sir," Susanna answered. "It is *not* true!" Her eyes were bright, and when Willing stopped in shocked surprise, she said, "I took an oath to tell the truth. That oath was to God, and I would not lie to save my son's life!"

"I suppose you'd let him hang?" Willing sneered.

Susanna faced him squarely. "Many mothers have given their sons for the Confederacy, Captain Willing. I love God, and my son would despise me if I denied my faith to save his life. Isn't that right, son?"

Burke said clearly, "Yes!"

At once Colonel Hill said, "You will not speak to the defendant, Mrs. Rocklin. And you, Mr. Rocklin, will have your turn to speak! Now are there any more questions from you gentlemen for Mrs. Rocklin?"

"Mrs. Rocklin," Lieutenant Carleton asked in a subdued tone, "I believe you have relatives who are in the Union Army?"

"Yes, Lieutenant," Susanna said, nodding. "My husband's brother Mr. Stephen Rocklin has a son in the Army of the Potomac—Colonel Gideon Rocklin. The colonel has two sons in the Union Army."

"Well, do you think it possible, since some of your family are in the Union, that your son Burke might have sympathies with the North?"

"No, sir, I cannot think so. My son took an oath to the Confederate States. He was not always a good son, but he was never a liar."

Lieutenant Carleton seemed to find this answer sufficient. "I have no more questions, Colonel Hill."

As soon as Susanna left the room, Colonel Hill asked, "Major DeQuincy, do you have other witnesses?"

"Yes, sir, I have one. I call Burke Rocklin."

DeQuincy stood up but moved to the side of the room so that the court had a clear view of the defendant. "Mr. Rocklin, will you please relate your experience to this court. Begin with the Battle of Second Manassas."

Burke nodded and began at once to tell his story. He spoke of the battle but said, "I was struck down on the battlefield and have no memory of anything that took place between that time and the time I woke up in the Armory Square Hospital in Washington."

"Now please tell the court of your time in that hospital," DeQuincy said.

Burke spoke carefully, omitting no detail, explaining all he experienced, including the time he'd spent at the Swenson farm.

He makes a fine witness, DeQuincy thought, *but wait until Willing gets at him!*

Finally Burke finished, and DeQuincy thought quickly. Ordinarily he would have drawn the witness out, but he knew nothing could improve on what Burke had said, nor the manner in which he had said it.

"Gentlemen, I have nothing to add to my client's statement. Captain Willing, your witness."

Willing leaped up, and for the next two hours he slashed at Burke's testimony. Burke kept his head, never losing his temper, and DeQuincy knew it was better for him to stay out of it.

Finally Willing said, "So we have your word, Mr. Rocklin, that all of this happened?"

"Yes, sir."

"Your word? But nothing more?" Willing turned to the court and made a solid speech regarding 'reasonable doubt' and the necessity of facts over hearsay. As he listened, even DeQuincy had to admit to himself it was good stuff. Finally Willing said, "If there were only *one* witness, I would not be so adamant. But you gentlemen know that the most heinous crime in any army is desertion and joining forces with the enemy. By all the *evidence*, this is exactly what Burke Rocklin has done. I know not his reasons, but there is *no* justification for this behavior."

DeQuincy studied the faces of the men on the court and knew he was licked. *Even the younger men can't let him go—not with evidence so piled against him!*

"We will hear the closing arguments after a short recess," Colonel Hill announced. The members of the court got up and filed out, and DeQuincy rose and accompanied Burke to the room that was his cell. The lawyer sat down, lit up a fresh cigar, and then looked at his client.

Burke caught the look, then shrugged. "You didn't have much to fight with, Major."

"Now don't be handing down any verdicts, Burke," the lawyer admonished. "We've still got a chance."

But late that afternoon, when DeQuincy emerged from the courtroom to speak with Clay and Susanna, his face told the story. Even before he could speak, Susanna said, "He was convicted, wasn't he?"

DeQuincy nodded slowly. "If we could only hear from your husband—!"

Clay felt his stomach knot up. "We've got to do something! It can't end like this!"

DeQuincy knew that things *did* end just this way—often— but he only said, "We'll hope for clemency in the sentence. I'll try for life imprisonment instead·of execution."

"No!" Susanna said at once. "That's worse than death, to be locked up for life!" She was pale, but her eyes were not defeated. "We will believe God! In the shadow of the gallows, I'll believe God!"

CHAPTER 22

"GIVE LOVE A CHANCE!"

$\mathcal{M}$elora pulled her horse up in front of the mansion, slipped to the ground, and handed the reins to the servant who came to take them. "Thank you, Moses," she said with a nod. As he took the lines, she asked, "Has your father come back?"

"No, ma'am, he ain't." Moses was the tall son of Dorrie and Zander. His high-planed face was sober, and he shook his head, adding, "Sho' is miserable 'bout Marse Burke!"

As the slave led her horse away, Melora turned and mounted the steps. When a young maid opened the door in answer to her knock, she said, "Hello, Lutie. Is Mrs. Rocklin here?"

"Yassum, Miss Melora. She's in de parlor wif Marse Clay. I guess you knows de way."

"Thank you, Lutie."

Melora went down the long hall to a small room and knocked lightly on the tall double doors. When she heard Susanna's voice bidding her to enter, she opened the door and stepped inside.

Clay got up at once and came to her. She put out her hands to him, saying, "I just heard, Clay."

"I knew you'd come," he said. He wanted to take her in his arms, but turned as his mother stood and came to Melora. The two women embraced, and then Susanna said, "You two sit down. I'll go make tea."

She left the room, and Clay summoned a sad ghost of a smile. "How'd you hear about Burke?"

"Tad Greenaway heard about it when he was in Richmond. He knew we'd want to know."

"It'll be in the paper today," Clay muttered. He looked pale and ill, Melora noted. Catching her glance, he shook his head. "It's hit me harder than I thought anything could, Melora."

"Come and sit down," she urged.

"No, I've been sitting here for hours. Is it too cold for you to walk?"

He got his coat and forage cap and helped her on with her heavy coat, and the two of them left the house.

"Your mother will wonder where we are," Melora said.

"No. She'll know," Clay said. He led her to a path at the side of the house, and the two of them walked down the narrow road that led to the summerhouse. The air was very cold, and he asked, "Are you warm enough?"

"Yes. I love cold weather."

They walked for half an hour, past the summerhouse where Clay had lived alone until Ellen had died. As they moved deeper into the woods, Melora thought of all that had happened in the last few months and knew that Clay's thoughts were on this, too.

The snow was packed down into hard plates of ice, and they walked carefully to keep from slipping. When they came to a small creek, Clay said, "Let's cross over. The ice will hold us up."

They edged carefully across the ice, grabbing at saplings to pull themselves up on the far bank. Clay went first, then reached back and pulled Melora after him. Her feet slipped, and she grabbed wildly, but he caught her and pulled her to firm footing, holding her close.

She had cried out as her feet flew out from under her, but when his arms closed around her, she held on tightly. Clay pulled her closer, and she looked up quickly. She knew he was going to kiss her and could have pulled away...but she did not. She surrendered to the pressure of his arms and rested against him, lifting her face.

The feel of her in his arms and the sight of her soft lips raised to his were enough for Clay. He held her tightly, and their kiss was wildly sweet. For that one moment, he forgot about Burke and the war and the children. There was only the joy of being with this woman he'd loved for so long and the solace of that love.

Melora clung to him, her hands going up to pull him closer. A tumultuous rush of love rose in her, and she gave herself to him completely, yielding herself to him with a sweet willingness.

Finally Clay lifted his head, but he did not let her go. "Melora, I love you so much!" His voice was husky with emotion.

"I know!" Melora whispered. "I know, my dear!" Reaching up, she cupped his cheek with her hand. "And you're the only man I've ever loved!"

They stood there clinging to each other, shut off from the world. Finally she took his hand and drew him down a narrow path that followed the creek. They said no more until he drew her to a stop, turned her around, and asked with torment in his fine eyes, "Melora, what are we going to do?"

"We're going to be faithful to God and to each other," Melora said at once.

"But—"

"I know, Clay," she broke in. "I know all that stirs within you, because it's in me, too. We're older; you could get killed in the war—" Her voice broke, and she shook her head. "It's all true, but God knows our hearts, and through Him, we'll always have each other. Do you believe that?"

"I only know I want you," Clay said simply. "But with Ellen dead so short a time and with a war to fight—"

"I'll be here, Clay," she said softly. "When the time is right, I'll be here."

He groaned and held her close again. "Oh, Melora! If we could just run away from here, just you and I! If we could find someplace where we could just be together and love each other."

Melora's lips curved in a tender smile, and she let him hold her for a time, then pulled back. "You'd never run away, Clay Rocklin, not in a million years!" Pride was in her eyes, for she knew this man well. "You'd let yourself be pulled into pieces before you'd run away from your duty!"

Clay peered at her closely and then smiled. "I never knew I was such a noble cuss," he said. "Tell me more."

She talked with him, telling him of her love and the reasons for it, and so took the sting out of Clay's sorrow. By the time they got back to the house, he realized what she had done. Just before they went inside, he took her hand and kissed it. "Came to get the old man out of the grumps, didn't you?"

"You're not an old man!"

"Well, old or young, I am a grateful man," he answered. "You know me pretty well, I guess."

"Clay, let's take what we have and be grateful for it." Melora turned her face upward to him, and Clay knew she was sweet beyond anything he'd ever known. "It's too soon to talk of anything permanent between us, so let's just take every moment we do have and savor it."

She kissed him lightly, then went inside. Clay followed her, and as soon as Susanna saw them, she knew what had happened and was glad. She, too, longed for the day when this son of hers could claim the joy he'd been waiting for.

After Clay left to go back to camp, Susanna and Melora sat for a long time, speaking some—but also sharing the silence in the way fine friends often do. Finally Susanna said, "Melora, you're the daughter-in-law I've always longed for.

Has he asked you to marry him?"

"No, it's too soon."

Susanna shook her head, a wistful smile on her face. "It's often too late for love, but never too soon, Melora! I'll pray God will help that foolish son of mine see that!"

A few days had passed since the verdict, and still no word came from Thomas Rocklin. With each passing day, the hopes of the family were dimmed. "He must be sick and unable to speak," Susanna said finally.

Burke had stood before the court for his sentencing and listened as they sentenced him to death—but the judgment had come only after a stormy session in which Lieutenant Powell Carleton almost managed to get himself court-martialed!

Lieutenant Carleton literally blew up when he saw that the court was going to hand out the death sentence. He turned pale, then stood up and said, "No! He's not going to hang—sir!"

Colonel Hill was taken completely aback—even more so when young Carleton refused to be admonished. A wild session ensued, in which Carleton had cried, "I won't be a part of it! He may be guilty, but I'm not convinced of it. The least we can do is hand down a life sentence so that there's a chance to straighten things out!"

"Straighten things out!" Colonel Hill grew incensed. "Are you telling me we're unjust?"

"You're not God, are you, Colonel?" Carleton demanded—and if the other members of the court had not intervened, it is likely that Lieutenant Carleton would have been Private Carleton and in the guardhouse!

Finally Burke was brought in and the sentence was pronounced by Colonel Hill. But Lieutenant Carleton stood up and stared straight at the colonel, stating flatly, "I want it on record that I oppose this sentence as being overly harsh!"

"Sit *down*, Lieutenant!" Colonel Hill almost shouted. He calmed himself, then looked at Burke. "You have been found guilty of treason and this court sentences you to be hanged. You will be taken from this place to a place of confinement, and at dawn on February 14, you will be executed by the provost marshall."

Burke said nothing to the colonel. He only looked at the young lieutenant and smiled. "Thank you, Lieutenant," he said softly, then turned and followed the sergeant out of the court.

George Willing came over to stand beside DeQuincy. The captain had a great admiration for DeQuincy and said with a certain sadness, "Too bad. But there was never any real chance for him, was there, DeQuincy?"

DeQuincy kept his head down as he stuffed his briefcase. Finally he lifted his eyes, which where hot with anger. "Willing—I hate to lose!" he gritted between clenched teeth.

"Why, Gaines, I believe you think the fellow is innocent!"

DeQuincy snatched up the briefcase, and as he stalked toward the door, Willing asked, "Where are you going?"

Major Gaines Franklin DeQuincy stopped and turned his head. "I'm going to get drunk," he announced, then did an abrupt about-face and marched out of the courtroom.

Captain Willing stared after him, then shouted, "Hey! DeQuincy! Wait, blast it all! I'm going to get drunk with you."

*

Burke was moved from the city jail to the stockade immediately after he was sentenced. He was treated kindly enough and spent most of his time writing. For the first two days he had visitors, but he pulled Clay aside to say, "On the last night, don't let Mother come. Or anybody else."

Clay said, "I'm coming, and that's final."

Burke grinned at his brother. "Just the two of us, then. All right?"

"If you say so."

And so the two days went by, and on the last night, Clay came and the two men sat and talked. Clay marveled at his younger brother's coolness and finally said, "Burke, I couldn't take it like—like you are."

Burke had been sipping coffee but lowered the cup. He stared at the other man for a long time, then said, "Clay, you were wrong."

"Wrong? About what?"

"About my not being an actor. That's what you told the court." He sipped the coffee, then stared into the cup. "I'm an actor, all right. Because I'm scared. Have been ever since

767

this thing blew up." He looked up and caught Clay's look of amazement. "Oh, come on, Clay!" He smiled briefly. "It's like before a battle. Everybody's scared, but no one wants to show it. Isn't that right?"

Clay nodded slowly. "It's the way it happens to me. I get so scared I can't swallow, but of course you can't show that in front of the men."

Burke grew silent, then asked with some difficulty, "It makes a difference, doesn't it, when a man knows God?"

Clay answered carefully. "Christians get scared just like men who don't know God. But—it's a different kind of fear, I think. Before I became a Christian, I was in a few spots that looked like the end, and I was plenty afraid. But after I got saved, why, I was scared, but it wasn't the same."

"Tell me about it, if you can, Clay."

"Well, a lost man doesn't have much hope. He's afraid of two things—death and what comes after. But a Christian, he *knows* he's all right after he dies, so it's just that fear of the unknown that gets him. And I think some of that's built into us, Burke. Self-preservation. Some men get close enough to God so that they lose even that. Men like Stephen, in the Bible, the man who was stoned." Clay's eyes grew thoughtful as he added, "Now *there* was a man for you! Praying for his enemies as they killed him!"

The lamp outside the cell threw yellow bars that fell across the faces of the two men, and as Clay studied Burke, he saw the younger man's fear. "Burke, I've never believed much in shoving people toward God. Always thought God could do the drawing and a man could do the giving up."

The shadow of death lay on Burke, and he looked down into his cup for a long time before finally saying, "I've—wanted to call on God, Clay." He looked up with misery in his dark eyes. "But it seems like such a—a *rotten* thing to do!"

"Calling on God, rotten?" Clay blinked in astonishment. "How could that be?"

"I've never called on Him before, never listened to Him when I had the chance. Now I'm in trouble and need Him. It seems so cheap and insincere, Clay!"

Clay shook his head. "You're making a big mistake, brother. You're thinking of God as if He were a man. God doesn't act like we do. He's God, and He acts like God."

"I don't see what you mean."

"Well, when somebody hurts you, what do you do? Hurt them back if you can, right? But that's because of what we've become. God didn't make us like that, Burke; sin makes us like that. Adam wasn't like that, not before he fell away from God's grace. He was like God. The Bible says that God said, 'Let us make man in our image.' That really means God made man like Himself."

"I haven't seen much of God in people," Burke said quietly.

"Yes, you have." Clay nodded. "You see it in Mother and in Raimey and in Melora. And you saw it in Jeremiah Irons. Isn't that right?"

Clay saw that his words hit Burke hard.

"Yes, I did!" he answered thoughtfully.

"And you saw it in that young woman, Grace Swenson, didn't you? I know you did, Burke."

Again Burke nodded. "You're right, Clay. She was full of God!" Then his lips drew into a harsh line. "But I'm not like them, Clay!"

"They're what Jesus Christ made them, Burke." Clay drove home the words, and for hours the two men talked. For Clay it was like one of the battles he'd taken part in. Sometimes he seemed to forge ahead, winning ground, and then Burke would counterattack, and he'd fall back. It was hard, agonizing work, for he knew he was wrestling for the very soul of his only brother.

More than once Burke cried out, "Leave me alone, Clay! It's no use! I've gone too far!"

But Clay never gave up. He read scripture after scripture. He prayed as he'd never prayed before in his life! And all the while he knew that some power was flowing into him, for he found himself quoting verses he didn't even know!

It's Melora and Mother—they're praying for me! he thought with certainty. And that realization encouraged and energized him, helping him as the night wore on and he pressed the matter on Burke.

Burke was holding himself together by will alone. He was terribly afraid, more afraid than he thought a man could be. He wanted to weep and beat the walls with his fists, but he sat in the chair trying to believe what Clay was telling him. "Do you mean that all I have to do is *ask*—and God will save me?"

"If you ask *rightly*, you'll be forgiven," Clay answered. When he saw the bewilderment in Burke's eyes, he said quickly, "Many people call on God who don't mean it. They want *something*, but they don't want God Himself."

"Well, I want to live," Burke said.

"I think you want more than that," Clay said. "You talked a lot about that preacher woman. I'm thinking if you lived, you would want her. Is that right?"

"Yes!"

"Well, you know you'd never have her as you are, don't you, Burke? And why do you want her? You may think it's because she's a woman and because she cared for you. But I will guarantee you that what drew you to Grace Swenson is the fact that you saw God in her! *That's* what drew you, for there is no greater lover than the Lord. Now if you could walk out of this cell and go to her, you know what she'd say?"

Burke nodded wearily. "She'd never have a man who didn't love God." He shook his head. "If only I could believe like she does. . .if I could know God the way she does—" He broke off suddenly, blinking in surprise at what he'd just said. Then he turned wondering eyes on his brother, eyes that were beginning to fill with understanding. "Why, maybe I *have* wanted God, Clay! Ever since I met Grace, I wanted what she had! The peace and the strength. . .the capacity to love and love. . ."

"It's Jesus, Burke. Grace has Jesus," Clay said with warmth. "And that's what you want. I believe you don't just want to live.

I think you really want to live the kind of life that you've seen in Grace Swenson."

Burke sat silently, then said, "I—I guess you're right. And I think I see what you mean, about asking God to forgive me."

"Then you must ask Him!"

Burke's eyes and voice filled with anguish. "I don't know how."

"Just talk to Him, as you're talking to me. You don't have to be afraid to ask God for forgiveness," Clay said gently. "He wants to give it to you even more than you want to receive it. He's been after all of us all our lives. And if you ask God what He wants in return, why, He'd say, 'I don't want anything you have, My son; I just want *you!*'"

Tears came to Burke's eyes as Clay spoke. He made no attempt to wipe them away as they ran down his cheeks. He leaned forward and whispered, "I can't imagine why *anyone* would want me, much less, God!"

Clay knew his brother was being convicted by the Holy Spirit. He spoke gently about God's mercy and finally said, "There's no secret formula to asking God to save you, Burke. People ask in different ways—the way doesn't matter to God. It's what's in the heart of the one who asks. Your heart is hungry for God, isn't it?"

"Yes!"

"Then we will pray. As I pray for you, you tell God you're tired of your old life. Tell Him how bad you feel about what you've done. Tell Him anything that's in your heart. He'll listen.

And when you've told Him that, just ask Him to pardon you, to forgive all your sins. Claim the protection and redemption of the blood of Jesus, Burke! Claim the blood! God always hears when we claim the blood of His Son!"

Clay dropped his head and began praying. He prayed fervently, his own tears falling down his face, and finally he heard a sound. Opening his eyes, he saw that Burke had fallen to his knees and was pressing his face against the floor, his shoulders shaking with sobs.

At once Clay knelt beside his brother, and the small room was filled with angels—or so it seemed to both men. After a time, Burke lifted his head, and Clay saw that his brother's eyes were free of the fear and anguish that had filled them. Instead they were filled with peace.

"You're really part of the family now, Burke!" Clay cried, throwing his arms around his brother, and he held him as the two rejoiced.

Finally they sat down, and Burke let his hands fall on the table. "You'll tell Mother?" He laughed, feeling like a child, so full of happiness. "Of course you will!" Then he smiled at Clay, wonder in his eyes. "It's so *different*, Clay!"

"Are you afraid, Burke?"

Burke Rocklin thought hard; then a smile came to his lips. "I've been burdened down so long...and now it's all fallen away! I guess I might have a little fear about the thing itself—the hanging—but the awful fear is gone! It's gone, and I feel like I'm free for the first time in my life."

"That's what Jesus does for us all, Burke; He sets us free!"

They sat there talking softly for a long time, and then Burke asked abruptly, "You're in love with Melora, aren't you, Clay?"

"Yes, I am."

Burke leaned forward, his eyes intent. "And you were faithful to Ellen all those hard years?"

"By the grace of God, I was, Burke."

Burke struggled with his thoughts, his brow knitted in a frown. Finally he asked, "Why don't you marry her, Clay?"

Clay had not been expecting such a question. "Why, Ellen's been dead less than a year! People would never understand. Besides, I may not live through this war. Melora would be left alone."

"Who cares what people say?" Burke demanded. "It's your life, and Melora's! You know Mother and Father love her dearly!"

"But if I die—!"

"If you die before you marry her, she has nothing. But if you marry now, she'll have *something*! And she deserves it, doesn't she? She's waited for you for a lot of years, years when she could have married a dozen times. It's not fair to her!"

"Burke, I can't—"

"Listen, brother." Burke spoke earnestly. "It makes a man see some things pretty clearly, being in a spot like I'm in. And what I see is that every one of us ought to give love a chance. My only regret now is that I'll never be able to show Grace how much I love her! But if I could get out of here, I'd marry her in a second, even if I knew it was going to last only a month!"

Clay sat like a man who had been struck in the stomach. Burke's words seemed to beat against him, and he could not move or think clearly.

Burke watched as Clay struggled with himself, and finally there came the moment when his brother seemed to collapse. His face broke and his hands trembled so much that he held them together tightly.

"Maybe it's so, Burke," he whispered. "Maybe it's so!" He gave Burke a look of wonder. "I've been so blind—so very blind!"

CHAPTER 23

WITNESS FOR THE DEFENSE

Wha—!" Colonel Ransom Hill struck at the hand that was pulling at him. He'd slept poorly and thought he was having a nightmare.

"Sir, a message from the secretary of war!"

The words drove sleep away from Hill. He sat upright and peered at the lieutenant who had come into his tent. "What's that? The secretary of war?"

"Yes, sir! I thought you'd want to see it at once."

"Light that lamp!" Colonel Hill threw the covers back and fumbled on the table for his reading glasses. Settling them on his nose, he took the envelope the lieutenant handed him and slit it with a knife he kept for that purpose. Drawing out a single sheet of paper, he read it carefully. His eyes widened, and he turned to the soldier standing nearby.

"Lieutenant, go find the other members who served on the court-martial for Burke Rocklin. Tell them the court will

776

reconvene at eight o'clock."

"Yes, sir. You mean—*this* morning, sir?"

"Yes, blast your eyes! Get moving!"

When the lieutenant scurried out the door, Hill read the message again carefully, aloud: " 'You are hereby ordered to reconvene the court and reconsider your verdict concerning Burke Rocklin. There is new evidence, and President Davis wants you to be certain that it is properly considered.' " It was signed "James A. Seddon, Secretary of War."

Although it was only five o'clock, Hill knew that he would sleep no more. He dressed and sat in his tent waiting for reveille. When it came, he got on his horse and rode slowly to the courthouse. He was two hours early, and there was nothing to do but wait.

Finally the doors opened, and he went at once to the courtroom. He took his seat at the table, and the other members of the court came in, sleepy-eyed and puzzled. He waited until the last of them appeared, then said, "We have been ordered to reopen the case of Burke Rocklin."

"By whose authority, sir?" Major Patterson asked.

Colonel Hill gave him a frosty stare. "President Jefferson Davis."

Patterson's mouth dropped open; then he shut it and swallowed hard. Hill could see the man's mind working. *If Patterson thinks the president wants the man declared innocent, he'll do it like a shot!* He had nothing but contempt for Patterson and was himself determined not to give an inch. Let the secretary of war and the president step inside his courtroom in person—he would not budge!

❧

Burke and Clay were waiting for the sun to come up, but at six they heard steps, running footsteps. The door opened and a lieutenant came in, his eyes open wide. "Burke! It's not what you think—I mean, something's happening!"

"What is it, Fred?" Clay demanded.

"Well, I can't say, Captain," the lieutenant said. "But I got orders to have the prisoner in the courtroom at eight o'clock."

Clay cried out, "Praise God!" He grabbed Burke and nearly lifted him off his feet. "It's got to be good news, Burke!"

"Better get shaved, Burke," the lieutenant said. "I'll be back to get you in half an hour." He grinned nervously. "Wouldn't want to be late for this, would you?"

Burke stared after him, then looked at Clay. "Maybe Father's come back with the papers from the hospital." He began to shave using cold water and then shrugged into his coat. It seemed a matter of minutes until the lieutenant came and led him away. When Burke entered the courtroom, he saw the court assembled. DeQuincy and Willing were standing up, and DeQuincy came to him at once. "Good news, Burke—"

"The court will begin proceedings!" Colonel Hill stared at DeQuincy and said, "Major, I understand there is new evidence to be offered?"

"Yes, if it please the court."

"It does *not* please the court, Major," Hill said coldly. "But it seems we have no choice. Present your evidence."

DeQuincy moved to stand before the officers at the table and saw that for once in his life, he was speaking to a *live* court! All five of the officers were staring at him avidly. "Gentlemen, I regret the inconvenience you've been put to, but the new evidence came at midnight. It took a visit to the president to get the court reconvened, but I think you'll not be hard on us after you hear what we have."

"Bring on the evidence, then, Major," Hill snapped. "It's too early for speeches."

"Of course, Colonel." DeQuincy nodded. "This case rests on one question: Did the defendant actually suffer a loss of memory? Once that is proven, the verdict can be nothing other than for acquittal. And I will admit that the defense was unable to prove this beyond a reasonable doubt before now." DeQuincy was a shrewd man. He knew enough to take the guilt from the shoulders of the court, to allow them to have some room to maneuver.

"Naturally you gentlemen brought in the only possible verdict you could, but let me now present you with some facts." He walked to the table, picked up a sheaf of papers, and brought them back to the court. "If you gentlemen will examine these papers, you'll find clear evidence that the defendant was indeed suffering from a complete loss of memory when he was taken off the battlefield. These are statements from the personnel of Armory Square Hospital—surgeons, nurses, orderlies—all swearing that from the moment the man we know to be Burke Rocklin became conscious, he had no memory at all of his past!"

DeQuincy watched the officers reading the papers with great interest and took the opportunity to turn and wink broadly at Burke.

"How are we to know these are reputable people?" Hill demanded. "We know none of them."

"You'll find a covering letter verifying all these statements. It's signed by one Dr. William Alexander Hammond, who is the surgeon general of the Union Army. He is a personal friend of the surgeon general of the Confederate Army, who will be happy to testify to this court both as to the validity of the signature and as to the character of Dr. Hammond."

"I see," Hill said, nodding slightly. He read on, then exclaimed, "This letter is from Miss Dorothea Dix!"

"Yes, sir. All the world knows that Miss Dix is a woman of unquestionable character. She is willing to come to this court and swear that this man, known to her as John Smith, was in her hospital because he had absolutely no memory of his past."

"Why, this puts quite a different light on things!" Major Lentz spoke up. He stared at the documents, then asked, "How were these obtained, may I ask?"

"They were brought by one of the staff who arrived in Richmond last night. Would the court care to hear a personal testimony by this staff member of Armory Square Hospital?"

Colonel Hill knew he was whipped. "Why, yes, of course!"

"Thank you, Colonel Hill." DeQuincy walked to the door, opened it, and said, "Will you come in, please?"

Every eye was on the door as a young woman in a gray dress stepped in. DeQuincy spoke to the officers, hard put to keep the triumph out of his tone. "This is Miss Grace Swenson, the nurse who treated Burke Rocklin when he was taken to the hospital in Washington. And, I believe, the person responsible for bringing him back to health."

Burke was on his feet, staring at Grace—and when she turned to meet his eyes, every man on the court saw his lips form her name. DeQuincy let the moment run on, for he was a man who loved drama, and a quick glance at the court told him that at least part of the officers of the court were the same!

Colonel Hill cleared his throat, saying in a gruff tone, "Mr. DeQuincy, please escort your witness to the stand. And, Mr. Rocklin," he added in a reproving tone, "you will take your seat, sir!"

Burke didn't mind the order, for he wasn't sure his legs would hold him up much longer anyway. He sat with a thud, amazement and longing warring in his expression.

Grace followed DeQuincy to the stand, then turned and took the oath. When she was seated, DeQuincy said, "Miss Swenson, what are your credentials as a nurse? Tell us about yourself."

"I was trained by Miss Dorothea Dix as a nurse, Major DeQuincy. Here are her recommendations. Would thee care to read them?"

At the use of *thee*, the officers on the court sharpened their attention. As Grace continued to speak, they grew fascinated by her demeanor and mannerisms. Finally she paused, and Captain Wells asked, "You are of the Friends, I take it?"

"Yes, Captain."

"Would you tell us how the man you called John Smith behaved when he first came to you?"

"Of course. He knew nothing, not even his name—"

The officers listened as Grace spoke, and DeQuincy knew they were captivated. And why not? He was fascinated himself!

That woman is something! What a witness! he thought with admiration.

Finally Grace finished, and DeQuincy gave the prosecuting attorney a slight bow. "Do you have questions, Captain Willing?"

Willing was stubborn, determined, and a poor loser. But what he was *not* was stupid. He saw at once that his goose was cooked and decided to make the best of it.

"Why, no, Major DeQuincy," he said blandly. "If this evidence had been in the hands of the court earlier, I feel certain that there would have been no trial." He turned boldly to Colonel Hill and took his political and military future in his hands. "Colonel, the prosecution recommends that the case be dropped."

"Second the motion! Second the motion!" young Lieutenant Powell Carleton yelped, jumping to his feet, and from Captain Wells came a rousing "Hear! Hear!"

Colonel Hill was not a fool, either. He glanced at Burke,

then smiled and said, "Do you gentlemen concur with me that the recommendation of the prosecuting attorney be followed and the case against Burke Rocklin be dropped?" He took only one look at the expressions of consent, then turned to face Burke.

"Mr. Rocklin, you are hereby released from this court. The case against you will be dropped from the records."

Burke heard the words Colonel Hill spoke but could make no response. His eyes were fixed on Grace, and everything in him screamed at him to go to her—but he could not seem to move.

It was Gaines Franklin DeQuincy, the incurable romantic, who nudged him roughly in the side and whispered, "Go to her, you young idiot!"

And then he was moving, bolting from his chair, not even noticing pieces of furniture that he pushed aside. . .and she was in his arms. The court pretended to be busy with their papers, but when Burke lowered his head to tenderly kiss the tall young woman, a cheer went up from the irrepressible Lieutenant Powell Carleton.

DeQuincy stood there, a silly grin on his face, watching as the couple recovered their senses enough to walk through the door—though neither one released his or her hold on the other. Willing came over to his opponent and said, "Let's go get drunk again, Gaines! And after the war, I may want you to come to work for my law firm!"

DeQuincy slanted a look at him. "Willing, I *may* permit you to come to work for *my* firm after the war, but if I condescend to do so, you will have to watch your drinking habits!"

Thomas Rocklin died four days after his son was set free. The trip to Pennsylvania and back had been too much for him, but he was totally content. Burke seldom left his father's side, and during the times his father was completely conscious, they talked together, sharing their hearts. It was those times that Burke was to remember all his life. And he knew he would never forget the tears of joy his father shed when he told him of his finding the Lord.

On the final day, Burke awoke from a nap in his chair to find his father's mind clear. He moved his chair until he was next to the bed and gravely met Thomas's gaze. "Father, you saved my life. How can I ever thank you?"

Thomas was very tired, but the words seemed to bring new life into his eyes. He looked over at his son and whispered, "You will have a son. Name him Thomas. Pour yourself into him!"

It was almost dawn when the family was called to Thomas's bedside. Susanna was holding her husband's hand as Thomas said his farewell to his daughter, Amy, then to her children, Grant, Rachel, and Les. He did the same for Clay's children; then he whispered, "Clay—?"

"Here!" Clay stooped beside the frail form and took his father's hand. "You've been a good father, sir!" he whispered.

"These last years—you've held me up when I couldn't find myself!"

Thomas smiled. "I–I'm glad, son. You've been—a proper son. Look after your mother—" Then he said, "Burke?" When his youngest boy came to him, the dying man asked, "Where is Grace?"

"Here, Father." Grace dropped to her knees and took the thin hand in hers.

"We did well. . .didn't we, daughter?"

"Thee did it all, Father!"

"Well, well. . ." Thomas closed his eyes, then opened them with an effort. "Marry him—have his children—!"

Grace's eyes filled with tears as her heart overflowed with love. "Yes! I will marry him!"

Pleased, Thomas gazed upon them all; then his body arched. "Susanna—!" he cried out.

"I'm here, Tom."

Thomas looked into her face, smiled beautifully. "You have been my darling—wife!"

Then he took a deep breath, his eyes closed slowly, and his head fell to one side. Susanna brushed his hair back, and for the first time tears came to her eyes.

"Good night, Tom," she whispered, bending over to kiss him. "We'll meet in the morning."

Three days after the funeral of Thomas Rocklin, Clay rode up

785

to the Yancy cabin. He was met, as usual, by the tribe of young Yancys, but when Melora came outside, he said, "Melora, put your coat on. I want to look at the hogs."

Melora looked at him uncertainly. "Why, all right, Clay." She slipped into her coat, and the two of them made their way to the hog pen. Once there, Clay turned quickly, saying, "Seems like this hog pen is the only private place around here."

"What is it?" Melora asked, trying to read his expression but failing. "Is something wrong?"

"No." Clay was watching her in a peculiar way, and Melora demanded, "You didn't come here to look at hogs, Clay Rocklin! Now what is it?"

Clay said slowly, "That night before we thought Burke was to be hanged, I was with him in his cell—we both thought it was the last night he had." His eyes grew thoughtful, and he spoke of how Burke had gotten saved.

"That's beautiful!" Melora smiled. "You must be very happy."

"Yes, we all are."

When he said no more, Melora asked gently, "Will you tell me what is troubling you, Clay?"

He took her hand, smiling. "I couldn't keep anything from you if I tried, could I? You know me better than I know myself. Well, Burke asked about us, about you and me and our feelings for each other. When I told him I loved you, he—" Clay broke off, and Melora was surprised to see a tinge of red flow into his face. "Well, he told me to do something about it. He said that everyone ought to give love a chance."

Melora stood very still. Her heart seemed to be beating very rapidly, and she had the feeling that if she looked down she could see it beating against her chest.

Clay watched as her eyes searched his. "I'm too old for you, Melora. I've got a family, and when I'm old, you'll still be young and beautiful. I may die in battle, or come home blind or maimed—" He halted uncertainly.

"What are you saying, Clay?"

He took a deep breath, then spoke the words he had despaired of ever being able to speak—the words that filled him with a great joy and wonder: "I'm asking you to marry me, Melora."

Melora stared at him with amazement. She had expected anything but this. Oh, she had been sure it would come someday, but not now, not so soon. "But—what about your family. . .and the community?"

Clay took both her hands in his and drew her close, his eyes never leaving her. "I don't care about anyone but you. My family loves you—and who cares what Sister Smellfungus says?" He slipped his arms about her, and she rested her hands on his firm, strong chest. "So I ask you again, will you have me as your husband, Melora?"

Light seemed to explode within Melora as she answered, "Yes, Clay. I'll have you. . .and you'll have me!"

Their lips met, and they clung to each other desperately.

Nothing else mattered, nothing else existed in that moment in time—for they finally had their dreams in their arms.

It was sometime later when Clay lifted his head to whisper, "Oh, Melora! I've got the world in my arms!"

CHAPTER 24

THE OREGON TRAIL

Spring came to Independence, Missouri, early that year. The warm breezes melted the snows, and the first golden buds appeared like tiny hearts.

The wagon train that pulled out of Independence, the first one of the year, was not large—only seventeen wagons—but there was a happy spirit about it that seemed to affect everyone. The train followed the Kansas River for two days, then turned north on the Little Blue. A few days later, the scout lifted his rifle and shouted, "There she is, the Platte—a mile wide and an inch deep!"

A cheer went up from those in the wagons, and they lurched forward, anxious to make Fort Kearney off in the distance.

On the seat of the third wagon, Burke Rocklin sat loosely, his eyes searching the horizon.

"Can thee see Oregon, husband?"

Burke turned to Grace, reached out a long arm, and drew

her to him. Ignoring her protests, he kissed her thoroughly. When she pulled away, looking around to see who might be watching, he laughed at her.

"You're a married woman, Grace. You can kiss all you please—as long as you're kissing me."

"Has thee no shame?" Grace scolded. She pouted—which only made him want to kiss her again—and for all her protestations, she had a gleam in her eyes that she could not hide.

"Nope, not a bit," Burke said, shaking his head. "What should I be ashamed of? You've got the most beautiful lips for kissing I've ever seen," he declared. Then he grinned and reached for her again. "As a matter of fact—"

"Burke, thee must stop!"

Grace pushed him away, but then he winked at her, saying, "You won't get rid of me that easy when we make camp!"

"Burke!"

He laughed out loud, saying, "I love to see you blush. Makes you even more delectable."

"Thee talks like a fool!"

"Why, no, I talk like a man in love."

Grace closed her mouth and moved closer to her husband. They had been married two months, and she was enjoying every minute of learning to be a wife. Now she said, "Burke, I feel so—so shameless!" Dropping her eyes, she whispered, "Do I make you happy, husband?"

Burke had discovered at once that his new bride had a fear that she would not be a good wife. He had learned that she needed to be told over and over that she was beautiful and desirable and that he adored her. And it was not difficult, for it was all true.

"Thee is the most beautiful and loving wife a man ever had," he said, smiling at her, then drew her close. "Every day I thank God for giving you to me."

"Truly?"

"Truly!"

She sighed and leaned against him with contentment. Finally she asked, "Do you feel lonely?"

"Lonely? Why, no! Not with you here, Grace!"

"I mean, thee is leaving thy home, husband, and all thy people. Will you not miss it?"

He smiled at the way she called him "husband"—it was something she had done often since their marriage, almost as if to reassure herself that he was hers. He touched her face tenderly. "I'll miss my people, Grace," he answered thoughtfully. "But I don't believe in the war. I think the South is going down, and no able-bodied man can live in Virginia and not believe in the Cause." He turned to face her. "Are you afraid, Grace? Of leaving your home? Oregon is a pretty rough place."

Grace took his hand and held it. "No. I'll never be afraid. But what will we do in Oregon?"

"Don't know," Burke admitted cheerfully. "I always wanted to see it, though. We'll just have to wait until we get there and see what happens."

They rolled along, contented and happy. That evening, they

joined in the circle of wagons, cooked supper, and listened to the songs that went up from around the fires.

When it grew late, he looked up at the sky and pointed. "Look, there's Orion."

She looked up at the spangled night until she found the star he indicated. She leaned back against his chest, and he held her close. "You smell good, like a woman should," he whispered.

The compliment brought tears to her eyes—what a miracle God had worked in giving her this man to be her love and her companion! "Come, it's time for bed," she said and pulled him to his feet. "We've got to get a good night's rest. It's a long way to Oregon."

"You go on," Burke said. "I'll take care of the chores." She got inside, and he fed the stock, saw that they were well tied, then put out the fire. When he climbed inside the wagon, she drew him down at once.

"Husband," she whispered. "Does thee truly love me?"

"Yes! Truly!"

He kissed her, and she held him tightly.

Overhead Orion and his fellows did their great dance as the moon turned the canvas on the wagon to silver. A coyote yelped soulfully somewhere in the distance. The small stream bubbled over rounded stones, making a friendly sound. And finally—

"And will thee love me forever?"

"Yes, wife—forever!"

THE SHADOW
OF HIS WINGS

To James and Murlene Golden—
our Golden Missionaries.
You have given Johnnie and me so much
over the past years!
All of us need to see the gospel
walking around, and to us,
you two have demonstrated Jesus Christ
and the power of His gospel
to transform lives.

PART ONE

Rooney

❦

CHAPTER 1

FLIGHT FROM VICKSBURG

$\mathcal{F}$or most people, terrible dreams come in the dead stillness of the night. They lie awake longing for the morning when they can escape into the world of reality.

For Rooney Smith, however, night was a welcome refuge where she escaped from the nightmarish days. She spent her waking hours fighting off men who moved through the slums of Vicksburg, for at the age of seventeen, she was a very attractive young woman. All day long she cleaned hotel rooms on Beacon Avenue, the worst street in the worst section of a river town noted for violence and vice. By the time she reached home, she was sick of the vile remarks and the grasping hands of men.

But no matter how bad the days, when she closed the door to the two-room shack she shared with her mother, Clara, and her brother, Buck, the nightmare ended and she could rest. Her mother worked in a bar called the Gay Lady and usually came home at dawn—when she didn't stay out for several days. So

795

each night Rooney closed and barred the door, making a safe haven for her and Buck. The two of them read together, played games by the hour, and—most important—were safe in the dilapidated shanty.

Late one Thursday, Rooney arrived home and shut and barred the door. Weariness flowed through her so that she leaned back against it, closed her eyes, and let the fatigue drain out of her. As usual, it was not the physical labor that debilitated her, but the feeling of uncleanness.

Opening her eyes, she shook her shoulders, then made a fire and heated water. Buck would not be home for half an hour, so she took a bath in a number ten galvanized washtub, sluicing herself with the warm water, and when she stepped out, dried off, and slipped into a clean dress, she felt most of the bitter, distasteful memories of the day slipping away.

Dark was falling fast, and she looked out the small window for Buck. He worked for a butcher, and she'd warned him to be home before dark. She began to put a simple meal together, and when the knock came at the door, she went at once, a smile on her face. Lifting the bar, she opened the door with a smile, saying, "It's about time you—"

But it was not Buck, and a chill ran through the girl as she saw the big man with pale blue eyes. Quickly she tried to shut the door, but he put out a big hand and seized it. "Now this is something I like!" he sneered. "Come to see Clara—but reckon you'll do better." He stood there holding the door as Rooney tried to force it shut, and with no effort he pushed it back.

Rooney backed away, saying as calmly as she could, "My mother's not here. You'll have to go now." When she saw that he made no move to leave but grinned more broadly, she lifted her chin. "You get out of here!" she said.

"Now don't be like that, sweetheart." He was a tall, heavily built man with yellow hair and a wide mouth. "I'm Dement Sloan. Know your ma *real* well." The catfish mouth drew upward into a leer, and his pale blue eyes shone with a glitter Rooney had seen in many men. "Now you and me, we can have ourselves a good time!"

Sloan let his eyes run up and down the girl's trim figure, took in the oval face, the short-cropped, curly auburn hair, and the large dark blue eyes now wide with fright. The fear in the girl pleased him, for he'd rather see women's fear than try to earn their admiration or love. Stepping inside, he kicked the door shut with his foot and stood there staring at her. "I brought us a bottle," he said, taking a brown bottle from his inner pocket. "We're gonna have us a real good little party, little girl!"

Rooney backed away, her eyes darting around, but there was no way of escape except through the door that Sloan blocked. "You—you better leave or I'll scream!"

Sloan set the bottle down on a battered table and advanced toward her. He was drunk and had come to find Clara Smith, having enjoyed her favors in the rooms over the Gay Lady. He was a handsome brute and a womanizer, though his taste ran to the coarser types found on Beacon Street. The sight of the young girl brought a surge of lust, and he grinned as he moved toward her.

Rooney twisted, moving behind a chair to escape the man, but he seized it and threw it aside. "You need a man, sweetheart, and I'm the man you need!"

Fear shot through Rooney, and she made one desperate attempt to fling by Sloan, but he caught her by the arm. "Come on, honey, don't be so shy!"

Suddenly the man released her arm and crumpled to the floor. Rooney was startled to see Buck suddenly standing in the room.

"It's me, sis," Buck said. Rooney blinked, and her eyes focused on the face of her brother. "You okay?"

"Buck! What—" Rooney stopped speaking as she looked at the form of Sloan on the floor. He was lying on his back, and his eyes were wide open. A wound gaped like an open mouth on his scalp, just over his left ear, and blood dripped steadily onto the wooden floor. Wildly Rooney looked up to stare at the small form of her brother.

He met her gaze, then suddenly tossed down the heavy iron poker he'd been holding. It clattered on the floor, startling Rooney, and he said in a frightened voice, "I—I think I killed him, sis!"

Rooney stared at Buck, then dropped to her knees beside the still form. Fearfully, she put her hand on the broad chest, then looked up to whisper, "No—he's alive!"

The explosion of violence had robbed Buck of all but fear. "I come in and he was hurtin' you, Rooney." He was an undersized lad with brown hair and large brown eyes, his cheeks now pale as paper. "I had to stop him!"

Seeing the boy's panic, Rooney got to her feet and drew him close. "I know, Buck! I know you did!"

He began to tremble, his thin form shaking in her embrace. "Will—will they hang me for it?" he whispered. Pulling his head back, he stared at her, his eyes wide with fear. "Will they, sis?"

"No! No, they won't!"

"If he dies, they will!"

Rooney said quickly, "He's not going to die." But looking down, she saw that the man was well dressed, obviously not a drunk or a bum. He'd come to Beacon Street, as many men did, for drink and women.

The police will believe him—not Buck and me! The thought flashed through Rooney, and instantly she knew they had to move him. "We've got to get him out of here, Buck."

Buck was almost paralyzed with fear, but he was a quick-witted boy. He had to be to survive among the dregs of Vicksburg! "Yeah, that's right," he said with a nod. He glanced down and shook his head. "He's so *big*, Rooney."

"I know, but we've got to do it!"

Turning quickly, she moved to the door, opened it, and stared outside. "It's pretty dark outside. We have to get him into the alley."

"When he comes to, he'll tell on us, sis."

"Maybe not—maybe he won't remember. He's drunk, and he's been hurt."

Hope touched Buck's eyes, and he nodded. A thought came

to him, and he exclaimed, "I know. We can use Tip's cart!"

At once Rooney nodded, relief in her face. "Go get it, Buck!"

The boy left the shack in a flash, and Rooney stood there staring down at the still, pale face of Sloan. Her knees were weak, and she was nauseated with fear, but she forced herself to remain calm. Soon she heard the sound of iron wheels rolling and opened the door.

"I got it. Lucky Tip left it here." He was pulling a low four-wheeled wagonlike affair used by a neighboring bricklayer to haul his bricks. It was only a little over a foot off the ground and had sides no more than four inches high.

"Come on, let's get him on it," Rooney whispered. The two of them advanced on the unconscious man, and she said, "Grab this arm, and I'll take the other one." She hated to touch him, but fear of what might come to them from the law was greater than her revulsion. They took a strong grip on the man's arms and tugged with all their strength. He weighed at least two hundred pounds, and by the time they had gotten the still form to the door, both of them were gasping.

"We'll never get him into the cart, Buck!"

"Lemme put the wagon up to the door so we don't have to drag him any farther than we have to."

It was the only way they could have managed it, and as they tried to lift his massive body into the cart, his head struck the edge of the wagon with an ugly sound that made Rooney cry out, "Be careful!"

But Buck ignored her. "Come on, sis!" he gasped. "We've got to get him outta here!"

As soon as Sloan's body was loaded, Rooney grabbed the tongue of the wagon, and the two of them dragged it down over the cobblestones. The loud rattle it made sounded like thunder to both of them, and Rooney expected someone to appear at any second. However, they reached the small opening that led between two of the shacks in the dilapidated row without a sign of anyone on the street. Quickly they wheeled the vehicle into the alley. "We'll have to roll him off," Buck whispered. "Got to take Tip's wagon back."

"All right." Rooney cradled the lolling head of the helpless man as they pulled him off, then carefully placed it down. She felt a wetness on her palm and knew it was fresh blood.

"Come on, sis—we got to get outta here!"

Rooney swallowed hard, then rose and followed Buck. As they stepped out of the alley, a voice cried out, "Hey! What you doin' there?"

Glancing down the street, Rooney saw the form of a man emerging from the darkness. Panic ran through her, and she wheeled, crying, "Run, Buck!" But Buck was already fleeing, and she ran with all the speed she could muster.

"Stop! Stop right there!"

The voice broke the stillness, and doors began to open, but the man was heavy, and the youthful pair ran like rabbits, dodging through alleys that Buck knew as well he knew his own hand. They crossed two streets, then burst onto a street occupied by warehouses and other large buildings.

"I. . .can't run any farther, Buck!"

"Me neither!"

They stopped and looked around the dark street. The windows of the warehouses caught the gleam of a few flickering streetlights. To Rooney they appeared to be opaque eyes staring at them. "Can you hear anything, Buck?" she gasped.

Buck listened hard, then shook his head. "No. I—I guess we got away."

The two stood there holding their breath, listening hard. The silence of the street washed over them. Faintly they heard the sound of a wagon rattling over cobblestone, but it was blocks away. Fear and the hard run had drained them both, and now they felt a tremendous sense of fatigue.

"What'll we do, sis?"

Rooney stared at Buck's pale face, noting that his lips were unsteady. She was stiff with fear herself but managed to say calmly, "We've got to get away from here."

His eyes grew wide with shock. "You mean. . .leave Vicksburg?"

"We can't stay here. That man will have the law on us."

"But where'll we go?"

Rooney had no idea of how to run away. She had no money on her, and they had only the clothes they stood in. But she had to do *something*! "Let's go see if anybody's at the house," she said finally.

"What for?"

"I have a little money, and we can get our clothes." She saw him hesitate, then said, "We'll look real careful, and if anybody's there, we won't go. But if the coast is clear, we can run in, grab our stuff and the money. Then we'll see."

It was not a good plan, and she dreaded going back to the house, but they had to have *something*. "After we go there, we'll have to go and tell Ma what happened."

"All right, sis."

Her brother's agreement came quickly, and she knew he was afraid. Putting her arm around him, she squeezed him. "It'll be all right, Buck. We'll get away."

Rooney was a resourceful girl, but this assurance was for her brother. She felt hollow inside and dreaded to go back to the house. She also was terrified of what her mother would do, but she could think of nothing else. "Come on, Buck," she urged. "We'll make it!"

❦

Alf Swanson, the bouncer at the Gay Lady, stepped out into the alley to catch a fresh breath of air. The smoke-laden interior of the saloon aggravated a hacking cough that had troubled him for days, and he coughed, hawked, and spat on the ground, glad for the relief. It was well after midnight, and he couldn't leave until the place closed down.

"Mr. Swanson!"

The burly bouncer started, for the voice caught him unprepared, seeming to rise out of the ground. He'd thought the alley deserted, and he growled suspiciously, "Who is it? Who's out there?"

"It's me—Rooney."

Swanson had thrown himself into a defensive position at the sound of the voice, but as the form of a young girl appeared out of the shadows to his left, he relaxed, dropping his fists.

"It's you, is it?" he said, surprise in his gravelly voice. "What in the world are ye doing here this time of night?"

"Buck and me are in trouble, Mr. Swanson."

Swanson stared at the girl, then looked over her shoulder and saw the boy. He was a hard man but had admired the way Rooney had fought to keep herself above the level of her mother. "Trouble? What kind of trouble?"

Rooney hesitated, but she had learned to like the big man. He had always been roughly kind to her and Buck. He had never tried to touch her and had given her some protection from time to time. Swanson was not a man who liked the law, Rooney knew, and she had no other way to turn. "A man named Dement Sloan came to our house a little while ago. . . ."

Swanson stood there listening, saying nothing, but when the girl finished, he shook his head. "Too bad you got caught," was his only remark.

"We have to get away from Vicksburg," Rooney said quickly. "Can you get our mother to come out here so we can talk to her?"

"I'll do that. Wait here—and keep out of sight."

Swanson stepped inside the saloon and walked directly to

Clara Smith. She was sitting at a table with a man who looked bored. "Clara, got to talk to you," Swanson said.

"Can't you see I'm busy?" A harsh note was in the woman's voice, but it was no harsher than her appearance. She had been an attractive woman once but had grown gross and hard. Her hair was dyed a brassy yellow, and any natural color her cheeks might have had was buried under a layer of paint. Her lips were a wide gash of scarlet, and her eyes were sunk back into her head, giving her an unhealthy appearance. She wore a low-cut green dress, but she had lost weight and looked thin and bony.

The man drained his drink and got to his feet, saying, "I got to leave anyway. See you next time, Clara."

As the man walked away, Clara cursed Swanson, but he snapped, "Shut up and come with me."

"Come where?"

But Swanson took her arm and piloted her out of the bar. When they were in the hall that led to the alley, he stopped and related what Rooney had told him. "And they got to get out of town, Clara—you, too."

"Me? I ain't done nothing!"

"The man was put down in your place. His name is Dement Sloan, a swell from uptown. He'll have friends, the big people up there," Swanson snapped. "You on such good terms with the law you can convince them you had nothing to do with it?"

Anger grew in Clara Smith until she trembled—and she began to curse and rave, her hands outstretched like the talons of a monstrous bird, her nails red as blood. "I'll *kill* those crazy kids!" she cried, her eyes bright with rage.

"Shut your mouth!" Swanson took the woman's arm, and his iron grip closed on it like a trap. "The fellow was attacking your daughter! Don't that mean nothing to you?" But he didn't wait for her answer. "Listen, you're drunk, but not so drunk you can't understand. The judge told you the last time you was up if you came before him again, it'd be the pen for you. You want to go there, Clara?"

Fear touched the woman's sunken eyes, and she shook her head and shivered. "No! I'd—I'd die in that place!"

"All right, then you got to get away."

"And go where?" Despair came into her thin face, and she began to cry. The tears ran down her cheeks, leaving tracks in the caked makeup. "I ain't got no money!"

Swanson released his grip. Reaching into his pocket, he pulled out a roll of bills. Peeling off several of them, he thrust them into her hand. "That'll be enough to tide you over until you can get another place."

"But *where*, Alf?" She saw the look that crossed his face and asked, "What is it? You think of something?"

"Maybe I have." Swanson was not a quick thinker. He took an idea and chewed on it before speaking it. Clara had learned this and waited nervously until finally the big man said slowly, "Richmond. . .that's where you better go."

"Richmond? Why'd I want to go there?"

"Because it's the capital of this here Southern Confederacy, that's why." When Swanson saw the blank look on her face, he snapped with irritation, "There's a war, ain't you noticed? Richmond's got thousands and thousands of men in the army there to protect her—a ton more than around here. And men is your business, ain't they, Clara?"

Swiftly the thin face of Clara Smith changed, for she understood this kind of reason. "Lots of soldiers there in Richmond?"

"Be purt' near a million, I guess." The tough, battered lips of Swanson twisted in a humorless grin. "Get every one of them boys to give you a dollar, and you'll have a million dollars, Clara."

"Well, I dunno—"

Impatiently Swanson swore. "Clara, you ain't young, and you're sick. Time was mebbe when you could call your shots. But now. . ." He shrugged and said evenly, "You need to be where the men ain't so particular."

For one moment anger brightened the woman's eyes—and then they dulled. "You're right, Alf, but Richmond's a long way."

"I got a friend works in the boiler room on the *Natchez Belle*," he said. "She'll be pulling out at dawn. I'll get him to stow you somewhere—no fare. She'll dock near Memphis, and you can get a train from there to Richmond—as long as the trains are still running."

"But I ain't got no clothes—nothing!"

"All right, I'll go to your place. If it's clear, I'll get your stuff." Alf stared at her. "Now, you know—?" He broke off suddenly, thinking hard, then said, "Listen, Clara, I got a friend in Richmond—at least, he was there last I heard. Got a place, sort of a hotel and bar. About like this one, I reckon. His name's

Studs Mulvaney. Won't be hard to find him and his joint. Look him up and tell him I said to give you and the kids a break."

"All right, Alf—and thanks."

"I'm doing it for the kids, Clara." Turning, he led her to the alley, then called out, "Hey, Rooney!"

When the girl and boy appeared, he said, "You and your ma's leaving for Richmond. Let me get my coat and gun; then we'll coast down and see if we can get your stuff, Clara."

Swanson left them alone, and Buck said, "Ma, I'm sorry, but I had to hit him."

Clara stared at the thin face of the boy. For one instant she almost flared out at him, but she was too tired. She shook her head, saying only, "One place is as good as another, I guess."

Several hours later, the ghostly form of the *Natchez Belle* slipped away from the docks. The smooth brown water of the Mississippi dropped in a shining waterfall from her paddles, catching the first rays of the rising sun. The engines throbbed, the drivers sending the huge paddle wheel into its rhythmic pattern, churning the water to a white froth.

Deep inside in a storeroom filled with flour, potatoes, and cans of food, Clara sat on a stool, her head down. Rooney saw that she was sick and came to stand beside her. Timidly she put her hand on her mother's shoulder. "It'll be all right, Ma."

Clara looked up, despair in her eyes. "No, it won't." She shook off her daughter's hand and turned her back to stare at the bulkhead.

Buck was staring out a porthole, entranced. "Look, Rooney!"

he whispered. When she joined him, she saw the shoreline slipping by very rapidly. "We must be going real fast," he said, his eyes large. "Wish we could stay on this ol' boat for a long time!"

Rooney, filled with dread at the specterlike thought of the future, nodded and put her arm around him.

"So do I, Buck!" she whispered sadly. "So do I!"

Chapter 2

Lowell Meets a Pair of Generals

*C*lay Rocklin stood idly under one of the towering oaks that lined the driveway leading up to Gracefield. He could hear the sound of laughter from the big white house and had been thinking of how unlikely it was that the Rocklin family would ever gather in exactly the same way. *The war is wearing us all down,* he thought sadly. *There'll be empty places here by the time it's over.* He was happy for the lull that permitted the Rocklins to gather at Gracefield for a brief time before the spring campaigns drew the Army of Northern Virginia away.

He half turned to go inside and join the others when a rider suddenly appeared on the road leading from Richmond. At first he thought it might be a courier with a message from regimental headquarters recalling them to duty, and then he saw that it was a civilian. He waited until the rider turned into the circular driveway, then exclaimed in surprise as he recognized his uncle Mark Rocklin. Moving forward as his uncle drew up, he called out to him, "Mark!"

Mark Rocklin pulled the bay stallion to a halt, glanced around, and came out of the saddle. "Clay, how are you?" He wore an expensive black suit that suited his tall figure, and despite his fifty-two years, he was still lean and strong. Clay could not speak the thought that leaped into his mind as the two shook hands: *The best-looking of the family—and he's wasted his life!* Mark had been the wild one of Noah Rocklin's sons, leaving home at an early age and never returning except for brief visits. Clay knew he'd been a riverboat gambler—and worse—but had always felt a strong affection for Mark.

"You came just in time, Uncle Mark," Clay said. "We managed to sneak a family reunion before the army gets goin' full steam again."

Mark studied the uniform Clay wore and remarked, "You're a captain now. I didn't know that. Are your boys all in the army?"

"Dent and Lowell are in my company. David's taking care of the home front." Something about Mark's appearance disturbed Clay. Lines were etched around his lips, and a somberness in his dark eyes revealed some sort of tragedy. But Clay knew that he could not ask what had aged his uncle. *He'll tell me if he wants me to know, and wild horses couldn't drag it out unless he's ready.* "Come on in. Everybody will be glad to see you."

"The prodigal returns home?" Mark smiled slightly. He turned to Clay, saying, "I couldn't get here for your father's funeral...."

Clay recognized that this was Mark Rocklin's apology for

many things and said, "I understand, Mark. We can't always do what we'd like, can we?" Then, wanting to break the moment, he said, "Come on! Let's join the crowd."

When the two entered, Clay called out loudly, "Set another plate! We've got another Rocklin to feed!"

Clay's mother, Susanna, was the first to get to Mark. She greeted him with a fierce hug, and the rest of the family waited for their turn. Clay watched as Mark smiled as he greeted each of them, thinking, *Something's wrong with Mark. There was always some sort of shadow over him, but it's worse now.*

After the greeting of Mark, the men were gathered in the drawing room while the women were in the kitchen. Food was the answer to many problems for women, and they gave themselves to it. The house was filled with the smells of fresh bread and pastries, and Dent said, "Raimey says there's been enough food cooked to feed a whole company." Glancing at his father, he said soberly, "I wish we could save some of it. We'll need it when we go out to fight the Yankees."

"Oh, Dent, we'll make them run next time—just like we did at Fredericksburg!" Lowell Rocklin spoke up from where he stood beside the fireplace. He was shorter and more muscular than his father and his brothers and perhaps for this reason held himself very straight. He had brown hair and hazel eyes that reflected his indignation. Seeing doubt on David's face, he lifted his voice, "Isn't that right, Father?"

Clay shook his head. "Depends on a lot of things, Lowell. The Army of the Potomac's got one hundred thousand men.

We can't match that."

Lowell gave the classic Southern answer in a confident voice. "Any Confederate can whip five Yankees!"

Dent Rocklin grew sober, and he touched the scar that marred his face. "You don't still believe that, Lowell? At Manassas those Yankees fought like wildcats when they were cornered. Every battle since then, too."

The talk went on for some time, Lowell standing erectly, stating that the Yankees would turn around and run for Washington as soon as the action started. The others were less certain, and it was Mark Rocklin who said, "Hope you're right about it, Lowell." He gave Clay a strange look, saying abruptly, "Can you use another soldier in your company, nephew?"

Clay blinked in surprise, caught off guard. "Why, I think we can find a place for you, Uncle Mark. The Major needs an aide, and you'll look the part."

"Meaning I'm too old to carry a Springfield along with the young fellows? Probably right." Mark nodded. He saw the doubt in their faces and gave a brief explanation. "I guess you've all felt that I didn't care about the South. I've given you cause enough to think that. I've been a pretty worthless fellow—but when a man gets older, he wants to be a part of something more permanent. For me, it's this family. I–I'd like to join it. . .belatedly."

"You've never been out of it, but now you'll be right in the middle of the Rocklin mob!" Clay knew that his uncle would never say much about his past but that this was his appeal to be accepted. "It'll be good to have you, Uncle Mark."

David had said little, but now he spoke up. "And I'd like to join, too, sir." He spoke to Clay, and there was an unhappiness in his eyes. "I can't stay home and grow potatoes while the rest of you fight!"

"David, we've been over this," Clay said slowly. "Somebody *has* to stay here and see that the food gets grown. The army can't fight unless it can eat."

"Anybody can run this place!"

"No, they can't, David." Dent spoke up. "*I* couldn't. You were working and learning how to run Gracefield from the time you were twelve years old. And what was *I* doing?" He lifted his hands in a gesture of helplessness. "I was out raising the devil!"

Mark kept quiet but was troubled over David. *He's always been the quiet one; Dent the colorful twin,* Mark thought. *Now he feels left out. I wish Clay would change his mind. The boy needs a chance.* But he knew that he'd forfeited his right to direct the family by his own irresponsible behavior, so he said nothing.

Finally David fell silent, and it was Lowell who looked now at Dent, his commanding officer, and grinned. "You think the Bluebellies will run, don't you, Dent?"

Dent returned the grin. "I'm no expert. We'd better get Stonewall Jackson in here to settle the question. . . ."

Clay slipped away as the talk turned to the coming battles and went to the kitchen. His mother was stirring a large pot filled with something that smelled good. He put his arm around her, asking quietly, "You all right?"

"Yes. Are you?"

Clay gave her an odd look, for she knew him better than he knew himself. "No, but that'll pass, I suppose. Things like this are always hard." At that moment Melora came through the door accompanied by Rena. She was in the midst of a story, and Clay was glad to see the smile on his daughter's face.

"I started home," Melora said, "but I had an idea, so I turned around and came here. I wanted to talk to Rena."

"What are you two plotting?" he asked. "You look like you're up to some outrage."

"Rena's coming to our house," Melora answered. A smile turned the corners of her full lips upward. "I'm going to teach her how to raise pigs."

"Can I, Daddy?"

Clay looked at Rena, nodding at once. *Be good for her to be with Melora,* he thought. "Why, sure. Every cultured Southern belle should learn the gentle art of raising pigs." He gave her a hug, adding, "Be sure you take a bath before you come back."

"Oh, Daddy!"

Clay and Melora watched the girl flounce away, and Melora said, "You shouldn't tease her so much, Clay."

He grinned suddenly. "I always teased you when you were a little girl. You turned out fairly well."

Melora tried not to smile, then gave it up. "I was a lot tougher than Rena."

"You were, for a fact," Clay said thoughtfully. He glanced

at Melora and then noted that the other women had gone to deliver the food to the men. "Melora, watch out for her, will you? With me having to go away and her mother gone, she needs someone to talk to, to trust."

"I know. That's why I asked her to come and spend some time with me."

"Besides, she'll have to get used to you being her new mama!" Clay teased, winking at his beloved.

"Rena's fine," Melora stated evenly. "It's *you* I believe who needs some mothering!"

Clay chuckled. "You have a way of rapping out with the truth. You always did that, even when you were ten years old."

"I did it when I was six," Melora returned, her eyes twinkling with the memories of the days when he'd first come into her life. She'd been only a child, but she'd fallen in love with Clay Rocklin from the beginning. She knew one day soon she'd be his wife—but that day was not now.

"Let's go join the others, Clay," she said. "When do you and the other men have to be back?"

"Dent will have to leave tomorrow. Lowell and I have a little job to do in Richmond, so we'll have a little more time."

"Bring Rena tomorrow. We can all look at the pigs."

He smiled at her, and they went into the drawing room to join the others. Clay felt a sense of relief that Melora had stepped into the responsibility of caring for Rena. He had discovered that Rena was very dependent on him, and now that Ellen was gone and he would be away on duty for yet another summer, she needed someone. *Nobody better for that than Melora,* he thought.

☙

General Jeb Stuart pulled his horse up shortly and put his direct gaze on the two men who had halted their own mounts to let him pass. He was headed out of Richmond, but the general always had an eye for a good horse. "Well now, that's a right pretty animal you've got there, Private," he observed.

"Thank you, General," Lowell said, returning the salute, then added boldly, "That's a pretty fair animal you're riding."

Clay had recognized the officer riding beside Stuart at once as General James Longstreet. Longstreet pulled a black cigar from between his teeth and laughed softly. "The boy sounds mighty confident, General. And that *is* a nice mare he's riding."

James Ewell Brown Stuart bridled. "She can't beat Skylark!" Jeb Stuart was a colorful figure, and he was also the leader of the Confederate cavalry. He was proud of his ability—and his horse. "Private, you're not thinking your horse can beat mine, I hope."

"Yes, sir, I'm afraid I am."

Longstreet laughed in delight. He himself was a plain man, and the flamboyant Stuart sometimes aggravated him. He gave Clay a look, seeing the resemblance at once between the two men. "Your son, Captain?"

"Yes, sir. I have two sons in the Richmond Grays."

Longstreet was impressed. "Have you, now?" he murmured. "That's admirable." He considered Clay, then the mare Lowell was riding. "Are you of the same opinion as your son—about the mare?"

Clay grinned. "She's never been beat, sir!"

Stuart saw the sly look of amusement on Longstreet's face. "Well, sir," he announced firmly, "that record is about to be broken!"

"You're not going to race an enlisted man, are you, General?" Clay asked with alarm.

Stuart's face was hidden behind the bushy black beard, but his eyes twinkled with humor. "I do it all the time, Captain," he said gleefully. "That's how I enlist my cavalry." He looked at the terrain, then lifted his gauntleted hand, pointing to a single tall pine in the middle of a pasture. "To that tree and back, Private—what's your name?"

"Lowell Rocklin, sir, and this is my father, Captain Clay Rocklin."

"General Longstreet, you give the signal," Stuart commanded. He brought his big stallion around so that he faced the tree, and Lowell did the same. As soon as they were in position, Longstreet shouted, "Go!"

As the two horses exploded into action, Clay said nervously, "Sir, my son is in a no-win situation. If he loses, his record with that mare is broken, but if he wins—well, nobody ever made any money beating a general!"

Longstreet looked at Clay, puffed on his cigar, and nodded.

"That's pretty wise, Captain Rocklin, but don't worry. Your boy won't beat General Stuart."

Clay watched uneasily but saw with some relief as the two horsemen made their return that Longstreet was right. Stuart beat Lowell by three lengths. Lowell pulled up, crestfallen, but General Stuart said heartily, "You have a fine animal, young fellow, and you're a fine rider." His blue eyes gleamed. "Jine the cavalry! Nothing like it!" He gave Longstreet a caustic grin, adding, "Any yokel can dress up and march around with a musket, but I need young fellows like you! We're the eyes of the army. Why, General Lee wouldn't make a move without me and my boys!"

Lowell was fascinated by the colorful Stuart and glanced at Clay. "Sir? Do you think I might?"

"Have to ask Colonel Benton for a transfer, I guess."

Stuart suddenly lifted his plumed hat, waved it, and shouted, "Do it, Private!" He spurred the stallion and drove off shouting with a wild whoop.

Clay stared after Stuart, then put his gaze on Longstreet. "Sir, he's quite a man, isn't he?"

Longstreet nodded. "For what he does, there's nobody better."

"Do you think General Stuart really wants me in the cavalry, sir?" Lowell asked.

Longstreet smiled. "Every young fellow in Virginia wants to join Jeb Stuart, and if he extended the offer to you, he means it." He nodded to Clay. "Come along, tell me about those boys of yours, Captain Rocklin."

Clay was flattered by the general's interest, and he gave a brief sketch of his boys. "This one is the best horseman of us all—best in the county." Clay smiled at Lowell, adding, "In my opinion, General, the best *anywhere*!"

Longstreet noticed Lowell flush at his father's praise. "Don't be embarrassed, Private. We're going to need the best from everyone to hold off the Yankees."

"May I ask your opinion of the enemy force, General?" Clay inquired cautiously.

Longstreet shrugged. "I expect you know he's coming with as big an army as has ever marched on this continent. He's got everything he needs—guns, ammunition, artillery—even balloons."

"Even *what*, sir?" Lowell asked with surprise.

"Balloons, Private." Longstreet nodded. There was a sober quality in the man, a steadiness that controlled all that he did and said. He was, Clay knew, the most reliable of all the Confederate generals, and Lee put much confidence in him. "Fellow named Thaddeus Lowe has come up with a new idea. Makes big balloons out of silk, fills them with hot air. They have baskets underneath, and the Federals send up an officer to get the position of the opposing troops."

"I haven't heard of that, sir," Clay said with interest. "Does it work?"

"They tell me it does, though I haven't seen it myself." Longstreet took the cigar out of his mouth, studied it, and added, "I hope it doesn't, Captain, because they have them and we don't!"

"Just a big balloon filled with hot air?" Lowell asked with surprise. "Why, that shouldn't be much trouble, General."

Longstreet turned his head to study the young man. "We had one last spring for a few days, and we sure could use every advantage we can muster. Private, if you want to serve the Confederacy, you make one of those things for me. I'll promote you on the spot to sergeant."

"Really, sir?"

Longstreet nodded. "You'd be a lot more use to the Cause doing that than riding around with General Stuart—" Longstreet suddenly realized what he had said and added hastily, "Of course, we couldn't do without General Stuart and his boys, but when the Yankees hit us, how are we going to know where they are? They'll know where *we* are! They'll have spotters up in those blasted things telling them where every man we have is located."

Lowell stared at General Longstreet, his eyes narrowing. "Sir, I can do it!"

Longstreet had not been serious, but at the intent look on Lowell's face, he grew sober. "Do it, then!" he snapped. Looking at Clay, he nodded, saying, "If your boy can come up with an observation balloon, it might make a big difference when we go into action." He nodded shortly, then rode off toward Stuart, who was waiting impatiently up the road.

"Never thought we'd be talking with two generals, Father!"

821

"Nor did I." Clay gave Lowell a quick look. "Did you hold your mare back?"

"Sure did! I've got more sense than to beat a general at anything!"

Clay laughed loudly. "Come on, son; we've got work to do."

As they rode into Richmond, Lowell said suddenly, "I could make that balloon, sir."

Clay was startled, for his mind was on other things. "Why, I guess you could, Lowell. You were always good at inventing things." He considered this intent young son of his carefully. "You going to try it?"

"I'd like to, sir."

"Well, I'll ask Colonel Benton to give you some time for this project. Shouldn't be too hard since Old Pete asked you to work on it."

"I'm going to have a try at it." Lowell's hazel eyes glowed. "Say, wouldn't that be something?"

"Wouldn't *what* be something?"

Lowell pointed up to where a red-tailed hawk was sailing high in the air. "To be up there with that fellow!"

Clay glanced upward, studied the steady flight of the bird, then nodded and smiled. "Yes, that really *would* be something, son!"

CHAPTER 3

CHIMBORAZO

Studs Mulvaney, owner of the Royal Hotel, was not a man prone to granting favors. But he'd taken Clara Smith on as one of his "hostesses"—dance hall girls—only because Alf Swanson had asked. Studs had given the woman a room on the second floor—a room that would be used to entertain men. She looked so ill and tired after her hard journey from Vicksburg, Studs had surprised himself by saying, "Take a few days to rest up, kid." Afterward on his way to his office, he'd had second thoughts. Looking over to Bugs Leggett, his one-legged swamper who was cleaning up, he remarked, "She won't make it, Bugs, but I got to do it. Owe Alf a big one."

"Wot about the girl and the kid?" Bugs demanded. "Pretty girl like that, she'll be trouble if she don't come across."

"Yeah, I guess that's right. Go get her, will you, Bugs?" After the swamper thumped out on his wooden leg, Mulvaney leaned back and stared at the picture of the coyly smiling nude on his wall, though not really seeing it. He was a huge man, well over six feet, with the battered features of an ex-prizefighter. He was nearing fifty now and growing fat, but was still rough enough to serve as his own bouncer. And the Royal Hotel needed a tough bouncer, for although it might qualify as a hotel insofar as it had rooms that could be rented, it was more of a saloon and a dance hall than anything else. And the rooms upstairs, where men followed the women, were paid for in bribes to the police each month.

When a slight knocking on the door drew his attention, he got up and walked to the door. Opening it, with a nod of his head he motioned in the two who stood there, then closed the door behind them. Staring down at the pair, he stated bluntly, "This ain't no place for kids."

Rooney said quickly, "Mr. Mulvaney, Buck and me can work. You got to have cleaning, and we're real good at that." She was frightened but held her head high. "Just give us a corner someplace to sleep in, and we'll work for our room and board."

Mulvaney had made up his mind to get rid of the pair, but he liked the girl's spunk. Taking the stub of a foul-smelling cigar out of his mouth, he stared down at them uncertainly. The boy, Buck, piped up, "And I can take messages and run all your errands—and I can do anything else you need done."

"Can you, now?" Jamming the cigar between his battered lips, the big man thought hard. *I can use the boy, but the girl could be trouble if any of my customers get an eyeful of her.* Still, he liked the girl's steady look and asked abruptly, "You're a good girl, ain'tcha?"

Rooney's cheeks reddened, and she nodded. "Yes, sir."

"Well, I'll do what I can for you." He thought hard, his eyes almost hidden in their sockets. A thousand blows had formed scar tissue that pulled his thick eyelids down so that he was slit eyed, but Rooney had learned to know the looks of men. Studs Mulvaney, she was sure, though hardly a civic leader, wasn't one of the bad ones.

Mulvaney reached a decision. "C'mon, I'll show you what I got. Might work out, might not."

Rooney and Buck followed the big man out of his office. It was only the middle of the afternoon, and the saloon was almost empty as he led them through it to the stairs near the back. They creaked under his weight, but he ignored the sound, turning at the top to his left. The hall was lined with doors, and there was a strange, thick odor that both young people noticed. At the end of the hall Mulvaney opened a door, and Rooney looked cautiously inside. It was some sort of storage room with mops, buckets, chamber pots, and other equipment piled carelessly around.

"See that ladder?"

Rooney and Buck saw a ladder composed of two boards nailed to the wall with two-foot-long pieces nailed across to form a rough sort of ladder.

"Yes, sir."

"Well, up at the top there's a room—sort of. Go up and

look it over; then come back down here."

At once Buck scrambled up the ladder, and Rooney followed, trying to keep her skirt around her legs, but glancing down, she saw that Mulvaney was staring down at the floor.

At the top of the ladder, she stepped off and found herself in a garret room—more or less. It was composed of a floor, four walls, and a peaked roof. Someone had boarded up the attic of the Royal Hotel and slapped a door in one side and a single window in the outer wall that looked down on Sixth Street. The walls were covered with yellowing newspaper, and the furniture consisted of two cots, one table, a chair, and a battered washstand.

Buck stepped over and pulled the window open. "Hey, we can see everything from here, sis!"

Rooney stared around at the room, and a great relief came to her. *It's like a little tree house,* she thought. *We'll be safe here!* Aloud she said, "We'll make us a real home here, Buck."

As she descended the rungs of the ladder, her mind was already working on how to fix up the room. Stepping to the floor, she said, "Oh, Mr. Mulvaney, it's just what Buck and me need!"

"Pretty rough for a young woman, ain't it?"

"Oh no!" Rooney's eyes were glowing, and she spoke with excitement. "Buck and me can fix it up fine! Can we work for you?"

"I reckon so." Mulvaney saw the two exchange happy glances and shrugged. "Guess we can round up some bedding and stuff.

Buck, go find Bugs and tell him to see what he can dig up." As soon as Buck disappeared, Mulvaney looked down at Rooney.

"See that door?" He shoved some boards aside and with a grunt opened a door that had been concealed behind them. "It goes out to some stairs, see? Used to be a fire escape, I reckon. Somebody made this closet and closed it off." Puffing blue smoke like a miniature engine, he considered Rooney, then said, "Wouldn't be too safe for a young girl to be in the hotel. You better use these stairs."

Rooney was relieved and said, "That'll be nice, Mr. Mulvaney."

"Can you cook?"

"Oh yes! I can bake biscuits and cook just about anything, if it's not too fancy. I worked for a café once, just washing dishes at first, but then I got to help the cook all the time."

"Guess that's what you'll do, then. C'mon, I'll show you the kitchen."

When they had descended the stairs, Rooney followed the owner through the bar into a dining room that held half a dozen battered wooden tables flanked by an assortment of chairs, then through a swinging door. "Hey, Chin, this is your new helper. Her name's Rooney."

Rooney faced a small, thin Oriental with a smooth yellow face. "Looney?" he said in a sibilant voice. He bowed three times, saying, "Wely nice, Looney!"

"It's *Rooney!*" Mulvaney growled but turned to the girl with a smile. "He can't talk American good, but he's a pretty

827

fair cook. You give him a hand."

"I'm glad to know you, Chin." Rooney smiled. She had never known a Chinese, but she felt that she would be safe with this one. That was always the test with any male: *Will I be safe with him?* "Maybe you can teach me to make Chinese food."

"Ah yesss!" Chin's head bobbed up and down, and he grinned, exposing yellow teeth. "You be glate hep to Chin, Looney!" The thin, undersized cook had never mastered the *r* of the English language, but he said, "You know how to fix pot loast?"

"He means pot *r*oast," Mulvaney said, grinning. "Come on, we'll see if Bugs and your brother got anything fer your room."

Rooney perched on a high stool, peeling potatoes with quick, efficient motions of a small knife. Across from her, Chin chopped meat into small strips with swift, accurate blows of a razor-sharp cleaver. This never failed to amaze Rooney, for the diminutive cook used his left hand to position the meat, his nimble fingers shoving portions of the rich red beef into place. Chin never seemed to look at the meat and withdrew his bony fingers just in time for them to escape being cut off by the blows of the heavy cleaver. He jabbered constantly as he worked, and Rooney had grown fond of him.

"You're going to chop all your fingers off one day, Chin," she remarked when the cook slammed the gleaming cleaver down, missing his fingers by a fragment of an inch, slicing the tough beef cleanly.

"Ho! Chin nevah miss!" As if to show his helper the truth of his words, he sent a staccato echo as he struck the beef a rapid series of blows. Each blow, Rooney saw with amazement, sliced a thin section of raw beef from the bone, and when the sound stopped, Chin held up the slices, triumph in his black eyes. "No fingas!" he crowed, then laughed silently at the girl. "You tly now?"

"No!" Rooney smiled, shaking her head. "I'll stick to peeling potatoes. What kind of pies do you want me to make for supper, Chin?"

"Ah—thlee apple and two laisen." Gathering up the beef, Chin proceeded to pull down pots and pans, making a terrific clatter, while at the same time raising his shrill voice to ask, "You like it heah, Looney?"

"Yes. Buck and I both do."

"I glad," Chin pronounced. "You fine young womans! Make good pies." His wise eyes came to rest on her as he tossed the ingredients for the meal together. He was a lonely man, cut off from his homeland by thousands of miles, and there were only a handful of Orientals in Richmond. He had lost his wife and children to an epidemic of cholera that had broken out aboard the ship bringing them to America and had never married again. His only interests were reading a small collection of books printed in his native language and playing cards. He was an inveterate gambler, and he had been overjoyed when Rooney had accepted his offer to play cards. He was, Rooney quickly discovered, a terrible gambler. She never played with him for money, of course, but even over their simple games Chin got so excited that she learned to beat him easily. "Don't get excited when you have a good hand," she had cautioned him. "And sometimes just *act* excited when you have a bad hand." But Chin was incurable and lost his wages at the gambling tables as soon as he received them. "You're really working for nothing for Mr. Mulvaney, Chin," she censured him more than once. "He pays you for working, and you turn right around and give it back to him at the card tables."

"I beat him next time!" was his inevitable reply.

Rooney had learned to survive the dangers of the Royal— primarily by keeping herself out of sight as much as possible. She worked hard in the kitchen, only going out to serve in the dining room when necessary. And she *never* went to the bar or the second floor—*never*! It was not so dangerous for Buck, so he sometimes went up the inner stairs, but Rooney had learned caution in a hard school. Always she left the kitchen by the outer door that opened into the alley and climbed the rickety stairs that led to the small closet, then climbed the ladder to the small room she shared with Buck. She had said once to Buck, "Let's make a rope ladder; then we can come up here and pull it up after us. Nobody could ever get to us."

"Aw, that'd be too hard," Buck had answered. He had learned to fit into the world of Richmond's lower denizens, the men and women who roamed the raw streets and alleyways. He was a sharp lad and was earning money, making himself useful to Mulvaney and other saloon owners along the street. There was always need for someone to take a bottle or a message, and men were careless with their money.

Rooney was aware that Buck was being hardened by the life they were forced to live, and despair came to her when she could find no way to protect him. She worried over his future, wanting him to have more than he did. All the love she could not lavish on parents, she gave to him. Until recently he had remained fairly innocent, but he was growing up, Rooney saw, and the boys he was beginning to spend time with were a bad influence.

She sat there peeling potatoes and listening to Chin tell about his youthful days in China. It was quiet in the kitchen, and she liked being in the kitchen with the little cook. Rooney had learned to enjoy the simple things, savoring them for the moment. Her life had been a tightrope, and only by some sort of miracle had she been able to keep her purity of body and mind in the midst of a raw and violent world.

The door swung open abruptly, and Rooney's mother came in. "I gotta have some money, Rooney," Clara demanded. "I know you got some, so let's have it."

Rooney reached into her pocket and took out the three dollars she had left from the small amount that Mulvaney paid her. She handed the sum to her mother, who snatched it and stared at the girl suspiciously. "This all you got?"

"Yes, that's all."

Clara stuck the bills into her bodice and started to speak but was seized by a coughing fit. Her thin body was racked by the deep, tearing coughs, and Rooney leaped up and ran to get a glass of water. Holding it toward her mother, she said urgently, "Mama—drink this!"

Clara seized the glass, and the water spilled over her chin as she tried to gulp it. Finally she sputtered and the coughing grew milder. Taking a shallow breath, she stared at Rooney with hollow eyes. "I got to go to the doctor," she muttered hoarsely. "I ain't feeling good."

"Maybe he'll give you some medicine for your cough," Rooney encouraged her. Timidly she placed her hand on her mother's shoulder, adding, "Maybe you should take a few days' rest."

Clara gave Rooney a look of anger mixed with despair. "There ain't no rest in this business." She turned to Chin. "You got any cough medicine, Cookee?"

"Ah yesss." Chin bowed with a sharp, jerky motion, turned, and went into the door that led to his small room just off the kitchen. He came back at once with a brown bottle in his thin hand. "Vely good for you," he insisted, then added a warning, "but make you sleep long time!"

The sick woman stared at the bottle, pulled off the cap, and sniffed at it. Blinking her eyes, she gasped, then looked at Chin. "Smells bad enough to be good. Thanks, Cookee." She gave Rooney a weary glance, asking, "You feelin' all right?"

"Yes, Mama."

Suspicion came to Clara Smith's faded eyes. "Stay away from these men. None of them is any good."

"I will."

Clara lifted the bottle, drank two swallows, then lowered it. A contortion twisted her features, and she gasped, "What is this stuff, anyway?"

"Vely good for sick womans," Chin insisted, his head bobbing up and down. Concern came into his smallish eyes as he added, "Not much. Too much and womans die!"

His words caught at Clara, turning her face suddenly still. She lifted the brown bottle, stared at it, then muttered, "There's worse things than dying, Cookee." She gave Rooney a look filled with bitterness, turned, and left the room.

"She vely sick," Chin said quietly, shaking his head. "Not a good place for sick womans!"

All afternoon as Rooney helped Chin with the cooking and later when she washed dishes, she thought about her mother. She had been ashamed of what her mother did for a long time, but there still remained a love for her. Finally she said good night to Chin, left the kitchen, and climbed the stairs and then the ladder up to her room. Carefully she lit the lamp, then took off her dress and undergarments and washed as well as she could, using a large enamel washbasin. All the water had to be hauled up to the room, but Buck had devised a method so that both of them could bathe. He'd found a twenty-gallon wooden barrel and—with Mulvaney's help—had hauled it up to the tiny room. The difficulty was in filling it with water, but he and Rooney had solved that by hauling up water from the alley using a rope and a two-gallon wooden bucket. Now as Rooney bathed herself with fresh water, she relaxed. When she was clean, she dried off, put on a thin dress she used for a nightgown, and went over to sit down at the makeshift desk— really a part of a door over two boxes. Picking up a book, she sat there and read until she grew sleepy, then put the book down. It was a story about an orphan named Jane Eyre, and somehow the book spoke to her. She read poorly, making the words out slowly, but even so, the plight of the young English girl touched her heart. *Funny that I can feel so sorry for a girl who's not even alive,* she mused as she sat hunched over the book. *With all my troubles, it's silly to read about somebody else's.*

Going to her cot, she lay down but didn't go to sleep at once. Finally fatigue caught up with her, and she drifted off. The noise of Buck climbing the ladder woke her instantly. She sat up and waited until he stepped inside, then said with a touch of rebuke, "It's too late for you to be out, Buck."

Buck shrugged and tossed his cap on the floor. He began undressing but made his defense by saying, "Big poker game across the street at the Chez Parée, sis. Some big wheels in it." He stripped off his shirt and, as he washed, added, "I took them some whiskey and sandwiches, and then one of them sent me downtown with a message. Gave me five dollars."

Rooney didn't like it but knew that both of them had little choice. "What was all that noise earlier tonight?"

"New bunch of soldiers come in—from Alabama, I think." Buck pulled off his trousers, then his shoes and socks. Stretching out on the narrow cot, he closed his eyes.

"Do the men say the Yankees will come here?" Rooney's world was delicately balanced. Any small event could send it rocking, and as poor as her condition was, she clung to it desperately. She knew little about the war. For her the only issue was: Will the Yankees come? If they came, she might lose her place, and she could not face that.

"Dunno, sis." Buck opened his eyes and said, "There's been lots of our men hurt in battle so far. One of the men in the poker game was a soldier—a doctor."

"What did he say?"

"Said it was real bad. He said he'd cut off arms and legs until they made a pile high as his head!"

"How awful!"

"Some of them wuz Yankees, though."

Rooney tried to shut the image of such a bloody scene from her mind. "Where do they take the wounded soldiers, Buck?"

"The officer said they haul them back to Richmond in wagons. Said lots of 'em are took to houses, and the people take care of them." He thought hard, then added, "He said there's a big hospital here, out on the edge of town. Can't say the name of it right. . .Shimboozo—somethin' like that." He was very sleepy and muttered, "He said they ain't no space or near enough doctors, and some of the wounded have to be put on the floor. Says some of 'em will just die with nobody to take care of 'em. . . ."

Rooney glanced over and saw that Buck was asleep. Rising,

she went to him, leaned over, and kissed his cheek, then turned and blew out the lamp. For a long time she lay in bed thinking of the wounded men who were dying because there was nobody to take care of them.

"I could at least get them water and wash their clothes." She lay still, and a determination came to her. "I'm goin' to that place. If Mr. Mulvaney will let me!"

Phoebe Yates Pember, matron at Chimborazo Hospital, looked up from the raw stump where a leg ended and stared at the youthful girl who'd come into the infirmary. The ward was packed with cots, and some of the men with less serious wounds were on blankets on the floor. The smell of blood, urine, and sweat filled the room, and there was a constant low muttering from men in pain.

"Well, what is it?" she demanded, staring at Rooney. Mrs. Pember had not slept well in a long time, and her nerves were ragged. It was not only the constant strain of men dying for the lack of simple care, but the opposition she had received from the doctors. They had let her know that male nurses were needed, not female! But she had a letter from President Jefferson Davis stating that he would be pleased if the medical department would give Mrs. Pember charge over a ward—and none of the doctors had the nerve to deny that letter!

But the staff had made Mrs. Pember as uncomfortable as possible, withholding supplies and giving her the most worthless of the male nurses and orderlies. And they had assaulted her verbally if not physically, making their talk around her as crude and rough as possible.

But Phoebe Yates Pember had forged ahead, throwing herself into the work of saving wounded Confederate soldiers. Ignoring the opposition of the staff, she had struck Chimborazo Hospital, Ward 12, like a small tornado. When her energy had produced the smallest death rate in her ward of any in the entire hospital, the doctors were forced to shut their mouths, though her success seemed to anger instead of please them.

Some help had come from the women of Richmond, but not nearly enough. Mrs. Pember looked at the girl with large blue eyes and snapped again, "Yes, what is it?" The stump she was working on was not well done, and she silently raged against the carelessness of the "surgeon" who had done such a poor job on the soldier.

"I've come to help with the soldiers, ma'am."

Mrs. Pember began to bandage the stump; then, looking up, she spoke more gently. "Help with the soldiers? Are you a nurse?"

"Oh no! I—I just thought I might do something. I could feed them and get them things—maybe help with the washing."

"What's your name?"

"Rooney Smith, ma'am."

"Do your parents know you're here? You're very young, and this is rough work."

"My mama...won't care." Rooney stumbled over the words,

then lifted her chin and stated, "I'm used to rough living. All I want to do is help."

A smile came to Mrs. Pember. "All right, Rooney. I'm glad you've come. How much would you like to work?"

"Oh, I can work all morning, Miz Pember! I cook in the afternoons, so I couldn't work then."

"That will be fine. Now if you'll just stay with me, I'll show you how to change bandages." She hesitated, then said, "Some of the wounds are very bad. Do you think you can do it?"

"I don't know, ma'am," Rooney answered quietly. "I'll try."

Mrs. Pember liked the girl. She distrusted people who made rash promises, and Rooney's reply pleased her. She turned to face the young soldier with the missing leg. "Think you'd like to have this pretty young woman for a nurse, Billy?"

The soldier was no more than eighteen. He was so thin that his eyes looked enormous in his face. But he smiled faintly and nodded. "Sure, Miz Pember. I'd like her just fine."

"Get Billy some fresh water, will you, Rooney? And try to get him to eat a little soup."

"Yes, ma'am," Rooney agreed. Quickly she got the water, then sat down and smiled at him. "This looks like good soup, Billy. I'm going to sit here and feed it to you, so just make up your mind to it!" He reminded her of her brother, Buck, and Rooney was glad to see him smile weakly.

"Yes, Miss Rooney, I'll sure do my best," he whispered. Billy Cantrell had been thinking of his own sweetheart, Ruth Wentworth—wondering how she would feel when a one-legged man came back to her. He'd been thinking about how Ruth loved to dance, and the thought had brought despair to him. Somehow it helped that this young girl was willing to sit with him. Maybe Ruthie would have him with one leg after all!

Chapter 4

Shadow Bluff

The Richmond Grays fought savage battles since their baptism of fire at Bull Run. Their ranks were thinned, and the shock of battle had dulled their spirits. The entire Confederate Army was shrinking from combat losses, and General Lee sought desperately to fill the empty ranks and garner supplies for the coming onslaught of the Army of the Potomac.

But even in that "slack" period between fall and spring, there were skirmishes all along the borders of Confederate territory. One of these involved a small Federal force that suddenly appeared along the northern border of Virginia. A daring young officer, Major Phil Ramsey, had obtained permission to raid the scattered troops now guarding that area. He had planned a surprise attack, but his force had been detected by scouts who had relayed the news to Richmond. The Richmond Grays were part of the force that had been sent to deal with the attack and had engaged in a sharp battle with Ramsey's men at dusk. They had fought themselves into a stupor, and all were thinking of what would happen at dawn. Lowell looked up bleary-eyed at a large hill or plateau that rose more than a hundred feet high ahead of them. "What hill is that, Sarge?"

Sergeant Waco Smith was sitting down, his back against a tree. A bloody rag was tied around his forehead, but he looked more alert than the members of his squad. "I dunno," he said, shrugging. "This is your country, ain't it? You're supposed to know it better than me." Waco was a Texan, and his heritage showed in the .44 he kept strapped to his side, just as he'd worn it when he was a Texas Ranger. He looked past Lowell to Clay, asking, "You know that hill, Captain?"

Clay Rocklin nodded, then came to sit down in front of the fire. "I think it's called Shadow Bluff," he said. He had impaled a piece of beef on his bayonet and held it over the fire. When it started to sizzle, he eyed it critically. "Looks good. I'm hungry as a wolf."

"Not enough meat for our company, Clay." Lieutenant Bushrod Aimes had come over and squatted down beside Clay. " 'Course, there's not as many of us eating now. The Yankees whittled us down some this afternoon."

Clay nodded. He and Aimes were old friends and shared many memories. "Guess that's right." He looked over at the sleeping men, adding, "Leo didn't make it, Bushrod."

"How many of us does that make?"

Clay shook his head, counting silently. "I don't know the count for sure, but I'd say about a dozen."

Bushrod stared at him, his eyes red rimmed and his face drawn with fatigue. "That's almost a quarter of the company. We can't take much more of this, Clay." He stared up at the looming face of Shadow Bluff and shook his head. "I hope we don't have to take that hill tomorrow."

"I think we'll have to try." Clay pulled the meat out of the fire, tore off a morsel, and tasted it. "About right." He cut the meat into portions and called out, "Lowell, you and Mark come to supper. Enough for you, too, Bushrod."

"I've eaten." Aimes got up and walked over to where the first platoon was camped, saying, "Watch yourself in the morning, Clay. Don't let any of your boys be heroes!"

Mark Rocklin had come over to sit beside Clay. He looked dark and saturnine in the gloom, his face highlighted by the flickering tongues of yellow flame. He had served as an aide to Colonel Benton since enlisting but had wrangled permission from the colonel to accompany the attacking force. Taking a portion of the meat, he chewed it, watching as Clay dealt out slices to Lowell and Waco. He felt old and out of place among these young men, though at the age of fifty-two he was able to outmarch many of the younger men. He was a handsome man, his features patrician and his hair almost as black as that of his nephew Clay Rocklin. Glancing over at Lowell, he asked, "Still thinking about joining the cavalry, Lowell?"

"In a minute if I had the chance," Lowell said with a big grin. He had always admired his uncle Mark, and the two of them had grown very close since Mark had enlisted. "Don't see many dead cavalrymen, do you?"

Mark laughed suddenly and nudged Clay. "You didn't teach this young whelp much respect for tradition, did you?"

Clay smiled at Lowell, but his eyes suddenly became serious. "I'm going to teach him some respect for those Yankee sharpshooters." He waved his chunk of meat at Lowell, adding, "You keep your head down tomorrow, Lowell." He'd had to pull the young man down more than once in the battles and had seen too many go down for good.

Lowell grinned, jibing at his father, "You always stay down, don't you, Captain Rocklin? Never see you moving around when the lead starts flying." He enjoyed the look on his father's face, for Clay was always moving about when the situation was worst.

Waco, seeing the expression on Clay's face, remarked slyly, "Seems like I been through all this before. Remember Bull Run? The three of us—and Lieutenant Rocklin, too—was staring at the Yankee guns jist like we are now."

Lowell nodded. "I never will forget the way you charged up that hill to get Dent, Father. Right in the teeth of the Bluebellies. You remember that, Waco?"

"Sure do!" the Texan said with a grin. "I was saying hello to Saint Peter all the way up. Bob Yancy was with us, too, as I think on it."

Lowell grasped his knees, his face rapt as he thought of that battle, shook his head slowly, and gave his father a look of admiration. "I don't think Dent would have made it if you hadn't led us up that hill."

Clay was uneasy as always when anyone referred to that time. He himself saw nothing heroic about that wild charge—not for him, at least. It was his own son who was in danger, and a man could do no less.

Clay said brusquely to Mark, "Keep this young firebrand under control, will you?"

"Do my best, but you know how these Rocklins are—stubborn as blue-nosed mules!"

All three of them laughed at Mark's definition, and Waco watched them with interest. "Must be nice to have kin beside you," he remarked.

"Not very smart," Clay answered at once. "We ought to be scattered out so that we'd have less chance of all of us getting hit."

Waco looked up at the hill in front of them. The Federal campfires winked out of the darkness like malevolent eyes, and the Texan shook his head. "I got a feeling about goin' up that blamed hill in the mornin', Captain." He shaved off a morsel of meat with his bowie knife, put it in his mouth, and chewed it slowly. "I shore don't want to go up there. Let the Bluebellies have it!"

Clay looked at the bulky mass of Shadow Bluff, and a chill ran through him. "I guess we don't have much choice, Sergeant. They're there, and we've got to drive them back."

At dawn the attack began, and Clay had time to say to Waco, "We're going to get hit hard. Watch out and try to save as many as you can!" Then he advanced at the head of the men into the raging battle. He lost sight of Lowell and thought, *I hope Mark takes care of him!*

But both Mark and Lowell were in the front of a line that hit the Union center. Mark held Lowell back for a while, but the younger man ran straight at the enemy. Mark cried out, "Lowell—you fool, get down!" When he saw that Lowell was not going to stop, he ran after him.

The Federals opened up with a volley that tore huge gaps in the gray-clad ranks, with salvo after salvo of exploding case shot. Mark saw Lowell go down, and with a wild cry he ran to where the young soldier had fallen. But before he got there he was struck in the stomach by a force that lifted him off his feet and threw him backward. The sun seemed to explode, and as pain ripped through him, he thought, *My God! I'm being killed!* And then he fell into a blackness that blotted out pain and thought instantly.

Clay's face was black with powder, and he called out, "Don't press the attack, men. They're retreating, and that's what we came for."

As the battle finally ended, Waco turned to Clay and said, "Your boy Lowell and Mark got hit, Captain."

The two of them hurried to where some of the wounded had been placed under a towering elm. Clay stumbled toward them, bent down, and saw that Lowell's eyes were open. "Son!

Are you hurt bad?"

Lowell licked his lips but seemed fairly alert. "N–no, I don't guess so. Just got sliced across the shoulders. But Uncle Mark, he's in poor shape."

Clay took a deep breath and squeezed Lowell's hand. He turned to Mark and saw the crimson blood that stained the gray uniform—and his heart sank. *A belly wound. He'll never make it!*

But Clay regained control quickly, saying, "Go back to that farmhouse, Sergeant. Commandeer all the wagons they've got. We've got to get the wounded to the hospital!"

As Waco dashed off to obey the command, Clay looked at the wounded men who were groaning and writhing on the ground. His eyes were filled with grief, not only for his own kin, but for all of them, Northern and Southern men alike. He bent over and whispered, "Son, I'm taking you and Mark into Richmond. You'll be all right."

Lowell nodded weakly. "We gave 'em the best we had, didn't we, sir?"

Clay nodded wearily. "Yes, Lowell, you did real fine! All of you boys did real fine!" Then he took a deep breath and rose to his feet. The battle was over, but as always, the suffering was only beginning.

The trip back to Richmond was hard on the wounded. Three of them died on the way and were buried beside the road. Finally they reached Chimborazo, and Clay got the wounded admitted. He waited outside until the surgery was over, then moved into the ward where Lowell and Mark were lying on cots.

The surgeon was still there, and Clay asked, "My son and my uncle—Doctor, how are they?"

The doctor was a short, heavy man with tired eyes. Glancing at Lowell, he nodded. "He's not bad. He'll make it." His eyes turned to the still form of Mark, and he shook his head. "I'm not hopeful about your uncle. Took a minié ball in the belly. I dug it out, but you know how bad a stomach wound can be."

"What are his chances, Doctor?" Clay asked, his eyes fixed on the two still forms.

"God knows." The doctor shrugged wearily, then turned and walked away.

CHAPTER 5

"JUST A FEW SCRAPS OF SILK!"

*W*ithin a week Chimborazo had become the biggest thing in Rooney Smith's life. She did her work with Chin in the afternoon and spent her evenings in the tiny room over the Royal—but she lived for the mornings.

Rising early, she dressed quietly, descended from the garret room to the alley, then made her way through the deserted streets of predawn Richmond to the hospital. Chimborazo Hospital was a sprawling affair perched on a high hill near the western side of Richmond. It eventually numbered 150 wards, each under the care of an assistant surgeon. The wards were housed in one-story buildings, 30 feet wide and 100 feet long.

At first Rooney had been confused by the jumbled fashion in which the wards were scattered but quickly learned that they were all grouped into five divisions, or hospitals. Mrs. Pember was in charge of Ward 12 in Hospital 2, and it was in that ward that Rooney worked.

As she climbed the steep incline leading to the hospital, she thought of how quickly she'd learned to help with the soldiers. Mrs. Pember had only let her clean at first, but when it became obvious that Rooney was a natural nurse, able to clean patients and change bandages quickly without flinching at the dirt, the smells, and the awful wounds, the matron had at once used her in this capacity.

The sun was creeping over the city, bathing the white hospital buildings in a golden red glow as Rooney entered the building where Mrs. Pember had her office. She passed through the center of the ward, speaking to men who were awake, remembering some of their names. Their eyes followed the slender young girl as she moved down the aisle, but there were no rude remarks.

She paused beside the bed of one of the patients who was sitting up staring at her. "Hello, Claude," she said, coming to stand beside him. He was a new patient, having come in only three days earlier, and he was, on the whole, a rather sorry specimen. He was lean as most of them were, but his hair lay over his shoulders in lank strands, and his fingernails were long, like claws.

"Claude, when are you going to let me cut your hair and your nails?"

The soldier stared at her and blinked with determination. "Never!" he spat out. "I done promised my ma I wouldn't cut my hair till the war's over. And I use my fingernails 'cause I couldn't get a fork when we wuz on the march."

Shaking her head with amusement, Rooney said, "Why, Claude, your mama would purely *thrash* you if she saw that dirty ol' greasy hair! And we've got plenty of forks here—you know that!"

But Claude shook his head stubbornly, and Rooney gave up. "If you'll let me clean you up, I'll write that letter you've been after me to do."

The eyes of the soldier brightened, and he sat up straighter. Then he seemed to consider this a weakness because he slumped down and shook his head. "I promised my ma," he muttered.

"Let me know if you change your mind."

Rooney left, and the man on the bed next to Claude, a pale young man of eighteen with one arm, jibed, "Claude, you ain't got good sense! That purty young thang wantin' to purty you up, and you laying there sulled up like a pizen pup! I allus knowed you Georgia crackers wuz dumb!"

Rooney didn't hear this remark, but later when she came out of the supply room with fresh water and bandages, Claude said abruptly as she passed, "Wal—I reckon you can do it, then."

Rooney wanted to laugh, but she had learned that most of the young men were highly sensitive, so she said only, "That's fine, Claude," and set about cleaning him up. As she worked with a pair of scissors, cutting his hair carefully, Claude's friends began calling out advice. "Don't let them things slip and cut his ears off, Miss Rooney. He's ugly enough as he is!" "Save them fangernails, nurse. They're the purtiest thing they is about ol' Claude!" "Better hose 'im down with turpentine, Miss Rooney!"

Rooney smiled at them, knowing that it was a lonely life

they led. Most of them were from Georgia and had no visitors. There was nothing to do for those who were bedfast except lie there and stare at the ceiling, and even the more mobile of the wounded could only talk or play endless games of cards. Her heart went out to them, and when she wasn't actually tending to their physical needs, she usually sat and talked to the worst cases or wrote letters home for the men.

"There!" she announced finally, rose, and stepped back to admire her work. "Don't you look nice! Wait—I saw a mirror in the office." She disappeared through the door and was back soon with a small round shaving mirror. "Look at yourself," she commanded.

Claude cautiously held the mirror up, as though it were a musket that might explode in his face. Billy Willis jibed, "Thet mirror is doomed! It'll break into a million pieces with a mug like that lookin' into it!"

But Claude had fixed his eyes on the mirror. He held silent and still for so long that the room grew quiet. Finally he lowered it and stared at Rooney. "Did you do all *that*?"

"I guess so, Claude. Do you like it?"

There was a long pause, and the tall, lean soldier stared at Rooney with astonishment and admiration. *What in the world is he thinking?* Rooney wondered.

Then Claude lifted his hand, stared at the neat nails. He moved his fingers as if to be sure that they actually *were* his own. Finally he crooked his index finger at Rooney in a gesture of command.

When Rooney leaned forward, Claude's voice dropped to a low pitch. "Air you married?"

"No, I'm not, Claude."

Claude Jenkins rose higher in the bed. He pushed his hair with one hand into a semblance of a wave. A faint color fluttered over his hollow cheeks, and stretching out a long bony finger, he gently touched Rooney's arm and with a constrained voice whispered mysteriously, "You wait!"

Rooney giggled, and hoots went up from the patients. As Rooney moved down the ward, changing bandages, she was pleased at the way she'd handled the matter. Later, when she met with Mrs. Pember to get instructions, she found that the matron had heard of the incident.

"I suppose you'll be leaving us, Rooney," Mrs. Pember said, catching the girl off guard.

"Why. . .why, no, ma'am! I don't have any thought of such a thing!"

Mrs. Pember's face was placid as a rule, but now she smiled, which made her look much younger. "You won't be marrying Claude, then?"

"Oh, Mrs. Pember," Rooney exclaimed, her face rosy, with a smile on her lips. "That's just some of his foolishness!"

"The whole ward was talking about it. I'm glad I'm not going to lose my best nurse." The matron noticed the flush of pleasure that came to the girl's cheeks at the compliment and wondered again about Rooney's circumstances. She was a woman of quick discernment and knew most of her staff well, but Rooney came and left, saying nothing of her life on the outside. A sudden thought came to her, and she asked cautiously, "You're not married, are you, Rooney?"

"Oh no, ma'am."

"I thought not, but girls are marrying very young these days. Too young, I'm sure." She studied the smooth cheeks of the young woman and asked, "None of the men have. . .bothered you, have they?"

"Oh no, Mrs. Pember," Rooney replied instantly. "They're all so sick, and most of them are real scared. A few of them try to flirt with me, but they don't mean anything by it." A soft compassion appeared in Rooney's large dark eyes, and she added thoughtfully, "I have to nurse my little brother when he gets sick. He's only thirteen, and these are grown men, but somehow some of them remind me of him—kind of like they are little boys."

"You've done fine work with them, Rooney. Not only with the bandaging and other work, but they all like you." A weariness came to Mrs. Pember's black eyes, and she said softly, "They need a woman's gentleness, and they see that quality in you."

"Well—it'd take a pretty mean person to treat them bad," Rooney said. "They got hurt fightin' for the South, so the least we can do is to take good care of them."

"Please, just don't marry Claude!"

Rooney giggled, then asked, "I'll bet some of them try to take up with you, don't they, Miz Pember?"

"Why, I wouldn't allow such a thing!"

The matron's reply was sharp, but the next day Rooney was

going through the ward with her when Mrs. Pember got a taste of male admiration.

After showing Rooney how to apply a particularly difficult type of bandage, the matron straightened up to find a tall, rough-looking soldier staring at her directly. Rooney noticed the man, too, and wondered if he would speak to Mrs. Pember.

The soldier was evidently on a visit, for he looked healthy and strong. And he had a pair of bold gray eyes that he fixed on Mrs. Pember, giving her his full attention. Mrs. Pember gave him stare for stare, but if she hoped to embarrass the tall soldier, she was not successful.

Without taking his eyes from the matron or saying a word, he began to walk slowly around and around her in a narrow circle. His sharp eyes took in every detail of Mrs. Pember's dress, face, and figure, his eye never fixing upon any particular feature but traveling incessantly.

Rooney wanted to laugh, so comical was the soldier's rapt attention, but she didn't dare. *Let's see how she handles this kind of thing,* she thought. She watched as Mrs. Pember moved her position, but the soldier shifted his to suit the new arrangement—again the matron moved, but the tall soldier, his eyes fixed upon her, moved constantly. Rooney would not have been surprised if he had asked her to open her mouth so he could examine her teeth, but he never said a word.

Finally the men lying on the cots began to laugh, and Mrs. Pember's cheeks began to glow. She'd never been bested in such a contest, but her stern glare had not fazed the soldier, who was now twisting his neck like an owl.

"What's the matter with you?" the matron demanded. "Haven't you ever seen a woman before?"

"Jerusalem!" the soldier whispered in a slow Texas drawl, keeping his eyes fixed on Mrs. Pember. "I never did see such a nice one. Why, you're as pretty as a pair of red shoes with green strings!"

The compliment almost destroyed Mrs. Pember's dignity, and she wheeled and almost fled from the ward.

Rooney stared at her dumbfounded, for she had admired the woman's strong spirit. She had seen Mrs. Pember stand up to officers who tried to humiliate her and send them away feeling the barbs of her speech. But the Texan had done what they had failed to do, and Rooney said to the soldier, "You sure did get a good look at Miz Pember."

"Wal, now," he breathed, still staring at the door through which the matron had fled for refuge. "I been to six battles, three county fairs, and two snake stompings, but I ain't never seen nothin' like her!"

Rooney expected Mrs. Pember to comment on the Texan, but she never referred to it. It pleased Rooney to know that this woman she admired so much could be—well, just a *woman* after all!

∾

Lowell awoke with a terrible headache and a tongue that felt like a piece of raw rope that had been soaked in tar. His lips were so dry that when he tried to lick them, they felt rough even to his swollen tongue.

Dimly he was aware that there were a large number of men in the long room, and as he lay there trying to sort it all out, he remembered the battle.

I've been shot!

Fear ran along his nerves, and he checked his limbs, noting with a weak relief that he had the usual number. Then he tried to sit up, and vivid slashing pain caught him across the back. It was as if a whip made of fire had been brought across his shoulders, bringing an involuntary cry of pain from his throat.

"Now you don't be moving so much." Cool hands were on his forehead, and Lowell peered up to see the face of a young woman.

"Where. . .is this place?" he gasped.

"Chimborazo Hospital. Now let me help you sit up, and you can have a drink."

Her strong hands lifted Lowell to a sitting position; then a glass of water was placed at his lips. Grasping at the glass, he downed it thirstily, then begged, "More—please!"

"You can have all you want," the young woman said. As she held another full glass to his lips, she said, "Be thankful you don't have a belly wound. They can't have water, just a wet cloth on their lips."

The water, tepid as it was, seemed to Lowell the best thing he'd ever tasted. "Thanks, miss," he whispered. "That was sure good!"

"You feel like lettin' me bandage your wound?" The girl, Lowell saw, was very young—and pretty, too!

"Are you a nurse?"

"No, just a helper, but the doctor wants your bandage changed. He said to clean the wound out, too."

"I guess you'd better do it," Lowell said, nodding. He was wearing a shirt that she pulled from him very gently. Her hands were cool and very steady as she removed the old bandage. "Is it bad?"

"No, not bad," she assured him. "Bullet plowed a sort of ditch across your shoulders. I'll bet it hurt when you got shot."

"Not so much at first," Lowell said, remembering. "Kind of knocked me out—but it got to hurting later. I think the doctor gave me some medicine to make me sleep."

"Laudanum, I'd reckon. Say if I hurt you."

Light as her hands were, the raw flesh was painful. Lowell endured it, however, and once when she had to bend over to bring the bandage under his arm, he was startled when her firm body pressed against his side. Quickly he looked at her, noting the curly hair and the clear eyes, as well as the smoothness of her cheeks. After seeing little but rough, bearded men for days, the girl looked like an angel.

"What's your name?" Lowell asked as she helped him put on a clean shirt. "I'm Lowell Rocklin."

"My name is Rooney Smith," she said. Looking down at him, she said, "Your pa, he was here earlier. Guess you didn't know it, though."

"Father was here?" Lowell remembered a little then of how his father had brought him and Mark back to Richmond in a wagon. And then he demanded, "My uncle Mark—is he here, too?"

"Well. . .yes."

Noting her hesitancy, he was afraid to ask, but he had to know. "How is he?"

"He's alive," Rooney said slowly. "The doctors, they operated on him again after they brought him here. I heard one of them tell your pa he didn't have much hope for your uncle."

Lowell sank back on the bed, his eyes cloudy. "He can't die!" he muttered.

Rooney looked down on him with pity. She'd seen so many die, yet she had not become hardened to it. Each death was a fresh grief to her, and she knew that the young man on the cot was suffering.

"He's real dear to you, your uncle?"

"Yes, he is." Lowell looked up at her, somehow anxious to talk and to explain how he felt. "He's always been good to me, and he's had a bad life."

"He married? Got children?"

"No. He never married." Lowell lay there silently, then said, "I guess that's why he always seemed so. . .well, sort of *left out*, you know? A man's not whole all by himself."

Lowell's statement came as a surprise to the girl. Her lips grew tight as she thought, then she nodded. "That's nice, Private Rocklin," she whispered. "I guess none of us are much without somebody to love."

She turned suddenly and disappeared before Lowell could thank her. He had no idea of the time and could only lie there until the sun rose. All around him he could hear the slight cries of pain as men moved on their beds, and he wondered if one of them was Mark. He made up his mind to talk to the doctor the first chance.

Father—he'll know about Mark, he thought. *I'll bet he'll be back tomorrow.* Then he thought of the young woman, wondering who she was. *She sure knows how to treat a fellow gentle.* The thought stayed with him, and he found himself looking forward to seeing her in the clear light of day.

She looks pretty in this dark, he thought sleepily, *but she's probably real homely in daylight.*

Clay came down between the two lines of beds, turning to speak to the patients. He'd gotten to know many of them during the five days he'd been coming to visit Lowell and Mark, and he paused long enough to stop beside a bed that bore a young soldier with both legs cut off above the knee. "Brought you that book I told you about, Thad," he said, smiling. "See how you like it."

"Thanks, Captain." There was no light in the young soldier's eyes, and he put the book down, then closed his eyes.

Clay hesitated, then said, "I'll see you later—before I leave." He felt helpless in cases like this—but always made the attempt. Shaking off the gloom that had come to him, he went to the section where Mark's bed was located and found Matron Pember there, speaking with one of the doctors.

"Oh, this is Captain Rocklin," Mrs. Pember said. "This is Dr. Jarvis, Captain. He's just been looking at your uncle's wound."

Clay glanced down and saw that Mark was awake. His face was sunken, and his eyes, always so brilliant, were dull and had no luster. "How are you, Mark?" Clay asked quietly.

"All right." Mark's voice was a hoarse whisper, and he had a fever that was dragging his vitality from him day by day.

Dr. Jarvis motioned with his head, and Clay followed him down the hall, saying, "Be back soon, Mark."

Dr. Birney Jarvis was a small man with pale green eyes. He stood there silently, dry washing his hands, then shrugged, saying, "Your uncle is in poor condition. The operation was almost too much for him. None of us expected him to survive it, but we had to try."

"Did you get all the metal out, Doctor?"

"Can't say." There was a clipped brevity in the doctor's voice, and he seemed almost unconcerned about his patient. *Probably got too many of them,* Clay thought. *And he's seen a lot of them die.* Clay judged the man's mannerisms and attitude, and a strong feeling came over him. He disliked and distrusted this man. There was no evidence or proof, but Clay knew that Jarvis would be of no help to Mark, and Clay determined right there to have another physician look at him.

"Our family doctor told me he'd come and see my uncle. Would that be all right, Doctor?"

"If you feel we're not competent, I suppose you can do so."

Clay tried to mollify the man, for he'd be over Mark's case and in a position to do him damage. "It's not that, sir, but Dr. Maxwell has taken care of all us Rocklins for a long time. Even if he couldn't do anything medically, it might make my uncle feel better to see him."

"Do as you please," Jarvis said coolly. "He's not going to make it in any case."

"The Lord can raise him up."

Jarvis sneered at that. "Then you'd better have the Lord come and take over the case."

Clay held a tight rein on his temper, saying only, "Thank you, Doctor," then turned and walked back to Mark's bedside. He found Mrs. Pember still there and drew her aside. "What's wrong with Dr. Jarvis? He's not at all concerned about my uncle."

"I can't comment on that, Captain," Mrs. Pember answered. "All I can say is that we'll do our best for Mark Rocklin."

"I know you'll do that. I've been meaning to compliment you on your excellent treatment of the men. I'm very grateful to you. My son is doing very well."

"Why, yes, he is. He'll be released soon." She looked across at Mark and shook her head. "I'm afraid we'll have your uncle with us for some time."

Clay talked with Mrs. Pember, then sat down and spent two hours with Mark. The sick man could not talk much, but it seemed to comfort him to have Clay there. Finally he took his leave, promising to return the next day and to bring Susanna with him.

Leaving the ward, he moved to the next building, where he found Lowell sitting up in a chair and talking with the pretty young woman Clay had noticed before. When Lowell introduced her, he said, "If my son gives you any trouble, Miss Smith, you tell me. I've had to paddle him before."

"You sure did!" Lowell agreed. He turned to Rooney, who was staring at his father. "Don't cross him, Rooney. He's a bad man!"

Clay saw that Lowell was in excellent spirits, and before he left he said, "Miss Smith, thank you for taking such good care of my boy. He's very special to me."

Rooney almost said, "To me, too," but choked it back. "He's doin' real good, sir."

After Clay left, Rooney said, "Your pa is sure a handsome man!" A mischief came to her, and she added, "Too bad you didn't take after him."

Lowell looked down at his hand. "You're right. My brothers, David and Dent, look just like him. I'm the runt of the family."

Rooney was shocked at his answer and put her hand on his. "Don't be foolish!" she said quietly. "God makes us like He wants us."

Lowell looked up quickly. "You believe that?"

"Yes, I do."

Lowell shook his head. "I'm glad, Rooney. I hope you always do."

Rooney changed the subject quickly. "When will you be

going back to the army?"

"Not for quite a while—maybe a month. Once I get out of here, I have a special assignment to work on for General Longstreet." He shifted on the chair and muttered, "Never could stand to be still. Wish I hadn't caught that bullet." He saw her eyes go to Billy Reynolds, who had no legs, and flushed. "Shouldn't have said that," he muttered. "It's just that I get restless."

"What is it? A spy mission or something like that?"

"Well, I'm going to make a balloon." He saw her look of surprise and quickly related General Longstreet's offer. He grew excited as he spoke—but when he finally finished, he lapsed into a gloom that drew his shoulders down. "Aw, I'm just dreaming. Since I've been lying here, I've realized that it can't be done."

"Why not? Don't you know how to make one of those things?"

"Oh, I could figure it all out," Lowell said quickly. "The trouble is there's nothing to make the canopy—the big balloon itself—out of. The Federals have lots of silk, but there's none in the South that I know of. That's all I need, Rooney—just a few scraps of silk!"

Rooney stared at him in disbelief. "Why, that's not right, Lowell! There's *lots* of silk right here in Richmond."

Lowell stared at her as if she'd lost her mind. "What in the world—"

"Silk *dresses*, silly!" she said, laughing aloud. "There must be *hundreds* of silk dresses in this town."

"Silk dresses? Why—" Lowell's eyes grew round, and he whistled. "Why, that's right, isn't it, Rooney!"

"Sure it is. Could you use silk dresses to make your balloon, Lowell?"

"I don't see why not—but. . ."

"What is it?"

"How would I *get* the dresses?" Lowell stared at her blankly. "I can't go around asking women to give me their dresses! I'd get shot by a jealous husband."

Rooney smiled, and her eyes were brighter than Lowell had ever seen them. "I can get them for you."

Lowell's face grew very intent as excitement built up in him. "Would you do that, Rooney?" He reached out and took her hand, squeezing it hard and not even conscious of it. "Why, we could do it—you and me!"

Rooney was *very* conscious of his hand holding hers. She had spent so much of her life fending off men that it felt strange to receive a touch from this young soldier without feeling fear.

She smiled, her dark blue eyes shining as she said, "We'll do it together, Lowell! We'll make a balloon together!"

CHAPTER 6

A VISIT TO GRACEFIELD

As Lowell turned the carriage into the long sweeping drive lined with massive oaks, Rooney's heart seemed to contract. Every day he was in the hospital, Lowell had *insisted* that she visit his family, and after making every excuse, Rooney finally conceded. So the day Lowell was released, he rented a carriage and then drove up in front of Chimborazo to pick up his new assistant.

Now as the horses drew up in front of the tall white house with massive white columns spanning the front and side, she wished heartily she'd never let him talk her into coming. She'd evaded all his inquiries concerning her home and family, inventing a story that involved an imaginary family in Natchez, Mississippi, and an aging and ailing aunt in Richmond whom she'd come to nurse. Lowell had hinted broadly that he'd be pleased to visit her at home, but she told him "Aunt Lillian" was too ill for *any* excitement—even a visitor.

Now as Lowell leaped to the ground and handed the lines to a tall black man, she wanted to cry out, "Take me back to town!" However, it was too late for that. Lowell reached up, and she had no choice but to let him help her to the ground.

"Come on, Rooney," Lowell said happily. "I'm anxious for you to meet my family." He was wearing a fine gray suit, for his uniform was too tight for comfort on his wound. His hazel eyes were gleaming, and his brown hair fell across his forehead, making him look very handsome and youthful. Holding to her arm, he said, "You're going to love my grandmother—everybody does."

Rooney was too frightened to answer. If his hand had not firmly grasped her arm, she felt that she would have whirled and dashed out into the woods that flanked the house. As they reached the top of the steps, the massive front door opened, and a heavy, white-haired black man greeted them.

"Marse Lowell!" The affection in the slave's voice was evident, and he seemed to have trouble speaking. Swallowing hard, he cleared his throat, saying roughly, "Whut you mean gettin' yo'self shot and scarin' Miz Susanna half to death! Ort to be ashamed!"

Lowell laughed and stepped forward to give the man a hard hug. "Don't you start fussing at me, Zander! I'll get plenty of that from Grandmother." Turning to the girl, he said, "This is Miss Rooney Smith, a new friend of mine. And this is Zander, Rooney. He and his wife, Dorrie, are the real bosses here!"

"I'm glad to know you, Zander."

"You come in now, Miz Rooney," the butler said, smiling.

"Miz Susanna, she out in the scuppernong arbor."

"Have Dorrie fix the blue bedroom for Miss Rooney, will you, Zander?"

Lowell passed into the house with the girl in tow. She had time only for an awed glance at a spacious foyer and a broad stairway that divided the lower part of the house. She caught a glimpse through a door of walls lined with books, and across the hallway, maids were cleaning the largest room she'd ever seen in a house. "That's our ballroom, Rooney," Lowell remarked. "Maybe we'll have a ball before I have to go. You like balls, don't you?"

The only dancing Rooney had ever seen was of the crude dance hall variety, so she only murmured, "They're very nice." She followed him out a side door and saw a building made up of white lath and covered with green vines. "There's my grandmother," Lowell said, and Rooney saw the woman who was moving among the flowers that surrounded the arbor.

"Lowell!"

Susanna Rocklin lifted her head to catch sight of the couple and put down a basket, coming to them at once with her arms outstretched. She embraced Lowell, kissed him firmly, then turned to examine the young woman. "And who is this you've brought to see us?"

"This is Rooney Smith," Lowell said. "She's going to help me build a balloon to fight the Yankees with."

Susanna smiled and put her hand out to Rooney, saying, "I'm so glad you've come, my dear. Clay's told me all about your kindness to Lowell and Mark."

As Rooney responded with her eyes lowered, Susanna studied her carefully. Her visits to Chimborazo had been in the afternoons, so she had never met the young woman, but she'd heard much about Rooney Smith! Not only Clay but Mark had sung her praises. And Lowell! Well, he'd talked of her with such excitement that Susanna had been very curious. *"Lowell interested in a young woman? That's something new!"* she had remarked to Clay.

What she saw was a young girl of no more than seventeen, with dark blue eyes shaded by impossibly thick black lashes. Her skin was close to olive and her complexion was smooth and fresh. The girl's hair was in a style that Susanna had never seen—cropped very short, it was a cap of rich auburn curls that framed her oval face. She was not tall, no taller than Susanna herself, and her figure was slender with the curves of young womanhood. She was wearing a simple blue dress and a pair of black shoes, both rather well-worn.

Susanna was surprised at the girl's beauty and at her obvious poverty. But many in Richmond were wearing their shoes and clothing to the point of thinness, so she smiled now and said, "Come into the house." She took Rooney's arm and, as they turned and walked toward the house, said, "We'll have something to eat, and then you can tell me all about this outlandish contraption my grandson's gone so daft over."

❧

Breakfast was served in the "small" dining room—which to Rooney was not small in any way. She had been informed by Lutie, one of the maids who had awakened her by simply entering the room, "Miz Rocklin, she say you come down for breakfus' when you gets dressed."

Rooney had brought no nightgown but had found one in the top drawer of a polished chifforobe. It was made of pale yellow silk, finer than any garment she'd ever owned in her life. She had worn it only because Lowell's grandmother had said, "Use any of the clothing you find in the room, Rooney." She had washed off in hot water that Lutie had brought to the room and dried off with a thick, fluffy white towel, and then—she'd experimented carefully with some of the powder she'd discovered in a china container on the washstand. It had smelled so heavenly that she'd dusted herself with it. Then she'd gone to bed, buried in the huge featherbed. She'd never slept on anything but a rough shuck mattress—and sometimes on worse!—and for a long time she'd lain there clean and sweet-smelling and floating on air, or so it seemed.

When Lutie called the next morning, Rooney bounded out of bed feeling like a princess. Quickly she dressed and went downstairs. Mrs. Rocklin was waiting for her, saying, "We'll have a nice breakfast all to ourselves, Rooney. Lowell was up before dawn. He went to his uncle Claude's to ask about borrowing some machinery of some sort. But he promised to be back by noon."

Rooney had taken a seat at the large oak table across from Susanna. Through high windows she could see the spacious grounds roll away toward the road and the woods.

Rooney said little, letting her hostess do the talking, and when the food came, she was amazed—scrambled eggs, fresh hot biscuits, thick-sliced bacon, grits, white gravy, and four different kinds of jelly.

"This one is made from the grapes in the scuppernong arbor," Susanna offered. "I like it the best."

Susanna Rocklin was sixty-one years old, but there was only a slight graying of her auburn hair. She had a patrician beauty that had only grown more fragile with age. Her eyes were an unusual blue-green that showed intelligence and kindness.

"Lowell kept you up too late, Rooney," Susanna said, a smile on her lips. "I gave up at eleven. Did he talk about balloons all night?"

"Oh no, ma'am." Rooney shook her head, sending her curls into a light dance about her head. "He told me all about how it was when he was growing up here. About all the Rocklins and the people who live here in the country."

"He loves his home, doesn't he?" Susanna said, sipping the strong black coffee in a delicate cup. "He always did."

"Are his brothers like him?"

"Oh no, child! Dent and David are twins, of course. They look like their father. Lowell looks. . .well, more like me, I suppose."

"He really does," Rooney murmured, struck by the sudden realization that the face of Susanna Rocklin had been mirrored in her young grandson's face. Except for the color of the eyes, they looked much alike. "What was he like when he was a little boy?"

That question prompted an answer that lasted until the sun was over the trees that lined the road. Susanna spoke of her family for a long time, then blinked and laughed in a half-embarrassed fashion. "Good heavens, Rooney. I've done what I always hated for grandparents to do."

"What's that, Miz Rocklin?"

"Bored you to death talking about my grandson!"

"I wasn't bored," Rooney said, offering a shy smile. "You have a wonderful family."

"What about your own family, Rooney?" Susanna inquired.

"Oh, there's just my ma and my brother, Buck, back in Mississippi. . . ." Rooney stumbled through her story, little knowing that the sharp mind of Susanna Rocklin was learning more about her than she would have liked for the woman to know.

"You're very fond of your brother, aren't you, Rooney?" Susanna asked gently. "I can tell by the way you talk about him."

"I guess so." Rooney faltered and wanted to tell this beautiful and kind woman how much she was worried about Buck—about his future. But she didn't dare for fear that she might give herself away.

Fortunately for her, Lowell came through the door breezily, saying, "Well, you didn't wait for me to have breakfast! I thought a poor wounded soldier would get better treatment!" He was smiling and went to kiss his grandmother, then sat down. "Dorrie!" He lifted his voice in a loud cry and, when a heavyset black woman came through the door, said, "Dorrie, are you trying to starve me to death? Bring me some of those

871

wonderful biscuits of yours!"

Dorrie laid her severe brown eyes on the young man. She was the wife of Zander and did more toward keeping the Big House running than Susanna Rocklin herself. "If you'd come to the table on time," she said with a sniff, hiding her affection for Lowell behind a stern look, "mebbe you'd get breakfus'. I got more to do than wait on lazy menfolks!"

But Lowell charmed the woman, Rooney saw, and soon she brought in a heaping platter of food. He caught at her as she went by and pulled her close. "Do you remember the time I killed your prize rooster with my slingshot, Dorrie?"

"I remembers it. Do *you*?"

Lowell squeezed her, laughing down into her ebony face. "I guess I do! I've still got scars from the pounding you gave me with that peach-tree switch!"

The thick lips of Dorrie turned up into a grin, and her old eyes shone. "Humph!" she snorted. "If you don't behaves yo'self, Marse Lowell Rocklin, I jes' might do it *again*!"

The three of them sat there for an hour, Lowell eating heartily, talking excitedly with his mouth full. He was full of schemes for building the balloon and had become very excited after his visit at Hartsworth, the plantation of Claude and Marianne Bristol. Marianne was the only daughter of Noah Rocklin, the founder of the Virginia Rocklins.

"Box can do all the metalwork here," Lowell said, "and Uncle Claude's got a wagon I can have to make the gas-making machinery."

"To make what?" Susanna demanded.

"Oh, Grandmother, I've explained all that," Lowell exclaimed. "We have to make gas to fill the balloons."

Susanna had no head for science and shook her head. "I don't understand any of it."

Lowell reached over and squeezed her hand. "You don't have to. All you have to do is give notes to all your friends."

"Notes? What sort of notes."

"Notes asking them to give Rooney their old silk dresses—and underwear."

Susanna stared at him in astonishment. "What did you say?"

Lowell was enjoying himself. He had a playful streak in him that David and Dent lacked, and he loved to tease his grandmother. "I said we've got to have silk dresses to make the balloon. I can't go barging in asking women to give me their dresses, can I?"

"But *underwear*? Really, Lowell!"

"Well, women do wear silk underwear."

"And how do *you* know so much about women's underwear?" Susanna demanded, her fine eyes flashing like fire.

Lowell leaned back and tried to put an innocent look on his face. "Oh, I hear some of the fellows talking. That's what they say, that women have lots of silk underwear. It's true, isn't it?"

"Rooney, I'm embarrassed for my grandson," Susanna said, her lips pressed tightly together. "He's got no manners at all!"

Rooney had heard much worse talk than Lowell's all her life but could not say so. She sat there watching Lowell, amazed at how he could tease his grandmother. *It's nice,* she thought. *How close they are—how much they love one another!*

"I will *not* write such a note, Lowell Rocklin!"

"Aw, now, you *have* to do it!" Lowell grew alarmed, his face falling. "I mean—how else can I get the silk? There's none in the whole Confederacy. And General Longstreet really needs this balloon!"

It took a great deal of persuasion, but Lowell was set on the matter. Susanna felt the business would be undignified. But finally she said, "I'll not write a letter, Lowell, but I'll go with Rooney and introduce her to some friends in Richmond. Rooney can do the collecting and see the things get to you."

"I knew you'd do it!" Lowell stood up, stepped over, and hugged Susanna.

She took the embrace, then stated, "But no underwear! I'm firm on that. I won't have those Yankees staring at the underclothing of Virginia's ladies!"

Lowell winked at Rooney, saying, "See how she is? Can't do a thing with her!"

Susanna laughed and turned her smile on Rooney. "He's spoiled rotten, Rooney! I hope you don't let him get around you the way I do. Make him behave!"

Rooney looked at the two, both so fine-looking—and so filled with love. She said, "I don't think I'll be able to do much with him, Miz Rocklin. You've taught him how to get what he wants."

"Right!" Lowell nodded. "After all," he added, "I don't want much—just my own way!"

The two women laughed at his absurd statement, and even Lowell had the grace to blush. "Well, I guess that sounds a little conceited." Then he looked at Rooney, and his eyes were filled with pride as he said, "But with a partner like Rooney, this thing's got to go! General Longstreet, here we come!"

CHAPTER 7

LOWELL FAILS THE TEST

$\mathcal{M}$ ark Rocklin's world had contracted to a single cot in a ward full of wounded and dying men. Pain was to him what water was to a fish—an element that surrounded him. He slept and awoke, but both states were vague and uncertain so that at times he was confused as to whether what he saw was reality or dream.

Time passed, but it had no meaning for him. Vaguely he was aware that men came and either got well or died. One night he came out of sleep to see two orderlies bundling a stiff body into a blanket. One of them said, "Graveyard's getting crowded. May have to start a new one."

The words of the orderly had taken root in Mark's confused mind. He dreamed of a huge graveyard with thousands of tombstones lined up rank on rank as far as the eye could see. They seemed to stretch out into the blue ether of the skies. But then a sinister figure draped in a robe that covered a specterlike countenance came to him, saying, "No room! No room for Mark Rocklin!"

Suddenly the scene faded, and he realized that someone was speaking to him, calling his name. He opened his eyes and saw that it was the young girl who often tended to him. *What is her name? Clay said she was taking care of Lowell. . . . Rooney! That's it!*

"Mr. Rocklin!" Rooney whispered. Her eyes were wide, and she had placed her hands on his chest. "Are you all right?"

Mark Rocklin blinked his eyes, and the last of the nightmare faded from his troubled mind. "Sure," he muttered through dry lips. "I'm okay, Rooney."

Rooney's gaze reflected her anxiety. "You were having a bad dream. I hate those things!" She studied him, then asked, "Can you eat something?"

"Not hungry."

"You've got to eat."

Mark lay quietly as she turned and disappeared. He was exhausted, and the pain in his side was ruinous. Sometimes it went away, but then it would tear through him unexpectedly, taking his breath and shutting off everything else. At other times it was a dull, throbbing ache, bearable but robbing him of ease. *Like having a toothache in my stomach!*

He'd been an active, healthy man all his life, and the days he'd endured since getting shot down had been terrible for him. *Better to be dead,* he thought bitterly, staring up at the ceiling. *I wish that minié ball had taken me right in the head!*

And then Rooney was back, drawing up a chair and holding

a spoonful of hot soup to his lips. Obediently he swallowed it, though he was not hungry. He managed to get down half of it before saying, "I can't eat any more."

"You did fine, Mr. Rocklin." She put the dish down and sat beside him, looking down into his face. "The doctor said you were doing a little better."

"He always says that."

"No, he doesn't." Rooney shook her head. "He tells the truth every time. If he says you're better, he believes it's so."

Not wanting to argue, Mark asked, "How's Lowell?"

"Oh, he went home a week ago. Don't you remember?"

"No. Guess I'm losing my mind."

"Don't say that, Mr. Rocklin!" Rooney was distressed and began to encourage Mark. He seemed better, more alert, and she found herself telling about her visit to Gracefield.

When she paused, Mark looked at her with a peculiar expression. "You went to my home, to Gracefield? How did that happen?" He saw her cheeks glow and listened as she explained about how she was helping Lowell with the construction of a balloon. He was truthfully more interested in Rooney's going to Gracefield—especially with Lowell—than in their project, but he listened as she spoke of the endeavor.

"And we're doin' real good, Mr. Rocklin," Rooney said, her eyes glowing with pleasure. "Mrs. Rocklin, she took me to meet some of her friends, and they got real interested. I go by and collect the dresses every couple of days. And when we get enough, Lowell will pick them up. And I'm going to help sew the balloon together."

"How's the collection going?" Mark asked. "Getting plenty of dresses?"

"Well—we did at first, but things have sorta gotten slow." Rooney bit her lip, then added, "I guess some ladies don't want their dresses up where everybody can see 'em. Then, too, there just aren't as many dresses as before the war. Lots of old dresses have been used for other things—bandages and like that."

"And since no new silk dresses will be coming in," Mark murmured, "lots of ladies want to hold on to those they have."

"I guess so."

The two talked for a long time, and Rooney noted that her patient looked better. She guessed that he was bored like many of the badly hurt soldiers. Finally she said, "I have to go to work now."

"Work? What sort of work do you do? Or did I ask you that?"

"No, you didn't. I'm a cook, and I've got to go get supper on." She hesitated, then murmured, "You sure do have a fine family, Mr. Rocklin." Then she turned and left.

That afternoon Susanna Rocklin came to visit Mark. The two talked quietly, and finally Mark asked about the girl. He listened carefully as Susanna related the visit of Rooney and how she'd gotten involved in the balloon project. Finally he asked, "That Rooney—is Lowell interested in her?"

"Oh, I don't know, Mark. Lowell's caught up in this balloon thing. He likes Rooney, but he's never thought of her as a sweetheart."

"She's not of our class, is she?"

"No, but she's very quick, Mark." Susanna shook her head almost sadly. "She's falling in love with Lowell; I can see that much. I'm afraid it will end badly for her."

"There are more important things than class, Susanna."

Startled at his remark, Susanna looked at him carefully and thought, *I know so little about this brother-in-law of mine! He's the strange one. Something has hurt him dreadfully—and he'll never speak of it.*

Then she said aloud, "I think you're right, Mark. With a little education and love, she could be a real lady."

"Well, give it to her, Susanna!" Mark mustered up a smile. "You could never marry me off, but maybe you'll have better luck with Lowell."

"You should have married, Mark," Susanna said simply, love for him filling her eyes. "You have so much to give a woman and children."

Mark stared at her, then shook his head. "Too late now," he said roughly. Then he made himself smile. "We'll both work on Lowell. He can give you a room full of great-grandchildren!"

"I'd like that!" She nodded, and they sat there talking until he grew weary and she left the hospital.

"You and Uncle Mark have gotten real close, haven't you, Rooney?"

"Why, I guess so, Lowell. I hurt for him so bad sometimes,

but he never complains."

Rooney and Lowell were in a small barn that was used for grain storage. Rooney was sitting in the midst of a pile of colorful dresses she was separating. Against the dull grays of the sacks of feed, the yellows, greens, and scarlets of the dresses lent a holiday atmosphere. There had been not so much as a square inch of space to be had in war-crowded Richmond, so Susanna had insisted that they do their work at Gracefield. "You can work on that old wagon with Box, and Rooney and I can do the dresses."

It had worked out very well. Box, the elderly blacksmith at Gracefield, had taken over the construction of the wagon and machinery that made the gas, and it amused both Susanna and Rooney to watch the tall, dignified slave boss Lowell around in a lordly fashion. Lowell didn't care, for he admired Box. "That man's got more sense than Jefferson Davis's whole cabinet!" he had often said of Box.

Rooney had managed to keep her identity and her poor background a secret, but she lived in fear that she would be found out. Buck had been puzzled by her long absences, and she had not enlightened him. Studs Mulvaney had interrogated her, but she had told him only that she was helping with the wounded men at Chimborazo. This satisfied the big man, for he knew the hotel wasn't a place for a girl such as her. But he had given her a warning: "Better take a stick to Buck. He's running with some pretty tough boys."

Now as Rooney sat surrounded by the colorful silk dresses,

she thought of her brother. *I've got to stay home more, spend more time with him.* She spoke her thoughts to Lowell, saying, "I've got to stay close to home for a while."

"Your aunt's not doing so well?" he asked at once.

"N–no," Rooney stammered. She had always hated lies and deceit, and it hurt to be dishonest with Lowell. She had come to know the Rocklins enough to know that they were people who put a great premium on truth and honor. But she could not think of another way. *It'll only be for a little while,* she thought. *Then he'll get his balloon made, and he'll never see me again.*

This thought hurt her, and she turned to the dresses, saying, "I'll have to take all the stitches out of all of these. It's going to be slow, but I'll do the best I can."

"We'll have to get you some help." A thought came to Lowell, and he said, "I know. We'll get Rena. She's due home this afternoon. Been on a visit with Melora Yancy." Suddenly he snapped his fingers. "What's wrong with me? We'll ask Melora and her sister Rose to come and help." Reaching down, he pulled Rooney to her feet, saying, "We need a little vacation anyhow."

Rooney protested but was glad to get outside. Lowell took the big carriage, and Susanna was excited by the idea. As they drove out, Lowell said, "Grandmother needs more company. She thinks a lot of Melora and Rose."

"Who are they? Do they own a plantation?"

"Oh no, just a small farm. Father and Buford Yancy are raising hogs together." He hesitated, wondering how much to tell this girl about his father and Melora. It would not do to tell her about the tangled skeins of his family history. He had known of his father's love for Melora Yancy for a long time, but he knew, as well, that his father had been completely faithful to his mother. The thought of his mother, Ellen, was painful, for she had been a weak woman. Finally he said, "My mother died nine months ago. And now my father and Melora are engaged."

Rooney asked, "Are the Yancys planters?"

"The Yancys are poor, but proud as any princes. Most of the older boys are in the army. Only four left at home now. Melora, she raised the whole bunch after her mother died."

Just before noon they arrived at the Yancy place. Melora came out, and Rooney saw at once that she was much younger than Clay Rocklin. She had never seen a prettier woman, however, and as soon as she got down and was introduced, Melora smiled at her, saying, "I'm glad you've taken this young man in hand, Rooney. His father's about to give up on him." Then she laughed and gave Lowell a resounding kiss. "I guess if I'm going to be your stepmother, I've got a right to do that!" Then she turned to say, "Don't you do that, Rose; he's a ladies' man." Rose Yancy was a seventeen-year-old image of her older sister. She smiled shyly at Lowell, who laughed at her and gave her a hug despite her protests. Another girl of thirteen named Martha came to greet them, and a boy of eleven.

"Where's Buford?" Lowell asked Melora.

"Down with the hogs." A dimple appeared in the dark-haired woman's face, and she added with a light in her fine eyes, "I think Pa's prouder of any of those hogs than he is of us." She motioned toward the rear of the cabin, saying, "Rena and Josh are with him. Why don't you go take a look at the critters, Lowell? I'll entertain Rooney."

Lowell set off for the hog pen accompanied by the children, and when he was out of hearing, Melora asked, "How is he, Rooney? His wound?"

"Oh, not bad at all, Miss Yancy. It hurts some, but soon he'll be good as new."

"That's good news—and call me Melora." She smiled and shook her head. "That young man has got you in on some wild scheme, Clay tells me. Come on in and have some fresh milk while you tell me about it."

Never had Rooney felt so at ease with a person as she did with Melora Yancy. There was something in the dark-haired woman's manner that made her feel comfortable. At Melora's urging, she related her experience in the hospital, including her care of Lowell and Mark.

Melora had the gift of silence and sat across the table listening carefully, her full attention on the girl. Clay had told her about Rooney, and others had mentioned her, too, so she was pleased to find that they had not exaggerated the girl's simple manners and fair beauty.

Finally Rooney ended her tale. "And so we've got to make this balloon for General Longstreet, and Lowell's come to ask if you and Rose can come and help with it." She hesitated, then added, "I don't think that's really the reason he wants you to come, though."

"No?"

"I think he sees how lonesome his grandmother is since her husband died. She needs some friends around to get her mind off her grief. And since you will be family. . ."

Melora smiled. "Did Lowell tell you how his father and I met?"

"No, he didn't," Rooney answered. Her eyes grew big. "Was it romantic?"

"Oh my, no!" Melora paused. "Well, not in the normal sense of the word. We met twenty-three years ago when I was just a little girl. He was real sick, and my family and I nursed him back to health."

Melora continued for twenty minutes, filling in the details of their lives from that first encounter to Clay's troubled marriage, his life as a wanderer, and his prodigal return to Gracefield. "He joined the army to prove to Lowell that he wasn't unfaithful to Ellen," Melora said. Then she looked full in Rooney's face. "I've been in love with Clay Rocklin since I was six years old, and I always will be. He's the best man I know, Rooney. He and I have nothing to be ashamed of. We're both Christians and have kept our friendship through a lot of trouble. You'll hear gossip, of course, but I can come to Clay as his wife knowing that both of us were faithful to God."

Rooney was entranced. She'd never heard anything like what Melora had just told her. "I hope you'll both be happy," she said quietly. "Will you—" She broke off as voices came from outside and only had time to say, "Thank you for telling me."

She had a fine time, and as she and Lowell left in the late afternoon, they had Melora's promise to be at Gracefield in two days. She smiled at Rena, who was standing beside Josh. "That is, if we can get Rena out of the pigpen. Josh has made a farmer out of her." She added quietly, "Josh is smart—but he stutters so that he hardly says a word. Rena's been good for him."

Rena Rocklin had come as a surprise to Rooney. She was like Clay, but still unique. They had spoken once when they'd gone to the well for water. Rena had asked about Mark, then had said, "Have you seen my father?"

There was a note in the girl's voice that caught Rooney's attention. *She's very close to him,* she thought. *Guess she's even a little afraid now that she doesn't have a mother.* "I haven't seen him for a week, but Lowell said he'll come when you get there." She saw the relief wash over Rena's face and knew her guess had been right.

Lowell put Rooney in the carriage, and they pulled out, waving good-byes and nodding at the Yancys' promises to be at Gracefield soon.

"That was so nice, Lowell."

"The Yancys are the best there is," Lowell answered. He kept her entertained for most of the journey by telling her tales of hunts and good times the Rocklins and the Yancys had enjoyed.

When they were five miles from home, darkness caught up with them. Lowell stopped at a creek to let the team drink and then turned to her. "Are you tired, Rooney?"

"Oh no. I never get tired."

They sat there, and the silence fell over them like a soft blanket. Far off a dog barked, and in the thicket next to the creek, something moved through the thick brush. Overhead the darkening sky was spangled with what seemed to be millions of cold, twinkling lights. Lowell looked up at them in silence, then said quietly, "God outdid Himself making all those, didn't He?"

"I've never seen so many!"

They sat there listening to the faint sounds that floated to them. They spoke rarely, and finally Lowell said, "I'm glad you're not one of those talking women, Rooney—one of those who can't bear a minute's silence."

She turned to him, and her large eyes caught the reflection of the moon. "I like it quiet," she said and smiled at him.

He put his arm around her and gave her shoulders a squeeze, much as he might have done with a young male friend. "You've helped me a lot, Rooney. I've been meaning to tell you how much I appreciate it."

"Why, I haven't done anything, Lowell." She was acutely conscious of the pressure of his arm on her shoulder, but felt strangely safe with this young man.

"Yes, you have," he contradicted her. "You took care of me in the hospital, and of Uncle Mark. And you came up with the idea of dresses for the silk. And you've been good to my grandmother." He nodded and squeezed her arm, adding, "That's a lot, Rooney!"

"I like doing things that please you, Lowell."

Her face, glowing in the silvery moonlight, filled his sight—and he became aware that the shoulder on which his hand rested was firm and rounded and warm—not at all like that of a hunting companion. Her face was only inches away from his, and he thought of Rooney Smith as an attractive and desirable young woman, not as a helper in a scheme!

Her hair was fragrant with soap, and her body lay firmly in the simple dress she wore. A vitality came from her, and her smile had a warmth that had some sort of promise. It was not the easy manner of some young women, for there was a virginal freshness about this girl that was very attractive in his sight. He'd not been much for girls, partly because most of them he'd courted had been too casual and even easy.

But not Rooney. She faced him with open eyes, and he put his free hand on her arm, pulling her around to face him. She watched him with surprise dawning in her eyes, but there was no fear. He drew her in and kissed her, his mouth resting lightly on her soft lips. He felt her innocence, yet there was a response in her lips that told him that she was a woman who had love to give.

When he drew back, he watched the expression pass over her face; he saw the generosity of her mouth, the glow of her eyes, and since he was a young man keenly aware of beauty, he found it hard to speak.

"You're a sweet girl, Rooney," he whispered finally. He released her at once as she drew back, and he asked, "You're not afraid of me, are you?"

"No—never of you." Rooney's voice was gentle and warm

in the night air, and though she said no more, Lowell knew that she had been stirred by the kiss—as he had.

Speaking to the team, he drove down the silver ribbon of road, and when he let her out at the front door, she smiled at him, saying, "Good night, Lowell. Thank you for taking me."

He nodded, said good night, then put up the team. It was late, and his grandmother was in bed. His wound hurt, but that was not what kept him awake. He thought for a long time about that moment at the creek—and knew that he would never forget it.

❧

President Jefferson Davis had proclaimed March 27, 1863, to be a national day of fasting and prayer. When that day came, all over the South men and women met in groups or sought a place of solitude to seek God. Never had the people faced such a crisis, and they responded by calling on God with fervor.

Lowell had found the streets of Richmond relatively bare and was told that most people were home praying. He went at once to Chimborazo, where Matron Pember welcomed him into her small office. When he asked about Rooney, she said, "Why, I can't say, Mr. Rocklin. She hasn't been in for three days now." A slight frown crossed her brow, and she added, "It's not like her. She's always been so faithful."

"Do you know where she lives?"

"Why, I don't really. She's never spoken of her home life. I thought *you* might know."

Lowell shook his head. "All I know is that she lives with an invalid aunt. And I don't even know her last name—Aunt Lillian is all I've heard Rooney call her."

Mrs. Pember was sympathetic and even worried. "Your uncle misses her greatly, as do all the men in the ward."

"Maybe she told him her aunt's name," Lowell said hopefully. He bid Mrs. Pember good-bye, urging her to get in touch with him if Rooney came back to the hospital. He went at once to see Mark and found him sitting up in a rocking chair. "Well, you're looking spry as a spring chicken," he said at once.

"I'm better, I guess. But still not able to get out of here."

"Do you know where Rooney lives?" Lowell burst out. "I haven't seen her for nearly a week."

"Why, no, Lowell, I have no idea." Mark's face was drawn with pain, and when he moved, it was slowly and with care. "Do you think something's happened to her?"

"Oh, I've got no reason to think that, but it's got me worried." His uncle, he saw, was concerned, too, and he put the best face he could on the problem. "Maybe Aunt Lillian needs some extra care at home, and Rooney can't get away. . . ." Lowell visited for an hour, then left the hospital.

All the next day he roamed the streets, visiting old friends and always asking if they knew a sickly woman named Lillian. He had no success and on the second day gave up. He was preparing to go back to Gracefield and carry on with the work, but before he left, he ran across an old friend, Dan Whitter. Whitter was a reporter for the Richmond *Examiner* and insisted that the two of them have dinner.

"Got to go by the court first, Lowell," Whitter explained. "Got a big case comin' up, my first time to cover one. Won't take long, though; then we'll go eat."

Lowell agreed, and the two of them made their way through the streets of Richmond. It was a crowded, bustling place filled with soldiers on leave, businessmen, and workers from the factories. Whitter led Lowell to the courthouse, which was not as crowded as the bars and saloons.

"Wait here, Lowell." Whitter nodded at one of the many empty seats in the courtroom, where a small scattering of visitors watched the processes of the court. "Won't be but a few minutes."

"Sure, Dan. Take your time."

Lowell settled down on one of the worn benches, pulled a copy of the *Examiner* from his pocket, and began to read. It was filled with stories of the war and little else. Jefferson Davis, he saw, was under attack—which was not unusual; the president of the Confederacy was a man who made firm friends and hard enemies. Vicksburg continued to resist Union naval attacks. Lowell thought, *As long as Vicksburg stands, we still can get supplies. If it falls, the Federals will have control of all of the Mississippi River—and cut our Confederacy in half.*

A woman's angry voice interrupted the stillness of the courtroom, and Lowell looked up to see a hard-faced woman with dyed hair being brought in forcibly by one of the officials. The judge said angrily, "You just behave yourself, woman! You're in trouble enough."

The woman screamed an obscenity at the judge, who shouted, "I hold you in contempt of court and sentence you to pay a fine of ten dollars! Now set her down and gag her if she don't shut up!"

The bailiff took the judge's words literally, forcing the woman to sit down and stating loudly enough for everyone to hear, "If you don't shut, I'll shut you!"

Lowell shook his head, for the sordid scene displeased him. He had lifted his paper and was about to begin reading when another bailiff entered with two prisoners, a young woman and a small boy.

The world suddenly seemed to stop—for the young girl was Rooney Smith! Lowell had been stunned no more by cannon fire at Malvern Hill than he was by the sight of Rooney! He dropped the newspaper, and his face grew pale as the judge began to read out the charge of attempted homicide. Clara Smith had been involved in a knifing at the Royal.

After reading the charges, the judge asked, "Do you have a lawyer, Clara Smith?"

"No, I ain't."

"Well, the court will have to appoint one." He looked at the young people. "Who are these children?" he asked. The bailiff coughed and said, "Children of the accused, Your Honor."

"Well, the case is put off until a lawyer can be found. Put it down for two weeks from today. The woman will remain in custody."

Clara Smith began shouting but was taken out at once by

the heavyset bailiff. Rooney turned to follow her, but the bailiff said, "You can visit her in jail, miss."

Rooney turned and spoke to Buck, and the two of them walked slowly down the aisle toward the door. When they were halfway there, Rooney saw Lowell—and stopped dead still. Her lips began to tremble, and her eyes were tragic.

Lowell stared at her but could not bring himself to say a word. He was shocked so deeply that all he could do was stare at the two. He saw her waiting, and for one instant he was on the verge of going to her. She looked so tiny and so vulnerable! Then he thought of what it would seem like to the citizens of the court, and word would get back to his family. Of course his unit would hear of it—there was no secrecy in this sort of thing.

Rooney saw the struggle going on in Lowell, saw his face draw with shame and anger. Her heart beat faster as he seemed almost ready to come to her.

But he dropped his head—and Rooney knew it was over. "Come on, Buck," she whispered and led him away. She held her head high, and her eyes were dry—but sorrow and shame were cutting her inside like a razor!

"And you didn't go to her? You let her walk out of that courtroom without speaking?"

Lowell blinked his eyes in shock as Mark Rocklin's words slashed at him. He went to Chimborazo the morning after the trial, and when he reported the event to his uncle, fire burned in Mark Rocklin's eyes. Scorn dripped from his pale lips as he gave Lowell Rocklin a tongue-lashing such as that young man had never received!

"You're so *holy*, aren't you!" Mark stabbed with his voice as he might have lunged with his fists if he'd been able. "You've never done anything wrong, not the great and pure Lowell Rocklin!" On and on he spoke until Lowell was pale and his hands trembled.

When his uncle stopped speaking, Lowell cleared his throat and blurted, "Well, I just couldn't *think*, Uncle Mark!" He hadn't slept a wink, and all night long he'd wrestled with anger at Rooney—and guilt for doing just what Mark accused him of. Now he took out his handkerchief and wiped his brow. "I mean, why didn't she *tell* me what kind of—"

"And you've shown *exactly* what you would've done if she had, haven't you, Lowell." Mark had been a rough man, and now his eyes were deadly. He loved the young man who stood trembling before him, but he was angry to the bone. The pain struck his stomach, and he paused, holding his breath as it tore through him.

Lowell saw the face of the older man stiffen and asked, "Is it bad?" knowing that it was. When Mark didn't speak, he sat down on a chair and twisted his hands, his brow knitted. "I—I was wrong, Uncle Mark."

Mark saw the trouble on the boy's unlined face. *He's still young. He thinks everyone is just what they seem to be.* The pain subsided, and Mark took a slow breath. "You made a mistake, my boy. But we all do that." Bitterness twisted his lips, and he said, "I've done much worse. But the difference is that I can't do anything about mine—you *can*!"

Lowell looked up hopefully and, seeing the compassion in Mark Rocklin's dark eyes, said, "I will, Uncle Mark! I'll find her and help her all I can!"

"Do it quick, boy! That girl needs help!"

Lowell stood up and left almost at a run, leaving Mark exhausted and wrestling with the pain. *Don't run from your woes, my boy!* he thought. *I found out a long time ago that's a sure way to ruin your life—and the lives of everybody around you!*

❧

"I need to see Miss Rooney Smith."

Studs Mulvaney looked down at the young man who'd come into the saloon and asked for the manager, took his cigar from his thick lips, and demanded, "What for?" It was only ten in the morning, and the saloon was empty—only Bugs was up and moving slowly around.

"Why. . .I–I'm a friend of hers," Lowell stammered. "She's in trouble, and I want to help her and her brother."

Mulvaney considered the fine clothing and the clean-cut face of the young man. He knew that Clara would be in jail for some time, and he had worried about Rooney and Buck. *This young fellow,* he thought, *could give some help.*

"Come on," he said abruptly.

Feeling as self-conscious as he had ever felt, Lowell followed the big man up the stairs. They passed several women who stared at him hard-eyed, but he ignored them as best he could.

Mulvaney opened a door leading into what appeared to be a closet, called out, "Rooney, come down here." He turned to glare at Lowell, his cigar making a circle as he shifted it. "Be careful with these kids, sonny," he said quietly. "I wouldn't like them to get in no trouble. They got enough of that as it is."

Then Rooney appeared, and her face grew still as she saw Lowell. Studs glanced at her, saying, "This a friend of yours, Rooney?"

"I. . .know him."

As soon as Mulvaney moved away, Lowell said hastily, "Rooney, you can't stay in this place!"

"Buck and me don't have anyplace else to go."

Lowell had made no plans for helping the pair. He had come out of shame heaped on him by his uncle. Now that he stood there, he found himself with a blank mind. "I. . .didn't mean to ignore you—at the court, I mean." When she didn't answer, he hastened to add, "I had no idea you were in trouble."

"There's no way you could have known." Rooney was confused but said the one thing she wanted to say to the young man. "I lied to you. . .about my family. I'm sorry for that."

Lowell blinked and said instantly, "Oh, don't worry about that!"

"I never wanted to lie to you, but. . ."

She looked very young and helpless, but Lowell couldn't

forget that she *had* lied to him. *I'll help her—but it won't be the same,* was the thought that came to him.

"Look, you can't stay here. This is no place for you—nor for your brother." Desperately he tried to think of something. "I know! You can stay at Gracefield."

"No, I can't go there!"

The vehemence of her reply startled Lowell. "Why not?"

"I—I couldn't face your family!"

Lowell said, "Rooney, it was Uncle Mark who told me to come and find you. My grandmother loves you, and so will the others."

Rooney was in a terrible position. She hated the thought of staying in the hotel, though Mulvaney had assured her she could. It was Buck she feared for the most, not herself.

If I could just get Buck out of here and on a farm, just for a little while!

"You and I could finish the balloon," Lowell said quickly. "It might not be forever, but for now you and the boy ought to get out of here."

"I'll have to do it," Rooney whispered. "When do you want us to come?"

"Why, right now!" Lowell answered. He wanted to get the two out of the Royal as quickly as possible. "We can be at Gracefield a little after noon."

Rooney looked startled but knew that it might be best. "I'll get Buck," she said.

When she turned to the ladder, Lowell said quickly, "I guess we'd better understand one thing, Rooney." She turned to look at him, and he knew he had to say the thing clearly. "About us—you and me—we'll just be working together. You know what I mean?"

Rooney looked at Lowell. "Yes," she said quietly, "I know what you mean, Mr. Rocklin."

She left him then, and somehow there was a rebuke in her words. *"Mr. Rocklin."* Why was her use of that name so hard? She was back soon with the boy. "This is my brother, Buck. This is Mr. Rocklin, Buck."

Lowell nodded to the boy, forced a smile, and said, "You'll be staying with us for a time, Buck. I hope you'll like it there."

"Yes, sir." Buck said nothing more but just watched Lowell very carefully.

Lowell led them to the buggy he'd brought to town, and they rode out of town at a fast trot. None of them spoke, and the silence grew heavy and uncomfortable.

Lowell glanced at Rooney and saw that her cheeks were pale as she stared straight ahead. *I've hurt her, but she's hurt me, too!*

But the thought didn't give him any comfort, and as the team carried the buggy out of Richmond, Lowell was filled with uncertainty.

Got to get that balloon built and get back to the real war, he thought as he sat awkwardly on the seat, trying not to touch the girl who sat beside him.

PART TWO

Lowell

CHAPTER 8

DRESSES FOR THE CAUSE

Rooney would never forget the day she and Buck arrived at Gracefield. The trip from Richmond had been strained and silent, with Lowell speaking only briefly. Buck, Rooney knew, was gripped with apprehension, and as she sat beside him, she took his hand and squeezed it. He gave her a worried smile but said nothing all the way to the Rocklin plantation.

When they pulled up in front of the house, Rooney felt the boy stiffen. "It's all right, Buck," she whispered as Lowell got out and handed the lines to Highboy. "These are real nice people—you'll see!"

Lowell hesitated, wondering how to break the news of these two guests to his grandmother. *I hope she's not going to be too mad*, he thought. *I have to see her alone.*

"Rooney, you might like to show Buck around the place while I go find Grandmother."

"All right." Turning to Buck, she said, "Come on. I'll show

you the horses." As they walked away, Buck looked fearfully over his shoulder as the man disappeared into the house.

"Rooney, they won't let us stay here!"

Now that they were actually on the grounds, Rooney privately thought the same. She let none of her doubt show, however, but made herself say cheerfully, "Don't worry. You'll like Miz Rocklin, Mister Lowell's grandmother. Come on, now, let's look at the horses. I'll bet Mister Lowell will let you ride one of them."

Buck shook his head doubtfully, saying, "I don't think they'll let us stay. We'd better go back to the Royal." His thin face grew tense, and he asked, "What if Ma comes back and we're not there?"

She won't come back—she'll be in jail, Rooney thought. Rooney had spoken with Studs, who knew about such things, and he'd told her that Clara would be sentenced for a short term. "Not too long," he'd added, seeing the stricken look on her face. "Jail's too small, and she didn't actually kill the fellow. You can stay here, Rooney. Don't worry about that."

Rooney set out to convince Buck that they would keep in touch with their mother, but the burden was heavy on his thin young shoulders. "Mr. Mulvaney promised to send word when Ma gets back," she said, then added brightly as they came to the pasture, "See that big black horse? That's King. Isn't he something. . . ?"

Inside the house Lowell had found his grandmother sewing in the library. Without preamble he said, "Grandmother, I've got something to tell you."

Susanna looked up quickly and, seeing the worry on her grandson's face, put her sewing down and said quietly, "Sit down, Lowell, and tell me about it."

Lowell was too tense to sit down, but walked up and down as he related the history. From time to time he cast a worried eye at the woman but saw nothing but serenity there. Finally he got to the end. Drawing his handkerchief out, he wiped his brow, saying nervously, "I—I didn't know what to do, Grandmother. I hated to leave them in that terrible place, so. . ."

When Lowell broke off, struggling for words, Susanna said calmly, "Well, Lowell, I hope you had sense enough to bring them here. I would love to have them."

A look of relief swept across Lowell's face. "I did, Grandmother. But I was sort of afraid to tell you." Now that the worst was over, he came over and sat down beside her on the horsehair couch. "I mean—it's asking a lot to take in two youngsters for I don't know how long—"

"Nonsense!" Susanna said firmly. Placing her sewing basket to one side, she reached over and took Lowell's hand, pressing it warmly. "I'm proud of you, Lowell. You have a good heart."

Lowell flushed, thinking of how he'd turned from Rooney in the courtroom. "Well, I–I'm not sure about that," he muttered. Then he shrugged his shoulders, asking, "Do you want me to bring them here?"

"No, I'll go with you." She got to her feet, and compassion shone in her eyes. "The poor things! What a terrible thing for them to go through! We'll have to be very kind to both of them, Lowell."

The two of them went out on the porch, and Lowell said, "They're looking at the horses, I think." He led the way, and turning the corner of the big barn, he said, "There they are."

Susanna studied the pair who turned to face them. The boy was thin and tense, with a look of defiance in his dark brown eyes. When Lowell introduced her, she said at once, "My, how nice it'll be to have some new faces around! I get so lonesome on this old place." Smiling at Buck, she said, "Most of my menfolk are gone to the war, Buck. Do you think you could learn to drive me to town in the buggy?"

Buck blinked with surprise, and some of the tension left him. "Oh yes, I can drive some, Miz Rocklin!" he replied eagerly.

"Well, you and I will be going quite a bit, I expect." Susanna turned to Rooney and, seeing the humiliation in the girl's dark blue eyes, set herself to put the girl at ease. "Rooney, Lowell tells me you're going to have a long visit with us?"

"Y—yes, ma'am."

"Well, I think that's grand! And I know just the place for you." Turning to Lowell, she said, "The old summerhouse, Lowell."

"Why, that's just the thing!" Lowell felt a wave of relief come over him and turned to say to the girl, "It's real private, Rooney. You and Buck can fix it up however you want. Come on, I'll take you there."

"I'll just go along. Rooney and I can see what the inside

needs," Susanna said. "You and Buck here can do the man's work." She smiled at Buck, saying, "It's down that little lane there. Suppose you drive us all there?"

Buck nodded eagerly, "Yes, ma'am!" he said, color tinging his pale cheeks. When the four of them returned to the buggy, Lowell helped his grandmother into the front, then gave Rooney a hand into the back. She kept her eyes from him, saying quietly, "Thank you."

Buck scrambled into the driver's seat, unwound the lines, and looked at the lane. "Down through them trees, Miz Rocklin?"

"Yes. Now don't go too fast," she said, smiling at him. She complimented him on his driving skill and was pleased at the way she found to make him feel more comfortable. *Poor little chap,* she thought as they passed through the lane formed by huge oak trees. *How little he has! But he's got good stuff in him— and so has Rooney!*

At the end of the lane, Rooney saw a small frame house nestled under a grove of pines. Buck pulled the horses to a stop and turned to Susanna. "Did I do all right?" he asked anxiously.

"Why, I should say so! I don't know of a man who could do better! I'd trust you to take me to Richmond right now!" Susanna patted his arm; then Lowell leaped to the ground and helped the women down. Looking around, Susanna shook her head. "Grounds need work—and the inside might be a mess."

At that moment a big dog dashed out of the woods, barking excitedly. "Get down, Buck!" Lowell snapped as the huge animal reared up and pawed at his shirt with muddy paws. "Now look at the mess you've made!"

"His name is the same as mine?" Buck asked Susanna with surprise.

"Yes, he's my granddaughter's dog."

"Can I pet him?"

"Of course, but he'll worry you to death."

Buck loved animals, and when he put his hand on the big dog's broad head, that was all it took. The dog leaped up, licking his face and pawing at him frantically.

"You two can do some hunting together," Lowell said. "He's a pretty good coon dog when he wants to be." Still feeling awkward with Rooney, he suggested, "Maybe you and I could tag along, Rooney."

"That would be nice!" Rooney was so pleased at the place and at Buck's pleasure that she forgot some of the painful interview she'd had with Lowell at the Royal.

Then they entered the cabin, and Rooney gasped. "Oh, this is so *nice!*" she exclaimed. It was small with only one main room. It housed a small kitchen off to one side and had a door leading to a bedroom. The main room was well furnished with a couch, a table, and several bookcases. "This is where Clay lived for a while," Susanna said. "He and Rena made it over like it is now. It's been pretty much empty since the beginning of the war, but Rena still comes here from time to time to read."

"Oh, I wouldn't want to put her out!"

"She'll be glad to have you. She and the dog will be with

you half the time. You two girls will have a good time, and you'll have to look out for them, Buck—and take care of your namesake, that pesky dog!"

"I'll take care of him!" Buck spoke up at once. "Can I go outside and play with him?"

"Of course! Lowell, you go with them. Show Buck. . .well, I guess we'll have to rename one of you." Susanna smiled. "When I call for Buck, I don't want that old dog coming to answer me."

"I'll be Buck Number One," Buck said. He smiled happily, the first smile Lowell or Susanna had seen from him. "That ol' dog can be Buck Number Two!"

Susanna and Rooney went over the small cabin after Lowell and the boy left. Susanna said nothing about the circumstances that brought them, speaking only of practical things about the summerhouse.

But when they had gone over the place, Rooney slowly turned to Susanna, saying, "Miss Susanna—I lied to you and Lowell."

Susanna knew better than to cut the girl off. People, she knew, had to get things out sometimes, so she stood there listening as Rooney struggled through her confession. *Better to let her get it all out—then we can put it behind us.*

When Rooney finished, saying miserably, "I didn't want to lie, but it just—it just came out that way," tears came to her eyes, and she whispered, "Maybe you don't want a liar livin' on your place!"

Susanna moved forward and took the girl in her arms. At

once Rooney threw her arms around the older woman and began to weep. Susanna held the slight form of the girl, patting her shoulder and murmuring sympathetic phrases. Susanna Rocklin was a strong woman, but part of her strength was her compassionate heart. Now as the girl's body was racked with sobs, she thought, *She's never had a mother to love her. I'm glad she's come here. She needs me!*

Finally the sobs diminished, and Susanna took a handkerchief from her pocket. "Now that's over!" she announced firmly, drying the girl's face. "We women have to do things like that once in a while, don't we?" A wry smile touched her lips. "I wish men had sense enough to cry things out!"

"Nobody ever was so kind!"

"No more of that!" Susanna turned the mood quickly. "What do you think about these curtains? I've got some in the attic that will look a lot better than these. Come along, and we'll go see what we have...."

"But—but, Father, think what it *looks* like!"

Clay stared at Lowell, who had appeared in the study of the Big House. "I don't see any problem," he said shortly. He had been assigned recruiting duty and had found it almost worse than battle! But it did enable him to get home, so he didn't complain much. He'd come into the study to work on the books when Lowell had burst in, anxiety on his face, saying, "Do you know what Rooney's doing?" Then without waiting for an answer, he'd exclaimed, "She's going around to the dance hall girls in Richmond asking for their dresses!"

That was when Clay had stared at Lowell. "Well, you have to have them, don't you?"

"Well. . .yes, sir, we do, but not from—from *those* women!"

Clay put his pencil down, leaned on the desk, and studied the agitated face of this son of his. Lowell, he knew, had more family feeling than the twins—that is, he was more concerned about the position of the Rocklin family. *He worries too much about how things look,* Clay thought, hoping Lowell would be able to cease thinking about what other people thought, just as he had eventually learned to do. He was tempted to tell Lowell he was too fussy but knew that wouldn't do.

"Look, Lowell," he said calmly, "in a war we have to do all kinds of things we wouldn't think of doing in better times." He saw the stubbornness on Lowell's face and said a little more stridently, "You ever think your grandmother would be digging up old outhouses?"

This was being done all over the South, for niter for gunpowder could not be imported, and there was no other source. Noting the embarrassed look on his son's face, Clay said gently, "Do you think I *like* having my mother involved in things like that?"

"No, sir, of course not!"

"So Rooney is just doing what you asked her to do, isn't she? Getting silk for your balloon?" Clay leaned back in his chair, his face lined with fatigue. He took his job as a captain in

907

the Richmond Grays seriously and had missed many hours of sleep trying to put C Company back together after battles. "I think you ought to commend her for finding a way to make the project happen," he commented quietly.

Lowell dropped his eyes and, after standing silently, looked up. "I suppose you're right, sir—but it's humiliating!"

Clay rose and came to put his hand on Lowell's shoulder. "I know, son, but it's for the Cause. Try to think of it like that." He smiled, his teeth very white against his tanned skin. "I'm proud of you for doing this. Most wounded men just sit around and wait—but you've worked hard on this idea."

The praise brought a flush to Lowell's cheeks, but he said only, "Well, guess I'll go tell Rooney to go ahead with the crazy scheme." A wry smile touched his lips, and as he left, Clay heard him mutter, "Doesn't matter much—that stubborn girl's going to do it anyway!"

As the two men were talking, Rena and Rooney were in the barn, sitting among billowing silk. Assisted by Rose and Melora, they had cut the dresses carefully into the patterns laid out by Lowell. Now with the Yancy women back home, the sewing fell to Rena and Rooney. Rena looked up from a seam she was working on and put her gaze on Rooney. "Do you think Lowell will let you go get more dresses from Richmond? He was awful mad at you for going to those places!"

"We have to have the silk, don't we?"

Rena studied the face of Rooney thoughtfully. She had grown very fond of her but was puzzled by her at the same time.

"What's it like in those places—the bars and saloons, Rooney? Do you ever see any of the bad women?"

Rooney's hand slipped, and a flush came to her cheeks. "Didn't you know, Rena? My mother is a dance hall woman."

A gasp came from Rena's lips, and her face contorted with embarrassment. "Why, Rooney!" she whispered in agony. "Nobody told me!"

"I should have told you myself," Rooney said. She looked up and saw Rena's face. "Oh, Rena!" she cried and then leaped up and went to the girl, for tears were running down her cheeks. "Don't cry! It's nothing to cry about!" She sat down beside Rena, assuring her over and over that she wasn't hurt. "I'm used to it, you see. It's the only life I've ever known." Then to avoid future problems, she quickly sketched her family history for the girl, ending by saying, "I'm so grateful to your brother for helping Buck and me. So don't you be sad, you hear?"

Finally Rena calmed down, and the two girls sat there working on the silk that slipped through their fingers sibilantly. Rooney was aware that Rena was troubled but waited quietly for her to speak of it. Finally Rena said with her eyes dropped to her hands, "My. . .my mother wasn't a good woman!"

"Oh, Rena!"

"She had. . .men friends," Rena said, and when she did lift her eyes, there was misery in them. "And I hated her—and now she's dead!" This was a thought that never completely left this girl, and no matter what anyone said, a heavy guilt lay deep inside her spirit.

"Do you want to tell me about it, Rena?" Rooney asked gently. And then, perhaps because Rooney had the same problem, Rena opened herself, speaking of her miserable childhood. She'd never been able to talk to anyone fully—they were all too close. But Rooney was her own age, and she talked for a long time. Finally she said, "Do you think God will ever forgive me, Rooney?"

"Oh, Rena, I don't think God holds it against you!"

"I hope not," Rena whispered. Then she heard someone coming and said quickly, "Thanks for listening to me, Rooney—it's a help!"

And then the door opened and Lowell entered. He saw the expression on his sister's face and thought, *She's been crying*, but said nothing. *She's probably been thinking about Mother again.* Then he saw that there was a light expression on Rena's face that had been absent, and it came to him that it was good for her to have a girl her own age to talk to.

"Well, you can go get the dresses, Rooney," he said, then blustered, "but I'm going with you!"

Rooney stared at him, knowing how angry he'd been at her actions. "Why, you don't have to do that, Lowell," she said. "Buck and me can do it."

"No, if it's got to be done, I'm going with you. Get ready, and we'll go this morning."

Lowell turned and left, and Rena said, "Lowell's about as stubborn as a man can get. I didn't think he'd ever change his mind about those dresses." A smile touched her lips, and she nodded. "I'll bet Daddy shamed him—or maybe Grandmother."

"I guess so." Rooney dropped a bright green section of silk, rose, and said, "It makes me feel bad, Rena. I hate to humble him, going to all those places."

"He wouldn't do it if he didn't want to, not Lowell." Rena stared at the girl across the table and nodded. "He likes you a lot, Rooney. I can tell."

Rooney looked up at the girl quickly, then shook her head. "No, I don't think so, Rena." Then she turned and left, saying, "We'll get enough to finish it—and he'll be glad when I'm gone!"

CHAPTER 9

ROONEY TAKES A RIDE

I hope the Yankees don't have any spies around here," Susanna Rocklin remarked. "If they do, they won't have any trouble getting a report on this contraption of yours, Lowell."

The field in which Rocklin stood was crowded with spectators, so many of them that Lowell had been forced to beg them to move back so that they wouldn't interfere with the launching of the balloon. There had been no announcement of the event, but somehow word had gotten out so that even before Lowell and Rooney had appeared, neighbors had arrived.

Lowell, who was working on the gas-generating machinery, looked around at the onlookers, then muttered to his grandmother, "I wish they'd all go home!"

"That's not very likely. People around here, they've been talking about my eccentric grandson for days now. None of them's ever seen a man fly, and they wouldn't miss it for anything." She stared at the wagon with its maze of iron pots and winding coils of copper tubing, adding laconically, "To tell the truth, I'm about as skeptical as the rest of them."

"It's got to work," Lowell said stubbornly. "We've tried it on those small balloons. You saw them fly, didn't you?"

"Well, yes, but that's different from all *this*!"

Lowell turned to look at Rooney and Buck, who were carefully spreading the canopy on the ground as if it were a monstrous bedspread. *Come to think of it,* he thought, *it looks like one of Grandmother's quilts!*

Made completely of small pieces of silk dresses, the canopy in the sparkling sunshine seemed to glitter with every color of the rainbow: scarlet, green, blue, yellow—every hue imaginable! Since it was finished, he thought of the long, arduous hours that the women had put into the project—especially Rooney, who had worked tirelessly on the canopy. She had been adamant about examining every seam, always insisting on double stitching them for strength, and often had rejected some of the work, declaring, "It's got to be *stronger!*"

Lowell shifted his gaze to Rooney, who was wearing a light blue dress trimmed with white lace, and a white straw hat. Excitement made her dark blue eyes flash, and she was chattering like a magpie to Buck as they moved around, pulling and tugging at the colorful material. *Couldn't have done it without those two,* he thought—and regretted the coolness that had come between him and Rooney. He missed their early camaraderie, and a vague sense of regret came to him as he studied her happy expression. *I've got to try to make it up to her,* was his thought, but then he turned his mind to the business of filling the canopy.

"Rooney! Are you and Buck ready?"

"Yes, I think so."

"All right—let's get started."

Lowell checked his gauges, then nodded to Josh, who was standing a few feet away. "All right, Josh, take that hose over and help Rooney and Buck."

"Y–yessir!" Josh exclaimed and, leaping forward, picked up the free end of the flexible tube used to carry the gas from the generating machinery to the canopy. As the lanky boy went into action, Lowell said to his grandmother, "That's a real smart young man. He invented that hose himself."

"Did he, now?" Susanna stared at Josh Yancy and shook her head. "Clay's always said young Josh could make anything under the sun. We'll have to see about giving him some more training, Lowell."

"I think that'd be good. He's got too much potential to spend his life raising pigs." As he watched the boy bend over to insert the end of the tube into the opening in the lower section of the canopy, he chuckled. "That hose has to *bend*, and I couldn't figure out a way to do it. We were talking about it at the Yancy place, and Josh finally came up with the idea of using silk and stiff cord. So I figured he earned himself a spot on the balloon team."

Susanna stared at the six-inch tube that twisted like a snake as the boy maneuvered it into position. "How in the world did that work?"

"Josh got the idea of building it around a small tree. He cut down a six-inch pine and took all the bark off. Then he put some lard all over it and took some pieces of silk that Rooney had left over and covered it with them. Then he wound baling twine around the silk and covered that with glue, and he laid strips of silk over that." Lowell shook his head with admiration. "I never thought it'd work, but when it dried, we grabbed the end and it just slipped right off! Easier than skinning a catfish!"

"He *is* a clever young fellow," Susanna exclaimed. "What happens now?"

"We fill the canopy," Lowell said. Taking a deep breath, he called out, "All ready?"

"All ready!" Rooney answered. She and Buck stood beside the brilliant silk, ready to hold it into place as it filled with gas.

Lowell reached out and moved the lever that allowed the gas to escape from the chambers and felt the tube give a sudden jerk. "Here it comes, Josh!" he called out. Steadily he kept the valve open, watching the gauge for a moment, then turned to look at the canopy.

"It's working!" he exclaimed, seeing the quiltlike layers of silk suddenly rising in the center. A mutter went around the people who were watching, and Lowell grew tense. *Got to be just right—can't go too fast or too slow.*

Rooney and Buck moved quickly around the edges of the canopy, lifting folds to make the inflation easier. Josh held the entry port tightly affixed to the exhaust tube, his face intent as he tried to let none of the gas escape. It had been the best time

915

of his life, working with Lowell and Rooney on this balloon, and he now knew that he would never be happy as a farmer. As the canopy swelled and grew like a small mountain before him, he struggled to his feet, aware that somehow he was going to do things like this—not feed pigs!

"Look at that thing!" A cry went up from Buford Yancy, who had brought his whole family over to watch the show. Buford was tall, lanky, and stronger than most young men, and his mouth dropped open as the balloon swelled before his eyes. "I never seed such!"

Neither had the crowd, for a babble of voices filled the air as the balloon grew larger. They were all simple people, accustomed to only the simplest machinery, and they stood there mystified. And the slaves! Superstitious to the bone, they moved back with fear, one elderly woman muttering, "It's de *debbil*! Dat's whut it is!" But she was not frightened enough to leave, for this was far too exciting to miss, so she moved back a few feet, her eyes fixed on the sight before her.

"Watch the harness!" Lowell called out. He'd seen that as the balloon began to rise, the ropes that held the observation basket were getting tangled. "Grandmother—hold this handle right here!" he ordered.

"What's that?" Susanna was so startled she could hardly speak, but Lowell gave her no chance to object, so she gingerly grasped the handle, staring at it as if it might blow up in her face.

Lowell leaped to free the lines and, seeing that his grandmother seemed to be doing the job, called out, "Hold it right there! I'll help with getting it up!"

Rooney, her heart beating with excitement, ran around freeing the silk. The folds were now free, and she could see that the seams were holding well. "It's working, Buck!" she cried out, and the two of them grinned at each other wildly.

Now the silk canopy was rising, swinging to an upright position. It was not round, but fuller at the top than at the bottom. Lowell had figured out that such an arrangement would give more lift, and there would be less opportunity for the gas to escape.

The slight breeze caught the flowering canopy, and Josh yelled, "I c—can't hold it!" He held on desperately but was losing his hold, Lowell saw.

Lowell yelled, "Highboy! Box! Give a hand!" He'd given careful instructions to these two, who in turn had enlisted ten of the huskiest men on the workforce, and at once they ran to grab the suspension ropes. "Hold it down!" Lowell yelled, wild with excitement. He waited until Josh cried, "She w—won't take any m—more, Mister Lowell!"

"All right!" Lowell leaped back to the wagon, reached around his grandmother, and shut the valve. Then whirling, he leaped back to grab one of the ropes. Rooney and Buck, he noted, were hanging on to ropes along with the slaves.

"Let it go up—slowly, now!"

As they played out the ropes, the balloon rose ten feet into the air, and the small gondola made of woven willow limbs was jerked aloft.

"Let me go up, Lowell!" Rooney cried, her face alive with excitement.

"No!" Lowell had decided that on the first flight there would be no passengers. Instead he had placed four fifty-pound sacks of feed in the gondola. "Nobody's going up the first flight—and I'll be the first one to fly! Now let it go—real slow, now!"

At Lowell's direction, the men played out the suspension ropes. Cries went up from the crowd, and Lowell himself wanted to shout as the balloon rose slowly into the air.

It works! he thought, and he'd never in his life had such a feeling of exultation. The rope slipped through his hands, and he kept the men steady as the balloon rose. Finally it was over a hundred feet in the air and would have gone higher if he had not called out, "That's high enough! Hold it there!"

Carefully he tested his rope and discovered that the slaves held it with ease. Dropping the line, he moved back and stared up at the graceful shape of the balloon as it swayed in the breeze. He discovered that he'd moved close to Rooney, who was staring upward, and without thinking, he suddenly put his arm around her and gave a squeeze.

"We did it, Rooney," he breathed. "We did it!"

Rooney was startled by the sudden hug, and for one moment, she surrendered to it. Looking up, her eyes sparkling, she whispered, "We did, didn't we, Lowell!"

For that one moment, he forgot the balloon, the crowd, and everything else. He was only conscious of the firmness of her shoulder as his hand lay on the thin dress she wore and of the creamy smoothness of her cheeks. Her lips were parted slightly, and her dark blue eyes were enormous.

And then she pulled away, her expression changing, and Lowell felt the wall that was between them—and knew that he was the one who had built it. Hastily he turned his attention to the balloon, and Rooney moved quietly back to stand away from the little group.

Only one person had noticed the scene between Lowell and Rooney—Susanna Rocklin. Her sharp eyes had taken it in, and she had not missed the manner in which Rooney Smith had moved away from her grandson's embrace. She said nothing but on an impulse went to stand beside the girl. When Rooney looked at her, she smiled, saying, "You must be very proud, Rooney."

"Oh—"

"Lowell told me this morning that he could never have done it if it hadn't been for you."

"I didn't do all that much."

Sensing the hurt in the young woman, Susanna said quietly, "He's a very different sort of young man, Lowell is. He's trying to find his way, and that's never easy, is it, Rooney?"

Rooney sensed that Susanna was trying to tell her something. She bit her lip and dropped her head for a moment, then lifted her eyes to face the older woman.

"No, it's not easy," she murmured, and then her eyes went to Lowell, who was staring up into the blue sky. "I guess growin' up is never easy—for anybody!"

"You're not going up in the balloon—and that's *final*!"

The argument about who would make the ascent in the balloon began immediately after breakfast. Lowell had gone outside to study the wind and the weather, and he had come back to announce with satisfaction, "Everything is good. Just a little breeze, not enough to matter."

Rooney had said almost nothing during breakfast, but she followed him so that the two of them were standing on a small patio just outside the dining room. It was very early, the crimson rays of the rising sun casting a glow over the landscape. She looked across to the field where the balloon wagons were outlined and said abruptly, "Lowell, I should be the one to go up."

That was when he'd stared at her and stated flatly, "You're not going up in the balloon, and that's *final*!"

Rooney shook her head, the action swaying her curls. "I thought about it all last night. If you're up in the gondola, what would happen if something goes wrong on the ground?"

"Nothing will go wrong!"

"Something went wrong yesterday."

Lowell flushed but shook his head stubbornly. "That won't happen again." He thought of the end of the flight, when the slaves had grown confused as a gust had shoved the balloon to one side. Several of them had dropped their ropes, which caused the remaining slaves to be dragged off their feet. The balloon would have gotten away if Lowell had not acted quickly to get extra help on the lines.

"It might," Rooney insisted. "And what if something happens and you get hurt?"

"What if *you* got hurt?"

"Why, if I got hurt, the balloon can still be used for the army to help General Longstreet. But if *you* broke your leg or something, it's all over. It'll all have been for nothing."

Lowell stared at her with consternation. He was a logical young man and realized that there was some logic to what she was saying. But he had set his heart on going up, and he didn't give up easily.

The argument went on in one fashion or another until ten o'clock, the time for the launch. At one point Lowell had said flatly, "Rooney, I don't want to hear any more!"

He spoke roughly and saw that his tone hurt her, but she had merely said, "I think you're wrong, Lowell. When you get somebody trained to do the work on the ground, you should go up. But you haven't done that."

The balloon was filled, and the crowd, much smaller this time, was composed of the slaves, who would work the ropes, and the family, who stood watching. They knew this flight would be with a passenger, and there was a tension in the air as Lowell put his hand on the basket and stood there for a moment.

Rooney stood beside Buck, saying nothing, and was shocked when without warning Lowell turned and said, "All right, Rooney. You win. Get into the basket!"

Susanna gasped. "He's sending that. . .that *child* up in that thing," she said angrily to no one in particular. "What's he thinking of?"

Rooney looked at Lowell's face, saw the disappointment etched on it, and said, "I know you want to go, Lowell," she whispered so that only he could hear, "but I think this is best."

Lowell shrugged, saying only, "Well, you got your way. Now get into the basket." She thought he was angry, but as she slipped inside, he suddenly grinned. "I'm a bad loser, Rooney!" And she felt a warm feeling for him.

She would have spoken, but he stepped back and nodded at Josh, who stood beside the gas machine, calling out, "Let her go, Josh!"

Rooney stood in the fragile wicker basket, watching as the bag began to swell. Soon it was a small mound, and then it swung upright. She stared upward at the swaying canopy and then heard Lowell call out, "Let go—slowly, now!"

The basket jerked, causing her to grab wildly at the rim, but then there was a smoothness, and she knew she was separated from earth!

Fascinated, she watched as the figures grew smaller. She could see the anxiety on the faces of the Rocklins—and the envy in the countenances of Buck and Josh.

Up, up she went, until the people looked very small. *They look like dolls!* she thought with pleasure. There was no fear, and when Lowell called out, "Are you all right?" she leaned over and waved at him.

"I'm fine!" she called back. "Let it go higher!"

For the next hour Rooney was ecstatic. She called out what she could see, her voice faint but clear to those below. "I can see the river—and there's the Chapman farm—and, oh, there's a mail rider coming! He must be five miles away, but I can see him!"

When Lowell finally brought the balloon down, Rooney leaped out and in her excitement grabbed his arm. Her eyes were flashing as she cried, "It's wonderful! You can see *everything*!"

Lowell stood there with the rest, listening as Rooney spoke, and when he finally was able to get a word in, he said wistfully, "It sounds great, Rooney."

Rooney stared at him, realizing what a sacrifice it had been for the young man to let her take his place. Instantly she said, "I know how much you wanted to go up, Lowell. Now let's get everything straight about what to do on the ground." She wanted to please him and added, "I'll bet we can settle that today; then you can go up last thing this afternoon!"

Lowell's face brightened, and he laughed out loud. "Lord help the man who gets you, Rooney Smith! You'll have him jumping through hoops!"

Susanna had moved closer, and now she saw the two young people standing close together. She noted the sweet expression on Rooney's face and saw Lowell suddenly laugh and reach out to pat her shoulder.

A smile touched the lips of Susanna Rocklin, and she nodded to herself as an idea touched her mind. As she turned away, she thought, *I wish you were here to see this, Thomas.*

CHAPTER 10

CAMP MEETING

General Silas Able looked up at the young private who'd somehow managed to get past his aide. "Well, Private, what is it?"

Lowell Rocklin said quickly, "General, I know you're busy, but I've been working on the balloon that General Longstreet wanted to see made."

"Oh...yes, I remember. The general mentioned the balloon to me in a correspondence when I came to the corps." General Able's division had been serving in Tennessee, but Lee requested his presence in Virginia. General Longstreet had been sent southeast to lay siege to Suffolk, Virginia, and Able was his replacement. He resembled Longstreet in appearance, being a blunt man in form as well as manners. He had heavy features, a high domed forehead over a pair of level blue eyes. A full beard and heavy mustache covered the lower part of his face, and he looked durable as stone. "What's your name, Private?"

924

"Private Lowell Rocklin, General. My father, brother, and I are in the Richmond Grays, serving under General Jackson."

General Able nodded and demanded bluntly, "And this balloon—you've actually got one?"

"Oh yes, sir. It's ready to go. And I'd guess that there'll be a chance to use it pretty soon."

The general's eyes glinted with humor. "You don't have to be very smart to see that the army's getting ready to move out."

"No, sir."

Chewing on the stub of a cigar, General Able considered Lowell. His mind was filled with the ten thousand details that generals must attend to. But Able tried to put those things behind him as the prospect of what a balloon would mean to the Army of Northern Virginia played in his mind. "I'd like to see what you've done, Private. Where is it?"

"Outside the camp, sir," Lowell said eagerly. "I wasn't sure if you wanted the troops to see it. It's down by the east road, near where the cavalry's stationed."

Able nodded and turned to his aide. "Jenkins, I'm going with this man. I should be back in a couple of hours." He mounted his large bay, and the two men rode through the center of the camp. It was a beehive of activity, and Lowell kept silence, awed by being in the company of such a high-ranking officer. But General Able began asking questions, and soon he'd discovered a great deal about Lowell. Able was an officer who liked to know his men as well as possible and was impressed at the ingenuity and drive of this young private.

"Your wound still bothering you, Private?" he asked, his sharp eyes taking in an artillery unit being prodded by a loud lieutenant.

"No, sir, hardly at all," Lowell said quickly. "I'm able to rejoin my regiment, but I thought I might do more good working with the balloon."

"If you can give us the Yankees' position, you'll certainly be useful. What's it like up there?"

"Oh, General, it's *fun!*" Lowell flushed, then said, "I know that's not what it's for, but it's the closest thing to flying there is, and I guess all of us have watched the birds and wished we could do what they do."

"I suppose so. Can you see a long way?"

"Why, sir, it's amazing!" Lowell began to describe the things that could be seen, and General Able listened carefully. One of the most difficult problems of a commander was finding out what was happening. The only method available was the courier, but that was slow and often inefficient. The courier had to make his way to some point of the battle, where he might get killed. If he didn't get killed, he had to be intelligent enough to grasp the details of the battle. He often had to find an officer who was wounded or dead or who had moved to another part of the field. Then, after gathering his information, he had to make his way back to his commander and deliver the message. But by that time the situation usually had changed completely.

"God knows we need some help with intelligence," the general said when Lowell paused. "We're going to have to do all we can to stop the Yankees."

"We can do it, sir!"

General Able glanced at the open face of the young man and hoped that the rest of the army was as confident. "That's the way to talk, Private," he said with a nod.

As the two rode along, the general spoke of the importance of getting information in battle, and Lowell absorbed it all. By the time the two of them pulled up beside the two wagons, Lowell had learned more than most knew about the battle to come. "I know we can help you, General!" He swung off his mount, followed by the general, and gestured. "There it is, sir!"

General Able stared at the wagons, which looked much like any other wagons—except for the solid high sides on one of them. Turning to Lowell, he said, "I guess I expected to see the thing all ready to fly. How long will it take to get it up in the air?"

"Oh, about an hour, sir, but we'll have to have some men to hold it down."

"I can commandeer whatever you need. I'd like to see how the thing works."

"Yes, sir!" Lowell motioned to Rooney, saying, "Let's get started—" And then he realized that Able was staring at the girl, as were many of the soldiers who were in the area. "Oh, this is Miss Rooney Smith. Miss Smith, General Silas Able."

Able removed his cigar, then his hat. "I'm happy to meet you, Miss Smith." He studied the girl, noting that she was wearing a man's clothing—a pair of brown trousers and a white shirt. They fit her loosely, but her slim figure left no doubt as to her sex. "I didn't know we'd have such an attractive young lady on our staff."

Rooney colored and said, "I'm just a helper, General."

"Don't believe that, sir," Lowell stated quickly. "There wouldn't even *be* a balloon if it weren't for her!"

General Able listened carefully as the young soldier related how getting the silk had been the young woman's idea and then said, "Well now, that's the way our Southern ladies are, always able to find a way to do what has to be done."

Lowell and Rooney quickly prepared the balloon. General Able simply pointed at ten cavalrymen, and they leaped at the chance to help Rooney spread out the canopy. As she kept them from trampling on it in their eagerness, Lowell worked on the gas-generating machinery. General Able stood right beside him, his sharp eyes taking in every move.

Finally Lowell called out, "Rooney, let's fill it." Then he directed the cavalrymen, showing them how to hold the ropes. He turned the valve, saying, "General, would you hold this valve open so I can give a hand with the balloon?"

"Of course."

General Able stood there, his hand on the valve, watching carefully. *If this thing would only work!* Finally he saw the balloon right itself and rise ten feet into the air. Lowell called out, "Shut the valve, General." And when the general shut the valve, Lowell grinned. "Be glad to have you come with me, sir!"

General Able was tempted but knew that Lee would have a heart attack if one of his officers did such a risky thing. "I'll stay here, Private," he answered, a smile hidden behind his beard.

"You fellows do just what Miss Smith tells you," Lowell said. As he got into the gondola he heard one of them say, "Thet little lady kin tell me to do *anythang*!"

Then at Lowell's command the balloon rose, with Rooney directing the men. It soared high into the air, and when it was about seventy-five feet in the air, Lowell called out, "I can see your camp, General! And there's a long line of wagons coming in from the south."

General Able was convinced. He stood there listening as Lowell described everything within a five-mile radius. When the young man called for Rooney to bring him down, Able was standing right beside the gondola. A cheer went up as he shook Lowell's hand, and he turned to see what seemed to be Jeb Stuart's entire cavalry surrounding them. They were waving their hats and calling out, "Just show us where the Yankees are, soldier!"

"Come along, *Sergeant* Rocklin," General Able said and saw the surprise in the young man's face. "General Longstreet informed me that he promised to make you a sergeant if this contraption worked. You've done a great thing, and I want to let General Lee hear about it."

"Yes, sir!" Lowell suddenly remembered Rooney and said, "But I'll have to help Miss Smith put the balloon to bed."

"Looks like she has plenty of volunteers," General Able remarked. "But you come to camp tomorrow—and bring her with you. Bring this thing with you, too. I want General Lee to see it in action."

As General Able rode away, Lowell made his way to Rooney. She was surrounded by a close-packed ring of rangy, sunburned troopers who were all trying to speak to her.

"Now, men, let Miss Smith get her work done," Lowell said firmly.

A tall sergeant turned to him scowling. "Hey, jine the cavalry, you duck-footed infantry!" Lowell bristled and would have made an argument out of it, but Rooney intervened.

"Thanks, Sergeant, for your help. I hope you'll be around when we go up to spot the Yankees."

Dazzled by the bright eyes of Rooney, the soldier capitulated. "Wal now, if you ever cut loose from this feller, miss, you can be *our* balloon lady, can't she, boys?"

A shout went up, and finally the sergeant herded his squad back to their campground. "Blasted fellow didn't have to be so—so *familiar*!" Lowell fumed. "You'd better watch out for these soldiers, Rooney. They're a bad lot."

"You're a soldier," she replied. In fact, she had enjoyed the teasing of the men, for they were nice, not like others she had known. A thought came to her, and she gave him a quick glance. "You're not *jealous*, are you, Lowell?"

"Jealous! Why, don't be silly!" Lowell threw his head back and drew his lips tightly together. "I'm responsible for you, and I'm going to see that nothing happens to you. Jealous!" He snorted and turned to begin taking the balloon down. She watched him for a moment; then her lips turned upward as she smiled.

They camped that night where they were. Lowell told Rooney, "Better get a good night's sleep. No telling how hard we'll have to travel when the army moves against the Yankees."

But they didn't get an early sleep, for the tall sergeant came over to say, "You two religious folks?"

Lowell was surprised and grunted half angrily, "You think we're heathens? Of course we're religious!"

The sergeant grinned at Lowell's indignation. "Revival goin' on. Stonewall's sure to be there. Pretty good preacher, too—just a little heavy on the fire and brimstone." He looked at Rooney and said innocently to Lowell, "If you're too busy, I'll be happy to escort the lady to the meetin'."

"I'll see to the lady, Sergeant!" Lowell said stiffly. After the cavalryman left, he turned to Rooney and asked, "Do you want to go?"

"Yes, but not in these clothes." Rooney turned and disappeared into the wagon. Lowell secured the gear in the gas-generating wagon and, when he was finished, found that Rooney was waiting for him.

"You...you look very nice," he said abruptly. She was wearing a light green dress with a white collar and lace on the sleeves. It fit her snugly, and he added, "Pretty dress."

"It's one of Rena's," Rooney said, smoothing the sleeve with her hand. "I didn't think of bringing a dress, but she told me I might need one. She's so nice!"

"Sure is. Well, let's get to the meeting."

They were soon among the crowds of soldiers hurrying to

931

an open field, where they found a place near the wagon that had been converted into a pulpit of sorts. The soldiers formed ranks around the speaker's platform, and Lowell suddenly nudged Rooney, whispering, "There's Stonewall!"

Rooney turned to catch a glimpse of the famous warrior, and as chance would have it, he turned at that moment. His eyes were the palest blue that she had ever seen, and they fastened on her. Able was standing beside Jackson, and seeing Stonewall looking at Rooney, he leaned closer and said something to him. Stonewall nodded and said something to a young major beside him. Instantly the young officer turned toward Rooney and started across the open space.

"Miss Smith, General Jackson would be pleased if you and the sergeant would join him for the service."

Rooney gasped and looked wildly at Lowell. He took her arm firmly, saying, "Thank you, Major. We'd be honored." Stepping out, he towed Rooney toward the officer, whispering, "Come *on*, Rooney! We'll never get a chance like this again." When they reached the generals, he dropped Rooney's arm and saluted smartly. "Sergeant Lowell Rocklin, General, and this is Miss Rooney Smith."

Jackson removed the old forage cap that had been pulled down over his eyes. He had an unusual face, rather youthful, and his voice was pleasant as he replied, "General Able has been telling me about the work you two are doing. I commend you for it." When the pair responded, Jackson asked about Lowell's family and was delighted to find out that they were in his command. "A father and *two* sons—what a testimony for the Southern Confederacy!" he exclaimed. Then he turned to Rooney and thanked her for her efforts. He was about to inquire into her family when the service began, and he said quickly, "You'll enjoy the service. The Lord is moving mightily among our men."

The service began when a heavyset young lieutenant began with a prayer, then led a song service that lasted for half an hour. Lowell knew all the songs, having heard them from his childhood, but they were all new to Rooney.

The men sang loudly such songs as "All Hail the Power of Jesus' Name," "Amazing Grace," "How Firm a Foundation," and a host of others. As song after song pealed on the soft April air, Rooney felt very peculiar. The words of the songs moved her, and as she looked around at the joy on the faces of some of the young soldiers—and of the older ones, as well—she wondered, *How can they be so happy when they may be dead in a few days?*

The last song began, and Stonewall Jackson, who had kept time with his hand, though not singing much, leaned over and whispered, "This is my favorite hymn, Miss Smith!" The words were clear, and Rooney listened hard as the song floated over the assembly:

There is a fountain filled with blood
Drawn from Immanuel's veins;
And sinners, plunged beneath that flood,
Lose all their guilty stains.

The words caught at Rooney as no words from a song ever had. She had no understanding of their meaning, but she was filled with grief and fear—and at the same time with a faint conception of joy such as she'd never known. Closing her eyes, she strained to catch each word as the song went on:

The dying thief rejoiced to see
That fountain in his day;
And there may I, though vile as he,
Wash all my sins away.

Dear dying Lamb, Thy precious blood
Shall never lose its pow'r,
Till all the ransomed church of God
Be saved, to sin no more.

E'er since by faith I saw the stream
Thy flowing wounds supply,
Redeeming love has been my theme,
And shall be till I die.

Rooney heard Jackson say fervently, "That's it! That's it! Redeeming love!" Hot tears suddenly burned her eyes, and her sight was so blurred she could not see except in wavy images. She had no handkerchief, but a hand touched her shoulder, and Jackson's voice said, "Here, daughter—use this!"

Blindly Rooney groped for the handkerchief, but no sooner

had she wiped her eyes and looked up into Jackson's eyes than her own filled again.

"Do you know the Lord Jesus, my dear?" Jackson leaned forward to ask. When Rooney shook her head, he asked, "Would you like to know your sins are forgiven?"

Rooney thought of her life, how awful it had been, and whispered, "I–I'm too bad!"

"We are all sinners," Jackson said. The preacher had mounted the wagon, and Jackson said, "After the sermon I would like to have a talk with you. Perhaps I can help point you to Jesus."

Rooney never forgot the next hour. The preacher, a tall, gangling man in the uniform of a chaplain, preached on the love of Jesus for sinners, and by the time the sermon was over, Rooney was weeping freely. When the preacher asked for those who needed salvation to come forward so that he could pray with them, Jackson spoke to Rooney quietly. He quoted a few simple verses that seemed to go straight to Rooney's heart like swords, and then he asked if she would let him pray with her. She had nodded at once, and the general began to pray—not loudly but very quietly.

Lowell was uncomfortably aware of all of this. He looked worried, but Able touched his arm, whispering, "Don't worry, Rocklin. Stonewall is doing what he loves best." Lowell nodded and watched as Rooney moved her lips and then lifted her head. He saw that her cheeks were stained with tears, but her eyes were brilliant as stars.

Jackson peered into the young woman's face, and a smile touched his thin lips. "You've been touched by Jesus," he said. "Never forget this moment, daughter. It's a holy time."

Much later Lowell and Rooney arrived at their wagon. The stars were out and the moon was full. Rooney had said nothing all the way back to their wagon, and when they got there, Lowell hesitated, then said, "Well, that was something, Rooney."

"I've never been to church, Lowell, never once in my whole life."

The announcement shocked Lowell. He had been brought up with church being such a part of his existence he couldn't imagine life without it. True, it had made no big impact on him, but it was *there*. He turned to Rooney, saying, "I never knew that."

"It's wonderful, isn't it, Lowell?" She took a deep breath, expelled it, and then said, "Why didn't you tell me being a Christian was so good?"

Lowell stared at her, unable to say a word. He had taken his religion for granted, but now he saw such a peace in Rooney that he became uneasy. "I don't talk much about it," he mumbled.

Rooney looked at him for a long moment, then nodded. "Nothing will ever be the same for me, Lowell." Then she turned and entered the wagon, leaving the young man as disturbed as he'd ever been in his life!

CHAPTER 11

A TIME TO FIGHT

*L*owell was chomping at the bit for a chance to see action, dreaming about the moment when he could prove the effectiveness of the balloon. Finally General Able sent word that scouts had reported enemy movements. "Keep that machine of yours ready, Sergeant. I'll be taking a force out to meet the Yankees. I think it's some sort of diversionary movement, but it'll be a good chance to test your balloon out before we get into a really big fight." Two days later word came to Lowell and Rooney that General Able was pulling out with a rather small force. When Lowell got to the general's tent, Able said brusquely, "Sergeant Rocklin, stay close to me. Chances are I won't have time to waste when I need your balloon."

"Yes, General!"

Lowell and Rooney took their place in the short line of supply wagons, almost suffocating with the fine dust raised by the feet of marching men and plodding mules. They were dead tired when they pulled off the road with the rest of the weary drivers to rest briefly for the night. They cooked a quick meal and afterward wandered to General Able's headquarters, hoping for news. They didn't see the general; however, they did speak with one of his aides, who told them, "The enemy was sighted by scouts, Sergeant. We'll engage them tomorrow."

"Better get some sleep, Rooney," Lowell said when they'd returned to their equipment wagon. "I think we'll be seeing some action tomorrow."

Rooney sat down by the fire and stared into it silently. Lowell came to sit across from her, saying, "I can never sleep before a battle." He looked at her curiously, then asked, "Are you afraid?"

Rooney looked up, and the yellow blaze sent a reflection to her eyes. "Why—I don't think I am." This seemed to puzzle her, for she poked at the fire with a stick, lost in thought. Finally she said, "I'm not very brave, you know. I've been afraid of things all my life. But somehow I'm not afraid of what's going to happen tomorrow."

"That's good," Lowell said, nodding. "No sense worrying about what you can't help."

But Rooney shook her head. "I don't understand it, but I know it's got something to do with what happened at the revival." She suddenly smiled at him, her face serene and happy in the glow of the fire. "I was always afraid to die. I had bad dreams lots of times. But now if I die, I'll be in heaven, won't I, Lowell?"

"I guess so."

She seemed fascinated by the thought—and pleased. She gave the hot glowing coals a poke with her stick, sending tiny yellow sparks flying. "What's heaven like, Lowell?"

He stared at her blankly, then shook his head. "I don't know. Never thought about it much." Her words seemed to disturb him, and he knew that he had never had the sort of experience that Rooney had. *Grandmother's got it—and father. And Dent and Raimey. But I've never had any sort of. . .of feeling like Rooney's got.*

"Good night," he said and, rising from the ground, went to his blankets and rolled into them under the wagon.

Rooney was surprised at his abrupt manner and disappointed. She wanted to talk, but Lowell was obviously troubled. She rose and got into the wagon. She slipped off her boots and went to sleep fully dressed, but first she prayed for Buck, then for all the Rocklins and the Yancys. She was not used to praying, but somehow she found the words flowing from her lips. And finally after she had asked God to keep all of them safe, she began to thank God. She had so little to thank Him for, but now it was as if a river were loosed inside her, and she whispered her thanks to God and her praises until they seemed to fill her spirit with joy. She fell asleep, her lips uttering praise and thanksgiving—and she felt very close to God!

The noise of cannon was deafening, and Lowell could hardly hear General Able. "Sir—I couldn't hear you!"

Able lifted his voice. "I said we've got to know what sort of force is over that hill. Can you get that thing up in the air and have a look?"

"Yes, sir!"

"I'll send Major Hankins, my aide, with you. Tell him what you see—and be sure you count the battle flags. That way we'll know how many regiments we're facing. Take ten men with you to help."

Lowell turned, and Able's aide and the men he had selected followed him. When they reached the balloon, Lowell called, "All right, Rooney. Let's get going!"

Rooney had everything ready, and soon the balloon was ten feet in the air. As Lowell got into the basket, Rooney leaned forward, her face pale. "Don't stay up too long," she said.

Lowell laughed at her, excited by the chance of helping in the battle. "Just don't let those fellows turn me loose," he said. "The wind's blowing toward the Yankee lines, and I don't want to report on their supply lines! Now let's get up there."

The balloon began to rise, and Rooney watched anxiously as the men played out the lines. Higher and higher it rose, and then the aide said, "They'll spot this thing, those Yankee gunners. Makes a perfect target."

Lowell watched avidly as the balloon rose above the tops of the trees, and when he saw what seemed to be a sea of blue, he yelled, "Major, I see them!"

"Where are they massed? How many are there?" Major Hankins yelled back. As Lowell called down the positions of the Federal troops, the officer jotted the information down in a brown notebook with a pencil.

"Cavalry over to the west—maybe two troops," Lowell yelled. "And they're moving four batteries of guns up over that little ridge. They'll have the range of our headquarters when they get there!"

"I'll take all this to the general," Hankins yelled, his voice almost blotted out by the sound of cannon that seemed to be growing stronger. He turned and left at a run, dodging among the men who were coming up to meet the enemy.

Just as he disappeared, a shell exploded not twenty feet away from where Rooney stood. She was deafened by the explosion and saw men blown into the air. She closed her eyes against the blast, but when she opened them, she saw the lower part of a man's body up against a tree where it had been blown.

"Lowell! You've got to come down!"

"No, I'm all right!" he shouted.

One of the men holding a rope said, "Miss, they've got the range. We'd better get out of here."

Rooney hesitated, then looked up to where the balloon was swaying in the breeze. "Lowell, we've got to pull out of here—"

But even as she called out, she saw with horror the gondola take a hit.

"Reel him in!" she cried, and at once the men began hauling the balloon down. But even as it came down, another shell exploded just above the colorful canopy. The silk was rent in a hundred places, and the men found the ropes limp in their hands.

"Get out of the way, lady!" a sergeant cried and came to pull Rooney to one side. She fought him, and then the gondola hit the ground and was covered at once by yards of tattered billowing silk.

"Lowell!" Rooney cried out, and jerking away from the soldier, she leaped to the fallen balloon and began tearing at the silk.

"Let me help you!" The sergeant fell in beside her and, pulling out a knife, slashed at the thin material.

Rooney seized the silk and pulled at it in a frenzy. She tore her fingernails and felt nothing. Then she saw a patch of gray uniform. "He's here! Help me get him out!"

The two of them pulled the silk away, and Rooney saw that Lowell was crumpled up in the bottom of the basket. His face was turned up, and she saw his eyelids flicker. "He's alive!" she cried. "Get him out!"

The soldier took a look inside, and his hand suddenly fell on Rooney's arm. She stared at him, tried to pull free, but he said, "His leg—it's bad!"

Rooney looked down and saw that Lowell's right leg was shattered above the knee. Scarlet blood was pumping steadily in a fine mist that had already made a puddle on the floor of the gondola.

"Let me get him!" The soldier reached down and pulled Lowell out of the basket, gripping him under the arms. He laid him down and stared at the leg. Without a word, he whipped off his belt and wrapped it around the wound in the leg. "He's lost a lot of blood," he muttered, shaking his head. "Got to get him to the doctor, but I can't let go of this belt."

Rooney leaped up, ran to the wagon, and got a blanket. When she returned, her face was pale as death, but her voice was strong. "You men, put him on this; then get three on a side. Sergeant, you hold on to that belt while we're moving him!"

"Do what she says, boys," the sergeant ordered. The men leaped to it, and almost at once they were hurrying away toward the field hospital. They passed new troops coming in but paid no heed to them, and in ten minutes the sergeant said, "There it is."

Rooney had been walking beside the sergeant, but now she ran ahead. An officer standing beside an ambulance stared at her, exclaiming, "A woman! What in the name—"

"Doctor, we've got a badly wounded man," Rooney broke in. "Where do you want him?"

The doctor stared at her, then at the soldiers carrying the bloodstained blanket. "On the table—here. Give them a hand, Lester, you and Tyrone!"

Rooney stayed as close to Lowell as she could. His eyes opened, and he muttered, "Rooney. What—"

"Here, get out of here, young woman!" the surgeon snapped. He was glaring at her, and then he looked at the leg. "Got to come off," he said gruffly.

"No!" Rooney whispered. "Please!"

The doctor stared at her. "This your husband?"

"N—no, sir."

He gave her a closer inspection and saw the fear in her eyes. In a kindlier voice, he said, "I'm sorry, but the bone is shattered. Actually there *is* no bone right here." He indicated the terrible wound above the knee. "It's the only way to save his life," he said. Then without more ado, he said, "Tyrone, take this young lady out for a walk."

"But I want to stay!"

"No, you don't," the doctor said firmly. "You can be of help to him afterward—but for now, he needs me."

Rooney stared at the doctor, swallowed hard, then nodded. She felt the touch of the man called Tyrone, who led her away. She found the sergeant waiting and went to him at once. "Thank you, Sergeant," she whispered. "You saved his life."

The sergeant shook his head, saying, "Well, I hope things go good for him—and for you, too, miss." He turned and called loudly, "All right, let's go get into this here fight!"

Rooney said to the man who stood waiting for her, "I'll go wait over under those trees. Come and get me when it's over!"

"Yes, ma'am. And don't worry. He'll be all right."

"Yes."

Rooney moved leadenly across to the grove. When she got there, she found herself praying. She was so stunned by what had happened that she found it almost impossible to think, and her words seemed strange and disjointed. The sun was hot, and the noise of the cannon throbbed, accompanied by thousands of muskets being fired.

Finally a voice said, "He's fine, miss. You can see him now."

Rooney whirled and followed the man to where Lowell lay on a cot. He was covered by a blanket, and the surgeon was looking down on him. When Rooney came to stand beside him, he said gently, "I did a good job. He'll have a good stump, with lots of muscle on it." He didn't say anything about the gangrene that killed many men who were wounded, for he was a kindly man.

"Your man?" he asked softly.

Rooney looked down at Lowell's face, so still and white. "He doesn't know it yet," she said, "but he's going to be."

The surgeon grinned and patted her shoulder. "You know what I think? I think he's a *very* fortunate young man!"

CHAPTER 12

"I'll Never Believe in Anything!"

After the engagement, the road to Richmond was jammed with wagons loaded with wounded. Men with major wounds were placed on the hard boards without even blankets, and as they were tossed from one side to the other, cries began to be heard: "Put me out—let me die! I can't stand this!"

Rooney had left the gas-generating wagon where it stood on the battlefield and had made a comfortable bed in the other one. She'd gathered the shredded balloon canopy and used the silk to make a thick mattress.

The second day after the amputation, she'd faced the surgeon, whose face was gray with fatigue, asking, "Doctor, can I take him to the hospital?"

"Yes. Get him there soon." His eyes were bitter as he looked at the men lying under trees with no cover at all. "Most of these will die before they get there—and some of them even afterwards."

"If you'll have the nurses put him into the wagon, I'm ready to start," Rooney said. She ran at once to the wagon and drove it back to the hospital. Going to Lowell, she said brightly, "Lowell, we're going home!"

Lowell was lying on a cot with a blanket over him, pulled up to his chin. A pallor had drained all the natural color from his cheeks, and his eyes were dull and listless. He looked up at her and gave a brief nod but said nothing. The shock of the operation had been great, and he had lost far too much blood. After he had regained consciousness and looked down at the stump of his right leg, he'd clamped his lips together and said nothing. When the surgeon had tried to cheer him up by saying, "You'll be up and around on a brand-new leg before you know it," he had stared at the man with bitterness.

Soon Rooney was on the road, which was crowded with marching men; now and then a troop of cavalry rode by, sending clouds of choking dust into the air. She stopped after an hour of this and pulled off to the side. Holding a canteen, she stepped into the wagon and knelt beside Lowell. Taking a handkerchief, she soaked it and removed the film of dust from his face. "This dust is bad, but we ought to be out of it soon," she said. When his face was clean, she asked gently, "Does it hurt much, Lowell?"

"No, it's all right." His tone was flat and spare, and his features were fixed as he stared up at the top of the wagon cover.

Rooney wanted to do more, but there seemed to be no way to comfort him. Pouring some of the water from the canteen into a cup, she said, "Drink more water, Lowell. The doctor said for you to drink as much as you can." He lifted his head and drank half the water, then muttered, "That's enough."

Rooney put the canteen beside him, then returned to the wagon seat and spoke to the horses. They resumed their plodding journey, and Rooney kept them at it all day. She paused at noon, pulling the wagon off to the side of the road, beside a muddy stream. The horses were thirsty, but she didn't let them drink too much. She fed them a little grain, then climbed into the wagon. Lowell looked at her blankly, and she tried to show a cheerful spirit. "I need to check your bandage, Lowell," she said.

"It's all right."

"Now don't be that way. The doctor said to check it often." She ignored his argument and looked carefully at the bandage. It was caked with dried blood, and she said, "I think it's all right. The bleeding's stopped."

It was hot under the wagon cover. Lowell's face was oily with sweat and plastered with the fine dust that fell over everything. She poured some water into a basin, soaked a square of cloth, and cleaned his face. "It'll be cooler when the sun goes down," she encouraged him. "I'll pull off the main road to make camp." She paused for his reply, but he closed his eyes without speaking, and she left and resumed the journey.

In midafternoon she crossed a wooden bridge and saw that the creek under it ran into a grove of hickory trees. A dirt trail followed the stream on the far side, and it looked solid, so she turned the team to follow it. Sixty yards from the main road, the trail entered the trees, and at once she found a spot beside the brook wide enough for the wagon and shaded by the towering trees.

Jumping to the ground, she unhitched the team and took them to a small meadow intersected by the creek. The grass was dry but would do for forage, and she tied the horses separately by long ropes to sturdy trees. They could reach food and water easily and would be fresh in the morning.

Returning to the wagon, she pulled the bolts that held the back section of the main frame and lowered it. Lowell, she saw, had pulled himself to a sitting position and was watching her with listless eyes.

"Lowell, this is a good place to camp. I'll make you a bed, and then we can get you out and you'll be more comfortable." She pulled several of the blankets from the floor and made a neat pallet not five feet from the back of the wagon. Moving him would be difficult, but she knew he needed to get out into the cooler air. *Don't let him see how scared you are,* she told herself fiercely. Hiding her apprehension, she moved to the rear of the wagon.

"Can you pull yourself over here, or should I get in and help?"

"I can do it."

He twisted around and carefully pushed himself forward with his hands until he was on the edge of the wagon bed. She took his good leg and carefully lifted it over the edge, then said, "Now you hold on to me and let down—be careful you don't bump your wound."

Lowell stared at her. He had fever and was filled with bitterness at the loss of the leg. But the intense heat of the wagon had been terrible, in addition to the pain the rough ride sent through him. He glanced at the stream with its cool shade and nodded. Through pale, tense lips he muttered, "I'm too heavy for you."

"You're only going right there. Just come down and put your arm around my shoulders."

Lowell had a fear that if he moved he might tear the stitches free—but at the same time didn't much care. He shrugged and slowly moved over the edge. It proved to be easier than he had thought, for he held himself carefully, bracing against the bed of the wagon, and his single foot touched the ground. Then she was against him, her arms bracing him tightly, and he moved one arm around her neck.

"That's it! Now let's just move right there to those blankets—just two steps. . . ."

Lowell let go of the wagon and the world seemed to reel. But Rooney held him tightly, saying, "That's it—just one step—good! Now another—now let yourself down."

She handled him very well, but it was with a grunt of relief that he sank down on the blanket. Looking up, he grunted. "Good to be out of that wagon."

"I know. Why don't you sit with your back against that tree? I know you're tired of lying down."

Lowell agreed, and it felt very good to be sitting up on solid earth without the jolting of the wagon. As soon as he was comfortable, she ran to the wagon and found a cup. Going to the creek, she filled it with fresh, cool water and brought it back to him. "This will be better than what we've had," she said with a smile.

His mouth was parched, and the cool water was the best drink he'd ever had. He sipped it slowly, letting it drain into the dried tissues of his mouth. He'd heard the wounded who couldn't be brought in cry for hours for water, and now he knew what torment they had been going through.

The coolness of the water—and of the slight breeze that came through the trees—refreshed him, and he sat there sipping the water and watching Rooney work. Procuring a hatchet, she chopped some dry wood from a fallen hickory, built a quick fire, and then began to throw together a meal. She worked rapidly and efficiently, and once when she looked up and met his eyes, she smiled, saying, "I'm going to fix us a *good* supper!"

When the meal was ready about an hour later, she carefully ladled some of the rich stew she'd made into a bowl and brought it to him. "No white tablecloth and silver tonight," she said cheerfully. "No time to make biscuits, either, but we've got half a loaf that's not too bad."

Lowell accepted the bowl of stew and the spoon and took a bite. It was very hot, and he sputtered. Blowing on a fresh spoonful, he tasted it and looked at Rooney, who was watching him. "Good," he said briefly. "Real good!"

Rooney was pleased. "I made lots of it, so eat all you can."

The two of them sat there eating slowly, and Lowell found

that he could not eat more than half of his portion. "Just not very hungry," he muttered.

His face was flushed, and Rooney thought, *He's got fever.* It was what the doctor had warned her of, but she said only, "You can have some more later. Let me get you some fresh water. We've got plenty of that."

The sun went down slowly, and after Rooney cleaned up the dishes and stored the stew in a closed pot, she said, "I'll just take a little walk—see what's down the creek."

"All right."

She walked away and followed the creek for two hundred yards. There she stopped to wash her face and tend to her personal needs. It was growing darker, and she stood beside the stream, praying for God to take the fever away.

Finally she turned and made her way back to the small camp and discovered that he was lying down and had fallen asleep. She moved softly to the wagon, got a blanket, and made a bed for herself across the fire. It was early and she was not sleepy, so she sat there quietly. She could hear the traffic on the road, but it was muted and did not disturb Lowell.

Overhead the leaves of the hickory trees rustled, seeming to whisper secrets to each other, and through the leafy fringe she could see the star-spangled sky that covered the earth.

Once she got up and moved to kneel beside Lowell. Touching his cheek lightly, she was shocked by the heat of his body. *Bad fever! I've got to get it down like the doctor said.*

She went to the wagon and grabbed some of the silk scraps.

Finding a gallon bucket, she went to the creek and filled it with cool water, then went back to Lowell, who was tossing now with a fitful mutter.

"Lowell. Wake up." She had to call his name several times, and when his eyes opened, they seemed blank. "I've got to get your fever down," she said. He only stared at her, and she began taking off his shirt. He blinked but made no resistance. When his shirt was opened, she took a square of the silk, dipped it in the cool water, and then removed it. Wringing some of the water out, she opened the cloth and spread it over Lowell's body. He jumped at the touch of the cold material, and she murmured, "Be still, Lowell. It's all right."

For two hours she kept up the treatment, getting cool water from time to time. His body was so hot that the cool, wet fabric was heated almost at once, but she worked on doggedly.

At one time he grew delirious, calling for his grandmother. "Is that you, Grandmother?" he would mumble and try to reach for her.

"Yes, Lowell, this is your grandmother," Rooney would whisper. "Lie still now, and Jesus will take care of you."

He would peer at her through fever-bright eyes and then seem to be reassured, only to go through the same thing a few minutes later.

Finally the fever went down, and Rooney breathed a shaky prayer of relief. "Thank you, Lord!" she said, then dried Lowell and put a dry shirt back on him.

She went to her pallet, tired as she had ever been, and fell to sleep at once. Time passed over her, and she had no sense of it. Finally she heard Lowell speak and came awake at once.

"Yes, Lowell?" Rooney was groggy but got to her feet and went to kneel beside him. "Are you all right?"

Lowell's head was down, but as he lifted his face to her, she saw the despair in his eyes by the light of the stars and the moon. He had always been a young man with a cheerful air, but now he was filled with bitterness.

Glancing down at his stump, he stiffened, then looked at her. "I wish it had killed me!" he stated flatly.

"No, that's not right, Lowell!"

"Right? What does that mean? Is it *right* for a man to creep around for the rest of his life a hopeless cripple?" His eyes were deep wells of anger as he whispered bitterly, "Don't talk to me about what's *right*!"

Rooney reached out to touch him, but he shoved her hand away roughly. "Leave me alone!" he said, his voice thick with anger.

"Lowell—don't be like that!"

"I'll be what I please—and I'll tell you one thing, Rooney. . ."

When he paused and looked down at his leg, he seemed to have forgotten what he had meant to say, so that Rooney asked, "What is it, Lowell?"

Lifting his head, he clenched his right fist and shook it at the heavens above. Then he said in a grating tone, "I'll never believe in anything again!"

PART THREE

Rena

CHAPTER 13

CLAY GOES RECRUITING

In 1863 spring came to Virginia so suddenly that it caught people by surprise. The sullen cold that had lain over the land seemed to leave overnight, bringing warm breezes. So sudden was the change that it was almost like walking out of one room into another. The grass that had been touched by September's frosty hand emerged in short emerald tongues. The woods put on their summer greenery, and the rivers ran clear within their banks.

But if relief had come to Virginia in the form of warm weather, wounded and dying men from old battles filled the hospitals and many of the homes of the land. Death became as familiar as birth, and almost every family struggled with the loss of a young man, cut down by the bloody scythe of war.

The Confederate Army had enjoyed a brief respite, for the Northern army had withdrawn to Washington—but only to prepare for another onslaught as soon as the problems of winter warfare were behind them and thinned ranks could be filled by the new recruits. Lee well knew that the Army of the Potomac would be back in greater force than ever—and he knew also that such tactics could only end in defeat for the South. He began to think of forcing the war, of leading his Army of Northern Virginia north. He well understood that he would have to fight the politicians who would scream that he was leaving Richmond unprotected—but there was no greater gambler in Virginia than Robert E. Lee. As the crippled army began to rebuild, more and more he turned his mind toward the North, hoping that one successful attack would carry the message of total war to the people who had never heard a shot fired.

But as Lee began to move in his mind toward launching an attack, the South had to go on. It was more difficult now, for they were cut off from their supplies. The sea route was closed by a vigilant U.S. Navy, which had thrown a tight net around most of the coast. Only a few fleet clipper ships were able to run the blockade, and they could not bring in the enormous supplies required to keep the South fed and clothed. Coffee and tea were gone—many were drinking "Richmond coffee," which might be made from roasted acorns. Household stores vanished, and only what could be grown locally was found in the almost-empty stores of Richmond.

The Southern army had to depend on a very few factories— and on captured arms. The cavalry did good service here, and General Jeb Stuart captured so many Federal supply trains that he was insulted when some of the mules he captured were of poor quality. He sent a message to President Lincoln:

> *President Lincoln:*
>
> *The last draw of wagons I've just made are very good, but the mules are inferior stock, scarcely able to haul off the empty wagons; and if you expect me to give your lines any further attention in this quarter, you should furnish better stock, as I've had to burn several valuable wagons before getting them in my lines.*
>
> *(signed) J. E. B. Stuart*

But humor was not common in most of the South, for the war had become a long, drawn-out affair that was not going to the Southern advantage.

In the wards of Chimborazo, packed to the walls with wounded men, the doctors and nurses worked so hard that it was difficult to keep a cheerful face. Mrs. Pember was one who managed to achieve this, for she understood that the wounded needed more than physical care. She spoke of this once to Rooney during a brief respite one evening. Rooney left Buck at Gracefield and had come to the hospital to offer her services again now that the work on the balloon was sadly behind her. She shared a tiny room with another nurse, and her presence helped relieve the overworked staff.

"I'm glad you've come, Rooney." Mrs. Pember nodded, a tired smile on her thin face. "You're always so good for the men."

"They're so scared—most of them," Rooney answered. She took a sip of the sassafras tea, then shook her head. "Lots of men would rather die in battle than come to a hospital."

"I know. They're young, and many of them have never been sick nor away from home. Now they're thrown into this big place where they get very poor care, though we do our best!"

"Some of them cry when they think no one is watching."

"Yes. And so do I." Mrs. Pember saw that the girl was surprised and asked, "Don't you, Rooney?"

"Why. . .yes, ma'am, I do," she confessed. She was tired after a long day, but there were still things to do. "Billy Rosemond died last night. I've got to write his mother, and I don't know what to say."

"That's always hard," the older woman said heavily. "All we can do is tell them their men died easily."

"Billy didn't!"

"I know, but what good would it do to tell his mother that?" Mrs. Pember laid her dark eyes on Rooney and said gently, "Sometimes kindness is better than the truth."

The two women sat in the small office, quietly drinking the strange-tasting tea and speaking from time to time. Finally a knock at the door caused them to look around. "Come in," Mrs. Pember said.

The door opened, and both women were startled to see Clay Rocklin enter. "Why, Captain Rocklin, come in!" Mrs. Pember said, rising to greet him. "I didn't know you were back in Richmond."

"Good evening, Mrs. Pember. Hello, Rooney. I came in to try to get supplies for the company." Clay nodded, and they saw that he was worn thin, his eyes weary. "I hate to bother you at this time of night, but I've got a problem."

"Sit down, Captain."

"No, I can't stay," Clay said quickly. He looked at the two women, then shook his head. "I've just come from my home, and I'm worried about my mother."

"I thought it might be about your uncle Mark or Lowell." Both men had been taken to Gracefield for extended care. The hospital was so crowded and nourishing food so scarce that Mrs. Pember had suggested to Susanna Rocklin that they would get better care at home.

"Well, Matron, I guess I really have come about them." He took a deep breath, and Rooney could see how worried he was. Fine lines had appeared around his mouth and eyes, and he was keeping himself upright only by a concerted effort. "I think it was the right thing for both of them to come home, but it's more than my mother can handle." He shook his head, adding, "She's not young anymore, and with the shortages and us Rocklin men in the army, it's about all she can do to manage the home."

"What do you need, Captain?" Mrs. Pember asked quickly.

"Well. . ." Clay hesitated, then turned to Rooney. "I guess I need Rooney Smith," he said. Then he added, "I know you need her here, too—"

"Of course we do," Mrs. Pember broke in. "But your mother

must have help, as well. As you know, Miss Smith is only a volunteer here, and I cannot force her to stay—or to leave." She turned to Rooney. "Would you be willing to go, Rooney?"

"I hate to leave you and the men here, Matron, but the Rocklins have done so much to help me and my brother. I just can't say no."

Clay expelled a deep sigh of relief. "I'm glad to hear that!" he exclaimed, and Rooney saw that her words had indeed lifted a load from his shoulders. His smile lightened the heaviness of his drawn face, and he added, "I'll be leaving tomorrow for a time with the company, but I can take you now—if that's not too soon for you."

"I'll get my things."

Clay spoke with Mrs. Pember for five minutes, expressing his appreciation for the fine treatment the men of his company had gotten from her, and then he and Rooney left the hospital and were on the road toward Gracefield.

"Will there be more fighting soon, Mr. Rocklin?" Rooney asked. She glanced at him as he sat loosely on the seat beside her, thinking of how tired he looked.

"I'm afraid so, Rooney."

"Will your company be in it?"

"Well, nobody knows for sure," Clay answered slowly. He was drowsy, but the cool air was like wine, and as they moved into the country, he felt the pleasure that always came to him when he was in the open. He turned and smiled at the young woman, adding, "Some regiments have gone through the whole war and never heard a gun fired. Others, like ours, have had so many losses they're only a fraction of their size at Bull Run."

Rooney looked very pretty, the fresh air making her cheeks rosy, and her blue eyes were enormous—or seemed to be. She considered what he said, then shook her head. "That doesn't seem fair," she commented.

"No, I guess not. But wars are never fair."

"I wish it were all over," she said quietly, her lips growing tight. "One of my patients died this morning—Billy Rosemond. He was seventeen years old—the same age as me." A brooding came into her expressive face, and her voice was tinged with both anger and grief. "His home was in Arkansas, in the mountains. He had a sweetheart there he talked about all the time. Her name is Sue Ellen Grantly, and they were going to be married when he got home."

A battery of field artillery came thundering down the road, sending up a cloud of dust. Clay drew the wagon off to the side of the road and waved a salute at the youthful officer who rode before the guns. He waited until the unit passed, then spoke to the team and moved them back onto the road. "That young fellow had better save his horses," he commented.

Rooney, however, was still thinking of the young soldier. "He won't be going home now, Mr. Rocklin. They took him out and buried him in that big graveyard close to the hospital." Dropping her head, she stared at the floor of the wagon, fingered the material of the brown cotton dress she wore, then looked at him to ask, "Will she remember him in five years—or twenty-five?"

"I think so, if she really loved him."

Rooney was caught by Clay's reply and pondered it as the wagon rumbled along. Finally she said, "She'll be alive and she'll marry—have children, maybe. But Billy's missed it all. He'll never be a husband or a daddy. In a few months he'll be nothing but bones. He won't ever have anything."

"He will if he was saved, Rooney," Clay said gently. He had learned to love this young woman, admiring her courage and her steadfast determination to keep herself pure in a terrible world. "Death seems like the end of everything to us who are left. But to those who die, it's not that way." He sat in the seat, tired to the bone but suddenly anxious to bring some of the faith that was in him to the heart of Rooney. Clay Rocklin had been an impetuous young man, but time, grief, and experience had tempered him. He had passed through a crucible of hardship that had fashioned him into a mature man of wisdom.

"You're not the only one to think as you do, Rooney," he said, his voice even and steady. "Most people do, I guess. I know I've spent a lot of my life wondering about God and trying to figure out how there can be a world that's such a mess with God able to do anything. And I don't have all the answers. Nobody does. But I've studied the Bible, I've listened to men and women of God, and I've come to understand that most of our grief for the dead is wrong."

"How can it be wrong to grieve?"

"It's not wrong like it's wrong to hate or hurt someone," Clay answered. "It's—well, it's more of a *mistake*, I guess you'd say. I'm talking now about grieving for those who died believing in Jesus Christ." A frown passed over his face, and he shook his head sadly. "Those who die lost. . .well, I don't know how to speak of that, Rooney. It's the worst thing I can think of. But if a person is saved, what happens to him when he dies?"

"He goes to heaven, doesn't he?"

"That's right. And what is heaven?"

Rooney shifted uncomfortably on the seat, for she had some doubts on that subject. "Well, from what I understand, it's a place where there's no pain and no problems—where people never die."

"That's part of it," Clay agreed, "but there's more to it. I may get in trouble here, Rooney," he said, smiling at her. "Don't tell the preacher on me, but I'm not sure that heaven is exactly like most of them preach. I mean, most people take their ideas of heaven from the book of Revelation, and it tells about heaven like it's a big city, full of gold streets and high walls with gates of pearl."

"You don't believe that?" Rooney was shocked, for she had gotten the idea that good Christians believed all the Bible.

Clay held up his hand quickly, saying defensively, "Hold on, now; don't shoot!" He was amused at her reaction and assured her, "It may be like that, Rooney. I don't really know—and don't really care. The important thing to me about heaven is not what the streets are made of, but who's there."

"You mean Jesus?"

"Yes! If Jesus is there, I don't care if the streets are made out of gold or dirt! He's the center of that place, and He never made anything that wasn't good, did He?" Then Clay waved his brown hand in an expressive gesture that swept the rolling fields and the low foothills. "As for me, I'd rather heaven looked like Virginia in the spring—like this! I wouldn't give one spoonful of Virginia dirt for any big city in the world!"

"Why, I never thought of that!"

Clay laughed and suddenly reached out and grabbed Rooney's hand, so that it was almost swallowed. "Don't let me lead you astray," he said. "Believe every word in the Bible, Rooney. It's the Word of God without error. I believe that with all my heart; it's just that I don't understand all of it."

Rooney liked his ease in holding her hand. Once she would have fought like a wildcat if a man in this isolated spot had done that, but she had learned from Lowell and Clay Rocklin that not all men were evil. It was a good feeling to let herself trust the big man beside her, and when he released her hand, she said thoughtfully, "I guess you mean that we'll miss Billy Rosemond, but he's in a better place."

"Have to think that, Rooney," Clay said. "I've seen lots of good men die in this war, but I'll see them again someday. That's what it is to be a Christian."

"Then. . .Christians never say good-bye, do they?"

Clay was struck by the words of the young woman. "Why, I never thought of that! But by heaven, it's *so*, Rooney!"

The two of them moved in a leisurely fashion all evening, stopping once to rest the horses, and then continued their journey. Rooney had never enjoyed a trip more, for she had a tremendous affection for Clay Rocklin. She had admired him for some time, but now she thought, *He's the best man I ever met! I wish every man in the world was like Mr. Clay Rocklin.*

Finally as they moved into the driveway of the Big House, she asked, "How are Mister Mark and Lowell doing?"

"Not very well, either of them. Mark isn't getting any better, and there's nothing much a doctor can do."

"And Lowell?"

"He's doing well physically, Rooney, but. . ."

Rooney glanced at him sharply, then said, "I know. He's real bitter."

Clay noted how quick the girl was, then said slowly, "He'll survive the loss of the leg, but I'm worried about him in other ways. I've seen it before, Rooney. Some men get so angry when they take a bad injury that they never have any joy or peace in them." He bit his lip and added in a whisper, "I pray to God that doesn't happen to Lowell!"

Rooney, without knowing it, reached over and put her hand on his arm. "We won't let him, Mister Clay! You and me and Miz Susanna, we'll pray and pray for him!"

Clay felt a warmth go through him, and his eyes suddenly burned with unshed tears. He'd seen so much misery and so much selfishness in his world—and now the gentleness of Rooney Smith touched him.

"God bless you, girl!" he whispered huskily. "That's exactly what we'll do. And God will help us!"

Melora came out of the house when she heard a team and wagon approaching. When she stepped onto the porch, she paused at the sight of Clay Rocklin driving up to her front door. She was a strong woman, but for years the very sight of Clay had brought her a peculiar weakness. She had loved him for so long! First as a small child, she'd loved him as children love some adults. Then as she'd made the passage from childhood into adolescence, she'd fought against the confusing emotions that had warred in her bosom, knowing that she could never have him, for he was married, and yet she was drawn to him in a powerful fashion. Finally, as a mature woman, she'd come to know that she'd never have another man. *If I can't have Clay, I'll live alone. I love him too much, and I couldn't rob another man of his right to a wife's love!*

For years now, she had carried this love locked away from everyone. While Clay's wife was alive, Melora and Clay had remained close friends, each knowing of the love in the other, but both aware that God would never let them have one another. Now that Ellen was dead and Clay was free, Melora was aware that he was now hers. The sight of him brought a pleasure to her, and she called out, "You must have smelled my pies baking all the way in Richmond."

Clay laughed, hauled the team to a stop, and leaped out of

the wagon. For a big man, he was agile and light on his feet, and now he tied the team, then came to her, his face lightened at the sight of her. He had spent years mourning the fact that he'd thrown away the best part of his youth married to a woman he didn't love and knowing that he could have had Melora. But he'd learned to accept that, and now he came to stand before her, admiration for her dark beauty in his face.

She was twenty-eight now but looked no more than eighteen. Her large almond-shaped eyes were green, and her black hair hung down her back to her waist. As always, he wanted to touch her but refrained. "Well, you may have an exalted idea about those pies of yours, Miss Yancy," he said. "A man might have other reasons for coming this way."

Melora's eyes sparkled as she shot back, "Oh, you don't want any pie, then? Well, I suppose Pa and the children can finish it off." She smiled demurely, adding, "It's only blackberry cobbler anyway."

Clay's jaw dropped, and he held up his hand in alarm. "Wait, now—don't be so blasted quick!" He nodded and tried to look unconcerned. "Maybe I could eat just a *small* portion of that cobbler!"

Melora burst into laughter, a pleasant sound in the afternoon air. "You liar! I'll never believe another word you say!"

Clay shrugged his shoulders, looking crestfallen. "Well, I guess I wouldn't blame you. I can resist anything except temptation—and Melora Yancy's blackberry cobbler!" Then he grinned and put his hand out, taking hers and saying, "I'm a man in a poor condition, woman."

"Really?" She loved these games he played with her and waited for him to come out with the thought that was to be plainly seen in his dark eyes.

"Yes. And you'll never know if I love you for yourself—or for your pies!"

Melora grew still, her form straight and her face clean and strong in the fading light. "I know already." She spoke simply and without any reservation. It was the way with this woman to be so open with her feelings, and Clay loved her for it. He stepped forward and took her in his arms, and she came willingly. When his lips fell on hers, there was a wild sweetness in the kiss, and the touch of her strong body pressing against him brought strong hungers. Her hands pressed the back of his neck as she pulled him closer, and all of the years of waiting seemed to evaporate. Now there was nothing to keep her from loving him with all the ardor that she had repressed for so long. Melora had long known that there was a fierce side of her nature, and now she loosed it, clutching Clay with her strong arms, savoring the strength of his lean, muscular body and the roughness of his caress. Then she felt her control slipping and pulled her head away, whispering, "Clay—I want you!"

Clay felt with Melora as he had never before felt with any other. "We'll be married, Melora! I have to have you!"

"When, Clay?"

"I can't say for sure, Melora. As soon as this war ends." They stood there looking into each other's eyes, thinking of what had passed—and what each knew was to come.

"The others are in the field, but they'll be back soon." She spoke quietly, then asked, "Can you stay for a while?"

"Yes."

"Then we've got time for a walk. Let's go down to the creek before supper."

They had their walk, Clay telling her of the family, she listening quietly. Always they had enjoyed each other's company, even when she was a child and he a full-grown man. The years had ripened this union, so that now there was complete ease and trust in each of them. They both knew that the love of the other was so true that nothing could change it, and the security of this warmed them both.

Finally they went back, and Clay was greeted by Buford and the children with enthusiasm. He was, to the children, more or less a favorite uncle, for he had always been good to them. To Buford he was a good friend, and the older man looked often at Clay over the supper table with affection in his greenish eyes. Most men, Yancy realized, would have taken advantage of a girl like Melora, but Clay Rocklin had been true as steel.

Finally when supper was over, they sat around the cabin, Clay enjoying the time immensely. After the tension and rigors of battle and bloodshed, it was a haven where he could rest and forget.

Finally the younger children left, but Clay said, "Josh, I'd like to talk to you."

Josh had turned to leave but now wheeled and asked,

"M—m—me? Why, s—sure, Mister Clay." The children all called him that, for it was what Melora had called him for years— still did on occasions.

Buford and Melora turned to Clay, not knowing what to expect, and Josh looked startled.

"Josh, we're short of help at my place. I'd like for you to come and help—if your father can spare you."

Buford said at once, "Why, shore, Clay! One of my nephews is coming to stay with us, my brother's boy. He's 'most sixteen now, and he can do the spring plowing while the others take care of the hogs."

Clay nodded, then looked at Josh. "I'll pay you full-grown man's wages, Josh. Our overseer is gone for a time, so you'll have to work hard to fill in until he gets back."

"I c—couldn't oversee n—nobody!"

Clay laughed, then rose and clapped the boy on the back, noting the strong muscles that lay on Josh's lean frame. "Didn't expect that," he said. "Just pitch in with the animals—you're real good with that. And you can help Box with the blacksmith work."

"I'd l—like that!"

"Thought you might," Clay said, grinning. "Just don't forget there's other work to be done. You'd stay in there fooling with some invention or other the whole day long, I think."

Josh idolized Clay Rocklin and nodded his head. "I kin g—go right n—now, can't I, Pa?"

Buford gave his consent, and Josh scooted off at once to get his clothes. "Sorry to rob you of a hand, Buford," Clay apologized.

"Ain't no never mind," Buford replied with a wave of his hand. "Do the boy good to be there." He got up then, saying, "I'll git his tools from the barn."

When he left the room, Clay rose and went to Melora. "This was good," he said simply. Pain came to his eyes, and he said briefly, "I wish I didn't have to go back."

"Someday you won't have to leave me."

Clay stared at Melora, then nodded. "That'll be the best thing in the world, won't it?" He took her hands in his, held them gently, studying her face, memorizing it, she knew, for the time ahead when he would be gone.

Swiftly she lifted her face, and he kissed her. His lips were firm as he held her in his arms, and she felt again the desire in him. She felt it in herself, as well, but she had long ago learned that her longing for Clay Rocklin had this element. She was not ashamed of it but was proud that he was strong enough to release her.

"Someday soon, Mister Clay," she whispered, "you won't have to go!"

CHAPTER 14

"You Learn a Lot on a Coon Hunt"

Josh Yancy liked and respected Lowell Rocklin deeply. Indeed, except for his own father and Clay, there was no man he thought more of. For this reason he had jumped at the chance to go back to Gracefield—so that he could spend more time with him.

But it hadn't worked out that way. Clay had taken him to the room that would be his, a snug room built off the barn. Then Clay had taken the tall young man around and lined out his work. Afterward Josh had said, "C–can I go see M–Mister Lowell now?"

"Yes, Josh, I wish you would." Clay held the boy's eyes, adding, "My son is pretty depressed. He needs all the friends he can get. I'd appreciate it if you'd spend a lot of time with him."

"Why, s–sure I w–will!"

Josh went at once to the Big House, and Susanna had greeted him warmly. "Why, Josh, I hear you're going to be taking over some of the work around here. That's good to hear. We need a good man on the place!" She had smiled at his embarrassment, then asked, "Did you come to see Lowell?"

"Y–yes, ma'am."

"Come right along. I'll take you to his room."

Josh had yanked off his floppy hat and held tightly to it as he followed Susanna down the hall. He had been in the Big House before, but it always made him feel awkward and out of place. Susanna turned through one of the doors, and when Josh entered, he saw Lowell sitting in a wheelchair staring out the window.

"Look who's come to visit with you, Lowell," she said brightly.

Josh stepped forward and was shocked to see how pale and thin Lowell Rocklin was. He hid his thoughts, however, and said, "H–hello, Mister L–Lowell. I'm g–glad to see you."

Lowell looked up, but he didn't smile. "Hello, Josh," he said briefly. His eyes were flat, and his mouth was pulled tight as if he'd tasted something sour. His attitude was more of a shock to Josh than his physical appearance, for Lowell Rocklin had been one of the most cheerful people the boy had ever seen.

"Now, Josh, you sit down and you two can talk," Susanna said quickly. "I know you must be hungry, so I'll have Dorrie fix up something for you both."

"Don't fix anything for me," Lowell said flatly.

Susanna hesitated, then left the room. Josh stood there uncomfortably, for Lowell hadn't invited him to sit down.

Finally he eased into the chair facing Lowell and said, "I'm g–gonna be w–working here, Mister L–Lowell."

Lowell glanced up at the boy without interest, nodded, and muttered, "That's good."

Josh was not good at small talk—his speech impediment kept him quiet with most people. But in the past he'd been so excited working with Lowell that he'd talked as much with that young man as he ever had with anyone. But for the next half hour, he was absolutely miserable. Lowell sat in his chair silent as a stone, not even answering the questions the boy asked him—merely nodding as if it didn't interest him much.

Josh grew desperate and finally asked, "What w–was it like... the b–battle, I m–mean?"

Lowell had glared at Josh, and for the only time in the conversation, some life showed in his eyes. He gestured down at his stump, then said acidly, "It was like that!"

Josh had been crushed and fell silent. The two sat there, Josh longing to leave but not knowing how. When Susanna came to the door to say, "Come along, you two," he was on his feet in an instant. He looked at the wheelchair and asked, "C–can I help you to the d–dining r–room, Mister Lowell?"

"No! I don't need any help!"

Susanna saw the boy's head move as if he'd been struck. She touched his arm, saying, "Go along to the kitchen, Josh. I'll be there soon." He went with a gust of relief.

When he was in the kitchen, he found that Dorrie had put a plate of hot food on the table and a big glass of cool buttermilk.

He began to eat, and she stood at the end of the table for a time. Her eyes were dark and brooding, and she finally said, "Mister Lowell, he bad off. Gonna take the hand of Gawd to help dat boy!"

Josh looked at her, startled, then nodded. "I r–reckon so, D–Dorrie," he said slowly. He was thinking, *This ain't gonna be as much fun as I thought,* but he kept that thought to himself, and when Susanna entered, he saw she was troubled.

"You'll have to be patient with Mister Lowell," she said quietly. "It's very hard for him."

"Yes, m–ma'am."

"He's always been so strong and able...the best horseman in the country, the fastest at the races the boys ran." She shrugged her shoulders, then turned to face the boy. "You two were very close, Josh. He thinks a lot of you. . .as if you were a younger brother. Please try to help him all you can."

"I sure w–will!" Josh nodded. He hated to see the Rocklins so torn by the tragedy and said hopefully, "H–he'll be f–fine, you'll s–see!"

Susanna gave him a thankful look, then began to speak of other things. But after the boy left, she and Dorrie sat down. The black woman knew Susanna well. "Doan you be frettin' now, Miz Susanna," she said firmly. "Gawd is gonna bring us through dis. . .lak He done brought us through befo'."

Susanna felt the force of the woman's love and loyalty and put her hand out. When the hard, work-worn hand of Dorrie closed around hers, she felt a rush of gratitude and said, "I don't know what the Rocklins would do without you, Dorrie."

Rena missed her father more than ever. Ever since he'd come back from his wanderings, she'd clung to him fiercely, and when he'd gone to the army, it had been terrible for her. Susanna had done her best, but her need for a strong man was something that no woman could give. Her own mother had given her so little love, and now even she was gone. Rena felt more alone than ever.

She visited Melora and had gotten very close to Rose, but the visits were rare. So Rena was left with much time on her hands. She did her best to help with the nursing and spent many hours with Uncle Mark. He was cheerful at times, but his wound was a constant drain on his strength, and she could only sit beside him, reading to him a great deal.

As for Lowell, after a few determined efforts to pull him from the despair that was eating his life away, she gave up but helped with his food and other slight chores. She longed to talk to Lowell, for the two had been close once, but now he was closed off behind some sort of wall that Rena could not penetrate.

When Rooney came, Rena was happy, for she got along well with the girl. But Rooney was busy helping Susanna and Dorrie and taking care of Lowell. Buck spent much time in the fields learning about crops, so Rena was alone.

She read for hours, the same books that Clay had read with her when he'd first come home. She loved to remember those days when she'd had him all to herself! They had been the best days of her life—just she and her father alone in the summerhouse, with books and a fire and lots of time in the crisp nights and then in the cobwebby mornings. How she longed for those days!

But they were gone. And now dark thoughts pushed aside the good memories. She no longer dreamed of days past but rather had terrifying nightmares. They were always the same, and they always woke her with a fright that made her heart beat like a trip-hammer.

They were brief dreams, lasting only a few seconds. She was in the summerhouse when a horse came down the lane. She would rise from her chair and go outside—and fear would sweep over her. The horse was black as night, and the rider was dressed in dark clothing. A black hat was pulled over his eyes, and his face was concealed behind a black neckerchief. Rena would stand there as this frightening horseman drew close, fear crawling though her mind. When he arrived, his great horse drawn up before him, he leaned forward, and Rena saw that he had no face, just a skull-like feature with burning eyes that seemed to scorch her skin and shrivel her where she stood.

She would try to run, but she was paralyzed. Then he would speak in a voice that rattled like chains, and his breath was like an open grave as he said with a vile laugh, "Your father is dead!"

Then Rena would scream and come out of her sleep, gasping and weeping. It would take hours for her trembling limbs to grow still, and she came to dread the night for fear of the nightmare coming again.

She'd had the dream the night before she went downstairs to find Uncle Mark sitting at the table. He could move around very little and always with great pain, but he covered his discomfort by saying, "Good morning, Rena. Come and eat some of these good pancakes Dorrie fixed for you and me."

"I'm not very hungry," she said but sat down, and when Dorrie put a golden brown pancake on her plate, she cut it into neat morsels and began to eat. Mark noted her wan face but said nothing. *Missing her father,* he thought and set out to take her mind off Clay.

"Gracefield has a new hand, did you know that?" he said, smiling.

"A new hand?"

"Yes, young Josh Yancy. You know him, don't you?"

"Oh yes. He helped Lowell with the balloon."

"He's quite an interesting boy. Clay was telling me how handy he is with tools." Mark forced himself to eat another bite of pancake, then added, "Ought to be company for you. You're about the same age."

"He's very shy," Rena remarked. "I guess because he stutters so bad."

"I think he might get over that," Mark said. "Some people do. Has he always stuttered?"

"Oh yes. I've known him for a long time—all my life, really. But he's a strange boy." She sipped the cocoa from the china mug, then said thoughtfully, "You know, Uncle Mark, now that I think of it, he's always avoided me. Every time I've gone to visit Melora, he always stayed out hunting. And he'd come in late, after I was in bed. The only time he'd talk to me was when we were out with the pigs—and then he only talked about those dirty animals!"

"What does Melora say?"

"I asked her about Josh once, and she talked about him a long time. I could see she was worried about him." Rena chewed a bite of pancake thoughtfully, then said, "She told me some people seem to be born feeling they're not as good as other people. She said Josh was like that. Even though he could do so many things so well, like making things and hunting and shooting. But she said she thought he stuttered because he felt like he is inferior."

"I've heard of things like that," Mark murmured. "But if he ever finds out he's not inferior, he might not stutter at all."

"I guess so." Rena looked at her uncle, then asked, "Do you think Lowell will get better, Uncle Mark? I mean—the way he acts?"

Mark frowned, for he had put this question to himself many times. He hesitated, not wanting to discourage the young woman, and finally said, "His problem is sort of like the one Josh has, Rena. He thinks because he lost a leg he's not the equal of other men. That's not unusual, I believe. Not true, of course, but with a strong young man like Lowell, it must seem that way. He's thinking nobody will ever love him—no woman, that is. And that's hard on a young man."

The two sat there talking, and Rooney joined them, and finally Susanna. They talked carefully around the subject of Lowell's condition, and finally Rena rose, saying, "I'm going riding if it's all right."

Her grandmother agreed, and she went at once to change into a riding habit that Clay had bought for her, one with a divided skirt that had made her the object of considerable gossip. But she loved to ride the horse Clay had gotten her and could not bear the sidesaddle most women used.

When she got to the stable, she found that all the stable hands were gone and set out to saddle the mare herself. But Candy was a difficult horse to manage, and finally after half an hour, Rena was exhausted and furious.

"You dumb ol' horse!" she cried angrily. "I ought to beat you with a stick."

"C–can I h–help you, M–Miss Rena?"

Rena whirled to find that Josh had come across the field and was watching her. Suspecting that he might be laughing at her, she snapped, "No! I'll get this saddle on if it kills me!"

Josh started to leave, but he couldn't just leave Rena to struggle with that all day.

He was, in fact, more afraid of Rena Rocklin than he was of almost anything—and always had been. Clay had brought her to his home often when she was only a child, and Josh remembered every visit! He didn't remember, however, the moment when he'd grown so tense around her that he avoided her. All he knew was that she was so beautiful and so far above him that he could not bear the thought of being humiliated by her. She'd never made fun of his handicap, but he was terrified that she might—and he didn't think he could stand that!

But now he forced his timidity to one side, came forward, and picked up the saddle. Ignoring her protests, he moved toward Candy, murmuring her name. The mare watched him suspiciously but allowed him to grasp her bridle. He tied her to the rail fence, then slapped the saddle on her. He tightened the cinch, then turned to say, "Y–you just h–have to let her kn–know who's boss."

Rena smiled suddenly and said, "Thanks, Josh." She mounted and took the reins. But instead of riding away, she asked, "How do you like living here, Josh?"

Josh had turned to leave but, at her question, stopped and turned to face her. "F–fine, Miss R–Rena," he replied. As always his mind went into some sort of paralysis, and he cursed himself. *After she's gone, I'll think of all kinds of stuff to say!*

Rena waited for him to say more; then when she saw that he was silent, she said, "You ought to go hunting. I know you and your father love that. My father said the woods are stiff with coons this year."

At once Josh's face brightened. "I'd l–like that! I'll f–find me a d–dog and go t–tonight!"

A whim came to Rena, born perhaps out of the boredom of her life—or perhaps out of a desire to spend her night free of the nightmare. "Take me with you, Josh," she said impulsively.

"Why, I c–can't do that!"

"Why not?"

"B–because. . ." Josh wanted to say that aristocratic young ladies didn't go running through the woods with poor white boys, but he couldn't manage all that. He stood before her helplessly, not knowing what to say. Finally he shook his head. "Miz R–Rocklin—she wouldn't like it!"

Rena grinned at Josh. "You haven't been here long enough to find out how spoiled I am! I can get anything I want out of my grandmother." While not far from the truth, Rena knew that she would have to maneuver carefully to do anything as wild as this! "I've even got a dog," she said. "The slaves borrow Buck sometimes to go coon hunting. You have to take me, though, to get Buck." Rena laughed at the shocked expression on Josh's face, then added, "Buck and Rooney will probably want to go. They don't know any more about hunting coons than I do, so you'll have to teach us all. What time do we leave?"

They left at dusk, Josh still in shock. He had never for one moment believed that the Rocklins would let Rena go on a coon hunt, but Rena had produced her grandmother with a flourish, bringing her to the blacksmith shop, where Josh was helping Box.

"My granddaughter tells me you fancy yourself a coon hunter, Josh," Susanna Rocklin had said at once. "Is that right?"

Josh had blinked in surprise, appalled. *That fool girl has got me in trouble right off,* he'd thought. "W–well, I've g–got a few, ma'am."

"Well, it's not very ladylike. But I can't think of a better reason than that for her not to go, so you take her along. Take Rooney and Buck, too." Susanna had smiled fondly at Rena, then instructed Josh, "Don't let them get chewed up by a bear or some other wild creature, you hear me?"

Josh had been too surprised to do more than nod, but at dusk he was joined by the three, who were all happy at the thought of spending the night in the woods.

Josh had said at once, "Go put on warmer c–clothes, and bring a bl–blanket!" He had gone to the kitchen and gotten enough food from Dorrie, who glared at him.

"Boy, you watch out fo' dem young folks!"

"I w–will, D–Dorrie," he muttered, then left the kitchen to go to the barn. He tied the sack on a mule named Revelation, and when the others came with blankets, he strapped them on.

"We can't all ride one mule, Josh," Buck piped up.

Josh grinned suddenly. "Nope. We w–walk, just l–like he does."

Rooney laughed at Buck, saying, "You wouldn't know a coon if you saw one!"

"Would, too!"

Rena was happy as she said, "Let's go, Josh. Buck's ready!"

The big dog sensed the excitement and ran ahead as they left the grounds. Josh spoke to him, and Buck came at once to his call. Rena was surprised. "Buck won't mind most people like that," she said. "How do you do that—make him mind?"

"Don't know." Josh shrugged. "M—most dogs seem t—to mind me."

Josh had been careful to talk to some of the slaves who hunted and had gotten good instructions. He led them to a spot about five miles from the house and then said, "Here w—we are."

Buck looked around, asking, "Where's the coons, Josh?"

"More to c—coon hunting th—than you might think," Josh said with a grin. "Let's m—make a fire."

The three of them ran to find wood, and by the time Josh had unloaded Revelation, they had enough to build a large fire. "Can I start it, Josh?" Buck asked. "I know how to build a fire."

"Fly at it, B—Buck!"

Josh let the three do the work, and when the fire was crackling, he pulled out a blanket and sat down on it close to the fire. Rena stared at him. "When do we get the coons?" she asked.

"Not for a l—long time," Josh said. Clasping his legs, he looked at the three who were all ready to start killing coons with both hands. "The b—best part of a hunt is sittin' around the f—fire," he said mildly.

The three looked rather foolish but joined Josh. They slowly unwound, and finally they began to talk freely. Josh said almost nothing, but Rena found it pleasant to talk and to listen. The darkness closed in, and there was something cozy about the flickering fire that scored the darkness. She was wide awake and happy, glad that she'd organized the hunt.

After two hours, Rooney said abruptly, "I'm hungry!" Rena and Buck echoed this, and they scurried around getting the food out of the sacks. There were potatoes and steaks—but nothing to cook in.

"We can't eat these raw, Josh!" Rena said reproachfully.

"I'll show you." Leading them to a small creek nearby, Josh showed them how to wrap the potatoes in mud, then how to bury them in the hot ashes. Then taking his sheath knife, he cut four saplings with forks on the end, peeled them, and showed the others how to attach the steaks to the forks. They went to the fire, and soon the smell of cooking meat filled the air.

They ate the steaks and the biscuits that Dorrie had donated like famished sharks. Later they dug the potatoes out of the ashes, but the three looked doubtful. "Eat those old black things?" Rena asked.

But when Josh opened them with his knife and dug the firm, white, steaming flesh from the blackened hulls, they devoured them with relish.

Finally about midnight, Josh rose, saying, "Buck! Go!" The big dog bounded into the darkness, and Josh yelled, "Well, you w–wanted to hunt c–coons, didn't you? C–come on, then!"

Rena would never forget that wild chase! She plunged through the woods, stumbling into holes, running into saplings that struck her across the face, out of breath and half afraid. But always she was aware that Josh was beside her, grabbing her arm to keep her from falling. "How can you *see*, Josh?" she gasped. "You must have eyes like an owl!"

Rooney and Buck were floundering through the thickets, both afraid of getting lost but having the time of their lives. Finally Josh called, "He's treed!"

Not five minutes later he led them to an open spot with one huge tree in the middle of it. By the light of the moon, they could see Buck clawing at the tree, baying in a hysterical fashion.

"Persimmon t–tree," Josh informed them. He peered upward, then said, "Big 'un!"

"How do we get 'im down, Josh?" Buck cried out, his eyes big with excitement.

Josh was staring up into the tree. "Go up and shake h–him down, B–Buck!" he commanded. "We'll l–let the d–dog take him!"

Rooney protested, but Buck went up the tree like a squirrel. As he moved upward, he sensed the coon moving and cried out, "He's goin' out on a limb, Josh! I'll shake him down! Get ready!"

Standing beneath the shadowy form of the animal, Josh waited, and soon the limb began to move violently up and down. "Watch out!" he yelled to the girls—and at that moment he saw a dark mass falling right at him!

Rena could not see clearly, but she saw the coon hit Josh, knocking him to the ground. She screamed, "Josh!" but all she could see was the blurred form of Josh rolling on the ground. He was shouting, "Git off me!"

After a few moments of frenzied action, part of the bulk scooted into the dark, pursued instantly by the dog.

"Josh, there's another one up here!" they heard Buck yell. "Want me to shake him down?"

"No! That was a bobcat you shook out on me—not a coon!"

"Oh, Josh!" Rena cried out and ran to where he was coming to his feet. She misjudged the distance and ran into him, upsetting him so that he fell down—and she with him. For one moment her face was close to his, and she whispered, "Are you hurt bad?"

"No!" Josh said, terribly conscious of Rena as she was crushed against him. Struggling to his feet, he pulled Rena up, then shouted, "Buck, don't shake *nothing* else out of that tree! It might be a grizzly bear!"

Rena and Rooney found that extremely funny and began giggling hysterically. Buck came scooting down and stopped to stare at the two; then he, too, began laughing. "I'll bet you looked funny when that ol' bobcat landed on you!" he said.

Josh stood there, embarrassed and ready to put up his wall of silence, but he found that he could laugh with them. All four of them laughed until they cried, and finally Josh said weakly, "Well, I g–guess we scared every c–coon away for t–ten miles!"

He led them back to the fire, and they stayed awake for hours, talking and singing old songs. Rooney sang one of the songs she'd heard the soldiers sing in camp:

Soft blows the breath of morning
In my own valley fair,
For it's there the opening roses

With fragrance scent the air,
With fragrance scent the air,
And with perfume fill the air,
But the breath of one I left there
Is sweeter far to me.

Soft fall the dews of evening
About our valley bowers;
And they glisten on the grass plots
And tremble on the flowers,
And tremble on the flowers
Like jewels rich to see,
But tears of one I left there
Are richer gems to me.

The sweet voice of the young woman seemed to lay a charm on the dark woods, and a quietness followed. Soon Rooney and Buck rolled up in their blankets and were fast asleep.

Josh thought that Rena was asleep, too. He sat staring at the fire until Buck came out of the woods, his tongue hanging out. Rena spoke, breaking the silence, saying, "Come here, Buck." The dog moved to her, flopped down, and then Rena said, "Josh, I never had so much fun in all my life!"

"Well, it is f–fun."

"You know something?" When Josh looked at her, she said softly, "You never stuttered when you were fighting with that bobcat."

She had never mentioned his impediment, and Josh's face reddened. He stared into the fire without answering, and she came out of her blankets and moved to sit beside him. "Don't be afraid to talk about it, Josh," she said. "It's nothing to be ashamed of, and someday it'll be gone."

"No, it w—won't never!"

He turned his face from her, but she wouldn't be denied. "You have to believe things, Josh. I do, anyway."

"B—believing won't m—make nothing happen!"

"I think it will." She hesitated, then found herself telling him about her dream. She had never told a soul, but somehow the darkness and the quietness seemed to make it easy. The fire sputtered as she spoke, and when she was finished, she was embarrassed. Half rising, she muttered, "Guess you think I'm crazy!"

He turned and caught her arm, pulling her back. "No, I d—don't," he said faintly. "You're the s—smartest girl I kn—know, 'cept for M—Melora."

She smiled at him, and he felt an odd feeling go through him. He was suddenly aware that he was holding her arm and dropped it abruptly.

"Josh—are you afraid of me?" Rena asked abruptly. "I mean—you've always avoided me. Don't you like me at all?"

Josh dropped his head and cleared his throat. "S—sure I l—like you, but. . ."

When he didn't finish, Rena knew what he was thinking. "Don't be afraid to be friends, Josh," she said quietly. "I told

989

you about my nightmare, and I haven't told it to anyone else. I thought I could tell you, and you wouldn't think. . .that I was silly."

"I would never th–think that!"

He turned to her and smiled, a full smile that she'd never seen, and she said, "Will we be friends, then? Real good friends?"

Josh swallowed and nodded without speaking. He was too full for speech and finally cleared his throat. "What did y–you mean about b–believing something?"

"I have to believe Daddy will come home and not get killed." She shivered at the words, and fear came to her, but she shook her head and said, "It's like—as long as I believe it, it'll happen, but if I stop. . ."

She broke off, and the two of them sat there in the flickering light of the fire. Finally she said, "Josh, let's both try to believe that my daddy, Dent, and your brothers will come home safe and that some day soon you won't stutter anymore."

Josh Yancy had never met anyone like this girl! For years he'd watched her, but shyness had kept him from approaching her. Now he was sitting beside her, looking into her dark eyes— and she was asking him to be her friend!

"I—I th–think that would be. . .r–real nice," he managed to say.

The two sat there, conscious that they had been given to one another. Finally Josh smiled at Rena, shaking his head. "You learn a lot on a coon hunt, d–don't you, R–Rena?"

CHAPTER 15

"I'll Never Be a Man Again!"

After the coon hunt Rena continually pressured Josh to take her again. He put her off on that but took her several times after small game—rabbits and squirrels. She was never able to hit much, and she hated it when Josh did. The first time he knocked over a plump rabbit and picked up the limp, bloody carcass, Rena had taken one look and cried, "Oh, the poor thing!"

Josh had given her an astonished look, then asked, "W–well, did you think I was g–gonna *kiss* it, R–Rena?" She had refused to look at it and begged him not to shoot another one. "What about th–that bacon you had for b–breakfast?" Josh had grinned slyly. "You think that p–pig died of old age?" But Rena had prevailed, and they had spent the afternoon tramping through the woods.

David had noted that Rena was constantly begging Josh to do something or other and one morning commented on it to

Susanna. The two of them were walking along the lane that led to the main road when Rena and Josh appeared at the edge of the woods, the girl's clear laughter sounding on the fresh April air. "She keeps that boy hopping, doesn't she?"

Susanna glanced at the pair and nodded. "He's been very good for her, David," she said. "She's been lonely for a long time."

"I know. Glad Dad thought of hiring the boy. He's as hard a worker as I ever saw—and he can make anything under the sun, I do believe!"

They ambled down the lane, enjoying the brilliant colors of the oaks and maples, then turned at the edge of the woods and made their way slowly along the split-rail fence. Abruptly David said, "Lowell's no better." His face was lined with pain, and he shook his head with desperation. "Just sits in that room and broods. You'd think he'd at least talk to his brother about it."

"He won't talk about his injury to anyone, David."

"I know, and that's bad. You know how some of the men are at Chimborazo? They make a joke about their wounds."

"Lowell will have to learn to accept this, but he's all shut up in himself. Your father is worried sick, and I guess I am, too."

David looked at her, and a startled expression came to his face. *If Grandmother's worried, things are even worse than I thought!* He took a few more steps, then halted and turned to her. "I wish I were a stronger man," he said, a sad note in his voice. "More like my brother Dent."

"Don't you ever say that!" A fierce light came to Susanna's

eyes, and she seized his arm and shook him angrily. "I won't have you talk like that, David!"

He blinked at her in astonishment, for she was not given to such outbursts. He smiled suddenly, then reached out and wrapped his hands around hers, holding them tightly. "Always take up for me, don't you, Grandmother?"

"You're who you are, and God made you that way, David. I don't want to hear you put yourself down again!" She saw that her sudden outburst had stunned him and made herself wait until she grew calmer. "I'm not Belle Boyd, the glamorous Rebel spy, but you don't want me to be, do you?" When he burst into laughter at the absurdity of her statement, she touched his arm, saying, "God made you, and He made Dent. He needs both of you, so let's hear no more foolishness!"

❧

"Oh, come on, Josh!" Rena begged. She had nagged him into taking her into the woods to look for the eggs of wild birds for her collection, but as they emerged, she'd asked him to take her fishing.

"I don't have t–time, Rena," Josh had protested. Looking across the field, he spotted Susanna and David Rocklin and said guiltily, "Now l–look, there's y–your grandmother and your brother!"

Rena gave a careless look at the two, then shook her head, her long dark hair swinging over her back. "They don't care what I do." She tugged at his arm and turned her eyes up at him—a tactic that she'd discovered would make him do almost anything she asked. "Come on, Josh, let's go!"

But Josh shook his head stubbornly. "No, I c–can't do it. I g–got work to do!" But when she continued to hold his arm and plead, he said finally, "W–well, we can go l–late this afternoon, I guess."

"Good!" Rena's eyes gleamed with victory, and she turned and ran away, saying, "I'll go dig some worms, and we can get some liver from Dorrie for catfish bait!"

Josh stared at her, then shook his head, mumbling, "I got t–to quit g–givin' in to that g–girl!" Then he hurried after her, turning to go to the forge, where he spent an hour working on various chores. Box, the elderly blacksmith, grinned at him as he worked, saying slyly, "Glad you fin' a little time to work, Josh." He was seventy-two and had been the blacksmith for the Rocklins since he was a young man. His hair was white as cotton, but his upper body was as powerful as ever from years at the forge. His world was no larger than Gracefield, and he wanted it that way. "Guess making a wagon wheel ain't as much fun as runnin' around with a purty gal, is it, Josh?"

Josh looked up from the forge, his face glowing from the heat. He knew Box was teasing him, but he didn't mind. Box was his teacher, and he had become fast friends with the slave. He looked at the piece of steel critically, then took it over to the anvil and picked up a hammer. Box watched as the boy began to strike the white-hot metal, nodding with approval. *He's a good one. Don't nevah waste his strength none. Always hits jes' right.*

When Josh finished the job, he put his tools away, saying, "I've got to go see Miss Rooney, Box. See you later."

He left the shop and went to the Big House, where he found Rooney in the kitchen shelling peas with Susanna. "Hello, Josh." Rooney smiled at him as he entered. "Come on and help us shell peas." She knew how he hated that kind of work and said quickly, "Just teasing." She rose and put the peas on the table, saying, "Something's wrong with Lowell's wheelchair. It's hard to roll."

"I'll t—take a look."

"I'll go with you. I'll be back to help with the peas, Miz Rocklin."

The two of them moved out of the kitchen, and the boy asked, "How is he?"

"His leg is healing well, but. . ." Rooney didn't finish, and Josh understood her anxiety. The two of them entered the room and found Lowell in the bed. Several magazines were scattered on the coverlet, but he was simply staring out the window.

"Josh has come to fix your chair, Lowell," Rooney said. "You need to get outside and get some of this good spring air in your lungs."

Lowell merely looked at her, then said, "Hello, Josh."

"Hello, M—Mister Lowell," Josh answered quickly. *He looks better than the last time I saw him,* he thought. He let his eyes drop to the brightly colored spread that covered the injured man, and marked the flatness where Lowell's leg should have been. Quickly he averted his eyes, turned, and walked to the wheelchair. As he examined the chair, he listened as Rooney tried to carry on a conversation with Lowell. But it was hopeless, and Josh thought of how miserable it had been trying to speak with him.

He looked at the chair, then turned to say, "N–needs a new axle."

"Can you fix it, Josh?" Rooney asked.

She was wearing a yellow dress that Josh had never seen before—one of Rena's, he guessed. *She sure does look nice,* Josh thought. *If lookin' at her don't pick up Mister Lowell's spirits, I don't know what will!* "Oh sure," he said. "Have to t–take it with m–me, though."

Lowell had been looking down at his marred outline. Now he lifted his head and said bitterly, "Go on, take it. I'm not going anywhere."

"You will be, Lowell," Rooney said quickly.

"Where would I go, to a ball? I could charm all the ladies with my new one-step waltz!"

There was such anger in Lowell's voice that Josh wanted to help him. "Aw, Mister Lowell, you'll b–be gettin' around soon."

"In a wheelchair? No thanks!"

Josh spoke before he thought, but he had grown very fond of Lowell during the days they had worked together. "You can g–get a new leg. L–lots of men—"

"Shut up!" Lowell glared at the boy, his eyes hot with anger. He had kept to his room, refusing to leave except on rare occasions, and his nerves were ragged. Night after night he had lain awake, hoping to die, and when that hadn't happened, he had searched for something to do with his life.

But there was nothing—or so he had decided. All his life he'd been active riding, hunting, and fishing. And none of those things could be done by a man with one leg. Sometimes he'd have a quick, vivid memory of a dance, of gliding around the room easily, looking into the eyes of a young woman, and a terrible fury would come, sweeping over him like a red tide. He'd taken his health for granted, and now that he was crippled, there was nothing in him, no resources to fall back on.

And so he lay in his bed—or sat in a chair—and stared out the window. And he treated people miserably! He lashed out at his grandmother, at Rooney, and at the slaves, shouting with a rage that rose in him unbidden. He let the loss of his leg turn him into a monster.

Now he stared at Josh, who had dropped his head, and felt shame. But he could not apologize, so he said, "Go on, fix the chair. I can sit in it and look out the window."

Josh left without a word, and Lowell glanced at Rooney, expecting her to berate him for his shameful outburst. But she merely began cleaning up the room, and finally her silence grated on him. "Well, go on and say it!" he growled.

Rooney turned to face him, her voice gentle. "Say what?"

"Tell me I'm an ingrate!" He ground out the words. His lips were contorted in an expression of self-loathing, and his eyes were filled with misery. "Say it! I could have been killed. Or tell me that other men have lost their legs without turning into. . . sullen beasts!"

Rooney's eyes filled with compassion, and she sat down on the edge of the bed. "You mustn't think such things, Lowell," she said gently. She wanted to put her arms around him and hold him as she'd held Buck when he was small and had come to her with his hurts. But she was wise enough to know that this was not the time—not yet. "You've had a bad time—worse than most men. Nobody can blame you for. . ."

When Rooney halted, Lowell suddenly grinned—the first sign of any humor she'd seen! "Acting like a spoiled brat?" he said. "Oh, don't be afraid to say it, Rooney. Don't you think I know how ungrateful I've been?"

"You mustn't—"

He waved his hand impatiently, cutting off her words. "I know what you've done, coming here and nursing me and Mark. But Mark's easy to take care of. I'm the one causing all the trouble." He had been sitting up, his back braced against the pillows. Now he slumped, and the anger and bitterness seemed to fade—at least for a time. He sat there silently, then looked up at Rooney, saying in a tightly controlled voice, "Other men have handled this, Rooney, but I can't. I never will."

"You will, Lowell!" Rooney could no longer refrain from touching him. She took his hand in hers, looking directly into his troubled eyes. Hope glowed in her eyes, and her lips parted softly as she spoke. "I know it'll be hard. There'll be some things you won't be able to do as well, but some things you'll learn to do better than before!"

Lowell stared at her. "What could a one-legged man do

better than one who's got both legs?" he demanded.

"Why, Lowell Rocklin, I expect you could do just about anything you wanted to do!"

Her statement shocked Lowell, and then he demanded again, "What could I do better with only one leg?"

Rooney was very quick, and she at once replied, "Why, you could invent something." She read the surprise in his eyes and rushed to say, "I know you don't like to talk about the balloon, but it was wonderful, Lowell, the way you made it! General Able told Mister Clay that he wished you'd make another one. He said it wasn't your fault that it got hit by a shell!"

"Not enough silk in Richmond for another one—even if we used ladies' underwear!"

His faint attempt at humor encouraged Rooney, and she squeezed his hand. "I guess not. But you could make something else for the army. And Josh and I would help!"

Lowell's eyes grew thoughtful, and he was very much aware of the firmness of her hand, which held his tightly. He could smell the faint lilac perfume that she used, and the sun shone on her hair, catching the gold glints in the auburn tresses.

For a moment she thought he was about to agree, and her spirit soared. But then he sighed and turned his head away from her. He pulled his hand free and muttered, "No, I'm just a cripple."

His words destroyed the brightness of her smile, and she whispered, "No, Lowell!"

But he turned to face her, and she saw that his eyes had

gone dead. He shook his head slowly, saying, "I'll never be a man again, Rooney—not a whole one, anyway."

"You can try, Lowell!" she pleaded.

"No! If I can't be a whole man, I don't see any use in anything." He rolled over, turning his back to her. Slowly she rose and without a word left the room.

Lowell lay on his side, sick at heart. Outside his window he could hear a group of blackbirds making their raucous cries. He kept his eyes tightly shut, trying to shut out the world. A vision of Rooney's face rose before him, and he heard her whisper, *"You can try, Lowell!"*

But he lay there facing the wall and knew that he would never be what others wanted him to be. *I can't do it!* he cried silently. *It'll all be pity, and I can't take that!*

CHAPTER 16

MARK AND ROONEY

"Look, Buck, the army's like a pyramid," Clay explained to the boy who sat beside him in a weathered cane-bottomed chair. The two of them had come in from a quick tour around the plantation and now were waiting for Josh to bring the buggy up from the barn.

Buck had been asking Clay question after question about the army, and Clay had answered them patiently. He was looking rested now; all the strain of battle that recent skirmishes had etched into his face was gone. A notebook was on the seat of an empty chair beside him, and he tore a page out of it, fished in his pocket for a pencil, then began to draw a diagram of a pyramid.

"Right here at the top is General Lee. He's the commander of the Army of Northern Virginia. But that army is divided into two parts, what we call *corps*. General Longstreet commands one and General Jackson the other."

Buck studied the page, then asked, "Which corps are you in, Captain?"

"Jackson's corps," Clay said. "But a corps is divided up into *divisions*—usually two or three, each one commanded by a general. A division's usually got somewhere between two to four thousand men."

"That's a lot!"

"Yes, it is—too many for one man to keep up with. So each division is divided into *brigades*. See?" Clay drew on the paper and watched the boy follow it intently. *He's a bright boy—reminds me of David.* He drew more lines, saying, "And each brigade is divided up into what we call *regiments*, usually about five hundred men."

Buck glanced up at Clay, admiration in his sharp features. "It's really complicated, ain't it?"

"Sure is, but it has to be this way. Sometimes the army has to move quick, Buck, and it can only do that if the privates know what to do." He leaned back and smiled at the bright-faced youngster. "Now General Lee can't come and say to every private, 'Soldier, get ready to march!' No, that wouldn't do. So he tells his corps commanders, and they tell the division commanders under them; then they pass the word along to brigade commanders, and they yell at the officers of the regiment—that's the next unit on the pyramid. Every regiment has ten *companies*. And I think, Buck, the company is the most important unit of all."

"Why is that, Captain?"

"It's small enough so the captain over it can know every man. He's like a father to them, sees after them, you know? And most of us, when we're asked which unit we're with, will name our company—like I'll say, 'I'm in C Company.'"

"And what does a lieutenant do in the company?"

"Look here, Buck," Clay said, pointing at the pyramid.

"Here's C Company, and there are two platoons. My son Lieutenant Denton is over the First Platoon." He leaned back and watched the boy study the chart, then nodded. "That's pretty well the way all armies are made up, Buck. Think you understand it?"

"Sure!"

Clay smiled and tore out a fresh sheet of paper. "All right, let's see you draw that pyramid." He took the pencil sketch, folded it, and watched as Buck fell to drawing, his whole attention on the paper. Josh pulled up in the buggy, and Clay said, "I'll go up and say good-bye to Lowell, Josh. Wait for me."

Josh nodded, then slipped out of the buggy and mounted the porch as Clay stepped into the house. Clay walked quickly down the hall, opened the door, and entered. "Came to say good-bye, son," he said to Lowell, who was sitting in his wheelchair holding a book. Not wanting to tower over Lowell, he sat down quickly in the straight-backed chair, studying the boy's face. *He's pale as a ghost, and he's lost too much weight*, was his thought, but he said only, "Hate to leave, but the army's moving right away."

Lowell said, "I wish you didn't have to go."

"Well, it'll be over someday, Lowell." Clay leaned back and sighed deeply. "The world's upside down, but it's been that way before and it'll be that way again. The thing to do when that happens is just to hang on until it comes right again."

"I guess so."

Lowell's reply was without energy, and for the entire ten minutes that Clay sat there, he replied to questions but offered nothing of his own. Finally Clay despaired, hating to leave but knowing that he must. Leaning forward, he said intently, "Son, I know this has hit you hard, but you've got a lot of life ahead of you. You can't hide in this room for the next thirty years." He spoke passionately and with compassion, but it was useless. Finally he saw that he was speaking to a man who'd given up on life, so he rose and moved to stand over Lowell. He bent down, embraced him, and said huskily, "God keep you, my son!" Then he waited, but Lowell only stared at him, saying nothing except, "I hope you come back safe—and with both legs."

Clay turned and walked from the room defeated and frustrated. He found Buck on the porch holding out his sheet of paper, asking, "Is this right?"

Clay stared at it blindly, then made himself focus on the drawing. "Yes, Buck. Exactly right. You'll make a good soldier someday."

"Maybe I can go with you now," Buck piped up eagerly. "Some of them drummer boys ain't no older than me!"

Bitterness came to Clay as he stared at the boy's youthful countenance, but he mustered a smile. "Stay here and take care of your sister, Buck. You're only a boy once, and there's no going back to live it again." He reached out and shook the boy's hand, then turned to say, "Let's go, Josh."

"Yes, sir!"

The two men got into the buggy, and Josh slapped the reins, startling the team into an abrupt trot. Getting to the main road, he turned their heads toward Richmond. For several miles neither man spoke. Finally Clay pulled himself together and turned to say, "I appreciate your driving me to camp, Josh." When the boy muttered that it was no trouble, Clay studied him more closely.

All the Yancy boys look like copies, he thought, then said, "I think Lonnie will make sergeant pretty soon. He's a fine soldier, but so is your other brother." Lonnie was in Clay's company, and Bob had just rejoined the company after recuperating from the leg wound he received at Fredericksburg.

"I g–get to thinkin' I ought to b–be in with them, C–Captain."

"No, you're too young! And besides, you're doing an important job."

"Raising p–pigs?"

"Doesn't sound like much, but the army will starve if it doesn't get food. And some fools are so busy raising cotton they won't have a thing for the soldiers!" Clay had made a cause of this, trying to get his fellow planters to see that the docks were full of cotton that could not be sold. *Why grow more?* he'd asked but had been ignored. All most Southern planters could think of was cotton, and they'd plant it until the bales reached the heavens.

Shrugging off his anger, Clay leaned back and thought about his family. Finally he said, "You've been good for Rena, Josh." He noted the boy's nervous glance and chuckled, slapping him on the shoulder. "You afraid I'd be a mad father, jumping all over you for taking my girl hunting?"

Josh colored but turned to face the big man squarely. "Y—yes, sir, that's about w—what I expected."

"You should know better," Clay said. "You've known Rena since you were children. And you know that since her mother died, and since I'm gone, she gets lonesome."

"I seen that." Josh wanted to say more but felt decidedly awkward. The distance in Southern society between a poor white farmer and a plantation owner was much like the distance between stars.

But Clay said, "You're an honest young man, Josh. I didn't hire you just to do the work." He was amused at Josh's look of astonishment and added, "I wanted you to be there to help Lowell. And now I see I was wiser than I knew. Because now it's pretty clear that Rena needs someone, too."

"I—I think the w—world of both of 'em, Mister Clay!"

"I know that, Josh, and it takes some of the pain out of leaving just to know that you'll be around." He hesitated, then said, "Lowell isn't easy to be with, but I hope you'll try to spend time with him. Get him interested in something—anything! He's got to get out of that room!"

Josh nodded sharply. "Miss Rooney and m–me talked about th–that."

"That's a bright young woman, Josh. What'd she say?"

Clay listened carefully as Josh slowly spun out the scheme that he and Rooney had put together. It took some time, for Josh halted often, angered by his impediment. The words were there, but they seemed to get lodged in his tongue. Finally he said, "So we h–hope it'll help him, C–Captain."

"You know, it just might!" Clay sat up, his back rigid with excitement. "It just might work!" He slapped his thigh hard and shook his head angrily. "I hate to go! By heaven, I do!" Then he caught himself and took a deep breath. Expelling it slowly, he said evenly, "But nobody wants to go off and fight—unless he's a fool!"

"Where w–will you be f–fighting, Captain?"

"I don't know for sure, Josh," Clay said slowly; then his eyes turned north. "Somewhere north of here. Maybe even Maryland again."

Josh looked in the direction Clay had indicated, then shook his head. "Tell Lonnie and B–Bob to be c–careful." He paused and added shyly, "And you, t–too, Mister Clay!"

"It's in God's hands, Josh," Clay said heavily. "All we can do is pray!"

❧

The good days were full of dull, throbbing pain—something a man could bear. One could bear a toothache for a day, and if

Mark thought of it like that, it seemed easier: *A toothache in the side, that's all it is.*

But the bad days were different. The pain came at unexpected moments, such as when he was lifting a spoon of hot chicken soup to his lips. He'd never been stuck with a bayonet, but the pain was like that—or so he thought—a sliver of hot steel stabbing without warning into his side! There was no controlling it—his whole body would arch in protest, sending the soup spoon flying. *If it would only begin easy, I could get ready for it!* Mark would think, but it never did. Always it was unexpected, and it never failed to send him into a gasping spasm.

Some days they didn't come—and the day that Clay came to say good-bye was one of his good days. The pain gnawed dully at his side and stomach, but he could bear that and covered it with a smile on his pale lips. He'd talked with Clay, urging him not to make a fool of himself by rushing into danger, then had halted abruptly. "But it does no good to warn you, Clay. I know you better than to think you'll take care of yourself." He'd spoken of Lowell, promising to do what he could, but neither man had much hope.

After Clay had left, Mark had gotten out of bed and moved carefully to the window, where he'd watched the two men leave for Richmond. Carefully he straightened up, and a surprised look crossed his thin face as there was little pain.

"Well, you're going to behave yourself, are you?" He had gotten into the absurd habit of speaking to his wound, addressing it as if it were a familiar enemy. "Well then, I'll just take advantage of your good behavior by getting dressed and getting about a bit."

He walked into the kitchen half an hour later, and Dorrie stared at him with a startled expression. "Whut you doin' outta dat bed!" She snorted. "Miss Susanna ain't said nuffin' 'bout you gettin' up!"

"Had to have some of your good cooking, Dorrie," Mark said with a smile. "My sister-in-law won't bring me anything but soup with weeds in it."

"Dem ain't weeds!" Dorrie snapped. "Dat's *parsley*, and it's good fo' you!"

Mark had been fond of Dorrie for years and had always loved to tease her. "Now, Dorrie, I know a weed when I see one," he insisted. "I'm not here for soup with weeds in it, anyway."

"Well, whut *does* you wants?" Dorrie demanded.

Mark closed his eyes as if thinking and counted off the items on his fingers: "A chicken-fried steak with lots of mushrooms. Some hush puppies and fried catfish, with lots of hot sauce to go on it. Oh yes, some oysters covered with black pepper—"

"Mister Mark! You done los' yo' mind?" Dorrie stood in the center of the floor, staring at the tall man aghast. "Why, dat stuff would kill you daid!" At that moment Susanna and Rooney entered, and Dorrie informed them of the demands the sick man had made. She didn't see the wink he gave the two women, but was outraged and refused to have anything to do with it!

"I'll fix something for him, Dorrie," Susanna said, smiling, and Dorrie huffed off breathing dire prophecies about what would happen if the patient was allowed to eat such things!

"It's wonderful to see you're feeling better, Mark," Susanna said with a bright smile. "Sit down, and I'll fix you something good. Rooney, you eat with him." When Rooney started to protest, she said firmly, "Am I the mistress of this house? Do as I tell you!"

Rooney sat down but was not afraid. She had learned that there was nothing to fear from Susanna Rocklin. And she was quick enough to know that Susanna wanted her to spend time with her brother-in-law, so she began speaking at once, and soon Mark was resting in a chair, listening as Rooney related the tale of the coon hunt.

"I'd like to have seen that bobcat and Josh rolling around on the ground," he said when she had finished. "Did Rena like it?"

The two sat there until Susanna brought a plate of fluffy eggs and dry toast with the crust removed. "You can't have anything with grease, Mark, but I've got some fresh dewberry jam, the kind you like so much."

Mark ate only a little but enjoyed the company. He said so later when he and Rooney went out for a short walk—orders of Mrs. Susanna Rocklin.

"I'm glad to get outside," he said, breathing the fresh warm air. "Didn't know how much I liked the outdoors until I couldn't have it."

"It is nice. I've always loved spring best of any time of the year," Rooney said. "I grew up in the city, so I never really got to enjoy all the flowers and budding trees." She thought briefly of those days, then said shortly, "I hope I never have to go back there again!"

They were passing the scuppernong arbor, and Mark was growing tired. "Let's sit and rest here." When they were seated, he said idly, "You didn't like the city, Rooney?"

"Oh, I hated it! But there wasn't anyplace else for me to go...." Without meaning to, she began to speak of her life. She was not aware of how skillful the man who sat beside her was at drawing people out, and it was with a shock that she suddenly realized that she had told him more than she'd intended.

"Oh, I didn't mean to go into all that!"

Mark smiled at her, saying, "I'm glad you told me about yourself, Rooney." His cheeks had some color in them, and the pain was mild—for the moment. "It was a difficult life—for you and for Buck, too. And I'm sure you'll never have to go back to that sort of thing."

But his words caused Rooney's brow to crease, and her eyes grew cloudy with doubt. "I worry about that," she said quietly. She had not confessed this to anyone else, but somehow the man sitting beside her was so kind! "We can't stay here always," she added. "I love my mom, but when she's out of prison, I don't think we can go back to living the way we did. This place has been so good for Buck. Who knows what would happen if he started hanging around those bad men again. But I don't know what else we can do."

Mark began to offer her reassurance. "Maybe when your

ma gets released, she'll see how much better this place is for you than a saloon. And Susanna needs you, Rooney. Even after the war, she'll need you. I think. . ."

He spoke quietly and was rewarded by seeing that his words were giving comfort to the girl beside him. But just as she seemed to be fully at peace about her future, the pain came to Mark. He was saying quietly, "And Buck will be able to go to school—"

Then it hit him, like a white-hot saber driven to the hilt into his side. He gasped and grabbed at his side, his face drained white as paste.

"Mister Mark!" Rooney saw him falling to one side and quickly leaped to hold him. At first she was afraid he was dying, but he managed to gasp, "Don't. . .worry! Just a. . .bad spell!"

Rooney saw Highboy working on a window of the house and cried out, "Highboy, help me!" When he came galloping up, she said, "Help me get Mr. Rocklin to his room!"

Highboy practically carried the stricken man up the steps, and Rooney moved ahead, opening doors. When they got to Mark's room, Rooney said, "Be easy, Highboy. Put him on the bed."

The two of them eased him down, and Highboy asked nervously, "You wants me to fetch Miz Susanna?"

"No, Highboy. Thank you, but it's all right now."

The slave left, and Rooney pulled off Mark's shoes, then began to loosen his clothes. Then she looked at his contorted face and turned at once to the washstand. Taking a brown bottle from the shelf, she poured a few ounces into a small glass, then returned and placed it to his lips. He swallowed it, and she replaced the bottle. She had grown efficient in taking care of large men and soon had his clothing off. Carefully she removed the bandage on his side and saw that his wound was draining an unhealthy stream of yellowish fluid. Quickly she cleaned the wound, dressed it, then sat down beside him, saying, "Are you feeling better, Mister Mark?"

The opiate was taking effect, and he moved his head slowly toward her. The searing pain had subsided, dulled by the drug, and his eyes were heavy lidded.

"Yes," he whispered. "Thank you, Rooney!" He licked his lips, then shook his head. "That was. . .a very bad one!"

Rooney rose and got a pan of cool water and a cloth and bathed the sweat from his face. He lay still with his eyes closed, and she thought he had passed out. But then he opened his eyes and stared at her. She could not read the expression in his dark eyes, and finally she asked, "What is it, Mister Mark? Can I get you something?"

He didn't answer but continued to examine her through drug-dulled eyes. Finally he whispered, "How old are you, Rooney?"

"Why, I'm seventeen."

He found that interesting and after a long pause whispered, "Seventeen. . .and a fine young woman."

The clock on the wall tolled the seconds, and once again he began to slide away into unconsciousness. But again the eyes opened, and his lips moved.

"I was in love with a young woman once."

"You were, sir?"

"Oh yes. . . ." His eyes began to droop, and he forced them up with an effort. His lips were dry, and she gave him a drink, then put his head down.

Rooney knew a little of the Rocklin family history. She knew that Lowell had told her that Uncle Mark had never been married. *Maybe he married her and kept their marriage secret from everyone,* she thought. Rooney asked, "What was her name?"

"Her name was. . .Beth." Mark gazed at Rooney through haze-filled eyes. "You. . .you remind me of her. . . . So beautiful."

"What happened to her, sir? Did you marry?" Rooney asked quickly, for she could see Mark slipping away again.

"She. . .she. . .so beautiful." And then Mark was unconscious.

Rising, she slipped out of the room and went to find Susanna, who was alarmed over the incident. "Oh, he's asleep now," Rooney assured her. She and the older woman spoke about the care he'd need, and then Rooney asked, making her tone casual, "Did Mister Mark ever marry?"

"No. We all hoped he would, but he never did."

"That's too bad," Rooney said. "He would have made some woman very happy."

CHAPTER 17

"LET US CROSS OVER THE RIVER"

General Robert E. Lee led the Army of Northern Virginia, determined to hit the Union Army such a blow that the Peace Party in the North would force Lincoln to end the struggle.

Clay Rocklin and the members of C Company of the Stonewall Brigade saw him as he rode by on Traveler. "Look at him. That's Bobby Lee!" Lonnie Yancy breathed. "Ain't he somethin' now? And look at that hoss!"

The horse was iron gray, sixteen hands high, with a short back, deep chest, and small head. His delicate ears moved constantly as he bore his burden proudly. He was the jewel of his master's hands, guided by word and not by rein.

The rider, too, was iron gray, his hair and beard now frosted. Lee had a broad forehead, deep-set eyes, straight nose, firm lips. He was all grace and symmetry, and unlike Stonewall Jackson, whose strength was hammered, his was beneath the surface. He was loved and idolized as no other general on either side, one of those men who can cause other men to follow him to their death. He was a firm Christian, believed in his country with all his soul, but he could not lift his sword against his native state. Virginia was home and family, and he threw himself into what he knew was a losing struggle because of his love for this land.

Clay watched Lee ride past with his staff, then turned to Lonnie Yancy, saying, "Yes, he's something, all right."

"Don't see how we can lose," Lonnie said, eyeing the general ride down the line of march. He was so much like his father that Clay thought of Buford. He had the same lanky strength and green eyes and the same determination. Lonnie had joined the army before Bull Run and had fought in every engagement. Clay had tried to get him to stay home and take care of his father's farm, but Lonnie had said stubbornly, "No, sir, I'm gonna fight for mah rights!"

Now Clay looked at this tall man and thought how typical he was of the army that now wound around between two hills like a butternut-colored serpent.

His rights? Why, Lonnie doesn't even know what they are! he thought almost wearily. *He never owned a slave and never will, but he's going to war to fight for the right to own one.*

But the Army of Northern Virginia was composed of men like Lonnie Yancy. It was an army of hunters, riders, walkers—men who lived close to the ground. They were rebels against the new age of the machine birthed in the North, loving the dirt of the South fanatically.

Clay's eyes ran down the ranks of his own company, noting

how *different* they were. His eye fell on Sam Griffin, who had come to war with nothing but his pants and shirt—and a rifle one of his ancestors had used at King's Mountain in the American Revolution. His eyes moved to James Huger, who'd first come to the Grays with a haircloth trunk full of fine shirts and a body servant to mend them. Clay smiled at how Huger had been tormented until he'd shared the shirts and sent the slave home. Now he wore the same rough clothing and floppy hat as Sam Griffin.

"Think we'll whip the Yankees, Clay?"

Turning quickly, Clay looked up at his brother-in-law, Major Brad Franklin, who was mounted on a fine bay stallion. He was dressed in a new uniform and looked every inch a soldier, his intense face smiling with anticipation.

Clay liked this man and nodded. Knowing that his men needed to hear him speak positively, he answered, "We'll wear them out, Major. My boys are ready for a scrap!"

Franklin looked at the lean, tanned faces of the men of C Company and nodded. "I think we'll do them in this time, Captain. Never saw the army so fired up." His face grew serious. "Keep your head down, Clay." He grinned, then spurred his horse and rode down the line, pausing to speak to the men from time to time.

"We got some good officers, Captain." Waco Smith, the ex–Texas Ranger, had moved up to walk beside Clay. He was a tall man who still wore a .44 in a holster on his thigh. He had the most direct gaze of any man Clay had ever seen—and was a tiger in battle.

"Got the best noncoms, too," Clay said fondly. "You mind what the major said, Waco. Don't get yourself shot." He added lightly to cover his concern, "Too hard for me to break in a new sergeant."

Waco Smith shot a quick glance at Clay, then grinned. "I was fixin' to say that about officers," he remarked dryly. The two marched along, speaking quietly of the affairs of the company. For both of them it was, for now, the center of their worlds. The men who marched with them were their concern, and each knew that when the battle was over, some of the men who walked with them would not be there.

Thinking, perhaps, of this, Waco finally shook his head. "Bad about Lowell. But at least he won't get killed." Both of them knew of men who had shot their hands off to get out of going into battle, and Waco added, "Lowell's going to make it, ain't he, Clay?"

"Yes." Clay's voice was slow, and he added, "But he's taking it bad, Waco."

"Figured he would. Young fella like that, he wants to be best at things. But he'll be all right." Waco looked back over the line, studied it, then shrugged. There was a streak of fatalism in the Texan, and he remarked, "Guess we'll lose some, Captain." The thought stayed with him, and his eyes were half hooded as he finally asked, "Why do some of us get killed and some don't?"

"No man knows the answer to that, Waco," Clay responded.

He had wondered himself about this but had come to believe that such questions had no answer. "A man can only do his best, and the rest is up to God."

The answer didn't satisfy Waco Smith, and as they moved along toward the north, he said, "Don't seem to fit, Captain, but it's shore the way things are." He had the old soldier's habit of putting such philosophical quandaries into some deep recess of his mind, and he became more cheerful. "How strong you think we are? And how many Bluebellies aim to stop us?"

"We've got about sixty thousand men, I think," Clay answered. "Don't know how many we'll be facing."

Smith looked through the clouds of dust raised by the feet of thousands of marching men. "Wal, there'll be more of them than they is of us." He spoke almost lightly, without concern. The veterans of the Army of Northern Virginia were accustomed to long odds. But they felt as Waco did as he dismissed the superior numbers, saying, "As long as we got Bobby Lee and Stonewall, I don't keer how many of them we got to fight. . . ."

Neither Waco, Clay, nor even General Robert E. Lee could see into the future—no more than could General Joe Hooker, who was leading the Army of the Potomac to meet them. Hooker had replaced Burnside after the Union failure at Fredericksburg.

The new general, forty-nine years old, was a graduate of West Point and a veteran of the Seminole and Mexican wars who had served in the Regular Army until 1853. At the outbreak of the Civil War, he had been commissioned a brigadier general and had fought with distinction in several battles, earning the nickname "Fighting Joe." He had a reputation for loose living, loose talk, and insubordination, but his bravery and aggressive spirit were beyond question. In Lincoln's opinion, these qualities outweighed his defects.

Hooker waited until April of 1863 was almost over, and the men knew that as soon as the roads were dry, the new campaign would begin. After months of inactivity, they looked forward to it.

Lee's army still occupied its defensive position overlooking Fredericksburg. Hooker knew from Burnside's disastrous experience that a frontal attack would be fatal. Instead he planned a wide sweep around Lee's left flank, leaving a third of his army to cross the Rappahannock and hold Lee in his entrenchments. The Confederate commander, with 60,000 men—compared with Hooker's 134,000—would be in danger of annihilation if the Union movements succeeded.

The battle began on May 1. Lee, with characteristic audacity, divided his army and attacked Hooker's advancing force. The Union commander, having heard that Lee had been heavily reinforced, faltered, and the day's fighting ended inconclusively.

That night Lee and Stonewall Jackson decided upon a bold movement. Having found a guide who knew the way through the tangled wilderness, Lee sent Jackson with twenty-six thousand men across the front only two or three miles away to strike at Hooker's exposed right flank. It was a terrible risk for the Confederate Army, for if Hooker struck Lee's remaining force, he would destroy it.

◈

The men of the Richmond Grays saw little of the overall strategy of the battle of Chancellorsville. When Clay awakened them just before dawn, it was still too dark to see, but they could hear firing, skirmishers in heated dispute with the Federals.

They ate a hurried breakfast, and at six o'clock they heard the first artillery fire. Soon rolling clouds of powder smoke rose slowly, and the furious ripping sound of small arms in volley ascended. Through the tangled wilderness, they saw balloons of smoke and points of muzzle blast from Federal gun positions.

Lonnie Yancy, standing beside Clay, stared at the blue forces that were gathering for the charge. "I didn't know there was so many of 'em!" he whispered.

They could hear their shouts of command, see the froth coming from the hardworking artillery horses as battery after battery was wheeled up, unlimbered, and run out, muzzles toward the Confederates. The Union flags snapped in the breeze, and mounted staff officers in clusters watched the army prepare.

"You wanted Yankees," Waco Smith said, grinning at the men. "Well, there they are—and hyar they come!"

The bugles sounded, and the blue carpet began to move, unrolling to the hoarse coughing of the cannons. They splashed across the small creek, some falling to turn the water crimson, but their places were filled by others.

Clay called out, "Fire by volley!" and he waited until the approaching wave of soldiers was fifty yards away before yelling, "Fire!"

The blue line suddenly was scattered and tossed by the hot lead. Clay yelled, "Come on, C Company!" He leaped forward, holding his pistol, and glanced down the line to see that Dent was leading his own men in the charge.

Lonnie Yancy had knocked down a soldier with his first shot, then reloaded and scrambled into the line. He knew no fear. That came before the battle—or afterward. He heard the high-pitched wailing, sustained and carried through the other noise like the screaming of animals, and realized that he was yelling along with the rest.

A blue-clad soldier appeared—undulating, weaving in the smoke—and he felt the shock of the rifle butt against his shoulder without even being aware that he had raised it. He bit off the end of the next cartridge, rammed it home, hammer back and cap pressed onto the nipple, then fired again. The blue haze ahead took shape, showing faces and arms and bright brass belt buckles.

Beside him he was aware of Sergeant Smith, and ahead was Lieutenant Dent Rocklin, taking aim and firing as calmly as if he were taking target practice at home. Major Franklin rode by on his fine horse, screaming and waving them forward, and other officers joined him.

Clay sent his last shot at the blue horde, then turned and picked up a musket dropped by Zeno Tafton, whose face was shot away. He loaded, fired, then reloaded.

At that moment he saw Brad Franklin ride forward and then reel in the saddle. "Brad!" he shouted and saw him fall to the ground, the horse running away in terror. Clay wanted to go to him, but there was no time.

Wrenching himself away from the scene, he saw that the Yankee line had begun retreating and yelled, "Keep firing!" He kept them at it until the Federals were back across the creek, but even as he ran to Franklin, he heard a slight cry to his right. Wheeling, he turned to see Lonnie Yancy drop his rifle and fall to the ground.

Clay called out, "Lonnie!" but when he bent over the man, he saw that a musket ball had struck him in the temple, killing him instantly.

How will I tell Melora? He was her favorite!

"Captain, Major Franklin's pretty bad!"

Clay looked up to see Waco standing over him, his face bloody and his eyes quick with anger. "We gotta get him to the hospital."

"Is he alive?" Clay demanded as he ran back to where the officer lay.

"Yeah, but gut shot."

Clay saw that Brad Franklin was conscious, but he saw also the pool of blood that poured through his fingers. "They...got me this time, Clay!" Brad gasped.

"You'll be all right," Clay answered. Both men knew the chances of surviving a belly wound were almost nil, but Clay said, "We'll get you to the surgeon."

"Clay. . .tell Amy. . .I've always loved her. . .just in case, you know."

Clay nodded but was filled with a sudden birth of faith. "Brad, I'm no prophet, but I think God's giving me a promise. I believe He's telling me you'll make it."

"Is that right, Clay?" Franklin stared through pain-filled eyes at his brother-in-law, whom he trusted greatly. He gasped, "Then I'll just go on your faith. . . ."

Clay directed the men as they picked Franklin up and carried him off to the hospital. Then he turned and walked down the line to where Bob Yancy was helping a wounded comrade. "Bob?"

Young Yancy glanced at him, and his face grew pale. Rising, he came to stand before Clay. "Is it Lonnie?"

"Yes, Bob." Clay put his hand on the young man's shoulder, adding gently, "He's gone, Bob. Gone to be with Jesus."

Tears sprang to Bob Yancy's eyes. They had always been close, and the war had brought them even closer together. Memories of childhood and hunting trips flashed through his mind. But he dashed them away and cleared his throat. "I don't know if I can go on without him here in the company."

"We'll all miss him, Bob," Clay said. "And we've got each other to lean on. Remember that."

Bob Yancy gave Clay a grateful look, then said, "I'll take care of him."

At that moment General Jackson came riding up, his eyes pale. The soldiers called him Old Blue Light because of this.

"Major Franklin is wounded?"

"Yes, sir. I've had him removed from the field," Clay answered.

Jackson wore an old forage cap pulled down over his eyes. He paused for one moment, then said, "I will pray for his recovery. You will take his place. I appoint you brevet major. Take the field, sir!"

The Grays saw little action the rest of that day. And the second day of battle was spent mostly marching through the wilderness to get into position. At twilight Jackson struck General O. O. Howard's Eleventh Corps on the extreme left of the Federal line. Howard's men broke in confusion. Except for the falling night and an agonizing misfortune, a complete rout would have followed.

The misfortune came as Stonewall Jackson rode forward on the turnpike toward Chancellorsville followed by several of his staff. He surveyed the enemy's position, then headed back toward his own lines.

As he rode near to the Confederate troops just placed in position and ignorant that he was in front, the nervous soldiers opened fire on Jackson's party. Two of the number fell from their saddles dead. Jackson spurred his horse forward where he was met by a second volley. The general received three balls at the same instant. One penetrated the palm of his right hand, a second passed around the wrist of his left arm, and a third ball passed through the left arm halfway from shoulder to elbow. The large bone of the upper arm was splintered to the elbow joint, and the wound bled freely.

Jackson reeled in the saddle and was caught by his aide, who laid him on the ground. Dr. Hunter McGuire came at once and saw to the general's removal. As he was carried away, Jackson called out, "General Pember, you must hold your ground, sir!"

At midnight Jackson's left arm was amputated near the shoulder. He made a good recovery at first, but pneumonia struck him and he weakened. On May 10 he died, a smile on his face. He said quietly and with an expression of relief, "Let us cross over the river and rest under the shade of the trees."

The day after Jackson was wounded, the battle resumed. Hooker lost control of himself and never was able to strike a hard blow at his enemy. By the end of the fighting, he concluded there was no chance of success. Once again a much stronger Army of the Potomac had been vanquished by a smaller force under a superior general.

After the battle Clay walked beside the wagons loaded with wounded, some of them begging to be killed as they were jolted on the rough roads.

We've lost so many men, he thought, and the faces of the men in his company who had fallen rose in his mind. *This army will never be the same. I just don't see how we can win.*

The promotion to major meant nothing to him. He thought of Lonnie Yancy, buried in a shallow grave, far from the Southern fields he loved so well, and bitterness at the waste of it all rose in his throat. He thought of Brad Franklin, alive but just barely, and could only pray as he trudged along.

He saw in his mind more clearly than he had with his eyes the shattered forms on the field, the gaping wounds, the scattered arms, feet, and legs outside the surgeons' tent, the blood-soaked ground, the staring wide-eyed faces turning black and bloated almost before they could be buried.

He had always hated the war, but now he despised it with an intensity that shook him. But he could not turn back and so swept it from his mind, going from man to man to give what encouragement he could.

CHAPTER 18

TO BE A ROCKLIN

The Army of Northern Virginia came home, and Richmond once again was filled with wounded men, for the wagons daily unloaded their bloody bodies at the doors of the hospitals. Chimborazo overflowed, and Mrs. Pember worked night and day caring for the shattered remains that were often dumped unceremoniously at the front of the ward. She longed for the help of people such as Rooney Smith, but knew that the young woman had her hands full at Gracefield.

Clay had come to Chimborazo to visit the members of his squad and, after spending time with each of them, went to Brad Franklin and his sister, Amy. Brad had amazed the entire staff by not dying from the worst type of body wound, and he had shown such improvement that he clamored to be sent to his home. Amy patted his hand as she pleaded with the doctor for this. She won her case, and Clay had volunteered to drive them to the Franklin plantation. He borrowed a wagon and took Brad and Amy home.

Before he could return to Gracefield, Clay had to stop at the Yancy place, for he knew he had to tell the family about the death of Lonnie. When he drove up, he was greeted with enthusiasm by the children, but with restraint by Buford and Melora. Clay said nothing about the death for a time, but finally when the three of them were alone in the cabin, he broached the unpleasant topic. He left nothing out, and the two listened intently. Finally he said huskily, "He was the best soldier in the regiment, Buford. Always up front, never shirked a duty. We'll all miss him greatly."

Buford Yancy sat loosely in a cane-bottomed chair, and his sharp face grew tense. He had watched Clay's face during the recital, and now he said softly, "Lonnie was always a dutiful boy. Never was a better son." He said no more, and it was Melora who came to stand behind him and put her hands on his shoulders. The two of them were so still, Clay thought they looked like a portrait.

Then Melora looked at Clay, pride and sorrow mingled in her eyes. "Thank you for telling us, Clay."

That was all. He left soon afterward, promising that he'd give Bob a furlough as soon as he got back. "He's taking this hard, and I think you all need each other right now."

Melora had walked to the wagon with him, and when he got in, she looked up and asked, "Will you be leaving soon for another battle, Clay?"

"Not right away," Clay said. "The army's not ready. I'll be at

Gracefield for at least two days. Will you come and visit while I'm there?"

"Yes. I'll come."

Just the promise was enough to lift his spirits, and he smiled, saying what had become a familiar refrain to them: "Soon I won't have to go away, Melora!"

"Soon, Clay," Melora echoed and stood there long after the wagon had jolted away down the rutted road and disappeared behind the line of trees.

When she went back inside, she found her father still seated in the worn chair. He gave her a peculiar look; then when she poured two cups of sassafras tea and brought them over, he asked unexpectedly, "Are you happy to marry him, Melora?"

Melora looked up quickly, aware that the pain of his loss was sharp. *He's worried about me,* she thought, and then she nodded. "Yes, I am, Pa."

Buford took in the clean sweep of Melora's cheek, the erect figure, and the air of sweetness. He'd lost a son, and now there was an emptiness in him. Nobody could ever take Lonnie's place. Vaguely he was stirred with a desire to see more of the Yancy line, not to take Lonnie's place, but. . . He couldn't explain his feeling but finally made an attempt of sorts. "I hate to see things wasted," he murmured. "God put everything on this earth to be used. . . ."

He broke off, unable to find words to frame the emptiness inside him. But Melora understood. She was a woman of great discernment, and now she put the teacup down and put her hands over his.

"I know, Pa." She waited until his eyes came to meet hers, then nodded. "Don't fret about me. I've had a good life, and I know I'll be happy as the wife of Clay Rocklin."

"I should of made you marry a long time ago."

Melora smiled, and a dimple appeared on her cheek. "Cut a switch to me?" she asked.

Buford smiled at her. Melora could always make him smile. "I guess that wouldn't have worked. But you've give up your girlhood to raise these younguns."

"It's what God wanted me to do, Pa," she said simply. Then she squeezed his hands hard, saying, "But they're about raised now, and Clay is free." Her eyes suddenly grew warm, and she whispered, "One day, Pa, you'll have another boy child to hold—mine and Clay's."

She had never spoken like this, but somehow the thing had come to her—not in fragments and bits, but whole and entire. She was as sure of this as she was sure that the sun was in the sky, and the knowledge burned in her with a holy fire.

Lowell tried to force himself to be pleasant to his father. Clay had come home as soon as he could and for two days had moved about the plantation, mostly outside with Josh and the hands going over the work. But several times he'd come to sit with Lowell, and it had not been easy, for Lowell's reticence was like a stone wall.

Finally on the second day, Clay said to Rooney, "I can't break through to him, Rooney. It's like he's crawled into a deep cave and won't come out."

"I know," Rooney replied. She and Josh and Rena had tried everything to get Lowell to open up, but nothing had worked. Rooney had accepted Lowell's harsh remarks meekly, never answering in kind, but even that response seemed to anger him. Looking up at Clay, she said suddenly, "Maybe if we could get him to go to just *one* thing, it might get him out of that cave."

Clay stared at her, the idea taking root. "You have an idea, Rooney? About someplace to take him?"

"Well, he got a letter yesterday. It was from a soldier named Jimmy Peck."

Clay's eyebrows went up. "Why, Jimmy's the drummer boy of our company! I saw him at the hospital before I came here."

"Is he hurt bad?"

Clay nodded, pain in his dark eyes. "I'm afraid so, Rooney. He's only fifteen years old, an orphan lad. He took some bad wounds, and Mrs. Pember told me he wasn't going to make it."

A cloud crossed Rooney's face. "Poor boy!" she whispered. "Only fifteen. That's younger than Josh and Rena!"

"What did the letter say?"

"He didn't write it himself. One of the women did. He asked Lowell to come and say good-bye to him."

Clay stiffened, and he shook his head, asking at once, "What did Lowell say?"

"He didn't say anything—not to me, anyway," Rooney admitted. Then she looked at him hopefully, adding, "But he didn't say he *wouldn't go*, Mister Clay. Up until now, nobody could even *mention* his leaving the house without making him mad."

"He and Lowell were great friends," Clay said slowly, thinking back. "The two of them were always into something together. Jimmy was such a fun-loving boy. Lowell looked on him as a younger brother, I think."

"Why don't you offer to take him, Mister Clay?"

"I will!" Clay's jaw grew tight, and he nodded emphatically. "I'll put it to him that he owes it to Jimmy, which he does." Hope came to him and he said, "You come along, Rooney. You'll have to drive him back home."

Clay went at once to Lowell's room, and as soon as he was inside, he said, "I just heard about Jimmy wanting you to come and see him."

Lowell gave him a startled look. He was sitting up in bed, reading a book, and for one moment couldn't answer. "I can't go to the hospital."

"Why can't you?" Clay demanded. He put his black eyes on Lowell, adding, "You're able to travel."

Lowell turned pale, and Clay saw that the fear of going outside of the room was torture to the young man. He ached for this son of his but knew that the greatest kindness he could show was to force him out of the self-imposed prison Lowell had designed. "You're going, Lowell," Clay said evenly. "Make up your mind to it."

A flash of anger leaped to Lowell's eyes. "I'm not a child! You can't make me go!"

Clay said softly, but with a trace of iron in his tone—a tone that Lowell had encountered in the past—"I can't make you behave decently toward Jimmy, but you're going to face him, son."

"I can't do it!" Lowell's face contorted with fear, and he grabbed at the first excuse that came to him. "My wound! It could start bleeding! I could die!"

This sort of thing had worked with Susanna, but Lowell saw at once that it meant nothing to his father, especially since the wound was mostly healed now. Clay Rocklin's eyes drew half shut, and he said, "Son, I'd rather see you die than go on being the sort of man you've become! You're a Rocklin! I know you lost a leg. Well, I'm sorry for that. But it doesn't give you the right to curl up like a whipped dog and whimper about how pitiful you are!"

"I don't—"

"Lowell, you're going to that hospital and saying good-bye to Jimmy. Now do you want me to help you get ready?"

Lowell glared at his father with hatred, but he saw that the tanned face was set. *I've got to go,* he thought with a sickness in his stomach. *If I don't, he'll pick me up and throw me into the wagon like I was a sack of meal!*

Lowell knew his father, knew the iron will that had carried him through half a lifetime of difficulties that would have killed most men. He'd seen him set his jaw in just the manner he saw now, coming back to face shame and disgrace and never once turning back. He'd seen his father maintain a marriage with his mother when almost any other man would have broken free from her. And he'd seen that expression in battle when Clay Rocklin had stepped into the hail of fire as though bullets were soft drops of summer rain!

"I–I'll get ready," Lowell whispered.

"Fine. I'll go get the wagon hitched. We'll put the wheelchair right in the wagon bed so you'll be comfortable."

Clay turned and left the room, aware that his fingers were trembling, and there was a nausea in his stomach. He had hated the scene! He hated to speak like that to Lowell, yet at the same time he felt a surge of hope. When Rooney came to face him, he nodded. "Get ready, Rooney; Lowell's going to say good-bye to his friend."

"All right, Lowell, hold steady now."

Lowell grasped at the arms of his wheelchair, and his father and a thick-bodied hospital attendant rolled it over the back edge of the wagon. He had made the ride in comfort physically, but the dread of being thrust into the busy world had so possessed him that he could not think. Now as the wheels touched the ground, he wanted to flee, but he was helpless.

"Thanks," Clay said to the attendant. "We can handle it from here." Clay stepped behind the chair, saying, "It's getting dark. I'll put you two inside, then go find us a room someplace."

"We can stay at the hospital," Rooney volunteered. She was acutely aware of Lowell's silence, and a feeling of dread had come over her as she thought, *Won't he ever say anything?*

Lowell's throat was constricted, and he found it difficult to breathe. As his father tilted the chair back and placed the front wheels on the sidewalk that led into the ward, he gripped the chair arms so tightly that his fingers cramped. Rooney stepped ahead and opened the door, and as soon as they were inside the long building, Lowell heard his name called!

"Hey! It's Lowell!"

"Well, look at you. Got an officer to shove you around! What an operator!"

"And got Miss Rooney waitin' on him! Lowell, you ort to be proud!"

Lowell felt the chair slow down, and as his father pushed him down the aisle, he saw familiar faces—men he'd fought beside in many battles. "H–hello, Ralph," he managed to say to a small soldier who had no hands. He thought of how many times Ralph Prentiss had entertained them all by playing on his banjo at a hundred campfires. Ralph saw that Lowell was struggling to find something to say and grinned. Waving his stumps, he winked. "Got to learn to play with my feet, Lowell!"

Lowell couldn't answer but managed a small smile. He spoke to other members of his company, and finally the chair halted next to a bed where a man with his eyes bandaged sat, his head cocked alertly to one side. "That you, Lowell?" he asked.

"Yes, it's me, Bailey."

"Well, I'm glad you come by, Lowell," the soldier said. "How you doin'?"

Lowell shifted uncomfortably in his chair but said quickly, "All right, Bailey."

"Heard you lost a leg," Bailey remarked. "Now thet's too bad, a dancin' man like you." Then he nodded confidently, adding, "But they make good legs fer fellers now, so they say." He paused and then shook his head. "Wisht they could make a pair of eyes fer me, but thet's past wishing fer!"

Clay said quickly, "I'll bring Lowell back later so you can visit, Bailey."

"Shore, Captain!"

When they moved out of that section of the ward, Lowell asked faintly, "Both eyes gone? No hope at all?"

"Minié ball tore them both out, son," Clay answered. His answer seemed to cause Lowell to settle into his chair, and he said no more.

At the end of the building, the matron came out and put her eyes on Lowell. "How's the stump, Lowell?" she asked briskly.

Lowell licked his lips and nodded. "It's healing, Mrs. Pember."

"Fine! You'll be up soon." She noted that Lowell didn't respond and said briefly, "You came to see Jimmy. He's been asking for you for a week, ever since he was brought in."

"How. . .how is he, ma'am?"

Mrs. Pember stared at him. "Why, he's dying. I thought you knew that, Lowell."

"No hope at all?"

"No." There was a stark quality in Mrs. Pember's voice, and Lowell looked up to see that her lips were drawn tightly together. "The wound was too high to amputate—in the hip, really. Dr. McCaw did the best he could, but there was really nothing he could do."

Lowell asked faintly, "Does he know he can't live?"

"Yes, it was only just to tell him."

Lowell was aware that the three of them were watching him closely. His head felt thick, and the pain from his stump had suddenly struck as it did at times, though not as often now. But he asked, "Can I see him?"

"Of course. He's back in the small ward. Come this way." She led them through a door that opened into a room with four beds, all of them occupied. "It's a little crowded for all of you," Mrs. Pember said. "Captain, would you put Lowell's chair close to Jimmy? Then we can let them have some time."

"Yes, Mrs. Pember." Clay maneuvered the wheelchair into position beside the cot holding the small form of Jimmy Peck, then stepped back. "Rooney and I will visit the others, son."

Lowell was not even conscious of their leaving. He was staring at the skull-like features of the young man on the cot. *He's nothing but a skeleton!* His eyes went to the blanket that covered the shattered hip, and he saw that it was black with blood.

Then the eyes opened, and a thin, reedy voice piped up, "Why, hello, Lowell!"

Lowell reached out and took the thin hand that the boy extended, saying, "Hello, Jimmy." He could say nothing for a moment, for his throat was constricted. "I'm. . .glad to see you."

Jimmy stared at him with fever-bright eyes. "I. . .been holdin' on, Lowell." He gasped for breath and then whispered, "Wasn't sure. . .I could do 'er!"

Lowell's eyes suddenly burned with tears. For the first time since he'd awakened to find himself missing a limb, he forgot about his own injury. The thin hand held to his, and he thought of the many fine times the two of them had had—and some bad ones, as well. Jimmy had been so healthy, so full of life! He had been as agile as a squirrel, and his bright eyes filled with fun and laughter no matter how bad things had gotten. Now he was poised at the door of death, and Lowell felt he could not bear it!

"Tell me. . .what you been. . .doin'," Jimmy gasped. Lowell had no desire to speak of himself. The thought of how he'd been sulking in a room, refusing all help, came to him bitterly, and he choked and lied about how well he was doing. Finally he gave up his feeble attempts and whispered, "Jimmy, I never thought it would come to this!"

The dying boy moved his head and fixed his eyes on his friend. "Why, shoot, Lowell. . .don't you worry none. . .about me!" He coughed a great tearing cough and then, after he got control, whispered, "Ain't got too long, Lowell. Got to tell you. . .something!"

The life was running out of the boy, and suddenly Lowell

looked down and saw that the blood on the blanket was turning scarlet. He ripped the blanket back and saw that crimson blood was escaping in a small jet.

"Mrs. Pember!" he called out, terrified, and at the same time he reached out and put his finger on the little orifice.

Soon Mrs. Pember appeared, followed by Clay and Rooney. "Don't move your finger, Lowell," she said quietly. "He'll bleed to death if you do."

"Do something!" Lowell pleaded. "Get the surgeon!"

"I'll send someone," Mrs. Pember said, then turned and left the room. "You stay with them, Rooney!"

Then they were alone, and Lowell's blood seemed to beat in his ears. He kept his finger on the boy's artery, trying to pray and failing.

Jimmy whispered, "I got to tell you. . .that I wanna meet you in heaven, Lowell."

The simple statement struck Lowell Rocklin as hard as a minié ball. He stared at the dying boy, then nodded. "I'll do my best, Jimmy."

"Do you know Jesus?"

Lowell clamped his jaws together and then shook his head. "No, Jimmy. I don't."

"Well. . .kin I tell you how to git saved?"

Rooney stood there transfixed as the pale lips of the boy moved. He spoke of how he'd repented and called on Jesus. Then in a fast-failing voice, he begged Lowell, "You. . .do it, too, Lowell. . .please!"

Rooney saw the tears on Lowell's face and prayed, *Oh God, save him!* Then she saw Lowell's lips moving and heard his words faintly, ". . .just a sinner—but save me, like You saved Jimmy and Rooney, for Jesus' sake."

Rooney could not see, but she heard Jimmy gasp, "Did. . . you do 'er, Lowell?"

"Yes, Jimmy!"

Then the surgeon, Dr. McCaw, was there, and Jimmy looked up at him. "How long. . .can I live?" he gasped.

Dr. McCaw's face was lined with fatigue, but there was a deep compassion in his voice as he answered, "As long as Lowell keeps his finger on that artery, my boy."

Jimmy stared at the doctor for a long moment, then turned his wan face toward Lowell. He whispered, "Are you. . .saved, Lowell?"

"Yes, I'm saved, Jimmy!"

And then Jimmy Peck gave a deep sigh. He reached over and put his hand over Lowell's, the one keeping his life in. A peaceful smile touched his thin, pale lips. "You can let go, Lowell."

But Lowell didn't let go. For two hours he sat there holding back the flow of blood. When his arm grew dead with the strain, the others tried to help, but Lowell refused, saying, "No, he's my friend!"

And then it ended. Jimmy opened his eyes and looked at Lowell. His pulse had grown so erratic that the doctor could not even find it. "He's lost too much blood. He's going!" the doctor had said.

Then Jimmy Peck stroked Lowell's hand, smiled, and whispered, "I'll see you. . .again, Lowell." Then his eyes closed.

Dr. McCaw said huskily, "He's gone, Lowell."

Lowell straightened up and sat upright in the wheelchair, staring at the small pale face. "Good-bye, Jimmy," he murmured. Only Rooney heard him add, "For now."

Rooney leaned down and said, "It was fine, Lowell! Just fine!"

And then Clay bent down and embraced Lowell, whispering, "I'm proud of you, my boy!"

Slowly Lowell looked up at them. His face was drawn with the struggle, but there was something in his eyes that had not been there before. And when he spoke, the hopelessness that had marked his tone was gone.

"I want to stay until Jimmy's buried," he said quietly.

"Of course," Clay answered. "I think that's what you should do."

Rooney was staring at Lowell's face, marveling at his expression—so different! She asked quietly, "And what then, Lowell?"

Lowell looked at her, then at his father. His face was pale, but there was a determination in his eyes. "Then I'll go home. And start living again!" He caught the hand that Clay held out, and Rooney took the other. Looking up at them, he felt so tired but so rested. Finally he said, "I'll meet Jimmy someday. I know that! But until that time, I've got to learn how to be a Rocklin!"

Clay stared down at his son, and pride laced his voice as he smiled and exclaimed, "You *are* a Rocklin, Lowell!"

And it was Rooney who bent over and kissed his cheek, whispering, "And now we can begin, Lowell! Begin all over again!"

PART FOUR
Josh

CHAPTER 19

TWO WOMEN

I never saw such a change in a man!" Susanna's eyes were bright with pride as she spoke of Lowell to David. "Ever since he went to the hospital to visit his friend, he's been a different person."

"It's wonderful, isn't it, Grandmother?" Shaking his head, he added, "It's like he's risen from the dead!"

Susanna laughed softly. "You always did have a knack for overstating things!"

She left him then and entered the dining room. "Hello, Grandmother," Rena said. She asked without warning, "Grandmother, you told me once that Grandfather came when he was courting and serenaded you, didn't you?"

A smile touched the older woman's lips. "Yes, he did. Couldn't carry a tune in both hands, but he did it!"

Rena leaned back, staring at her grandmother almost enviously. "I think that's wonderful!" she sighed. Then she picked up her fork, nibbled thoughtfully on the fragment of pancake, and asked, "Grandmother, do you think any man will ever serenade *me*?"

Rena's expression was so woebegone that Susanna's heart went out to her. "I'm sure they will, lots of them," she said. Then she proved her wisdom by saying, "Oh, when I was your age, I thought I was plain and that no boy would ever like me. I had myself all primed to be an old maiden aunt living with my nephews—something dreadful like that!"

"Really?"

"All girls think that at a certain time, Rena." Susanna smiled and saw that her words had touched a fear that the girl had struggled with. "Of course! Didn't you know that?"

"No. I—I thought I was the only one."

Susanna sipped the last of her tea, rose, and went around to squeeze the girl's firm shoulders. "No, all of us feel like that, but you'll feel different soon. Why, I expect your father will have to run off some of your suitors with his pistol soon enough!"

Rena giggled and took an enormous wad of pancakes into her mouth. She felt a rush of relief and got up to embrace her grandmother, saying around the mouthful of pancake, "Oh, I *love* you, Grandmother!"

Susanna thought, *She needs so much encouragement—this war's robbed her of so much that I had!*

As Rena ran from the room, Dorrie came from where she'd been washing dishes. She'd heard the exchange and was not in the least ashamed of listening. Everything that happened to the Rocklin family was her business, and now she said, "Dat chile is growin' up, ain' she?" Her wise old eyes were sober, and she added thoughtfully, "Things ain't the same, is dey? Not lak when you was her age."

"No, Dorrie." Susanna thought of the days of her youth—carefree, happy times—times that would never come again. But she was too strong to grieve over what could not be changed. "She's a good girl, Dorrie, but she's had a hard life. And now she worries about losing her father."

Dorrie nodded but said strongly, "She's a Rocklin, ain't she? She gonna do *fine*, so doan you be worryin' yo' head. Gawd, He's knowin''bout all this! You heah me now?"

Susanna laughed and gave Dorrie a hug. "All right. Now let's go to work!" She looked out the window, saying, "There goes Josh. If Rena sees him, she'll make him take her fishing or something."

But Josh didn't see Rena that morning. He made straight for the backyard, where he found Rooney cooking lye soap. She was stirring the mixture in a big black pot, and when Josh rounded the corner and came to her, she greeted him eagerly. "Hi, Josh! Are we ready?"

"I g–guess so, R–Rooney." He lifted a small black bag, saying, "I got what we n–need."

Rooney looked across the yard to where two of the young slaves were talking. "Lucy, come and finish this soap, will you?" She waited until the two girls came and got their instructions, then said, "Come on, Josh."

As Josh followed her, a worried expression came to his face. The wind blew his hair over his eyes, and he brushed it back with his free hand, saying, "I'm a little n–nervous, Rooney."

Rooney glanced at him quickly, then said with a reassurance she didn't quite feel, "It'll be all right, Josh." As they approached the door, she slowed down and then turned to face him. Her mop of auburn curls had been blown so that they formed a soft crown, and her wide eyes were thoughtful. "Lowell's changed. You've seen how *different* he is, haven't you?"

Josh nodded, but there was a reluctance in his tone as he answered her. "Yeah, but I ain't sure h–he's changed *this* much!"

"Come on, Josh. I'm sure it'll be fine."

The two entered the house and moved toward Lowell's room. Rooney knocked on the door, and when Lowell called out, "Come in," the two of them entered. Lowell looked at the pair with surprise, for both of them wore rather strained expressions. "Well, you two look like you've come to cut my other leg off!" He saw Rooney blink with shock, and Josh looked as if he wanted to turn and run back out of the door!

Lowell watched them but was thinking, *Guess I've made some progress—got to where I can make a joke about it, anyway.* He noted that his mild remark had shaken them and said, "Well, come on in, both of you."

Rooney moved closer, and Josh followed, both of them as nervous as they'd ever been. Lowell noted this; then his eye fell on the bag in Josh's hands. "What's that you've got, Josh?

You bring your lunch?"

Josh swallowed but could only shake his head. He gave Rooney an agonized glance, and she said, "Lowell, we've...been meaning to talk to you...Josh and me." Her face was pale, and she had trouble with her words.

Lowell stared at the pair, then said quietly, "Look, whatever it is, you don't have to be scared out of your wits. I'm not going to shoot you." He smiled, adding, "I've yelled at you enough since you got here so that at least you know my bad behavior won't kill you. Just tell me what the trouble is."

His manner was so mild that Rooney was encouraged, so she took a deep breath and began. "Lowell, Josh and me have been thinking, ever since you got hurt, that we might be able to...to help."

Lowell nodded, and a smile touched his lips. "You have helped, Rooney, and you, too, Josh. Anybody else would have left me to wallow in my own pity a long time ago." He saw that his words made them both feel more comfortable, so he said, "Now I guess your visit has something to do with what Josh has in his suitcase?"

"Well, yes, it has," Rooney replied. "You see, we got to thinking awhile back about those legs that soldiers get when they...lose a leg."

Josh spoke up. "I c–can make one, Mister Lowell!"

Lowell stared at Josh, his face filled with surprise. "Make an artificial leg?"

"S–sure! I c–can do it!"

Lowell stared at the two, affection coming to his hazel eyes. "Why, I never doubted you could make anything you set your hand to, Josh, but—"

"We thought of it right after you got back, Lowell!" Rooney's eyes were alive with excitement. Now that she was certain that Lowell was not going to be angry, she threw herself into convincing him. "First we went to Richmond to see about having you one made. And there's only two places where you can get a leg."

"Guess they must be pretty busy," Lowell commented.

"That's the way it was," Rooney said with a nod. "They both said they'd have to put us on a list, but it'd be a long time before they can get to us."

"B—but I looked around while I was th—there," Josh said, his thin face stubborn. "And I s—seen how they made them l—legs!"

Lowell gave Josh a fond look but said doubtfully, "I guess that's a pretty specialized kind of work, making artificial legs. Not like making a plow or a table."

But Josh was adamant. "I asked th—the man about making one m—myself." Josh was the mildest of young men, but Lowell had noted from the first that when he got a notion in his head, he became stubborn. Now the boy's chin was stuck out, and he said, "He t—told me I couldn't do it—but I can!"

Rooney said quickly, "I asked him to let Josh come and watch him, just to learn how."

"What did he say to that?"

"He said no, but I kept after him until he agreed!"

"Sh-she shore did, Mister Lowell!" Josh grinned broadly at Rooney. "She d–did it for sure!" Then he laughed as Rooney tried to make him stop. "She t–turned them b–big blue eyes of hers on that f–feller and let her l–lips go tremblin', and then she said, 'B–but my sweetheart n–needs this so b–bad!'"

Lowell shot an astonished look at Rooney, who blushed furiously. "You didn't!" he exclaimed.

"Well, he made me do it!"

"You should have s–seen her, Mister Lowell!" Josh crowed. "She had h–him almost crying!"

Rooney's fair cheeks were red as roses, and when Lowell burst into laughter, she pouted, "Well, it worked, didn't it?"

"I guess so," Lowell finally answered, then added with a wink toward Josh, "But I'll be on my guard with you from now on, Rooney. A woman like you can get about anything she wants from a man!"

"Oh, don't be foolish!" Rooney snapped. She had begged Josh not to tell Lowell of the incident, and it had embarrassed her. But now that she saw that it had amused Lowell, she felt better. "Now let's get down to business," she said. "Josh spent almost a week there, and he learned just about everything. Tell him, Josh!"

Josh began to speak, and both Lowell and Rooney noted that his stutter grew less noticeable as he became immersed in the explanation. Lowell glanced at Rooney, and she caught his eyes, nodding slightly. *How does she know what I'm thinking?*

Lowell wondered. *Have to be careful around this girl!*

"...and so I *know* I c–can do it," Josh ended.

"Well, let's get started," Lowell said at once, and his willingness pleased the young man—and Rooney, as well. "What's first?"

"First, Mister Lowell," Josh said quickly, "we g–got to make a wax model."

"A model? Of what?" Lowell asked.

"Of your. . .s–stump." Josh faltered over the use of the word *stump*, but he and Rooney had already decided that they'd have to use the term. He saw a flicker of embarrassment in Lowell's eyes, so he hurried with his explanation. "Your whole weight w–will rest on it, see? So the s–socket of the new l–leg's got to fit just right."

"I guess I see that," Lowell said slowly. "Did you see them do this—at the shop, I mean?"

"Oh, sure," Josh said, nodding. "Ain't nothin' to it. Just take wax and h–heat it. Then put the stump in so's it l–leaves an impression."

"Well, I guess we'd better do it, Josh."

"I'll heat the wax," Rooney said instantly and, taking the small case from Josh, left the room.

"That g–girl's a caution, M–Mister Lowell!" Josh said, shaking his head with obvious admiration. "Ain't n–nothing stops her when her m–mind's made up!"

"Tell me again about how she wheedled that leg maker into letting you stay," Lowell begged. He sat there letting Josh retell the story, then urged him to give more details about the leg. They were interrupted when Rooney entered, bearing a basin with a cloth over the top.

"It's too hot, Josh," she said, placing the basin on the washstand. "We'll have to let it cool a little."

As the pair worked on making the cast, Lowell was so absorbed in the process that he realized with a shock that he was not embarrassed by the presence of Rooney. This was partly, he realized, because she had cared for him and was accustomed to his handicap. *With any other woman this would be hard,* he thought. *She makes it so easy!*

Finally the cast was made to Josh's satisfaction. "I'll g–get started on this," he announced and left the room.

"That's an amazing young man," Lowell said thoughtfully. He had settled back in his chair after dressing, and his eyes were thoughtful. He turned them on her, saying, "And you're an amazing young woman."

Rooney was making his bed but looked at him with a startled expression. She was not accustomed to compliments and said only, "Why, it's good to be able to help."

Lowell considered her, then asked, "Do you think you could manage this chair? I'd like to go out for a while."

"Oh, that would be nice!" She gave the coverlet a final tug, then came over. "You can see the new colt."

Lowell caught her wrist as she moved to step behind him. Rooney broke off her remarks and gave him a startled look. He held her firmly, looked up, and said, "Rooney. . ."

And then he could not find the words to express what was inside him. He struggled for a long moment, then, taken by an impulse, lifted her hand to his lips and kissed it.

"Oh—Lowell!" Rooney gasped, and her lips trembled. No man had ever kissed her hand, and something about the gesture brought a sudden rush of happiness to her. Finally she took a deep breath, then smiled tremulously, saying, "Let's go outside, Lowell."

She took him outdoors, and the warm May breeze blew against her face—but she knew the weather was not the cause of the flush her cheeks felt as they moved along the walk.

CHAPTER 20

MAN IN THE SADDLE

The Confederate Army had won the battle of Chancellorsville, but at a ruinous cost. The Army of Northern Virginia lost veterans, and there were no replacements. Supplies were exhausted, and the leaders of the Confederacy were aware that the Army of the Potomac would be back—larger and more powerful than ever.

One hope burned brightly for the South—the hope of recognition from Europe. England made a pretense of neutrality, but the aristocracy and ruling classes sided with the South. Agents of the Confederate government reported that if General Lee could establish his army firmly on Northern soil, England would at once acknowledge the independence of the South. This meant that ample loans could be obtained from that country to shore up the failing resources of the Confederacy.

At this same time an antiwar movement called the Copperhead movement was gaining strength in the North. President

Davis hoped that it would cause the North to falter, perhaps even to declare the war over.

Lee had informed the president that an offensive against the North was the only hope for the South. "If we wait for them to come to us," he'd said, "we'll be surrounded, and we cannot win a long siege."

So as spring gave way to summer, men were looking north, and the Army of Northern Virginia felt the stirrings of far-off battles. . . .

❧

"Well, h–here it is!" Josh stood before Lowell holding the new leg in his hands. "Sure h–hope it works."

Lowell had waited anxiously for Josh to finish the work on the leg, but now that the moment had come, he felt an unexpected rush of fear shoot through him.

What if it doesn't work?

He tried to banish the thought, but there was such uneasiness in his expression that Josh said quickly, "We m–might have to work on it a l–little, but I *know* it'll work!"

Josh's assurance seemed to brace Lowell somewhat, for some of the tension left his face. "All right, Josh, let's see how she goes."

Lowell stripped off the robe, and Josh came to help him fit the device. He'd been to the hospital with Rooney, and the two of them had studied the way the limbs had been strapped into place. Josh had also taken his workmanship back to the shop in Richmond, where the owner had been highly impressed. "Excellent job! You can come to work for me anytime!" he had said. He'd given Josh a few suggestions but had indicated that there were few improvements to be made.

Now Josh knelt and fastened the limb into place. He had worked with Lowell, taking measurements and making sure that the straps were exactly right. Finally he looked up and asked, "That too tight?"

Lowell was staring down at the leg. It was made of cork and was very light, but he was filled with doubt. "Let me put my pants on, Josh," he said.

"Sure!"

Lowell had not worn trousers since arriving at the hospital. Such a garment would have made it difficult to dress his stump and would have been uncomfortable in any case. Now, however, the urge came to him, and he struggled into the trousers with Josh's help.

"There you are." Josh nodded and stood up. "Ready to t–try it?" He was nervous, for he'd thought of little but getting Lowell on his feet ever since he'd started the project. Now that the time had come, he wondered what he'd do if his work didn't measure up.

Lowell sat still, looking down at himself. There was no difference in the legs, he saw at once. Josh had used his remaining leg as a model, carving the artificial limb to exactly the same measurements.

His voice was hoarse as he said, "Feel like I'm about to get on a wild horse, Josh." But he shook his head, mustered up a grin, then said, "All right. Here we go!"

Josh put his hands out. Lowell took them, then heaved himself to his feet. For one moment he looked surprised, then gripped the young man's hands hard. "Room is going around like a top!"

"J–just hold what you g–got, Mister Lowell," Josh urged. "You been down f–for a long time."

Lowell nodded and stood there until the room settled down. Cautiously he swayed back and forth, then side to side. It was a strange sensation, completely unlike anything he had ever experienced. He seemed to be balanced on his remaining leg, and there was no feeling of having the other foot on the floor. Looking down, he assured himself that both feet were planted, then gave Josh a crooked grin. "Seems to be working... so far," he muttered.

"Does it h–hurt?"

"Well, a little bit," Lowell agreed. "Not too bad, though."

"The man in the shop said you'd toughen up. No w–way to do that except to u–use it a lot."

"Like forming a callous on your hands, I guess," Lowell said. Then, taking a deep breath, he nodded. "Hang on, Josh. I'm pretty shaky." Gripping the hands of the boy, he placed his weight on his sound leg, then twisted his body as Josh had tried to instruct him. He leaned forward, and the artificial limb swung into place. Then he tried to put his weight on it while swinging his other leg. But he had no confidence, so he staggered and loosed his grip on Josh's hand. He waved his arms wildly, then fell into Josh, who caught him about the waist and kept him from falling.

Josh held him, saying, "Hey—don't w–worry! I've g–got you!"

"Put me back in the chair!" Lowell gasped.

"Mister Lowell!"

"Put me back, blast you, Josh!"

Josh helped his friend to move backward, and when Lowell was seated, he saw that his face was pale and perspiration covered his brow. He waited, knowing that this was a critical time. The limb maker in Richmond and the nurses at the hospital had warned him that many men simply gave up and refused to use the limbs, choosing a wheelchair instead.

"I can't do it!" Lowell whispered. "I can't do it, Josh!"

Josh was in a strange position. All his life he'd looked on men like Clay Rocklin and his family with awe. They were rich and influential, far above his station. Josh still felt that way, but he had thrown himself into helping Lowell walk, and despite his shyness, there was a stubborn streak in him. He came from hill people who took the back of no man's hand, and now as he looked down at Lowell, courage rose in him. He knew that gentleness would not do here—that Lowell Rocklin had to be pushed!

"Mister Lowell, you g–got to do it," Josh said. And when the man shook his head stubbornly, the boy said, "You ain't a coward, are you?"

Lowell looked up at Josh abruptly, as startled as if the boy had slapped him across the face. He reddened and cried, "Get out! Leave me alone!"

"No, sir, I c–can't do that!" Josh's face was pale, but his jaw was set, and he stared right into Lowell's face. "I guess if any of the Rocklins are cowards, n–nobody ever found out about it. Are you aimin' to b–be the first?"

Lowell stared at the boy, anger rising to choke him. He wanted to throw himself at the boy, to strike him down with his fists! How did he dare!

And then Lowell thought of the sacrifices the boy had made—all to help him. And now he saw Josh was almost trembling, though he held himself upright and taut. *It took a lot for him to speak up to me that way,* he thought. *He's got plenty of nerve—more than I have!*

Josh watched as the anger seemed to drain from Lowell's face, and Josh said in a pleading voice, "I don't l–like to talk to you bad, but you just g–gotta make it!"

Lowell let his eyes drop to his hands, then to his legs. He understood clearly at that moment that he had come to a fork in the road, and his choice would follow him the rest of his days. *I'll either get up and try again—even if I fall a thousand times—or I'll crawl into bed and be helpless for the rest of my life!*

Seldom had any choice been so clear to Lowell. And he thought of Jack Bailey, who had said, *"They make good legs fer fellers now, so they say. Wisht they could make a pair of eyes fer me, but thet's past wishing fer!"*

That thought put a desperate courage into Lowell Rocklin,

and he prayed silently, *Oh God, don't let me give up!*

Josh saw Lowell look up, and he was filled with encouragement, for there was a defiant look in Lowell's hazel eyes. And then he grinned faintly, saying, "Well, you're a pretty good preacher, Josh. Now let's try it again!"

"I knowed you w–wouldn't give up!" Josh took the hand of Lowell Rocklin, heaved him up, then said, "N–now we'll take it r–real easy. . . ."

❧

While Lincoln fumbled in his attempts to find a commander who would fight, the Confederate Army repaired itself, knowing that the onslaught would soon come.

Colonel Taylor Dewitt called Clay to his headquarters one sunny morning, giving him an order. "Major Rocklin, I've got a hard duty for you." Taylor's eyes gleamed with humor, and he laughed aloud. "Doggone it, Clay, I wish you were the colonel and I was the major!"

"Don't think I'd like that, Colonel," Clay said, smiling. "What's the duty?"

"Recruiting," Taylor said. "Our ranks are stretched too thin. Get out there and get some men for us. You'll be close to your people, so tell them all hello from your colonel!"

Clay had drawn a horse, and after listening to the moans from Dent—with broad hints about favoritism from his "old buddy Taylor Dewitt"—he rode out of the camp and made his way back to Richmond. He made several stops on the way and was surprised at winning several young fellows over to signing up. He was not a high-pressure salesman, but something in his quiet manner made the young men want to be in his company. Several of them were afraid the war would be over before they could get in it, and Clay didn't argue, though he knew better.

When he got to his own county, the recruiting went even better. He was known by most of the planters, and the Yancy boys had spread the word about the Richmond Grays. It had been filled with young aristocrats at first, but now Clay was looking for hard fighters, not dancers!

Finally he drew up in front of Gracefield just after noon on Tuesday. He'd worked hard and had a good catch, enough to please the colonel, so he had no guilt over taking a couple of days at home. Highboy met him, white teeth gleaming, and when Clay threw him a piece of hard money, his head bobbed up and down violently. "Sho' is good to see you, Marse Clay!"

"Grain him good, Highboy. I've ridden him hard." He pulled a large sack from behind his saddle, dismounted, and made his way up the steps.

He was met on the porch by Rena, who threw herself into his arms, nearly knocking him off balance. "Whoa! Be careful with an old man!" he protested but grasped her around the waist and swung her around so that her feet flew out. She objected, but it was a game he'd played with her for years, and she loved it!

"Now I'm out of breath," he said, putting her down but keeping his hands on her waist. "You're getting fat," he announced.

"I am not!"

"Are, too!" Then he kissed her and whispered, "You're the best-looking woman I've seen in these parts!"

Clay picked up his sack, and the two went into the house, Rena chattering and hanging onto his free hand. Clay was relieved to see her so happy. He'd been concerned over leaving her, but she'd finally cast off the heavy burden he'd seen on her after Ellen died.

As they moved inside, the family all came to greet him, and Dorrie said, "Come on and set down. Dinnuh's ready."

Clay went to her, put his arm around her ample waist, and said, "I've got a present for you in my bag here."

Dorrie gave him a look that was at the same time avaricious and suspicious. "Whut you done got me?"

"I'll show you." He opened the sack, rummaged through it, then pulled out a thin package. "Here you are."

Dorrie took it, saying her thanks, but when she started to leave, Clay shook his head. "None of that! Open it and see if it fits."

Dorrie looked around, grumbled, then opened the package. She took one look inside, her eyes flew open, and then she hurriedly closed the package before the rest of them could see what was inside.

"What is it, Dorrie? I couldn't see," Rena protested.

But Dorrie merely shut her lips tightly and shook her head. Then she looked at Clay, who was grinning broadly and who prompted her, "Don't you like it, Dorrie?"

The tall black woman drew herself up and clutched the

package firmly. Then she stared at the tall man whose eyes were laughing at her, and she said, "Mister Clay—you is *bad*!" Whirling, she left the room.

Clay said, "Never saw such ingratitude!"

Susanna was laughing, for she had caught a glimpse of the present. "That would have made a good piece for your balloon, Rooney."

Then they all went in and sat down at the table, and Clay began passing out gifts for everyone. "Just my way of saying how important you all are to me," Clay said in explanation for his generosity.

Dorrie and Lucy began bringing in the food, and Clay looked around for Rooney, for he didn't notice her leave the room. Then she entered, smiling at him in a rather mysterious fashion. Clay said, "Come and get your gift, Rooney."

But she didn't come to him as Clay expected. He glanced at his mother and saw that she, too, had a look of excitement on her face. Everyone, in fact, had that same expression.

"What's going on?" Clay asked, looking around. "You all look like the cat who swallowed the canary."

"We've got a gift for you, too, Mister Clay," Rooney said.

"A gift for me? Well, let's have it," Clay insisted.

Rooney moved back toward the double door she had passed through and whispered something that Clay couldn't hear. He couldn't imagine what was going to happen but knew that for some reason everyone was grinning broadly.

And then he heard steps—a strange tread that somehow

didn't seem exactly right. Something about the rhythm of it. . .

And then Lowell appeared!

Clay had never been struck so hard in his life. He'd spent sleepless nights praying for—for exactly what he was seeing now! Lowell was wearing a fine gray suit with a white shirt. He held a cane in his right hand, and there was a proud smile on his lips. "Hello, Father," he said and then began to walk across the floor.

Clay had wisdom enough to stand and wait. He wanted to run and grab Lowell but knew instinctively that this would be wrong. Lowell moved across the floor, swinging his right limb and planting it firmly. It was awkward and ungainly, but Clay didn't care! As Lowell came to stand before him, Clay's eyes filled with tears. He made no move to hide them, and if he had looked around, he would have seen that he was not the only one so moved.

"Lowell," he whispered. "I. . .I can't tell you. . .what this means to me!"

"You'll have to thank Josh and Rooney, Father," Lowell said unsteadily. He cleared his throat and thrust his hand out. "Welcome home, sir!"

Clay grasped the hand, then could not restrain himself. He put his arms around Lowell and held him fiercely. Then he released him, turned, and pulled out a handkerchief. Blowing his nose, he waited for a moment, and when he turned around, he said evenly, "Well, let's eat!"

It broke the tension, and all during the meal, Lowell spoke

of how it had come about, always giving the credit to Josh and Rooney. He had a different spirit, and Clay did not miss the expression in Rooney's eyes. She never took her eyes from Lowell for more than a few moments, and when she saw Clay observing this, she flushed and dropped her eyes.

Finally the meal was over, and Lowell said, "Father, I want some of your time."

"Of course."

Clay rose and followed the young man outside. Lowell led him out the side door, for it was only one step—much easier to navigate than the front porch. Clay walked along, adjusting his pace to Lowell's, and found himself at the pasture where the horses were kept. Lowell leaned against the fence, put his fingers in his mouth, and whistled shrilly.

"I could never do that," Clay stated. Then he saw Midnight, Lowell's favorite mount, appear from around the barn. The beautiful horse came up to the two men, and Lowell gave him a bit of biscuit he pulled from his pocket. "Beautiful animal! Never saw a finer one."

Lowell patted the smooth muzzle, then turned to face his father. His face was as earnest as Clay had ever seen it, and he began to tell Clay how he'd struggled to learn to walk. Once again, he gave Josh and Rooney all the credit. "I must have fallen a thousand times, but they always picked me up," he said quietly.

"We'll always owe them for that. They're quality." He was aware that Lowell was framing something, trying to find a way to ask him something. "What is it, son?" he asked. "I'll do anything I can for you—you must know that."

"All right, I'll tell you." Lowell put his hazel eyes directly on Clay and took a deep breath. "I want to stay in the army." He saw the surprise on Clay's face and quickly went on: "I know it'll be hard, but I can do it, sir."

Clay was troubled and showed it. His brow furrowed, and he said, "Why, Lowell, you know what the army's like. It'd be too hard for you. You'll learn to walk much better, but I don't think you'd be able to keep up over some of the terrain we'll be marching through."

"I know, but I want to be a courier." Lowell saw the idea make a change in his father's face. "I can't march, but I'll be able to ride as well as any man."

Clay nodded slowly, then said, "Well, now that's so, I guess." He stood there letting the idea sink in and finally said, "Nobody will look down on you if you don't go, son. You've done your share."

Lowell shook his head stubbornly. "I've got to do it, sir!"

"And you want me to find you a place?"

"Yes, sir!"

"Well, I'll do it." A thought came to him, and he exclaimed, "Why, General Stuart—he'd be glad to have you, Lowell!"

"I never thought of that!"

"He was very impressed with you," Clay replied. "I'll be glad to speak to the colonel about you transferring and not being mustered out."

"Do you really think he'll have me?"

Clay looked on Lowell's eager face, and pride swelled in him. He gripped Lowell's arm tightly, then said, "Son, *any* general would be glad to have you on his staff!" Then he laughed and shook his head. "Well, I'm a little prejudiced, I guess." He looked at the black horse and then at Lowell. "When do you want to go, son?"

Lowell thought, then said, "Josh and Rooney will help me. And it won't be as hard as learning to walk." He did some fast figuring, then said, "I'll be ready in two weeks, sir."

"Two weeks," Clay said thoughtfully. He did some addition of his own, then smiled briefly. "That'll be plenty of time, I think."

"Where will the next battle be?" Lowell asked.

"I think it'll be in the North. We've got to hit the Yankees on their own ground."

"I'll hope to be with you, sir!"

Clay suddenly asked, "What about Rooney?" He smiled at the startled expression on Lowell's face. "You can't take her with you, as you did last time."

"I—I guess not," Lowell stammered. Then his face brightened. "But she'll be here when I get back."

Clay didn't respond, but even as he turned the conversation toward the probable tactics of General Hooker, he was thinking, *He's in love with that girl—and I don't blame him!*

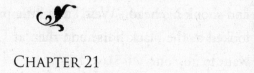

CHAPTER 21

RENA LOSES A FRIEND

"Easy, Midnight!"

Lowell held the reins firmly as the black horse snorted and tossed his head. He had always been a difficult animal to mount, requiring strength and great agility, though he was quickly obedient once a rider was on his back. He was not in the least a vicious horse, but for some reason he refused to stand quietly as a rider stepped into the stirrup.

Lowell had saddled Midnight in the barn, then led him outside into the brilliant sunlight, stopping in the center of the small corral built of split rails. Although he did not take his eyes off the prancing stallion, he was aware that he had an audience. Behind him Highboy and two other hands were standing at the door to the barn, and to his left he knew that Rooney, Buck, Josh, and Rena were standing outside the tall fence.

They had all seen him ride Midnight. For two weeks he'd left early in the morning every day for a ride, but he'd always been helped into the saddle by Josh or one of the hands. What they didn't know was that Lowell had gone several times to practice getting into the saddle with only Highboy present.

And those sessions had been disasters! Even now as Lowell held the horse fast, he thought of the many falls he'd taken, and he heard Highboy whisper, "Oh, Marse Lowell. . . be keerful!" The tall slave had begged the young man not to attempt mounting on his own, saying, "I'll go to the army wif you, Marse Lowell! Lots of soldiers takes dey body servants, and I can hep you git on dat hoss every time!"

After Lowell had been tossed to the ground several times, he'd been sorely tempted to accept Highboy's offer. But he'd shaken his head grimly, saying, "No thanks, Highboy. I'll get on my own horse or I won't go!"

Finally he'd managed to pull the trick off once—and was elated. It wasn't the end of the thing, of course, for Midnight had no intention of reforming! However, he'd stayed at it until he could manage getting astride the horse at least nine times out of ten, so he'd announced at breakfast that everyone was invited to watch.

Now as he hauled in on the reins, he was aware that if he got thrown, he'd look like a fool and a failure, but he was ready to risk it. There were rumors about the army moving into the North soon, and Lowell was determined to be a part of it.

"Easy, boy," he said gently but firmly. As he pulled the horse's head down, he moved to the side, his movement somewhat jerky. Keeping Midnight's head down, he leaned under the glossy neck, tossed the reins over, and caught them, then held them tightly. Midnight tried to toss his head and prance away, but Lowell jerked him into place almost roughly.

The trick was to mount quickly, he had discovered. One false move and Midnight would be sidling off to one side or giving that little half-buck that made it impossible for him to throw his artificial leg over the saddle. *Good thing it was the right leg instead of the left,* he thought. *I'd never be able to balance in the stirrup on the cork one.*

Giving the reins a steady pull, he stepped to the side and balanced on his artificial leg—and this was the critical moment! He had learned that if he could hold that balance, lift his left leg, and jam it into the stirrup, it was possible to lift himself with one surge of power and throw the other leg over the saddle even if Midnight tried one of his tricks. But if he missed the stirrup with his left foot, he was helpless and usually was dragged to the ground in an ignominious fall.

Now he jerked down on the reins to hold the horse steady for one moment, lifted his left foot, and stabbed at the stirrup—and was elated when his boot entered! He'd had Josh enlarge the stirrup so that it was easier to insert the toe of his boot, and now as it hit home, he instantly grabbed the saddle horn with his right hand, gave a sharp heave, and threw his right leg up and over the broad back of Midnight. Just as he did, Midnight gave a forward lurch, but the momentum of his effort carried him into the saddle, and he knew he was safe! He heard Highboy yelp shrilly and identified Rooney's voice as she cried out, "That's the way, Lowell!"

As he pulled Midnight up sharply, he glanced down to his right and lifted his body, shoving the toe of his boot into the stirrup, which had been specially designed by Josh so that it hung low enough to allow his leg to lock. Josh had also taken the forward sway out of that stirrup by means of carefully designed strips of white oak. This device prevented the stirrup from swaying forward when his boot hit and also held the leg firmly in place.

Flushed with his success, Lowell turned Midnight's head toward his small audience and swept off his hat. "Guess I'll be able to get a job with a circus!"

They all laughed, and he wheeled the horse around and called for Josh to open the gate. Then he gave a shrill cry and sent the sleek animal out at full speed. Leaning forward, he exulted in the speed of the animal, and a joy he thought he'd never know again came to him. *I'm as good as any man when I get in the saddle!* He drove the horse at a breakneck speed, then turned him sharply and was pleased that he'd mastered that trick. There was some loss of response, perhaps, but so little that he knew he could still do the job.

He put the horse through every difficulty he could devise, then slapped him on the neck fondly. "If I do as well as you, boy, I'll get a medal!"

When he returned to step down from the tired horse, he saw that Rooney was waiting. "Take good care of him, Highboy," he said fondly. "We've got a long way to go, him and me!"

Rooney came to meet him as he moved through the gate. She took his arm, and Lowell knew that it was partly to help him, for she had learned to serve as a brace for him since he'd almost given up his cane. He still used it, but now he put his arm around her waist and smiled. "Maybe I could take you along when I go back. You could cook for me and wash my clothes, just like in our ballooning days."

Rooney gave him a swift glance, longing in her face. "Oh, Lowell, I wish I could!"

She had such a woebegone expression that Lowell almost laughed. "Well, I doubt if the general would favor that."

"I don't see why not." They were walking along the open space that separated the barns and outbuildings from the main house, and Lowell gazed at the place, realizing how fond he was of Gracefield. He knew that he might never see it again, for no one was safe in battle. He'd grown up here and knew nearly every stone and blade of grass, and it gave him a wrench to think this might be his last glimpse of it.

"When will you be going?"

Startled, he looked down at her. "Why, day after tomorrow, I guess."

They had come to the scuppernong arbor, and the white lath work was covered with vines, most of them returning to the green of summer. Rooney stopped abruptly and turned to him, and he saw that she was very serious. Her blue eyes contained some sort of sadness that was rare, for she was a happy girl as a rule. Something was in her mind, he saw, for her lips were pursed as they were when she was making a decision, and there was a hesitancy in her manner.

"What is it, Rooney?"

"Oh, I don't know. . . ." She was not tall and had to tilt her head upward to look into his face. Lowell admired the freshness of her skin, the clearness of her eyes, and her long, thick lashes. "I wish you weren't going!" she said abruptly. Then she took the lapels of his suit coat and suddenly leaned against him.

Lowell was taken by surprise, for he had not seen this side of Rooney for a long time. She had been the strong one, always giving him confidence and never showing fear. He put his arms around her, thoroughly aware of the intense femininity that he held in his arms. Finally, without drawing back, she lifted her face and said simply, "I love you, Lowell!"

And then Rooney Smith did something that she would not have dreamed of doing only a few months before: She released her grip on his coat, reached up, and pulled his head down, kissing him firmly on the mouth.

For Lowell, there was a wild sweetness in her gesture, and the softness of her lips stirred him, so that he gripped her and pulled her closer. He half expected her to draw back, but instead she pressed herself against him with an impassioned gesture as if she were afraid she would lose him. He could smell the sweetness of the scent she wore, and her hair brushed against his cheeks, stirred by the wind.

There was no reserve in Rooney, and it was as if all the fears she'd had about men had never been. As Lowell held her, it was a natural thing, and she had no other thought but *I love this man!*

Finally she drew back and shyly dropped her eyes—and then raised them. She waited for him to speak, and though she had almost no experience with real love, she knew that Lowell felt some of what was in her so powerfully. Finally he whispered, "And I love you, Rooney!"

She laughed then, and when he kissed her again, it was as if she'd come home to safety after a long and difficult voyage. She pulled back, drew him to the bench, and, when they were seated, began to speak of how she'd fallen in love with him. He listened, charmed by her honesty and openness as much as by her fresh, youthful beauty. Finally she stopped and reached out to stroke his cheek. She started to speak and halted, a troubled look in her eyes.

"What is it, Rooney?"

"I–I'm not the kind of girl men like you. . .care for," she said quietly.

He read her thoughts and caught her hand. Holding it firmly, he said, "Yes, you are! You're honest and brave and beautiful. What else is there for a man?"

Rooney said with difficulty, "My family!" She could not say more and turned her face away. "When my mother gets out of. . . jail, I'll have to help her. You—you wouldn't want a woman like that in your—" She almost said, "in your family," but realized that Lowell had said nothing about marriage. She thought of the long line of Rocklins, men and women of distinction, and fell silent.

"Rooney, I can't say much right now," Lowell said quietly, then paused, thinking, *How much has changed in just a few weeks! When I had two legs, I'd never have thought of marrying a girl in her social class. Now it's what I want more than anything in the world!* He had not himself realized this fully, and the suddenness of it shocked him. He'd been firmly fixed in his own little world, but the blast of a cannon had completely destroyed his dreams and ideals. Now, looking at Rooney, he understood that he'd let go of them along with the bitterness that had filled his spirit. *I want her more than I ever wanted all those things I set such store by! Why, I can't even think of the future without her in it!*

Carefully he said, "Rooney, it's you I love. I've got only one leg, and you've got a mother with terrible problems. We have to take each other with the difficult things as well as the good things." He stroked her hair, for he loved the wild soft curls that crowned her head, and he began to tell her how much she'd come to mean to him. He'd never done this, but the words came easily, without effort. She kept her eyes fixed on him, her lips half parted, and there was such trust and joy in her expression that finally Lowell said, "You're the one woman in the world for me, Rooney!"

"Oh, Lowell!"

"But I've got to go," Lowell added. "It's something I have to do. When I get back. . .well, we'll have lots of plans to make."

"Yes, Lowell." Fear came to Rooney, as it did, perhaps, to all women who sent their men off to face the cannons, but she kept a smile on her lips. "I'll be waiting for you."

He got to his feet and, when she rose, embraced her briefly, then said, "That makes all the difference, sweetheart!"

If the pair had known they were under careful observation, they might have behaved differently, but neither of them realized that a pair of sharp eyes was watching them from the door of the hayloft.

Rena had persuaded Josh to take her rabbit hunting, and she'd joined him in the loft, helping to throw down hay for the farm animals. Josh had been pleased that Rena was going, but he turned to see her staring out the window instead of helping throw down forkfuls of the fragrant hay. Curiously he stepped behind her and peered over her shoulder. One glance and he pulled her around, "You ain't g–got no business watching such!"

"Lowell is kissing Rooney!"

"W–well, is it any of your b–business?"

Rena saw that Josh was angry, but she wanted to see more. She tried to pull away, but he held her arm so tightly that she couldn't move. "Let me go!" she cried angrily.

"No! It's not right spying."

Rena flushed with anger—and guilt. She'd known it wasn't right to watch the pair, and now that Josh had caught her at it—and refused to join her—it made her very angry. Without thought, she swung her arm and slapped him on the face, the blow making an ugly sound.

Josh stared at the girl, conscious of the stinging blow, but hurt worse by Rena's act than anything else. He was terribly sensitive, and it had been a new world when Rena Rocklin had shown him such kindness. Now as the sound of the blow seemed to echo in his ears, his eyes grew bleak. Dropping his grip on her arm, he turned and walked away. Without a word, he leaped from the loft into the pile of hay, caught his balance, then ran out of the barn.

Rena was transfixed, unable to move. She had not *meant* to strike Josh! It had been her pride that had made her do it, and she leaped forward to the ladder, crying, "Josh! Josh! I didn't mean it!"

But he was gone, and though she searched for him everywhere, she couldn't find him. Finally she went to her room, fell across her bed, and wept until she was weak.

When she went downstairs, Susanna saw at once the trouble that lurked in her granddaughter's eyes. "What's wrong, Rena?" she asked.

Rena stared at her with tragic eyes and began to tell Susanna what she'd done. By the time she'd finished, her voice was trembling and tears were brimming in her eyes. "I was so mean to him, Grandmother! He was right, and I was wrong!"

Susanna remembered how small things were enormous to the very young. She'd seen that the young man had been good for Rena, and now she saw that the girl's affection for Josh ran deeper than she'd thought. Putting her arms around the girl, she murmured, "It'll be all right."

"I've got to find him. . .tell him I was wrong." She looked up and saw that her grandmother had an odd look in her eyes.

"What is it?" she whispered.

"Josh has gone home for a little while, Rena," Susanna said, pity in her tone. "He told David he had to help his father with the work there."

Rena's face turned pale, and she whispered, "He's mad at me! And he's right!"

Susanna stood there trying to comfort the weeping girl but knew that there was little she could do. *When you're sixteen, a thing like this is as big as a mountain,* she thought. Aloud she said, "Rena, he's hurt, but he's a good young man. He'll get over it, and you two will be friends again."

"No, he won't come back," Rena said, shaking her head. "You don't know how shy he is—but *I* knew it! He's so ashamed of his stutter that he doesn't make friends, Grandmother. And. . . and I was his friend!"

Rena tore loose from Susanna's hands and ran out the door, disappearing around the corner of the house, shaking with the sobs she tried to hold back.

Susanna stared after the girl, then picked up the tray of food and made her way to Mark's room. "I've fixed you one of those omelets you like, Mark," she said, setting the tray down.

Mark Rocklin knew this woman very well. One glance at her and he demanded, "What is it, Susanna? Bad news about the boys?"

"Oh no." Susanna hesitated, then sat down and related the problem to him. When she had finished, she sighed and looked at him, weariness in her eyes and in the lines of her face. "She thinks it's the end of the world, Mark."

"The young always think that." He toyed with the omelet, then looked at her with a tired smile. "You carry so many people on those small shoulders, Susanna." And then he added, "You've always been the finest woman I've ever known."

His praise shocked Susanna Rocklin, bringing a tinge of red to her cheeks. "Why, Mark—" She started to protest, but he cut her off.

"It's true. I should have told you years ago. And Rena's like you," he added. "She's had a pretty bad knock, but she'll make it."

"I think she will, but it's good to have someone else tell me." Susanna leaned over and stroked Mark's hand, noting with a sudden fear how frail it was. The two of them sat there speaking quietly, and somehow they both felt a closeness that had been gone for years. Neither of them knew how to speak of it—and neither did. But when Susanna rose to take his tray back to the kitchen, she gave a sudden sigh of relief. "You've made me feel better, Mark."

"I'm glad. Good to be of some use." He caught himself, saying, "That sounds like self-pity, and there's nothing I hate worse than that in a man!" He hesitated and for one moment seemed on the brink of telling his sister-in-law something.

Susanna caught the look on Mark's face and asked, "What is it, Mark? I've thought for some time you've wanted to tell me something. I'd like to hear it."

Mark Rocklin had spent his life alone for the most part. Only a few times had he been able to speak his mind and heart to another, and he longed to speak now. But the habits of a lifetime were strong, and he found no words to express what was in his heart.

"Sometime I'll tell you, Susanna," he said and then wearily lay down and turned his face to the wall.

Susanna stared at him, then shook her head and left the room without a word. Going to her sewing room, she closed the door and sat down in the worn rocking chair. She began to rock, and the motions of the old chair were as even as the tides or the spinning of the globe. She picked up the worn black Bible but did not open it. Holding it in her hands, she closed her eyes and her lips began to move. "Dear Lord, hear my prayer. . . ."

CHAPTER 22

"Jine the Cavalry!"

Some officers were so colorless that they could pass through a crowd without being recognized. General Ulysses S. Grant was one of these. He wore the uniform of a private at times, the only mark of his rank being the stars pinned to his coat. Grant was so plain in appearance that once when he was boarding a gunboat, smoking a cigar, the guard, a new private in the army, stopped him and addressed him roughly: "You—throw that cigar away!" Grant had smiled, tossed his cigar away, then passed by, saying, "I like to see a soldier who does his duty."

General James Ewell Brown Stuart was definitely *not* one of these drab officers! The general—better know as Jeb Stuart—would never be overlooked in any crowd. His uniform consisted of a pair of thigh-high black boots, tan breeches, a flowing cape with scarlet lining that rippled in the wind as he rode his horse at a full gallop, and a black ostrich plume crowning his rakish hat. Stuart surrounded himself with men only slightly less colorful than himself, and his entourage included one man called Sweeny, who had been a professional minstrel. Wherever Stuart camped, one could hear the lively plunking of the banjo and the laughter of his men.

As Lowell guided Midnight through the ranks of tents that practically surrounded Richmond, he was seized by a sudden tension. *I must be crazy doing this! Every young fellow in the South with a horse wants to ride with Jeb Stuart. He can get all the men he wants with two legs. No reason for him to take me.*

As he moved past the line of tents that marked the camp of the infantry, he heard the tinny, plinking sound of a banjo. Drawing closer, he heard a fine tenor voice singing:

We're tenting tonight on the old camp ground;
Give us a song to cheer
Our weary hearts, a song of home,
And friends we love so dear.

Many are the hearts that are weary tonight,
Wishing for the war to cease;
Many are the hearts looking for the right
To see the dawn of peace.
Tenting tonight, tenting tonight,
Tenting on the old camp ground.

Rows of small tents framed the background of the cavalry encampment, but Lowell made his way to a large Sibley tent set out in front. The conical canvas shelter could accommodate twenty soldiers, but by the ensign flying from the polished pole beside it, Lowell knew that it housed General Jeb Stuart.

Pulling Midnight to a halt, he spotted the general at once. Stuart was in the midst of a circle of officers who were being served a meal by two black servants. Lowell noted at once that there was a holiday air about the group and decided that all he'd heard about Jeb Stuart's ability to draw men and hold them was true.

"I'm Lieutenant Collins. What can I do for you?"

Glancing around with a start, Lowell looked down at a tall, long-legged lieutenant who had advanced from his left and now positioned himself directly in front of Midnight. He was wearing a heavy Dance revolver, a Confederate copy of the Colt .44 Dragoon and the favorite weapon of Stuart's troopers. "Why, I'd like to speak with General Stuart, Lieutenant." He fished an envelope out of his pocket and extended it to the officer. "I have a letter from Colonel Benton of the Richmond Grays."

"Wait here," Collins replied, then eyed Midnight with a practiced eye. "Better keep your eye on that hoss. Some of our folks might decide to requisition him."

Lowell grinned and nodded, then watched as the long-legged officer approached Stuart. He saw the general glance at him, then tear the envelope open and scan the single sheet of paper inside. He nodded and waved Lowell forward. The officers surrounding the general watched the new arrival curiously, and Lowell felt a moment of awkwardness. *I can't ride Midnight through the middle of them, but if I get off, they'll know I've got a wooden leg.*

Setting his teeth, he slipped off Midnight and moved forward. No matter how much practice he'd put in, he was acutely aware of the halting gait he was forced to use. He was also aware that Stuart was watching his progress thoughtfully. But the general smiled, wide lips almost hidden behind his ferocious beard and moustache. "Well, Sergeant Rocklin, we meet again!"

"I'm surprised you remember, General."

"I might have forgotten you, but I never forget a good horse." He put his bright blue eyes on Midnight, then shot at Lowell directly, "I'll buy him from you, Sergeant—name your price."

Lowell shook his head. "Sorry, General, but I couldn't sell him."

Stuart nodded his approval. "I'd have been disappointed if you had." He put that thought aside, then studied Lowell carefully. "Too bad about that balloon getting destroyed." He glanced at his staff and gave them a brief history of the balloon. When he finished, a chunky young major eating from a tin plate said, "I wish we had some of those things. They'd come in handy."

Stuart nodded absently, still engaged in some sort of thought. "That's right, Major Malone." He studied Lowell, then said, "You took a pretty bad wound. General Able told me about it."

"Yes, sir, I lost a leg," Lowell said instantly and was aware of the scrutiny the staff officers gave his legs. He knew that this would be the issue and wanted to get it into the open. He had hoped to see the general alone, but there was no chance of that now.

"Your colonel writes that you want to jine the cavalry."

"Yes, sir, more than anything!"

"Well, Sergeant, I admire your grit, but we're a pretty rough bunch." Stuart hesitated, seeking for the best way to put what was in his mind. Finally he shrugged and said bluntly, "Lots of men with two legs can't stay up and take the punishment we have to take. It would be difficult for a man with only one."

"If I fall behind, take my horse and leave me!"

A mutter of approval went around the circle, and Major Malone observed, "A man can't say fairer than that, General!"

Lieutenant Collins put in slyly, "Be a good way to get another good hoss, sir."

Stuart looked over Lowell's shoulder at the fine lines of Midnight and hesitated. Then he shook his head firmly. "I'm mighty tempted, but it wouldn't be fair. I'm sorry, Sergeant. I admire your spunk, but—"

Sensing rejection coming, Lowell said quickly, "General, I can give you two reasons why you should take me."

Stuart had already settled the matter in his mind, but Lowell's statement caught at him. "And those two are?"

"The first is that I can play a harmonica as well as Mr. Sweeny there can play a banjo."

Sweeny was a short man with a bushy head of black hair and a pair of bright black eyes. "Why, let's have a sample, Sergeant!

If you can do what you say, I'll be on your side. Some of these so-called musicians in this troop can't tell one note from another!"

Lowell had learned to play the harmonica from Box. He had a great deal of natural ability and had spent long hours making up tunes and acquiring new skills. Knowing of Stuart's love of music, he'd stashed his harmonica in his pocket, hoping for just such a chance as this. Pulling it out, he put it to his lips and began playing a lively tune, employing the trills and half notes he'd learned. Sweeny listened critically for the first few notes, then nodded gleefully. "The man can do it!" he cheered; then his hand began to move across the strings of his banjo.

The two instruments formed a wonderful harmony on the stillness of the air, and Stuart, Lowell noted, enjoyed the duet. He beat his thigh with a hard hand and moved his head in time with the music. When the two reached the end, giving a run of staccato notes as a final flourish, he led the loud applause that went up and said loudly, "Never heard better mouth organ playin' in my whole life, Sergeant!" Then he added regretfully, "But a man's got to be more than a musician to ride with me. What's your second reason?"

Lowell knew his last chance had come. "Why, General, I don't see how you can turn down a man who can beat anybody in your whole cavalry in a horse race!"

"Ho! That's pretty big talk!" Stuart blinked. Memory came to him, and he said, "As I recollect, we settled that awhile back. Me and Skylark beat you and that black horse right smartly!"

Lowell suddenly grinned. "No, sir, all we settled was that any private should have enough sense *not* to beat a general in a horse race—or anything else!"

A shout of laughter filled the air, and Major Malone's voice rose over it. "He's got you there, General! Why, even a *major* knows better than to win against his commanding officer!"

Stuart's genial expression gave way to a sudden flare of anger that brightened his eyes. "That's the squeal of a loser!" he exclaimed, his pride touched. "Man that can't win has to blame it on something!"

Lowell said carefully, "Sir, I don't suppose you'd give me and Midnight another chance?"

Stuart understood at once what the sergeant was up to. He could not suppress a grin. "I can guess the stakes," he shot back. "If you beat me, I let you into the troop."

"Yes, sir!"

"What do I get if *I* win?"

"Why, you prove to your staff that you've got the best horse, General."

"Don't see how you can refuse the man, General Stuart," Major Malone urged slyly, winking at his fellow officers.

"Well, by George, I'll have to show you clodhoppers *again* what a real horse is!" Turning his head, Stuart yelled, "Turner, saddle Skylark!"

The officers all ate hastily, and in the background Lowell could see the troopers had gotten word of the race. He stood talking with Major Malone, who asked about his background and then listened intently. "I've met your father," he said, nodding. "Fine officer!" Then he glanced at Stuart, who was swinging into the saddle. Leaning forward, he whispered, "Make the race half a mile or more. Skylark can beat anything on four legs for a quarter of a mile, but that black gelding of yours looks like he's got more bottom!"

"Thank you, sir!" Lowell nodded gratefully. He stepped into the saddle, aware that eyes were taking in his actions critically. When Stuart rode forward, the two of them moved together along the line of tents into the large open field where drill took place. It was occupied now by a lieutenant drilling his company, but when he saw Stuart and Lowell followed by the staff—and by many of the troopers who hurried to see the race—he called out loudly, "Let's take a break, men. We can watch them imitation soldiers play with their hosses!"

Lowell grinned, for he himself had made fun of the easy life of the cavalry. Then Stuart pulled up to say, "Now I don't want any excuses after we get this thing done, so you can pick the distance and the route, Sergeant."

Lowell was prepared and lifted his arm. "How about to that big tree and back, sir?"

Stuart blinked at the choice and gave Major Malone a hard glance. The major returned his stare blandly, and the general nodded shortly. "That's half a mile to that tree."

"We can make it shorter, sir," Lowell said, "if that distance is too much for your horse."

A muffled laughter ran around the men who watched, and

Stuart glared at them furiously. "That will be fine—to the tree and back. Major Malone, you can give the start. We go on the count of three!"

Lowell guided Midnight forward, and the big horse knew as well as his rider what was happening. He quivered with eagerness, the powerful muscles bunching as the two horsemen brought them side by side. Lowell held the eager animal in check as Malone's voice rang out, "One—two—*three*!"

Midnight shot forward, but Skylark was faster. As Lowell had expected, by the time they had reached the tree, the smaller bay was four lengths ahead of the big gelding. Stuart rounded the tree and shouted as the two passed, "Too bad, Sergeant!"

Lowell leaned into the turn, and when he faced the crowd of cheering men across the field, he leaned forward, shouting, "Midnight, get him!" He felt the surge of power that pulled him back as Midnight lunged forward, and he let out a wild cry as he saw the gap begin to close.

General Stuart cast a look over his shoulder, a startled expression crossing his face as he saw the big black coming up fast. Whirling, he began to lash his horse with the reins, but it did no good. As Lowell pulled up even, Stuart's face was swept with chagrin.

Lowell urged Midnight on, but as he approached the starting point he was tempted to pull the animal back. *No, I'll beat him as bad as I can!* When he shot into the gap left by the spectators and glanced back, he saw that he'd beaten Stuart by three lengths. Pulling Midnight to a stop, he slipped to the ground, where he was surrounded at once by a group of admiring troopers who beat his shoulders in congratulations.

Major Malone took Skylark's reins as Stuart came to the ground and tossed them to him. "A good race, General," he stated. "The boy has a fine animal."

Stuart stared at him accusingly. "Did you give him any advice, Malone?"

"Why, yes," the major confirmed. "I told him that he'd better choose a long distance because no horse alive could beat Skylark in a quarter of a mile."

"Why, you...you *scoundrel*!" Stuart almost stuttered, anger in his flashing blue eyes. For one moment Malone thought he was about to be transferred to the infantry, but then Stuart's good humor won out. He stared at the group of admiring troopers and officers who surrounded the big black horse and laughed aloud. "Well, he'll be your responsibility, Major. See that he keeps up—or I *will* have that black horse!"

"Yes, sir," Malone said, grinning, knowing his man. "And I think we'd better have another race. . .this time for a shorter distance."

"Right! Can't have a mere private beating his commanding officer!"

"Why, Rocklin's a sergeant, General!"

"Not anymore," Stuart slyly stated. "He'll have to earn his stripes all over again. Come along, Major."

Lowell turned from speaking with the men who pressed in to shake his hand and stroke the sides of Midnight. He waited for the general to speak, fearful that he'd lost his chance despite winning the race.

But Stuart smiled, and Lowell's heart seemed to leap as the bearded general said, "Well, looks like you jined the cavalry, Private Rocklin. Now let's see if you can keep up!"

Lowell didn't miss the fact that he'd been demoted, but that meant nothing to him. "Thank you, General!" he responded quickly. "I'll do my best to do that."

"You'll serve in Major Malone's troop, and we'll have a race tomorrow." Stuart's bright blue eyes twinkled as he added, "This time for just a *quarter*!"

"Yes, sir!"

As Malone walked away with Lowell to show him his quarters and acquaint him with his sergeant, he said, "Private, I don't think I'd win that race tomorrow if I were you."

The words were gently spoken, but Lowell understood at once that he was being given what amounted to a command. "No, *sir*," he said vigorously. "Midnight never does well two days in a row, especially against generals!"

Malone laughed and then sobered. "I'm not sure I did the right thing, helping you get back into this war. We'll be leaving shortly to join General Lee."

"We'll be going north?" Lowell asked, excitement in his voice.

"It's no secret." Major Malone's rugged face was suddenly tense, and he shrugged his thin shoulders. "Everybody seems to know what's coming. I just hope Hooker doesn't know what

Lee is up to."

"Major, thank you for helping me!"

Malone had a sudden vision of this eager young man lying dead on a battlefield. *It'll be all my fault if that happens, but I can't think on that.* "Your home is just outside of Richmond?" he asked suddenly.

"Yes, sir."

"I wish mine were! Well, there's no time for training you. You can serve as a courier for the general. That means you'll be a messenger boy, but I don't have to tell you how important that is."

"I understand, sir. It's great just to be here!"

Again a picture of this keen-eyed young man lying bloodied in a distant field flashed through Malone's mind, and he said impulsively, "After the sergeant gives you your instruction, take what time there is and be with your people. We won't pull out for four days—be back by then."

"What about the race, Major?"

"Wait until the general beats you," Malone answered with a dry smile. "Then go see your people." They were almost to the spot where a sergeant stood watching them, and he added quietly, "Enjoy your time with your family. It may be the last you'll have for a time."

❧

Mark and Rooney had grown very close, and Rooney often thought of what the tall man had said about loving a woman named Beth. She had said nothing about the matter and was certain that he had no memory of it. But she had grown fond of him and wished that he would confide in her. One afternoon she was sitting with him, reading from a novel called *Ivanhoe*, and when he seemed bored, she put it down. Idly she asked, "You never thought of marriage, Mr. Rocklin?"

Her question troubled him, she saw, and he hesitated before saying, "Yes, I did think of it once." He let the silence run on, then shook his head. "I wish now that I had married."

"Why didn't you?" Rooney asked quietly.

Mark stared into the fire, his dark eyes grown moody. When he spoke, it was in a low voice, almost a whisper. "Pride, I guess. She wasn't of our class—" Suddenly he realized what he was saying and gave Rooney a startled glance.

He's thinking I'm not of Lowell's class, Rooney knew instantly. She saw that he was embarrassed and said, "It's all right. I understand."

A look of relief washed across his face, and he said, "You're a discerning young woman, Rooney."

She was exactly that, and as she sat there listening to the fire crackle, the missing pieces of Mark Rocklin's life fell into place. His family all realized that he was a man who was incomplete. He'd been a driven man, traveling much and coming home to Gracefield as if it were a safe harbor, but restless and unhappy even when there.

He fell in love with a poor girl but wouldn't marry her because of his family, Rooney thought. *I wish he'd married. He's been so unhappy!* Then she asked, "What became of her, Mr. Rocklin? Did she marry somebody else?"

"No, she died." The words were harsh and almost grim, and Rooney knew the door had slammed shut. She began to speak of other things, but she understood Mark Rocklin's unhappiness now, she felt, more than his own family did.

Buck suddenly burst into the room, crying, "It's Lowell! He's ridin' in!"

Rooney threw down the Sir Walter Scott book and ran through the door, closely followed by Buck. They found Rena, Susanna, and David on the front porch, and there was Lowell riding in on Midnight!

"Lowell!" David exclaimed as the young man dismounted. "We didn't expect you back."

"Well, I left a sergeant and came back a private, David, but I'm serving under General Stuart!"

Susanna could not have cared less about his rank but simply put her arms out. He gave her a fierce hug, then did the same for Rena. "Dad'll be home soon. I met him in Richmond." Then he turned and clapped his hand fondly on Buck's shoulder, saying, "I've got a present for you in my saddlebags. It's a Yankee officer's pistol. Go get it, but don't shoot anybody!"

Buck leaped off the porch with a yelp and was soon brandishing the pistol wildly. "I hope it's not loaded," David said, grinning at Buck.

"No, it's not." Lowell turned to Rooney then, and there was a sudden silence. Susanna broke it, saying, "Rena, you come and help me fix this man something to eat."

Rena started to protest, but Susanna gave her arm a sudden pull toward the door. "David, take Midnight to the barn." She herded Rena inside, pausing at the door to give Rooney a sly smile. "Bring him in when you're through with him, Rooney," she said.

Lowell smiled suddenly and took Rooney's arm. "My grandmother is a smart woman." They stood there looking at each other, and then he demanded, "Come with me."

"Where are we going?"

"To the scuppernong arbor," Lowell said, a sly grin forming. "That's where us Rocklin men take pretty girls to kiss them!"

Rooney blushed but then said, "All right, I'll do it." He laughed at her red face, then led her around the house to the arbor. When they were inside, he looked around. "I wasn't joking about this place, Rooney. My father said he got more kisses here when he was courtin' than anywhere else. He even proposed to Melanie Benton right on this very spot."

"She turned him down and married your uncle Gideon, didn't she?"

"That's right. You've really boned up on my family history." He reached out and took her by the arms, but when he tried to embrace her, she resisted. "What's the matter?" he asked. He'd looked forward to this moment, but now she was apprehensive. Thoughts had come to him, such as *No woman wants a man with only one leg!* And now he stood there waiting for her to tell him that she'd changed her mind.

But Rooney was thinking about what Mark had said. *"She wasn't of our class."* Rooney slowly lifted her eyes and said, "You come from a proud family—"

At once Lowell expelled his breath. "Never mind the family!" he said almost roughly. "I'm not asking you to marry the family. I'm asking you to marry *me*! If they don't accept you, we'll go make our own place!"

Rooney's eyes filled with unbidden tears, for it was what Mark should have said to that girl years ago. Throwing her arms around him, she cried out, "Oh, Lowell, I love you so!"

He held her fast, kissed her, and then said huskily, "My father said he'd horsewhip me if I let you get away—and my grandmother is just about as bad!"

They stood there relishing each other's company for close to an hour—until Buck's head poked around the corner. "You two gonna stay out here all day? Come on, Lowell. You gotta show me how to load the pistol, and Miz Rocklin wants to see you." He frowned at Rooney, adding, "You sure are selfish, Rooney, hoggin' Lowell so the rest of us can't have him."

Rooney laughed at Buck, then went to him and asked, "Do you know what a brother-in-law is. . . ?"

❦

Mark awakened himself by uttering a short cry, the result of a ragged pain that tore across his stomach and brought him out of a fitful sleep. Cool hands touched his brow, and he heard Melora's voice saying, "Drink this, Mr. Rocklin." He swallowed the bitter liquid she held to his lips, then lay back on the bed.

"Sorry to be such a baby," he muttered. "You don't have to sit up with me, Melora."

"I'm not sleepy." Melora pulled the oak rocker by the window up to the bed and began knitting. As she worked, she talked quietly of the small affairs that made up the lives of the Rocklins and the Yancys. Not the war—she didn't speak of that. She spoke of the new calf, the fox that Box had killed carrying off a chicken, the church supper that had been such a success.

Mark lay there rigidly until the pain subsided, then relaxed as the room grew fuzzy. Her voice was warm and soft and pleasant. As she spoke and he felt sleep dragging him down, something came to him. At first he thought, *It's none of my business,* but the thought persisted. So he said carefully, "Melora?"

"Yes, Mr. Rocklin?"

"When are you and Clay getting married?"

"Why, we haven't decided."

Mark felt a sharp disappointment at her answer. He fought off the drowsiness that fogged his mind, opened his eyes, and struggled to sit up. Then Melora blinked and said, "What's wrong? Is it the pain?"

"No, it's not that." Mark had pulled himself into a sitting position, and Melora leaned forward, anxiety in her eyes. "Melora, don't put it off! Marry Clay as soon as you can—tomorrow!"

Melora was startled by the passion in Mark Rocklin's voice. She knew him to be a man who kept his emotions under strict control, but now his face was set in a grim expression. "Why do you say that?"

"Because I waited too long once. There was. . .a girl I loved. And I let her slip away." Haggard lines creased the sick man's face, and he reached out to Melora. When she took his hand, he said hoarsely, "Nobody has tomorrow, Melora. All you and Clay have is *now*. I know Clay thinks it would be unfair to marry you until he's back safely from the war. But if you love him, give him what time there is. If it's only a day, that's better than missing love altogether!"

The medicine hit Mark then, and he lay back. His eyes closed, and he muttered a few words before dropping off into a deep sleep. Melora remained to be sure that he was all right, then rose and left the room. It was after midnight, and she knew that he would sleep, so she went to her room. For a long time after she went to bed, she thought of Mark's words: *"All you and Clay have is now."*

The next morning she rose early and said little to anyone. Mark seemed not to remember the incident, and she did not mention it. All morning she worked; then in the afternoon she changed and went for a long walk in the woods. As she moved across the soft earth, following the path beside the creek, she thought of the times she and Clay had walked there in earlier days.

Finally she turned and walked back down the path, and when she came out of the timberline, she saw Clay riding down the road. He saw her at once and spurred his horse. Dismounting, he moved toward her, and she put her arms up. Clay said with surprise, "Melora, what is it?" She was not a woman to parade her emotions, but now she held him tightly, lifting her face. He kissed her and as always was totally aware of her femininity.

"Clay, I want to get married—now!"

Clay's face stiffened with surprise. "Why, Melora—" He began to protest, but she cut him off by placing her fingers over his lips.

"I know. You're afraid you won't come back. That I'll be a widow. Clay, I've waited for you too long. I want you, even if it's only for a day or a week!"

Clay was amazed at Melora's intensity. Her dark eyes pleaded with him, and her lips were soft yet firm with purpose. "But what if there's a child?"

"Then I'll have something of you, Clay. I love you, and we have little time. All we have is now. Let's not let it slip by!"

Clay pulled her close, kissed her again, then lifted his lips. "Day after tomorrow you'll be my wife, Melora!" Then he laughed, and there was a joy in him that Melora had never seen. "Come on. Let's go tell Mother to start baking the wedding cake!"

Hand in hand they ran like children down the road, and Clay's mount threw his head up, puzzled at this sudden freedom. Then with a whicker, he moved into the field and began cropping the tender blades of emerald grass.

CHAPTER 23

NOW IS FOREVER

*C*lay walked out of the house and headed for the barn. The sky was painted a hard bright blue, and clouds white as cotton sailed majestically overhead. He'd never felt better and had given Rooney a tremendous hug, stating firmly, "I'd have horsewhipped this boy of mine if he hadn't proposed to you!"

As he moved toward the stable, he heard a voice and turned to find Rena running out the front door. "Daddy, are you going to the Yancys'?"

"Sure am. I'm taking your grandmother's wedding dress to my bride-to-be."

Rena looked pale and hesitated slightly. "Take me with you, Daddy."

"Why, sure! Come along. You're going to be the maid of honor, so you and Melora can make all the plans." He'd spoken with his mother, asking why Rena was so subdued. She'd said, "She and Josh had a spat," and Clay had thought little of it, saying, "They'll make it up."

Now as he climbed into the buggy, he noted the girl's pale face and asked, "Are you sure you want to go, Rena?"

"I have to go with you, Daddy," she said, lifting her chin defiantly.

Clay hesitated, for on this trip he wanted to be alone. But there was a vulnerability in his daughter's wan face that made him say, "Why, sure, Rena. I'd have asked you if I'd known you wanted to go."

Rena climbed into the buggy, and soon Gracefield was left behind. "I've missed you," Clay said, turning to smile at her. "And Dent said to tell you that you and your grandmother will be staying with Raimey after the wedding." He put his arm around her, squeezed her, then added, "You've got to go see that my grandson gets raised the right way!"

Thomas Denton Rocklin had been born to Dent and Raimey in early March, and no one at Gracefield had had the opportunity to spend much time with the newest Rocklin.

Rena tried to pull away, but he held her fast. She really liked to be held and was glad that he kept his arm around her. "Daddy...," she said tentatively, "I was horrible to Josh...."

As the girl poured out the story, Clay understood how important this thing was to her. She was sensitive—too much so, he thought at the time—and the boy had been someone her own age to talk to. Susanna had told him how fond Rena was of Josh, and now he listened, then said carefully, "Too bad! Nothing much worse than hurting a friend, is there?"

"He hates me!"

"No, he doesn't," Clay said firmly. "Josh has too much sense for that. His feelings are hurt, but he'll get over it."

As they drove along, he talked to her easily, keeping his arm around her shoulder. He had a very special love for this daughter of his and knew that she was very dependent on him. He had never escaped the sadness over the loss of the years when he'd been away. He'd missed so much of her girlhood, and she'd missed having a father. Now he was determined to make it up to her. The war had come, and he had to do all he could during the fleeting times that they were together.

Finally they drove into the opening where the Yancy cabin sat and saw the smoke pouring out of the chimney. Clay said, "Hope that smoke means Melora's cookin' up somethin' good!"

As he stopped the team, the door opened and Buford stepped outside, followed by Melora and the others. "Well, I never!" he exclaimed. "Comin' round at dinnertime again!"

Clay stepped down, then turned to help Rena. Melora came over to put her arm around Rena. "I'm so glad you came with your father, Rena. You've got to help me plan everything."

Clay reached into the buggy and brought out an oblong box. "I hope you're the same size as my mother was when she married. She says you are."

"I won't be as beautiful as she was, Clay."

"That's your opinion, not mine." Clay smiled warmly and winked at Buford. "How much dowry do I get for taking this old maid off your hands, Buford?"

"Daddy!" Rena exclaimed. "You ought to be ashamed!" But Clay only laughed at her and sat down with his host to drink some fresh buttermilk. He was exuberant in a fashion that none of them had seen before, and for the next ten minutes kept them all smiling as he spoke of how he was robbing them of their cook.

Rena watched Josh, who said not one word—and had not even looked at her. All of the younger Yancys crowded around her, and she smiled and talked with them, but she felt a sharp despair when Josh retired to a dark corner of the room and sat with his face turned down.

Clay had observed this, too, and thought quickly. "Melora, do you still have that case of books I sent—the old ones?"

"Why, yes, Clay." Melora had been watching the little drama, not missing the misery on the faces of both Josh and Rena. She understood at once what Clay was up to and said, "They're up in the bedroom in the loft."

"Josh," Clay said, "hop upstairs and find me a book called *The Last of the Mohicans*, will you?"

"Yes, s–sir."

Melora waited until Josh had disappeared up the steep ladder and exclaimed, "I forgot. I put that book in another box. Rena, go tell Josh to look in the small box, not the big one."

Rena blinked and cast a nervous look at Clay, who said, "Go on, daughter, do what Melora tells you!"

When Rena reached the top of the ladder and stepped into the large room, she saw Josh turn toward her. She had dreaded this moment—yet longed for it for days. At once she walked across to him and whispered, "Josh, I'm. . .I'm sorry I hit you! You were right, and I was wrong!"

Josh was stunned, and as he looked down and saw how afraid she was and noted the tears beginning to gather in her eyes, he swallowed, saying hoarsely, "Aw, it w–wasn't nothing."

"Yes, it was!" Rena tentatively put her hand on his arm, and her voice was so low that he could hardly hear her as she said, "Will you be friends again, Josh?"

Josh had been miserable since leaving Gracefield. He'd gone about his work with a dullness and lack of interest, so that his family knew that something was very wrong with him, but he had not spoken of his problem.

Now as he looked down and saw Rena's dark eyes looking at him in a woeful manner and her soft lips trembling, he couldn't stand it. "I'd like that," he muttered, then added fervently, "I missed you something awful, Rena!"

"Did you, Josh? Really?" Rena suddenly threw her arms about the boy and held him closely. "I was so miserable I thought I'd die!"

Josh was shocked almost witless by Rena's embrace. He stood there awkwardly, not knowing what to do with his arms. The pressure of her form against him sent a shock through him, and he stood there stiff as a ramrod. Then he put his arms around her and patted her on the shoulder. "Let's never fuss again, Rena!" he said.

Rena drew back suddenly. "Josh! You're not stuttering!"

Josh blinked and realized that she was right. "I guess you scared it out of me!" he marveled.

"Oh, Josh!" Rena was so excited that without thinking, she leaned forward and kissed him on the lips—and then she froze, realizing what she'd done. Josh, she saw, was staring at her, and finally she said, "Well, it was only a little kiss! Didn't you ever get kissed before?"

Embarrassed by her boldness, she turned away and started for the door, but he leaped after her, caught her, and whirled her around. "Not by such a pretty girl," he said. And then he heard himself saying, "But I like it fine, Rena." And he leaned forward and kissed her cheek.

He drew back, and they stared at each other wordlessly. Finally Rena said, "Will you come back, Josh? And take me coon hunting and fishing?"

Josh nodded, answering at once, "Sure I will." He stared at her, then said again, "I've missed you a heap, Rena!"

Clay and Melora noted the expressions on the faces of the two young people when they finally returned with the book. Clay couldn't resist saying, "Must have had to look hard for that book, Josh."

But Melora said, "Now stop that, Clay." She rose and headed for the door, saying, "You can come and help me feed the stock."

"I'll do that," Buford protested, but Melora gave him a warning look, and he mumbled, "Well, I guess not."

Clay walked with Melora, taking her hand. "I guess Rena and Josh made up," he remarked. "She was miserable."

"So was Josh."

They fed the stock; then she took his hand and led him down past the barn to the small pond. They stood there looking at their reflection in the still water. "Remember when the snapping turtle bit me and wouldn't let go?" she said with a smile.

"I remember."

Clay let his mind go back and thought of the twelve-year-old Melora, her eyes filled with tears as he'd worked to get the small turtle to release her. "It must have hurt like the dickens, but you didn't cry out loud."

"No, I didn't, did I?" Melora was caught up in the memory and said gently, "We have lots of memories, don't we, Clay?"

Clay Rocklin took her in his arms and saw her eyes widen. He bent his head and kissed her, savoring the softness of her lips. Then he lifted his head and said, "Melora, I love you."

"I love you, too, Clay." *I've loved him since I was a little girl,* she thought. *He may not come back from the next battle. I want to have all of him I can—and to give him all that a woman can give a man.*

"Melora!" Clay stroked her black hair, and he held her in his arms. The still green water of the small pond mirrored their image, and there was a holy quietness over the earth.

Finally he said huskily, "I can't promise you how long—"

Melora put her fingers over his lips and lifted her face, saying, "Now is forever, isn't it, Clay?"

CHAPTER 24

"With This Ring I Thee Wed"

"Clay, for heaven's sake, sit down!" Colonel Taylor Dewitt had joined Clay in the pastor's study. The faint sound of the organ filtered through the door, and Clay had been pacing the floor like a caged lion. As Clay's best man, Taylor felt it his duty to keep the bridegroom from exploding, and he said in disgust, "It's only a wedding, man! Why, you didn't get this nervous at the Bloody Angle!"

Clay halted abruptly and glared at his friend. "This is worse than going into battle, Taylor," he muttered grimly. "I'd rather get shot than go out there!"

The two had been friends for years, and Taylor came to lay his hand on Clay's broad shoulder. "I guess I was the same when I got married. Goes with the territory, I suppose—" He broke off as a short man with fair hair and intense blue eyes entered. "Glad you came, Pastor. The bridegroom's about ready to make a run for it."

Rev. John Talbot, pastor of Faith Church, the largest in Richmond, was accustomed to nervous bridegrooms. "Quite natural," he said, smiling. "But let me tell you this, Major Rocklin—fifteen things may go wrong when we go out there. The maid of honor may fall flat, one of the guests might drop dead of a heart attack, the roof might fall in. . . ." Rev. Talbot paused dramatically, his lips lifting in a smile as he added, "But when you walk out of that church, you'll be a married man!"

Clay laughed, amused by the short minister. "I trust you for that, Rev. Talbot. But all the same I'd just as soon we'd eloped."

"And rob the women of a chance at a good cry?" Dewitt jibed. "Not likely! Anyway, you couldn't cheat Melora out of a big wedding."

Clay knew that Taylor was right. He himself had wanted to have the ceremony at the small church near Gracefield, but the pastor was serving as a chaplain with Lee's army, and the church would never have held the crowd. Clay had stood outside watching the crowd arrive, and the sight of what seemed to be half the people in Richmond and the surrounding countryside shook his nerve.

"Let's go over the ceremony one more time, Reverend!" he pleaded.

"Now, Major, there's no reason for that. You just do what I tell you, and everything will go all right. Colonel Dewitt, you have the ring?"

"Ring?" Taylor stared at the pastor blankly, then snapped his fingers. "I left it at camp."

"You did *what*!" Clay shouted. "Why, I should have known better than to—"

Taylor laughed loudly and pulled the ring from his pocket. "Of course I have the ring! Now calm down, Clay. It'll soon be over, and it won't hurt a bit."

"You make getting married sound like pulling a wisdom tooth!" Clay glared at him. His nerves were frayed, and he asked nervously, "What time is it?"

At that moment the organ music swelled, and Pastor Talbot said, "That's our signal. Now you two just follow me."

Clay walked stiffly through the door behind the minister. As he took his place with Dewitt standing beside him, his jaws were tightly clenched, and he swallowed hard. The church was illuminated by bright waves of pale yellow sunlight that streamed in through the high windows. Clay forced himself to relax, and slowly he took in the crowd that had gathered in the large sanctuary.

His mother sat in the first row to his right. Susanna Rocklin was a serene woman, but her fine eyes were filled with satisfaction as she smiled at him.

David, dressed in a fine gray suit, sat next to Susanna, and next to him were Dent and Raimey. Dent's face was turned so that his scar was invisible to Clay, but when he turned, the jagged slash was obvious. Clay glanced at his daughter-in-law—blind but lovely as a young woman can be! And nestled in her arms was Clay's infant grandson, Thomas. Clay didn't think he was biased when he thought that this was the most beautiful baby in the whole world. And then his eyes fell on Lowell and Rooney, both of them beaming at him.

Clay noted briefly the other members of the Rocklin clan—the Bristols and the Franklins with all the younger ones. Then far back in the balcony, the black faces of Dorrie, Zander, Box, and the slaves he'd known for years.

On the other side, he saw the pews were filled with Yancys and their kin. Most of the men were gone to the war, but the women and children were there, dressed in their cotton dresses and Sunday shows. And throughout the church he saw faces of friends. He also was shocked when he recognized some of the leaders of the Confederacy—including Alex Stephens and Jefferson Davis!

Then the great organ swelled, and everyone in the building rose and turned to see Miss Rena Rocklin, the maid of honor, as she came down the aisle. She wore a light blue gown that Clay had never seen, and there was such joy on her face and such grace in her figure that he could hardly believe what he saw. *She's become a woman, and I'll never have that little girl again!* Glancing to his left, he saw Josh standing with his family, and there was an expression on his youthful face that was close to worship. *He loves Rena, and I wouldn't be surprised—*

But he never finished his thought, for once Rena was in place, the great organ filled the sanctuary with the beginning chords of Mendelssohn's "Wedding March." Clay's head turned to the entrance, and there she was—Melora!

She wore a dress of pure, shimmering white silk with a high

lacy bodice and a long train. The dark sheen of her hair was set off by a filmy veil, and her beautiful green eyes glowed as they met Clay's.

Buford Yancy, wearing a worn black suit and a string tie, was at her side. Melora took his arm, and the two of them made their way down the aisle. A calmness enveloped Melora, a serene air that was a reflection of her spirit. She was smiling slightly as she came to stand before Rev. Talbot, but Clay saw that her eyes glistened. She looked at Clay, handsome and tall in his ash-gray uniform, and thought, *He's the only man I've ever loved!*

"Who gives this woman in marriage?"

Buford Yancy swallowed hard, then nodded. "Reckon I do." He did his part by placing Melora's hand in Clay's, then went to the front pew and seated himself.

As the minister began to speak, Clay could feel the pressure of Melora's hand. He returned it and found it strong and warm. The moment he took her hand, all nervousness left him, and he listened carefully as Rev. Talbot spoke of marriage and the sanctity of it.

When it came time for the two of them to say their vows, Melora's voice was not loud but so firm that those in the balcony heard her clearly. *"I, Melora, take thee, Clay, to be my wedded husband. . .to have and to hold. . .to love and to cherish. . .in sickness and in health. . . ."* She turned to look at Clay, and diamonds were in her beautifully shaped eyes. Then as he spoke the old words to her, her lips quivered but still were soft with a smile.

"With this ring I thee wed."

Clay slipped the gold band on Melora's finger and then lifted her hand and kissed it. The unexpected gesture brought a sigh from the women in the audience, and the pastor smiled. "Very well done, Major. I hope you will be doing the same on your golden anniversary!"

Clay looked at him, then put his eyes on Melora. "You may be sure of that, Reverend!"

"By the authority vested in me by the sovereign state of Virginia, I pronounce you man and wife! Major, you may kiss your bride!"

Melora turned her face upward, and her lips were tender and yielding as Clay bent to kiss her. For one instant she clung to him, then stepped back. "Now, Mister Clay," she whispered, using her familiar old name for him, "you finally belong to me!"

Then the music swelled, and the couple made their way to the back of the church. They could not leave, of course, for a reception had been planned. "We have to be patient," Melora whispered, seeing the anguish on Clay's face. "Everyone wants to wish us well."

For over two hours the newlyweds were subjected to well-wishing. Clay's back was slapped and his hand was shaken until it was sore, and Melora was the recipient of many kisses.

The first to come brought a shock, for it was none other than Jefferson Davis and his wife, Varina. The president shook hands with Clay, saying, "Congratulations, Major! My prayers will be with you!" Then as Mrs. Davis bowed to Clay, murmuring her congratulations, Davis moved to Melora. He was an austere man, not given to gestures. But perhaps it was the face of Melora, so peaceful and full of joy, that moved him to lean forward and kiss her on the cheek.

"Why, Mr. President!" Varina Davis exclaimed. "You're becoming quite a courtier!" And then she, too, stepped forward and kissed Melora, whispering, "I hope you will love your husband as well as I love mine!"

Finally the line ended, and Melora and Clay had one brief moment with Susanna. She kissed them both, then stepped back, saying, "I wish your father were here to see this. Now be on your way!"

Clay and Melora were struck by a hail of rice as they stepped outside. Both of them were startled when a command rang out: "Draw sabers!"

Clay got a glimpse of his old comrade Bushrod Aimes standing at the end of a double line of gray-clad troopers. A grin adorned his round face as the men drew sabers. The gleaming sabers flashed in the sunlight, and the sound of clashing metal broke the stillness of the morning. Clay and Melora moved under the canopy of bright steel, and Clay noted the grinning faces of his comrades-in-arms as they held the sabers rigid.

When they reached the end of the line, Bushrod stuck his hand out. "Get out of here quick, Major! There's talk of one of those fool shivaree things!"

"Thanks for the warning, Bushrod," Clay said, grinning. He helped Melora into the buggy and took the lines, and when he spoke sharply, the team leaped instantly into a fast gallop.

Watching the dust, Bushrod said to Taylor Dewitt, who'd come to stand beside him, "Looks like they're in a hurry, don't it?"

Taylor watched the dust rising from the wheels of the buggy and shook his head. "I don't blame them," he murmured. "They've only got a few days. I don't reckon they want to waste a second of them!"

"Oh, Clay! It's perfect!"

Clay had helped Melora out of the buggy, and the two had entered the small cabin nestled on the bank of a small lake. "It's not the Majestic Hotel in Charleston," Clay said quickly. "Actually it's a hunting lodge, but it's private."

Melora was delighted as they entered the cabin. "Look, Clay, everything is so neat—and someone filled the cupboard with all kinds of groceries!" Clay smiled as she dashed around the room, making new discoveries. Finally she turned to ask, "How did you do all this?"

"Well, actually I hired Mort Jenkins and his wife to get it ready. They live about five miles from here." A humorous light touched Clay's eyes, and he said, "Let me show you the rest of the place." He moved across the room and opened the door, and when Melora came to stand beside him, she looked inside to see a large double bed. A brightly colored bedspread was turned back to reveal freshly starched sheets. Melora felt her cheeks grow warm, and she refused to turn and look at Clay. He said nothing, and finally she turned and met his eyes. "It looks. . . very comfortable," she managed.

"I'm sure it is."

Melora suddenly giggled and, giving Clay a gentle shove out of the room, said, "Get my bag. I need to change out of this wedding dress." When Clay's face brightened, she rolled her eyes. "Mind yourself, Mister Clay. I'm going to put on another dress so you can show me the lake. . . ."

They roamed the trails of the dense woods holding hands, and the sound of their laughter frightened a small herd of deer. As they fled away, Melora cried, "Oh, look, Clay—a fawn!"

Later they moved around the path that bordered the edge of the lake. "We can dig worms and come fishing," Melora said. When Clay remarked blandly that he might find better things to do, she pushed him suddenly so that he couldn't catch his balance and fell into the water. He came out and ran after her, catching her in his arms and threatening to toss her in. But she clung to his neck and begged, so he shook his head and put her down. "You treated me much better when you were nine years old!"

Melora gave him a slanting glance—infinitely feminine—and murmured, "Oh, I don't know. I may treat you better than you can imagine, Mister Clay!"

Clay's eyes grew wide in anticipation—and surprise at Melora's forwardness. "Why, Mrs. Rocklin!" he said in mock innocence. He reached for her, but she ran away and he pursued.

Later she cooked supper, and they ate by candlelight. When

they had finished, he helped her with the dishes, and then they went outside to walk beside the lake. The moon glowed brightly in the sky, then came down to repeat itself in the glassy surface of the pond. Crickets sang their monotonous song, and a frog they startled cried, "Yikes!" and plunged—*kerplunk*—into the water. They watched the circles spread over the pond, and when the lake was finally still, Clay said quietly, "I wish we could stay here forever, Melora!"

She reached up and touched his face, then announced, "We'll come here often. It'll be our place." She hesitated for one brief moment, then said quietly, "Give me a few minutes, Clay."

He watched her as she moved back toward the cabin, then turned and breathed the air laden with the scent of earth and water and evergreens. Old memories flooded him, but he shut them out. *This is a night to think of the future!*

Finally he turned and walked slowly back and entered the cabin. Melora stood in the kitchen wearing a white silk gown. Her eyes seemed enormous as she gave him a look that he could not understand.

He took her in his arms, marveling at the incredible smoothness of her skin, savoring the scent of violets—but stronger than that was the fragrance that was simply Melora—feminine and mysterious.

She was trembling in his arms, and Clay whispered, "Are you afraid, sweet?"

"Just a little." But then she put her arms around his head and whispered fiercely, "But I'm your wife now, Clay. All that

I am is yours!"

Clay said huskily, "Melora, I'll never stop loving you—never!" When he found her lips, they were soft and vulnerable but at the same time firm and willing. He then led her to their bridal bedroom.

❧

"Are you going to sleep all day?"

Clay woke up with a start to find Melora standing over him pulling his hair. He caught her arm and pulled her down. She struggled, but he ignored her efforts. "No, I'm not going to sleep *all* day."

Melora's cheeks were bright with color, and she couldn't meet his eyes for a moment; then she gave his hair a jerk so hard that he yelped. "Do you want breakfast or not?" she demanded.

Clay rubbed his head, then smiled. "Come here, wife!" he commanded.

Melora colored even more brightly, but she came to sit beside him. "I must be an obedient wife," she whispered against his chest as he held her.

Clay stroked her back, then said, "You know, I've often thought that you had a tiger in you—but now I know there's a whole menagerie!"

"You're *awful*!"

"You didn't think—!"

Melora leaped up and ran out of the room, crying, "I'm going to throw your breakfast out the door!"

"Hey—don't do that!" Clay yelped in alarm. "Give a man a chance to get his pants on!" He struggled into his clothes, then went into the other room to find his breakfast on the table. "Pancakes and bacon!" he said with satisfaction. "You always did make the best pancakes in the world!"

They ate; then Clay rose and said, "Come on. Let's go fishing."

"Now?" Melora asked in surprise. "Let me do the dishes first."

Clay said, "Fishing is more important than washing dishes." He paused then and came to her. Taking her hand, he studied the ring on her finger, then kissed the hand as he had during the wedding ceremony. Then he pulled her close, and when she was enfolded, he whispered, "Melora, I love you more than life. I. . .I feel like a man who's wandered in some kind of. . .of deep dark woods, who finally finds his way home. Wherever you are, sweetheart, that's home to me!"

Melora rested against him, feeling the steady, strong beating of his heart.

"Clay, let's always be that—a home for each other!"

"We don't have long."

Fiercely she clung to him, and as her arms tightened about him, he heard her whisper, "We have *now*, Clay—and now is forever!"

ABOUT THE AUTHOR

Award-winning, bestselling author, Gilbert Morris is well known for penning numerous Christian novels for adults and children since 1984 with 6.5 million books in print. He is probably best known for the forty-book House of Winslow series, and his *Edge of Honor* was a 2001 Christy Award winner. He lives with his wife in Gulf Shores, Alabama.

If you enjoyed

APPOMATTOX SAGA

(PARTS 1 AND 2)

then don't miss

APPOMATTOX SAGA

(PART 3)

AVAILABLE FALL 2009